Maxim Jakubowski is a Lon...
editor. He was born in the UK...
Following a career in book pu...
world-famous Murder One bookshop in London in
1988. He compiles two acclaimed annual series for the
Mammoth list: *Best New Erotica* and *Best British Crime*.
He is a winner of the Anthony and the Karel Awards, a
frequent TV and radio broadcaster, crime columnist for
the *Guardian* newspaper and Literary Director of
London's Crime Scene Festival. His latest thriller is *I
Was Waiting for You*.

May 2013

THE MAMMOTH BOOK OF BEST BRITISH MYSTERIES

Volume 10

EDITED BY
MAXIM JAKUBOWSKI

ROBINSON

RUNNING PRESS
PHILADELPHIA · LONDON

Constable & Robinson Ltd
55–56 Russell Square
London WC1B 4HP
www.constablerobinson.com

First published in the UK as *The Mammoth Book of Best British Crime 10*
by Robinson, an imprint of Constable & Robinson Ltd, 2013

Copyright © Maxim Jakubowski, 2013
(unless otherwise stated)

The right of Maxim Jakubowski to be identified as the
author of this work has been asserted by him in accordance
with the Copyright, Designs & Patents Act 1988.

All rights reserved. This book is sold subject to the condition
that it shall not be reproduced in whole or in part, in any form or by any means,
electronic or mechanical, including photocopying, recording, or by any information
storage and retrieval system now known or hereafter invented, without written
permission from the publisher and
without a similar condition, including this condition, being imposed on the subsequent
purchaser.

A copy of the British Library Cataloguing in Publication
Data is available from the British Library

UK ISBN: 978-1-78033-793-7 (paperback)
UK ISBN: 978-1-78033-794-4 (ebook)

First published in the United States in 2013 as
The Mammoth Book of Best British Mysteries 10
by Running Press Book Publishers, a Member of the Perseus Books Group

All rights reserved under the Pan-American and International Copyright Conventions

Books published by Running Press are available at special discounts for bulk purchases
in the United States by corporations, institutions, and other organizations. For more
information, please contact the Special Markets Department at the Perseus Books
Group, 2300 Chestnut Street, Suite 200, Philadelphia, PA 19103, or call (800)
810-4145, ext. 5000, or e-mail special.markets@perseusbooks.com.

US ISBN: 978-0-7624-4810-4
US Library of Congress Control Number: 2012942534

9 8 7 6 5 4 3 2 1
Digit on the right indicates the number of this printing

Running Press Book Publishers
2300 Chestnut Street
Philadelphia, PA 19103-4371

Visit us on the web!
www.runningpress.com

Printed and bound in the UK

CONTENTS

INTRODUCTION   1

THE BONE-HEADED LEAGUE   4
Lee Child

THIS THING OF DARKNESS   11
Peter Tremayne

BIG GUY   30
Paul Johnston

THE CONSPIRATORS   35
Christopher Fowler

SQUEAKY   53
Martin Edwards

FISTS OF DESTINY   69
Col Bury

NAIN ROUGE   76
Barbara Nadel

THE KING OF OUDH'S CURRY   86
Amy Myers

LONDON CALLING   101
Ian Ayris and Nick Quantrill

THE CURIOUS AFFAIR OF THE DEODAND   105
Lisa Tuttle

GOD MOVING OVER THE FACE OF THE WATERS   137
Steve Mosby

STARDUST   144
Phil Lovesey

HE DID NOT ALWAYS SEE HER   159
Claire Seeber

METHOD MURDER   165
Simon Brett

THE MAN WHO TOOK OFF HIS HAT TO THE
  DRIVER OF THE TRAIN   184
Peter Turnbull

TOGETHER IN ELECTRIC DREAMS   193
Carol Anne Davis

LAST TRAIN FROM DESPRIT   202
Richard Godwin

THE MESSAGE   211
Margaret Murphy

TEA FOR TWO   229
Sally Spedding

SAFE AND SOUND   238
Edward Marston

CONFESSION   251
Paula Williams

TEN BELLS AT ROBBIE'S   257
Tony Black

WILKOLAK   263
Nina Allan

WHO KILLED SKIPPY?   301
Paul D. Brazill

INHERITANCE   311
Jane Casey

A MEMORABLE DAY   330
L. C. Tyler

LAPTOP   338
Cath Staincliffe

BLOOD ON THE GHAT 354
Barry Maitland

VANISHING ACT 384
Christine Poulson

THE BETRAYED 398
Roger Busby

TURNING THE TABLES 415
Judith Cutler

HANDY MAN 432
John Harvey

THE INVISIBLE GUNMAN 444
Keith McCarthy

THE GOLDEN HOUR 468
Bernie Crosthwaite

THE HABIT OF SILENCE 483
Ann Cleeves

THE UNKNOWN CRIME 495
Sarah Rayne

THE LADDER 506
Adrian McKinty

THE HOSTESS 523
Joel Lane

COME AWAY WITH ME 528
Stella Duffy

BEDLAM 549
Ken Bruen

4 A.M., WHEN THE WALLS ARE THINNER 555
Alison Littlewood

THE CASE OF DEATH AND HONEY 570
Neil Gaiman

ACKNOWLEDGEMENTS 589

INTRODUCTION

FOR TEN YEARS now it's been my privilege to edit this collection of short stories presenting the best of British crime and mystery fiction, and I've been afforded the opportunity of publishing over 400 stories by some of the most outstanding writers in our field. Almost all the "big" names amongst our local authors in the British Isles (and beyond, as some have moved to the Antipodes during the course of the series' career) have been included in our pages: Ian Rankin, Derek Raymond, Val McDermid, Mark Billingham, Simon Kernick, Peter James, Reginald Hill, John Mortimer, Alexander McCall Smith, Andrew Taylor, Anne Perry, Roger Jon Ellory, Liza Cody, amongst others, and it has been a pleasure to feature them.

Stories published in *The Mammoth Book of Best British Crime* have won some of the most prestigious awards in the field, including the Crime Writers' Association Short Story Dagger, the Mystery Writers of America Edgar Award and the Anthony Award, while countless others have featured on the respective shortlists.

The present volume is no exception as it features Peter Turnbull's Edgar-winning story, Margaret Murphy and Cath Staincliffe's CWA Dagger Short Story joint winners, and a further two short-listed tales from diverse awards. In addition, Lee Child makes a welcome new appearance and an old friend of mine, Neil Gaiman, with whom I used to sit on the SF Foundation committee meetings in the years when he wasn't quite as famous as he is now, also makes his debut, with a delightful Sherlockian tale, miles away from his more customary and splendid worlds of fantasy.

Other return offenders, and most welcome they are as ever, include Paul Johnston, Edward Marston, Judith Cutler, John Harvey, Amy Myers, Christopher Fowler, Simon Brett, Peter Tremayne, Ken Bruen, Barbara Nadel, Martin Edwards, Barry

Maitland, Adrian McKinty, Ann Cleeves, Phil Lovesey, and countless other regulars. But again, one of my greatest reasons for pride in the series is the fact that I'm able to introduce new writers who, in all likelihood, will also become household names in the years to come: take your bow, Nina Allan, Claire Seeber, Joel Lane, Lisa Tuttle (whose excellent writing in other fields is not to be missed), Paula Williams, Roger Busby (a veteran on the comeback trail), Jane Casey, Alison Littlewood and Richard Godwin.

I hope that in this busy past decade our series has ably demonstrated the strengths and attraction of British crime writing in all its diversity, ranging from the cosy tale of detection to the noir borderlands of mayhem and destruction and the deep nooks and crannies of psychological suspense and terror. Crime writing is a many-sided art in which our writers tempt you in sly and clever ways, offering you puzzles to solve, asking ever-worrying questions about the world we live in but, most of all, providing first-class entertainment along with the thrills.

As the market for short stories and anthologies changes, its retail profile changes too, and there is, sadly, a strong possibility this may be the final volume in our series (although our primary publishers wish to debut another crime project, which may involve many of our loyal authors, as an Internet/digital replacement). But ten years is a long time, and I rest assured in the knowledge of all the enjoyment these pages have brought to so many readers over that period.

So, this is also the time to thank many of the people who have been instrumental in bringing these ten volumes to date to you, the readers, in addition of course to all the writers who have made these volumes so exciting. A vote of thanks then to David Shelley, who gave the project its first go-ahead, to Susie Dunlop, and then, at Constable & Robinson, who've supported me through thick and thin, Nick Robinson, Peter Duncan and Duncan Proudfoot, and in the USA Kent Carroll, Herman Graf and Christopher Navratil. Without them, we would not have lasted anywhere near so long.

Every year, our authors have kept on surprising me with the sparkle of their imagination and the fluidity of their writing. This volume is no exception. Expect to be surprised, scared, charmed, intrigued, shocked even.

And we'll meet again, at some stage in the future, in a murky field where death, ghosts of the past, villains and detectives, cops and sleuths, fight their ongoing battle; where good and evil are never black or white but come in a hundred shades of grey. There are some pretty black stories here too: Wilkolak, Come Away With Me, The Hostess, etc.

It's been a great ride!

Maxim Jakubowski

THE BONE-HEADED LEAGUE

Lee Child

For once the FBI did the right thing: it sent the Anglophile to England. To London, more specifically, for a three-year posting at the Embassy in Grosvenor Square. Pleasures there were extensive, and duties there were light. Most agents ran background checks on visa applicants and intending immigrants and kept their ears to the ground on international matters, but I liaised with London's Metropolitan Police when American nationals were involved in local crimes, either as victims or witnesses or perpetrators.

I loved every minute of it, as I knew I would. I love that kind of work, I love London, I love the British way of life, I love the theatre, the culture, the pubs, the pastimes, the people, the buildings, the Thames, the fog, the rain. Even the soccer. I was expecting it to be all good, and it was all good.

Until.

I had spent a damp Wednesday morning in February helping out, as I often did, by rubber-stamping immigration paperwork, and then I was saved by a call from a sergeant at Scotland Yard, asking on behalf of his inspector that I attend a crime scene north of Wigmore Street and south of Regent's Park. On the 200 block of Baker Street, more specifically, which was enough to send a little jolt through my Anglophile heart, because every Anglophile knows that Sherlock Holmes's fictional address was 221b Baker Street. It was quite possible I would be working right underneath the great detective's fictional window.

And I was, as well as underneath many other windows too, because the Met's crime scenes are always fantastically elaborate.

We have *CSI* on television, where they solve everything in forty-three minutes with DNA, and the Met has Scene-of-Crime-Officers, who spend forty-three minutes closing roads and diverting pedestrians, before spending forty-three minutes shrugging themselves into Tyvek bodysuits and Tyvek booties and Tyvek hoods, before spending forty-three minutes stringing Keep-Out tape between lamp posts and fence railings, before spending forty-three minutes erecting white tents and shrouds over anything of any interest whatsoever. The result was that I found a passable imitation of a travelling circus already in situ when I got there.

There was a cordon, of course, several layers deep, and I got through them all by showing my Department of Justice credentials and by mentioning the inspector's name, which was Bradley Rose. I found the man himself stumping around on the damp sidewalk some yards south of the largest white tent. He was a short man, but substantial, with no tie and snappy eyeglasses and a shaved head. He was an old-fashioned London thief-taker, softly spoken but at the same time impatient with bullshit, which his own department provided in exasperating quantity.

He jerked his thumb at the tent and said, "Dead man."

I nodded. Obviously I wasn't surprised. Not even the Met uses tents and Tyvek for purse-snatching.

He jerked his thumb again and said, "American."

I nodded again. I knew Rose was quite capable of working that out from dentistry or clothing or shoes or hairstyle or body shape, but equally I knew he would not have involved me officially without some more definitive indicator. And as if answering the unasked question he pulled two plastic evidence bags from his pocket. One contained an opened-out blue US passport, and the other contained a white business card. He handed both bags to me and jerked his thumb again and said, "From his pockets."

I knew better than to touch the evidence itself. I turned the bags this way and that and examined both items through the plastic. The passport photograph showed a sullen man, pale of skin, with hooded eyes that looked both evasive and challenging. I glanced up and Rose said, "It's probably him. The boat matches the photo, near enough."

Boat was a contraction of *boat race*, which was cockney rhyming slang for face. Apples and pears, stairs, trouble and strife, wife, plates of meat, feet, and so on. I asked, "What killed him?"

"Knife under the ribs," Rose said.

The name on the passport was Ezekiah Hopkins.

Rose said, "Did you ever hear of a name like that before?"

"Hopkins?" I said.

"No, Ezekiah."

I looked up at the windows above me and said, "Yes, I did."

The place of birth was recorded as Pennsylvania, USA.

I gave the bagged passport back to Rose and looked at the business card. It was impossible to be certain without handling it, but it seemed to be a cheap item. Thin stock, no texture, plain print, no embossing. It was the kind of thing anyone can order online for a few pounds a thousand. The legend said *Hopkins, Ross & Spaulding*, as if there were some kind of partnership of that name. There was no indication of what business they were supposed to be in. There was a phone number on the card, with a 610 area code. Eastern Pennsylvania, but not Philly. The address on the card read simply *Lebanon, PA*. East of Harrisburg, as I recalled. Correct for the 610 code. I had never been there.

"Did you call the number?" I asked.

"That's your job," Rose said.

"No one will answer," I said. "A buck gets ten it's phony."

Rose gave me a long look and took out his phone. He said, "It better be phony. I don't have an international calling plan. If someone answers in America it'll cost me an arm and a leg." He pressed 001, then 610, then the next seven digits. From six feet away I heard the triumphant little phone company triplet that announced a number that didn't work. Rose clicked off and gave me the look again.

"How did you know?" he asked.

I said, "*Omne ignotum pro magnifico*."

"What's that?"

"Latin."

"For what?"

"Every unexplained thing seems magnificent. In other words, a good magician doesn't reveal his tricks."

"You're a magician now?"

"I'm an FBI special agent," I said. I looked up at the windows again. Rose followed my gaze and said, "Yes, I know. Sherlock Holmes lived here."

"No, he didn't," I said. "He didn't exist. He was made up. So were these buildings. In Arthur Conan Doyle's day Baker Street only went up to about number eighty. Or a hundred, perhaps. The rest of it was a country road. Marylebone was a separate little village a mile away."

"I was born in Brixton," Rose said. "I wouldn't know anything about that."

"Conan Doyle made up the number two hundred and twenty-one," I said. "Like movies and TV make up the phone numbers you see on the screen. And the licence plates on the cars. So they don't cause trouble for real people."

"What's your point?"

"I'm not sure," I said. "But you're going to have to let me have the passport. When you're done with it, I mean. Because it's probably phony too."

"What's going on here?"

"Where do you live?"

"Hammersmith," he said.

"Does Hammersmith have a library?"

"Probably."

"Go borrow a book. *The Adventures of Sherlock Holmes*. The second story. It's called 'The Red-Headed League'. Read it tonight, and I'll come see you in the morning."

Visiting Scotland Yard is always a pleasure. It's a slice of history. It's a slice of the future, too. Scotland Yard is a very modern place these days. Plenty of information technology. Plenty of people using it.

I found Rose in his office, which was nothing more than open space defended by furniture. Like a kid's fort. He said, "I got the book but I haven't read it yet. I'm going to read it now."

He pointed to a fat paperback volume on the desk. So to give him time I took Ezekiah Hopkins's passport back to the Embassy and had it tested. It was a fake, but very good, except for some blunders so obvious they had to be deliberate. Like taunts, or provocations. I got back to Scotland Yard and Rose said, "I read the story."

"And?"

"All those names were in it. Ezekiah Hopkins, and Ross, and Spaulding. And Lebanon, Pennsylvania, too. And Sherlock Holmes said the same Latin you did. He was an educated man, apparently."

"And what was the story about?"

"Decoy," Rose said. "A ruse was developed whereby a certain Mr Wilson was regularly decoyed away from his legitimate place of business for a predictable period of time, so that an ongoing illegal task of some sensitivity could be accomplished in his absence."

"Very good," I said. "And what does the story tell us?"

"Nothing," Rose said. "Nothing at all. No one was decoying me away from my legitimate place of business. That *was* my legitimate place of business. I go wherever dead people go."

"And?"

"And if they *were* trying to decoy me away, they wouldn't leave clues beforehand, would they? They wouldn't spell it out for me in advance. I mean, what would be the point of that?"

"There might be a point," I said.

"What kind?"

I asked, "If this were just some foreigner stabbed to death on Baker Street, what would you do next?"

"Not very much, to be honest."

"Exactly. Just one of those things. But *now* what are you going to do next?"

"I'm going to find out who's yanking my chain. First step, I'm going back on scene to make sure we didn't miss any other clues."

"*Quod erat demonstrandum*," I said.

"What's that?"

"Latin."

"For what?"

"They're decoying you out. They've succeeded in what they set out to do."

"Decoying me out from what? I don't do anything important in the office."

He insisted on going. We headed back to Baker Street. The tents were still there. The tape was still fluttering. We found no more clues. So we studied the context instead, physically, looking for the kind of serious crimes that could occur if law enforcement was distracted. We didn't find anything. That part of Baker Street had the official Sherlock Holmes Museum, and the waxworks, and a bunch of stores of no real consequence, and a few banks, but the banks were all bust anyway. Blowing one up would be doing it a considerable favour.

Then Rose wanted a book that explained the various Sherlock Holmes references in greater detail, so I took him to the British Library in Bloomsbury. He spent an hour with an annotated compendium. He got sidetracked by the geographic errors Conan Doyle had made. He started to think the story he had read could be approached obliquely, as if it were written in code.

Altogether we spent the rest of the week on it. The Wednesday, the Thursday, and the Friday. Easily thirty hours. We got nowhere. We made no progress. But nothing happened. None of Rose's other cases unravelled, and London's crime did not spike. There were no consequences. None at all.

So as the weeks passed both Rose and I forgot all about the matter. And Rose never thought about it again, as far as I know. I did, of course. Because three months later it became clear that it was I who had been decoyed. My interest had been piqued, and I had spent thirty hours doing fun Anglophile things. They knew that would happen, naturally. They had planned well. They knew I would be called out to the dead American, and they knew how to stage the kinds of things that would set me off like the Energizer Bunny. Three days. Thirty hours. Out of the building, unable to offer help with the rubber-stamping, not there to notice them paying for their kids' college educations by rubber-stamping visas that should have been rejected instantly. Which is how four particular individuals made it to the States, and which is why three hundred people died in Denver, and which is why the others were executed, and which is why I sit alone in Leavenworth in Kansas, where by chance one of the few books the prison allows is *The Adventures of Sherlock Holmes*.

THIS THING OF DARKNESS

A MASTER HARDY DREW MYSTERY

Peter Tremayne

"This thing of darkness.
I acknowledge mine."

William Shakespeare, *The Tempest*, V, i

MASTER HARDY DREW, Constable of the Bankside Watch, stood regarding the blackened and still smoking ruins of the once imposing edifice of the house on the corner of Stony Street near the parish church of St Saviour's. There was little left of it as it had been a wood-built house, and wood and dry plaster were a combustible mix.

"It was a fine old house," Master Drew's companion said reflectively. "It once belonged to the old Papist Bishop Gardiner."

"The one who took pleasure in burning those he deemed heretics in Queen Mary's time?" asked Master Drew with a slight shudder. He had not been born when Mary had been on the throne but he knew it to be a strange, unsettled period when, during those five short years, she had earned the epithet of "Bloody Mary".

Master Pettigrew, the fire warden, nodded.

"Aye, Master Drew. The same who condemned some good men to the flames because they would not accept Roman ways."

"Well, it is not infrequent that buildings catch alight and burn. You and your sturdy lads have put out the flames and no other properties seem threatened. Why, therefore, do you bring me here?"

Master Pettigrew inclined his head towards the smouldering ruins.

"There is a body here. I think you should see it."

The constable frowned.

"A poor soul caught in the fire? Surely that is a task for the coroner?"

"That's as may be, good master. Come and examine it for yourself. It is not badly burned," he added, seeing the distaste on Master Drew's features. "I believe it was not fire that killed him."

He led the way through the charred wood and the odd standing wall towards what must have been the back of the house and into an area that had been partially built of bricks and thus not much harmed in the conflagration.

Master Drew saw the problem straightway. The body of a man was hanging from a thick beam by means of iron manacles that secured his wrists and linked them via a chain over the beam. He breathed out sharply.

"This is a thing of darkness. A deed of evil," he muttered.

The constable tried not to look at the legs of the corpse for they had received the force of the fire. The upper body was blackened but not burned for, by that curious vagary to which fire is often prey, the flames had not engulfed the entire body. The flames seemed to have died down after they had reached the corpse.

The body was that of a man of thirty or perhaps a little more. Through the soot and grime it was impossible to detect much about the features.

Master Drew saw that the mouth was tied as in the manner of a gag. The eyes were bulging still and blood-rimmed, marking the struggle to obtain air that must have been filled with smoke and fumes from the fire.

"You will observe, Master Drew, that the upper garments of this man speak of some wealth and status, and the manner of his death was clearly planned."

The constable sniffed in irritation.

"I am experienced in the matter of observation," he rebuked sharply.

Indeed, he had already observed that, in spite of the blackened and scorched garments, they were clearly those affected by a person of wealth. His sharp eyes had detected something under the shirt and he drew the long dagger he wore at his belt and used it to push aside the doublet and undershirt. Beneath was a gold chain on which was hung a medallion of sorts.

Master Pettigrew let out a breath. He was probably thinking of the wealth that he had missed, for being warden of the fire watch around Bankside did not provide him with means to live as he would want...or not without a little help from items collected in the debris of fires such as this.

Using the tip of his dagger, Master Drew was able to lift the chain over the head of the corpse and then examine it. Master Pettigrew peered over his shoulder.

"A dead sheep moulded in gold," he breathed.

Master Drew shook his head.

"Not a dead sheep but the fleece of a sheep. I have seen the like once before. It was just after the defeat of the Spanish invasion force. They brought some prisoners to the Tower and I was one of the appointed guards. One of the prisoners was wearing such a symbol. When a sergeant wanted to divest him of it, our captain rebuked him, saying it was the symbol of a noble order and that the prisoner should be treated, therefore, with all courtesy and respect."

The warden looked worried.

"A nobleman murdered here on the Bankside? We will not hear the last of it, good constable. A noble would have influence."

Master Drew nodded thoughtfully.

"A nobleman, aye. But of what country and what allegiance? This order was set up to defend the Papist faith."

Master Pettigrew looked at him in horror.

"The Papist Faith, you say?"

"This is a Spanish order for I see the insignia of Philip of Spain on the reverse."

"Spanish?' gasped Master Pettigrew. "There are several noble Spaniards in London at this time."

Master Drew's features hardened.

"And many who would as lief cut a Spaniard's throat in revenge for the cruelties of previous years. Were there no witnesses to this incendiary act?"

To his surprise, Master Pettigrew nodded an affirmative.

"Tom Shadwell, a passing fruit merchant, saw the flames and called the alarm," returned Master Pettigrew. "That was at dawn this morning. My men managed to isolate the building and extinguish the flames within the hour. Then we entered and that was when I found the body and sent for you."

"Well, one thing is for certain, this poor soul did not hang himself nor set fire to this place. To whom does this building now belong?"

"I think it must still belong to the Bishop of Winchester for he has many estates around here. Such was the office of Bishop Gardiner but he has been dead these fifty years, during which it has remained empty."

"That's true," Master Drew reflected. "I have never seen it occupied since I came here as Assistant Constable. No one has ever claimed it nor sought to occupy it."

"Aye, and for the reason that local folk claim it to be haunted by the spirits of the unfortunates that Bishop Gardiner tortured and condemned to the flames as heretics."

Master Drew pocketed the chain thoughtfully and glanced once more at the body.

"Release the corpse to the charge of the coroner, Master Pettigrew, and say that I will speak with him anon, but to do nothing precipitate until I have done so."

He was about to turn when he caught sight of something in the corner of the room that puzzled him. In spite of the fire having damaged this area, he saw that the floorboards were smashed and that, where they had been torn away, a rectangular hole had been dug into the earth. He moved towards it.

"Is this the work of your men, Master Pettigrew?" he asked.

The warden of the fire watch shook his head.

"Not of my men."

Master Drew sniffed sharply.

"Then someone has excavated this hole. But for what purpose?"

He bent down, peered into the hole and poked at it with the tip of his long dagger.

"The hole was already here and something buried, which was but recently dug up and removed and…" He frowned, moved his dagger again and then bent down into the hole, carefully, trying to avoid the soot. With a grunt of satisfaction he came up holding something between thumb and forefinger.

"A coin?" hazarded Master Pettigrew, leaning over his shoulder.

"Aye, a coin," the constable confirmed, scraping away some of the soot with the point of the dagger.

"A groat?"

"No, this is a shilling, and an Irish shilling of Philip and Mary at that. See the harp under the crown on the face…and either side, under smaller crowns, the initials P and M? Now what would that be doing here?"

"Well, Bishop Gardiner was a Papist during the time of Mary and approved her marriage to the Spanish King Philip. It is logical that he might have lost the coin then."

Master Drew looked down at the hole again. He knew better than to comment further. Instead, he slipped the coin into his pocket and moved towards the exit of the blackened building. Outside, groups of people were already gathering. He suspected that some of them had come to forage and pillage if there was anything worth salvaging.

"Where are you away to?" called Master Pettigrew.

"To proceed with my investigation," he replied. "I'll speak to the fruit merchant who first saw the conflagration."

"He has the barrow at the corner of Clink Street, selling fruit and nosegays to those visiting the folk within the prison."

The constable made no reply but he knew Tom Shadwell, the fruit seller, well enough and often passed the time of day with him as he made his way by the grim walls of the old prison.

"A body found, you say, good constable?" Tom Shadwell's face paled when Master Drew told him of the gruesome find. "I saw only the flames and had no idea that anyone dwelt within the building. Had I known, I would have made an effort to save the poor soul. So far as I knew, it had been empty these many years."

"You would have been too late anyway," replied Master Drew. "It is murder that we are dealing with. Therefore, be cautious in your thoughts before you recite to me as much as you may remember."

Tom Shadwell rubbed the bridge of his nose with a crooked forefinger.

"The first light was spreading when I came by the corner of Stony Street to make my way to my pitch. I was pushing my barrow as usual. It is not long after dawn that the prison door is opened and visitors are allowed to go in. I usually start my trade early. I was passing the old house when I saw the flames…"

He suddenly paused and frowned.

"You have thought of something, Master Shadwell?" prompted the constable.

"It is unrelated to the fire."

"Let me decide that."

"There was a coach standing in Stony Street, not far from the house. Two men were lifting a small wooden chest inside. It seemed heavy. Even as I passed the end of the street they had placed it in the coach, then one climbed in and the other scrambled to the box and took the reins. Away it went in a trice. I then crossed the end of the street towards the old house and that was when I heard the crackle of the fire and saw its flames through the window. I pushed my barrow to the end of the street, for I knew Master Pettigrew, warden of the fire watch, dwelt there. I was reluctant to leave my barrow – prey to thieves and wastrels – but there was no one about, so I ran along to his house and raised the alarm. That is all I know."

"This coach, could you identify it?"

Shadwell shook his head.

"It was dark and the two men were clad in dark cloaks."

"Well-dressed fellows, would you say?"

"Hard to say, Master Constable."

"And which way did this coach proceed? Towards the bridge?"

Shadwell shook his head.

"In this direction, towards Clink Street or maybe along to Bankside, not towards the bridge."

Having ascertained there was nothing more to be gathered from the fruit seller, Master Drew turned past the Clink Prison to the adjacent imposing ancient structure of Winchester Palace that dominated the area just west of the Bridgehead. Southwark was the largest town of the diocese of Winchester. In the days when Winchester was capital of the Saxon kingdom, before London reclaimed its Roman prominence, the Bishops of Winchester were all-powerful. Even after Winchester fell into decline as a capital, the bishops remained within court circles and therefore had to be frequently in London for royal and administrative purposes. So the grand Winchester Palace was built on the south bank of the Thames.

Master Drew explained his business to the gatekeeper of the palace and was shown directly to the office of Sir Gilbert Scrivener, secretary to His Grace, Thomas Bilson, Bishop of Winchester.

"The house on the corner of Stony Street? We have large estates in Southwark, Master Drew, as you know. But I do vaguely recall it. Unused since Bishop Gardiner's decease."

"You have no personal acquaintance with the house, then?"

"My dear constable," replied Sir Gilbert, "I have more things to do with my time than personally to acquaint myself with all the properties controlled by the diocese. As for the burning of this building, and the murder of foreigners, it is not to be wondered that they and empty houses are treated in such manner – since it is so, it may be a blessing for it has long been His Grace's wish to rebuild that crumbling edifice and set up on the site something more useful to the church and the community."

"So you *are* acquainted with the house?" replied Master Drew sharply.

Sir Gilbert spread his hands with a thin smile.

"I said, not personally. But I am His Grace's secretary. I fear you do but waste your time for do we not live in Southwark, and is it not said that these mean streets are better termed a foul den than a fair garden? Its reputation is best described as notorious. Bankside itself is a nest of prostitutes and thieves, of cut-throats and vagabonds."

"And playhouses," smiled Master Drew grimly. "Do not forget the playhouses, Sir Gilbert."

The secretary sighed impatiently.

"I cannot spare you more time, Master Constable. I wish you a good morning and success with your endeavours."

Outside the gates of Winchester Palace, Master Drew paused, frowning, one hand fingering the golden chain that reposed in his breeches pocket.

He sighed deeply. It was going to be a long walk to where he felt his next enquiry was going to take him. His allowance as Constable of the Bankside Watch would not stretch to what the justices of Southwark might deem the unnecessary expense of a wherryman to ferry him across the river. So, with a shrug, he set off for the entrance to the London Bridge. He was walking towards it when a voice hailed him.

"Give you a good day, Master Constable."

He glanced up to see old Jepheson, the tanner, guiding his wagonload of hides towards the bridge. Master Drew knew him well for he had prevented the old man and his wife from being attacked and robbed one summer evening in their tannery in Bear Lane.

"Good day, Master Jepheson. Whither away?"

"To deliver these hides to The Strand."

Master Drew smiled broadly. Here was luck indeed.

"Then I will seek the favour of a ride there with you for it will save me an exhausting walk and the wear of my shoe leather.'

"Climb up and welcome. I am already in your debt."

Master Drew obeyed with alacrity. While old Jepheson prattled on, the constable could not help but dwell on the meaning of the golden chain in his pocket. A Spanish noble order found on the corpse of a murdered man... All England knew that the long war between England and Spain was coming to a negotiated end. Envoys from the two kingdoms were even now meeting in the palace built by the Duke of Somerset. Since 1585 the war had continued, with no side gaining any advantage. With the death of Elizabeth and the accession last year of James VI of Scotland as James I of England, it was felt the time had come to end the long and wasteful war. The old enemy, Philip II of Spain, was also dead and Philip III now ruled there. Six leading Spanish noblemen had arrived with their entourages to conduct the negotiations that would, hopefully, lead to a peace treaty.

Somerset House was on the north bank of the River Thames. Southwark was south of London Bridge and therefore a separate jurisdiction from London. It owed its importance to this position at the farther end of the only bridge spanning the Thames, making it the main thoroughfare to the south. It had further increased its prosperity and population by making itself a pleasure ground for the more law-abiding citizens of the north bank of the Thames. It had been only in 1550 that the City of London had decided to attempt to control the lawlessness of Southwark by setting up Justices and Constables, such as Master Drew, to impose order there.

But Southwark still felt separate and would not be forced into obedience to the Justices of London. It became the headquarters of the rebel Sir Thomas Wyatt in 1554, when he raised an insurgent force to move on London and prevent Queen Mary's intended marriage to Philip II of Spain. Only the fortification on the northern end of London Bridge and the training of the cannons of the Tower of London across the river on the homes and churches of the people of Southwark, had forced the withdrawal of the insurgents.

It was because of this "independence", this freedom and laxity in the laws, that the Bankside area became the place where playhouses had sprung up, beyond the restrictions placed on their neighbours on the northern bank. The Bankside had become a haunt of prostitutes, pimps and thieves. Master Drew's remit was to impose order upon them, but because of the separation in jurisdiction he realized he would be unable to exercise his authority on the northern bank.

Master Drew left Jepheson and his wagon of hides in The Strand and walked to the gates of Somerset House. In the courtyard an officer of the guard stopped him and shook his head when Drew said he wanted to see one of the Spanish delegation or their secretaries.

"You have no jurisdiction here, Constable," replied the officer. "I can let no one through without legal authority."

"Master Drew?" a sharp voice suddenly called behind him.

The constable swung round. A man of small stature, crookback, with a tawny-coloured beard and hair, and sharp green eyes, was examining him. He had apparently emerged from a nearby doorway. The officer of the guard stiffened and saluted while Master Drew performed a clumsy bow as he recognized the Lord Chancellor of England, Sir Robert Cecil.

"I thought it was you," Sir Robert said, with a soft, malicious smile. "I never forget a face. What business brings you hither?"

Master Drew tried to repress thoughts of how Sir Robert had come perilously close to having him arrested for conspiracy to High Treason while Elizabeth lay dying the previous year.

"A matter that may be one of national importance, Sir Robert."

The Lord Chancellor raised his eyebrows and then waved away the officer of the guard.

"Then, come walk with me, and tell me what you mean."

As they paced the courtyard, Master Drew, with few wasted words, explained what had happened and ended by presenting Sir Robert with the gold chain.

The Lord Chancellor frowned as he examined it.

"I have seen the like before and recently. You have in mind that it belongs to one of the Spanish delegation?"

"And even worse," agreed Master Drew, "that the owner of the chain and the body in the house on Stony Street may be one of your Spanish nobles. If it is so and one of the ambassadors has been murdered at such a fraught time..." He shrugged.

The diplomatic implications were not lost on Sir Robert.

"If so, then indeed we face perilous times," he said softly. He turned back to the officer of the guard and called to him.

"Go to the apartment of His Grace, the Duke of Frias, and ask him if it would not be troubling him too much if he could attend me in my chamber. I pray you, put as much courtesy and politeness into the request as you can."

The officer went off on his new errand.

Sir Robert guided Master Drew into the building and through to a chamber where a fire crackled in the hearth.

"I have seen the Duke of Frias returning from his morning ride, so I know he is safe," confided Sir Robert. "He is chief ambassador of the Spanish and should be able to assist in this matter."

It seemed only a short time passed before there was a knock on the door and the officer of the guard entered and stood to one side.

"His Grace Juan de Velasco Frias, Duke of Frias, Constable of Castile," he announced solemnly.

A tall, dark and elegantly dressed man entered and made a sweeping courtly bow to them.

Sir Robert went forward to greet him.

"Your Grace, forgive me for disturbing your morning's preoccupations, but we must ask for your advice and information on a matter of pressing concern to both our nations."

The Duke smiled with a cursory movement of his facial muscles. His dark eyes looking enquiringly at Master Drew, taking in his more shabby clothing and appearance, which clearly did not place him as a courtier or officer of state.

"It is what I and my compatriots are here for, Sir Robert. But I have not had the pleasure of this gentleman's acquaintance."

"This is Master Drew, a Constable of the Bankside…"

"*Master* Drew? And a Constable? I am Constable of Castile. Do you not have to be of the knightly rank to be a Constable in this kingdom?"

"There is a difference in office, Your Grace," Sir Robert explained hurriedly. "Suffice to say, Master Drew is much in our confidence. Tell me, have you seen all your compatriots this morning?"

The Duke frowned.

"All? Indeed, we breakfasted together to discuss some points to raise at our sessions later today. Why do you ask?"

"Master Drew has something to explain."

Master Drew cleared his throat and repeated his story and then held out the chain for the Spaniard to inspect.

"The Order of the Golden Fleece," the Duke whispered softly. "It bears the insignia of His Majesty, Felipe III." The expression on his face told them he recognized the significance of this discovery. He turned his dark eyes to Sir Robert. "Can someone ask the Count of Villa Medina to join us?"

Sir Robert glanced towards the officer of the guard who had remained by the door, and issued instructions.

When he had gone Master Drew asked: "Does Your Grace think that this belongs to the Count of Villa Medina?"

The Duke of Frias shook his head.

"I know that the Count of Villa Medina is not a member of this noble order. However, he will, I am sure, be able to cast light on the person who held this honour."

Again, it was not long before the door was opened, to a nervous man whose movements reminded Master Drew of a bird, quick and unpredictable. He possessed the habit of running his hand swiftly over his small pointed beard each time he spoke.

This time, the Duke of Frias explained in rapid Spanish and then turned to Master Drew and asked him to hold forth the golden chain.

The Count's face paled as he examined it.

"I can identify the owner of this," he said slowly. He spoke a fair English but without the fluency of the Duke.

"And the owner is...?" queried Master Drew.

"My secretary, the Chevalier Stefano Jardiniero y Barbastro."

Master Drew frowned.

"Stefano Jardiniero?" he echoed.

The Count made a motion with his hand, stroking his beard rapidly.

"He is of an English family who fled to Spain on the death of Mary, former Queen Consort of Spain."

Sir Robert sniffed in embarrassment as he explained.

"Stefano Jardiniero was a nephew of Bishop Stephen Gardiner. That is why the name is familiar. I recall the family."

Master Drew tried to hide his surprise.

"Bishop Gardiner of Winchester?"

"The family was granted asylum by the late King Felipe who gave them an estate in Barbastro," added the Count of Villa Medina. "The Chevalier proved his nobility and loyalty in the King's service and so was ennobled by the court and made a member of this order."

Sir Robert glanced keenly at Master Drew.

"I am aware that Bishop Gardiner sent several worthy men to the flames as martyrs for the Protestant cause. Therefore there may be some who would see the death of one of his family as just retribution. But before we reach such a conclusion, let us seek out the facts. I presume the Chevalier is currently unaccounted for?"

The Count looked embarrassed and nodded.

"I sent for him this morning to discuss notes appertaining to the treaty but was told he was not in his chambers and that his bed had not been slept in. He has not been seen since last evening."

"And why has an alarm not been raised?"

The Count of Villa Medina shrugged.

"The Chevalier is still a young man and there are many distractions in this city to preoccupy him."

Master Drew looked sharply at him. The manner of his speech was careful to the point where it seemed obvious that he was withholding something.

"If I am to expedite this matter, I need to know all the facts."

The Count was hesitant but the Duke of Frias spoke to him sharply in Spanish.

"It is true," the Count said, as if answering the Duke but in English. He turned to Master Drew. "Very well, the facts it shall be. The Chevalier said he had to go out last evening, as he wanted to collect an old… how do you call it? *Una reliquia de familia.*"

The Duke translated for him.

"A family heirloom. He spoke to the Count of this within my hearing. He mentioned no further details."

Master Drew sighed deeply.

"I would be grateful if the Count would accompany me across to Bankside in order that he may formally identify the body. After all, it may not be the Chevalier's. But if it is, let us confirm it. Perhaps, Sir Robert, you might provide a coach to take us south of the river? I cannot ask the Count to walk with me."

"Even better," replied the Lord Chancellor, "there is a boat by the quayside at my constant disposal that will make your journey shorter." He turned to the officer of the guard. "Captain, take you two good stalwarts of your guard and accompany Master Drew and the Count. You are the constable's to command and his commands may be given in my name. Is that clear?"

The officer saluted and turned to fulfil his task.

A moment later the Count and guards were seated with Master Drew in the boat, whose four oars were manned by men in the livery of the Lord Chancellor. It pushed off from the north bank, making its way swiftly over the dark waters of the Thames, south towards the less than salubrious quays and wooden piers that lined the Bankside.

An elderly man limped forward to help tie up the boat in the hope of receiving a coin for his trouble. Master Drew recognized him as one of those unfortunates who regularly frequented the quays to scavenge or pick up the odd job here and there. A thought suddenly came to him.

"Were you about the quays last evening?" he demanded sharply.

The man touched his cap awkwardly.

"That I was, Master Constable. I do be here most times unless the ague confine me to the pot room at the Bell, wherein I do be given a place by the fire by the good office of the innkeeper."

"Did you notice a boat similar to this one?" He jerked his head towards the boat they had arrived in. "Did a young man land here last night?"

"There be many young men come to the Bankside, good Master. You know as well as I. Young rakes in search of a good time at the taverns or theatres and the company of low women."

Master Drew took out a penny and fingered it before the man's eyes.

"This man would have been well dressed and foreign withal."

"Foreign, you say? Spoke he like a Dago?"

Drew's eyes narrowed.

"You spoke with him?"

"By my soul, I did. It was late and I was about to go back to the Bell. There were few folk around. He came from the quay and asked if I could direct him to Stony Street, which I did. He then asked if I knew whether the Gardiner house still stood. That I could not say for I had never heard of it. But when he confided that Gardiner was once the bishop here, I said he had best call at Winchester Palace and enquire there. I told him where that was and he gave me a coin and went his way. That's all I do know."

Master Drew dropped the penny into the man's hand and instructed the boatmen to stand ready to transport the Count back to Somerset House. The mortuary was not far away and, as soon as the Count had confirmed that the body of the young man was, indeed, that of his missing secretary, the Chevalier Stefano Jardiniero, he was despatched with one of the guards back to the boat, with assurances that his murderer would soon be found.

With the officer and the other guard in attendance, Master Drew made his way directly to Winchester Palace and went straightway to the gatekeeper, who was the same man who had been on duty earlier.

"Who was on watch here last night between dusk and midnight?" he demanded without preamble.

The man looked nervously from the constable, whom he knew, to the liveried soldiers behind him.

"Why, old Martin, Master Drew."

"And where shall I find old Martin?" snapped the constable.

"About this time o' day, he'll be in the Bear Pit Tavern."

It was a short walk to the tavern, which was on the quayside, and old Martin was soon pointed out.

Master Drew seated himself opposite the elderly man.

"Last evening you were the watch at the entrance to Winchester Palace." It was a statement and not a question.

Martin looked at him with rheumy eyes.

"I cannot deny it."

"A young foreign gentleman called there?"

"He did, good master. That he did. He asked me if the Gardiner House on Stony Street still stood."

"And you told him?"

"I told him that all the houses belonged to the diocese of Winchester, and which did he mean? He was trying to explain when Master Burton came by and took him aside to offer his help. They were deep in conversation for a while and then the foreign gentleman... well, he went off looking quite content."

"You saw no more of him?"

"None."

"And who is this Master Burton?"

"Why, he be manservant to Sir Gilbert Scrivener."

Master Drew sat back with a curious smile on his face.

Within fifteen minutes he was standing before the desk of the secretary to His Grace, the Bishop of Winchester, with the officer of the Lord Chancellor's guard at the door. Sir Gilbert was frowning in annoyance.

"I have much business to occupy me, Master Constable. I trust this will not take too long, and only condescend to spare the time as you now say you come on the Lord Chancellor's business."

Master Drew returned his gaze steadily, refusing to be intimidated by the man or his office.

"I would tell you a brief story first, about one of the Bishops of Winchester. Fortunately for him he died in the time of Queen Mary and so did not have to account for the Protestant souls he cast into the flames to cure them of what he deemed to be heresy. He was a wealthy and influential man and owned many houses here when he occupied this very palace. One particular building was used to interrogate and torture heretics. You know it... the one that was burned down last night.

"It seems he gathered together some wealth, a chest of coins, that, if Mary lost her throne and the Protestant faction came in, would help him escape to Spain and ease his exile. In the end, Mary outlived him and it was members of his own family who later had to flee to Spain. Before his death, he seems to have written instructions to his family there as to where they could find that chest of coins. But war between Spain and England prevented any member of the family seeking it... until now, nearly twenty years later, when it so happened one of his family was appointed secretary to the Spanish ambassadors who are now in this country to agree the peace.'

Sir Gilbert looked stony-faced.

"Are you coming to a point, Master Constable?"

"Last night this scion of the Gardiner family, now known as Chevalier Jardiniero y Barbastro, came in search of the Gardiner house wherein the box was buried. He made the mistake of being too free in his enquiries."

"Are you saying that someone decided to kill him for vengeance when they knew he was the relative of Bishop Gardiner?"

Master Drew shook his head.

"Not for such a lofty motive as vengeance was he killed, but merely of theft. He was followed and watched, and when he dug up the box of coins, they attacked, bound him so that he could hardly breathe and left him to the tender mercy of the fire that they had set. They hoped the conflagration would destroy the evidence of their evil. They had a coach waiting and set off with the strongbox. That much was seen."

Sir Gilbert raised an eye, quickly searching the constable's features.

"And were they thus identified?"

"When the young man came here asking directions, he was told the way by Master Burton," Master Drew went on, avoiding the question.

"Master Burton? My manservant?"

"Where is Master Burton?"

Sir Gilbert frowned.

"He set out this morning in my coach with some papers bound for Winchester."

"And with the chest of money?"

"If he is involved in such a business, have no fear. I will question the rogue and he shall be punished. You may leave it in my hands."

Master Drew smiled and shook his head.

"Not in your hands, I am afraid, Sir Gilbert. Master Burton had an accomplice."

"And do you name him?" Sir Gilbert's jaw tightened.

"You were that accomplice."

"You cannot prove it."

"Perhaps not. But you revealed yourself earlier when I was asking you about the ownership of the house and spoke of the body found there. I had not mentioned anything about it or the possibility of its Spanish identification – yet you said to me that the burning of a house and murder of a foreigner was not to be wondered at in this city. How would you know that the body found was that of a foreigner unless you shared Master Burton's secret?"

Sir Gilbert's eyes narrowed.

"You are clever, Master Drew, and with the tongue of a serpent. But when all is said and done, I am an Englishman with good connections, and the young man was a foreigner and a Spaniard at that."

"The war is over, Sir Gilbert, or will be when this treaty is signed."

"My answer to any charge will be that I was retrieving what is rightfully the property of the Bishops of Winchester from theft by a foreigner. I shall say that he tried to make away with this treasure and Master Burton and I prevented him and reclaimed it for its true owner."

Master Drew paused and nodded thoughtfully.

"It is, perhaps, a good defence. But there is one aspect that may not sit well with such a plea; that is, the Chevalier Stefano Jardiniero y Barbastro was a member of the delegation currently negotiating the treaty. True, he was but a secretary within the delegation, and there are arguments to be made on both sides as to whether the treasure to which he had been directed was his family's property or whether subsequent Bishops of Winchester had a right to it. And, of course, we will have to ascertain whether Master Burton has gone directly with the chest to the Bishop of Winchester or whether he may have cause to rest with it awhile in your own manor at Winchester Town.

"And, even when these arguments are all set in place, it will come down to a simple matter of policy. How badly do the Lord Chancellor and His Majesty desire this treaty ending the twenty years of war with Spain? The Spanish ambassadors may seek to be compensated for the murder of one of their number before agreement can be reached."

* * *

It was at the end of August of that year of 1604 that the treaty of peace and perpetual alliance between England and Spain was finally signed in Somerset House. Two weeks before the agreement, a certain Master Burton was taken from Newgate in a tumbrel to Tyburn Tree and hanged. A year later a prisoner in the Clink caught typhoid, in spite of the payments he had been able to give the jailer to secure good quarters for himself during his incarceration. He was dead within three days. It was common gossip in the prison that he had once been a man of some status and influence and had even dwelt in the grand palace of the Bishop of Winchester, adjacent to the prison.

BIG GUY

Paul Johnston

So I'm on the train back from Oxford, where I've been signing copies of my latest novel. The staff in Blackwell's and Waterstones were about as interested as Hollywood producers are in actresses over fifty, so it didn't take long. Then again, the seventh in my series featuring the maverick, eighteen-stone muscleman Storm Waters (yes, unaccountably, I like Pink Floyd) got only one review in the national press and that was less than complimentary: "Andy Stewart's Waters series is about as lively as a dried-up lake these days. Give us a break, mate – preferably terminal." And I bought the tosser a ludicrously overpriced drink at the Taunton Crime'n'Cider Fest last summer.

I peer through the rain and make out the stained concrete cooling towers at Didcot. Already the honeyed walls of my alma mater seem leagues away. Ha! Like I went to Oxford. It was the university of life for me – left school at sixteen with no GCSEs, worked in various burger bars for more years than I can remember, wrote unsolicited album reviews until one (of Bowie's *Reality* – think hatchet) finally got picked up by an ever-so-cool (they thought) monthly, worked behind the bar at far too many music festivals, drank a lot, smoked even more etc., etc. But I also read, widely and carefully. I did my research, I calculated what sold. And then I wrote the first Storm novel. You know the clichéd advice, "Write what you know"? Screw that. I'm five foot five in my DMs and have never been over nine stone, even when I binged on burgers and beer. I used my imagination and uncaged the big guy – ex-Royal Marine, ex-SBS, now freelance fist-for-hire, Storm Waters. He takes the fight to the bad men and saves the world. Frequently. Kind of James Bond with bigger abs and biceps, plus a much bigger weapon or three. Naturally, the women go wet for him. More surprisingly, they've gone for me too. I've had publicity girls, editors, bookshop managers, journos, TV interviewers and even a supermodel (admittedly well past her prime) in my pants. Then there are the fans. Don't, whatever you do, get me started on my fans...

I'm reading a film mag and listening to Radiohead on my iPod when I realize something's going on further down the carriage. It's one of those crappy trains where the first-class section is small and only for City wankers. Besides, I like to go steerage. It keeps me in touch with my readers though, disappointingly, I've seen no one reading a Storm novel all day. Anyway, from the way the white-haired ticket collector's head is going back and forward, it's obvious he's having a go at a passenger. I unplug and listen in.

"That's only a single," he's saying. "You'll have to pay full price to cover your return journey."

The punter, a young guy with unwashed hair and a scabby leather jacket, starts mouthing off, not too loudly. I still catch several F-words. So do other passengers in the vicinity. One of them's a well-dressed old woman with blue hair.

"Do you mind?" she says, in a voice that could cut crystal from long range. "Some of us don't appreciate that kind of language."

Leather Jacket ignores her and keeps unloading on the ticket collector, whose cheeks have gone what I think is puce – I've never been much good at anything other than the basic colours. Maybe that's why I'm a noir writer.

"If you don't pay, I'll have to issue a penalty notice and put you off the train at Reading," the official says. There are beads of sweat on his forehead and suddenly he looks well past retirement age.

The kid doesn't care, he just keeps on fucking and buggering, his head down. I wonder if he's ingested illicit pharmaceuticals. Or maybe he's a diabetic having a hypo. Someone should take a look at him.

Blue Perm's on her feet now, having a good old rant. Three or four other passengers have joined her, surrounding Leather Jacket like a lynch mob. The sun comes through the clouds and I can see spittle flying from their lips.

I ask myself what Storm would have done. Probably grabbed the offender by the ankles, held him upside down and shaken him till the money for his fare fell out of his pockets. That's not an option I have. Although Leather Jacket's skinny, he's at least six inches taller than me. So I decide to play peacemaker.

"Excuse me," I say, from behind the ticket collector. "I'll pay his fare."

That makes them look round. The offender is the only one paying no attention, his chin resting on his chest as he keeps on spouting semi-audible abuse.

"You can't do that," Blue Perm says, the powder on her face shifting like snow before an avalanche.

"Yes, I can." I wave a twenty-quid note under her nose, then offer it to the official. "Keep the change..." I peer at the badge on his jacket "...Ken Burns, Customer Services Specialist."

It would have been the smile that did it. I've been told about it often enough, usually by women after the main event. Apparently it makes me look patronizing, arrogant, rude, vicious and self-obsessed, maybe all at the same time. Anyway, I'd successfully got everyone in the vicinity's goat. Except the kid's. At last he's quiet, maybe even asleep. Or has he passed out?

"The lady's right, sir," Ken says, pronouncing the last word with maximum disrespect. "Passengers are obliged to have a valid ticket on their person for all parts of their journey."

"Come on," I say. "I'm giving you the money for him." I look at Leather Jacket. He seems to be breathing regularly and his colour is normal. Probably stoned. "Just print out a ticket and we'll get back to minding our own business." I give Blue Perm a death stare.

"I hardly think you're minding your own business," she says, turning to her friend, Purple Furze, with a tight, triumphant smile.

With hindsight I shouldn't have stuck my tongue out at her, but it was the only way I could avoid upending a tanker-load of Storm Waters's notoriously esoteric vocabulary of abuse over her. I follow up with a pair of raised middle fingers that may have got a bit close to her nostrils.

Both Blue and Purple give strangled squawks of consternation, the former grabbing the Customer Services Specialist's sleeve with a vein-corded claw.

"That's it," he says. "I'm calling the Transport Police."

Then I hear my hero's voice.

"Is there a problem here?"

Everyone looks at the big guy – six foot four at least and built like Arnie before he did his Reagan act. He's got crew-cut blond hair and is wearing a green combat jacket. Storm Waters in the flesh! Am I dreaming? Did someone sprinkle hash over my Bran Flakes this morning? I feel a stupid smile spread over my face.

"This…man insulted me," Blue Perm says. Nothing about Leather Jacket, who's now snoring peacefully. "He…he…"

"Flipped you the bird in stereo," says Purple Furze, in an American accent.

Storm runs a disparaging eye – actually, two – over me. "We can't be having that, can we?" he says, in a voice with the same mixture of Cockney and parade ground as my man's. He grabs my shoulder and turns to the smirking official. "No ticket, eh?" He plucks the twenty quid from my hand and gives it to Ken. "That's no reason to cause trouble, sonny." He pushes me towards the end of the carriage.

I would have pointed out that I'm thirty-seven, but I'm struggling to keep up with his rapid pace. Plus the grip on my shoulder is vice-like.

"I…I write books," I say, trying to take the sting from the situation. "You're…you're in them."

The big guy stares at me as if I'm what pond life excretes. "Books? What do you mean, I'm in them?"

"Storm Waters," I say. "Ex-Marine, ex—"

"I've read one of those," he says, tightening his grip even more. "Or rather, a bit of one. Fucking shite, mate." He leans closer. "And I should know. I was in the SBS."

That's all we say. When the train comes into Reading, he frog-marches me to the doors. Ken's there, but the coloured-hair ladies are keeping their distance. Leather Jacket's still asleep.

"Easy to trip when you get off these trains, isn't it?" Storm says.

Less puce now, Ken smiles. "See it all the time."

The doors open and I go flying.

I wake up in hospital – a broken shoulder, three cracked ribs and severe concussion. I never find out what happened to Leather Jacket, but I'm not betting that Ken Burns, Customer Services Specialist Masturbator, used my money for his ticket. I could have set my lawyer after the big guy, but I believe in learning from experience.

Storm Waters – he's history. My new hero's a baronet with a monocle, and his mother has a blue rinse.

THE CONSPIRATORS

Christopher Fowler

A T THE NEXT table of the hotel restaurant, three waiters took their places beside the diners, and, with a synchronized flourish, raised the silver covers on their salvers. A fourth appeared, bearing a tray containing a quartet of tiny copper pots. Each waiter took a handle and proceeded to pour the sauces from the pots on to the salvers from a height of not less than eighteen inches. They might have been tipping jewels into coffers.

Court and Lassiter barely bothered to break off their conversation and look up at the display. They knew that these ostentatious rituals were the hotel's way of justifying the risible menu prices to tourists.

The waiters finished serving and tiptoed away, leaving the diners to warble and coo over their miniscule meals, some kind of cubed chicken in cream. The restaurant was designed with plenty of steel, glass and black crystal, with the occasional tortured twist of green bamboo providing natural colour. It was as hushed as a funeral parlour. Everyone seemed to be whispering.

Sean Lassiter had ordered a steak, medium rare, the only item on the menu that looked like meat. He had eaten it as if he was in an American diner, using only a fork. The steaks were so tender you could do that here.

"When was the last time you knew exactly what you wanted?" he asked Court, raising his whisky tumbler and studying his former business partner through the diamond-cut lattice.

Oliver Court's palms were dry, but he still pressed them against his thighs. Lassiter had once been his mentor, and was the only man in the world who could make him uncomfortable with a simple question.

"Come on, Oliver, I saw the look in your eyes the first day I met you. Nowadays I can't read them because you're wearing coloured contacts. I remember, you were so hungry and envious I thought you might actually start taking notes during our meal. I see that look a lot, but it's not usually so obvious. When members of my staff get that anxious, it usually means they're frightened of failure and they're scared of being found out. Well, I can't blame anyone for wanting to make the best of themselves. But you were prepared to leave behind an awful lot in order to be a success."

It was a gentle rebuke, but a rebuke nonetheless. Lassiter was old school; his compliments were backhanded and his criticisms were constructive. He knew the difference between perspicacity and merely being rude. For a businessman who had been on the road for the past forty years, he was immaculately groomed. His hair was sleek and white, his tan subtle, his suit quietly extravagant.

He's heard something about me, thought Court, shifting carefully on his chromium chair, which was too low. The central column of the table prevented him from stretching out his long legs.

"Have you got where you wanted to be?"

Court did not trust himself to tell the truth. From here he could see out through the curvilinear glass of the restaurant. In front of the hotel, trucks drove back and forth along the spotlit spit of land that projected into the blackness of the Persian Gulf. The Indian workers toiled around the clock in shifts, building ever further out into the sea.

They had kept the conversation light while they ate. Families, schools, colleagues, holidays, topics suitable for food. The serious part required a clear table and strong drinks.

There was only one other drinker at the bar, a nylon-haired brunette with long legs, a tiny waist and perfectly circular breasts, like a character from a video game. The décolletage of her tight black dress was cut to the aureoles of her nipples. Lassiter assumed she kept herself more carefully covered beyond the confines of the hotel. They were in the Middle East, after all. Seamed stockings, high heels, a brassiere that must have presented an engineering challenge, she was about twenty-three years old and blatantly selling herself. He wondered what the young Arabic barman thought of her.

Court caught him thoughtfully studying the call-girl's legs. "How long have you known me, Sean?" he asked, buying time.

"Long enough to see where you're going." Lassiter smiled. He'd had his teeth bleached. They shone peppermint white in the black light from the bar, and made him look like a game-show host. He noticed Court following his eyes to the girl. "It's just an honest question."

In truth, Lassiter had been disappointed by his apprentice. Court needed the approval of others, and as a consequence, his ambitions were displayed for all to see. He never took advice, so why was he here? Somewhere deep inside Lassiter an alarm bell rang.

Court knew he could not be completely honest, because there was too much at stake. "I think I've been pretty successful," he answered carefully. "There's still a way to go. That's why I value your advice."

Lassiter looked almost relieved. Perhaps he didn't want to have an argument with his former pupil. "Your division is doing very nicely, Oliver. You're about to expand it, you wouldn't be human if you didn't feel a little nervous. From what I hear, my directors will back you, but in these uncertain times you'll need to detail your long-term plans. Just don't be too eager. The English don't trust people who are anxious to please. It puts them off. They want negotiations to be tricky enough for their colleagues to see how hard they work."

"I can't remember a time when I didn't look up to you," said Court, catching the waitress's eye and sewing the air with his right hand, the universal sign for *check, please*. "You've always been my— "

"Don't say mentor, Oliver, it makes me feel positively ancient."

"I was going to say friend. I feel I can tell you anything and I'll always get a straight answer."

"So long as it works both ways."

"You don't have to ask that. I was still just a property agent when you gave me a job. Now I run the whole of the US division. I'd appreciate it if you could cast an eye over my proposals, just to get your feedback." Despite the difference in their ages, they were now almost evenly matched in terms of their careers within the company. Lassiter still gave the hotel chain class and respectability. Many considered Court to be an upstart, but he had made North America profitable again by building flashy boutique hotels aimed at kids with money.

Lassiter smiled at his glass, twisting it. "It would be my pleasure, you know that." Court was offering to show him his plans ahead of the directors' meeting? He'd want something in return, but what, and how badly?

Lassiter looked around at the empty bar, the midnight-blue carpet, the silver walls, the glittering star-points of light in the ceiling. He wondered if this was what Heaven looked like, without a bill at the end of the evening.

"Excuse me for a moment." Court rose from his chair and went to say something to the girl. After the exchange, she followed him back to join the table. "This is my friend Sean Lassiter," he said, introducing her.

"Hi, I'm Vienna." She tossed her hair back in a movement designed to help her avoid bothering with eye contact. She was American, he supposed, or had been taught English by one. "Look at this place. The Jews and Arabs agree so completely on soft furnishings, you'd think they could work everything else out from that." She had as much confidence as either of them, but Court knew that if they ignored her, she would drop out of the conversation. She was a professional. She had brought her own drink with her.

"Mr Lassiter here owns the hotel."

That wiped the smile from her face. "Is that true?" she asked, lowering her glass. Court could tell she was racking her brains to recall the name.

"Well, I'm the managing director of the consortium that owns it," said Lassiter, managing to make the role sound unimportant.

"He's being modest," said Court, "he owns the entire chain."

If Vienna was impressed, she was too smart to show it. Her deal was with the maître d'. She only cared about her direct contacts. "Is it owned by the Americans?"

"No, it's mainly Indian and Russian money."

"They charge non-guests an entrance fee just to look around the lobby of this hotel," she said, "but I guess you know that."

"I don't suppose that affects you." It seemed that, having made the effort to talk to the girl, Lassiter was happier talking to Court. "You're not staying at the Burj Al Arab, Oliver?"

"Even I can't justify that kind of expense. Besides, loyalty dictates that I stay here. I suppose you've got a suite."

"Penthouse sea-facing corner, but not the royal suite," said Lassiter. "That's reserved for heads of state."

"I heard quite a few of the rooms are empty." The Middle East was part of Lassiter's domain.

"It's not just here. There's been a lot of over-construction. Look out of the window along the coastline. Everyone's been affected by the bad publicity lately, those stories of raw sewage being pumped into the sea, but it doesn't stop them from building."

"You're not worried enough to reduce the cost of a room yet," Court added. "So, do we get to see your view?"

He wants to bring the girl, Lassiter thought in some surprise, *how will this work out?* "Sure, if you want."

Court paid without checking the total and stood up, placing his hand in the valley of Vienna's back. This small gesture was enough to seal the deal. She showed no reaction as she rose and left with them, the light from the neon bar-sign casting a crimson stripe across her neck that appeared to sever it.

"At these prices I thought you'd have your own elevator," Court needled gently.

"Only the royal apartment has that. For security purposes." Lassiter stabbed at the illuminated gold lift-button. "We need to invent something better than first class. The whole concept of privilege has become debased."

"I read somewhere that you need to earn six million per annum to live like a millionaire these days," said Vienna.

Court watched his boss against the dark golden glass of the elevator. Lassiter had started to put on the kind of weight he would never be able to shift. His new suit was already becoming too tight.

He was in his mid-sixties but showed no desire to stop working or even slow down. *Sharks drown if they stop swimming,* Court thought. *The only way he'll stop is if he dies. I'm surprised Elizabeth still puts up with it.*

He wondered if Lassiter went around telling people how he'd given Court a start in the hotel business. Mentors had a habit of doing that.

"Welcome to my world," said Lassiter without any obvious hint of irony as he held open the door for Vienna. The suite displayed all the accoutrements of wealth without any of the concomitant taste. A curved bar was lined with gold-leaf piping that rose to enclose a range of vintage whisky bottles presented on sheets of underlit crimson glass, like items of baroque jewellery.

"Want to try the whisky?"

"I'm staying with vodka."

Vienna watched until her own drink had been poured, then went to the bathroom.

"She's very beautiful," Lassiter conceded.

"She doesn't have to be here if she doesn't want to," said Court. "She's with your hotel, which presumably means she has quality control."

Lassiter walked to the glass wall and looked down to the beach. Spotlights picked out the tall wavering palms that had been transported fully grown and impatiently planted into the unfinished esplanade. The crystal blackness reflected every glittering pinpoint in the apartment, creating a second starscape above the sea. There was no natural sound audible in the suite, only the faint but steady hiss of cold ionized air pumped up through the ventilation system, and the settling chink of perfectly cubed ice on glass.

"Allow me," said Court, pouring a heavy measure of Scotch. "It's a nice view. Although I don't like to look at the sea. I'd prefer to be surrounded by buildings. City boy at heart."

Lassiter accepted the proffered drink and downed it in one. He had been drinking hard all evening. The New Business Model Seminar was so stultifying that everyone had been pushing their upper alcohol limits for the past three days, and there was still another day to go.

"Did you learn anything at all today?" Lassiter asked. "Spare me all those speakers from the Far East with their strangled English and aching politeness. Did you actually get anything out of it?"

"No, but I didn't expect to."

They studied the view. Lassiter pressed his chilled tumbler against his forehead. "Look at it. There's no one out there and nothing to see. You could be in Monte Carlo, Geneva or Madrid. That's the beauty of our European hotels, Oliver. Whichever one you use, there you are, home and safe again. Sometimes I wake up and have no idea where I am. And it doesn't matter."

"How's the seminar working out for you?"

"I'll go home four days nearer to my death with a sun-reddened face and a portfolio full of brochures my PA will eventually tip into the bin."

"It's not like you to be a cynic," Court observed. "I remember when you first saw potential in me, the things you taught me, all that practical advice and optimism for the future."

"I'm afraid my hopes atrophied somewhat when our so-called first-world society decided to hand over the reins of financial responsibility to a bunch of cowboy bankers." He drained his glass, the ice clinking against his white teeth. "I'm old enough to remember when selling was a challenge. These days I feel like a nurse spoon-feeding paralysed patients. Christ, I want to start smoking again, but these rooms are alarmed. Pour me another, will you?"

Court headed back to the bar. He picked up a matchbook, crested and labelled "Royal Persian Hotel, Dubai" and slipped it into his pocket. "How come there are no cameras in the corridors?" he wondered aloud.

"The Arabs are like the Swiss when it comes to issues of privacy. The rich need to treat each other in an adult manner because there are so many dirty secrets to keep tucked away."

Court was not familiar with this reflective side of Lassiter. The man who had elevated as many careers as he had destroyed was going soft. Men became vulnerable to strange fancies when they felt their sexual powers waning.

"The most powerful religious leaders emerge from desert states, have you noticed?" Lassiter mused. "Whereas political leaders nurture their theories in cities. One thinks of Pol Pot's agrarian revolution being discussed in smoky Parisian cafés. In my darkest nightmares I imagined a new business model, one where morals and decent behaviour are considered detrimental, where only grabbing the next million in the next hour commands any respect at all. And at some point – I'm not sure when – my nightmare became real. This is what we do, Oliver, and we all collude in the process. The definition of a conspiracy is the combination of any number of people in surreptitious agreement to commit a secret, unlawful, evil and wrongful act. Think about what we do and ask yourself if you really want to join the next level."

He's lost it, thought Oliver. *The great Sean Lassiter is stepping out of the ring to watch sunsets and talk hippy-dippy shit. This is too good to be true.*

"You've made your money, Sean. If you feel like this, why don't you just sell up?"

Lassiter regarded him from beneath hooded eyelids. "There's no one I trust enough. You want to know if that includes you. I groomed you, I knew what would happen. Give someone the benefit of your experience for long enough, and it stands to reason they'll eventually try to buy the company out from under you. I never held your success against you, Oliver."

"That's because your own success always remained greater. It's easy to be magnanimous when you're at the top. What if I really wanted to buy the company now?"

There it is, thought Lassiter, *the real purpose of dinner.* "I wondered when you would finally ask."

"You don't think I'd look after the staff."

"My people? I replace them like batteries." Lassiter looked towards the bathroom door. The girl seemed to be taking a long time.

"Then why not sell to me?" Court walked over to the balcony and unlocked the doors, rolling them silently back. The cool night air was a relief after the chemically conditioned atmosphere. "Hey, we can smoke out here. Doors and windows you can open forty floors up, they'd never allow this at home." He laughed, patting his pockets.

With one last glance back at the bathroom, Lassiter joined him on the balcony. He leaned over the edge and looked down. "You're right, there's hardly a light on in the entire building. We should be renegotiating the prices of the suites. Europe holds too many festivals and seminars at this time of the year. Half the salesmen in America leave home in March and don't get back until their house-plants are dead."

"Your profits are down, and I've heard the next quarter will be even worse."

"Maybe we did expand Europe too quickly. When a wolf is sick, the others decide what to do; whether you live or die depends on how important you are to the pack. You think we're going lame, one of the pack lagging behind?" He sighed wearily. "Are you going to bite me on the leg and drag me into the bushes? Why not... it's what I would have done."

The only sign of life came from the headlights of the gravel trucks swerving past each other in the distance, like tin toys on a track. Their thin bright beams shone into total blackness. Back along the coastline, a line of steel towers glowed through the sea-mist like a phantom stockade.

Court realized that to get an answer he would have to give one. "You asked me what do I want?" he repeated. "I want to reach the top of my profession."

"That's not a desire, it's an instinct, like releasing air from a diving tank." Given the amount he had drunk, Lassiter surprised himself with the analogy. It was true; his career was as lonely and claustrophobic as being under the sea.

"All right. Then I desire respect."

Lassiter turned to study him. "Surely you have that already. Don't you?" From the way he said it, Lassiter made it clear that Court had yet to earn it from his teacher.

"I suppose so. In that case, I don't know. That's the answer to your question; I really don't know."

"Fair enough. I suppose that's more honest than saying you want our hotels to be the finest in the world. You're still only in your thirties—"

"Thirty-four."

"You have time on your side. Now I suppose you want an answer to your question." Lassiter lit the proffered cigar and drew hard on it. "I can't sell you the company, Oliver."

"Why not?"

"It would be too obvious."

"What do you mean?"

"It's what you want. I can always tell what you're going to do next. You're positively metronomic in your habits. I can see inside your head, which means that from a business point of view I can always out-think you. And if I can, others will. That's not good."

"It's because I learned everything from you. You'll always be the one person who knows exactly what I think. You'll always outguess me."

The ocean air should have started sobering him up, but it was having the opposite effect. Lassiter struggled to understand what Court was saying to him. The air was completely still, and there was no sound. Even the distant trucks moved past each other in silence. If his wife were here he knew she would appreciate the beauty of the night, but she was asleep in London. It was late and he was still wearing his business suit, and polished black shoes that pinched.

"You know the story of the Caliph of Jaipur?" asked Court, draining his glass and setting it down on the balcony table. "He hired the finest painter in the land to create a fresco of heavenly angels for the walls of his harem. When it was finished, he asked the artisan if it really was the best fresco in all the kingdom. The painter told him that there was no finer artwork to be found beneath the horizons, nor would there ever be again until someone else could afford his services. So the Sultan had him beheaded."

Lassiter looked at him blearily. Only the whites of Court's eyes showed in the jet night, and then they were gone. A streak of silver sparkled in the ocean like a flash of static electricity, the signature of the moon. He felt tired and looked for a place to sit, but Court was crouching beside him. When he rose, he was holding Lassiter's right ankle. Court stood taller and taller, rising higher and higher, until Lassiter realized he could no longer remain upright. "You're not drunk," he said absurdly.

"I don't drink whisky." Court raised his old friend's ankle higher, until pain shot through Lassiter's thigh muscles.

"Vodka—"

"Because it looks like water. Sure you don't want to sell?"

"Over my dead body."

Court shrugged his shoulders. "That was the general idea." With both his hands clasped beneath Lassiter's foot Court leaned back suddenly, like a Scotsman tossing a caber, raising his arms smartly so that Lassiter lost his battle with gravity and found himself lifted cleanly into the air, over the barrier of the balcony. His mouth opened in shock, but only the smallest sound emerged. His fingers grasped at the air beyond the low rail, too late, and he tumbled silently down, past the empty dark floors. The first part of the fall seemed to last for ever, as if he were wheeling through the night in slow motion, like a firework that had failed to ignite, or a spaceman with a cut cord.

But then he hit his head on the concrete lip of the thirtieth balcony, and this sent him spinning madly out of orbit. His head turned from white to black, leaving a matching stain on the building wall. His leg hit another ledge, his arm another, his head again, his arm, his leg, until there was hardly a bone in his body left unbroken – and that was long before he hit the ground.

Court stepped back into the room. "You might want to come out now," he called. "We're alone." He heard running water stop.

The bathroom door was padded crimson with gold studs. It opened cautiously. Vienna emerged with her make-up refreshed, like a meticulously restored painting. She took in the suite, three glasses, one occupant less, an open balcony door, and decided to say nothing. Had she an inkling of what had just happened? Her face was a mask. Court's decision to act had been spontaneous. He knew she could not have seen anything, and Lassiter had made no noise. He doubted that she cared anyway. It was not her job to care. She worked in a service industry.

"My colleague had to leave. Thanks for coming up," said Court, feeling inside his jacket. He unclipped her handbag and dropped in a roll of banknotes. "Maybe we'll see each other again."

"I'd like that." Vienna's smile was unreadable. She turned and walked to the door, seemingly aware of exactly how many steps it would take. "You know where to find me."

And she was gone.

Court closed the window and rinsed the glasses, placing them back on the bar shelf. He had left no other mark in the suite. Letting himself out, he padded along the corridor and caught the elevator to his own room. He had paid the girl too much, but would not have been able to get Lassiter back to his suite without her. Everyone knew that even though the old man loved his wife, he still needed to prove himself with the ladies.

He would heed his mentor's advice and not suggest the buyout immediately; that would be crass. There were plenty of other preparations he could be making while the company came to terms with Lassiter's death. It would be interesting to see how long they could keep it out of the news.

Before the last day of the conference began, he took a stroll outside. The sky was a painful deep blue, sharper than knives. The pavements had been hosed down, and were already nearly dry. He circled the hotel but found no sign of any disturbance. Shielding his eyes, he squinted up at the balconies, trying to spot where Lassiter had hit the building, but realized that he was standing beneath the ledges, and would not be able to see anything.

The day dragged past in parades of PowerPoint bar charts, each more candy-coloured than the last, as if their radiance could make up for their dullness. At lunchtime he saw two men who looked like plainclothes police. They were standing motionless in the reception area, in mirror shades and shiny blue suits. By the time afternoon tea was served, even Lassiter's reservation had disappeared from the records. Clearly, the hotel's reputation was more important than its founder's demise. *The things we create outgrow us*, thought Court, shutting down his laptop. *One day you own the company, the next even your PA can't remember you. I thought*

*there would be repercussions. I guess Sean was right. It's all part
of the new business model.*

Two weeks later, Court found himself at Domodedovo Airport in
Moscow. He always seemed to be holding meetings in departure
lounges. In the business-class bar he had bumped into an old English
friend, a nervy, sticklike redhead called Amanda, and had invited her to
join him. Watching snow fall on airfields from behind picture windows
always had a calming effect on him. Amanda was a seasoned executive
with half a dozen personal communication devices in her briefcase and
no hint of a private life. She told him she was going to try internet
dating when she finally settled in one city long enough to do so.

"I was wondering what you thought about Sean Lassiter," she
said, slowly emptying another miniature bottle of Tanqueray into
her glass. "There's a rumour going around that Elizabeth was about
to leave him."

Court had no idea. Suddenly the lack of publicity surrounding the
death made sense. "I heard something to that effect," he said.

"They hadn't been sleeping together for years," she told him
knowledgeably. "I was reading an article in the *Economist* about
the similarities between successful businessmen and serial killers.
They share the same lack of compassion, the same selfishness and
determination to succeed. They exploit the flaws of their opponents,
and lose their ability to judge on moral grounds."

For a crazy moment he wondered if she had heard another, darker
rumour, but decided it was impossible. The buyout had only been
discussed with a handful of board members. It would not be made
public until after it was successful.

"I guess you're going on to St Petersburg," she said. "Where are
you staying?"

"The Grand Sovetskaya. How about you?"

"Oh, nothing so fancy. That was one of Sean's personal favourites,
wasn't it?"

"Well, it's part of the chain."

"I slept with him, you know. Our flights were cancelled and we
were stuck at the Espacio Rojo Hotel in Barcelona. I was really

sorry to hear he died. Or was it the Severine in Paris? They have this fabulous spa treatment where they wrap you in oil-soaked gauze and place hot stones down your spine…"

He listened without hearing. The image of the old man pumping away on top of poor bony Amanda while whispering sales figures in her ears was best left behind in the departure lounge.

The Grand Sovetskaya was an unashamedly old-world hotel in the French style, with green copper gables and crouching gargoyles. In the domed reception area hung a crystal chandelier the size of a skip. The rooms were filled with dark wooden dressers, sideboards and wardrobes, and were locked with huge brass keys. There were twenty-one floors of corridors that smelled of furniture polish and boiled cabbage, all identical and gently curved, like those of an ocean liner. Thick floral carpets and heavily lined drapes deadened all sound.

Best of all was the bar, a paradise for the serious drinker. The shelves were stacked with dozens of flavoured vodkas and an immense range of mysterious liquors, vaguely medicinal in appearance. Court suspected that the elderly hatchet-faced bar staff had arrived with the first guests. Heavy marble ashtrays lined the counter. This was clearly no place for lightweights.

Court was there to conclude the discreet negotiations with Lassiter's board, but if anyone asked, he was attending a forum staged by the Opportunities In New Business Development Commission. Discretion was second nature to him. He spent most of his life in hotels as quiet as libraries where the patrons were defined by the depth of their expense accounts. Lighting a cigar, he thought about Lassiter turning over and over in the warm night air, a tiny flailing puppet whose existence had been erased almost before he hit the concrete. How many Indian workers had been employed to scrub the blood from the stones before another harsh dawn flooded the hotel with sunlight? Had the manager posted Lassiter's luggage back to his grieving wife? Had Elizabeth pored over the spreadsheets, graphs and overlays, hopelessly looking for answers?

He felt no guilt. Lassiter's downward spiral had begun before Dubai. Court had saved him the incremental degradation a man feels when he realizes the company he has founded no longer needs or desires his advice. He waved aside the blue haze of cigar smoke and studied Vienna. She was seated in a red-leather horseshoe banquette between two short bald oligarchs. When she saw him looking, she momentarily forgot what she was saying. Her eyes lingered a moment too long.

Clearly, she was good at her job if she was travelling to international clients. For a second it crossed his mind that they might make an interesting team, but he knew that the best call-girls stayed at the peak of their trade by giving nothing of themselves to others. Even so...

It would have been unprofessional to send her any kind of message while she was working, so he smoked and waited, and treated himself to a golden Comte de Lauvia 1982 Armagnac. The Russians here were loud and unsophisticated, but Vienna never appeared bored. After an hour they were clearly drunk. Court had no idea what she said to them, but they suddenly fell into a sombre mood and rose together, bidding her goodnight.

She came over to him with her shoes in one hand, and he realized how much they added to her height. "However long your evening has been," she told him, taking a sip of his brandy, "I promise you, mine was longer." She licked her lips appreciatively and allowed her head to fall back against the red leather seat. "Mmm. Can I get one of those?"

The waiter appeared without being summoned, delivered and departed. She seemed content to drink and drift without making small talk. She wore another low-cut black dress, and a single strand of pearls. Her perfume had faded enough to allow a natural womanly odour, faint but arousing, to rise from her peach-coloured skin.

He relit his cigar and watched her, wondering how much she remembered of their last meeting. The bar was almost empty. It was 2.15 in the morning. "How long are you staying here?" he asked.

"Two nights. I'm entertaining those guys."

"They must be important."

"To someone. Not to me. It's a job."

"They left without you."

"I sent them away." She took the cigar from his fingers and smoked it for a minute.

"I'm here for— "

"I don't want to know why you're here." She studied the glowing tip of the cigar. "I'm sure you get tired of talking shop. I do."

"So, Vienna, what would you rather do?"

She turned her eyes to his. Her pupils were violet, the lashes long and black. "Shall I tell you what I would really like to do?"

He gave no response, but waited with a small catch in his breath.

"I would like to fall asleep in a great big soft bed with my head on your chest."

"We can do that." Then he remembered. "Wait, they screwed up my reservation. I have two singles. We can push them together."

"Thanks, but no thanks."

"Well, where are you staying?"

She held up the key. It was the first time he had seen a genuine smile on her lips. "I have the royal suite."

Now he was impressed. "How did you get that?"

"How do you think?"

They made their way to the twenty-first floor. As they followed the curve of the passage, Vienna entwined her fingers in his. *I don't have to tell this woman anything*, he thought, *she and I are the same kind*.

When she unlocked the door at the end of the corridor and turned on the lights, he was disappointed to see that except for an extra pair of curtains covering the end wall, the room was almost identical to his. It was unbearably hot. He removed his suit jacket, threw it on the couch and loosened his tie.

"Make me a drink,'" she told him, "I'll be back." She headed for the bathroom. Something made him uncomfortable. He heard the bathroom door shut, then silence. He poured two whiskies at the wet bar and thought for a moment. It was exactly what she had done in Dubai.

No, it wasn't.

Then she had waited until she had seen her own drink poured. Call-girls always did that, just to be careful.

She wasn't going to drink anything. Then why had she asked him to make her a drink?

"Vienna?" He knocked on the bathroom door, but there was silence beyond. He placed his ear against the wood and listened. Nothing.

The room was spectacularly hot. Vienna was obviously missing Dubai. There didn't seem to be a thermostat anywhere. Then he remembered; his was in the bathroom. "Vienna," he called, "turn the heat down, will you?"

The floor tipped, just a little, but enough for him to realize what had happened. He headed back to the bar and examined his drained whisky tumbler. There was some kind of white residue in the bottom of it. Sweat was starting to pour between his shoulder blades. The front of his shirt was darkening around his armpits and in the middle of his chest.

The carpet seemed to be pulling away beneath his feet. He needed cold air, fast. He reached the end window and pulled back the curtains, but there was just more wall behind them.

The big French windows were in the same place as the ones in his room. He lurched across to them and tried the right handle. It turned easily. He pulled the glass door towards him and a blast of sub-zero air filled the room. It was snowing hard. Almost instantly he began to sober up. He tried to think.

Stepping on to the balcony, he breathed in the stinging winter air, filling his lungs with ice. Fat white flakes settled on his eyelids, in his ears. His head was clearing fast but his reactions were still slow.

Too slow to stop the door from being shut behind him. Vienna was standing beyond the glass. She studied him blankly, as if watching an animal at the zoo. Her right arm was raised, her hand against the wall. She was pressing something. She wiggled the fingers of her left hand slightly, waving goodbye.

The steel shutter that fitted tightly over the windows was swiftly closing. He tried to seize its edge with his fingers, to push it back up, but it was so cold that the flesh of his fingertips, still wet from his whisky glass, stuck to the metal, pulling him down.

And then it was shut. He tore his fingers free, leaving behind four small scarlet patches of skin. The sweat on his back was already turning to ice. He hammered on the steel shutter, but was shocked by its thickness. It barely rattled. Old French-style hotels always sported European shutters. He moved around the edges of the metre-wide balcony. A sheer drop down, no lights on anywhere. The rooms on either side had bricked-up windows.

The bitter wind had risen to a howl. He was in his shirtsleeves, and knew he had but a short time to live. He had been drinking all evening; his blood was thin. He fell to the floor of the balcony and pushed himself into the wall, but the ice and snow still blew through the balustrade, settling over him.

His first instinct was to assume he had been subjected to a woman's revenge. Then he remembered she was merely an employee.

He tried to laugh when he understood what had happened, but the saliva was freezing in his mouth. Even his eyes were becoming hard to move. He fancied he could hear the ice forming beneath his skin. Tiny crackles like rustling cellophane filled his ears.

Staring out into the night beyond the balcony, the darkness was sprinkled with swirling white flakes that looked like stars. He could have been anywhere in the world.

They'll leave the shutters down for twenty-four hours, he thought, *just to be absolutely sure. Vienna will be back on a Dubai beach by then.*

His mind was growing numb. He remembered something from a history book he had once read. When the Persian matriarchs wanted to rid themselves of the most treacherous family members, they locked them away in sumptuous apartments and left them to die. From a business point of view, it made perfect sense to do so. He should have put forward the idea as part of his new business model, but, just as Lassiter had warned, someone else had thought of it first.

He found himself laughing as the freezing snow-laden winds whirled about him, and then he could no longer close his mouth.

SQUEAKY

Martin Edwards

"*LET'S GO INTO the forest,*" Squeaky said.

Adele glanced at Brendan. Her husband was hunched over the steering wheel, eyes fixed on the road ahead. Lips motionless. She looked over her shoulder.

Squeaky squatted on the back seat, grinning at her.

Something about Squeaky disturbed Adele, and in wilder moments, she fancied Squeaky knew it. Those widely spaced blue eyes weren't as innocent as they ought to be. They stared through Adele, as if her skull were made of glass, exposing her thoughts like scrawl on a postcard.

The car rounded a bend. Fields dusted with the first snow of winter bordered either side of the road. In the distance, a dark gathering of trees stretched as far as she could see. A brown signpost for tourists pointed the way, but the lane was deserted.

"*Let's go into the forest.*"

The scratchy, high-pitched voice made Adele's flesh tingle. She clenched her small fists. Brendan's lips were parted. She could see the pink tip of his tongue. The car jerked forward as he pressed his foot on the accelerator. They raced past the road-sign.

"*But I wanted to go into the forest.*"

"Shut up!" Adele muttered.

"*Oh, dear me!*" This was Squeaky's catchphrase.

"I told you to shut up!"

How shaming, to scream like that at Squeaky. Stupid and immature of her, too, but she couldn't help herself. Brendan threw her a glance. Was that dread in his eyes? The heater was buzzing – he had changed it to the highest setting – and the car's interior was stuffy. Sweat slicked his brow.

"Are you...okay?" His voice never used to falter like this.

"Fine," she said. "Yeah, I'm fine."

They drove on in silence for another twenty minutes, until they reached the hospice on the outskirts of the next town. While Brendan waited to reverse into a vacant space, Adele jumped out to buy a parking ticket. She took another look at Squeaky through the window of the car. Snub-nosed and straw-haired, with a red top and baggy blue jeans. A figure that might have walked out of a bad dream. Squeaky ought to find it impossible to scare a grown woman. But a tremor ran down Adele's spine as she shoved coins into the slot of the machine.

When she returned to stick the ticket on to the windscreen, Brendan had Squeaky over his shoulder, and the big canvas holdall in his hand. He pecked Adele on the cheek.

"See you later...Have a good shop."

Why couldn't he meet her eye? She strove for brightness. "Good luck. Hope the kids have a wonderful time."

As she walked towards the main road, Squeaky's piercing gaze seemed to track her movements. She felt naked, despite being wrapped up against the cold in a warm woollen coat and scarf. Squaring her shoulders, she looked straight ahead, determined not to spare Squeaky another glance. Though she itched to put her hands round that scrawny neck.

Drifting through the crowds in the shopping mall, she found it impossible to push thoughts of Squeaky out of her mind. Sometimes she thought there were three people in their marriage, not two. Whenever she tried to talk about her anxieties to Brendan, he was kind but intransigent. Squeaky had changed his life for the better, he said. Surely Adele understood? He'd found his true vocation. It wasn't as if his wife had any cause to worry.

After all, Squeaky was only a doll.

When Adele first met Brendan, at a party thrown by a casual acquaintance neither of them knew well or much liked, he told her he was a magician. After their first night in bed together, he confessed that his magic amounted to little more than a few conjuring tricks. He didn't even run to a glamorous assistant, he said with a mock-sheepish grin. For years, he'd worked as a quantity surveyor, but after the death of his wife he'd wanted to change his life completely. Adele knew how he felt.

They had plenty in common. Liked the same TV shows, laughed at the same jokes. He was marvellous company, charming and courteous, although Adele was perceptive enough to detect a streak of self-indulgence running through him. But that had been true of Josh, it was true of most men. Maybe all men. Brendan was a nice guy, but not the strongest of characters; forced into a corner, he'd put himself first. But you had to balance positives against the negatives. Brendan made her smile for the first time since Josh's accident when they were out boating in his native Australia, on the final day of the holiday of a lifetime to celebrate their fifth wedding anniversary.

Bereavement was another thing they had in common. Brendan made no secret of his devotion to the first Mrs O'Leary. Not that Adele resented this: jealousy wasn't one of her vices. She deplored the way Gilly had betrayed Brendan's trust. He still kept photos of her in an old suitcase in the loft, and the identical pout featured in every single one. Gilly was pretty and vain, the doted-on daughter of a widowed wealthy banker. When Daddy died, she needed someone else to spoil her rotten. It was clear even from Brendan's kind-hearted comments that she'd been flattered by his unfailing attentiveness, and relished having a good-looking man at her beck and call. And Brendan, tall and introspective, with a mop of dark hair and deep brown eyes, was a very good-looking man.

Adele lingered in her favourite fashion store, where Christmas carols sung by a kids' choir trilled over the loudspeakers.

Brightly shone the moon that night
Though the frost was cruel...

After that disturbing episode with Squeaky, she was in the mood for a treat. A skimpy designer nightdress caught her eye. The price was extortionate for something so insubstantial, but money wasn't a problem, and Brendan would love slipping it off her slim white shoulders. So: a treat for both of them. She carried her trophy to the till.

Poor Brendan deserved his fun. He was terrific in bed, but that hadn't been enough for vain and selfish Gilly. She'd started an affair with an old school friend called Hodgkinson, who contacted her via a social networking site. Hodgkinson was married to a woman disabled by some rare malfunction of her auto-immune system. Brendan knew none of this until the police came knocking at his door one Saturday afternoon, and told him that his wife had been found dead in a car filled with exhaust fumes. The car belonged to the man whose body was draped across hers. She and the school friend had perpetrated the ultimate in selfishness. A suicide pact.

> *'Sire, the night is darker now*
> *And the wind blows stronger*
> *Fails my heart, I know not how,*
> *I can go no longer...'*

She stabbed her PIN number into the credit-card machine. Brendan was quite open about the fact that the police had needed to check him out in order to make sure that he hadn't contrived an ingenious double murder. To a suspicious detective, the affair might seem to give him a motive to do away with Gilly and her lover, and to make matters worse, Brendan inherited all the money her father had left her.

Lucky he was a conjuror in his spare time. While Gilly spent her last hours with her lover, he'd risen bright and early to travel to a hotel in Bath where he'd been booked by a distant cousin to perform some table magic at her husband's fortieth birthday party.

It all made sense. Gilly was a flake, the other man was depressed about his wife's deteriorating health, and they couldn't see a happy future together. Two star-crossed lovers whose self-absorption knew no bounds.

And even if a suicide pact seemed an overreaction, what other explanation could there be? The lover's wife was immobile in a hospital bed, while Brendan had a perfect alibi.

***

It was so sad. Brendan explained to Adele that after Gilly's death, somehow he couldn't face performing magic tricks any more. She sympathized; he was a sensitive soul. The money he inherited enabled him to pack up his job, but he still yearned to become an entertainer. Six months after he and Adele returned home from a blissful honeymoon cruise in the Caribbean, he stumbled across an internet auction that seized his imagination.

Squeaky was for sale.

As a schoolboy, he told Adele, he'd practised mimicry from time to time, but magic was his first love. On the spur of the moment, he decided to acquire a dummy of his own and become a ventriloquist.

At first, Adele was delighted. Brendan needed to scrub the memory of magic – and Gilly's treachery – out of his mind. What better way than to discover a fresh interest? For a few weeks, because they believed in sharing, she even taught herself ventriloquism. Its mysterious nature intrigued her; the first ventriloquists had been shamans and gastromancers, and the idea of taking on another persona seemed attractive to her.

"You've got a knack for it!" he'd exclaimed in delight.

She'd tried to look modest. "I just believe a couple ought to share their interests, that's all."

All too soon, the novelty palled. As it did, she found herself disliking Squeaky more with every week that passed. How silly, to loathe a stuffed dummy. Yet she couldn't help feeling dismayed by the amount of time Brendan devoted to his hobby. Worse, he teased her by making Squeaky poke fun at her clothes and hair styles. All in good fun, of course, but Squeaky's sense of humour was sharper and less kindly than Brendan's. Once or twice, a barbed jest got under Adele's skin.

Was Squeaky a boy or a hoydenish girl? Brendan was vague, and the dummy's appearance and voice were oddly sexless. But there was no denying that Squeaky had a spiky personality, tainted by malevolence. He, she or it – whatever – seemed to glory in stirring up trouble.

Before long, Adele wanted Squeaky out of the house, but Brendan was better at ventriloquism than he'd ever been at magic, and he wouldn't hear of ditching the dummy. He started to pick up bookings: children's birthday parties, in the main, but he also performed in social clubs and rest homes. Today he was putting on a show for sick children in a hospice. Brightening their troubled lives.

When Adele pushed it, they had their first blazing row. Brendan's pleasant face turned pink with outrage. He wouldn't hear of getting rid of Squeaky. How could Adele possibly make a fuss about a doll who brought pleasure to countless people, kids and old folk in particular?

Adele found herself shouting, "Sometimes I think you care more about that fucking dummy than you do about me!"

"You're making a fool of yourself," he hissed. "Behaving like a spoiled brat."

He'd never criticized her before, and that came as such a shock, in the end she gave in. Usually, Brendan was master of his emotions. But she'd seen something new in him. A cussed determination that was proof against anything she might say. She saw that he found her objections to Squeaky mean-spirited and neurotic.

Shopping done, she decided a quick gin and tonic would fortify her for the return trip with Squeaky. She wasn't due to meet up with Brendan for another half-hour, so she made her way to the Spread Eagle, on the other side of the road from the hospice. It wasn't a salubrious locality, and the pub didn't have a good reputation, but who cared? Suppose some man chatted her up, she wouldn't start kicking and screaming. She could do with being made to feel good. To feel herself desired again.

Walking up to the bar, she glanced in a large oval mirror that hung above the counter. In the reflection, she saw Brendan. He was seated at a table, with a half-pint glass of beer in front of him, handing a padded envelope to a bulky man with a broken nose.

For God's sake. It was Gerard Finucane.

Adele didn't wait to be served. As Finucane put the envelope in the pocket of his coat, she turned on her heel and hurried out into the wintry evening.

* * *

Waiting in the car, Adele realized she'd have minded less if she'd caught Brendan groping a busty barmaid. Gerard Finucane was bad news. And wasn't he supposed to have gone back to Ireland after the trial?

Finucane was a builder, and Brendan knew him through work. They were friends, but made an odd couple, a quiet and nervy professional and a loud, egotistical extrovert. Finucane called himself an entrepreneur, but that was simply a synonym for a criminal. Brendan introduced Adele to him before the wedding, and when they went out for a drink as a threesome, she realized within minutes that this was a man who loved taking risks. Finucane didn't care, he simply couldn't help himself. Brazenly, he stroked her leg under the table while Brendan told a tedious anecdote about some job they'd worked on together. For a few minutes, she did nothing about it, but when Finucane's fingers strayed under the hem of her skirt, she gave him a fierce look and shifted her chair away. His response was a cheeky wink and an excessively loud guffaw when Brendan belatedly delivered an anti-climactic punchline.

Finucane hadn't made it to the wedding, because he'd been remanded in custody, accused along with a couple of thugs who worked for him of beating up a business rival and leaving him brain-dead. Reluctantly, Brendan admitted to Adele that Finucane had been inside more than once in his life. But the trial folded on the first day when the main prosecution witnesses failed to turn up. Had they been threatened? Nothing could be proved. Finucane and his henchmen walked away from court without a stain on their characters.

Even so… How could a decent, caring man like Brendan be friendly with a violent criminal like Gerard Finucane?

And what was inside the padded envelope?

"How was your afternoon?"

"Oh, it was great. The kids loved Squeaky."

Nothing much else was said on the way home. No mention of a trip to the Spread Eagle, though Adele's nostrils detected a beery whiff. Squeaky uttered not a word, but when Adele stole a glance at the back seat, Squeaky's grin seemed as triumphant as it was vindictive.

Brendan and Adele lived in a split-level house on a steep hill over-looking a fast-flowing stream. It was a new-build and obtaining planning permission in the green belt had been fraught with problems, but Brendan knew the right people and, for all Adele knew, greased the right palms. She didn't care if a few rules needed to be bent; their new home occupied one of the most desirable loca-tions in the north of England, and when it was finished it would be worth a fortune. A balcony was to be built on to the living room, from which in summer they would be able to look down on the stream and the woods beyond.

Before getting married, they'd talked about starting a family. Adele liked the idea of having kids; Josh hadn't been interested, but something was lacking from her life and she wondered if it might be motherhood. Not that she was starry-eyed about small children; she'd taken an unpaid position as a classroom assistant in a school in the next village, and she found the constant squabbling a bore. But you saw your own offspring differently from other people's.

A month ago, she had told Brendan she'd stopped taking her contraception, but since the row about Squeaky, they hadn't made love. Brendan wasn't a man for reconciliation sex – quite a contrast to Josh, and one of the few areas where the comparison favoured her first husband – and she was becoming frustrated by his continued lack of response. She had her needs, and one of the things that had most attracted her to Brendan had been his skill at fulfilling them.

"Shall we open a bottle of Chablis?" she asked before starting the meal. "I need a drink, how about you?"

Brendan frowned. He was fussy about mixing the grape and the grain. Now was the moment for him to mention that he'd had a quick half and a catch-up with Gerard Finucane.

He cleared his throat. "Lovely. I could do with a drop of alcohol myself. I love performing for an audience, but it does leave me shattered."

* * *

As they were undressing in their vast and luxurious bedroom that night, Brendan launched into a long and complicated explanation about the delay to the building of the balcony and the garage block. Adele hated mess, and yearned for the work to be finished. She was almost tempted to ask if he should bring Finucane in to speed it up. For all his faults, at least he was renowned for getting things done.

Adele lay in bed, waiting for her husband. He took an age cleaning his teeth. Did he want her to give up and fall asleep with boredom? She decided to go on to the offensive.

"Why did you let Squeaky talk like that in the car?"

Through the open door to the en suite bathroom, she saw Brendan freeze in the act of lifting his electric toothbrush.

"Just leave it, can you, please?"

"Brendan, I'm trying to help."

"You're not helping," he muttered.

"Why did Squeaky want to go into the forest?"

He spat into the basin and padded back towards their king-size bed. She saw that he'd developed some sort of tic in his left eye. Nerves? What did he have to be stressed about?

"I don't want to talk about it."

He clambered into bed and she stretched an arm around his waist.

"Brendan, it's not natural. We both know what happened in the forest. Why are you letting that bloody doll talk like that? What's going on?"

He lifted a hand and switched off the light. They never made love in the dark, she didn't know why. Her guess was that Gilly had preferred it with the lights out, and this was one of the changes Brendan had made in his life. New woman, new house, new adventures in the bedroom. He'd been so inventive, until the arrival of Squeaky.

"Goodnight."

"Brendan, we need to discuss this."

He wriggled out of her grip and did not reply.

"Brendan."

No answer. Was he trembling? And if so, why?

***

"*Let's go into the forest.*"

Adele woke in the early hours, hearing Squeaky's voice in her head. As a rule she was a sound sleeper; even when Josh died, she'd kept managing six or seven hours each night.

The forest meant only one thing to Brendan. Among the oaks and the firs was the lay-by where Gilly and her boyfriend had parked their car, not far from the cottage where the lover lived, before poisoning themselves with exhaust fumes.

Brendan was snoring. The sleep of the just? Adele couldn't help doubting it.

Was he giving money to Finucane in that padded envelope, and if so, why was payment due? Time to think the unthinkable. Suppose that, instead of being in Dublin, Finucane had sneaked back into England and killed Gilly and the man on Brendan's behalf. He was capable of murder, but surely Brendan wasn't? Not Brendan, the charming, introspective worrier she had fallen in love with.

Yet he had a powerful double motive. What if greed and jealousy had driven him to do something terrible – or rather, hire Finucane to do something terrible, and now he was tormented by guilt?

That might explain an obssession with the two deaths in that fume-filled car, and Squeaky's insistent demand:

"*Let's go into the forest.*"

No! There was a flaw in the theory. Relief flooded through her. Finucane was street-wise, in a way Brendan never could be. If Finucane had agreed to carry out a couple of contract killings, he'd have insisted on payment in advance. Or, at the least, half his money upfront, half on delivery of his side of the bargain. Inconceivable that he'd have waited until now to take his money. Brendan couldn't have been paying him for services rendered. Maybe there was something other than cash in the envelope, maybe...

Another thought struck her, and even snuggled under the thick duvet, she found herself shivering.

What if he wanted Finucane to undertake another job for him?

"Where's Squeaky?" Brendan demanded the next morning.

They were breakfasting in their magnificent new kitchen. Through the panoramic windows, Adele watched tentative snowflakes drift on to the York stone flags before melting.

"More toast?"

"Did you hear me?" Brendan's voice rose as he struggled to control his emotions. "What have you done with Squeaky?"

"*Wouldn't you like to know?*"

A good impersonation, even if Adele said so herself. Her lips didn't move at all, but she thought she'd captured Squeaky's provocative, malicious tone.

Brendan slipped off the high stool and advanced towards her. His eyes shone with anger, his shoulders were rigid with tension.

"For God's sake, what have you done?"

"*Oh, dear me!*"

Adele had climbed out of bed in the middle of the night, taken Squeaky from the bed in the room next door to theirs, and hidden the doll in a linen basket in the utility room. The temptation to throw Squeaky in the dustbin, or even go outside and toss it down into the stream, had almost overpowered her. Yet somehow she'd kept calm enough to resist the urge to be rid of Squeaky for ever.

And it was worth the effort, to see the truth revealed in Brendan's eyes.

He cared more for Squeaky than he did for her.

A week later, Adele was sitting in a restaurant, enjoying a turkey dinner with colleagues from the school where she worked, when a discreet waiter asked her to accompany him to the manager's office. There she found a young woman police officer with sorrowful eyes and a bad case of acne.

"Mrs Keane?"

"Yes, what is it?"

"I'm so sorry to interrupt your Christmas meal. Would you like to sit down, please?"

The restaurant manager, face etched with anxiety, pulled out a chair for her.

"What's happened?"

"I'm afraid I have some bad news for you."

Adele counted the pimples on the woman's cheeks. Said nothing.

"It's your husband. I'm sorry to say that he has been in an accident."

"Oh my God. Is he hurt?"

The policewoman bowed her head. "I'm afraid he died a short time ago."

Adele made a small yelping noise of incoherent distress.

"I am so sorry, Mrs Keane."

"What...what in Heaven's name happened?"

"He was hit by a motor vehicle as he left a public house."

Adele stared. "Yes, he told me he'd be popping out for a pint while I enjoyed myself with my friends."

The policewoman cleared her throat. "I have to tell you, the driver did not stop. We suspect he'd been drinking. There were eyewitnesses who said the vehicle swerved before it knocked down your husband, and then accelerated out of sight. The driver must have known he'd hit someone. But it's the time of year. In the run-up to Christmas, people drink far too much. It's appallingly irresponsible."

"Nice place," Finucane said a couple of nights later, as he looked around the living room. "No expense spared."

Adele was bored with playing the grieving widow. Putting her glass down on a glass-topped occasional table, she sat on the sofa and kicked off her shoes. "Nothing but the best, was Brendan's motto. He had the money, and he didn't mind spending it."

Finucane said something coarse about Brendan.

"I suppose we ought to talk about your fee," Adele said.

Finucane grinned at her. "You already made a payment in kind in the hotel, don't forget. I'm not some bog-standard mercenary, you know. We can come to an arrangement, you and me."

Adele chortled and lifted her glass. "Suits me, sweetie. So here's to – mutually satisfactory arrangements."

He swallowed some wine and fingered the brickwork of the exposed chimney breast. "Not bad," he said, with deliberate ambiguity. "Not bad at all."

"I want to know about Gilly."

He put a stubby finger to his lips. "Ask no questions and I'll tell you no lies."

"Come on, Ged. I'm dying to know the gory details. How did you do it?"

He laughed. "You're really something, you know?"

"Yes, I do know. Satisfy my curiosity, and then we can finish the bottle upstairs."

A theatrical sigh. "Women, eh?"

"Can't live with them, can't live without them?"

A broad grin. He wasn't handsome, not in Brendan's league at all in terms of looks, but she was conscious of a crude magnetism pulling her towards him.

"All right, if you really must know. When Brendan was away, Gilly had the house to herself. Once her feller, Hodgkinson, left his wife in hospital, he came around. They had a few drinks and smoked some dope before going to bed. I was waiting for my chance."

"Go on." She saw he relished having an audience. A bit like Brendan with Squeaky.

"I fitted a garden hose that Brendan had left out for me to the exhaust of Gilly's estate car, using a kid's feeding bottle which he'd cut in half. Wearing surgical gloves, I ran the hose through the garage and utility room and up a hole in the floorboards right underneath the bed. As soon as I switched on the engine, I nipped upstairs. The two of them were dead to the world. I pulled the duvet over Hodgkinson's nose and mouth, squeezed hard for half a minute and pushed the hose into his face with my right hand, and held it there until he was dead. Same with Gilly. She was stoned, and barely struggled. Not that she was strong enough to fight back, even if she'd realized what was happening. She was a tiny, frail woman. Big tits, mind."

"Not as nice as mine, though."

"No way, darling, you're one of a kind."

She licked her lips provocatively. "You'd better believe it."

"Anyway, I lugged both of them to the car and put them in the boot with a blanket over their heads. I'd put a folding bicycle in the car as well. After I'd driven to the forest, I dumped Hodgkinson in the driver's seat. Gilly stayed in the boot. I put some family photos that Brendan gave me next to her body, put earphones on her, and switched on her iPod, so it seemed she'd been listening to her favourite Leonard Cohen tracks. And then I connected a length of vacuum hose to the exhaust, put the other end in the boot, and switched on the ignition. Once the scene was set, I took out the bike and cycled away.

"We had a couple of lucky breaks. Hodgkinson had told his wife's nurse that he couldn't bear what was happening to her. She thought suicide was in his mind. And the detective leading the inquiry owed me a favour. Some of the forensic stuff was mislaid. Nothing could be proved."

Adele clapped her hands. "Amazing!"

He fondled her bare neck. "Yeah, that's me. Amazing."

"And it doesn't bother you...that you killed a couple?"

He exhaled. "It was a job. You can't be sentimental."

"Not like Brendan. His conscience bothered him."

"Not enough to stop him wanting you out of the way, sweetheart. Lucky you realized and got in touch."

"Lucky you were willing to change sides."

A raucous laugh. "No contest. I've always fancied you, Adele, you must know that."

"I suppose so," she said with a sweet smile.

"Brendan didn't know when he was well off."

"No." Adele ran her fingers through Finucane's hair. "Did he say anything about this...new relationship?"

"Nah, he made a mystery out of it. Whoever he was seeing, I bet she didn't compare to you."

Adele pictured Squeaky's weird eyes and red lips.

"You're right."

Finucane closed his eyes as her hand slid between his legs.

"*Ged, is that you?*"

Finucane sat up with a start, swearing wildly.

"What was that?"

Adele moved away from him, gasping in fear. "A voice... it sounded like...no, it can't be."

"Some kind of joke?" Finucane swore again. "You're not telling me Brendan's risen from the dead?"

"I think the voice came from outside." Adele pointed to the sliding doors. They hadn't pulled the curtains when they came into the living room. Outside, the night was black. Not a star to be seen.

Finucane sprang to his feet. "Some bastard spying on us? They'll be sorry."

"Ged, be careful!"

"Don't worry." He put his hand in his pocket and pulled out a small knife. "Nobody messes me around."

"I don't think I locked the doors," she said in a whisper. "He might...come in."

"Switch the light off," Finucane hissed.

With her finger on the switch, Adele said, "What are you going to do?"

"What do you think?"

The last thing she saw before the light went out was the glint of the blade in his palm. She heard him pull at the handle of the sliding doors, and then move through them. Moments later came the scream.

"*Oh, dear me!*"

She just couldn't resist it, as she switched the lights back on. Walking to the open doors, she looked down at the concrete fifteen feet below. Finucane's body was a heap of broken bones. Better check to make sure he was dead before she called the police to tell them about the intruder who had threatened her with his knife before falling to his death, unaware that the sliding doors gave on to a balcony that did not exist. Adele didn't believe in taking chances.

Five minutes later, after dialling 999, she made her way upstairs and went into the spare room. Squeaky was lying on the bed, staring at her. At least, Adele said to herself, her ventriloquial skills had come in handy tonight. Only one thing left to do now. Was that fear in the doll's eyes? If not, it ought to be.

She tore Squeaky's head off, and then the rest of its limbs.

Yes, it was childish, but strangely satisfying. Certainly she didn't feel a twinge of remorse as she waited for the police to arrive. She'd never fretted about tipping Josh out of that boat, the day after he told her he wanted a divorce, and she wouldn't waste any tears on Brendan or Finucane, let alone horrid, ugly Squeaky.

Leave the guilt to her dead husband, and his dismembered conscience.

FISTS OF DESTINY

Col Bury

IT WAS TIME. They were ready. In the modest living room of the red-brick council semi, Bill took a breath to compose himself and gazed into innocent eyes.

"Apologies for the swearing in advance, guys, but I want you to know the full story," he said, dipping his head, before recounting the events of the day evil visited Manchester...

The infamous Manchester rain gave way to a rare and stunning sun. It certainly wasn't a day to be stuck inside the biggest skyscraper in the UK outside London – the Beetham Tower.

The business conference was due to start at 9 a.m., but Steve being Steve, he was there half an hour before. The discipline and respect gleaned from his military days were still a big part of him, despite now being on civvy street. His punctuality and meticulously bulled shoes, so shiny you could check your hair in them, were a testament to that.

The droning increased as people filed into the Hilton Hotel conference room on the twenty-second floor, just under halfway up, and Steve wiped sweat from his brow with a hanky as he headed for the large windows to take in the sights.

He noticed a big Asian bloke wearing a puffy jacket, who took a seat on the front row. Steve briefly felt uneasy, wondering: *Why would somebody wear a padded winter jacket on such a hot day?* Quickly dismissing the thought, he smiled inwardly, realizing his army days had made him paranoid.

He gazed in awe at a panoramic view over half the vast city; the "capital of the north" they called it. In sheer contrast to the plush tower, he looked south at the clusters of gloomy high-rise flats in the distance, where buying drugs was as routine as popping to the corner shop for a loaf. Focusing on the "The Seven Sisters", a group of flats in Old Trafford, one of which Steve had managed somehow to escape, he could just make out the roof of his dad's old local, where, sadly now, heroin ran as freely as ale. The surrounding streets led to the notorious Moss Side, home of the tit-for-tat shootings that had resulted in the media giving the city its unfortunate epithet: "Gunchester".

On the flipside, Manchester's vibrant music scene, stemming from the likes of The Smiths, The Happy Mondays, Stone Roses and, latterly, Oasis, had given rise to another nickname: "Madchester". Steve recalled bopping on the dance floor of the Hacienda while brimming with amphetamines. Happy days...though long since tainted by unshakable images of his friends being blown up in Kabul, the guilt of survival still jabbing at his heart every day.

Below him, the bustling dots of city-centre shoppers and domino-sized cars signified the city's many decent folk going about their business. Scanning further, the Manchester Ship Canal and the River Irwell were like arteries leading to the heart of the city, the motorway network the veins, and the many rail-tracks the capillaries. The friendly Manchester folk were undoubtedly the blood running through the city, keeping it forever vital. However, one wrong turn from a naive visitor into the suburbs, and their experience of the so-called 'friendly city' would likely be one of hours spent at the local nick, telling a cop how they were beaten up for their possessions.

Surrounding the tower, numerous old red-brick warehouses – a reminder of the city's past as a leading powerhouse in world textiles – were now converted into snazzy designer outlets, coffee shops and apartments, including Steve's beloved Hacienda, where he'd met Lucy all those years ago. Lucy and the kids kept him going these days. They were the only antidote to the memories of comrades blasted to pieces, that sometimes brought him to the brink of suicide.

Steve ran a hand across the side of his heavily scarred neck, a constant reminder of the day he'd crawled from that burning tank... leaving his mates... screaming...

He shook those haunting screams away. He wasn't surprised to see a woman beside him gawping. He vaguely recognized her: about forty, wearing a pinstripe suit and more make-up than Coco the Clown. Embarrassed, she swiftly diverted her gaze, pretending to look out of the window. Steve wasn't too bothered; he'd got used to the staring years ago, and the name-calling – "Turkey Neck" being *their* favourite, not his. He followed the new direction of her gaze.

Outside, on a billboard, a huge poster, one half red, the other blue, advertising "United v City", epitomized the passion of this football-mad city. Unfortunately, on derby day the red and blue often represented blood and bruises, especially the evening after the match, when beer-fuelled exuberance could erupt into violence.

A tram caught his attention, faintly rumbling the girders of a bridge to his left, a mass of tiny commuters exiting like scurrying insects as it stopped at Deansgate station, bringing him back from his musings.

Inside the conference room, everyone was dressed formally, clutching their respective folders, briefcases or handbags. A group to his left were also taking in the view, debating whether they could see Blackpool Tower in the distance through the Majorcan blue sky. One know-it-all chap with a fake tan and designer suit raised a few eyebrows, suggesting that from the top you could see Jodrell Bank Observatory and even Snowdonia in Wales!

By now, everyone was vying for the best seats – not too near the front, mind, in case the spotlight was on you, such was the nature of these sales-training days. However, never one to shirk a challenge, Steve had already placed his suit jacket around a chair, front centre.

As the others took their seats, Steve looked around for a familiar face, checked his watch and then shook his head. *He's late as usual – typical!* He returned to his seat at the front, seeing that the big guy wearing the puffy jacket was actually sitting in the chair beside his.

Steve ignored the uneasy feeling again, and began flipping through one of the brochures that had been left on each seat. Apparently, the Hilton owned the first twenty-three floors, including 285 bedrooms, a restaurant and even a swimming pool. The floor above was Manchester's only "sky-bar", and from there up to the forty-seventh floor at the top were 219 privately owned apartments and sixteen penthouses, making the Beetham Tower the tallest residential building in Europe.

A gunshot blasted out, changing everything.

People screamed, some hitting the floor; others just froze, staring agog. Steve ducked and pivoted, seeing a skinny, olive-skinned chap running to the front of the room brandishing a revolver. He seemed pretty pissed off, his face contorted. Steve spotted the headband with the Pakistani emblem, and the uneasy feeling within him escalated. The screaming around him evoked unwelcome memories, but he shook them away again. *Not now!*

Steve hoped this was just a daring mass robbery but doubted it, wondering, *Why the headband?*

A few seconds later, the big bloke beside him tied a similar headband around his head and stood up, shrugging off his puffy jacket. The crowd gasped in unison. The man glared manically, holding up one clenched fist containing a detonator button, attached by dangling wires to a mass of explosives strapped to his ample body via ...*a suicide vest.*

IED...Improvised Explosive Device...probably packed with ball bearings, nails and screws, for maximum shrapnel effects on detonation...

Steve was now thinking, *9/11.*

He was two metres away, witnessing the sheer madness in Bombman's wide eyes and the sweat dripping from his brow. Steve bowed his head, picturing Lucy and his kids, as Pistol-man started barking out orders in broken English.

"Pass mobile phones to end. Anyone tries make call... I kill!"

It was surreal. People just did as they were told, but little involuntary bursts of sobbing and yelping from the crowd prompted Pistol-man again.

"Shut the fuck up! No noise. Phones now!" he shouted, training the handgun on the stunned crowd.

After taking his Nokia from his trouser pocket, Steve motioned to pass it along to a pretty girl of no more than twenty. He noticed her hands shaking, her face paler than the moon, her eyes tearfully pleading with him. As he gave her the phone, he gently squeezed her hand, softening his hard features as best he could in a bid to reassure her.

Biting his lip, he saw discreet movement to his left and spotted the woman who'd been staring at him earlier. She skulked low, dialling on her mobile, probably calling the cops.

Bad move.

"No, no...bast-aaard!" yelled Pistol-man, running past Steve. Without hesitation, he blasted out two slugs. The first triggered a loud, splintering crack in a window; the second hit the woman in the forehead. She jerked back momentarily before slumping forward in her chair. Shocked sales reps nearby were showered crimson, Steve feeling a light spray on his own neck. He gently ran a hand across it then looked at his palm, seeing the red smears. He clenched his fist tight, fighting to control his instincts. The girl to his right held her hands to her face, blocking out the madness while stifling breathless sobs.

Steve heard a faint mumbling directly behind him and briefly turned to see a balding, bespectacled chap with sad, red eyes. There was an unpleasant whiff and he saw that the man had pissed his pants.

The man whispered, desperately, "Please...no...I have children... they need me..." A bearded bloke beside him shuffled sideways in his seat, distancing himself from the stench of urine while wearing a look of confused dismay.

The shrieks and crying intensified from further behind, and the unwanted memories pumping through Steve were now strangely fuelling him.

An athletic-looking man in his early thirties tried to make a run for it towards a door at the front. With a grimace, Pistol-man shot him in the back. The man collapsed on to the plush carpet like a discarded rag doll, face first, arms outstretched.

"No more! You fuckin' hear me?" spat Pistol-man.

Everyone was still, silent but for the occasional burst of weeping. *Think!* Steve kept sneaking glances around him, from his bowed position. *Not yet.*

Bomb-man looked very agitated, sweat dripping down his face. His raised fist began to shake, the detonator protruding below his thumb.

Pistol-man tossed all the mobiles into a pile, the odd one bleeping, having not yet been silenced for the meeting. He climbed three steps on to the stage, and began a speech.

"Listen... you fuckin' infidels!" he shouted, pausing to spit at the crowd.

Interrupting him, U2's "It's a Beautiful Day" chimed, and Pistol-man snapped, firing two more shots into the pile of phones. People winced, jumping in their seats. Defiantly, the tune only finished when it was good and ready.

Subtly edging his body sideways and trying to keep his head still, Steve scanned the extremes of his peripheral vision, absorbing his surroundings. His eye-line eventually found the man he'd searched for earlier, sitting at the back. They knew each other well, and exchanged a brief, yet telling, glance and imperceptible nods.

Ignoring the rest of the bullshit speech, he managed to slip the photo of his kids out of his wallet. He gazed at the snapshot then kissed it, tears welling, heart leaden.

Amid Pistol-man's fragmented words ... "avenging... jihad... paradise... infidels..." Steve's mind drifted back to Kabul ... *Mad-dog Maguire ... Johnny Bartlett ... Davy McPherson...* and then he sprang from his seat, charging like a bull on speed.

His right fist impacted with Bomb-man's nose, bursting it, crushed tomato-style. Steve's momentum carried him on and he grabbed the stumbling Bomb-man's wrists. Pistol-man's cursing was now irrelevant, as he fumbled bullets from his pocket to reload the handgun. Steve and Bomb-man stumbled towards the windows, the detonator wire swinging between them. A cacophony of screams, both in the room and in Steve's head, drove him on.

He felt the terrorist's strength as they grappled face to face, two metres from the windows. The stench of his sweat, the taste of his blood, was sickening. But adrenaline and focus carried Steve forward, bundling Bomb-man nearer the glass with an encouraging headbutt.

They parted momentarily and Bomb-man took hold of the detonator. Steve lunged at him, thrusting him into the cracked window, shattering it. Giant shards crashed down and the would-be killer toppled backwards, his arms clutching frantically at nothing.

Time seemed to stop... then, as if in slow motion... Steve felt himself falling...

...the wind rushed noisily in his ears... distant screams... the beautiful blue sky somersaulting in his vision, alternating with the rapidly approaching streets... face-up, Bomb-man plummeted, just below Steve... a flash of an evil grin... a deafening blast... forever silencing those haunting screams...

Bill brushed a hand through thinning grey hair and gazed into little eyes that were bravely fighting back tears.

"Okay, guys?"

Nods of acknowledgement.

"That day twenty-two people died, most of them shoppers below. If it weren't for your daddy, the death toll could've been *two thousand*...and twenty-two."

First to speak was Holly, her voice faint, crackly. "So...my daddy...was a hero, Uncle Bill?"

"Yes, darling. Your daddy...*IS*...will always be...a hero."

Holly hugged her uncle tightly, her head resting against his paunch.

Jake spoke next, swallowing before clearing his throat. "But... what happened to Pistol-man, Uncle Bill?"

"That revolver only had six bullets, lad. Your daddy knew that too."

Bill smiled, and held up his own sturdy fist.

NAIN ROUGE

Barbara Nadel

RITCHIE WAS AS drunk as a sack when he first saw it out of the corner of his eye. Shuffling down Selden towards Woodward Avenue, it was talking and laughing to itself and knitting its tiny fingers in a nervous sort of a way. Ritchie's first thought was that he was seeing things. It had been a long time since he'd put away anything apart from the odd bottle of Bud, much less nine…or was it thirteen?…beefy great shots of vodka. His body was clearly in some sort of revolt at the violence he had done to it, but Ritchie's attitude was just simply, "Deal with it, bastard!" If his body didn't like the booze he'd tipped into it, then that was its problem. He had much bigger issues to deal with than whether or not his guts wanted to tolerate spirits, or whether his arteries were hardening every time he put a cigarette into his mouth. Now he was seeing the freaking Nain Rouge, which could only mean one thing. He'd lost his mind.

Through all of Detroit's many and various vicissitudes, Ritchie Carbone had always managed, somehow, to cling on to his business. It wasn't much! It *hadn't* been much. A Coney Dog joint on 2nd Avenue. Detroiters loved Coney Hotdogs. What wasn't to like? Nothing! So a lot of people had moved out of the Cass Corridor over the years? So there was a reason for that, namely drug-fuelled and gang-sanctioned violence, but, hey, it was Detroit! Tough city, tough crowd.

But then as Ritchie knew very well, that only worked up to a point. When some little shit who called himself 'Da Man' had pumped a bullet into old Freddie's head, that had been enough for Ritchie. That had been it…through, finished, gone. No more Coney Dogs on 2nd and a whole heap of trouble about how he was going to explain how he voluntarily made himself unemployed to Welfare. And now, to top it all, a crazy little mythical freak laughing at him from underneath a lamp post. Instinctively he put one hand up to his face so that it wouldn't be able to recognize him. But it was probably way too late.

Of all the many badasses that Detroit had endured over the centuries, the Nain Rouge, or Red Dwarf, had to be the baddest. It was just legend, of course, but it was a legend that went back a long, long way. A small, child-like creature with brown fur, red boots, blazing eyes and rotten teeth was said to have attacked Detroit's founder, Antoine de la Mothe Cadillac, in 1701. Shortly afterwards, Cadillac, a wealthy French businessman, suffered a downturn in his fortunes from which he never recovered. His altercation with the Nain is said to have rocked Cadillac to his core. But then the Nain Rouge was a creature that he would have recognized from his native country. A variety of lutin, the Nain Rouge was a common figure in the folklore, myths and legends of Normandy. Ritchie Carbone knew of it from the annual Marche du Nain Rouge, an old Detroit custom that had been revived in 2010.

His buddy, Jigsaw, had told him about it first. Jigsaw had been a Ford employee back in the day; now he made his living ripping copper and other metals out of derelict buildings to sell for scrap. He'd walked into Ritchie's place almost a year ago and said, "You heard they gonna banish the Nain this year?"

Ritchie had frowned; he remembered it well. "What? You mean they gonna have that march where everyone gets dressed up so they can fool some thing that don't even exist into walking into a fire?"

"That's the thing." Jigsaw had had his usual; a large dog, fries and a bottle of cherry pop. "Hey, Ritchie, this what you think they call gentrification?"

Reviving the old Marche du Nain Rouge was something that, to Ritchie, certainly smacked of middle-class people amusing themselves. Although most people with money had moved out of the city years ago, a new type of urban elite was trickling back into pretty old buildings like the Fyffes place on the corner of Adams Avenue and Woodward. They liked old customs like the banishing of the Nain Rouge every springtime. It was said that if the Nain could be banished on the nearest Sunday to the Vernal Equinox, the city would be safe from misfortune for another year. Heaven knew it needed it!

Ritchie Carbone, in spite of having a father from Italy, was Detroit through and through. His mother, Agnes, could trace her ancestry back to Cadillac's French compatriots and her folks, the Blancs, had stayed in the city ever since. At fifty-eight, Ritchie had seen the riots of '67, the many vicissitudes of the automobile industry, the urban ruins, and, more latterly, the first little flickers of possible city renewal. He knew that the place needed every bit of help it could get, and if that included banishing an evil fantasy figure from its streets then so be it. But that had been before that little shit Da Man had taken over large swathes of 2nd; before he'd put a gun to Freddie's head and pulled the trigger without Ritchie even having a chance to consider his offer of "protection".

Still with his hand in front of his face – to let the Nain see you was dangerous, lest it come back sometime to take its revenge – Ritchie yelled at the creature. "Hey, you!" he said. "Get out of my city! Don't you think we got enough problems, huh?"

But the little bastard just laughed, bared its rotten teeth at him and then began to scamper off at speed towards Woodward. Why Ritchie Carbone decided to stagger off after the Nain wasn't really clear to him at the time, apart from the notion that he was generally angry. But this was actually at Da Man as opposed to the mythical Nain. Not that that mattered a bean! Ritchie drained his last shot of vodka down to the very last drip and then he got up and ran.

Laughing all the while, the little freak quickly got to Woodward and then turned right. It was, or appeared to be, heading back into the city. Ritchie, adamant that that shouldn't be allowed to happen, followed. So, it was just some supernatural fairy or whatever – if it meant to sock what remained of Detroit in the guts once again, he was going to give it a hammering it would never forget. His mind had clearly gone, what the hell did it matter if he smacked around some bastard that wasn't really there! What did he have left to lose anyway? The business had gone, his wife had left him, the freaking gangstas had even shot his freaking dog, for God's sake!

Apart from the odd bus, the cars on Woodward seemed to fall into two categories: junk wagons just about held together by rust, and great big gleaming gangsta mobiles, brimming with blacked-out windows, guns, and the odd diamond-encrusted finger just glanced through the windshield. Someone like Ritchie couldn't relate to any of that! Apart from his friendships with junkies like Jigsaw and Black Bottom Boo, he'd always been a straight-down-the-line, middle-of-the-road kind of person. Being white in a majority black neighbourhood had never bothered him. He'd got on with everyone, just like he had when Cass had been largely white. God rest her soul, his momma had even had him take Coneys up to the hookers on Cass Avenue when he was little more than an infant.

"Those girls gotta make a dollar just like everyone," Agnes Carbone had said whenever she'd made up a bag of food for the ladies of the night. White, black, Jew or Gentile, she'd never cared and neither had Ritchie – until Da Man had come into his life. All swagger and crazy jewellery, tooled up homies and attitude, Da Man had started their "conversation" by calling Ritchie "white trash". For the sake of his customers, as well as himself, he'd taken it. Until Da Man had shot Freddie.

There'd been no need to kill the dog like that! Hound was old and blind and he hadn't known what the hell had been going on. The customers had high-tailed out, screaming. Not long afterwards Da Man and his crew left as well, but not before they'd told Ritchie that he had to somehow find a thousand dollars a week to pay for his own "protection". It had been after that that Ritchie had impotently thrown all of his hotdogs, his bread and his French fries after the gangstas. They'd just landed on the sidewalk, the waste inherent in their disposal making him want to weep. Since when had he become this hopelessly vulnerable and impotent old man?

The Nain started to cross over Woodward, dodging between the cars and laughing uproariously as it did so. Sometimes a Focus or a Hummer or a Jeep would look as if it was about to barrel into the

Nain, but it would always, somehow, evade a collision and come up smiling. At one point it even climbed on to the hood of some great big gangsta mobile and tapped its clawed fingers against the windshield, but then it slid off again and landed on the tarmac, giggling. The car went on its way, its driver seemingly oblivious to the danger he or she had been in.

Still on the sidewalk, Ritchie swayed on rubber legs, looking for a gap in the traffic. In New York crossing anywhere but a designated point would have had him up for jaywalking, but in Detroit nobody cared. He launched himself out into the wide road just before he got to Martin Luther King Jr Boulevard. The Nain, across Woodward now, flicked him the finger and Ritchie, at that moment, decided that, real or not, the Nain Rouge was history. Even if he couldn't prove his manhood with some teenage gangsta, he could at least vent his spleen on this little shit!

The Nain Rouge skipped, hopped and babbled its way into the old middle-class professional district of Brush Park. Once a place where doctors, attorneys, auto executives and lumber barons lived, Brush Park was now a wasteland of spectres, a graveyard for old houses that were rotten, abused, and haunted by the shades of lifestyles long since over with. Ritchie Carbone remembered it well. He'd had an old grade-school friend from Brush Park, a Jewish attorney's son called Ron Sachs. His family had moved out in the sixties and Ron had eventually gone to Harvard. Last Ritchie had heard of him, he'd been practising law in LA. Good for him.

Up ahead, the Nain stopped outside the moonlit remains of a Gothic mansion and bent double. Then it pulled its pants down and it farted at him. Infuriated by its rudeness, Ritchie could feel his blood-pressure go through the roof as his head began to pound with anger and with booze and with the unaccustomed exercise he was getting. His father had died from a stroke back in the eighties; he'd have to be careful. But what for? The Nain, fart over, shuffled on, grunting and babbling and laughing through its awful, cracked teeth.

What for? Ritchie thought again. *What am I breathing, what am I existing, what am I living for?* Even before he'd sold the business, his marriage had been on the skids. Maria, his wife, had been so over serving Coneys, she'd run off with a professional poker player back in 2008. Now, apparently, she and this Ralph were holed up somewhere outside Reno. Her kids wouldn't see her, but then neither Kathy nor Frank came to see Ritchie that often either and he was the so-called "injured" partner. No one lived in Detroit any more, no one dared.

Old Jigsaw had offered to buy him some apparently very fierce German Shepherd off a junkie from Eastern Market, but Ritchie had passed. Freddie hadn't been a guard dog, he'd been a friend. Ritchie didn't want to have some beast he was terrified of stopping him from leaving his own apartment.

He followed the Nain on to John R Street and then stopped to catch his breath. This part of Brush Park was completely gone to urban prairie. There was nothing. No wrecked houses, no vegetation – apart from grass – and no objects but litter. People reported seeing skunks in such places, even coyotes. The nothingness of it made Ritchie shudder. This was a district where he'd played as a kid, where he'd had tea with Ron Sachs and his family in his dad's elegant, turreted mansion. All gone. He looked around for the Nain and just saw a void. Even the creature that traditionally presaged doom for the city couldn't stand this. Maybe Brush Park represented "job done" to the evil little freak. After all, the destruction of Detroit was its final aim.

Over the centuries since Cadillac had founded the city, almost every disaster that had befallen it had been heralded by a sighting of the Nain. Back in '67 during the riots there had been a lot of sightings. Then Detroit had survived, but it had changed too. Black folks had had enough and so they'd expressed their anger and they'd forced change. Ritchie had cheered them all the way. So what Da Man had done to him hit still harder. As he'd tried to tell the boy at the time, *"This white trash has always been on your side!"* But it hadn't meant squat. Not to Da Man or to any of his crew.

There was a frigid late-February moon in the sky and the frost on the ground was so hard it was almost ice. Cold as unwilling charity, it was too bitter to snow and all but the most desperate addicts, the dying junkies, the most deprived of the deprived, were inside their homes, their squats or their crack shacks. No one was about and the silence, with the exception of the blood pounding through Ritchie's head, was complete. Come March it would be Nain-banishing time again – unless of course he could get the little prick dealt with early. But it had disappeared. Not that it had ever really been anywhere in the first place. A product of vodka shots, the Nain was just bile-scented vomit from his sick, tired and bitter mind. It wasn't Detroit that was falling apart, at least not completely and not yet, but Ritchie Carbone. With no savings, no pension and only a small apartment on Cass by way of assets, he was pretty much finished. With Welfare he could exist, but he couldn't live. His pa had died when he was only two years older than Ritchie was now, and he'd been ready to go. Agnes, his wife, had been dead for almost thirty years by the time old Salvatore died at sixty. Ritchie still remembered how the old man had cried for her every single day.

Then something sharp jabbed into one of his buttocks and he turned around to see the Nain, its vile fingers jabbing into his butt. When he looked at it, it screamed with laughter and Ritchie, furious, said, "You are so freaking dead!"

The Nain took off like a rocket back towards Erskine Street, whooping and chuntering and waving its disgusting furry arms in the air. It was having a high old time!

Heavy, breathless and now seeing stars in front of his eyes, Ritchie Carbone pulled his unwilling body after it, his mind seething with visions of carnage and revenge. Nobody jabbed him in the butt! Not even Da Man and his crew had stooped to that. Some freaky thing from his subconscious wasn't going to get away with it! He ran after the thing and was about to follow it into some rotting house when he recognized exactly where he was. He stopped. At one time there had been two turrets attached to the old Sachs house, now there was only one. But it was definitely where Ron and his family had lived. Ritchie put a hand up to his chest as he gasped for air and tried to deal with the shock. Mrs Sachs had been house-proud crazy! What would she make of the place now? Ritchie knew that it would break her heart and it made him want to cry in sympathy. Mrs Sachs had always made chocolate refrigerator cake, which had tasted so wonderful he'd closed his eyes with pleasure every time he'd eaten it. He'd been young and he and Ron had often talked about what they wanted to do when they grew up. Ritchie hadn't wanted to go into his Pa's Coney Dog business, he'd wanted to be a US Air Force pilot...not just a broken dream, but one literally hammered out of him by necessity, by recession, by the systematic destruction of his city.

As he ran up the teetering staircase to the place where the Sachses' front door had once been, Ritchie let out a howl like a wounded wolf. But then suddenly he stopped because it was in front of him. The Nain, scowling and spitting and yet at the same time laughing at him too. He wanted to pull its rotten head off, reach down its neck and pull its wicked heart out.

It laughed one more time and then he was upon it, tearing at its ghastly red flesh with his fingers and with his teeth.

In spite of the cold, Ritchie slept better in that terrible skeleton of the old Sachs house than he'd done in his apartment for months. The Nain had fought, of course it had, it was well known throughout history for its viciousness. But he must have prevailed because he was still alive even though his body hurt and he could see a spider's web of small scratches on his hands. Amazingly, to Ritchie, he'd had neither a stroke nor a heart attack. Maybe killing the Nain had somehow, magically, restored him to full health again.

But then what did he mean by 'killing the Nain'? Now that he was sober, there was surely no more craziness and so therefore no more Nain? He had a bunch of small cuts all over the backs of his hands, but then he probably got those scrambling up into the old Sachs place. How he'd remembered where to find the house after so many years, especially drunk out of his gourd, was hard to work out – until he remembered. He'd followed the Nain. But then that wasn't really possible, because the Nain Rouge didn't exist. It was just a folk tale.

Ritchie stood up and felt the rotted floorboards splinter underneath his feet. If he remembered correctly, the Sachses had had a basement. Ritchie moved as carefully as he could until he felt he was on rather more solid footing. He'd just congratulated himself on surviving that particular ordeal when his eyes were caught by the sight of a tattered, miserable bundle underneath the remains of a great bay window. It was very, very red, and although Ritchie knew that it couldn't possibly be the Nain, because the Nain didn't really exist, he knew that he feared examining it.

For what seemed like hours he tried to formulate an excuse he could give to himself for not seeing what the bundle contained. But he couldn't. On the one hand he never wanted to see what was in there, while on the other he wanted to do that more than anything else in the world. If it was the Nain all his preconceptions about reality and the world he thought he lived in would be shattered. If it wasn't...

As quickly as he could, before fear consumed him, Ritchie reached down with one shaking hand and pulled the thing apart. When his hands came away, they were covered in thick, crimson arterial blood. In slow motion, or so it seemed at the time, the tiny head rolled out of the rags that had once constituted the little girl's tattered clothes and fell to the floor at Ritchie's feet. Her long, thick, bright red hair had been hiding the terrible stump that had been her neck, that he had hacked and hacked and hacked at until it came away in his hands...

Ritchie Carbone dropped to his knees as the thundering of his own blood threatened to deafen him. She had to be seven years old at the most! A tiny child, probably the daughter of some spaced-out junkie, playing with him, taunting him, being the Nain Rouge and... But had it been like that, or had *he* made *her* run?

He didn't know! He couldn't remember! Not like that, not in any detail! He looked down into her glassy-eyed, horrified little face, and the hammering in his head became a wild, discordant cacophony. Suddenly weak, Ritchie Carbone tipped forward and lay across the tiny body, twitching and unable to speak. Later it snowed and so neither of them were discovered for well over a week. A ghastly and macabre tableau that the police, when they attended, could only speculate about.

Come the Vernal Equinox, the Marche du Nain Rouge still managed to banish the little horror for another year. Everyone saw the evil dwarf burn, in effigy, on a big bonfire in Cass Park, just minutes from where Carbone's old Coney Dog place used to be. A lot of the revellers said that it was a pity there was nowhere left in the Cass Corridor to get a decent Coney any more. But then they all agreed that it had probably been meant to be. Why, after all, should anyone get a lovely hotdog treat after burning even a mythical being, in effigy, to death?

THE KING OF OUDH'S CURRY

Amy Myers

So THIS WAS Oakham Manor. Auguste Didier was already having doubts about the wisdom of his journey. Not only had he come at great inconvenience to cook a banquet for a quiet but prestigious wedding, but the promised carriage to meet him at the Kentish railway station of Maidstone had not awaited him. Instead he had been forced to take an omnibus, alight some distance away and trudge the remaining mile with his baggage in what for England was extraordinary heat. Now at last he had arrived at the gates of the Manor with the delights of a refreshing tisane and then of preparing a sumptuous banquet before him.

"Are you the new chef?" an anxious voice enquired.

Intent on studying the façade of the Palladian mansion before him, Auguste had not seen the vagrant sitting propped up against the high brick wall to one side of the imposing iron gates. He looked to be a man of at least sixty, with tattered clothes which hung loosely on his shoulders, implying that his girth had once been considerably wider. Mild eyes in a wrinkled face, topped by a battered and old-fashioned white cook's hat, gazed up at him hopefully. Cook's hat? Could this sad-looking man be the former chef?

"Only for the next four days," Auguste replied truthfully.

The vagrant (or chef) shook his head sadly. "Four days ... I doubt if you'll last that long, sir. Why, I saw a chef go in these very gates three days ago, and he's gone already. Then there was William; he went after a month, and before him one called Tom spent only two days here."

"Why did all these cooks leave so suddenly? Were they dissatisfied with the kitchens?" Auguste was aghast. This sounded ominous. He had been relying on finding the very latest equipment there.

The vagrant looked perplexed. "They're all dead, sir, so I never asked them. If only they'd taken my recipe, it might have been different. But they wouldn't. I did tell them it was Sir Oliver's favourite... And now the latest has dropped dead. Let me see." He paused, deep in thought, then pronounced in triumph: "Alfred Hogg! That was his name. A gloomy sort of person. Unlike his late Majesty the King of Oudh, who was a very jolly gentleman."

Auguste began to feel distinctly uneasy. Nothing had been mentioned to him about this disastrous procession of chefs when Sir Oliver Marsh had so desperately begged him to cook the wedding banquet at the union of himself and his housekeeper. Such a ceremony was unusual enough in itself, without this vagrant's revelations. Who was he? Another chef, as he had implied? And what did the late King of Oudh have to do with Oakham Manor? Oudh had once been part of the Moghul Empire but was now a region of India and thus a province of the British Empire. Its late king, so far as Auguste could recollect, had been Wajid Ali Shah who died some years ago in the 1880s, and who had indeed been jolly but was unlikely to have travelled to Kent.

He decided to adopt a jovial tone. "I shall take great care not to drop arsenic into the soup."

There was no answering mirth, and perhaps, Auguste conceded, rightly so in the circumstances. Instead the vagrant looked most distressed. "Please do, sir. You will take my recipe yourself, won't you?"

"I beg your pardon?" Auguste stared at the grubby piece of paper that was pushed towards him.

"My recipe, sir. I do assure you, it is superb. If only they would have taken it, as I asked, all those chefs might still be with us."

"Recipe for what?" Auguste asked cautiously, taking the piece of paper.

"The King of Oudh's curry, sir. He gave this recipe to my father with his own royal hands. That's why he died."

"Who? Your father?" Auguste looked at the recipe in trepidation.

"No, sir, Prince Albert, Her Majesty's late husband. They must have mixed up the ingredients at Buckingham Palace and put arsenic instead of pounded mace in it. As one chef to another, sir, you'd agree that's not wise."

"I would," Auguste said hastily. He would have agreed with anything, provided he could speedily remove himself from here, in case this madman still carried a supply of poison. Prince Albert had died over thirty years earlier, but the death of the last chef of Oakham Manor had apparently been far more recent. Then he reproached himself. This poor man was mad and needed gentle understanding. "I'll certainly take your recipe, and try it, Mr... er—"

"Today I've decided that my name is Saxe-Coburg," was the grand reply. "And that is why I try to give the true recipe to every cook I meet. After all, the last one died only two days ago and I wouldn't like that to happen again. Suppose the King of Oudh were to attend the wedding ceremony? Not that that's likely. I recall he died in the early thirties, and that would be sixty years ago now."

"So he certainly won't be here for Sir Oliver's wedding," Auguste said jovially. The early thirties? This must be an earlier king than Wajid Ali Shah then. He had a faint recollection of reading of an eccentric gentleman on the throne of Oudh, with an excessive fear of being poisoned and a large harem (which perhaps accounted for the jolliness which the vagrant's father had attributed to him).

The vagrant sighed. "I believe not, sir, which is a great relief. Although of course it would be unfortunate if any of Sir Oliver's guests died, especially the Prince of Wales."

The Prince of Wales was to attend? Auguste was momentarily panic-stricken. The Prince of Wales had very definite ideas about his food – and about chefs. Surely he could not be among the guests? Sir Oliver would have warned him. Auguste tried to think logically, which was difficult as the glitter in the vagrant's eyes was now distinctly alarming. He forgot about trying to display gentle understanding, put the recipe in his pocket and made a speedy escape.

The forecourt of the Manor was already crowded with carriages, which was strange as the wedding was not to take place for another three days. He hesitated over whether to present himself at the front entrance of the mansion or the tradesmen's entrance – always a moot point for a master chef. Luckily the matter was settled for him as he saw a familiar figure walking towards him from the latter.

Auguste blinked. Egbert Rose? What was a detective inspector from Scotland Yard doing here? Surely this could be no social call – and yet the alternative was not pleasant to contemplate.

Egbert looked pleased to see him. "Well, well. Afternoon, Mr Didier."

"You're here to guard the guests, Inspector?"

"Not unless you're planning to bump them off," Egbert replied drily. "The cook's been murdered."

Murdered? This was growing worse, Auguste thought. Three men not only dead but murdered here? That surely suggested that more deaths might follow.

"Chap of the name of Alfred Hogg," Egbert continued, obviously pleased by Auguste's alarm. 'Came from Surrey. Used to work at a big house there with his wife. Had an eye for a pretty housemaid or two, they told the Yard, so his wife walked out, and after a year or two he decided he'd move on when one of the housemaids got in the family way. Never had time to start on the girls here; he was murdered the day after he arrived. The butler raised the alarm when he found him, and insisted on an investigation. He was right. Enough arsenic to wipe out the entire household."

Auguste's head spun with shock at this clear indication that the vagrant was no madman. Not completely anyway. The reason for Auguste's hasty summons to the Manor to cook for the wedding was apparent, but surely that would now be postponed? "How was the poison administered?" he asked faintly.

"In his food. A curry, the scientists tell us. The poor devil probably cooked his own death. There was a jar of rat poison in the kitchen."

Auguste reeled. *Curry*? This household seemed addicted to it. "Were the other chefs murdered too?"

Egbert looked startled. "What other chefs?"

"I was told Hogg's predecessors also died suspiciously soon after their arrival."

"First I've heard of it. Sure you haven't had a dose of the sun?"

"No. A dose of a former chef, whom I believe I had the pleasure of meeting at the gate."

Egbert grinned. "I've heard about old Isaac. So you're concocting a theory that he poisons off every new chef on their arrival, are you?"

Auguste paled. "No." That unpleasant thought had not occurred to him. "Fortunately I am merely a temporary chef."

"The others seem to have been temporary too. Make sure you're not next on the list."

"This menu of yours ..." Sir Oliver Marsh, a most merry gentleman when Auguste had met him previously at Plum's Club for Gentlemen, was looking worried. Surely there could be no problem with the menu Auguste had presented to him? It had been the result of many hours of anxious thought.

"Superb, Didier... superb! The turbot *à la Carème* is an inspired choice," Sir Oliver continued.

Auguste relaxed. Even so, he had expected to be told the wedding was postponed in view of the police presence and the chef's death. True, Mr Hogg had only worked here for a day, and he was not a family member, but nevertheless, Auguste thought, "Ask not for whom the bell tolls, it tolls for thee".

"So the wedding will still take place, Sir Oliver?" He glanced curiously at the prospective bride seated at Sir Oliver's side. Mrs Peak was in her middle years, and clad as befitted her current status in black bombazine. She looked as if she too might be merry by nature (unusual in housekeepers), but today she had other things on her mind.

"It will, Mr Didier," she assured him.

"It must," boomed Sir Oliver.

Mrs Peak had obviously noticed Auguste's surprise because she hastened to explain. "You are thinking of Mr Hogg's death, of course. That poison was meant for me, Mr Didier. I cannot be sure who is responsible, but there is no doubt that I was the intended victim. The curry that the police tell us killed him had been prepared for me by poor Mr Hogg. It is a favourite of mine, and I'd told him so."

"But why should someone wish to do such a terrible thing?" Auguste was even more appalled.

"I am afraid that there are those who do not approve of my marrying Sir Oliver."

He put a comforting hand on his wife-to-be's arm. "So the quicker the knot's tied the better, Didier," he said. "The wedding was always going to be a small one, but now we're overrun by police we've decided it will be even smaller. Good news, eh, Didier? Same money, not so much work. Much simpler food."

Auguste gazed at him in dismay. He could hardly believe that Sir Oliver expected him to be pleased by the news that he was being deprived of the opportunity to cook purée of partridges with quails' eggs, bisque of lobsters, civet of hare, and countless other delicacies.

"We'll have curry instead," Sir Oliver continued decisively. "Just the ticket. I took a fancy to it when I was a subaltern out in India. We'll have a few extras for the weaklings, of course. Roast beef, plain boiled trout, roly-poly pudding...you know the sort of thing."

Auguste did. His also knew that his art would be wasted on such unchallenging trifles. In addition to that, he was uncomfortably aware that his life might be threatened.

"Let me take you to meet Mr Carstairs, our butler, Mr Didier." Mrs Peak beamed at him. "I'm sure you are eager to begin your duties."

Auguste was not. In fact he realized that he was far more interested in the parade of his dead predecessors than he was in the preparation of such a mundane menu. And as it was Mr Carstairs who had raised the possibility of the last chef's meeting an unnatural death, Auguste would be interested to meet him. The demise of several chefs, however, would seem to conflict with Mrs Peak's belief that she was the intended victim. Pondering this, he followed her rustling skirts down the grand sweeping staircase, at the bottom of which stood a sour-faced lady of perhaps fifty, clad badly but so expensively that she clearly did not belong to the servants' quarters.

"I did not expect to see *you* on this staircase, Mrs Peak," she trilled shrilly.

The implication was clear. Housekeepers and temporary chefs should be using the servants' staircase. Mrs Peak was obviously well used to such attacks. "I have been discussing my wedding with Sir Oliver." A pleasant smile accompanied this reminder that soon the balance of power would be reversed.

If Auguste read the sour lady's expression correctly, that wedding would be no reason for her to celebrate.

"Poor lady," Mrs Peak commented to him as she swept along the next corridor. "Miss Lavinia Cartwright is merely a dependent cousin of Sir Oliver's late wife. I believe she had *hopes*, Mr Didier."

"Of what?"

"Of marrying Sir Oliver herself. She was employed out of sheer kindness as governess to his only son, and somehow he never had the heart to turn her out."

It occurred to Auguste that Mrs Peak could well find the heart to do so herself in due course. "His son lives here still?"

"Alas, tragically killed in the Zulu War. Sir Oliver's heir lives in the dower house on the estate – heir, that is, until Sir Oliver's and my wedding,' she added complacently. "Mr Ernest Marsh, I fear, is a young gentleman who lives on his expectations."

"So the estate is entailed."

"No." A beaming smile now. "It is for Sir Oliver to decide the future of his wealth and estates. I fear, Mr Didier, neither Miss Cartwright nor Mr Marsh cares for his happiness, only for their own future gain."

Auguste was beginning to understand why Mrs Peak believed herself to be the intended victim, and with reason. This posed an interesting question.

"Was the curry that killed Mr Hogg prepared only for you?"

"Yes. No one else has the taste for it in the servants' hall except me, but obviously the unfortunate Mr Hogg enjoyed it too. He was a newcomer, of course, and so whoever committed this terrible deed could not have known of his liking for curry."

"But you would have partaken of it yourself at dinner that evening."

"Indeed, but fortunately I was delayed by private business with Sir Oliver and could not eat with the other servants. I intended to dine later. By that time, the terrible news of Mr Hogg's illness made me suspicious of the curry."

"I gather other chefs here have died in similar circumstances," Auguste said tentatively.

She stopped short, and drew herself up indignantly. "Mr Didier, what can you mean?"

"One called Tom who died after two days, and William after a month."

Mrs Peak relaxed, and gave a merry laugh. "I do believe you've been listening to Mr Dickens."

"I beg your pardon?" Auguste could not recall the great novelist, even if he were alive, having much interest in chefs.

"Isaac Dickens, who often sits at the Manor gates."

Was that the vagrant's real name, Auguste wondered, or his chosen one for the day? "So it's not true about other chefs being murdered?"

"Of course not. William died of natural causes, and Tom simply disappeared, as cooks do from time to time. So distressing for Sir Oliver. A housemaid vanished at the same time, and we felt the two incidents might be connected. Very foolish. How could they get another place as good as Sir Oliver provides?"

Auguste still remained to be convinced of the pleasures of working at Oakham Manor. "Who *is* Isaac Dickens?"

"Isaac was chef here for many years, but he reached an age where the exigencies of cooking in such a prestigious household grew too much for him. He was pensioned off, but I fear he still likes to haunt the gates. He's quite harmless."

Auguste recalled the fanatical light in Isaac's eyes and was far from sure about this. "I agree it seems probable that the poisoner was trying to kill you, not Mr Hogg, and that must be frightening for you."

"It is." The housekeeper relaxed her guard a little. "I do try not to worry Sir Oliver too much about it, so it is a relief to be able to confide in you, Mr Didier."

Another problem still bothered him, but it was a difficult matter to raise. "Only a limited number of people would have access to that curry before it could be cooked and eaten," he began cautiously.

He need not have worried. Mrs Peak saw his point immediately.

"You are implying, of course, that the family, in which I include Miss Cartwright and Mr Ernest Marsh, would not normally enter the kitchen areas, which are in the servants' domain. You are correct."

"Then—"

Mrs Peak swept on. "There had been complaints, Mr Didier. The aroma of curry does not please everyone, and as Sir Oliver is fond of it a special kitchen was set up in a small outbuilding once used for storing apples. It has no connection either with the servants' wing or with the main house and so the smell of spices does not travel so quickly. Sir Oliver visits the kitchen himself, indulging in making his own blends of curry powder, and *anyone* – including Miss Cartwright and Mr Ernest – would be able to do the same. Even Mr Carstairs..." She hesitated. "I should explain, Mr Didier, that Mr Carstairs is not happy about my marriage. At one time, we had an understanding."

"That is easy to believe," Auguste replied gallantly. "He must have been most worried by your near escape from the poisoned curry."

"He was," Mrs Peak replied. "That is why he insisted on an inquest. 'There is more to this,' he said. 'The coroner must be notified about Mr Hogg's death.'"

Auguste was still struggling with a mental image of all those noble ladies and gentlemen beating a path to an outbuilding to indulge a passion for curry-powder blending. Curry, in his opinion, failed to woo the meat, fish or vegetables that it claimed to enhance; it merely tried to smother their taste out of existence.

Butlers were almighty beings in a household such as Oakham Manor, but then so were chefs, he reflected, as they arrived at the door of Pug's Parlour, the butler's sanctum. Nevertheless, as the door opened and a tall, thin, almost elegant gentleman peered out at him, Auguste decided to be wary. Butlers usually resented sharing power, and chefs, albeit temporary ones, might provide a threat to Mr Carstairs's authority, especially if he was upset by Mrs Peak's marriage to Sir Oliver. Luckily, Mr Carstairs had obviously overcome any inner turmoil and was gravely welcoming.

"An honour to have you with us, Mr Didier. So good of you to come at such short notice."

Auguste endeavoured to look flattered. "I am delighted to be here." Even to his ears his own voice lacked conviction.

"I have explained to Mr Didier," Mrs Peak said earnestly, "that we are a happy household here, despite the most distressing occurrence of Mr Hogg's death."

"An accident," Mr Carstairs assured Auguste. "As I explained to the inspector when he asked why I had called for an inquest. The idea of murder or suicide seemed far-fetched, and yet so did the idea of a natural death so soon after Mr Hogg's arrival. When I inspected the kitchen I realized that rat poison must have been used for its proper purpose and then not put back in its rightful place. The new chef must have confused it with rice flour or arrowroot."

Mrs Peak disagreed. "Or else someone placed it there purposely, having thrown handfuls of it into the curry. That, I feel, is far more likely. Mr Hogg was not the sort of person to confuse ingredients."

Mr Carstairs looked taken aback by her disagreement, and hastily murmured that she was no doubt correct.

"Which recipe did Mr Hogg use?" Auguste asked, remembering the dire prospect before him. He too would be cooking curry and endeavouring to make of it a dish suitable for a wedding banquet.

Mrs Peak smiled at him. "Mr Hogg asked me which was Sir Oliver's favourite curry, because, as he explained, he would need to practise. I therefore passed him the recipe."

Once established in the attic room that was to be his home for the next few days – with a key in the lock in view of the possibility of assassination – Auguste took the grubby piece of paper that Isaac

had given him out of his pocket. Flour was not one of the ingredients listed for Sir Oliver's favourite, the King of Oudh's curry.

He found old Isaac sitting peacefully at the gate contemplating a
cow in the field opposite and munching a lump of bread. In his other
hand he had a hunk of cheese, and a bottle of beer stood on the
grass beside him.

"I'm sorry to disturb you at lunch, Mr Dickens."

"You're still alive," Isaac commented with great disappointment.

"And intend to remain so," Auguste informed him. "I have to
cook the King of Oudh's curry for the wedding ceremony."

"My dear fellow, I am delighted." Bread and cheese were laid
aside as Isaac scrambled to his feet and pumped Auguste's hand in
appreciation of the honour. "At last someone has seen the beauty of
the recipe. Only Sir Oliver had paid due deference to it hitherto."

"I'm told that Alfred Hogg cooked this particular curry too, the
one that carried the poison in it."

Isaac looked puzzled. "I didn't give the recipe to him. He didn't
want it, and I was glad of it. He did not look a worthy sort of
person."

"Mr Hogg requested the recipe for Sir Oliver's favourite, and
Mrs Peak passed it to him. It seems to be generally known in the
household."

"But rarely cooked," Isaac said severely. "Sir Oliver is badly
served, I fear."

"Does your recipe carry flour of any kind in it?" If not, then an
accident with the ingredients was most certainly ruled out.

"Certainly not." Isaac was indignant. "The King of Oudh's is not
a commonplace curry, Mr Didier. King Nasir-ud-din was a most
superior person, so my father informed me. He was most enthusiastic about European culture, and indeed his favoured companion
was a European barber, a strange fellow called de Russett, who
tasted all his food and wine, lest it was poisoned. The barber
shopped in the markets to bring back only the finest and purest
ingredients and then cooked them himself for His Majesty. He is
hardly likely to have included flour amongst them. Now were it
some inferior curry, such as that known as Mr Arnott's curry, with

cabbage and apples, flour would no doubt be permissible, but with the King of Oudh's refined tastes, it would be totally out of place. I am speechless at the suggestion, sir, speechless."

Alfred Hogg might have confused flour with rat poison but he would not have added it to the curry, Auguste reasoned. That must have been done by a third party. But if so, he wondered, why did the killer leave the rat poison in the outside kitchen? Why not remove it? It seemed extraordinarily careless.

"So you're still alive."

Auguste whirled round in the middle of the extremely boring task of making a shepherd's pie for the wedding on the morrow. His spirits were very low and he was counting the hours until he could return to his beloved Plum's Club for Gentlemen, where his art was appreciated.

"As you can see," he said crossly. He liked Inspector Rose but was beginning heartily to dislike comments on his own continuing existence. He had tried to keep his mind on wedding menus, but this was hard when it kept moving back to the question of the dead chef. Partly, he admitted, because he had been obliged to cook such large quantities of the King of Oudh's curry in the two days that had passed since his arrival.

"Nice-looking pie, Mr Didier." Egbert Rose looked wistfully at it, and for a moment Auguste was pleased.

"Would you like one, Inspector? I can spare one for Mrs Rose."

"No arsenic in it, is there?"

"That is not an ingredient I'm accustomed to using," Auguste replied mildly. Jokes were all very well, but when they concerned his cooking they had to be put in their place.

The inspector had the grace to blush. "Thought you'd like to know we've put a guard on Mrs Peak. Those other dead chefs—"

"I understand their deaths or disappearances were not due to the King of Oudh's curry," Auguste broke in. "Or to any other curry or any third party."

Egbert looked disappointed. "So you know that, do you? Yes, it looks certain that Mrs Peak was the intended target."

"Have you talked yet to Miss Cartwright and Mr Ernest Marsh? They would seem to have plenty of cause to wish Mrs Peak harm."

"I have. Spitting fury, both of them. They'd have liked to have doctored her curry, but I can't prove either of them did."

"And Mr Carstairs, her jilted lover?"

"Same thing. Rather too eager to point out it must have been an accident. But you know what I think, Mr Didier?"

Auguste regarded him carefully. "That the curry is being pulled over our eyes?"

"What?" The inspector looked totally bemused.

It was Auguste's turn to blush. "I'm sorry, Inspector. I am somewhat dejected at present. I am not accustomed to cooking curry."

"What *is* this about a curry?"

"Not *a* curry, *the* curry. The King of Oudh's curry. Sir Oliver's favourite and the one that Alfred Hogg cooked that day. It doesn't have flour in it, which rules out the possibility of an accident with the jar of rat poison. That was deliberately left there to smother us."

Egbert regarded him sourly at this second slip. "Speak for yourself. I'm not smothered."

Auguste made another effort. "I apologize. It is the curry that smothers."

"Smothers what?" The inspector was getting irritated, and Auguste could hardly blame him.

"The curry's main ingredients are suffused with the strong flavours of the sauce."

"I'm not here for a cooking lesson, Mr Didier. I'll send along Mrs Rose for that."

Auguste tried again. "You – we perhaps – are losing touch with the main ingredient of this case."

"And what might that be?"

"The dead man, Alfred Hogg. There are several people who would no doubt like to kill Mrs Peak, but we forget who actually *was* killed."

"Who would want to kill him? He'd only been here a day."

"Exactly. So there could be only one person here who would wish to kill him."

"And who might that be?"

"Mrs Peak."

Egbert stared at him incredulously. "The blooming bride? Hell and Tommy, what for?"

"Only she could have a motive for leaving the rat poison in the curry kitchen after using it to flavour the curry to kill Alfred Hogg. She needed to show that others in the household, both family and servants, could not only have had reason to kill her, but also the means. If she'd moved the jar back to its proper place, it's unlikely that the connection could have been made that she was the intended victim, not the cook. If it turned out that there was an investigation into the death, she needed all the attention to be on herself, not on Mr Hogg. Once Mr Carstairs had raised the alarm, she quickly drew attention to herself... a task made easier because it could have been true. Three people could, theoretically, have wished her out of the way. She needed to act in a hurry after the shock she had received the day before."

Egbert Rose was still staring at him. "What shock? If you'd be so good as to enlighten me, Mr Didier?"

"Of seeing Alfred Hogg again, in view of their relationship. Sir Oliver would have appointed him, not her."

"What's all this about a relationship?"

"I think you will find that she is actually Mrs Hogg. She spoke of Mr Hogg in terms of knowing his habits. He was not the sort of person to confuse ingredients, according to her. And he had to be silenced quickly if her marriage was to go ahead."

There was a long pause. "All theory. No proof."

"I admit that."

Another pause, then: "I'll get my men on to it. Should be easy enough to prove."

"I hope so."

Egbert Rose paused on his way to the kitchen door. "By the way, Mr Didier. I was walking by that outside kitchen. The curry you've been cooking smells rather good. I'll have the recipe, if I may."

***

"It's all very well, Mr Didier, but what shall I do?" Sir Oliver looked piteously grey after Egbert Rose had broken the news to him. Auguste had immediately been summoned and his heart had been moved when he saw his temporary employer's anxious expression.

"I am sorry, sir," he said. "I'm sure Mrs Peak was genuinely fond of you."

"Eh?" Sir Oliver's face looked a little more like its usual merry self. "Nonsense, man. She was after my money. Lavinia said so all the time. Good girl, Lavinia. Might have a wedding after all. So what shall I do?"

"About what?"

"A cook. You said you're leaving."

"I am, sir." He couldn't stay in this spice-laden household any longer.

"Who's to cook my curry then?"

Auguste seized his chance. "There is an old gentleman at your gate ..."

LONDON CALLING

Ian Ayris and Nick Quantrill

King's Cross, London – 18.50

HAD ANOTHER EAR-BASHIN off the missus. "Hull?" she says. "Hull? What you got to go to Hull for?" "Business," I says. And it is. My business. She don't know nothing about what I do. She thinks I'm one of them blokes what pick up cars and drop em off places, you know, them geezers you see carryin number-plates round with em. She don't know I'm on the firm. Harry's firm. Harry Sullivan.

I been doin jobs for Harry ten years now. I'm what you might call, a specialist. Harry's got a problem, he phones me up, I clear it with the missus, and I sort the problem out. The problem's always got a name, and a place I can find em. In this case it's Tony Weathers. And he's in Hull. Apparently, so Harry says, this Weathers geezer owes him a large wedge and needs teachin a lesson. Only one lesson I teach. The hardest one there is. Harry's brother is based up there, but he don't trust him to sort it, even though he's Harry's number two. Can't say I blame him. Still, he's got us a lead on where Weathers is hiding out, so I have to play along.

So I'm on this train to Hull. Bound to be a dump. Up north, ain't it? It's all like that up there. Manchester, Liverpool, Leeds, Newcastle. Like goin back two hundred years. I been all over, doin jobs for Harry. But I'm gettin sick of it now. This is the last one. I've made me mind up on that. Tracey, that's me missus, she reckons I let Harry walk all over me. "Whenever that phone rings," she says, "and it's Harry, you're all, 'Yes, Harry, no, Harry, three bags full, Harry.'"

That's what she reckons. Not any more. Not after today. I'll show her. I'm gonna be the big man. Got a couple of fellas onside, high up in the firm, you know. Harry won't know what hit him.

Holderness Road, Hull – 19.50

Fuck's sake. You just can't get the staff in this business. I look around the staff-room. Lazy to a man. Playing cards, laughing and joking, like there's nothing better to do. I shake my head and close the door on them. Don't they realize we're in the grip of the biggest recession in living memory? I've given them jobs and roofs over their heads. Looked after their families. It's all right for them. They're not entrepreneurs like me. They're happy just to pick up their wages. Knobheads, the lot of them.

My office is upstairs. It's small, but it does me. My wife, Denise, helps out sometimes. She passes me some paperwork. I'm not really in the mood. I ask her to make me a coffee. She disappears. Reluctantly. I need to look over the accounts, make sure I'm making the right decision here. The best advice I ever got was from my brother. If you're standing still, you're going backwards, he told me. He was always the clever one. And the handsome one. And the more successful one. The only thing I got that he wanted was Denise.

I'm looking at the income and expenditure on the spreadsheet. It's giving me a headache. The figures don't add up, that's for sure, and I have to sort it. Times are tough and I've got a decision to make. This Weathers situation is an opportunity, and it's important to recognize opportunities when they present themselves. Denise breaks my concentration by putting a cup of coffee in front of me. I look up at her. He'll be here soon, she says.

Hull Interchange – 20.15

Hull station's just like any other in this god-forsaken country. Soulless. Fuckin soulless. Pretentious wankers even call it an "interchange" rather than a station. The place is fuckin empty. End of the line. Nobody just passes through here. There's even a statue of Philip Larkin. What kind of place celebrates an old racist? That said, I don't mind a bit of his poetry. I like a bit of culture.

Eddie said he'd meet me out front. Eddie Painter. One of my boys. Or he will be, give it a couple of weeks. Went to school together, me and Eddie. I trust him with me life.

Here he is.

"Hello, Pete. You all right? Bloody place this, ain't it?"

I nod. Grim. Gotta be distant when you're the boss. Enigmatic, you know.

"Motor's over here, Pete."

We get shiftin. He's parked down a side road. Good thinkin. CCTV's a bastard.

Turns out Eddie's got hold of a Merc. C250. Classy. That's what I like about Eddie. Comes across as a fuckin idiot at times, but the boy's got class.

So off we go. Through the streets of Hull. Fuck me, I thought the East End was a shithole, but this up here, it's a different fuckin game. But it ain't the time for no sight-seein, I gotta set me stall straight and then I'm home free. Me and Eddie'll drive back, then it's straight over to Harry's gaff to make him an offer he can't refuse. That's out *The Godfather*, that is. The first one.

Eddie pulls the motor into a sideroad and squeaks the kerb as he parks.

"You all right?" I says.

He nods his head. Says nothing.

"Is this it, then?" I says.

A Portakabin on an industrial estate. It might be time for Harry to learn the facts of life, but I've got to admit I still have some respect for the bloke. He's done a lot better than his brother, that's for sure. I shake me head. A fuckin Portakabin.

Holderness Road, Hull – 20.25

I hear a car pull up so I look out of the window. It's them. I tell Denise to disappear. She doesn't need to be about for this bit.

Eddie Painter leads them in. I nod to him. Decent bloke is Eddie. He's put the years in. Behind him comes Pete. I shake his hand, tell him it's good to see him. We all sit down. I'm behind the desk, they're both sat in front of me.

"It's a bit of a shithole up here, ain't it?" Pete says. "A fucking Portakabin on a building site?"

I shrug. It does me. Low-key. Keeps me under the radar. I tell him I know where Tony Weathers is.

Pete sits down and smiles at me. Horrible teeth. "I'm not interested in Weathers," he says.

I see him go to his pocket.

Eddie speaks. "I wouldn't do that if I was you, Pete." I watch as he turns towards his mate.

By the time he turns back to me, I've got my gun out. It's my turn to smile. "You thought you could come here and try to turn me against Harry? My own brother? Eddie told me all about your little plan."

My brother might be the blue-eyed boy, and I might be the one stuck up here, but there's a line you don't cross. He lets me get on with my thing, run my own sidelines up here. I know which side my bread's buttered on. Harry's not ready for the scrapyard just yet.

Eddie has a gun trained on him, too. "Sorry about this, Pete," he says.

"Do you think me and Harry don't speak?" I say to Pete. It's slowly dawning on him that he's been stitched up.

My mobile rings. I hold it up to him. The display says Harry. "London calling," I say. I listen as Harry talks and then tell him we're just about done here. Times are tough, but I've made my decision. "Blood's thicker than water," I say to Pete after terminating the call. "Much thicker."

And sometimes it's handy operating from a Portakabin on a building site. Plenty of foundations that need filling in.

THE CURIOUS AFFAIR OF THE DEODAND

Lisa Tuttle

O NCE IT HAD become painfully clear that I could no longer continue to work in association with Miss G— F—, I departed Scotland and returned to London, where I hoped I would quickly find employment. I had no bank account, no property, nothing of any value to pawn or sell, and, after I had paid my train fare, little more than twelve shillings to my name. Although I had friends in London who would open their homes to me, I had imposed before, and was determined not to be a burden. It was therefore a matter of the utmost urgency that I should obtain a position: I emphasize this point to account for what might appear a precipitate decision.

Arriving so early in the morning at King's Cross, it seemed logical enough to set off at once, on foot, for the ladies' employment bureau in Oxford Street.

The bag that had seemed light enough when I took it down from the train grew heavier with every step, so that I was often obliged to stop and set it down for a few moments. One such rest took place outside a newsagent's shop, and while I caught my breath and rubbed my aching arm I glanced at the notices on display in the window. One, among the descriptions of lost pets and offers of rooms to let, caught my attention.

—

Consulting Detective
Requires Assistant

Must be literate, brave, congenial, with a good memory, & willing to work all hours.

Apply in person to
J. Jesperson,
203A Gower Street

Even as my heart leaped, I scolded myself for being a silly girl. Certainly, I was sharp and brave, blessed with good health and a strong constitution, but when you came right down to it, I was a woman, small and weak. What detective would take on such a liability?

But the card said nothing about weapons or physical strength. I read it again, and then glanced up from the number on the card – 203A – to the number painted above the shop premises: 203.

There were two doors. One, to the left, led into the little shop, but the other, painted glistening black, bore a brass plate inscribed *Jesperson*.

My knock was answered by a lady in early middle age, too genteel in dress and appearance to be mistaken for a servant.

"Mrs Jesperson?" I asked.

"Yes?"

I told her I had come in response to the advertisement, and she let me in. There was a lingering smell of fried bacon and toasted bread that reminded me I'd had nothing to eat since the previous afternoon.

"Jasper," she said, opening another door and beckoning me on. "Your notice has already borne fruit! Here is a lady ... Miss ... ?"

"I am Miss Lane," I said, going in.

I entered a warm, crowded, busy, comfortable, cheerful place. I relaxed, the general atmosphere, with the familiar scent of books, tobacco, toast, and ink that imbued it, making me feel at home even before I'd had a chance to look around. The room obviously combined as office and living room in one. The floor-to-ceiling bookshelves, crammed with volumes, gave it the look of a study, as did the very large, very cluttered desk piled with papers and journals. But there were also armchairs near the fireplace – the hearth cold on this warm June morning; the mantelpiece so laden with such a variety of objects I simply could not take them in at a glance – and a table bearing the remains of breakfast for two. This quick impression was all I had time to absorb before the man, springing up from his place at the table, commanded my attention.

I say *man*, yet the first word that came to mind was *boy*, for despite his size – he was, I later learned, six foot four inches tall – the smooth, pale, lightly freckled face beneath a crown of red-gold curls was like that of an angelic child.

He fixed penetrating blue eyes upon me. "How do you do, Miss Lane? So, you fancy yourself a detective?" His voice at any rate was a man's; deep and well modulated.

"I would not say so. But you advertised for an assistant, someone literate, brave, congenial, with a good memory, and willing to work all hours. I believe I possess all those qualities, and I am in search of … *interesting* employment."

Something sparked between us. It was not that romantic passion that poets and sentimental novelists consider the only connection worth writing about between a man and a woman. It was, rather, a *liking*, a recognition of congeniality of mind and spirit.

Mr Jesperson nodded his head and rubbed his hands together, the mannerisms of an older man. "Well, very well," he murmured to himself, before fixing me again with his piercing gaze.

"You have worked before, of course, in some capacity requiring sharp perceptions, careful observation, and a bold spirit, yet you are now cut adrift—"

"Jasper, please," Mrs Jesperson interrupted. "Show the lady common courtesy, at least." Laying one hand gently on my arm, she invited me to sit, indicating a chair, and offered tea.

"I'd love some, thank you. But that's your chair, surely?"

"Oh, no, I won't intrude any further." As she spoke, she lifted the fine white china teapot, assessing the weight of the contents with a practised turn of her wrist. "I'll leave the two of you to your interview while I fetch more tea. Would you like bread and butter, or anything else?"

A lady always refuses food when she hasn't been invited to a meal – but I was too hungry for good manners. "That would be most welcome, thank you."

"I'll have more toast, if you please, and jam would be nice, too, Mother."

She raised her eyes heavenward and sighed as she went away.

He'd already returned his attention to me. "You have been in the Highlands, in the country home of one of our titled families. You were expecting to be there for the rest of the summer, until an unfortunate ... occurrence ... led to an abrupt termination of your visit, and you were forced to leave at once, taking the first train to London where you have ... a sister? No, nothing closer than an aunt or a cousin, I think. And you were on your way there when, pausing to rest, you spotted my notice." He stopped, watching me expectantly.

I shook my head to chide him.

He gaped, crestfallen. "I'm wrong?"

"Only about a few things, but anyone with eyes might guess I'd been in Scotland, considering the time of day, and the fact that I've had no breakfast, and that there are no foreign stickers on my portmanteau."

"And the abrupt departure?"

"I was on foot, alone, there not having been time for a letter to inform my friends – there is no aunt or cousin – of my arrival."

"The job is yours," he said suddenly. "Don't worry about references – *you* are your own best reference. The job is yours, if you still want it."

"I should like to know more about it, first," I replied, thinking I should at least appear to be cautious. "What would be my duties?"

"*Duties* seems to me the wrong word. Your *role*, if you like, would be that of an associate, helping me to solve crimes, assisting in deduction, and, well, whatever is required. You've read the Sherlock Holmes stories?"

"Of course. I should point out that, unlike Dr Watson, I'd be no good in a fight. I have a few basic nursing skills, so I could bind your wounds, but don't expect me to recognize the symptoms of dengue fever, or—or—"

He laughed. "I don't ask for any of that. My mother's the nurse. I'm a crack shot, and I've also mastered certain skills imported from the Orient, which give me an advantage in unarmed combat. I cannot promise to keep you out of danger entirely, but if danger does not frighten you—" He took the answer from my face and gave me a broad smile. "Very well, then. We're agreed?"

How I longed to return that smile, and take the hand he offered to shake on it! But with no home, and only twelve shillings in my purse, I needed more.

"What's the matter?"

"This is awkward," I said. "Unlike Dr Watson, I don't have a medical practice to provide me with an income ..."

"Oh, money!" he exclaimed, with that careless intonation possible only to people who've never had to worry about the lack of it. "Why, of course, I mean for you to get something more than the thrill of the chase out of this business. A man's got to live! A woman, too. How are you at writing? Nothing fancy, just setting down events in proper order, in a way that anyone might understand. Ever tried your hand at such a narrative?"

"I've written a few articles; most recently, reports for the Society for Psychical Research, which were published, although not above my own name."

His eyes widened when I mentioned the SPR, and he burst out excitedly, "C— House! By Jove, is that where you've been? Are you 'Miss X'?"

I must have looked pained, for he quickly apologized.

I didn't like to explain how hearing her name – one of her silly pseudonyms – when I was feeling so far from her, so safe and comfortable, had unsettled me, so I only remarked that I'd been startled by his swift, accurate deduction. "'Miss X' *was* the name assigned in authorship to my reports, but in actual fact I was her ... her assistant, until yesterday, when a disagreement about some events in C— House led to my sudden departure. But how do you know of it? The investigation is incomplete, and no report has yet been published."

Without taking his eyes from my face – and what secrets he read there, I didn't want to know! – Jesperson waved one long-fingered hand towards the desk piled with papers and journals. "Although not myself a member of the SPR, I take a keen interest in their findings. I have read the correspondence; I knew there was an investigation of the house planned for this summer.

"I am a thoroughly rational, modern man," he went on. "If I worship anything, it must be the god we call Reason. I'm a materialist who has no truck with superstition, but in my studies I've come across a great many things that science cannot explain. I do not sneer at those who attend séances or hunt for ghosts; I think it would be foolish to ignore the unexplained as unworthy of investigation. *Everything* should be questioned and explored. It's not belief that is important, but *facts*."

"I agree," I said quietly.

He leaned towards me across the uncleared table, his gaze frank and curious. "Have you ever seen a ghost, Miss Lane?"

"No."

But he had noticed some small hesitation. "You're not certain? You've had experiences that can't be explained in rational terms?"

"Many people have had such experiences."

"Yes," he drawled, and leaned back, a faraway look in his eyes. But only for a moment. "Tell me: do you possess any of those odd talents or senses that are generally called *psychic*?"

Despite the many times I'd been asked that question, I still had a struggle with my reply. "I am aware, at times, of *atmospheres* to which others seem immune, and occasionally receive impressions … sometimes I possess knowledge of things without being able to explain how I know. But I make no claims; I do not discount the effects of a vivid imagination allied with sharp perception and a good memory. Almost every so-called psychic medium I have ever met could achieve their results through looking, listening, and remembering, with no need for 'spirit guides'."

He nodded in thoughtful agreement. "I have performed mind-reading tricks myself. If I didn't feel obliged to explain how it was done, I suppose I could make money at it. So how do you explain ghosts? Aren't they spirits?"

"I don't know. I subscribe to the idea that the ghosts people see or sense are after-images, akin to photographs or some form of recorded memory. Strong emotions seem to leave an impression behind, in certain places more powerfully than in others. Objects also have their memories, if I may put it like that. Occasionally, an inanimate object will give off vibrations – of ill will, or despair – so that it seems to project a kind of mental image of the person who owned it."

He gazed at me in fascination, which I found a novel experience. Even quite elderly gentlemen in the SPR had not found me so interesting, but of course I tended to meet them in company with "Miss X", who was used to being the centre of attention.

I decided it was time to get back to business, and reminded him of his original question: "You asked me if I wrote. I presume you were thinking that I could write up your cases with a view to publcation?"

"Certainly the more interesting ones. Publication would have two useful ends. On the one hand, it would bring my name to public attention, and attract new clients. On the other, it would provide you with an income."

My heart sank. I had friends who survived by the pen, so was well aware of how much time and toil it required to scrape a bare living in Grub Street. Even if Mr Jesperson solved an interesting, exciting case every week (which seemed unlikely), and I sold every story I wrote … I was still struggling to work out how much I'd have to write, at thruppence a line, to earn enough to pay for room and board in a dingy lodging-house, when he said something that cheered me:

"Of course, I realize not every case would be suitable for publication. I only mention it so you wouldn't think you'd have to live solely on your percentage."

"What percentage?"

"That would depend on the extent of your contribution. It could be anything from ten to fifty per cent of whatever the client pays me."

Mrs Jesperson had entered the room while he was speaking, and I heard her sharp intake of breath just before she set down the tray she carried on the table. "Jasper?" she said in a voice of doom.

"I can hardly ask Miss Lane to work unpaid, Mother."

"You can't afford to pay an assistant."

Despite my discomfiture, I intervened. "Please, let's not argue over money. I must admit, it's still unclear what Mr Jesperson would be paying me *for*, apart from the sort of intellectual support and companionship any *friend* would freely give. And I should like to be that friend."

Now I had their rapt attention. "As you deduced, Mr Jesperson, I left my last situation rather abruptly, without being paid for my work. I came to London to seek, not my fortune, but simply honest work to support myself."

I paused to draw breath, rather hoping one of them would say something, and I took a quick glance around the room to remind myself that even if Mrs Jesperson felt they could not afford to pay an assistant, they nevertheless had all this – the fine china, the silver, the leather-bound books and substantial furniture, a whole houseful of things – by contrast with the contents of my single, well-worn bag.

"If I could afford it, I should propose an unpaid trial period, perhaps a month to discover the value of my contribution to your work. Unfortunately, I can't even afford to rent a room—"

"But you'll stay here!" exclaimed Mrs Jesperson. She frowned at her son. "Didn't you explain?"

Mr Jesperson was now serenely pouring tea. "I thought you might have deduced it, from the wording of my advertisement. The part about working all hours. Of course my assistant must be here, ready for any eventuality. It's no good if I have to write you a letter every time I want your opinion, or send a messenger halfway across London and await your reply."

"There's a room upstairs, well furnished and waiting," said Mrs Jesperson, handing me a plate of white bread, thinly sliced and thickly buttered, and then a little glass bowl heaped with raspberry jam. I saw that her tray also contained a plate of buttered toast, and a pot of honey. "And three meals a day."

***

The room upstairs was indeed very nice, spacious enough to serve as both bedroom and sitting room, and far more pleasantly decorated than any accommodation I'd ever paid for in London. Not a single Landseer reproduction or indifferent engraving hung upon the wall, yet there was an attractive watercolour landscape and some odd, interesting carvings from a culture I did not recognize. The furnishings were basic, but cushions and brightly patterned swathes of fabric made it more attractive, and I felt at home there at once, soothed and inspired by the surroundings, just as in the large, cluttered room downstairs.

I spent some time unpacking and arranging my few things, and writing letters informing friends of my new address, before I lay down to rest. I hadn't slept much on the train, but now established in my new position – even if it was nearly as problematic, in terms of remuneration, as my last – I felt comfortable enough to fall into a deep and refreshing slumber.

Dinner was a delicious vegetable curry prepared by Mrs Jesperson herself. They could not afford a cook, although they did have a "daily" for the heavier housework. That evening, as we sat together, I learned a little of their recent history, without being terribly forthcoming about my own.

Jasper Jesperson was twenty-one years old, and an only child. Barely fifteen when his father died, he'd accompanied his mother to India, where she had a brother. But they had been in India for only a year before going to China, and, later, the South Sea Islands. An intriguing offer brought them back to London more than a year previously, but it had not turned out as expected (he said he would tell me the whole story another time) and subsequently he decided that the best use of his abilities and interests would be to establish himself as a consulting detective.

He'd concluded three successful commissions so far. Two had been rather easily dealt with and would not make interesting stories; the third was quite different, and I shall write about that another time. It was after that case, which had so tested his abilities, that he decided to advertise for an assistant.

His fourth case, and my first, was to begin the next morning, with the arrival of a new client.

"Read his letter, and you may know as much about the affair as I," said Jesperson, handing a folded page across his desk to me.

The sheet was headed with the name of a gentlemen's club in Mayfair, and signed "William Randall". Although some overhasty pen strokes and blotches might suggest the author was in the grip of strong emotion, it might also be that he was more accustomed to dictating his correspondence.

Dear Mr Jesperson,

Your name was given to me by a friend in the Foreign Office with the suggestion that if anyone could solve a murder that still baffles the police, it is you.

Someone close to me believes I am at risk of a murderous attack from the same, unknown killer, to whose victim she was at the time engaged to be married.

I will explain all when we meet. If I may, I will call on you at ten o'clock on Wednesday morning. If that is inconvenient, please reply by return of post with a more suitable time.

Yours sincerely, etc.

I folded the letter and handed it back to Jesperson, who was gazing at me, bright-eyed and expectant.

He prompted. "Any questions?"

"The Foreign Office?"

"Never mind about that. It's only my uncle, trying to keep me in work. Don't you want to know what I've deduced about the writer of this letter? What unsolved crime affects this man so nearly? I believe I have it."

"I think I'd rather wait and hear what Mr Randall himself has to say, first. If you're right, well and good, but if you're wrong, you'll only confuse me."

He looked a bit crestfallen, making me think of a little boy who hadn't been allowed to show off his cleverness, and I said, "You can tell me afterwards if you were right."

"But you might not believe me. Oh, well, it doesn't matter."

I heard his mother murmur, "Party tricks." But if he heard, he at least gave no sign, and let me change the subject, and the rest of the evening passed quite pleasantly.

Mr William Randall arrived promptly as the carriage clock on the (recently dusted) mantelpiece was striking ten. He was a dapper young man with a drooping moustache, his regular features lifted from mere good looks into something striking by a pair of large, dark eyes that anyone more romantic than I would call soulful.

He refused any refreshment, took a seat, and began his story after the brief, hesitant disclaimer that "it was probably a load of nonsense", but his fiancée was worried.

"The lady I intend to make my wife is Miss Flora Bellamy, of Harrow." Her name meant nothing to me, but we both saw Jesperson straighten up.

"Yes, I thought you might make the connection. She was, of course, engaged to Mr Archibald Adcocks, the prominent financier, at the time of his terrible death."

"So she thinks his death was connected to the fact of their engagement? And that you are now in danger?"

"She does."

"How curious! What are her reasons?"

He sighed and held up his hands. "'The heart has its reasons, that reason knows not.' Women, you know, think more with their hearts than their heads. It is all too circumstantial to convince me, a matter of mere coincidence, and yet ... she is so *certain*."

Listening to them was frustrating, so I was forced to interrupt. "Excuse me, but would you mind telling me the facts of Mr Adcocks's death?"

Jesperson turned to me with a smile of secret triumph. *I could have told you last night!* said his expression, but he only remarked, "It was in all the papers, a year ago."

"Fifteen months," Randall corrected him. "He was attacked on his way to the railway station, not long after saying goodnight to Flora at her door. She wanted him to take a cab, because he had recently injured his foot, but he insisted that he could manage the short walk easily with the aid of a stick." He hesitated, then said, "He borrowed a walking stick from the stand beside the door."

"The injury must have been very recent," I suggested, and Randall gave me a nod.

"Not long after dinner, that same evening. He tripped in the hall and struck his foot, but although it was quite painful, he insisted it was too minor to make a fuss about."

"Not a man to make a fuss."

"He was no weakling. And quite well able to look after himself. Something of an amateur pugilist."

"Yet someone attacked him, unprovoked."

"So we must assume. He was found lying sprawled on the path, his head bloody from a terrible blow. He was barely alive, unable to speak, and died from his injury that same night, without being able to indicate what had happened. It may be that he didn't know, that the cowardly assault had come from behind."

"No one was ever arrested," Jesperson told me. "There were no suspects."

I frowned. "Could anyone suggest a motive?"

"It was usually assumed to have been an impulsive crime, not planned, since the murder weapon was his own walking stick."

"Not his own," Mr Randall objected. "Borrowed from Flora's house."

"Even so. It may be he was attacked by a gang of thugs who thought him an easy target because he limped. Yet, if they were intent on robbery, no one could explain why they did not take his wallet, stuffed with pound notes, or his gold watch, or anything else. He was found not long after he fell, lying in the open, near a streetlamp, and there were no obvious hiding places nearby.

Although one witness reported hearing a cry, no one was seen running away or otherwise behaving in a suspicious manner."

"Did Mr Adcocks have enemies?" I asked.

"He seems to have been well liked by all who knew him, including those who did business with him. No one obviously benefited by his death."

"Who inherited his property?"

"His mother."

Before I could say anything more, Jesperson resumed. "Mr Randall, you've suggested that Miss Bellamy believed his death was as a result of, or at least connected to, their engagement."

"No one else thought so."

"How did her family feel about it?"

He sighed and shook his head. "She has no family. Since being orphaned at an early age, Miss Bellamy has lived in the house of her guardian, a man by the name of Rupert Harcourt."

Although the even tenor of his voice did not change, when he pronounced this name I shivered, and knew we had come to the heart of the matter.

"Her parents named this man as her guardian?" Jesperson enquired.

Mr Randall shook his head. "They did not know him. He had no connection to the family at all. When Mr Bellamy died, the infant Flora was all alone in the world. A total stranger, reading of her situation in a newspaper, was so struck with pity that he offered her a home."

"You find that strange," I said, remarking his tone.

His eyes, for all their languid soulfulness, could still deliver a piercing look. "It is surely unusual for an unmarried, childless man of thirty-plus to go out of his way to adopt an unwanted infant. In fact, he never *did* adopt Flora, but set up some sort of legal arrangement to last until she married, or reached the age of twenty-one – a date still eight months in the future."

"She has money?"

"Very little. To give him credit, Harcourt never touched her small inheritance, yet she lacked for nothing; toys and sweetmeats, clothes and meals, books and music lessons, were all paid for from his own pocket. The money from her father was left to gain interest. I suppose it may be near one thousand pounds."

It sounded a lot to me, being used to managing on less than thirty pounds a year, but it was not the sort of fortune to inspire a devious double-murder plot.

"Has any attempt been made on your life?" Jesperson asked suddenly, and I saw Mr Randall wince and raise his hand to his head before he replied, "Oh, no, hardly – no, not at all."

Jesperson responded testily to this prevarication. "Oh, come now! Something happened to frighten your fiancée, whatever you may make of it. Don't try to hide it."

With a sigh, Randall lifted the lock of dark hair that half-hid his forehead and bowed his head to reveal a bruised gash, obviously quite recent, at the hairline.

He explained that a few days earlier he had been to dine with Flora and her guardian. After the meal, the two men had adjourned to Harcourt's study, a large room at the front of the house, with cigars and brandy, and there Randall had asked permission to wed Miss Bellamy.

"It was a formality, really, since she had agreed, but as the man was still her legal guardian, it seemed the right thing to do."

"His response?"

"He said, rather roughly, that young ladies always made their own decisions, but he had no objections. Then he asked if I knew she'd been engaged once before. I said that I did, and he gave an unpleasant laugh and asked me if that hadn't made me think twice. I didn't know what he meant to imply, but it seemed meant to be offensive. Trying not to take offence, I told him that I loved Flora, and that since she had been good enough to accept me, nothing short of death would induce me to part from her. And it was at that dramatic moment that a book fell off a shelf high above my head."

He winced. "It looked worse than it was – scalp wounds bleed profusely – but it was quite painful. I had never imagined a book as a lethal weapon."

"Where was Harcourt when this occurred?"

"He was facing me, standing farther away from the bookshelves. Before you ask, I could see him clearly, and while I suppose he might have contrived it, I was not aware of him doing anything that could have triggered the fall. In any case, he seemed completely shocked, and almost as worried about his book as my head. I should probably say *more*. If he'd meant to harm me, I don't think it would have been at the risk of any part of his collection."

"He's a book collector?"

"Nothing so benign," Mr Randall replied. "In fact, it was because of the collection that Flora rarely set foot inside that room. She found the morbid atmosphere more unpleasant than the scent of our cigars."

"R. M. Harcourt of Harrow," Jesperson said.

"You know of him?"

"I had not made the connection until this moment. He has written of his collection – at least, certain recent acquisitions – in a journal to which I subscribe."

Turning to me, Jesperson explained that Mr Harcourt took a particular interest in murder, and had, over the years, managed to acquire a goodly number of weapons – knives, guns, and a variety of sharp or heavy instruments – that had caused the loss of human life: a lady's hat pin, a piece of brick, a Japanese sword, an ordinary-looking iron poker. In addition, he had amassed a library on the subject of the crime, as well as what might be described as mementos of murder, odds and ends that were connected in some way with any famous – or infamous – crime: hair from the heads of murderers or their victims, blood-stained clothing, photographs of crime scenes, incriminating letters. He possessed poison rings, flasks, phials, bottles, and even the very cup in which Mrs Maybrick had mixed the arsenic powder with which she killed her husband.

"He's very proud of it," Randall said. "Occasionally, people call at the house to see the collection, or to offer new items they hope he'll buy. I was polite, but, frankly, I will never understand the appeal of such gruesome objects.

"After the accident, Flora became hysterical, and made me promise I'd never enter that room again. Then she decided that was not enough, and that I must not return to the house. She also suggested we should not announce our engagement, and wait until she's twenty-one to marry."

"She suspects her guardian?" Jesperson asked quietly.

Mr Randall hesitated, then shook his head. "She *says* she does not. But she feels I am in danger, through my attachment to her, and if she's right about that, who else could it be?"

"Forgive me, but...are there no rejected suitors?"

"Flora told me she received but two marriage proposals in her life, and she's never mentioned anyone...I've never heard of any other man, who might harbour such strong feelings for her," he replied. "But, in any case, she is wrong. Adcocks's murder, quite naturally, affected her nerves. She sees danger, an unknown assassin, lurking everywhere; an evil force behind every accident." He paused to take a deep breath.

"Shortly after the injury in the study, I chanced to stumble over an object in the hall – and I might have fallen and struck my head a second time if Flora hadn't been there to catch me. This was the same object that Adcocks had bruised his foot on, and this coincidence was too much. Her nerves are not strong. How can they be? She's suffered so much, has lost everyone she has ever loved – that's when she insisted I leave at once, and not come back. She imagined danger where there was none."

"And yet, whether or not *you* are in danger, someone killed Mr Adcocks," Jesperson said with heavy emphasis.

"Precisely. And if you can solve that crime, I hope her fears may be put to rest."

After Mr Randall had departed, Jesperson dashed off a letter to Mr Harcourt.

"I think it best that Harcourt has no reason to connect us to his ward or her fiancé," he told me. "Therefore, I shall present myself to him as a fellow aficionado of murder. And as he shows me his collection, it may be that, if he does know something of Adcocks's death, he'll give himself away."

"Won't he wonder how you've heard of it?"

"Not at all. It is quite well known in certain circles." He scarcely paused in his writing as he replied, stretching out his other hand and running it down the spines of a stack of journals on the desk beside him, as if he were one of those blind folk who read with their fingertips.

Abstracting one issue, he paused to flip through the pages until he found the one he wanted me to see.

It was a page of letters, with the headline *More Solutions to the Ripper Murders*. The letter indicated by his finger was signed *R. M. Harcourt, The Pines, Harrow*. Another, finishing in the next column, bore the name of *J. Jesperson, Gower Street*.

"So he may know who you are?"

"As you'll see by the date, this issue is a year old. I was still a mere student of crime and detection then, unknown to the public." Finished, he sealed the envelope and held it out to me. "Take this to the post office—" He stopped, with a look of chagrin. "Forgive me."

"For what? I am your assistant."

"My manner was too peremptory. I should have—"

I cut him off. "If we're going to work together, you must stop thinking of me as a female who'll be mortally offended if you forget to say *please*."

"It's not that."

I waited.

"I advertised for an assistant, not a servant. I hope we can work together as equals."

"Understood," I said, not revealing how pleased I felt. "Also understood is that when time is of the essence, politeness can go hang. And the only reason I am still standing here with this letter in my hand, rather than being halfway to the nearest post office, is that I don't know where that is."

Mr Harcourt replied with an invitation by return of post, so the next day found us on the train rattling through the north-western suburbs of London, at one time a familiar journey to me. Although I had not been in Harrow for more than ten years, it was the scene of my youth, my father having been a classics master at Harrow School until his untimely death.

However, we had lived in the village on the hill, whereas Mr Harcourt's house was almost a mile away, in one of the newer developments which had grown up following the extension of the Metropolitan Line.

Jesperson had said nothing in his letter about a companion, and we had decided my role would be that of Inconvenient Female Relative. Naturally, I would have no interest in the collection – indeed, if I knew what it was, I might well be shocked – so while the men were closeted together, I'd be free to conduct my own investigation. Randall had told Miss Bellamy to expect me.

The Pines was a mock-Tudor affair shielded from the road by the two namesakes that gave it a somewhat secretive and gloomy air. But that was nothing compared to the interior of the house. As I stepped across the threshold, I was gripped by panic. I am sensitive to atmospheres, no matter how much I try to blame it on imagination, and what I felt in that hallway was as bad as any haunted house. But it is difficult to describe to someone who has never experienced such things. If I were describing a smell, I could compare it to a tannery, a slaughterhouse, or a sewer. Only someone with no sense of smell could bear to live there.

Fighting the panic, I looked around for distraction. A large, attractive Chinese vase, green and yellow, had been put into service as a stand for umbrellas and walking sticks. Among the curving wooden handles clustering above the open top, the silver-capped walking stick stood out, commanding attention not simply by its different appearance, but by the grim air of menace it exuded, like a low and deadly hiss.

Of course, I knew at once what it was, and felt appalled. How could they have kept it? Why hadn't it been broken and destroyed, the wood burned to ash, the silver head melted down to be remade into something new?

Tearing my horrified gaze away, I spotted the hideous stone gargoyle crouching like a demon near the foot of the stairs, and shuddered at its baleful look before my partner's light touch on my arm recalled me to the present as he introduced me to the owner of these things.

Mr Harcourt was a portly, balding man with a luxuriant and well-tended moustache, and – for me, at any rate – a cold and fishlike stare. There was more warmth, and a twitch of a smile, in the greeting he gave Jesperson, leaving me in no doubt that my presence was unwelcome.

Relief came swiftly in the form of a young lady descending the stair. Slender and dark-haired, with a face that was handsome rather than pretty, she was dressed like a shop assistant or office worker in a crisp, white shirtfront and plain dark skirt. Even smiling warmly in welcome, she had a serious look, her eyes haunted by worry.

"Flora! Exquisite timing, as ever. Although if you had known to expect company you would have worn one of your pretty dresses, I hope," said Harcourt. He performed hasty introductions and rapidly withdrew with Jesperson behind a solid oak door, leaving us alone in the hall with its sinister atmosphere.

"Perhaps you'd like to see the garden," said Miss Bellamy, touching my elbow to guide me along a corridor towards the back of the house. As I passed through the door, leaving the house, the taste of fresh air was almost intoxicating.

"You are sensitive," she remarked, leading me away from the cold back wall of the house, through an arbour and along a path, into a sheltered rose garden.

"I claim no special powers," I said, "but the atmosphere in that house is … extraordinary. I have to wonder how you can live there."

She nodded slightly. "And yet, you know, most people feel nothing. Mr Adcocks never did. Mr Randall's mood alters when he visits, and I am aware of his unease, yet he will not admit it."

Although I had not said so to Jesperson, I had toyed with the idea that Miss Bellamy herself might be the killer we sought. The manner of Mr Adcocks's death seemed to indicate an attack by a strong and brutal man, an action impossible for most women; nevertheless, I had found that men tended to underestimate the female sex quite as much as they idealized it, and I could imagine a grieving fiancée who was in truth a cold-hearted murderer.

But that idea vanished to nothing as soon as I set eyes on her, a slip of a girl, and as we sat down, side by side, on a curving bench in a sunny green spot, the scent of roses and the warm hum of bees filling the air around us, I was utterly certain that this gentle, soft-spoken female, so concerned about the feelings of others, was incapable of killing another human being, by any means.

"How can you bear to live in that house?" I asked her.

"Don't forget, I've lived there nearly all my life," she said. "People can get used to almost anything. Imagine someone who must work in a slaughterhouse every day."

"I imagine such a person would be brutalized and degraded by his work," I replied. "If the comparison were to someone who must *live* in a slaughterhouse … well, I can't imagine many who would stick it for long. I'm surprised you never ran away. What was it like when you first came here? Were you terrified?"

She looked thoughtful. "I can't remember anything before I came here. I was not yet two years old. And back then, Mr Harcourt's collection was only small. It grew along with me. Over the years, as he added items, he told me the story of each one. So I became accustomed to tales of violent death and human wickedness from an early age. I was not at all attracted to those things, but I accepted their existence. Imagine a child growing up in a madhouse or a prison. Even the strangest situations become normal if one knows nothing else."

"But now, at last, you can escape," I said. "Have you set a date for your wedding?"

She stared at me. "Surely William told you? I think it's best we don't even speak of an engagement until after I'm of age, and can leave here."

"You believe your guardian doesn't wish you to marry?"

She gave a short, humourless laugh. "Oh, I believe he would like to see me married! A wife and a widow in the same day would please him very much!"

There was no point in beating about the bush. "Do you think he killed Mr Adcocks?"

She did not flinch. "No. Despite his fascination with the subject, Mr Harcourt is no murderer."

"Do you suspect someone else?"

She did not reply. I thought I saw something cornered and furtive in her look. "Miss Bellamy," I said gently, "however painful this is, we can't help unless you tell me what it is you suspect, or fear, no matter how slight or strange. Were you there, did you see anything, when Mr Adcocks was attacked?"

She shook her head. "I bade him goodnight and went up to my room. I thought he was safe ..."

"And your guardian?"

"He was shut up in his room, as usual."

I looked towards the house, but the ground floor was shielded from my view by shrubs and foliage. "Is there another exit? From his room?"

"No. And I would not have missed the sounds if he'd left the house."

"Who murdered Mr Adcocks?" I asked suddenly.

"No one."

"And yet he is dead."

"He was killed by a powerful blow to his head. The blow came from a walking stick. Can it be called murder, is it even a crime, without human intervention?"

I had seen objects levitate, hover, move about, even shoot through the air as if hurled with great force, although no one was near. Usually there was trickery involved; but not always. I had seen what I believed to be the effect of mind over matter, and also witnessed what was called *poltergeist* – the German for "noisy spirit" – activity. Yet I was deeply suspicious of everything attributed to the action of "spirits". I had yet to encounter anything that was not better explained by the power of the human mind.

"What are you saying?" I asked her gently. "You believe that the stick, an inanimate object, moved, and killed a man, of its own volition?" Yet even as I asked, the memory of the malignant power I had sensed in that very stick, only a few minutes earlier, made me much less certain that I was right to imply the impossibility of such a thing.

"Have you ever heard of a deodand?"

"I'm not familiar with the word."

"It's a term from old English law: *deo*, to God, *dandum*, that which must be given. It referred to any possession which was the immediate cause of a person's accidental death. The object was then forfeit to the Crown, to be put to some pious use."

I couldn't think of anything to say to that, and she smiled. "That walking stick was a deodand. Not officially; it's hardly that old. But it was the proximate cause of death to a young man almost seventy years ago – so my guardian told me.

"And the unpleasant stone gargoyle beside the stair? It fell off the tower where it had been placed many centuries before, and killed a mother and child.

"My guardian collects such things, along with his morbid keepsakes from actual murders.

"He gave Archie that stick, knowing what it was, and suspecting what it would do." She stopped and passed a hand across her brow. "What am I saying? Of course he didn't suspect. Why should he? None of them had ever hurt him, or me. Not even when I was a child who played with whatever took my fancy – he wouldn't let me touch anything dangerous, of course, nothing sharp or breakable. I whispered secrets in the gargoyle's ear, even used to kiss it, and it was that gargoyle—" She stopped, her hand to her mouth.

I waited for her to go on.

"It was in the wrong place, too near the stair. I thought perhaps, when the maid washed the floor, she'd pushed it out, but she insisted she never did. Yet it was not where it usually was, and that's why Archie stumbled against it, and wrenched his ankle.

"It happened again, just a few days ago, to Will. He fell over it, and if I hadn't caught him, he might have struck his head, might have been killed, just like Archie!"

"Someone moved it," I said, trying to inject a note of reason. "If not the maid, then your guardian, or a mysterious stranger. And if Mr Randall's stumble had resulted in a serious injury, even death, that would have been an accident; no one could possibly call it murder, even if someone moved the gargoyle.

"But that stick ... I really can't imagine that a stick, in Mr Adcocks's possession, could have caused his death without the intervention of another person. If you think your guardian was controlling it, willing it to strike—"

"No! Why would he do that? Even if he had the ability, why would he want to kill my fiancé when he was looking forward to seeing how *I* would cause his death?"

She had gone white except for two hectic splashes of red in her cheeks. I shook my head. "I don't understand."

"Of course not. Because you don't understand that I, too, am a deodand. I am the gem of his collection. My early history explains why he took me in. I killed my entire family before I was two years of age."

I gripped her hands. "Miss Bellamy—"

"I am utterly sane," she said calmly. "I am not hysterical. These are the facts. Being born, I brought about the death of my mother."

"That's hardly—"

"Unique? I know. Listen. Nine months later, my father was taking his motherless children on holiday when we were involved in a railway accident. In the crash, my brother, a child of two, was thrown to the floor, as was I. I landed directly on top of him, a fact which may have saved *me* from injury, but caused his death. I have never known whether he died of suffocation, or if my weight broke his neck."

"No one could call that your fault," I said, trying not to dwell on the image.

"I know that," she said, pulling her hands away. "Believe me, I am not such a fool as to think it was anything other than extremely bad luck. I have had many years to come to terms with my past. I do not require your pity. I tell you this only so you may understand Mr Harcourt's interest in me.

"My father was injured in the accident. Some months later he was still in an invalid chair, needing a nurse to help him in and out and wheel him about. We'd gone out for a walk— When I say 'we', I mean my father in his chair pushed by his nurse, a young man, and I in my pram, pushed by mine, a pretty young woman. We stopped at a local beauty spot to admire the view. My nurse put me down on a blanket on the grass, near to my father, who was dozing in the sun, and then I suppose they must have stopped paying much attention to anything but each other as they fell to flirting. I hadn't yet learned to walk, but I was getting better at standing up, and as I hauled myself to my feet, using my father's chair as support, somehow I must have let off the brake – maybe the nurse hadn't properly set it – and as he rolled away, I just watched him go, picking up speed, until I saw the chair carrying my last living relative go over the edge of the cliff, and bear him to his death on the rocks below."

I made no further effort to comfort her, unable to find the words. "So Mr Harcourt considers you as some sort of loaded weapon in his possession? Ready to go off when you are loved?"

"He has never said as much, but that's what I've understood by a gleam in his eye, and a quickening of interest, once I became of marriageable age. It was he who contrived to introduce me to a number of wealthy young men, until Archibald Adcocks took the bait. And he pressed me to accept, although I was inclined to wait."

"Regardless of what Mr Harcourt believes—"

"I know. And you're right, I don't believe it of myself. Mr Harcourt imagines, because he kept himself so coldly distant, repelling my natural affection, and sent me to day school rather than risk my becoming too close to a kind governess, that I never was loved, and never loved anyone, since my father died.

"But there was a girl at school … My guardian may have no idea how passionately girls can love each other, but I'm sure *you* will," she said, with a look that should have made me blush. Instead, it made me smile.

We looked at each other like conspirators. "I take it your friend remains alive and well?"

"Indeed, and still my dearest friend, although we're now more temperate in our emotions … or, at least, the expression of them. So, you see, I *know* my affection is not dangerous."

"And yet you seem to think that by becoming engaged to marry you, Mr Adcocks signed his own death warrant. And that Mr Randall is under threat for the same reason."

"Yes …" She looked thoughtful. "But not because of my feelings for him, or his for me. It's something else. Marriage to anyone would take me away from this house, would remove me from my guardian's collection. That's it!" she said, and stood up.

"What is it?"

"He thinks marriage is the only way he might lose me. He's never imagined I might simply decide to leave."

I stood up, too, to face her. "I don't understand."

"Mr Harcourt is scarcely sane when it comes to his collection. He cannot bear the thought of losing a single piece of it. He is happiest when gloating over it alone, and whenever he has a chance to add something new. Although he admits potential buyers, he only wants their envy and admiration as they view his objects – he will never agree to sell an item, no matter how much money he is offered.

"And while he has been talking about my marriage since I was sixteen, and began pushing me at eligible bachelors on my eighteenth birthday, driven by thoughts of what he thinks will happen when I am once more part of a family, greedily imagining how his collection will grow after the violent, accidental death of my husband... yet he knows this will be possible only if he lets me go. In his twisted mind, I am part of his collection, and the thought of losing me, even only temporarily, and in aid of gaining more, is terrible to him."

"His mind is divided?"

"I am sorry, Miss Lane. You should not have been brought into this. There was no need for William to enlist the aid of a detective. I should have realized that I am the only one who can end this madness."

She started back to the house and I followed. Although I had no idea what she intended, I felt that we were approaching crisis.

She raised her fist to rap on the heavy oak, but at the very first blow the door to her guardian's study swung open.

Harcourt was at the far end of the room, by the window, displaying something in a flat wooden box to Jesperson. They both looked around sharply as we entered, Harcourt startled and annoyed. Clearly, he had not expected us, and I could only assume that he had neglected to shut the door properly.

"What's the meaning of this disturbance?" he demanded, hastily shutting up the box.

"I must speak to you."

"Let it wait. We have company."

"I am happy to have witnesses." She took a breath. "I shall not marry."

I had tensed myself against the negative atmosphere upon entering the house, and had been particularly reluctant to enter Harcourt's study, expecting it to be the epicentre of the unrest, yet as I slowly followed Miss Bellamy, I found that what had been unpleasant and discordant was now harmonious. Using the metaphor of scent, consider bonfire smoke. A great waft in the face is horrible, but at the right distance, the scent of burning leaves and wood is pleasant.

"You've rushed in here to say that? I am at a loss to understand why," Harcourt replied coldly. "Your change of heart is of no interest to *me*. I suggest you write to Mr Randall."

"You don't understand. I mean I shall never marry."

His eyes bulged. "Are you insane?" Suddenly, he turned on me. "What have you been saying? What sort of mad rubbish, to turn her mind?"

"Miss Lane had nothing to do with it," Flora said swiftly. "I have been thinking matters over for the past several days, and only now decided to tell you—"

"Oh, very likely!" He had been casting a venomous glare on me, but now stared coldly at Jesperson. "I'm afraid I must ask you to take this female person away, immediately."

I could see that my partner was at a loss: should he leap to my defence, invent excuses, or pretend to a masculine solidarity that might leave the door open for future visits? Although I didn't want to leave Flora alone with Harcourt, I didn't know what we would achieve by trying to stay, so I left the room, just as Flora was demanding, "Am I not allowed to have my own friends?"

"As long as I'm your guardian, Flora, you will do as I say. You'll have nothing more to do with that female, and you will not break off your engagement. We'll forget you ever said anything about it. Mr Jesperson, if you please!"

As they emerged, with Flora in the lead, I was surprised to see the hint of a smile on her face. She winked at me before turning on her guardian again.

"So, I am to be your *object* and meekly allow *your* will to prevail in everything, until my twenty-first birthday changes everything?"

"That will change nothing," he said scornfully. "You don't imagine you'll be anything different than you are now? Than you've always been?"

She flinched, but held steady. "In the eyes of the law."

"The law." He snorted. "The law is an ass. It has nothing to say about *you*. It has no idea what you are." His gaze on her was horrible.

"I may as well go now," she said quietly.

"Go? What are you talking about?"

"You are right that a few months will change nothing. *You* are pleased with the situation; I am not. So I shall leave."

She looked from me to Jesperson, saying, "If it's not too much trouble ..."

He was swift to take her meaning. "Of course, come with us. Any help we can give—"

I heard the rattle, and saw that the Chinese vase was rocking violently back and forth, until it tilted too far and fell, shattering against the hard floor, and spilling its burden of umbrellas and walking sticks.

Only one of the sticks did not come to rest with everything else on the floor, but shot through the air, straight at Jesperson.

If it had struck where it aimed, against his throat, I have no doubt it would have killed him, but he was quick. Almost as if he'd expected the attack, he stepped lightly aside, his arm rising, fluid and graceful, to catch the handle.

Unlike an ordinary thrown object, the stick continued to move after it was caught, writhing and struggling to escape while he gripped it more firmly, frowning as he looked for a thread or wire and tried to work out the trick of it.

Certain there would be no invisible thread, I looked instead at Harcourt. His expression was nothing like those I'd seen on the faces of mediums or mentalists; he looked utterly astonished, and thrilled. If he had caused the stick's activity, it was through a power hidden from his conscious mind, something he did not suspect and could not control.

Then another movement, glimpsed from the corner of my eye, caught my attention, and as I turned to look, I heard the terrible grating, grinding noise made by the stone gargoyle as it ponderously rocked itself across the floor. Although no one was near enough to be at risk if it fell over, I nevertheless called out a warning.

Flora took one look and shouted: "Stop it! Stop it right now!"

The gargoyle stopped moving, and so did the stick, although Jesperson still kept a tight hold and a wary eye on it.

Harcourt took a hesitant step forward, his eyes still fixed upon the stick. "Give – give it to me, if you please, Mr Jesperson," he said. "That – that is the weapon that killed poor Mr Adcocks; and before that, a young man in Plymouth. If not for your exceptionally quick reflexes, you would have been its third victim."

After a reluctant pause, Jesperson handed over the stick, saying, "You expected this might happen?"

"Never," the man gasped, staring at the stick in his hands with an unhealthy mixture of lust and fear. "Who would imagine that the instinct to kill would be inherent?"

"You imagined it inherent in *me*," said Flora. "A mindless, killing force so powerful that it could use me – a living, intelligent being – without regard for my own free will?"

"No, no, certainly not," he said, without conviction. "You were a mere infant, with no ability to think or act for yourself, when fate used you to terminate the lives of three innocent souls. It is quite different now." He had been looking at her, but the lure of the object in his hands proved too much, and he soon returned to staring at it like a besotted lover.

"You've always thought of me as another piece in your collection," Flora said bitterly. "A mindless, soulless thing, and not even your favourite."

"Dear Flora, don't be absurd. I know you are no 'thing'. You have been like a daughter to me. Have I not always cared for you as best I could? Bought you whatever your heart desired? My only concern has ever been to see you safely and happily married to the man of your choice, when the time came."

While my sympathies were entirely with Flora, I recognized that to an outside observer she would seem hysterical, and Harcourt the sane one.

"Yet you must have wondered," Jesperson said, as if idly. "Eh, Harcourt? You surely wondered if your ward was intended by Fate for family happiness. Perhaps you saw her first engagement as a scientific experiment. The result was not as you *hoped*, but perhaps as you feared … ?"

They exchanged a look, man to man, and although Harcourt shook his head ruefully, I saw the smug satisfaction beneath the solemn expression.

"You're vile," Flora murmured. She cleared her throat and announced, "I can never marry. I won't put another life at risk."

This time, Harcourt did not protest. He shrugged and sighed, and said, "I would never force you to go against your will, no matter how foolish it seems to me."

"That's not all. I'm leaving your collection today, Mr Harcourt—"

"Oh, come now. Don't be childish. You can't blame me for what you are!"

"Not for what I am; only for what you've tried to make me. The atmosphere in this house is hideous, not because of the objects, but because of your gloating fascination with murder and violent death. I'm going. I won't set foot in this house again as long as you are alive."

Having stated her intention, she made straight for the door.

I felt the shudder that ran through the house even before her hand touched the handle; it was a sensation so subtle yet so profound that I thought at first I might be ill.

Harcourt yelled. His nose was bleeding; the walking stick had come to life again in his hand and seemed determined to beat him to death. He managed to remove it to arm's length, and struggled to keep it under control. The gargoyle, too, was shuddering back to life, and, from the variety of creaks and groans and fluttering sounds I heard coming from the next room, so were other pieces of the collection.

"Move," said Jesperson urgently, propelling me forward. "Get out of the house! Is there anyone else here?" Hearing the shouts, the little maid who'd let us in reappeared, and, although looking utterly bewildered, allowed him to usher her outside as well.

We met Flora at the front gate and turned back to look at the house.

"Where's Harcourt?" Jesperson demanded. "He was right behind me."

"He won't leave his collection," said Flora. "He'll have gone back for it. He used to worry aloud about what he should save first, if the house were on fire."

"But it's the collection itself that's the threat!"

On my own, I might have left Harcourt to his fate, but when my partner ran back inside, I felt it my duty to follow. Mounting the front steps, I was able to see through the window into the study, and what I saw brought me to a standstill.

Pale and portly Mr Harcourt was leaping and whirling like a dervish, holding the silver-headed stick away from his body like a magic staff, as he struggled to evade a flurry of small objects bent on striking him. Occasionally in his efforts he unconsciously pulled his arm in closer to his body, allowing the stick to give him a sharp crack on his leg or shoulder, and then he would shriek in pain or anger.

Books and other things continued to tumble from the shelves. Many simply fell, but others seemed hurled with great force directly at him, and these struck a variety of glancing blows against his body, head, and limbs. A glass-fronted display case shook fiercely, as if caught in an earthquake, until it burst open, releasing everything inside. A great malignant swarm composed of small bottles, jars, needles, pins, razors, and many more things I could not recognize enveloped the man, whose cries turned to a constant, terrified howling as they attacked him.

Feeling sick, I turned aside and went indoors to my partner, who was throwing himself bodily against the solid oak door of Harcourt's study, as if he imagined he could force it open. Seeing me, he stopped and rubbed his shoulder, looking a little sheepish.

I gave him one of my hairpins, assuming he would know how to use it.

As he fiddled with the lock, I listened to the horrible sounds that accompanied the violence on the other side: thuds and thumps, shrieks and wails and groans, and then a shocking, liquid hissing, followed by a gurgle, and then the heaviest thud of all, and then silence.

By the time Jesperson managed to get the door open, it was all over. Harcourt was dead. His bloody, battered corpse lay on the carpet, surrounded by the remnants of his murderous collection. Whatever life had possessed them had expired with his. There was a sharp, acrid stench in the room – I guess from the contents of various broken bottles – but nothing so foul as the atmosphere it replaced.

"Vitriol," said Jesperson. "Don't look."

But I had already seen what was left of the face, and it was no more shocking than the sounds had led me to imagine.

As I went out to give Flora Bellamy the news, and to send the maid to fetch the police, I already knew that this had not turned out to be a case I could write about for publication.

And, as it developed, it grew worse.

It was fortunate indeed that Jasper Jesperson had some influential relatives who moved in the circles of power, for otherwise I think the local police would have been pleased to charge him with murder, in the absence of more likely suspects, and if he hadn't done it, I was their next choice.

Even though we might argue we had saved his life, our client was so far from pleased with the outcome of our investigations that he refused to pay us anything. It was not Harcourt's death that bothered him so much as Miss Bellamy's insistence on releasing him from their engagement. She would give him no better reason for her change of heart than to say that she was reconsidering how she might best spend her life, and that she was inclined to seek some form of employment by which to support herself "like Miss Lane".

Flora Bellamy never set foot inside The Pines again. Even though her guardian was dead, she had decided to take no chances, and hired others to empty the house before selling it. In his will, Harcourt left everything to his ward, with only one caveat: although she could decide whether to keep or dispose of "the collection", she must do so as a whole, and not break it up.

This stipulation she decided to ignore.

"Perhaps I'm wrong," she said to me, the last time I saw her, "but I believe it could be dangerous. Individual objects are only things, but when gathered together, they became something more – first in Mr Harcourt's imagination, and then in reality.

"The concept in law of the *deodand* was that something which had once done evil could be remade into something useful, even holy, by good works. That was not allowed to happen in Mr Harcourt's collection. His use of those things was opposed to good; it venerated the evil deed."

Her way of redemption was to donate everything that remained in the house to a good cause. Being extra-cautious, she chose one so far away that she would not have to fear an accidental encounter with her former possessions, and had everything sent to a leper colony on the other side of the world.

I took it as a positive sign that she did not feel obliged to sacrifice herself in a similar way.

She decided to share a flat with her school friend, and embarked on a course of training in bookkeeping and office management.

Jesperson and I, naturally, discussed the details of this case – which began with one unsolved murder, and concluded with two – at great length when we were alone together, and also with Mrs Jesperson, but we were never able to agree upon how to assign the blame for the killings. We all agreed that both Adcocks and Harcourt were murdered, yet we also agreed that if there were no murderer, murder could not have been done.

I hope our next case will be less of a curiosity.

GOD MOVING OVER THE FACE OF THE WATERS

Steve Mosby

THE NIGHT BEFORE, I walked the coastline.

I didn't set out until after midnight, as I wanted to avoid the search parties. At that time, the sky, the sand and the sea in between were identical shades of black – indistinguishable except for the moonlight that caught the ridges of the waves, and a prickle of stars overhead. The beach was invisible. Pebbles crunched beneath my feet, the sound fading to the steady push of packed, wet sand as I reached the water itself.

Everyone feels small, facing the sea. It's the vast, open horizon, I think, and the sensation of how unimportant you are in the grand scheme of things. It's like standing on the edge of an alien world – or perhaps like staring into the face of God, and suddenly realizing how incomprehensible He actually is. How little He cares about you. If He even deigns to notice you at all.

The sea noticed me, of course. I felt it in the rush of hiss and retreat, and the sudden waft of ice in the air as it came rolling up the beach at me before pulling back its swift, foaming fingers. The water feathered impotently around my shoes. If I ventured in then it would take me without hesitation, because that is what it does, but right here I was safe.

I squatted down and flicked at the sea.

The contempt in my message was clear, and I heard a deep, chained-dog rumble from out towards the horizon: an angry folding of faraway water that longed to reach out and take me but couldn't.

A moment later, the smell of coconut filled the air. The contempt in the sea's reply was equally clear.

"Fuck you," I told it.

Then stood up, hitching my rucksack higher for comfort, and started looking.

The first coffee of the morning curdled.

I stared down at the tatters and shreds of cream on the surface. The milk was in date, so it was probably something else. Perhaps it was even the rucksack, which rested in the corner of the kitchen now, stinking of fish and rot. Whatever, I tipped the coffee away and made a fresh cup, this time without milk.

It was a little after 8.20; through the window, the sky was white as mist. I took the coffee out into the cold morning and wandered down the shivering grass of my back garden, opening the gate in the chain-link fence at the bottom. There were a few furrowed boulders out here, a short incline, and then the beach.

I sat down on one of the boulders, wrapping my hands around the steaming cup for warmth. Beyond the beach, the fluttering, blue-grey sea, gulls wheeling overhead like flies. It was still half-asleep right now, but grumbling to itself. Bruised, but too dozy to remember why.

I hoped it woke up soon.

I hoped it saw me up here and knew what I'd done.

In the meantime, I sipped my coffee and thought about Anna.

People often wonder why I never moved.

Sometimes they even ask me outright. The place must be so big for you now, they say, and it must contain so many difficult memories – and, surely, it's painful to wake up every day, after what happened, and see the sea?

They don't know anything, these people.

***

By the time I'd finished my coffee, I'd spotted the helicopter: a tiny orange speck hanging over the vast expanse of sea, the fluttering chop of its propellers sounding dull and insignificant, barely there. Down the beach to my left, a group of indistinct figures was moving steadily along.

I sloshed the dregs from my cup on to the rocks in front of me.

The sea had come to life a little by now. It was still groggy, pulling itself slowly up the beach, but I could sense the muscles it had: the tendons below the surface that were clawing this enormous, heavy thing up the sand towards me. It knew what I'd done. Eventually, it would tire and wash itself away again, drained of energy. For now, I enjoyed watching God struggling and crawling before me.

I'm not afraid of you.

Despite the disparity in their powers, the group of figures would reach me long before the sea did. Six policemen, with orange jackets over their normal uniforms, feeling their way slowly and uselessly along the braille of the coast.

Hague, of course, was one of them.

Eight months ago, a little boy went missing off the coast here. It was a familiar story. He was on the beach, playing with his older sister, and he went out too far into the waves. You can't get away with that here. This stretch of coast is notorious for its unforgiving currents, and you'll find few, if any, locals willing to swim in it. By the time the little girl alerted her parents, the boy had been swept out to sea and was presumed drowned.

Hague was involved in the search. He walked the coastline with different volunteers for a period of two weeks. He knew the boy was dead, but finding the body was important to him. Not understanding the whims of the sea, the parents held out hope – and would no doubt continue to do so until their son was found. So Hague walked the coast.

I watched him, day after day.

Finally, in the second week, I walked with him.

***

As they approached now, his expression was grim. The others looked the same. It was as though they'd passed around an emotion to wear before heading out this morning, like Vaseline at an autopsy.

I heard the scuff of their boots on the sand.

"Jonathan."

Hague nodded as he drew to a halt in front of me, his fellow officers grouping behind.

I nodded back. "Morning."

"It is morning, yes." Hague looked over my shoulder at my house. "It is that. But not a good one. You'll have been following the news?"

"A little."

"You've heard about Charlotte Evans?"

Yes. Ten years old, but she looked younger. Her photograph had been on the news the past few nights: curly blonde hair and plump, sun-red cheeks. She wouldn't look like that any more.

"I saw something on the television."

"It's been three days now."

"That's bad."

"Real bad, yeah. So it's not going to be a good result. But we're walking the shore for her. There's a lot of ground to cover."

"I don't think you'll find her."

I probably said that too quickly, but I didn't care. He was making me sad – this man who always kept looking – and I wanted him to go away.

Hague inclined his head. Looked at me curiously.

"You don't?"

"You know what the sea's like around here. It happens, and it's awful, but I think that she's probably gone."

"Well, maybe." He frowned. "Maybe not. People have a way of turning up in all sorts of different places. Don't they?"

"Do they?"

He looked at me.

"Sometimes they do. They sure do."

I heard the fluttering of the helicopter alter slightly as it moved away. The sea, behind the police, was making steady progress up towards us. For a long moment, Hague and I stared at each other. And then the spell was broken. He came back to life.

"Well, I guess we'd better get moving. You keep your eyes open, Jonathan. Let us know if you see anything."

I nodded. As they headed off, I watched him talking into his radio, and I knew that he suspected. *Something*, at least. Something that was too alien to make any real sense to him.

That's the way it is though.

In my own way, I'm as incomprehensible as God.

Eight months ago, when I volunteered to walk with Hague, it had been out of frustration. Every day, I'd watched him trailing alone along the shore, knowing the whole time he would never find the little boy. I'd wanted to make him understand. Or maybe, more simply, I'd wanted him to stop.

At some point, as we walked, I tried to explain the truth of the matter. *The little boy is gone*, I told him. *Because that is what the sea does. It only takes; it never gives back.*

We stopped walking.

"Not necessarily." He looked at me strangely for a moment, then shifted gears as empathy took over. "I mean, I know we never found Anna – but we looked. We walked then. I— "

I missed the rest of what he said. Memories washed the words under. Her soft, brown arms, clear beads of water clinging to her skin. The tangled dreadlocks of her wet hair. The coconut scent of her suntan cream. And then the look of fear on her face as the sea's strong fingers circled our waists and *pulled*.

Swim.

Jonathan – swim.

Her screams, after we were separated, the sound of them slashed apart by the waves.

The last I heard of her.

I interrupted him.

"It would be wrong, wouldn't it?"

"What?"

"It would be wrong. If it got to choose."

"Jonathan…"

I should probably have noticed how uncomfortable Hague had become, but I didn't, or else I didn't care.

"No," I told him. "It wouldn't be fair. If it took Anna and didn't give her back, for *no reason at all*, why would it be different for anyone else? Why should it?"

He stared at me, helpless, not knowing what to say, then gestured at the sea: a motion that didn't need accompanying words. It's chance, he meant. Chaos. It must make sense on some unfathomable level … but we can never understand. All we can do in the face of it is walk the shore.

Take whatever scraps are thrown our way.

That's what he meant.

I shook my head in disgust and walked away from him, not looking back. But I felt his gaze following me as I left. I don't know what he thought.

I do know that, after our conversation, Hague stopped looking for the little boy.

Later – after I'd put the stinking rucksack at the far end of the cellar – I went outside again and made my way down the beach. The police and helicopter were gone now, and the sea was retreating. I spent some time following it down, stepping on its angry edges. If I was swimming in it then it could and would take me. But the beach and the coast were mine. It needed to know that.

"Fuck you."

I kneeled down and flicked at the water with my fingers.

And I told it that it couldn't choose people and single them out. I wouldn't let it – and I didn't care if it didn't understand, or if it was angry about that. Here, on the cusp of incomprehensibility, we would meet each other halfway, or not at all. It could decide what it took; I would decide what it gave. And if it wouldn't give me Anna back then it wouldn't give anyone anything.

"Fuck you if you think she's going home."

As I stood up and walked away, I sensed a groan in the faraway water behind me, a melancholy whale-song of sound. The scent of coconut oil followed me as I made my way back up the beach. But there was no contempt in it this time. I understood deep down that it was simply giving me all that was left of her now.

I didn't acknowledge it – just kept walking.

The sea was giving me all it could. And perhaps, in its own vast, alien way, it was unable to understand why that wasn't enough.

STARDUST

Phil Lovesey

S OMEONE – IT DOESN'T matter who – once told me we're all stardust. Just strange organic composites of the carbon atom; walking, talking, loving, killing. Humanity reduced to powder. Perhaps it was the dull old spud who attempted to teach me science; maybe the warbled lyrics from a prog-rocker; or a TV presenter doing his best to enliven some sort of astrophysics documentary – like I say, it doesn't matter who – but the words, the *concept* of it, have remained with me since. Brought me comfort over the years at times, helped me sometimes to zoom out from the chaos, the injustices of life, see myself as merely a cosmic speck at the mercy of the universe and its frequent bitter ironies.

Pretty existential for a petty thief, I guess.

Then again, I have had the occasional six or nine months locked away with my thoughts and battered prison library paperbacks to think some of this stuff through. A not-very-good petty thief, in truth.

Anyway, back to the stardust and ironies ...

I'd just finished a short stretch at one of Her Majesty's less-than-salubrious hotels for the wretched, and had found myself fetched up in front of my new front door as sorted by the dear folk from the Probation Service. A good system this, for the serial offender like myself. Get given nine months, keep the old nose clean for five of them; smile, make the right noises, tell the panel how much you've changed, how nights wracked with remorse have brought about a life-changing conversion to go straight ... and hey presto, they're sorting you new digs, clothes and some cash in your pocket to tide you over.

Best bits of thieving I've ever done ... and all from the taxpayer. Shame on me, you might say. But seriously, in my shoes, you'd do the same. Your dust ain't no different from my dust.

It's a horrible door, in a horrible block of flats, in a horrible part of town. The probation guy tries to sell it to me as an "apartment", as if by his Americanizing the shabby place I'll not notice the damp, the cracked windowpanes, worn furniture, and bare bulbs. But I smile and thank him anyway. After all, I tell him, home's what you make it. Or what you take from others. He doesn't react to the quip. He's young, this one – would probably refer to himself as a "rookie" – and simply wants to go. I let him, knowing there's no banter to be had. He's too desperate to "check in for a burger and fries" some-where, the perfect twenty-something product of a life made bland by corporate domination.

Like I said, I've had a lot of time to read this sort of stuff.

Now, there's a drill for this sort of place. It goes like this – let *them* come to you. They always will. For where there's one shabby Probation Service flat in a block, there'll be others. And the occu-pants will soon know when the new bloke hitches up. And then comes sniffing, scratching, seeing what's to be had. It's just how it is – I've done it myself.

Sure enough, within ten minutes of the College Boy leaving, a bearded, lanky heap of methadone-using stardust is on my doorstep, trying to ingratiate himself, his pink eyes swimming in a pallid head that nods and twitches as he asks me for "a few quid – just for a few days, like". I invite him in, give him the money in exchange for some essential "local" information.

He's called Rambling Ian – apparently – and has served the usual amount of time in the past. We talk about various jails, wings, screws – not reminiscing but testing each other for truths, lies, connections, mutual friends and enemies we've made along our less-than-merry way. I think he's probably all right, and he goes on to describe himself as a "standard human road accident on the heroin highway".

I ask him about others in the block. He tells me we're the only two "insiders", the other flats housing the predictable assortment of single mothers, forgotten pensioners, unemployed divorcees, and immigrant workers. No rich pickings to be had here, then. But I'd guessed that already. Rambling Ian follows up with a few possible opportunities for a spot of nocturnal thievery just a few streets away.

"Big places," he says. "Fancy."

"And full of alarms," I reply, knowing where this is heading.

"Maybe, but with the two of us ... you know ..."

I smile. I'm not about to shatter his illusion that he's on the verge of hooking up with a latter-day Raffles, because however ridiculous the notion may be, I need him onside for a while; he may have his uses. So I tell him I'll think it over, and he makes for the door.

"'Course," he adds on his way out, "there's always Buzz on the top floor. He's an odd old geezer."

"Buzz?"

"As in Lightyear, from the kid's film. You know, all those toys comin' to life an' that?"

I shake my head. Children's films were never my thing, unless it was to try and pick a few adult pockets or rob a hassled mum's handbag in the gloom of the cinema. My spoils from the Hollywood film industry.

"American, he is," he goes on. "Crazy old fella. Lives on his own at the very top with just a telescope. Never lets anyone through the door. Rumour round here is that he used to be some sort of spaceman or something."

"Spaceman? As in an old druggie?"

My new "partner" looks a little hurt by this. "No. The real deal. That he went up on one of those Apollo missions back in the seventies. Walked on the moon, drove one of them buggy things, the lot."

"And, naturally, he ends up living on top of a crummy block of flats in South London."

"I'm telling you what folk say about him," he replies. "Never met the fella myself."

"Yeah," I say, trying to sound sympathetic. "Well, I reckon there're a few people pulling your leg, Ian."

"Ask around if you don't believe me," he insists. "They'll maybe even tell you about the moon rock he keeps up there. Size of your fist, it is, and he brought it back from the moon itself. Smuggles it out of NASA, brought it over here."

"Be worth an awful lot of loot for a lump of stone?"

"A moon rock," he replied, wide-eyed, clearly not getting it. "A sacred piece of the heavens."

"And right now," I said, closing the door, "I need to get a sacred piece of sleep."

Rambling Ian was right about one thing: we were the only two "probys" in the block. Indeed, from mostly law-abiding observations over the next few days, I began to realize that of the twenty-six flats, maybe a third of them were empty, boarded and shuttered. One day an Asian family moved out, the next day the boards and shutters appeared. The whole block felt like it was dying – a good thing, probably. I guessed that I was the last "resident" who had been allowed in, and now the powers that be were simply waiting until people moved out, or on to pastures new, in order that it could be pulled down without the cost of rehousing remaining residents. Robbery in its own way, but conveniently legal.

As for me, familiar urges were beginning to return, fuelled by dwindling money, lack of real employment opportunity for someone like me, and just ... let's call it old habits dying way too hard. It's not excusable what I do, it's not exciting – or glamorous – it's just what I do. And like I say, I'm not even that good at it. But just as some are born to be judges, I reckon some are born to be judged. Without us, there's no them. Universal balance, I guess.

Of course, the eternal problem for the burglar is cash conversion. Finding a trusted fence to whom to pass over your liberated goods in exchange for some of the lovely folding stuff. A dying breed, the local fences, literally. None of the youngsters see the opportunities presented by the profession, preferring the easier, more obvious routes. Granted, there'll still be a bloke in the local pub who'll mention that he'll give you a couple of hundred quid for a wall-mounted plasma television, but honestly, you try getting those things off the damn wall in the first place. I guess you could say I'm part of a dying breed, too. Forty-seven and too old to rob and roll ...

So, I'm looking for easier places, easier things to swipe. Never been good with any kind of vehicle, so they're out. Leaves me with houses – big ones, mostly, for obvious reasons. Not too big, though, as I've never had the know-how to bypass alarm systems. However, as most medium-sized places nearly always have unlinked alarms, they don't present the same problem an engine-disabled Mercedes does. In fact, as any competent housebreaker will tell you (and I do count myself as competent at breaking in, it's the getting out and away with it that tends to be a little more problematic), the appearance of an alarm box on the side of your home is the finest advertisement for opportunists like me. Forget a blaring siren, just have a recorded message that shouts: *Hey! Up here on the wall! Yeah, look at me! Lots of lovely stuff inside, and no one's going to give a damn if I start screaming! Get in, help yourselves!* The same with half-drawn curtains, lights blazing away inside. The genuinely rich got that way by saving money, not wasting it on electricity. Their curtains will be drawn, just one light in the room they're in. Couple of pointers from the other side for you, that's all. Happy to oblige.

Anyway, one night I'm returning after a little late-night work a few streets away from the block, not much of a haul, jewellery mostly, but enough to last another week if I can fence the stuff, when I get back to the flat and discover a note has been slid under the door:

> You went in the front downstairs window.
> Used a glass cutter. Turned the lights
> off once you were inside. You went to the
> front upstairs bedroom. Again, turned the
> light off. Then left three minutes later.
> I may have some work for you. Number 26.

I'd been spotted.

***

It was an impressive telescope. Very impressive. Not that I'm the least *au fait* with optical devices, but this was impressive because it didn't even look like a telescope. Not the normal kind, anyway, the type you might see jammed over a pirate's eye in a swashbuckling yarn. No, this was something you'd expect from a fifties sci-fi B-movie, a great white barrel of a thing, with pipes, meters, and humming electronic devices secured to it, mounted on a sturdy tripod. And, at this precise moment – pointing from its vantage point right at the house I'd just broken into.

I had my eye pressed to an insignificant-looking tube at its side, but the image was crystal clear. Made more impressive by the green night-vision.

By my side, the elderly American fiddled with a few switches. The image zoomed out a little, then flipped to a series of bodies and cars passing by in variegated red-and-orange tones.

"Thermal imaging," he said. "I followed your every move, then switched to night vision when you were inside. It's a good view from here, the house is nicely exposed."

I stepped back. "I guess I was, too. Exposed, I mean."

He nodded as I tried to decide his age – late sixties, early seventies? Small, compact, still reasonably fit. "You said you might have some work for me?" No point in beating about the bush.

Another nod as he moved a pile of papers so he could sit in a tattered old armchair, and they joined one of the many other piles on the floor. I guess that was what made the 'scope all the more impressive, a gleaming technical artefact in the obvious shambles of such a chaotic flat. Half-finished meals and abandoned coffee cups lay amongst the detritus. He offered me another chair, which even I refrained from sitting on. And as a bloke who's shared a cell with three other lags for twenty-three hours a day, that was really saying something.

"People round here," he began, "call me The Astronaut."

I shrugged, unimpressed. "I heard it was Buzz."

He smiled. "After Aldrin?"

"Lightyear," I corrected him. "Some character from a kids' film."

The smile wavered as he caught my eye-line wandering back to the 'scope. "If you're thinking of stealing it, I guess you should know it weighs close on a quarter of a ton. They winched it up the side of the building to get it in. And, in case you're wondering, it's worth well over a hundred thousand of your Brit pounds."

My Brit pounds. The old guy was obviously still smarting from the Buzz Lightyear thing. Granted, he sounded a bit American, but only in that sort of clichéd way anyone would if they tried to put on an accent. I probably do a more convincing effort after watching a couple of old *Star Trek* reruns.

I looked round briefly, tried to get some sort of picture of the bloke. Too much contradictory information. An old guy living in a dump like some sort of tramp (no doubt he'd have said "hobo" to try and add extra authenticity to the Yank thing), yet clearly able to afford the sort of sky-gazing kit Greenwich Observatory would have been proud of.

Other signs. No trace of a woman's touch, so presumably he lived alone. No evidence of any help from the Social Services – God, it'd have taken a crack team of their best cleaners even to begin to sort the place out. So – weird old recluse with access to expensive technology living in some sort of delusional fantasy world in which he once strolled about on the moon? Yeah, I know – it's where the word "lunatic" derives from.

And yet, something else about Buzz that Rambling Ian had told me stuck in my mind – *Lives at the very top with a telescope. Never lets anyone through the door.* But here I was, forty minutes after illegally entering one locked premises, and I'd seemingly gained effortless entry into another.

"Another great feature of my 'scope," he began, "is that it ..."

"Takes photographs?" I finished for him, already ahead. Not much of a leap to make, he'd been so keen to show me the means of my "capture", in all its technological excesses, it seemed logical Mr Spaceman would also have photographic evidence of my evening's work with which to blackmail me.

He nodded, a little too smugly for my liking. "I love this block," he went on. "Love living here – on top. I guess you could say that when you've been to the places I've been to, seen the things I have, it becomes very difficult for your feet ever to really touch the ground."

I ignored this, didn't want to be drawn into the fantasy. Point was, however odd, eccentric, or plain insane the man was, he had pictures that could stick me straight back inside. "You mentioned you may have some work for me?"

He smiled, and I knew that he knew he had me. Whatever was going to be played out, it would be at his pace, not mine. "I've lived here since 'eighty-three. Right here, on the top. 'Course, it was in better repair way back then. And I've loved it ever since. It gives me ... anonymity. Leaves me free just to watch."

"The moon, presumably," I replied, trying to hurry him along.

"No," he replied. "Seen enough of the moon in my time. Far too much."

"Rumour round here is you walked on it."

He smiled. "Lots of rumours round here. I use the 'scope to see the truth." He fixed me with his eyes. "I see a lot of things with the 'scope. Like you, for instance. The day you arrived with the young mutt from the prison services. Yeah, I thought to myself, here comes another one. Then, of course, there've been all your – how should I put this – night-time jaunts? Those illegal little excursions into the surrounding backstreets. What else could you be but just another common thief?" He paused, steepled his fingers.

I tried to bow in a slightly patronizing manner, but I think it just came across as a bow. No point in denying it, the man did have an unsettling presence. Would have made a good judge. "You have me at a disadvantage."

"I know," he replied.

"You want me to steal something for you."

He smiled, shook his head slowly. "Not for me. *From* me."

He waited for my reaction. After the aborted bow, I gave it a miss.

"There were," he continued, "several visits by the Apollo space programme to the moon. As is the way, the first is the most widely seared into public consciousness. By the time my mission went up, people were largely bored, and had begun counting the massive cost of the programme. They'd grown tired of watching men bounce on a dark, dusty surface a quarter of a million miles away. The so-called 'scientific value' of such missions was openly criticized. In consequence, I was one of the last human beings ever to walk on the surface of the moon."

"I heard it was just a movie set somewhere out in the desert," I tried.

"If only it was." He looked away, lost for a moment. "My life soon disintegrated. My marriage broke down, and I took to the bottle." He shrugged. "It's a recognized phenomenon. When you've experienced the heavenly beauty of that cold black solace; when you've looked back and seen how perfect the Earth really is, how it silently spins – just so magisterially – all else, all human experience, pales. You become ... nothing."

I watched him, sitting there amidst all the rubbish, a lonely old man with nothing but dreams. Delusional – well, he had to be, didn't he? And yet, something about the way he spoke about it all ...

"You still meet up with all your moon buddies?" I knew it was wrong to encourage the fantasy, yet a small part of me wanted to know more ... almost, perhaps, wanted to believe. The stardust thing, I guess.

He gave a short, contemptuous laugh. "Losers all," he said. "Every darn one of them. Opening crummy supermarkets to turn a buck. Jeez, the last thing I did Stateside was a series of commercials." He pulled a horribly insincere smile. "*Say please for Moon Cheese.*"

"Can't say I ever heard of it," I said.

"So I shipped up and away. Came here. To my tower in the sky. Spend what I can on the 'scope and live very happily."

"Do you have any friends?" I asked, feeling a little sorry for him. "Relatives? Visitors?"

He turned to me. "What for? I keep my own company." He pointed to the telescope. "I see all the people, all the things they do. I have no desire for their intrusion. It's what makes you and me so similar. We both crave the solitude and the darkness. For you, it's work. For me – personal."

"What's your name?"

He waved a hand. "Not necessary. Neither's yours. But, you know, on reflection, I do quite like the Buzz thing."

"Why do you want me to steal something from you?"

"Shouldn't the question be *what* do you want me to steal?"

I looked round briefly. "Well, Buzz, I'm guessing it won't be the 'scope. And frankly, I doubt there's anything else in here that would interest the scabbiest gull on the dump."

"Incorrect," he replied, standing and making his way slowly through the paper piles to a small, smothered chest of drawers, and bringing out a small ring box. "I brought something back. When I was there."

I found myself swallowing as he beckoned me over to a small table. No, I told myself, it *couldn't* be, could it? The rumoured moon rock? Here, in a shabby block of South London flats? And yet, the closer I got to the box, the more I wanted to open it.

"Is it …?" I asked.

He nodded, slowly opening the lid to reveal a small grey stone no bigger than the tip of my finger. "Interplanetary contraband. Smuggled just the same way those poor drugs mules do. Mind you, maybe more painfully. You try swallowing a wrapped piece of the moon in a zero-gravity space capsule."

I smiled at the image. "And they never found out?"

"The folks at mission control?" He shook his head. "Didn't have a clue. See, after splashdown, each Apollo mission had to spend time in a decompression chamber."

I nodded, briefly remembering newspaper images of astronauts smiling through thick glass windows.

"I'd imagine conditions inside were pretty similar to your penal experiences. Three men locked up with just some very crude sanitation facilities. And of course, when you're back here, gravity suddenly exerts itself very forcefully. Those little bits of rock we'd each swallowed became extremely heavy as they worked their way through."

I winced slightly.

"All we had to do was keep swallowing the rocks when they … reappeared. That, and pray we could withhold them during the debrief and subsequent release to the waiting world's press. I finally got this fella to myself two days after I'd made it home." He took the rock out. "Not many of us can say we've had a piece of the universe pass right through us three times. Guess he's made even more of a journey than me. You want to hold it?"

As an offer, he hadn't sold it that well. "I'll pass. No pun intended."

He snapped the lid shut, slowly scratched the side of his head. "You're thinking I'm insane, of course. That this is nothing more than some little pebble I picked up from the park."

"No, I'm thinking you've called me up here to do a job. I simply want to know what it is."

He slipped the ring box into a pocket, navigated his way back to the window, and begun turning wheels on the telescope. I watched as the large white barrel moved slowly to the left, still pointing down towards the darkened town many floors below. Satisfied he'd found the right spot, he beckoned me over. I pressed my eye to the soft rubber eyepiece; saw nothing until he flicked the night-vision switch. A green window glowed. A downstairs room, by the look of it, half-drawn curtains failing to obscure opulent trappings inside. I recognized it immediately, a large house less than fifty yards from the place I'd just relieved of its jewellery. Indeed, I'd been past it several times, had already considered its potential for easy pickings.

"You chose to ignore this place," I heard him say. "Why?"

I kept my eye tight to the rubber, making out more of the room. "The wall-mounted safe. It's just about visible from the street, if you know what you're looking for."

"A standard three-tumbler dial model," he said. "Surely not a problem for someone like you? And an indication of lucrative spoils inside?"

"Not this one," I said, taking a longer look at the small metal box mounted between two gilt-framed pictures. "Open the door on that sucker and all you'll find is a web camera looking right at you, linked direct to the security company. It's bait. Before you know it, there're a dozen police cars waiting outside." I stepped back from

the 'scope. "The whole place stinks of wire-traps and alarms.
Whatever they've got in there, they want to keep hold of it."

He nodded.

"But you're not going to tell me, are you?"

He shook his head.

"You just want me to do whatever it is you want?"

Another nod. It was like talking to a mute.

"You're going to have to try and help me with some words," I
tried. "Even better an explanation."

"His name is Saunders."

"The owner?" I asked.

"And not just of that house, either," he replied. "He owns this
whole place."

"The block?"

"And all its apartments, land and accesses."

"These flats, they're all rented?"

He nodded. "Cheques payable to Mr Mark Saunders." He
slumped back down in the ruined armchair. "His father's company
built the place. Joe Saunders – nice fella. Died last year, left the lot
to his son, Mark. His house, its contents, and this block."

I was beginning to get the picture. "And since then, his son's let
the place go to rack and ruin?"

"'S'about it."

"Let me guess," I said, thinking of the boarded-up doors and
windows. "Now he's about to sell? Have the place condemned as a
liability, eyesore, whatever; then pocket the loot before the demo-
lition teams arrive?"

Buzz nodded. "It's part of a so-called urban-renewal scheme.
They'll pay him millions to reduce this place to rubble."

"And you'll lose your home in the sky?"

He shuffled through some papers at his feet, threw a letter across
at me. "Their latest offer."

Headed "Dear Occupier", it was an offer to rehouse the old guy
in some new housing development. The words "ground-floor
retirement apartment" had been angrily underlined – presumably
by Buzz himself.

"I ain't moving," he said. "Just ain't."

"But if this place isn't safe …?" My eyes drifted to a paragraph detailing the owner's concerns about the central lifts, how it might be necessary to close them to residents. "It's going to make getting out of here pretty tough. You could be stranded."

He jabbed a finger. "What are you saying? That I'm too old to manage a few flights of lousy stairs if I need to? Jeez, I walked on the moon!"

It was getting out of control. "Show me the pictures," I said.

"Pictures?"

"The ones you took of me earlier tonight," I replied, pointing at the telescope, the only part of the situation that didn't fit my theory that the man was simply a lonely delusionist.

"Kick those papers out of the way," he instructed from his chair. "Underneath, there's a printer. Push the red button on the left."

I kneeled, did as he said, watching the linked printer come to life, then begin spitting out a series of shots of me about my earlier business. Green, pin-sharp, night-visioned evidence that I was there; outside and inside. Conclusive.

He chuckled softly. "I guess your big mistake was to take the hat and scarf off when you got inside. But I think I managed to get your good side."

"So the job is?" I asked, wondering if there was any way to rid the 'scope of the pictures. There had to be some sort of memory attached to it, an internal digital camera, perhaps. But where …?

"Your job," he said, "is to steal my moon rock, then break into Saunders's house and place it on the cocktail cabinet at the back of the living room, where I can be sure to see it."

I frowned. "The reason?"

"Because," he explained, as if talking to a small child, "when I get back from my weekly Astrological Society meeting tomorrow night and discover my apartment has been burgled, I shall be able to point the blame at Saunders."

"Just because there's a pebble on his cocktail cabinet?"

"No!" he snapped back. "Because it's the thing he covets the most. The moon rock!"

"Right," I announced, mind made up. "I'm going now. I'm sorry you're going to have to move, but – hey, there it is. But let me tell you this. If you think breaking into people's houses and leaving stones in their living rooms makes a jot of difference, then you're very wrong."

His face began to show panic. "I'll send the pictures to the police! You'll be back in the slammer with all the other scum!"

"Don't you get it?" I tried. "It's over. This building is falling down. It's had its time. They're trying to get you somewhere better, more accessible. You can't fight for this sort of stuff with bits of goddamned moon, Buzz. I'm sorry, but that's the way it is."

He blinked slowly. "I'll send the photos to the police."

"No, you won't," I said.

"Try me."

"I don't have to." I shook my head, walked towards the door.

"What makes you so sure, thief?"

I turned, looked at the confused, angry old man sitting in the detritus of his lonely delusions. "Because, Buzz," I slowly explained, "you'd have to give the police a signed statement. As, indeed, would I, wherein I'd detail exactly what has happened here tonight. There'd most like be some sort of court case. You'd be called as a witness; forced to swear on a Bible as to your name. Then it'd all come out, wouldn't it, Buzz? That you weren't who you claimed to be? That you were really an odd little bloke who needed a ground-floor flat and help from the Social Services."

He stared back, blank-faced.

"Put it this way, Buzz. You shop me, and we're both going down…"

I got to do a fair bit of reading in the next eight months, spent so much time reading about space and space travel that the other lags on the wing got to calling me Buzz, a name I was happy with, though I never let on precisely why.

The court case lasted for three days, and to be fair, in a slow news week, attracted a few columns in the tabloids. I guess it was simply the absurdity of it all. I'm not going to tell you his real name, but rest assured he wasn't an astronaut, which came as a bit of a disappointment, in a weird sort of way. His eyes never met mine as he gave evidence, and at no time during the trial did he ever mention any of the crazy moon stuff. He came out as a decent old star-gazing vigilante, photographing misdeeds from up on high – and I came out with eight months.

Rambling Ian came to visit, told me the case had attracted enough attention to warrant Social Services moving in on the old guy and "re-accommodating" him. Apparently a crowd had gathered to see the huge telescope being winched back down the side of the building, clapping and cheering. Buzz, he told me, had simply watched, tears in his eyes.

A few months later, I made the usual right noises to the panel, and left Her Maj's Pleasure a cosmologically enlightened man. Sure, I was going to be a thief again, always would, we all have to live, don't we? We're all stardust, after all.

True to form, the Probation set me up in a cosy little dump just south of the river. Three days later, returning from a midnight sortie, I found a note slipped under the doorway:

```
You walked south for four minutes. Turned
right, stayed outside number 27 for twelve
minutes until the owners returned. You
hid in a bush as they went inside. I'm
just wondering if you needed a former
employee of NASA's mission control to
help guide your mission status in a safer
and more profitable way? Between us, we
could reach for the moon.
```

Opening the front door, I scanned the horizon, looking past disused warehouses and over the river towards a distant tower block, its top-floor lights blazing.

I nodded, bowed – and I swear something winked back.

HE DID NOT ALWAYS SEE HER

Claire Seeber

JEFF HELPED OLIVIA choose the February book, steering her heavily towards Mary Shelley's *Frankenstein*. There were a few inward groans when Olivia had mumbled her idea at the last meeting. The group preferred modern books: they often enjoyed the *Daily Mail's* selection, or the ones that chat-show couple chose. But actually, they all agreed at the meeting, Shelley had hit on something with the creation of the monster. It was hard to imagine it being written by a woman. And, of course, they were most happy to be at Olivia's house with Jeff on hand, so charmingly attentive.

When the women left that evening, tapping out into the cold clear night beneath the few stars visible in Chiswick's busy skies, Olivia loaded the dishwasher, wiped all the worktops down, and went up to bed. Jacqueline had lingered; was taking a particularly long time to finish the oily Chardonnay Jeff had so thoughtfully provided, still simpering with spectacular adoration at his jokes. Olivia didn't worry that they'd think her rude for slipping off; her husband would be happy to see Jacqueline out.

Upstairs Olivia peeped in at her daughter, cleaned her teeth and then checked her son. Her heart turned over to see he'd slipped his thumb into his mouth, a habit long fought. His hair was slightly damp and his face flushed. Olivia turned the radiator down and gently tried to disengage his thumb, checking quickly over her shoulder. By the time Jeff had managed to steer an equally flushed Jacqueline out towards her enormous car, Olivia was asleep. He didn't want to have to, but Jeff woke her anyway. He was off on business for ten days early the next morning.

If you keep still for long enough, do you cease to exist? Olivia wondered as she stared out of the kitchen window. The late snow was melting slowly on the small green lawn until the patch looked rather like the Pacer mints she used to steal from Woolworth's as a child. Absently Olivia rinsed the last plate until it shone, gazing at the pathetic leaning ball of raisin eyes and carrots that had once been a snowman, the radio beside her rattling with a phone-in about women being ignored in the bedroom.

"If he doesn't see me as I want to be seen, do I not exist?" moaned a well-spoken academic-type called Miriam. "Do I simply not count in his eyes?"

The presenter murmured sympathetically and moved on swiftly.

Olivia felt a sudden urge to scream loudly. Instead she staunched the hot tap, sealing off the heat that aggravated the deep welts on her left hand. She stared down at the marks, labels of her own weakness. Her youngest wandered in, treading neat muddy footprints across the spotless floor.

"Can I have some crisps?" she asked, but she was already rifling through the cupboard where they lived, her auburn ponytail sleek against her back.

"Can you see me?" Olivia asked her daughter curiously.

"Dur!" her daughter replied, rustling plastic. "I'm not blind, Mum, you know. I don't have a white stick." She chose a packet of prawn cocktail flavour and wandered off again. They were ridiculously pink, Olivia observed vaguely, wiping down the sink. Prawns weren't naturally that pink, were they?

He came home early, before Olivia had a chance to clean the mud off the back step. "Hello," she said nervously. "Good trip?" He checked the kitchen in silence. She held her breath; she thought she'd got away with it – then he opened the back door to check. He looked at her just once, his handsome face inscrutable. In silence, he went upstairs; in silence he came down again, out of his shirt and tie now, wearing a blue tracksuit with white stripes down the side that showed off his tall frame nicely but was frankly horrible in Olivia's eyes. He wasn't the young boy she'd fancied from afar in the refectory any more; he'd taken up running recently to fight his paunch. She wondered if he thought the stripes would make him go faster. Not that she would offer such a frivolous opinion these days.

Olivia had cleaned the mud up now but it was too late, she knew. She also knew that if she crouched in the corner she only inflamed his rage, inflamed it 'til it bubbled; he saw her rather like a dog, cowering from its master. Well, she was a dog, to him.

"Bitch," he would snarl, his face contorted until he was positively ugly. So instead she chose to stay still when she recognized the signs.

Now she lay flat on the gleaming kitchen floor. She lay flat but her head felt fuzzy.

"What the hell are you doing?" he scoffed, opening the fridge and helping himself to a pork pie. It was very sturdy and compact, Olivia noted from her horizontal position. A small tight structure of pastry, meat and fat.

"I thought I'd save you the bother," she answered her husband quietly. She could see dirt, some old cat-hairs, a bit of fluff stuck in strange yellow muck on the skirting-board. Luckily he never got this low.

Her eldest walked into the room and stopped when he saw her. "Have you hurt your back again, Mummy?" he asked, but his eyes were anxious. He moved towards her.

"It's a bit sore, sweetie, yes. You go on now." She forced a smile. "Get on with your maths. I'll be up in a minute."

Her husband laughed mirthlessly, throwing his head back, spraying tiny fragments of pork pie across the sparkling worktop.

"Your mother's a daft bint," he spluttered to his son, eventually recovering himself. When he laughed, his tracksuit top rode up, showing the top of wiry dark-red pubic hair. Olivia felt quite nauseous. "Did you know that, Dan? A daft fucking bint."

"You shouldn't call her that," her eldest muttered, his eyes steadfastly on the floor.

Her husband stopped laughing. He stared at his son.

"Well, you shouldn't," Dan said, a little louder now, his pale face flushing with the effort of challenging his father. "It's horrible." He looked up this time, directly at the older man.

"Get out, Dan," Olivia said quickly, scrambling to her feet. She knew what came next.

As her husband made a lunge for Dan, the remnants of the pork pie smashing on to the shining tiles, Olivia thrust herself in front of her ten-year-old son. "Go!" she shouted at him. With a stifled sob, he went.

After the beating, a hot-eyed Olivia struggled to hold back the tears – but she wouldn't give him the satisfaction. Long gone were the days when he held her and cried himself, begging for forgiveness. Long long gone.

She had found that if she kept very still he did not always see her. Over time, a long and weary time that eventually amounted to most of her adult life, Olivia realized that this was likely to be her safest option. Not necessarily her salvation, but the best bet laced on a short string of bad ones.

She leaned against the worktop trying to quell her shaking; eventually she asked her husband, "If I leave you, what would you do?"

He regarded her calmly. He picked a bit of pork out of his teeth and spat it on the floor. "Him, for a start." He gestured with his head at the door their son had left through. He smirked at her, then trod the pork pie carefully into the small cracks between the terracotta tiles. "Little shit."

On his way out of the room he picked up the copy of *Frankenstein* stacked neatly with the cookbooks.

"And this was quite obviously written by her husband," he snapped, "stupid bitch." He chucked the paperback at Olivia's head; she didn't duck quite in time. Then he scooped up the phone to call his great friend Bert. "Booked the course, you hound?" Jeff barked with laughter at the response, and slammed the door behind him.

Olivia stared down at the squashed pork pie, his words reverberating round her throbbing head. "*Him for a start.*" The pork pie reminded her of her wedding breakfast, the time when love and hope meant more than empty promises. He hadn't hit her until a few weeks after the honeymoon. Until they were on the other side of the world; settling in Jakarta for his work. Until she made the wrong rice for his dinner; until she had no one familiar to turn to and no money of her own. Until she could only wander tearfully on the beach, stepping over the coconut-leaf offerings outside each Hindu home and wondering what she'd done; already sick and pregnant in the humid nights with her beloved son.

When the book club arrived for their next meeting at Olivia's house, they were surprised that Jeff was out. He was always there, welcoming them, pouring the wine, joshing them gently in the way they loved, flattering them and making them think: *If only*. He took so much more interest than any of their husbands; in fact, sometimes he even suggested the books that Olivia picked to read.

"Lucky Olivia," they'd sigh. "Such devotion. Such a family man. And still so handsome too." Olivia would smile wanly and deep down they'd think: *Stupid cow, she doesn't deserve him, such a cold woman, so difficult to get close to, so thin and brittle*. But they put up with her for Jeff. Lovely man.

This cold March night, Olivia had served up a proper treat. Bowls of glistening green olives, sparkling wine, thick pâté and creamy Brie, a plate of crusty, homemade-looking pork pies beside dark red tulips as the centrepiece. Olivia seemed different too. She had some colour in her cheeks for once; she didn't look quite so thin and she'd cut her hair to a sleek and shiny bob that hung just above her shoulders. If you looked closely you might have seen the small scar that marked her forehead, the exact shape of a book corner, but her new fringe hid it well.

"I thought Jeff loved your long hair?" Cathy asked quizzically.

"He did." Olivia took a big sip of her Prosecco. "But I hated it. So I had it cut right off."

"And where is he?" Cathy asked girlishly, looking through the open door into the hall as if Jeff might step in at any moment. "I quite miss him now he's not here."

"Do you?" Olivia smiled shyly. "I find it very – quiet now he's away on business."

"And where's he gone, the naughty man?" asked Jacqueline with a pained fuchsia smile, secretly ruing the two hours she'd spent that afternoon in Hair Flair having her thin hair bouffed.

"Back to Indonesia; they couldn't do without him, they found. He really is a telecommunications expert, it seems." Olivia drained her wine. "He might be gone some time." She picked up the plate of golden pastry with a steady hand, the little handmade leaves on top of each pie curling in the soft electric light, and offered it around. "Pork pie, anyone?"

METHOD MURDER

Simon Brett

As an actor, Kenny Mountford yearned to be taken seriously. Since finishing at drama school, he'd done all right. A bit of theatre work, but mostly television, which was good news because it paid better. However, a continuous round of small parts in *The Bill*, *Heartbeat* and *Midsomer Murders* had left him, by the time he reached his early thirties, with a deep sense of dissatisfaction. It wasn't celebrity that he craved, it was respectability. He wanted to be able to hold his head high amongst other actors when the discussion moved on to the issues of the "truth" and "integrity" of their profession.

And really that meant doing more theatre. For the more obscure and impenetrable the theatre work, the higher the integrity of the actors involved. This meant, in effect, working with one of a small list of trendy directors, directors who didn't pander to the public by making their work accessible or simply entertaining. So Kenny Mountford set out to meet and ingratiate himself with such a director.

It was a good time for him to make the move. A stint playing the barman on a successful sitcom had bolstered his income to the point that he had paid off the mortgage on his Notting Hill house. And, besides, his live-in actress girlfriend Lesley-Jane Walden was not only a nice bit of arm candy to satisfy the gossip columns, she was also making a good whack as the latest *femme fatale* in a long-running soap opera. Her hunger for celebrity was currently satisfied, they weren't in need of money, so Kenny Mountford was in a position where he could afford to pursue art for art's sake.

The latest *enfant terrible* of British theatre was a director called Charlie Fenton. Like many of his breed, he had a great contempt for the written word, rejecting texts by playwrights in favour of improvisation. In the many television and newspaper interviews he gave, he regularly pontificated about "the straitjacket of conformity" and derided "the crowd-pleasing lack of originality demonstrated by the constant revival of classic theatre texts". One somewhat sceptical interviewer had asked if this meant Charlie Fenton considered one of his improvised pieces to be better than a play by Shakespeare and, though hotly denying the suggestion, the director made it fairly clear that that actually was his view.

What Charlie Fenton was most famous for was his in-depth approach to characterization. Though claiming to have developed his own system, he owed more than he cared to admit to the pioneering work in New York of Lee Strasberg, the originator of the "Method". This was a style of acting which aimed for greater authenticity, and its exponents had included Meryl Streep, Paul Newman, Robert de Niro and even, surprisingly, Marilyn Monroe. Rather than building up a character from the outside and assembling a collection of mannerisms, a "Method actor" would try so to immerse himself in the identity of the person he was playing that he virtually *became* that person.

So if an actor were playing a milkman in a Charlie Fenton production, the director would send the poor unfortunate off to spend three months delivering milk. Someone with the role of a Muslim terrorist would be obliged to convert to Islam. An actress playing a prostitute would have to turn tricks in the streets around King's Cross (and almost definitely service Charlie Fenton too, so that he could check she was doing it properly). And one poor unfortunate had once spent three months in a basement blindfolded and chained to a radiator for a proposed production about hostage-taking. (It would only have been three weeks, but Charlie Fenton omitted to inform the actor when he abandoned the idea.)

Once his casts had immersed themselves in their characters, weeks of improvisation in rehearsal rooms would ensue, until the director edited what he considered to be the best bits into a script. After the production had opened, this text based on the actors' lines would then be published in the form of a book, for which Charlie Fenton took all the royalties.

The carefully leaked details of his rehearsal methods only added to the director's mystique, and very few people realized that ordering actors around in this way was just part of Charlie Fenton's ongoing power trip. The lengthy build-up to his productions was nothing to do with the quality of theatre that resulted; it was all about his ego. Also the total control he exercised over his companies proved to be a good way of getting pretty young actresses into bed. (He had a wife and family somewhere in the background, but spent little time with them.)

Awestruck accounts of the director's procedures, tantrums and bullying ensured that any actor in search of theatrical respectability was desperate to work with Charlie Fenton. And so it was with Kenny Mountford.

They finally met after a first night of a National Theatre *King Lear*. The play wasn't really Lesley-Jane Walden's cup of tea, but it was a first night, after all. Any occasion when there was a chance of her being photographed and appearing in the tabloids suited her very well indeed (though she had been a little disappointed by the lack of *paparazzi* down at the South Bank). As soon as the final curtain was down Charlie Fenton was at the bar, surrounded by toadies, who hung on every word as he proceeded to list Shakespeare's shortcomings as a dramatist. Kenny and Lesley-Jane had gone to the performance with one of their actor friends who had once spent six months picking tomatoes and learning Polish in order to take part in a Charlie Fenton production about migrant workers. And the friend effected the coveted introduction.

The director, who sported a silly little goatee and grey ponytail, favoured Lesley-Jane with a coruscating smile. "I've seen some of your work," he said. "It's amazing how a really good actor can shine even amidst the dross of a soap opera."

She blushed and smiled prettily at this. Which wasn't difficult for Lesley-Jane Walden. She was so pretty that she did everything prettily.

Kenny Mountford felt encouraged. If Charlie Fenton had recognized his girlfriend's quality in a soap opera, the director might look equally favourably at his work in a sitcom. But that illusion was not allowed to last for long. Looking superciliously at him over half-moon glasses, Charlie Fenton said, "Oh, yes, I know your name. Still paying the mortgage rather publicly on the telly, are you?"

"Maybe," Kenny replied, "but I am about to change direction."

"Towards what?"

"More serious theatre work."

"Oh, yes?" the director sneered. "That's what they all say."

"No, I mean it."

"Kenny, I don't think you'd recognize 'more serious theatre work' if it jumped up and bit you on the bum. You have clearly been destined from birth for a life of well-paid mediocrity."

"I disagree. I'm genuinely committed to doing more serious work."

"Really?" The director scrutinized the actor with something approaching contempt. "I don't think you could hack it.'

"Try me."

Charlie Fenton was silent for a moment of appraisal. Then he said, "I bet you wouldn't have the dedication to work with me."

"Are you offering me a job?"

"If I were, I'm pretty confident you couldn't do it."

"Again I say: try me."

Another long silence ensued. Then the director announced, "I'm starting work on a new project. About criminal gangs in London."

"What would it involve for the actors?"

"Deep cover. Infiltrating the gangs."

Kenny was aware of the slight admonitory shake of Lesley-Jane's head, but he ignored the signal. "I'm up for it," he said.

"I'll phone you with further details," the director announced in a magisterial manner that suggested the audience was at an end.

"Shall I give you my mobile number?"

"Landline. I don't do mobiles." Clearly another eccentricity, which was indulged like all Charlie Fenton's eccentricities. He flashed another smile at Lesley-Jane, then looked hard at Kenny, his lips curled with scepticism. 'If you can come back to me in three months as a member of a London gang, you've got a part in the show."

"You're on," said Kenny Mountford.

Lesley-Jane wasn't keen on the idea. If Kenny was going to go underground, he wouldn't be able to squire her to all the premieres, launches and first nights her ego craved. Their relationship was fine while he too had a high-profile television face, but she didn't want to end up with a boyfriend nobody recognized. She also knew that her own work situation was precarious. Young *femmes fatales* in soap operas had a short shelf life. One of the scriptwriters had already hinted that her character might have a fatal car crash in store. There was a race against time for her to announce that she was leaving the show before the public heard that she'd been pushed off it. And then she'd need another series to move on to, and there weren't currently many signs of that being offered. At such a time she'd be more than usually dependent on the reflected fame of her partner. (She had always followed the old show business advice: if you can't be famous yourself, then make sure you go to bed with someone who is.) The last thing she wanted at that moment was for Kenny to disappear off the social radar for some months while he immersed himself in gangland culture.

But Lesley-Jane's remonstrations were ignored. Her boyfriend's mind was now focused on only one thing: proving his seriousness as an actor to Charlie Fenton.

And to do that he had to infiltrate a London gang. Which actually turned out to be surprisingly easy. He didn't have to hang around Shepherd's Bush Green for long before he was approached by someone with a heavy Russian accent and asked if he wanted to buy drugs. After a couple of weeks of making regular purchases of heroin (which he didn't use but stockpiled in his bathroom cabinet), he only had to default on payments twice to be hustled into a car with tinted windows, blindfolded and taken off to meet the organization's frighteners.

They didn't have to hurt him to get their money. Kenny Mountford had the cash ready with him and handed it over as soon as his blindfold was removed. He found himself seated on a chair in a windowless cellar, loomed over by the two heavies who'd snatched him and facing a thin-faced man in an expensive suit. From their conversation in the car, he'd deduced that his abductors were called Vasili and Vladimir. They addressed the thin-faced man as Fyodor. All three spoke English with a heavy accent from somewhere in the former Soviet Union.

"So if you had the money all the time, why didn't you pay up?" asked the man in the suit, whose effortless authority identified him as the gang's leader.

"Maybe he enjoys being beaten to a pulp," suggested the heavy Kenny was pretty sure was called Vasili.

"Maybe," said Kenny Mountford with a cool that he'd spent three years at drama school perfecting, "but that's not actually the reason. I just thought this was a good way of getting to meet you, Fyodor."

"Do you know who I am?" the man asked, intrigued.

"I only know your name, but it doesn't take much intelligence to work out that you're higher up this organization than the two goons who brought me here."

Kenny felt the men either side of him stiffen and was aware of their fists bunching, but he remembered his concentration exercises and didn't flinch.

Fyodor raised a hand to pacify his enforcers. "You are right. I control the organization."

"And am I allowed to know what it's called?"

He smiled a crooked smile. "The Semfiropol Boys. From where we started our operations. Do you know where Semfiropol is?" Kenny shook his head. "It is in the Crimea. Southern Ukraine. Near to Yalta. I assume you have not been there?" Another shake of the head. "Well, we did what we could over there, but the pickings were small, and there were a lot of... entrenched interests. Turf wars, dangerous. In London our life is easier."

"And how many are there in the Semfiropol Boys?"

"Twenty, maybe thirty, it depends. Sometimes people become untrustworthy and have to be eliminated."

Kenny was aware of a reaction from Vasili and Vladimir. Clearly elimination was the part of the job they enjoyed.

"And do you just deal in drugs?"

Fyodor spread his hands wide in an encompassing gesture. "Drugs... prostitution...protection rackets...loan sharking...The Semfiropol Boys are a multifunction organization." Then came the question that Kenny knew couldn't be delayed much longer. "But why do you want to know this? Curiosity?"

"More than just curiosity."

"Good. If it was just curiosity, I think Vasili and Vladimir would have to eliminate you straight away." The gang boss smiled a thin smile. "They may well have to eliminate you straight away, whatever the reason for your enquiries. You could be a cop, for all we know."

"I can assure you I am not a cop."

"But that's exactly what you would say if you were a cop."

"Well, I'm not."

"Mr Mountford, I am not here to chop logic with you. I am a busy man." He looked at his watch. "I have a meeting shortly with a senior civil servant in the Home Office. He is helping me with some visa applications for members of my extended family in Semfiropol. Now please will you tell me why you are here? And why I shouldn't just hand you straight over to Vasili and Vladimir for elimination."

Kenny Mountford took a deep breath. There was no doubt that he had put himself in very real danger. But, as he had that daunting thought, he couldn't help also feeling a warm glow. Charlie Fenton would be so impressed by the lengths he had gone to in his quest for authenticity.

"I'm here because I want to join your gang."

"Join the Semfiropol Boys?" asked Fyodor in astonishment. Vasili and Vladimir let out deep threatening chuckles at the very idea.

"Yes."

"But why should we let you join us? As I said, you could be a cop. You could be a journalist. You could be a spy from the Odessa Reds." The reactions from Vasili and Vladimir left Kenny in no doubt as to what Fyodor was talking about. They might sound like a breed of chicken, but the Odessa Reds were clearly a rival gang.

"How can I prove to you that I'm none of those things? What are the qualifications for most of the people who join your gang?"

"Most of them have family connections with me in Semfiropol which go back many generations. At the very least, most of them are Ukrainian."

"I can sound Ukrainian," said Kenny, demonstrating the point. (He had made quite a study of accents at drama school.)

His impression didn't go down well with Vasili and Vladimir. They clearly thought he was sending them up. Two giant hands slammed down on his shoulders, while two giant fists were once again bunched.

But again a gesture from their boss froze them before the blows made contact.

"Anyone who wants to join the Semfiropol Boys," said Fyodor quietly, "has to pass certain tests."

"A lot of tests?" asked Kenny Mountford, maintaining his nonchalance with increasing difficulty.

The gang boss nodded. "The big one's at the end. Not many people get that far. But if you want to have a go at one of the starting tests…"

Kenny nodded. Fyodor leaned forward and told him what the first test was.

Like most actors, Kenny Mountford always felt a huge surge of excitement when he got a new part. However trivial the piece, hours would be spent poring over the script, making decisions about the character's accent and body language. The part that Fyodor had given him prompted exactly the same adrenaline rush, though in this case he had no text to work from. Kenny started reading everything he could find about the Crimean region, and Semfiropol in particular. He also tracked down recordings of Ukrainians speaking English and trained himself to imitate them.

The new direction his career was taking still failed to raise much enthusiasm in Lesley-Jane. From an early age her main aim in life had been to be the centre of attention, so she didn't respond well to being totally ignored by the man she was living with. But Kenny was too preoccupied with his new role to notice her disquiet.

The first test he had been given by Fyodor was relatively easy. All he had to do was to sell drugs in Shepherd's Bush, just like the dealer who had served as his initial introduction to the Semfiropol Boys. Apart from the work he was doing on his accent, Kenny also spent a considerable time sourcing clothes for the role, and was satisfied that the hoodie, jeans and trainers he ended up with had achieved exactly the requisite degree of shabbiness. He found it a welcome relief to be selecting his own clothes for a part, rather than having to follow the whims of some queeny Costume Designer as he would in television.

He needn't have bothered, though. The kind of lowlife he was peddling the drugs to didn't even notice what he looked like. The only thing they thought about was their next fix. But for Kenny Mountford as an artist – and a potential participant in a Charlie Fenton production – it was very important that he should get every minutest detail right.

After his first successful foray as a drug dealer, he got home early evening to find a very impatient Lesley-Jane Walden, dressed up to the nines and in a foul temper. "Where the hell have you been?" she shrieked, almost before he'd come through the door. "You know we're meant to be at this Tom Cruise premiere in half an hour."

"I'm sorry. I forgot."

"Well, for God's sake, get changed into something respectable and I'll call for a cab."

"I don't want to get changed." Kenny Mountford hadn't really formalized the idea before, but he suddenly knew that he wasn't going to change his clothes until Charlie Fenton agreed to give him the part in his next production. He was going to immerse himself in the role of a Semfiropol Boy until that wonderful moment. "And don't try to change my mind," he added in his best Ukrainian accent.

"What the hell are you talking about – and why the hell are you using that stupid voice?" demanded Lesley-Jane. "If we don't leave in the next five minutes, we'll have missed all the *paparazzi*. And if you think I'm going to be seen at a Tom Cruise premiere with someone dressed like you are, Kenny, then you've got another think coming!" Her face was so contorted with fury that she no longer looked even mildly pretty.

"Listen," Kenny continued in his Ukrainian voice, "I've got more important things to do than to—"

He was interrupted by the phone ringing. Lesley-Jane turned away from him in disgust. He picked up the receiver. A seductive "Hello" came from the other end of the line. The man's voice was vaguely familiar, but Kenny could not immediately identify it.

"Hello," he replied, still Ukrainian.

The tone changed from seduction to suspicion. "Who is this?"

Then Kenny knew. "Charlie," he enthused, reverting to his normal voice, "how good to hear you."

At the other end of the phone Charlie Fenton sounded slightly thrown. "Is that Kenny?"

"Yes. What can I do for you?"

The director still didn't sound his usual confident self as he stuttered out a reply. "Oh, I just... I was... um..." Then, sounding more assured, he said, "I just wanted to check how you were getting on with your infiltration process."

"I thought you weren't going to be in touch for three months."

"No, I, er, um... I changed my mind."

"Well, in answer to your question, Charlie, my infiltration is going very well. I'm already working for a gang."

"That's good."

"They're Ukrainian," he went on, reassuming the accent to illustrate his point. "And, actually, it's good you've rung, because there's something I wanted to ask you..."

"What's that?"

"How deep do you think I should go into this character I'm playing?"

"As deep as possible, Kenny." With something of his old pomposity, the director went on: "My style of theatre involves the participants in *total immersion* in their characters."

"I'm glad you said that, because I've been wondering whether I should actually be living in my house while I'm doing this preparation work. A Ukrainian gangster wouldn't live in a Notting Hill house like mine, would he?"

"No, he certainly wouldn't."

'So what I want to ask you is: do you think I should move out of my house?"

"No question. You certainly should," replied Charlie Fenton.

He took a grubby room in a basement near Goldhawk Road and, as he got deeper into his part, Kenny Mountford realized that he could no longer be Kenny Mountford. He needed a new identity to go with his new persona. He consulted Vasili and Vladimir on Ukrainian names and, following their advice, retitled himself Anatoli Semyonov. He also cut himself off from the English media. He stopped watching television, and the only radio he listened to on very crackly short wave was a station from Kiev. He bought Ukrainian newspapers in which at first he couldn't even understand the alphabet.

Meanwhile, the tests set by Fyodor got tougher. On top of the dealing, Kenny was now delegated to join Vasili, Vladimir and other of the Semfiropol Boys in some enforcement work. Drug customers dragging their feet on payments, prostitutes or pimps trying to keep more of the take than they were meant to... to bring these to a proper sense of priorities called for a certain amount of threatening behaviour, and frequently violence. In such situations, as with the drug dealing, Kenny – or rather Anatoli Semyonov – did what was required of him.

The thought never came into his mind that what he was doing might be immoral, that if he were caught he could be facing a long stretch in prison. Kenny Mountford was *acting*, he was researching the role of Anatoli Semyonov with the long-term view of appearing in a show created by the legendary Charlie Fenton. When such a conflict of priorities arose, Morality was for the petty-minded; Art was far more important.

As he got deeper and deeper under his Semfiropol Boys cover, Kenny saw less and less of Lesley-Jane. He didn't feel the deprivation. He was so focused on what he saw as his work that his mind had little room for other thoughts.

At the end of an evening with Vasili, Vladimir and some baseball bats, which had left a club-owner who was behind on his protection payments needing three weeks' hospitalization, the three Semfiropol Boys – or rather the two Semfiropol Boys and the one prospective Semfiropol Boy – reported back to Fyodor.

The gang leader was very pleased with them. "This is good work. I think we are achieving more since Anatoli has been with us." Vasili and Vladimir looked a little sour, but Kenny Mountford glowed with pride. He had reached the point where commendation from Fyodor was almost as important to him as commendation from Charlie Fenton. "And I think it is time that Anatoli Semyonov should be given his final test…"

Kenny could hardly contain his excitement. In his heavily Ukrainian voice, he asked, "You mean the one that will actually make me a fully qualified member of the Semfiropol Boys?"

Fyodor nodded. "Yes, that is exactly what I mean." He gave a curt nod of his head. Vasili and Vladimir, knowing the signal well, left the room. A long silence filled the space between the two men who remained.

It was broken by Fyodor. "Yes, Anatoli, I think you have proved you understand fully the role that is required of you."

Kenny Mountford could hardly contain himself. It was the best review he'd had since *The Stage* had described his Prospero as "luminescently compelling".

"So what do I have to do? Don't worry, whatever it is, I'll do it. I won't let you down."

"You have to kill someone," said Fyodor.

At first Kenny had had difficulty with the amount of vodka-drinking that being an aspirant Semfiropol Boy involved, but now he could match Vasili and Vladimir shot for shot – and even, on occasions, outdrink them. They tended to meet during the small hours (after a good night's threatening) in a basement club off Westbourne Grove. It was a dark place, heavy with the fug of cigarettes. Down there in the murk no one observed the smoking ban. And, having seen the size of the barmen, Kenny didn't envy any Department of Health Inspector delegated to enforce it.

He was always the only non-Russian speaker there, though his grasp of the language was improving, thanks to an online course he'd enrolled in. Kenny had a private ambition that, when the three months were up, he would return to Charlie Fenton not only looking like a Ukrainian gangster, but also speaking like one.

That evening they were well into the second bottle of vodka before either Vasili or Vladimir mentioned the task which they knew Fyodor had set Kenny. "So," asked Vladimir, always the more sceptical of the two, "do you reckon you can do it? Or are you going to chicken out?"

"Don't worry, *tovarich*, I can do it." He sounded as confident as ever, but couldn't deny to himself that the demand made by Fyodor had been a shock. Playing for time, he went on, "The only thing I can't decide about it is *who* I should kill? Just someone random who I happen to see in the street? Would that be the right thing to do?"

"It would be all right," replied Vasili, "but it would be rather a waste of a hit."

"How do you mean?"

"Well, if you're going to kill someone, at least make sure it's someone you already want out of your way."

"I'm sorry, I don't quite understand you."

"For heaven's sake, Anatoli," said Vladimir impatiently, "kill one of your enemies!"

"Ah." Kenny Mountford tried to think whether he actually had any enemies. There were people who'd got up his nose over the years – directors who hadn't recognized his talent, casting directors who had resolutely refused to cast him, actors who'd stolen his laughs – but none of these transgressions did he really think of as killing matters.

His confusion must have communicated itself to Vladimir, because he said, "You must have a sibling who's infuriated you at some point, someone's who's cheated you of money, a man who's stolen one of your girlfriends…"

"Yes, I must have, mustn't I?" Though, for the life of him, Kenny Mountford still couldn't think of anyone who was a suitable candidate for murder. He also couldn't completely suppress the unworthy feeling – which he knew would threaten his integrity as an actor in the eyes of someone like Charlie Fenton – that killing people was wrong.

The conversation became becalmed. After a few more shots of vodka, Vladimir announced he was off to get a freebie from one of the Bayswater working girls controlled by the Semfiropol Boys. "Got to be some perks in this job," he said.

But Vasili lingered. He seemed to have sensed Kenny's unease. "You are worried about the killing?"

"Well…"

"It is common. The first one. Many people find that. After two or three, though…" Vasili downed another shot of vodka "…it seems a natural thing to do. It might even seem a natural thing for an actor to do…"

Kenny was shocked. "You know I'm an actor?" Vasili smiled. "Do Fyodor and Vladimir know too?" Vasili shook his head. "Only me." Kenny Mountford felt a flood of relief.

There was a silence. Then Vasili leaned forward, lowering his voice as he said, "Maybe I could help you…"

"How?"

"There is a service I provide. It is not free, but it is not expensive… given the going rate." He let out a short cynical laugh. "There are plenty of Semfiropol Boys who have got their qualifications from me." Kenny Mountford looked puzzled. "I mean that they have never killed anyone. I have done the killings for them."

"Ah." Kenny couldn't deny he was tempted. He knew that, for the full immersion in his character that Charlie Fenton required, he should do the killing himself. But he couldn't help feeling a little squeamish about the idea. And if Vasili was offering him a way round the problem… "How much?" he asked, not realizing that, now the danger of his actually having to commit a murder had receded, he'd dropped out of his Ukrainian accent.

Vasili told him. It seemed a demeaningly small sum for the price of a human life, but Kenny knew this was not the moment for sentimentality. And he did still have quite a lot of money left from the sitcom fees. "So how do you select the target? Even more important, how do you make it look as if I've actually committed the murder?"

The Ukrainian dismissed the questions with an airy wave of his hand. "You leave such details to me. I have done it before, so I know what I'm doing. So far as Fyodor is concerned, it is definitely you who has committed the murder. So far as the police are concerned, nothing ties the crime to you. All you have to do is to get yourself a watertight alibi for tomorrow evening."

"Tomorrow evening?" Kenny was rather shocked by the short notice.

With a shrug, Vasili said, "Once you have decided to do something, there is no point in putting off doing it."

"I suppose you're right…"

"Of course I am right."

"But I'm still not clear about how you select the victim."

"That, as I say, is not your problem. Usually, I kill one of my client's enemies. That way, not only does Fyodor recognize there is a motive for the murder, the client also gets rid of someone who's bugging them. It is a very efficient system – no?'

"But if your client doesn't have any enemies…"

"Everyone has enemies," said Vasili firmly. Kenny was about to say that he really didn't think he did, but thought better of it. "So, Anatoli, have we got a deal?"

"Yes, we've got a deal."

Having checked with Vasili the proposed timescale for the murder and handed over the agreed fee the next morning, Kenny set about arranging his alibi. It couldn't involve any of the Semfiropol Boys, because Fyodor wasn't meant to know that he had an alibi. So, to keep himself safe from police suspicions, Anatoli Semyonov would have to, for one evening only, return to his old persona of Kenny Mountford.

He decided that a visit to a fringe theatre was the answer. A quick check through *Time Out* led to a call to an actor friend, who sounded slightly surprised to hear from him, but who agreed to join him in darkest Kilburn for an experimental play about glue-sniffing, whose cast included an actress they both knew. "You're not going with Lesley-Jane?" asked the friend.

"No."

"I'm not surprised."

"What do you mean by that?"

"Nothing, Kenny, nothing."

Normally he would have asked for an explanation of his friend's remark, but Kenny was preoccupied by his plans for the evening. Even if the audience were small, as audiences for fringe theatre frequently are, he would still have people to vouch for where he was at the moment Vasili committed his murder for him. Kenny Mountford felt a glow of satisfaction at the efficiency of the arrangements he had made.

The serenity of his mood was shattered in the afternoon by a call from Fyodor. "Anatoli, I want you to keep an eye on Vasili. I'm not sure he's playing straight with me."

"How do you mean?" asked Kenny nervously.

"I've heard rumours he's doing work on the side, not just jobs I give him for the Semfiropol Boys."

"What kind of work?"

"Contract killing. If you can bring me any proof that's what he's been doing, Anatoli, I will see to it that he is eliminated. And you will be richly rewarded."

"Oh," said Kenny.

He spent the rest of the afternoon trying to get through to Vasili's mobile, but it was permanently switched off. By the time he met his friend at the fringe theatre in Kilburn, Kenny Mountford was in an extremely twitchy state. There was no pretending that his situation wasn't serious. If Fyodor found out that he had actually paid Vasili to do his qualifying murder for him, Kenny didn't think it'd be long before there was a contract out on his own life. But he couldn't let anyone at the theatre see how anxious he was, so all his acting skills were called for as he sat through the interminably tedious and badly acted play about glue-sniffing and then, over drinks in the bar, told the actress who'd been in it how marvellous, absolutely marvellous, her performance had been.

His friend had his car with him and offered to drop Kenny off. As they were driving along they heard the Radio 4 Midnight News. The distinguished theatre director Charlie Fenton had been shot dead in Notting Hill at ten o'clock that evening.

"Good God," said his friend. "If you hadn't actually been with me, I'd have had you down as Number One Suspect for that murder, Kenny."

"Why?"

But his friend wouldn't say more.

Had Kenny Mountford not completely cut himself off from the English press and media, he would have known about the affair between Charlie Fenton and Lesley-Jane Walden. Their photos had been plastered all over the tabloids for weeks. He might also have pieced together that the director had never had any interest in him, only in Lesley-Jane – hence the request when they first met for their mutual landline, rather than Kenny's mobile number. How convenient for Charlie had been the actor's willingness to go under-cover and leave the field wide open to his rival.

Vasili, however, read his tabloids and knew all about the affair. He recognized Charlie Fenton as the perfect victim. The guy had gone off with Kenny's girlfriend! Fyodor wouldn't need any convincing that that was a proper motive for murder.

So Vasili had lain in wait outside the Notting Hill house, confident that sooner or later Charlie Fenton would appear. As indeed he did, on the dot of ten o'clock. A car drew up some hundred yards away from Kenny Mountford's house and the very recognizable figure of the director emerged, blowing a kiss to someone inside. Vasili drew out his favoured weapon, the PSS Silent Pistol which had been developed for the KGB, and when his quarry was close enough, discharged two bullets into Charlie Fenton's head.

Job done. Coolly replacing the pistol in his pocket, Vasili had walked away, confident that there was nothing to tie him to this crime, as there had been nothing to tie him to any of his previous fifty-odd hits. Confident also that Fyodor would assume that the job had been done by Kenny Mountford.

What he hadn't taken into account was Charlie Fenton's tomcat nature. No sooner had the director bedded one woman than he was on the lookout for another, and his honeymoon of monogamy with Lesley-Jane Walden had been short. She, suspecting something was going on, had been watching at the window of the house that evening for her philandering lover to return. As soon as Charlie Fenton got out of the car she had started to video him on her camera, and thus recorded his death. The footage, when handed over to the police, also revealed very clear images of Vasili, from which he was quickly identified and as quickly arrested.

Lesley-Jane Walden was in seventh heaven. To be at the centre of a murder case – there were actresses who would kill to achieve that kind of publicity. In the event, though, it didn't do her much good. The police made no mention of the help she had given to their investigation in any of their press conferences. They didn't even mention her name. And all the obituaries of Charlie Fenton spoke only of "his towering theatrical originality" and his reputation as "a loving family man". Lesley-Jane Walden was furious.

Her mood wasn't improved when Kenny ordered her to get out of the house. She moved into a girlfriend's flat and started badgering her agent to get her on to *I'm A Celebrity – Get Me Out Of Here!*

"You are a clever boy, Anatoli Semyonov," said Fyodor, when they next met. "To get rid of your girlfriend's lover and arrange things so that Vasili is arrested for the murder – this is excellent work. I have wanted Vasili out of the way for a long time. You are not just a clever boy, Anatoli, you are also a clever Semfiropol Boy."

"You mean I have qualified to join the gang?"

"Of course you have qualified. Now you will always be welcome here. You are one of the Semfiropol Boys."

So Kenny Mountford too thought: job done. Except, of course, having done that job was not going to lead on to the other job. Kenny had done what he promised – infiltrated a London gang – but the man to whom he had made that promise was no longer around. There would never be a Charlie Fenton production about London gangs. All Kenny Mountford's efforts had been in vain.

And yet the realization did not upset him. No one could say he hadn't tried everything he could to achieve respectability as an actor, and now it was time to move on. Time to get back to being Kenny Mountford. All that "Method", in-depth research approach to characterization might be all right for some people in the business. But, for him, he reckoned he preferred something called "acting".

When he finally spoke to his agent, she revealed that she'd been going nearly apoplectic trying to contact him over the previous weeks. The BBC was doing a new sitcom and they wanted him to play the lead! He said he'd do it.

But Kenny Mountford didn't lose touch with Fyodor and the Semfiropol Boys. As an actor, it's always good to have more than one string to your bow.

THE MAN WHO TOOK OFF HIS HAT TO THE DRIVER OF THE TRAIN

Peter Turnbull

OVER THE YEARS the story of the man who took his hat off to the driver of the train grew to have three parts. Three, George Hennessey mused as he walked a pleasant walk on a pleasant summer's evening, late, from his house to the pub in Easingwold for a pint of stout, just one before "last orders" were called. Yes, he thought, the story had three distinct parts. There was, he remembered as his eye was caught by a rapidly darting bat, the incident itself and the story therein, then there was the story as he had told it to Charles, then finally it was seeing the woman: again.

She had not grown old gracefully: she had refused to surrender to the years, and like so many women who pursue that policy she had, in the opinion of George Hennessey, quite simply made things worse for herself. Even if her figure had remained slender she could not at the age of fifty plus wear tee-shirts and jeans and trainers, and drink among the city's youth and hope to blend.

Hennessey was walking the walls from the police station at Mickle-gate Bar to the fish restaurant on Lendal, intending to take lunch 'out' as was his custom, when he saw her approaching him. She didn't recognize him and walked quickly, urgently, in such a manner that a casual observer would see her as a woman about a pressing errand, a woman going somewhere. But Hennessey, a police officer for the greater part of his working life, and now nearing retirement, was a keen student of human behaviour. He saw a rather frightened woman, speeding away from something, something within her, something in her past from which there was no escape, no matter how breathlessly fast she walked. He recognized her as she wove in and out of the tourists who strolled the walls but he could not immediately place her, except that he knew she belonged to his professional rather than to his private life. She approached him and swept past him, the sagging cheeks, the heavy make-up, glistening red lips and scraggy hair, and the quick, quick, quick, short, short, short steps along the ancient battlements, beneath a vast blue, cloudless July sky. On impulse, George Hennessey turned and followed her, quickening his pace to keep up with her.

She passed Micklegate Bar and left the walls at Baile Hill, turned sharp left into Cromwell Road and entered the Waggoner's Rest. Hennessey followed her into the pub. He was familiar with the Waggoner's Rest though he didn't often frequent it, knowing it to be a "locals" pub. Few tourists to the Faire and Famouse Citie of York find it and, further, it is in the evenings the haunt of a youthful set of locals, to which the woman clearly felt she belonged. By the time Hennessey entered the pub, the woman had purchased a large port and was sitting alone in the corner of the then empty lounge bar. Hennessey purchased a non-alcoholic drink and sat in the far corner, observing her out of the corner of his eye.

Olivia Stringer.

Of course, Olivia Stringer. Her name came to him suddenly. So this is how she has ended up, alone, wasted, probably a drunkard if not an out and out alcoholic, judging by her emaciated appearance. A massive glass of port wine and no food to be seen, and that in the middle of the day. And a day-to-day, hand-to-mouth existence too, judging by the threadbare denims and the shapeless green tee-shirt. But he felt no pity for her, no compassion, not after what she had done twenty years earlier.

The case, as Hennessey recalled, had unfolded when the driver of an Edinburgh to London express train had brought his train to a rapid but controlled stop and had reported to York control that he had had "one under", giving the approximate location. All railway traffic on the up line was halted, and the emergency services had sped to the scene.

George Hennessey, then a Detective Sergeant with the Vale of York Police, was asked to represent the CID at the incident, procedure dictating that a suicide has to be considered suspicious until foul play can be safely ruled out. By the time Hennessey had arrived at the scene, the body had been lifted from the track, a relief driver had taken the train on, and rail traffic was flowing normally.

"I always said if I had one under, that I'd look away." The train driver, still clearly shaken, leaned against the police vehicle and pulled heavily on a cigarette. Judging by the number of butts screwed into the dry ground at his feet, it was one in a long line of cigarettes he had smoked between the time of the incident and Sergeant Hennessey's arrival. "But you can't, you see," he appealed to Hennessey. "You can't look away." He was a small man, Hennessey recalled, and he remembered being amused to note that driving a locomotive capable of 125 m.p.h. clearly didn't involve the use of great physical strength. Up to that point he had always thought of train drivers as being large, brawny types. Clearly, he found, that was not the case. "I rounded the bend, sixty miles an hour at this point, not fast as fast trains go, but no time to stop before the impact. I brought the speed down as fast as I could but there wasn't enough track to stop. Reckon I hit him doing about forty."

"Fast enough."

"Oh, aye, fast enough all right, but we had eye contact, right till the end. I mean, he was looking right into my eyes and I was looking right into his. He just stood there. Other drivers say that their 'one unders' turn away before impact, or stand facing away from the train altogether, or attempt to jump to safety at the last minute."

"But not this man?"

The driver took one last desperate drag of the cigarette and tossed it to the ground and he stamped it into the soil whereupon it lay, with the others. "Not this man, oh, no, not this man. Not a bit of it. Have you seen him?"

"Haven't. Why, should I?"

"Only his appearance, not the normal 'one under', not shabbily dressed if dressed at all. One of my mates had a 'one under' who was totally naked, escaped from a psychiatric hospital, but this guy – well dressed, pinstripe suit, bowler hat – he looked like a bank manager or an accountant. And do you know what he did?"

"Tell me."

"Just before impact, he raised his hat to me and mouthed 'thank you'."

Hennessey sipped his tonic water and glanced across at Olivia Stringer, who sat staring into space and was now, courtesy of the Planet Earth's revolutions, bathed in a shaft of sunlight which streamed through the stained-glass window.

The "one under", that particular "one under", Hennessey had recalled as being very rapidly identified. What was his name? What was his name? It had an unusual ring to it, something … ordinary surname, but very unusual Christian name. Webster. That's it... Webster. What was his Christian name? Something... Webster?

Darius. That was it. Darius Webster. A bank manager of the Gillygate branch of the Yorkshire and Lancashire Bank, one of the last of the family-owned banks, as it is still fond of announcing. At first Hennessey had assumed that it was a hyphenated surname.

"No," Mrs Webster sitting in her very "just so" house had said. "No, it's a real Christian name. Darius, his grandfather, was called by that name, and he was christened with that name too. He wanted our son to bear the name but I refused, of course."

Hennessey sat ill at ease in the drawing room of the house which had a superficial "appearance is everything" feel about it. Even Mrs Webster's distress had not seemed genuine, and with the passage of time still didn't seem so. The French windows opened on to a mani-cured lawn on which two miniature poodles played and yapped at each other, so Hennessey had further recalled.

"I'm so pleased that Cyril was able to identify poor Darius, I'm sure I couldn't." Mrs Webster had sniffed and Hennessey couldn't help thinking that "Cyril" had been short-changed in respect of his

name. Given the choice, Hennessey would have preferred to be a
"Darius" rather than a "Cyril", especially if he had to grow up in
the gritty north of England where "Cyrils" can have an uncomfortable time.

"Could you think of any reason why your husband should have
committed suicide, Mrs Webster?"

"None. No reason." She had sniffed into a delicately embroi-
dered handkerchief. "He had everything. Me, two children, this
house. What more could any man want?"

George Hennessey watched as Olivia Stringer drained the glass of
port and staggered with the empty glass to the bar, fished out a
small plastic bag from the pocket of her jeans and from it tipped
coins on to the bar top. She counted out, in silver and bronze,
enough for another large port. She carried the drink unsteadily back
to the seat in the corner and began to sip it. She also began talking
to herself, as Hennessey's mind went back to the next stage in that
inquiry.

The next stage had been to visit Mr Webster's place of work. He
had found the mood among the staff sombre and subdued.

"We would have called the police in now." Mr Penge received the
then Sergeant Hennessey in Darius Webster's panelled office. "I'm a
caretaker manager," he explained, "here to look after the shop until
things get sorted out."

"Things?" Hennessey had asked. "Many things?"

"About half a million things." Penge, a tall man with a serious
attitude, sighed. "I confess, I never thought…a smallish family-
owned bank … we enjoy a lot of staff loyalty…"

"Half a million things?" Hennessey had pressed.

"Half a million pounds."

"Missing?"

"Well, yes. Not in the sense that we don't know where it's gone,
but missing in the sense that it's not where it should be. We don't
keep money like that in the vaults but rather it's been drained out of
a number of dormant accounts. Only found out when one account
was activated and we traced the money to Darius Webster's personal

account, from where it has been taken out in the form of cash. I confess, for a banker he left a trail any idiot could follow."

"When did you first notice something amiss?"

"About a week ago, which was when Mr Webster phoned to say he had 'flu and wouldn't be coming in to work. We did an investigation and have concluded what we have concluded…that Darius Webster, loyal employee of the bank, not long to go before retiring, has ruined his life by embezzling half a million pounds of customers' money. We were about to call the police but your timely arrival has saved a phone call. Suicide, you say?"

"Appears to be so. This morning on the railway line just south of York."

"Poor Darius. I knew him, knew him well. I always found him to be a man of integrity. I can't imagine what brainstorm he must have had to make him do that … then to kill himself … now that *is* the Darius Webster I knew, a man who'd rather take his life than live without integrity. But Darius Webster a thief … no … no way. He was a practising Christian. It must have been a period of insanity. If he had returned the money, it was something the bank would have managed … early retirement, I would have thought, something of that sort." Penge leaned forward and rested his forehead in the palm of his left hand. "Oh, dear… then this morning we received this in the post." He handed Hennessey a receipt. "It's a left-luggage receipt from York station. It came with this." He then handed Hennessey a second piece of paper which revealed itself to be a handwritten note. '*It's all there…so sorry…D. Webster*'. "It's Darius Webster's handwriting."

"You haven't collected it?"

"Well, as you see, we'd want the police with us anyway if he has put the half a million pounds in the left luggage. We wouldn't be happy walking through York with a bundle like that."

"I can imagine. So, shall we go and see what he has left us? I can arrange for a number of constables to bolster our numbers."

"Thank you."

Hennessey and Penge rendezvous-ed with three constables at York station's left-luggage office and presented the receipt. In return they were handed two large suitcases. Both were unlocked, and when opened both were observed to contain large quantities of banknotes.

"We'll escort you back to the bank with this," Hennessey said. "A police vehicle and a couple of constables."

"Appreciate it," Penge had said. "It's all going to be here. All half a million. Poor Darius...I know why he killed himself...he couldn't live with himself after doing this. But why, why did he do it in the first place?"

"I'd like to know that too," Hennessey had said.

By the time Hennessey had recollected this, Olivia Stringer was about halfway through the glass of port and staring into space, chatting quite amicably with herself. Hennessey couldn't remember who supplied the name: Mr Penge, or Mrs Webster, or one of the bank staff. Hennessey couldn't even remember the name, but it was the name of a man who was of Webster's age and he and Webster were described as being "like brothers". Hennessey met him the day after Webster's suicide by which time the man had heard the news and was in a state of shock. They sat together on solid wooden garden furniture in the pleasingly mature garden at the rear of the man's house in Nether Poppleton where, beyond the garden, there was a pleasant view across the meadows to the River Ouse.

"I should have seen it coming," the man said. "All those signals, clear as daylight in hindsight."

"Tell me."

"Well, it started, or stopped, whichever way you look at it, after the birth of their second child. After that Mrs Webster moved into the spare room, saying, 'He's got two children, no further point in our sleeping together.'"

"She said that?"

"Yes, in this house. Darius didn't know where to put himself."

"A man wants more than that."

"Of course he does, and a woman too, but not Mrs Webster. From that point onwards, her idea of keeping romance alive in her marriage was walking arm in arm with her husband to and from the ten o'clock service. So long as it all looked right, the reality didn't matter. And he stuck it too. For fifteen years more he put up with that charade. Then, maybe it was because he'd finally snapped, maybe it was because he'd found himself in a mid-life crisis, he told me that he'd found 'a girl'."

"A girl?"

"That was what he said. He was delighted, he could not contain his excitement, he was like an adolescent with his first real girl-friend. It was all a bit embarrassing. That was about three months ago."

"Did he mention her name?" Hennessey remembered that he had asked that question.

"Olivia. Never told me her second name. She's about thirty, that makes her twenty years his junior. Didn't like the sound of her really, seemed a bit of a good-time girl, not Darius's type at all. Then earlier on this week he phoned me. He said 'I've ruined my life' and then he put the phone down. I phoned him at his work, then at his home, he wasn't at either place. He was nowhere to be found."

Hennessey watched Olivia Stringer drain the glass and then look disappointed and lost. She stared at the glass as if willing it to refill by magic. He remembered meeting her for the first time.

"My boyfriend pays for it," she had said, smiling, designer clothes, designer jewellery. "This flat, it's rented, as is, furnished, but my boyfriend pays for it all. Well, he's older than me, a bit of a sugar daddy, I suppose, and I'm his sugar baby."

"I see," Hennessey growled disapprovingly.

"Men do what I want them to do," she said, twirling her figure. "I can make men do anything."

"Can you?"

"Oh, yes. I'm thirty, have to start thinking about settling down, so I told my sugar daddy that if he got some serious money, I'd go away with him and we'd settle down together. Anyway, how did you find me? And what do you want?"

So Hennessey had told her that her name had been found in her "sugar daddy's" address book. He also told her that just the previous day said "sugar daddy" had stood on a railway line and said "thank you" to the driver of the train a second before the impact despatched "sugar daddy" to the hereafter.

And that, Hennessey mused, as he drained his glass of tonic water, was the first part of the story.

The second part occurred some ten years later when George Hennessey and his son Charles, by then a student, had whiled away a winter's evening by burning faggots in the hearth of the living room of their home in Easingwold, and "jawing". George Hennessey's dear wife and dear mother to Charles had died sadly young some years earlier but had left a strong and a warm "ghost" in the house and garden, and father and son had bonded in her absence. It had grown to be George Hennessey's practice to tell his son of cases he had been involved in, never compromising his professionalism by naming names or cheapening their "jaw sessions" by relating salacious or sensational incidents, but rather choosing incidents which offered his growing son some insight into the human condition. The story of the man who took his hat off to the train driver was one such, and he had related the story one evening as the dried twigs crackled and flamed in the fireplace.

The third part of the story was a wholly unexpected exchange between Olivia Stringer and George Hennessey. That lunchtime an emaciated Olivia Stringer, focusing her eyes on Hennessey as the only other customer in the pub, had staggered over to him and said, "Can you buy me a drink, sir? I'm down on my luck, sir."

Hennessey had stood and said, "No, Olivia, I can't," and had walked away, out of the Waggoner's Rest, feeling Olivia Stringer's eyes burning into him, wondering who he was, and how he knew her name?

TOGETHER IN ELECTRIC DREAMS

Carol Anne Davis

FROM THE START, I did everything in my power to split them up, to make him exclusively mine again. But the bitch just wouldn't let go so I had to kill. The psychologist here at the prison thinks that I overreacted but she clearly hasn't loved enough...

I met him, of all places, on a sponsored walk for breast cancer. Both his mother and mine had died of the disease and it created an immediate bond between us. We were both forty, both divorced, both had one grown-up child who lived far away. Even our names sounded good together – Jack and Gill. My work as the assistant headmistress at a girls' school brought me into contact with very few men and his job as an aeronautics engineer meant that he worked with very few women. Neither of us had been dating for years so we were ready for action, fell hard.

Jack praised everything about me at the start – my looks, my figure, my somewhat dry sense of humour. He said that I was cute, that he loved my body, that I was very entertaining and that he loved spending time with me. I reciprocated with ardour, forever hugging and kissing him. He was always freshly showered and sweet-scented, so there was nothing that I wouldn't do...

And, at the onset, it seemed enough. He appeared to set out his stall, telling me that if he remarried, his wife would get his sizeable pension. He was disappointed that his first wife had had so little interest in his work. Many women hear the word "engineer" and turn away – they want a man with a job which they can understand, someone in sales or teaching. But I'd had friends in the engineering faculty when I studied English at university, simply because one of my sister's boyfriends was an engineer.

Throughout my course, I came to know these youths well, found that, if you looked beyond the initial awkwardness, they had good hearts and grounded personalities. They wanted what we all want, love and mutual support. They were the type of men who would hold their beloved in high esteem and would never cheat. Or so I thought...

I remember the first time I knew that something wasn't right. I'd been dating Jack for six months, and we were in love, when he went on one of his regular works nights out. By then, I'd met and socialized with most of his colleagues. Indeed, I often picked him up from the pub at the end of these evenings, sometimes joining him for the final round. But, on this particular evening, he was vague about exactly where they were going and said that he'd get a lift back from a mate.

The following day, I asked him which of the usual suspects were there. He reeled off a few names, hesitated, said "Becky", then added another few male names.

"Becky?" I asked. I mean, women in engineering are rarer than hen's teeth or at least they were when I was at uni.

"Mmm, she joined us about a month ago."

"Any good?" There had been one female engineer on my sister's boyfriend's course and she'd only survived by getting various blokes to help her with her course work. She was beauty without the brains. Her father had persuaded her to try engineering as she was his only child and he needed someone to take over the family firm.

"Yeah, she's okay."

We were curled up on the settee and I'd just switched on the television and was about to leaf through the TV magazine. All of a sudden he was staring intently at the screen, yet it was showing *EastEnders*, a programme we both despised.

"There's a documentary just starting on BBC4," I muttered, picking up the remote control but still watching him out of the corner of my eye.

"I'll make us a cuppa," he said, and catapulted off the couch.

I felt a growing unease as I waited for him to return. He'd always told me that he was a one-woman man and had given me no reason to doubt him. But the way he'd hesitated before mentioning her name...

"So, what does Becky do?" I asked when he returned with two overfilled mugs.

"She works for me."

"Did she come from Ashton's?" I knew that another engineering firm had recently paid off their staff and that several of them had been taken on by the company which employed Jack.

"No, she's straight out of university.'"

"A mere foetus!" I laughed, and waited for him to say that she was hopelessly callow.

Instead, he merely muttered another, "She's okay."

It would be a month before I saw them together but I knew that she was my rival long before that. Put bluntly, he changed, became more distant. He stopped holding my hand when we were out walking and he went from greeting me with a "Hi, gorgeous" to a mere "Hi". He also started to find fault with my appearance, pinching my waistline and asking if I'd gained weight. Ironically, I'd lost a few pounds as I was terrified of losing him, was often too upset to eat.

I decided to go to the gym and tone up, though it was a horrible thought after a day spent dealing with overwrought teachers, pushy parents and hormonal pupils. But I was suddenly competing with a girl of twenty-two.

What with skipping meals and working out on the ski machine after school, I went from a size fourteen to a twelve in a fortnight. Then I waited outside Jack's work one day and saw him leave, laughing, with Becky and she must have been a perfect ten. She had long blonde tresses which caught the light and danced around in the summer breeze – mine's a brunette pixie cut and I have my share of bad hair days. She also had the straight white teeth of an American actress, whereas I have molars courtesy of the NHS.

It hurts to get your teeth straightened. It really does. They play that part down when you go for a private consultation. Instead, they take your photo and show you what you're going to look like after your pegs are realigned. I signed up there and then and spent the next four months in pain, and still have ongoing discomfort. But they did look better, they really did. Even Jack said so, but he still didn't want me to pick him up from his works nights out.

I was getting slimmer, prettier, fitter, yet it wasn't enough. "It's surprising that you still get spots at your age," he said one day. In the bathroom a moment later, I looked in the mirror at the small red bump next to my gloss-enhanced lips and marvelled that my future happiness could depend on it. Dermabrasion helped, as did a lighter foundation, but I began to dread the run-up to my period when my complexion would be at its worst.

If you're a feminist, I bet that by now you're urging me to leave. And I should have done, I know, but he'd been so wonderful to me at the beginning. I kept thinking that if I tried hard enough, I could get the man who had loved me back. I mean, it's not as if he was nasty all the time – he still took me out three times a week and made love to me as if he really meant it. And he still made future plans.

So, for the first eight months after Becky arrived, I convinced myself that he merely had a crush on her, that it wasn't recipro-cated. After all, what would a twenty-two-year-old blonde beauty see in a forty-two-year-old man who was beginning to lose his hair?

She saw something, the bitch – maybe it was the thought of his pension or maybe she had a thing about father figures. Who knows? All I can say for sure is that I followed them from work one night and saw them go into an Italian restaurant. No boss. No colleagues. Just him and her, with their arms around each other's waists as they walked along the road and disappeared into the Venetian. I stood outside for a moment, feeling ill and afraid.

At first, I resolved not to mention it. I mean, what if he wanted to finish with me but just didn't have the guts? I'd be making it so easy for him to bring things to a swift conclusion. Instead, I decided just to hang on in there in the hope that she would find a guy of her own age and he'd return all of his affection to me.

My resolve lasted for two whole days, then I burst into tears.

"What's wrong? You're usually so calm," he said, taking his hand from my left breast where he'd been sending thrill after thrill through my nipple.

"I saw you holding hands with a blonde girl."

"Christ," he said, looking shocked, "I never wanted you to know."

I took a deep breath. "I thought that we promised to be exclusive?"

He swallowed visibly. "We did."

"So?" *Don't end it, don't end it, don't end it.*

"She… she's just so young and lively. She really gets under my skin. But at the same time, she can be overwhelming. I love being with you, it's so nice and restful here."

He made me sound like a day spa, but it was a start.

"At her age, her hormones must be all over the place?" I hoped against hope that she had wicked PMS.

"Tell me about it. For one week out of every month she snaps my head off and sometimes throws things at me!"

"And is that what you want?"

He shook his head. "It's exhausting. But the rest of the time, she's…" He seemed to realize belatedly who he was talking to. "I'm sorry, but she's really got to me."

"It's probably just lust," I said, trying to keep my voice from breaking again.

He shrugged. "Who knows? Maybe I'm having an early mid-life crisis."

I tensed every sinew in my body. "I'd like you to give her up."

"I can't."

"But we were so good together!"

"We still are. I don't want to lose either of you."

I took the deepest of breaths. "And if I issued an ultimatum?"

He looked down and played absently with my pubic hair. "I'd choose her."

So, there it was.

"Because she's new?"

"And different from everyone else that I've ever gone out with. I mean, my wife and girlfriends have always been traditionalists."

"But you are, too."

"I was, but she's made me think about things differently. She's sort of New Age but she's somehow tied it all in with quantum mechanics. It's fascinating stuff."

"I was something of a hippy at university," I said, somewhat desperately. In other words, I'd owned a couple of tie-dye outfits and an Afghan coat.

"She likes all these esoteric things, believes in the supernatural."

"But you're an atheist. We both are!"

"I think that I'd consider myself an agnostic nowadays."

I should end this, I thought, then breathed in his aftershave and faint manly sweat and knew that I couldn't. I wanted him in my bed and in my life every single day. Surely three days a week was much, much better than nothing? He made me laugh, made me think, made me orgasm twice in one night. She was offering the hurly-burly of the futon whilst I gave him the deep, deep peace of the king-size bed.

I made the next three months so peaceful that it's a wonder he didn't die of bliss. We had weekly home-cooked meals at my place, washed down by the finest wines and brandies. We lay in my Jacuzzi and listened to whale music, made love using a vibrating relaxing massager which I'd purchased online. On other nights, we went to see feel-good movies or enjoyed weekend trips to bird sanctuaries and nature reserves.

Would he really enjoy going clubbing with her once the novelty had worn off? Was being the oldest swinger in town truly his preference? Surely he'd tire of her monthly aggression and choose comparatively laid-back me?

"Shall we go to the Eden Project this weekend?" I asked. Eve had tempted Adam with an apple but I was using greenery and pastoral music as my offerings.

"Can't – Becky's no longer going to her parents' at the weekend so I'll be taking her dancing instead."

I felt as if I'd been hit.

"What's changed?"

"They've moved abroad."

"But she'd been seeing them every weekend?" I'd always thought that he mainly saw her straight from work, that he'd made an active choice to spend every Saturday and Sunday with me.

"Uh-huh. They were running a struggling bed and breakfast and she was helping out."

"So now you're going to switch between the two of us?"

He looked away then mumbled, "Not sure."

"What if she has PMS?"

"Oh, she's switched to a different pill. She's much better."

"Is she really?" I said, and a little acid came back up from my stomach and burned my throat.

Have you any idea how difficult it is to fill an entire weekend when you know that the man you love is having fun with your much younger rival? Oh, I resurrected my old social life with the hill-walking club and went for meals out with my neighbour, but nothing brought me pleasure any more. Now I lived for Monday, Wednesday and Friday nights which I spent with Jack, sometimes socializing and sometimes staying in. I tried so hard to please him on these nights – my conversation sweet, my laughter ready, my tongue bionic – but he still went to her every weekend and maybe even saw her on Tuesdays and Thursdays too. Plus they were together all day at work, had hours in which to build up shared jokes. I couldn't compete.

Eventually, it began to affect my health so badly that I'd lie there in the mornings unable to get out of bed. I felt literally weighted. This was particularly strange as by now I'd lost two stone, looked pale and weak. I also lost concentration when I did finally arrive at work, was called in front of the board of governors and warned that I had to shape up. But he was still touching her, licking her, doing all of the things that he was doing to me but doubtless preferring her silkier and perkier body. It was driving me mad...

After the sacking, I signed on but the Job Centre didn't offer a new start.

"Once you're over forty..." one of the other jobseekers said sadly.

"Everything's aimed at people in their twenties," I said savagely.

She had it all. I had less and less. We were reaching a showdown. It was then that I realized I had to kill.

It wasn't difficult. After all, I knew where they worked and lived, their day-to-day movements. I simply aimed my car and watched the body fly through the air. Afterwards, I ran over the cadaver as it lay on the ground, reversed and ran over it again numerous times. I was taking no chances, had to eliminate every breath.

I received a life sentence for his murder, of course. Does that surprise you? I mean, that it was Jack that I killed, my beloved? It surprised the prison psychologist.

"Why didn't you kill Becky, your rival?" she asked.

"Because there are new female graduates going into engineering all the time nowadays," I said sadly, remembering my recent research. "There would always be other young women tempting him away."

"So why not let him go?"

"I loved him too much, he meant everything to me. This way he's mine for ever. No one else can ever have him now."

"But you've given up everything in the process," she said sadly.

I was so glad that she cared.

She's right though – life can be pointless in here unless you have someone to think about all of the time. Fortunately I realized within days that she and I are meant to be together. We talk easily during our sessions and she always looks pained when she admits that our time is up. She, too, used to work in an all-girls school so we share a history. I imagine she's also had secret crushes on the older girls, just like me. And there's a synchronicity in our names – she's Lilian and, if I use my full moniker, I'm Gillian. It's rhyme and reason. It's fate.

There's only one problem: Raisa, who is on the extended privileges programme, likes Lilian too. She has more independence than me as she's a trusted prisoner, has free rein of the building. She's probably popping in to see Lilian whilst I'm in the workshop, stuffing soft toys.

Not for much longer, though. I've bought a knife from one of the metal-shop workers, had it honed to the sharpest point imaginable. I reckon it'll only take thirty seconds, during my one-to-one therapy, to cut the psychologist's throat. Lilian will always endure in my

memory, alongside Jack, and neither of them will ever again be
unfaithful. It's the ultimate ownership – I take their lives and they
become mine.

LAST TRAIN FROM DESPRIT

Richard Godwin

THE FLAMINGO BAR stood beneath the broken neon glow of a sign that read: "Make Money. Change Your Life Now". The words flickered outside the unwashed window, while the name of the company that was advertising hope to the desolate remained submerged in blackness. All that was visible were the letters LOSS beneath the slogan.

Joe Murray sat in the Flamingo one Monday when the lights went out in the small town of Desprit, which lay lodged like a thorn in the hungry side of Allen, South Dakota. He was reading an article in the *Rapid City Journal* entitled "Allen may be poor, but there's hope". As he looked at the latest statistics about the few who'd found jobs, the power came back on and the sign flickered into life. Glancing up, Joe deciphered the mystery that was the ad. "LOSS INSURERS NEVILLE TRADE INC, JOB VACANCIES", it read, "we're looking for employees. If you're honest, you're our man." It gave a phone number that he hurriedly jotted down on a matchbox with a pen he'd taken from the betting shop. Then he headed out into the yellow morning, found the nearest pay phone and made the call. Someone had scrawled "Wes The Trassh Of America" on the wall and Joe traced the illiterate letters with his eyes as he waited.

"Neville Trade, how may I help you?"

"I saw your ad and I'm ringing up about vacancies," Joe said.

"I'm not aware we've placed an ad. Where did you see it, sir?"

"It's on the sign outside the Flamingo."

"I'm sorry?"

"It's a bar in Desprit."

"Desprit?" she said, as if someone had forced a swear word into her mouth. "I'm sorry, sir, that ad is over a year old, we've asked for it to be taken down."

"Nothing works in this town," Joe said, as he hung up the greasy receiver.

Outside his feet felt leaden on the hard road. Turning the corner to Railyard Street he bumped into Rocco, with his salesman's eyes, hair greased back, collar up to hide the scar that ran in a red streak from his neck to his ear.

"Hey, Joe," he said. "Thought you'd left town, the amount of times I knocked on your door. How's Mandy?"

"I been busy, Mandy's good."

"I'm sure she is. You got work?"

"I heard you got out, I was going to visit you."

"All that time inside, Joe. I saw you only once. I been out for months." Rocco laughed. "It's OK. I got plenty of visits, from people a lot better-looking than you."

"I wondered how you been doing."

"Well, here I am, Joe. I got a job going if you're interested."

"I dunno."

"No killing involved. Shooting that cop was dumb. Shit, do I look like a cop killer?"

"Nah."

"Exactly. I got style…feel this coat."

Rocco offered his lapel and watched with canine eyes as Joe ran his hand across the material.

"Nice."

"Joe, there's a cool four K riding on this, you get half. Wanna be a loser all your life?"

He playfully jabbed Joe in the shoulder.

"Doing what?"

"Simple job, you'll be in and out quicker than a whore's snatch. What do you say?"

"Half, huh? Maybe I'll come round later and you can tell me more about it. I ain't promising nothing though."

Rocco straightened Joe's dirty collar.

"You need to smarten up, Joe, you look like shit."

Mandy was sleeping back at the damp apartment. Her naked legs were astride the night table, her arms sprawled out on the grey sheets. A train chugged by and the bedroom shook as Joe read the note she'd left him when she staggered in at five: "Either you get a job or I'm leaving. I ain't doing this no more."

He ran his eyes down her back and stared at the tattoo of a naked woman wrapped around a dollar bill that spread from her spine to her buttocks. He leaned and kissed the nape of her neck, admiring the shape of her breasts from the side as they squashed into the mattress. She'd gained some weight lately and he liked it.

"I'll buy you more tattoos, Mandy, you'll see."

He lay down and shut his eyes.

When he opened them it was dark. He rose and tried the light. There was no bulb in it. He navigated the room in the lurid beam shed by the streetlight, which illuminated the rusty water dripping down the back wall. Mandy's purse lay on the edge of the sofa. Joe reached inside and took out ten bucks. He walked two blocks to the store, where he bought some razor blades and a can of shaving foam. Back at the apartment he stared into his blue eyes in the tarnished mirror as he scraped the beard from his face, waiting for the revelation. He looked in his late thirties, and the struggle to survive showed in the lines around his eyes. He was putting his best shirt on when Mandy stirred and got out of bed.

"Hey, Joe, your beard."

"Darlin', I'm gonna get a job, I'm gonna get us out of here," Joe said, running his eyes down to the sculpted tuft of dark hair at her crotch as she put on her bra from the night before.

"An' how you gonna do that?"

"You'll see."

"Joe, we're only in our twenties and what have we got?" She fished her panties off the chair, which sported a broken spring. "This wet hole by a railway line that keeps us awake and drives us to drink."

He looked at Mandy and thought how with her deep green eyes and black hair she could have so many better men than him. Then her lightbulb crackpipe on the broken coffee table caught his attention.

"We're another bulb down," he said.

"I'll get a straight shooter later so you can watch me get dressed under the overhead light."

"Don't you want to be more than a crackhead?"

"What about you and your whisky?"

"I wish you wouldn't do that."

"What?"

"Put on your panties when another man's fucked you in them."

"They don't fuck me in them, baby, they fuck me butt naked. An' now's not a good time to get jealous."

"What does that mean?"

"I'm pregnant."

"Is it mine?"

"Sure it's yours, they all wear a rubber."

"Mandy?"

"It's yours."

He reached out and touched her arm and she turned her head away.

"I want it," he said.

"How we gonna bring a kid up?"

"I'll make money."

"Doing what? You ain't had a job in years, you got no qualifications, we live in the poorest town in America."

"This time it's gonna live, we're dying in Desprit. Sometimes when I lie awake at night this apartment feels like a coffin in the damp earth and the only living thing is a train rattling by."

"What future does our baby have, Joe? With you and me as parents to look after it?"

"Give up crack and it will live."

"I'll have to give up my career first."

"Do it."

"While you go and work in Wall Street?"

"Remember burying her, Mandy? That night, you and me over by the park with a stolen spade? Remember that tiny body in the cold ground? You puked your guts out."

"How could I forget?"

"I read your note."

"I ain't doing it no more."

"Give me till tonight."

He left her standing there and headed out beneath the rusted iron bridge which cast a constant shadow on their apartment. A train thundered by as Joe made his way to meet Rocco.

They sat on a leopardskin sofa at Rocco's apartment. Joe looked with envy at his lifestyle: the plasma-screen TV, iPod, clean furniture, new carpet.

"Where d'you get all this?" Joe said.

"Does it matter? I'm getting out of here, I'm getting out of Desprit, it should be called the town of no hope."

"So what's the job?"

"It's simple," Rocco said. "This friend of mine owns an office block. It's all legit, I got the keys."

"He wants you to rob his office?"

"He ain't got no insurance, wants out, he's given me the combination. We go in, get the cash out of the safe, and leave."

"Simple as that?"

Rocco laid a steady hand on Joe's shoulder.

"One thing I learned inside is not to go back in."

"So why do you need me, Rocco?"

"There's a security guard, I know the times he does his rounds. We get to the office by the back stairs, he never uses them, but I need you to keep watch while I'm getting the cash. My friend takes sixty per cent, and between you and me it's a straight fifty-fifty cut."

"That's kind of generous of you, Rocco."

"I'm a generous guy."

"It's like you're doing me a favour."

"Joe, I got responsibilities. My kids ain't getting all the things I'd like them to."

"I seen them, they're doing OK."

"You don't know. You ain't a father yet."

Joe thought of Mandy, of new tattoos, of another town away from Desprit, where he didn't feel like spitting at himself every time he caught his own reflection. He nodded and Rocco drew his cashmere coat around his broad shoulders.

Beneath a sullen moonless sky they made their way to the office block that stood out like a scar on a street teeming with restaurants and late-night bars. Raucous drunks staggered out on to the stained pavement, arms heavy on their women, who wobbled on high heels, spraying cheap perfume into the air. Joe and Rocco scurried by, collars, up, heads down in the anonymous night.

Rocco had a key to the back door and they scaled the iron stairs on rubber soles to an office on the top floor, assisted by the torches they held in front of them like stiletto knives. It all went smoothly as they moved silently within the building. The safe was set in the wall behind a painting of a man fishing in a lake, which Joe helped Rocco remove and set down on the floor. Rocco fumbled with the combination as Joe checked the hallway. All quiet except for the satisfying click inside the office. Rocco removed the cash and Joe helped him bundle it into two holdalls. Then they made their way downstairs.

"Easy, see?" Rocco said.

"We got away with it."

"Nothing could go wrong with this job, it was all planned out."

"We got money and that means a future."

As they were passing the second floor a door opened and a large security guard came out. He said nothing as he reached for his gun. Joe froze as Rocco pulled a Glock from his coat and shot the guard. He dropped to the floor like a wounded bull and Joe watched the blood pool by his head. Rocco headed outside, Joe following.

Back at his apartment Rocco handed out the cash.

"What did you mean about Mandy, Rocco?" Joe said.

"She's a good-looking woman, and you ain't gonna keep her if you don't develop some style."

"Is that what you got, style, shooting the guard?"

"Screw him."

"You can't help killing, can you? You just got out, you'll be first on their list."

"What you gonna do, Joe, tell 'em?"

"Have you screwed Mandy?"

A smirk began to crawl across Rocco's mouth as he looked away.

"I wouldn't do that."

"No?"

Rocco lit a cigarette and stared out at the black backdrop of night as Joe grabbed him by the shoulder and spun him round.

"You have."

He hit Rocco in the face, knocking him over a chair. The cigarette singed Rocco's lip and his nose opened up.

"That was a dumb thing to do, Joe, real dumb."

Joe grabbed his money, his hand burning, as Rocco stood and pulled a knife. He was by the door when Rocco slashed at his shirt. He looked down and saw the ripped cotton and the gash in his stomach. He held the bag in front of him to ward off the knife as Rocco came at him again, and he headed out the door and down the stairs, dripping blood on the ruined steps.

Mandy stirred in her sleep as Joe entered the apartment. He inspected the wound in the bathroom. It didn't look too deep and he bandaged it.

The next morning over coffee he said to Mandy: "Let's get out of here, you, me and the baby."

"Where we gonna go, Joe?"

"Anywhere. I got money."

"How?"

"It's a loan."

"There's blood on your shirt, Joe, I saw it in the trash. You're wounded."

"I'll see a doctor when we get out of here. Come with me, Mandy."

"Loan... You got involved with Rocco, didn't you?"

"Why do you think it's Rocco?" She looked away. "Is it mine, Mandy?" Joe said.

"It's yours."

They waited until night, avoiding each other in the wounded silence of the dripping apartment. They packed their few clothes into their tattered bags. And they got the last train out of Desprit, walking with the conviction of the hunted up to the platform on the creaking iron bridge that scowled down on Railyard Street.

As they waited, Joe clutched the holdall with the cash in it, as if he were clenching the slender promise of a future in his hand. He jumped every time someone walked up, but no cops came, and finally the last night train limped and wheezed down the line and they got on. They sat side by side watching the long line of misery that were the final houses of Desprit shrink and fade on the grey horizon. And the empty train rocked its way into the black unknown landscape outside.

"Where we going, Joe?" Mandy said.

"Anywhere. Away from here."

"Away from us, Joe? We're going nowhere, we ain't got nowhere to go. Look at this, it's like a ghost train, and we're the only two riders."

"I got cash. We got a future."

"Stolen cash, they'll find you."

"No, they won't."

"Joe, I been keeping us afloat by letting other men screw me. What does that make us?"

"It don't make us nothing. You're mine, all mine."

"Joe, you don't know yourself. You've separated who you are into bits, and the pieces you don't like are buried in a drawer."

Joe was clutching the arm of the faded seat with white knuckles as the train sped into the silent night.

"All I used to want was for you to embrace me, to hold me for ever, lay down and never go away. How come you don't hold me no more? It takes a piece away, Joe, it steals your hope. I tried to be your girl, I tried to belong to you, but what I had to do to support us made belonging impossible."

"It's in the past."

"We are the past."

"Leave it back in Desprit. There's a future growing inside you, Mandy."

"It got spread around, Joe. You're the great pretender, it's like you went deaf with despair."

"What did?"

"My hooking. You never heard them talking? I got used, everyone knew. All those men. It's killed something in me."

"Men like Rocco? Tell me, Mandy, are you carrying his baby?"

They passed through a tunnel and in the altered light Mandy's face changed. She looked older, harder, like someone else. As they came out of the tunnel she turned to Joe with cold clear eyes.

"Does it matter? It could be anyone's. What are you, Joe? A piece of Rocco's charity?"

"You fuckin' bitch! Nothing is ever good enough for you."

A stranger entered the carriage then and Joe looked at him in the bleak window of the moving train as he hit Mandy. He had no control over this other man who punched his soiled lover in the gut, doubling her over, as Joe tasted all the poisoned impotent years gathering like a black tide inside him. Then Mandy was screaming and Joe was trying to say her name, but his voice was torn in his throat, and no words came, only a gasp of despair like a howl erupted into the last train from Desprit.

Joe looked down at the littered floor. He noticed Mandy was bleeding and he reached for her, his hand falling through the air, as the train jostled on the broken track, knocking him against the side of the carriage. He put his hand to his side and it felt wet. As the train thundered on, Joe's wound opened up and all he and Mandy had left was the endless embrace of the black night around them.

THE MESSAGE

Margaret Murphy

R ULES OF THE game:

One, find your spot.
Two, stake your claim.
Three, warn off all comers.
Four, wait.

Vincent Connolly is keeping dixie on the corner of Roscoe Street and
Mount Pleasant. Roscoe Street isn't much more than an alley; you'd
have a job squeezing a car down – which means he can watch without
fear of being disturbed. He's halfway between the Antrim and Aachen
Hotels, keeping an eye on both at once. They're busy because of the
official opening of the second Mersey tunnel tomorrow; the Queen's
going to make a speech, thousands are expected to turn out – and the
city-centre hotels are filling up fast. It's the biggest thing the city has
seen since the Beatles' concert at the Empire on their triumphal return
from America in 1964. That was seven years ago, when Vincent was
only four years old – too young to remember much, except it was
November and freezing, and he was wearing short trousers, so his
knees felt like two hard lumps of stone. They stood at the traffic lights
in Rodney Street, him holding his dad's hand, waiting for the four
most famous Liverpudlians to drive past. As the limo slowed to turn
the corner, Paul McCartney noticed him and waved. Vincent had got
a lot of mileage out of that one little wave. He decided then that he
would be rich and famous, like Paul McCartney, and ride in a big
limo with his own chauffeur.

Now it's 1971, Vincent is eleven, the Beatles broke up a year ago, T-Rex is the band to watch, and Vincent's new hero is Evel Knievel. For months, he's had his eye on a Raleigh Chopper in the window of Quinn's in Edge Lane. It's bright orange, it does wheelies, and it's the most beautiful thing Vincent has ever seen.

He doesn't mind working for it. He's never had a newspaper round, or a Saturday job, but he is a grafter. October, he can be found outside the pubs in town, collecting a Penny for the Guy. From Bonfire Night to New Year, he'll team up with a couple of mates, going door-to-door, carol singing. Summertime, he'll scour the streets for pop bottles, turning them in for the thruppenny deposit – one-and-a-half pence in new money. Saturdays, in the football season, he'll take himself off to the city's north end to mind cars in the streets around Goodison Park – practically the dark side of the moon, as far as his mates are concerned, but Vincent's entrepreneurial spirit tells him if you want something bad enough, you've got to go where the action is.

He lacks the muscle to claim the prime spots – he's got the scars to prove it – so, for now, he's happy enough working the margins.

The Antrim is the bigger of the two hotels, and he angles himself so he's got a good view. A half-hour passes, three lots of tourists arrive – all of them, disappointingly, by taxi. He settles to a game of single ollies in the gutter for a bit, practising long shots with his best marble, just to keep his eye in. It's a warm, sunny June evening, so he doesn't really mind.

Another fifteen minutes, and the traffic heading out of town is lighter; Wednesday, some of the shops close half-day. By six, Mount Pleasant is mostly quiet. A bus wheezes up the hill, a few cars pass, left and right, but you can count the minutes by them, now. Things won't pick up again until after tea-time, when the pubs start to fill up. By six-thirty, he's thinking of heading back for his own tea, when he sees a car stop outside the Aachen, off to his right.

One man, on his own. He sits with the engine running while he folds up a map. *Tourist*.

'You're on, Vinnie,' Vincent whispers softly. He picks up his marbles and stuffs them into his pocket.

He's still wearing his school uniform, so he's presentable, but he's pinned an SFX school badge over his own as a disguise. He licks both hands and smooths them over his head in an attempt to flatten his double crown, then he rubs the grit off the knees of his trousers. Now he's ready, poised on the balls of his feet, waiting for the driver to get out so he can make his play.

In Vincent's book, you can't beat car-minding. It seems nobler than the rest, somehow, and it couldn't be easier – no special props required – you just walk up, say, "Mind your car, mister?" and agree your price. Ten new pence is the going rate, but he'll go as low as five, if the owner decides he wants to barter. It's a contract. The unspoken clause – the small print, if you like – is cough up the fee, or you might come back to find your car on bricks.

The man shoves open the door and hoists himself out of the driver's seat. He's not especially tall, it's just that the car he's wedged into is a Morris Minor, a little granny car. Vincent squints into the sun, taking in more details: spots of rust mar the smoke-grey paintwork, nibbling at the sills and lower rims of the door. Even the wheel arches are wrecked. He curls his lip in disgust; a heap of tin – hardly even worth crossing the road for.

The man is five-nine or -ten, and spare. Collar-length hair – dark brown, maybe – it's hard to tell from twenty-five yards away. He's wearing a leather bomber jacket over an open-necked shirt. He stretches, cricks his neck, left, right, goes round to the car boot, and checks up and down the street, which gets Vincent's spider-sense tingling.

He ducks deeper into the shadow of the alleyway, crouching behind the railings of the corner house. The man lifts out a vinyl suitcase in dirty cream. He sets it down on the road, reaches inside the car boot again, and brings out a small blue carry-all. He looks up and down the hill a second time, opens the driver's door and leans inside. Vincent grips the railing, holding his breath. The man straightens up and – *hey, presto* – the bag is gone.

Still crouched in the shadows, Vincent watches him walk up the steps of the hotel. The front door is open, but he has to ring to gain entry though the vestibule door. Someone answers, the man steps inside, and Vincent sags against the wall. The bricks are cool against his back, but he's sweating. He can't decide if it's fear, or guilt, or excitement, because he's made up his mind to find out what's in that small blue bag.

Taking money off strangers to mind their cars is a bit scally, but breaking into a car is Borstal territory. Not that he hasn't done it before – for sunglasses left on the dashboard, or loose change in the glove compartment – small stuff, in and out in less than a minute. But this isn't small stuff; the way the man had looked around before he ducked inside the car, it had to be something special in that bag. Money, maybe; a big fat wad of crisp new notes. Or stolen jewels: emeralds as green as mossy caves, rubies that glow like communion wine. Vincent sees himself raking his fingers through a mound of gold coins, scooping out emeralds and sapphires and diamonds, buried like shells in sand.

He is about to break cover when the lobby door opens and the man steps out. For a second he stands in the hotel doorway and stares straight across the road, into the shadows of the alleyway. Vincent's heart seizes. He flattens himself against the wall and turns his head, hiding his face.

For a long minute, he shuts his eyes tight and wills the man away. When he dares to look, the man is already heading down the hill, into the westering sun. As he reaches the bend in the road, a shaft of sunlight catches his hair and it flares red for an instant, then he is gone.

Vincent can't take his eyes off the car, almost afraid it will vanish into thin air if he so much as blinks. *Less than a minute*, he tells himself. *That's all it'll take.* But his heart is thudding hard in his chest, and he can't make his legs work. Five minutes. Ten. Fifteen. Because what if the man had forgotten his wallet in his hurry? What if he comes back? What if someone is watching from the hotel?

"And what if you're a big girl's blouse, Vincent Connolly?"

The sound of his own voice makes him jump, and he's walking before he even knows it – one moment he's squatting in the shadows, gripping the railings like they will save him from falling, the next, he's at the car, his penknife in his hand.

Close to, the rust is even worse. *Moggy Minor*, he thinks, disgustedly – *one doddering step up from an invalid carriage*. Still… on the plus side, they're easy: the quarter-light catch wears loose with age – and this one's ready for the scrapyard. He pushes gently at the lower corner with the point of the knife blade and it gives. He dips into his pocket for his jemmy. It's made from a cola tin, cut to one-inch width, and fashioned into a small hook at one end. The metal is flexible, but strong, and thin enough to fit between the door and the window frame. In an instant, he's flipped the catch, reached in and lifted the door handle.

A Wolseley slows down as he swings the door open. A shaft of fear jolts through him, and he thinks of abandoning the job, but the chance to get his hands on all that money makes him reckless. He turns and waves the driver on with a smile, sees him clock the fake school badge on his blazer and grins even broader. The driver's eyes swivel to the road and he motors on to the traffic lights.

Vincent slides inside the car, closes the door, and keeps his head down. The interior reeks of petrol fumes and cigarettes. The vinyl of the driver's seat is cracked, and greyish stuffing curdles from the seams. He reaches underneath, and comes up empty.

Certain that any second he'll be yanked out feet first, he leans across to the passenger side and feels under the seat. Nothing. Zilch. Zero. Just grit and dust and tufts of cotton. But the passenger seat is in good nick: no cracks or splits in the leatherette. So where has the stuffing come from?

Frowning, he reaches under again, but this time he turns his palm up, pats the underside of the seat. His heart begins to thud pleasantly; he's found something solid. He tugs gently and it drops on to his hand.

He's grinning as he barrels up the steps to his house. Vincent lives in a narrow Georgian terrace in Clarence Street, less than a minute's walk from where the car is parked, but he has run past his own street, left and then left again, crossing Clarence Street a second time, on the lookout for anyone following, before cutting south, down Green Lane, covering four sides of a square to end up back at his house.

The door is on the latch. His mum is cooking lamb stew: summer or winter, you can tell the day of the week by what's cooking; Wednesday is Irish stew. He scoops up the *Liverpool Echo* from the doormat and leaves the carry-all at the foot of the stairs, under his blazer, before sauntering to the kitchen.

"Is that you, Vincent?" His mother glances over her shoulder. "I thought you were at rehearsals." His class has been chosen to perform for the Queen.

"We were so good, they let us finish early."

He must have sounded less than enthusiastic, because she scolds, "It's a great honour. You'll remember tomorrow for the rest of your life."

Vincent's mum is a patriotic Irish immigrant. And she says *he's* full of contradictions.

"*The Echo's* full of it," he says, slapping the newspaper on to the table.

She balances the spoon on the rim of the pot and turns to him. Her face is flushed from the heat of the pot; or maybe it's excitement. She wipes her hands on her apron and picks up the paper. "Well, go and change out of your school uniform. You can tell Cathy, tea's almost ready. And wash your hands before you come down."

For once, he doesn't complain.

He tiptoes past his sister's bedroom door and sidles into his room like a burglar. He shuts the door, then slides the carry-all under his bed. He untucks the blankets from his mattress and lets them hang. They are grey army surplus, not made for luxury, and the drop finishes a good three inches clear of the floor. He steps back to the door to inspect his handiwork. He can just spy one corner of the bag. He casts about the room and his eyes snag on a pile of laundry his mum has been on at him to fetch downstairs. He smiles. Given the choice between picking up his dirty socks and eating worms, Cathy Connolly would reach for a knife and fork. Smiling to himself, he heaps the ripe-smelling jumble of dirty clothing on top of the bag.

* * *

He says hardly a word at the dinner table, evading his mother's questions about the rehearsal by shovelling great spoonfuls of stew into his mouth. All the while, his sister looks at him from under her lashes, with that smirk on her face that says she knows something. He tries to ignore her, gulping down his meal so fast it scalds his throat, pleading homework to get out of washing the dishes.

His mother might be gullible, but she's no pushover.

"You've plenty of time to do your homework *after* you've done the dishes," she says.

"But Cathy could— "

"It's not Cathy's turn. And she has more homework than you do, but you don't hear your sister whining about doing her fair share."

Cathy widens her eyes and flutters her eyelashes at him, enjoying her beatification.

He stamps up the stairs twenty minutes later, grumbling to himself under his breath.

"Where were you?"

His heart does a quick skip. Cathy, waiting to pounce on the landing.

"When?"

"Well, I'm not talking about when God was handing out brains, 'cos we both know you were scuffing your shoes at the back of the queue, *that* day."

He scowls at her, but his sister is armour-plated and his scowls bounce harmlessly off her thick skull.

"Mary Thomas said you went home sick at four."

"It's none of your business."

"Is."

He tries to barge past, but she's got long arms and she is fast on her feet. "You're a little liar, Vincent Connolly."

"Am not."

"Are. How would you know if the dress rehearsal went well? How would *you* know dress rehearsal finished early, when you *missed* the dress rehearsal?" She adds spitefully, "It's a shame, really. Miss Taggart says you make a *lovely* little dancer."

He feels the familiar burn of humiliation and outrage at the intrusion. She's *no right* to talk to his class teacher like he's just a little kid. He sees the gleam of triumph in her eyes and hates her for it.

Cathy is fourteen and attends the convent school on Mount Pleasant; she'll be at the big parade, too. But while she gets to keep her dignity, playing the recorder, Vincent is expected to make a tit of himself, prancing about in an animal mask. In an animal mask *in front of the Queen.*

"Get lost, Cathy."

Cathy pulls a sad face. "Now Miss Taggart says you won't be able to be in the pageant."

"You can have my mask, if you like," he says. "Be an improvement." Silly moo doesn't know she's just made his day. He makes a break for his room, and she gives way; it doesn't occur to him that she let him pass. He's thinking he'll buy that Chopper bike with the money in the bag, take his mum shopping, buy her a whole new outfit. He'll get his dad a carton of ciggies – the good ones in the gold packs. As for Cathy, she can whistle. *No* – he thinks, shoving open his bedroom door – *I'll get her a paper bag – a big one to fit over her big fat ugly head. No, a tarantula – no, two tarantulas – no, a whole nest of tarantulas. Six of them – a dozen – big enough to eat a bird in one gulp; evil creatures with bone-crushing jaws and fat bodies and great goggly eyes on stalks. I'll make a cosy den for them under her pillow and stay awake until she comes up to bed...* A whole hour later than him, by the way, 'cos Cathy's a *big* girl—

He loses the thread of his fantasy. His bed has been carefully remade, the blankets tucked in. The dirty linen he'd used to camouflage the bag is folded neatly at the foot of the bed. And the bag has gone. He feels its absence like a hole in the centre of him.

Horrified, he whirls to face the door, but Cathy has slipped quietly away. Her bedroom door is shut. He boots it open.

Cathy is sitting cross-legged on her bed, the bag in front of her.

"You bloody—"

"Thief?" she says, in that pert way that drives him crackers. "Takes one to know one, doesn't it, Vincent?"

"You give it back!"

She puts a finger to her lips and cocks her head. The front door slams. It's Dad. She whispers, "Anybody home?"

Their father's voice booms out, a second after, like an echo in reverse: "Anybody home?"

Her eyes sparkle with malicious good humour. "What would Dad say if he knew you'd been thieving?"

Vincent clenches his fists, tears of impotent rage pricking his eyes. He considers rushing her, but Dad would hear and come to investigate.

"Give me it. It's mine."

"Now, Vincent, we both know that's not true." She plucks at the zip and he wants to fling himself at her, to claw it from her grasp.

She shouts, "Is that you, Dad?" putting on her girly voice just for him.

Their father's footsteps clump up the stairs. "How's my girl?" he says.

"Just getting changed." She raises her eyebrows, and reluctantly, Vincent back-heels the door shut.

Their father passes her door and they hear a heavy sigh as he slumps on to the bed to take off his shoes.

Cathy is smiling as she unzips the bag, and Vincent wants to kill her. First, she looks blank, then puzzled, then worried.

"You can turn off the big act," he whispers furiously.

Only she doesn't look like she's acting. And when she finally turns her face to him, her expression is one of sick horror.

"Oh, Vincent," she whispers.

His stomach flips. The anticipated wealth – the bundles of cash, the glittering treasures of his imagination – all crumbles to dust.

Carefully, reverently, she lifts a Bible and a set of rosary beads out of the bag. The beads are dark, solid wood; a serious rosary, a man's rosary. She holds it up so the silver crucifix swings, and he stares at it, almost hypnotized.

She reaches into the carry-all again, and brings out a small package, wrapped in brown paper. Three words are printed in neat block capitals on the front of it: "FOR FATHER O'BRIEN".

They stare at it for a long moment.

"Vinnie, you robbed a priest."

"He *isn't*," Vincent whispers, his voice hoarse. He feels sweat break out on his forehead.

Wordlessly, she holds up the rosary, the Jersusalem Bible.

"He *can't* be – he was wearing *normal clothes*."

"Shh!" She looks past him to the bedroom door, and he realizes he had been shouting. They hold their breath, listening for their father. There's no sound, and after a moment she whispers: "He might be on his holidays."

"He was wearing a leather *jacket*, Cath."

She looks into his face, absorbing the information, but her eyes stray again to the parcel, as if pulled by a magnet. "So, maybe it's his brother, or a friend. It doesn't *matter,* Vinnie: that parcel is addressed to Father O'Brien. There's no getting away from it – you robbed a priest." She bites her lip. "And that's a mortal sin."

Cathy is in the Legion of Mary, and she's been on two retreats with the sisters of Notre Dame. She always gets an A in Religious Education – so if Cathy says it's a mortal sin, he knows for sure that the devil is already stoking the fires of hell, chucking on extra coals, ready to roast him.

"I'll go to confession, I'll do penance – I'll do a novena," he gabbles, trying to think of something that will appease. "I'll do the Nine First Fridays—"

The shocked look on his sister's face makes him stop. But the Nine First Fridays are the most powerful prayer he knows: a special devotion to the Sacred Heart, getting up at six o'clock on the first Friday each month for nine solid months to attend early mass and receive the Holy Eucharist – surely that will wipe his sin away?

"Vincent," she says, gently, "there's no penance for a mortal sin – and you can't receive Holy Communion with a big black stain on your soul: it would be like inviting Jesus into your home with the devil sitting by the fire in your favourite armchair."

When he was little, Vincent's mum and dad both had to work, and Cathy would take care of him after school, in the holidays – even weekends, if Mum got the chance of overtime. Between the ages of five and eight, Cathy had been his minder, his teacher, his best mate, the maker-up of games and adventures. But he'd got bigger, and by his ninth birthday he wanted his independence. He became rebellious, and she was offended and hurt and that made her superior and sarcastic. Now, feeling the devil squatting deep inside him, chiselling away at his soot-blackened soul, he feels small again, frightened and lost, and he wishes she would take charge.

"What'm I gonna do, Cath?"

She stares at the neat brown package as if it's radioactive.

"Vinnie..." She frowns, distracted, like she's doing a difficult sum in her head. "There's only one way to get let off a mortal sin." She turns her eyes on him, and they are so filled with fear that Vincent is seized by a terrible dread.

"What d'you mean, 'it's gone'?"

The man in the leather jacket is standing in a phone box, opposite the clock tower of the university's Victoria Building. The quarter chimes have sounded and the clock's gilt hands read 6.32; he should be in position by now. He closes his eyes. "Gone...vanished. Stolen."

"You lost it." His unit commander's voice is hard, nasal, contemptuous.

"I thought it would be safe in the car."

"Oh, well, that's all right then – anyone can make a mistake."

"It was well hidden."

"Not that well, eh?"

The man fixes his gaze on the gleaming face of the clock, willing the hands to move, but the silence seems to last an eternity.

"When?"

"Sometime between six last night and five this morning."

"*Twelve hours* you left it?"

"Wouldn't it draw attention if I checked the damn thing every five minutes?"

"Watch your tone."

The man grips the phone receiver hard. The sun has been up since 4.30 and the temperature in the glass box must be eighty degrees, but he daren't ease the door open for air.

"Is it set to go?"

"It's on a twenty-four-hour timer, like you said. It'll trigger automatically at three this afternoon." He takes a breath to speak again, but the voice on the line interrupts.

"Shut up – I'm thinking."

He waits in obedient silence.

"Whoever took it must've dumped it, otherwise you'd be locked up in a police cell by now."

"That's what I—"

"I'm speaking, here."

He clamps his mouth shut so fast he bites his tongue.

"Even so, you'd better not go back to the hotel. Leave the car, catch a bus to Manchester. I'll have someone pick you up."

"I have a weapon. I could still complete my mission."

"And how close d'you think you'd get?"

"I could mingle with the crowd. They won't even see me."

A snort of derision. "You've a whiff of the zealot about you, lad. They'll sniff you out in a heartbeat, so they will – be all over you like flies on shit." The man listened to the metallic harshness of the voice, his eyes closed. "This's what you get when you send a *dalta* to do a soldier's job."

That stings – he's no raw recruit. "Haven't I proved myself a dozen times?"

"Not this time, son – and this is the one that counts."

"It's a setback – I'll make up for it."

"You will. But not in Liverpool; not today."

"Look, I checked it out – the approach roads are closed, but there's a bridge—"

"What d'you think you'll hit with a thirty-eight-calibre service revolver from a bloody bridge?"

He wants to say he's been practising – that he can hit a can from thirty yards – but that would sound childish. A tin can isn't a moving target, and it takes more than a steady hand to look another human being in the face and fire a bullet into them. So he says nothing.

"No," his superior says. "No. They'd catch you. And make no mistake – they would shoot you like a dog.'"

"I don't care."

"Only fools want to be martyrs, son. And if *you* don't care, *I* do. I care that we've spent money on equipment and you let a scouse scallywag walk away with it. I *care* that security will be stepped up for every official visit after today – even if you walk away right now. Because there's the small matter of a package that will turn up at three p.m." He sighed angrily. "We'll just have to pray to God the thieving bastard left it somewhere useful, like the city centre."

He books his ticket for one o'clock and walks down to the docks to clear his head. They are still adding the finishing touches to the stands when he stops by the tunnel approach on his way back to the coach station. He joins a group of kids gawping through the wire mesh at the chippies hammering the final nails in the platform. He can see the plaque above the tunnel, draped in blue cloth. This is where the Queen will make her speech. A team of men are sweeping the road leading to the tunnel entrance and a dozen more are raking smooth the bare soil of the verges.

Attendance is by invitation only, but a man dressed in overalls and looking like he has a job to do might pass unchallenged and find a good spot under the stands. Only what would be the point? Without the device, it would be hopeless: even if he did manage to remain undiscovered, he would have to abandon his hiding place, walk out in front of thousands of people, place himself close enough to aim his pistol and fire.

Police are already clustered in threes and fours along the newly metalled road; there will be sharpshooters along the route – and, true enough, they would shoot him like a dog.

Father O'Brien hadn't been anyone important. He didn't have the ear of the bishop and he wasn't destined for Rome; he hadn't a scholarly brain nor a Jesuit's mind to play the kind of politics it would take to elevate him above parish priest.

But he was a good man. He came from the fertile chalklands of Wexford, around Bantry Bay, where they spoke in softer tones, and faces were more given to smile. He liked a drink, and would stand you a pint if he fell into conversation with you at the Crown Bar, but he wouldn't hesitate to tell a man when he'd had enough, and he'd tipped more than one out on to the street before he'd drunk his fill. The man's father and the priest had come to blows over that; he'd taken to drinking after he lost his job on the shipyard. Father O'Brien had kicked his da out of that bar every night for a fortnight, until on the last day, his da got murderous mad. He swung wildly at Father O'Brien, out on the street, but the priest ducked and dodged, light on his feet, deflecting and blocking, until at last, dizzy and exhausted, his da had sunk to the pavement and wept.

"Ten thousand men work at the Belfast shipyard, Father," he'd said, his words sloshing out of his mouth. "And just four hundred Catholics among them. You've a good education: can you tell me what makes a Protestant better at lugging sacks of grain than a Catholic? Is there some calculation that adds up the worth of a man and subtracts a measure of humanity because he was born a Catholic?"

Father O'Brien didn't have an answer, but he sat with the boy's father on the kerb, until he'd raged and wept the anger out of him, and then the priest walked him home. He knew this to be the God's honest truth, for the man had seen it with his own eyes as a boy of fourteen.

Father O'Brien didn't preach taking up arms against the oppressor. He wasn't affiliated to the IRA, nor even Sinn Féin. "My only affiliation," he would say, "is to God Almighty; my only obligation is to my flock." Which was how he came to die. Not in a hail of bullets, but in the stupidest, most pointless way imaginable. A macho squaddie – a bad driver trying to impress his oppos – lost control of his vehicle turning a corner. Father O'Brien had been visiting a house in the next street, delivering the last sacraments to an old man dying of the cancer. The armoured vehicle skidded, clipped the opposite kerb, spun one hundred and eighty degrees, and smashed into the end of a terrace decorated with a painting of the Irish tricolour. Father O'Brien was pinned against the wall and died instantly.

He had been a gentle man, and a modest one, yet the violence and futility of his death had made a spectacle of him: a thing to point to as evidence of the British army's lack of respect; a dread event for old men to sigh and shake their heads over; a lurid tale for children to whisper in the playground, of the priest who was cut in half by an armoured car. Father O'Brien was no longer remembered for the good he'd done in life – only for the notoriety of his death.

The man had meant to deliver a message: that Father O'Brien's death would not go unpunished, and in failing in his mission he had failed Father O'Brien.

Vincent and Cathy stand in the porch. It's just shy of seven o'clock, and the sun is shining hot through the top light of the front door. Cathy's face is pale.

"You know what you have to do?"

He nods, but he has a lump in his throat as big as a bottle-washer ollie, so he can't speak.

She straightens his tie and combs her fingers through his hair, staring solemnly down at him. He doesn't squirm; in truth, he wouldn't complain if she took him by the hand and walked with him down the street in broad daylight, because he does not want to do this alone.

She seems taller, today. Grown up.

"I'll tell Mum you had to go early to rehearsals."

He frowns, wishing he hadn't skipped rehearsals the day before; thinks that dancing in an animal mask seems small humiliation, compared with what he has to do now.

"I'll tell Miss Taggart you've got a tummy bug, in case it takes a while, so you'll have to make yourself scarce for the rest of the day. All right?"

He nods again.

She hands him the small blue carry-all and blinks tears from her eyes.

He hefts the bag and squares his shoulders, setting off down the street like a soldier off to war.

The car is parked outside the hotel, but he waits an hour and still the man hasn't come out. Another half-hour, and the manager appears on the doorstep.

"What're you up to?" he asks.

"Is the man here – the one that owns the Morris Minor?"

The manager is broad-faced, with small eyes. He jams his hands in his trouser pockets and says, "What's it to you?"

He's wearing grey flannel trousers and a matching waistcoat to hide his soft belly; Vincent reckons he could easy out-run him, but his great sin burns his soul like acid, so he stills his itchy feet, and composes his face into an approximation of innocence.

"Got something for him."

The manager lifts his chin. "That it?" He holds a hand out for the bag. "I'll make sure he gets it."

Vincent tightens his grip on the carry-all and takes a step back. "Is he in?"

"Went out early," the man says. "Missed his breakfast."

"I'll wait."

"Not here, you won't – you're making my guests nervous, loitering outside."

"You can't stop me. It's a free country." He feels a pang of guilt: he promised Cathy he'd mind his manners.

"We'll see what the police've got to say about that." The man narrows his eyes. "Anyway, shouldn't you be in school?" His small eyes fasten on Vincent's blazer pocket. He's forgotten to pin the SFX badge over the real one. He clamps his hand over his pocket and the man comes at him, pitching forward as he lurches down the steps. Vincent turns and flees.

He pelts up the hill and cuts right into Rodney Street, then dodges left into the Scotch Churchyard and ducks behind one of the grave-stones, hugging the bag close to his chest. He can't stop shaking. The gardens of the convent back on to the graveyard; he'll catch his sister in the grounds during break. He checks his watch – playtime won't be for another hour-and-a-half. He sits down behind McKenzie's pyramid to wait.

He would have gone – in fact, he was already on his way. If the bus hadn't been diverted. If the driver hadn't turned down Shaw Street. If the new route hadn't taken them through Everton. If he'd looked out of the window to his left, rather than his right.

If, if, if… He would have stayed on the bus and been picked up in Manchester and made his ignominious way home. But in Everton, Orange Lodge and Catholic sectarianism was as strong as on any street in Belfast. A long stretch of grey wall ran beneath the new high-rise blocks on Netherfield Road. If he had turned away, just for a second, bored by the monotony of grey concrete and dusty pavements… But something had caught his eye; he glanced right and had seen the insult, daubed in orange paint on a grey wall – ill-spelt, angry, hateful: "THE POPE IS A BASTERD".

He recoiled like he'd been spat at. All morning, a rage had smouldered, built from the tinder of grief and loss, fuelled by the shock of finding the device gone and, yes, by the mortification he had suffered in telling his commander. Now it sparked and flared, and he blazed with righteous fire.

He lurched from his seat to the front. "Stop the bus," he said.

The driver didn't even take his eyes off the road. "It's not a request service, Paddy, lad."

"Oh, good – 'cos this is not a request."

The driver swivelled his head to look at him. "And who d'you think you are?"

The man took hold of the driver's seatback and leaned in, allowing his leather jacket to fall open just enough to show the revolver tucked in his belt. "I'm the Angel of Death, son."

It's four minutes to three as he heads south-west down Birkenhead Road on the other side of the Mersey. He'd crossed the great wide dock of East Float and crossed it again, tracking over every one of the Four Bridges, lost. Forty-five minutes later, he'd fetched up at the Seacombe Ferry terminal, with just a handrail between him and the muddy waters of the Mersey. He could happily have thrown himself in, had a kindly ferryman not asked him if he was off to the parade, and given him clear directions to Wheatland Lane, where he might stand on the bridge and wave to the Queen. He barrels along, the little car's engine screaming, past a stretch of blasted landscape. His heart is beating like an Orange Man's Lambeg. It's two minutes before the hour. She'll give her speech on the Liverpool side, then motor through to Wallasey; giving him time to find a spot. He *will* deliver the message for Father O'Brien. He almost misses the sharp turn westward and wrestles the wheel right. The gun slides in his lap, and he catches it, tucking it firmly in his waistband.

He's driving full into the afternoon sun, now; it scorches his face, burning through the windscreen, and he yanks the visor down. A sheet of paper flutters on to the dashboard. His foot hard on the pedal, he picks it up, squints at it as he powers towards the bridge.

It's a note, written on lined paper, in a child's neat handwriting:

> Dear Mister,
>
> I came to see you at the hotel but you weren't there. I wanted to say to your face that I am truly sorry I stole Father O'Brien's present. My sister says it's a Mortal Sin to steal from a Priest. I waited for ages, but the manager told me to push off, and he would of got me arrested if I didn't so I couldn't stay. My sister said it would be OK if I wrote you a message instead. So I hope you will forgive me and ask Father to forgive me as well. I never opened it or nothing, so I hope it will be OK and that you will forgive me.
>
> Sorry.
>
> PS - I put it back ~~esae~~ exacly like I found it.

His eyes widen. He hits the brakes. The car skids, turning ninety degrees, sliding sideways along the empty road. He reaches for the door, but his fingers seem too big, too clumsy to work the handle, he can't seem to get a grip of the lever. He can't seem to—

The thin, electronic beep of the clock in the bag under his seat sounds a fraction of a second before the flash. Then the windows shatter and the grey bodywork blows apart like a tin can on a bonfire.

TEA FOR TWO

Sally Spedding

THE FUZZ AND me have never exactly been bosom pals, but for the last four months, I've been keeping my nose extra clean. Doing all right with my own space, some cash in the bank from knowing one end of a greyhound from the other, until I spotted an unmarked Escort hanging around my bedsit in Ennis Street by Bethnal Green Tube. Then this Suit got out – all six feet of him – and stared up at my fourth-floor window.

"I've not an earthly why we're doing this," I complained to him some five minutes later. "Waste of a good morning if you ask me."

"Just need to sort a few things out," he said, and not a lot since. So I reasoned with myself the sooner we got this over with, the sooner I could go to Walthamstow for the dogs, like I'd planned.

Now it's just me and this too-tight Suit in "The Box" at the local lockup, staring at a grainy black-and-white photo that's obviously been enlarged.

"Take me back to the beginning when you were a kid," he says. "And no short-cuts."

"Why?"

"Patience, Mr Dwyer. I'm the one asking the questions, remember?"

I swallow bile that's crept up my throat. I'm trying to keep calm.

"There I am, in the distance, walking away from them others," I say, pointing at the skinniest kid with the whitest legs. "See? D'you need a magnifying glass?"

"No, Mr Dwyer. Just some answers. Why were you walking away?"

"Fed up of being called Fatso, Big Ears and the rest. I remember thinking I'd better things to do than hang around taking shit like that."

"Just you?"

"Yes."

"Think again."

"I don't get it," I say. "You had a tip-off?"

"What about?"

This is a trick…

"Nothing."

I was brought here hot and sweaty, but not any more. Quite the opposite. I'm looking for my gloves to warm up my fingers, but they've gone missing.

"How about the evening of September the tenth 1950?" he goes on, and I can't help sneaking a look at his shaved neck. His clean, shiny skin.

Like I've said, I've never trusted the Fuzz. Why should I, given my history? But this one, young enough to be my own son, seems kosher enough. Even the brew he's brought in for me is drinkable. Although his smile is meant to crack my memory that's hardened like cement, you try recalling stuff that happened that long ago. It's no joke, 'specially since there's been so much water under the bridge – Tower Bridge, to be precise – more my home then than the one I was supposed to go back to every night.

162, Rosehill Street, Rotherhithe, if you must know. With not a bloody rose or a hill in sight.

"It's important you take me through exactly what happened." The Suit. Slips a new tape into his recorder. Clicks it on. The sound makes me jump, and he notices. "Are you comfortable? Or would you prefer a softer chair?"

I don't answer. His tone of voice has changed, making my pulse slow up and a growing shadow fill my mind. "You're suspecting me of summat, right?" I say. I can't help myself. It just comes out.

"And what might that be?" He smiles again; this time showing big white teeth. All his own. Lucky not to have had 'em out like I did as a kid, to save on dentists. Come to think of it, there's something about his expression that rings a bell, but for the life of me, I can't think why. He pushes the photo even closer towards me until it rests in a beam of sunlight from the one barred window. I need to be careful.

Then I remember that same sun beginning to drop in the late-afternoon sky, making our shadows longer than we were, and that rusty old barge – the *May Queen* – moored just off the stony beach, glow like the lippy my step-mum wore before her nights out.

"Freddie's the one on the right, bending down. Am I correct?" says The Suit.

"Yessir. Freddie Miles. Smiley for short. He were a right bastard."

My inquisitor's Adam's apple bobs up and down in his throat. I wonder if I've put a foot wrong. My warder in the Scrubs warned me to be deferential with the Fuzz at all times, to the point of actually browning my nose. So here I am, doing like he said.

"What's he up to in this photo?"

"Picking up the biggest stones. Then we'd make a right huge pile..."

"Why?"

"Ammo, 'course. Even though the war was well over, he'd pretend the Boche were still about to come up river, and he'd be Churchill, seeing them off."

"Are these other boys doing the same? The Thomas brothers – Geraint and Dafydd – and the Robinson triplets?" The Suit's chewed forefinger points at the left-hand side of the photograph where the other five lads are busy obeying orders...

If there's one thing I can't abide, it's people who eat their own skin. I wonder if he's been at it since he was a kid...He's remembered all the names, mind. Even though I've only told him the once.

"They was his slaves too," I explain. "His 'Gatherers'. Nobody took offence at that, 'cept me and Dafydd. Funny you mention the Thomases. Never saw hide nor hair of them after Guy Fawkes Night. Like they'd never existed..."

He gets up. Goes over to the bare noticeboard. If this is a ploy to help me remember more, it doesn't. "One of them vanished sometime before November the fifth. Did you know that, Mr Dwyer? It's been a cold case since then."

I'm trying not to blink. Nor show any emotions. Something else the Scrubs has taught me.

"Which one's that?"

"Dafydd. There he is. The smallest. And after that Christmas, having given up the search for him, the rest of the family emigrated. So we discovered. "

"Why pick on me? Where's the rest of 'em lads?"

"I'm not at liberty to say. Besides most of the gang have either died or live outside our jurisdiction." He sits down again and his nose catches the sun while the tape recorder makes a sudden hissing sound. He corrects it. Leans forward towards me with another question on his lips. But I beat him to it. Not to ask what jurisdiction means, but something far more important. "Who took this photo?"

"That's not for you to worry about."

"Has someone sent it you, after all these years?"

A nod.

"I'd like a lawyer to be present."

"That's not appropriate, Mr Dwyer. May I call you Carl? This is just an informal chat..."

With both chairs and the table between us welded to the floor? With another Fuzz hovering outside the door, and a large glass panel taking up most of the opposite wall? The kind you see on TV cop shows? Come on, mate, pull the other one...

"Another tea, Carl?" he asks.

"You're taking the piss. If you think I had anything to do with... with..."

"Dafydd's death?" He switches off his machine. Eyebrows raised. "When you were still in short trousers, but old enough to know better?"

Death? Jesus Christ...

"Then I'm using my right to silence."

"Up to you." He stands up for the second time and pockets the neat gadget with my answers still inside. I notice the carotid jumping in his neck. He's not as calm as he pretends. While the sun goes in, he taps on the door to be let out, then turns towards me. "Remember, from now on we'll be breathing down your neck, so no moving away, eh? No contacting any of the others, unless you want another *sojourn* in the Scrubs. Think about it, Carl."

And I do. 'Specially the slopping out...

For seven whole days, I avoided anywhere with fucking CCTV, which didn't leave me much choice, but now needs must. At Baba's Internet café, the Somalian guy takes my three quid and shows me into a pre-fab extension at the back, where I can work. I've done two IT skills courses in the past four years, so the internet's no problem. But Dafydd Thomas is. Nothing on him at all. Nor any of the others in the gang. More and more, I'm beginning to feel something's amiss.

Instinct tells me to try and find where those Taffies, who'd come from Port Talbot, ended up. Then I remember the 'death' word. Each death needs a certificate which is open to public scrutiny.

Rotherhithe Register Office is just a ten-minute bus ride away.

There's always someone happy to make you feel like a jerk, and the wanker in the reception area proves my point. For a start, he can barely be arsed to look up from his computer.

"It's Kew you want," he says at last, and I notice how his lips are cracked and dry. His skin like a map of red rivers. Quite different from that moisturized Suit who kept me on my own for a further half-hour to "have a rethink".

Bollocks.

"You'll need some ID. A driving licence, utility bill, etcetera," the geek goes on. "And it costs..." He then looks up at me and my crap clothes as if to say, "don't bother". I have to admit, he's right. There are too many obstacles. Time for that rethink, to get my memory up and running before it's too late.

I don't recognize the place at all. Hell, no. Tarted up with new shingle, and where us kids used to race each other on to it, is a bistro complete with red parasols fluttering in the hot breeze. I hesitate for a moment. It's not just the temperature sealing my nylon shirt to my back, but being there again.

"You OK, sir?" A uniform has suddenly materialized alongside me. One of those Community Police Officers. Some jobless git in fluorescent yellow fancy dress. "I can fetch you a drink of water..."

"I'm pukka, ta very much. Too old for this heat, mind."

He wanders off, ducking away from a gull about to dump on his peaked cap. Normally, I'd say "serve him right", but I'm too busy staring at the *May Queen*, uglier than ever. Now painted black to match her cabin.

Yes, the cabin...

It's cooler here under one of these parasols and, with a cold Stella in my hand, I feel those intervening years fold away from me like a collapsing pack of cards.

Night-time, and while the other lads have gone to the chippie, Smiley's dragging me and Dafydd towards the barge, by a rope round our necks. Neither of us can swim, but Smiley can. He can do everything, and I mean *everything*. Sometimes the Thames's tarry water fills my lungs, but does he care? Why should he? Me and Dafydd who'd stood up to him when he'd branded us "fucking snitchers" for telling our teacher at Gladebrook Primary how weird he was. Not that we went there much. But she wasn't frightened of Smiley and his rubbish family...

Dafydd's up on deck first. No screaming, not with that rag in his gob, while my heart's drumming so hard it feels about to burst. No moon or stars. No lights either except those feeble pinpricks along by St Paul's, and the pong of oil and damp and the shit dribbling down Dafydd's short trouser legs. Him with the cheeky grin and his Robertson's golly badge proudly pinned to his home-made jumper, lies tied to the rickety old table. His clothes chucked overboard.

"I want me mam," he grunts. "I want to go home..."

But what can I do?

Smiley's living up to his name all right. Smiling. He produces a knife he's nicked from somewhere and makes the first, bloody cut. "Tastes just like pork, Carl." He licks his lips as he lowers the fork and its pink morsel of shoulder over the lit stove. "Try some."

That's when I throw up, and as a punishment, I have to watch till he's eaten his fill.

How could I get any kip after that? 'Specially after doing three years for breaking and entering and GBH, which I never meant to do. Two hours a night, if I was lucky. Just as well, given the pond life I shared with. And, no, don't talk to me about ham...

I make myself a cuppa on my bedsit's gas ring. Nice and sweet. But why's my hand shaking? Why do I feel as if that same shite river water's rolling over my head again, like it did when I made my escape from the *May Queen,* my numb feet paddling back and forth for Britain? Because I'd just dreamed of teeth with bits of Dafydd trapped between them. The very same smile I'd seen a week ago...

The Suit had changed his name, hadn't he? Long before he and I first met. The coward. And been on leave from the can since midnight. There's a young Polish cleaner, Jana so her name tag says. I'd spotted her while he'd led me into The Box under false pretences. Trying to pin things on me. This time she's collecting her bike from the rack in the full staff car park. Once she's out of the CCTV's range, I make my move. Ask her where this Suit lives.

"54, Darcy Road. Near cricket ground. Something like that," she hisses, stuffing my three crisp tenners down her bra. I'm not fussed what she does with 'em. Worth every penny when you think of it.

Ten minutes later, I'm in number 54's whitewashed basement room, home to a half-full wine rack taking up most of one wall. Its owner a *bon vivant* no less. My, my, ain't he done well?

From the room overhead, I can make out a cricket match in progress on the TV. Then comes a wheezy cough. And another. I wasn't the best second-storey man in Catford for nothing, but if you're hoping I'll spill the tricks of my trade to you, you'll be disappointed.

Here we go, Carl. Amazing what a credit card and a hairgrip can do...

***

Smiley Senior's in a wheelchair now. One carpet-slippered foot in the grave already. His gob opens in surprise when he sees me come to join him in the lounge. Acrylic crowns, I notice. Not quite what I recall from way back, but easier to shift than the real thing. They look almost pretty, arranged on the rug like that, around his feet...

"Carl Dwyer," I announce myself. "Remember me?"

He's well hooked. "Can't say I do."

"I know why you took the fucking photo," I shout over the cricket commentator's gabble. "As a sick souvenir."

"What photo? What souvenir?" His red spit sprays in my direction. The cripple tries to get up. No joy. Not with my boot in his crotch. I zap his flat-screen. I want him to listen only to me

"The one your dustbin lid showed me in the can last week. Trying to stitch me up, he was, so you'd go free."

Smiley's Adam's Apple's like a captive frog between my hands. Another feature he's passed on. I smell his piss. Old, rank piss. You've no idea how long I've waited to hear *him* beg for mercy.

"Thomas's twat of a brother took it, if you must know," he glugs. "He wanted a souvenir of us Gatherers to take back with him to Wales..."

"You holy fucking friar. Only *you* could afford a Box Brownie."

Then three's suddenly a crowd with Junior himself pushing his way in. His police-issue Walther the added extra. But I'm tooled up too. Been busy practising.

"Put that down," he snarls at me. "And get out. If you do, I'll turn a blind eye. Pretend you've not been here."

"No deal. I'm staying. Why? Your dad owes you an explanation." I kick the nearside wheel of Smiley Senior's wheelchair. He topples one way then the other.

"C'mon, Freddie. Tell him about those shoulder steaks, the fried liver, the cobbler's awls... How you dealt with Dafydd's beating heart. How I wasn't allowed to breathe a word. "

Junior's turning green. Turning away from me to face the killer.

"You never... "

"He bloody did." And then, as if someone's just pulled the plug from my mind, I relive the rest of that terrible night.

The cook covers his head with his fat, red hands and shuts his eyes. But there's nowhere for him to hide. His kin, on the other hand, is all ears.

"As God's my witness, I don't know what he means," croaks the psycho when I've finished my tale. "Give it to him, son. Or I'll be wondering whose side you're on."

I recognize a saddo with in-built obedience when I see one. Junior's off guard.

Down on the rug, both knees gone, making way too much din. His dad's scattered teeth aren't white any more, but red.

His pistol's all mine now. Its full chamber giving it more weight than my Beretta, but I won't finish him off. Not just yet, anyway. Why? you might ask. Because all this has given me a real appetite. As has stripping off his trackies and dragging him towards the generous worktop next to the hot, new Aga.

Setting the kitchen table for two doesn't take a minute.

"Meals on wheels," I tell Smiley Senior brightly, propelling him into the kitchen where his tea lies waiting "You must be bloody starving."

SAFE AND SOUND

Edward Marston

New York City, 1868

THE ATTACK CAME when he least expected it. Henry Culver, a wealthy banker, was driving home in a cab through the gathering darkness of an April evening. He was in a contented mood. Having dined with some colleagues, he'd been able to mix business with pleasure and wash both of them down agreeably with the finest of wine. As the cab took him through a maze of streets, Culver dozed off happily. It was only when the horse clattered to a halt and the vehicle shuddered that he was jerked awake. He alighted, paid the driver and moved unsteadily towards his house. Before the banker reached his front door, however, a burly figure stepped out of the shadows, knocked off his top hat and cudgelled him to the ground.

Culver was a healthy man in his early fifties but he was no match for a seasoned ruffian. Exploiting the element of surprise, the attacker struck and kicked him unmercifully. All that the banker could do was curl up and try to cover his head with his arms. The assault was over as suddenly as it had begun. After drawing blood and inflicting severe pain, the assailant turned on his heel and ran off to a waiting horse. Henry Culver was left groaning on the sidewalk.

In the years that he'd been working as a private detective in the city, Jeb Lyman had watched a great deal of fear, grief and desperation walk through his office door but he'd never seen them so starkly embodied in one person before. Maria Culver was in a terrible state. She was trembling with fear, ashen with grief, her once-handsome face pockmarked with tragedy. Getting up quickly from behind his desk, Lyman helped her to a chair, poured a glass of water from a jug then helped her to sip it. Gradually, his visitor started to calm down.

"Do please forgive me,'" she said, dabbing at her eyes with a handkerchief. "I've been so *worried*."

"Perhaps you'd care to tell me why," he said, softly. "My name is Jeb Lyman, by the way. Whatever your problem, I'll do my utmost to help you solve it."

Maria took a deep breath and tried to compose herself. After giving her name, she told him what had happened to her husband the previous evening and how she'd found him, sprawled in a pool of blood, not five yards from his own doorstep. Listening patiently, Lyman deduced a great deal from her appearance, dress and educated vowels. Clearly, she was a loyal, loving wife from a privileged world into which crime had never intruded before.

Lyman was a stocky man in his thirties with features that were inexcusably ugly. Though he had the face of a desperado, however, he was intensely law-abiding and had an unshakable belief in the concept of justice. The more he listened to her story, the more he wanted someone to pay for the vicious assault on Henry Culver. As soon as she'd finished, he picked on a salient point.

"You say that nothing was stolen, Mrs Culver?" he observed.

"No," she replied, "that was the curious thing. My husband thought the man was after his billfold and his pocket watch but they were untouched."

"Robbery was clearly not the motive for the attack, then."

"I'm so frightened, Mr Lyman. Henry might have been *killed*."

"I very much doubt that. Since he had Mr Culver at his mercy, the assailant could easily have battered him to death but he drew back. It sounds to me as if he was administering a warning."

"Why on earth should he do that?' she asked.

"That's what we must find out," said Lyman, pensively stroking his chin. "I take it that you've reported the crime to the police."

"They were summoned immediately."

"So why have you turned to me?"

"That was my husband's idea," she explained. "Henry doesn't have much faith in the police. He thinks they reserve their best efforts for more serious crimes – though nothing is more serious to me than this, Mr Lyman. I can't bear to see him in such a condition."

"It must be very distressing for you."

"He remembered your name being mentioned by a close friend of ours – Thomas Reinhold. I believe you recovered some stolen property for him."

"I did rather more than that," said Lyman, recalling that he had also solved a murder in the process. "I'm grateful to Mr Reinhold for recommending me."

"Is there any hope of catching this brute?"

"Oh, yes – there's always hope, Mrs Culver."

"How will you go about it?"

"First of all, I'd like to speak to your husband. Is he in a fit state to answer questions?"

"Yes, Mr Lyman."

"Then let's take a cab back to the house," he suggested with a reassuring smile, "and I'll begin my investigation at once."

Propped up in bed on some pillows, Henry Culver was a sorry sight. His face was heavily bruised and two bloodshot eyes stared out from beneath the bandaging around his head. He had sustained cuts, abrasions and a cracked rib. The fingers on his left hand had been broken by a blow from the cudgel. His lips were swollen and some of his teeth had been dislodged. He was evidently in great pain but had refused to go to hospital.

Left alone with him, Lyman expressed his sympathy and asked him to recount what had happened. What he heard was substantially the version given to him by the wife but there were additional details. The banker remembered that his attacker had an Irish accent and had said "That'll teach you, Mr Culver!" before he fled.

"It was no random assault, then," noted Lyman. "He knew exactly who you were and when you were likely to return."

Culver was alarmed. "Does that mean I was *watched*?"

"It's more than likely, sir."

"Why?"

"Only you can answer that. Do you have many enemies?"

"None at all that I know of," said Culver, proudly. "Oh, I have business rivals, of course, and some of them stoop to disgraceful tactics from time to time but they'd never be involved in anything like this. It's unthinkable."

"Could it be that you've upset someone recently?"

Culver's eyes flashed. "There's no question of that, Mr Lyman," he snapped, "and I'll thank you not to make such suggestions. I'm a highly respected banker with years of service behind me. I didn't get to such an eminent position by upsetting people."

Lyman suspected that that was exactly what he'd done. Culver had the peremptory tone of a man who expects to be obeyed and who can't conceive that he's causing offence when he throws his weight around. The detective became less sympathetic towards him. On the other hand, Culver was retaining his services so a degree of politeness was obligatory.

"From all that I've heard so far," said Lyman, "it sounds to me as if someone was issuing a warning. Who might that be, sir?"

"I've no idea."

"I believe that you do, Mr Culver, and that you're deliberately holding something back."

"Damn your impertinence!"

"I'm only being practical," insisted Lyman. "Since I have so little to go on, I need every scrap of information I can gather. You, for whatever reason, are concealing something important. I can sense it. You obviously don't trust me and I, as a consequence, have lost trust in you. Goodbye, Mr Culver," he added, moving towards the door. "I think you need to find someone else to handle this case."

"Wait!"

It was a howl of pain. Lyman turned to look at him. Squirming in his bed, Culver wrestled with his thoughts for several minutes. When he eventually spoke, he lowered his voice to a whisper.

"My wife must know nothing of this," he emphasized. "Maria is hurt enough as it is. I want her spared any more suffering."

"I understand, sir."

"There *is* something you should know. The reason I didn't tell you about it before is that I'm rather ashamed. It shows me in a foolish light."

"Go on," invited Lyman.

The banker sighed. "I received a letter," he admitted.

"A threatening letter, I daresay."

"It didn't seem so at the time, Mr Lyman, that's why I didn't take it seriously. It simply informed me that I should be very careful from now on. That's all. I thought it was some silly joke designed to give me a scare so I decided to ignore it – how stupid of me!"

"Did you keep the letter?"

"No, I tore it up and threw it away."

"That was unfortunate."

"I thought no more of it until this arrived today." Reaching under the pillow, he extracted an envelope and handed it over. "Like the other one, it's unsigned."

Lyman took out the letter and read it aloud. "'*Does that change your mind, Mr Culver?*'" He looked up at the banker. "It couldn't be more explicit than that, sir. Was this written by the same hand as the first letter?"

"Yes, Mr Lyman – I'm certain of it."

"Then I'll hang on to it, if I may?"

"Please do. I'd hate my wife to find it." Culver shook his head. "I've never had trouble of this kind before. I know that the city is a dangerous place but I keep well clear of bad neighbourhoods. I've always felt perfectly safe, walking down my own street at night. That's why I was completely off guard." He heaved another sigh. "I'm beginning to think that Hazelhurst may be right."

"Hazelhurst?'

"He's an acquaintance of mine – William Hazelhurst. When I met him recently, he told me that he employed a bodyguard to drive him home after dark and to keep an eye on the house."

"Where does this gentleman live?"

"Four blocks away from here, Mr Lyman."

"I would've thought this was a relatively safe neighbourhood."

"That's what I believed – until last night."

"I think I'd like to speak to Mr Hazelhurst," Lyman decided.

"Then you'll have to go to his office on Fifth Avenue. He's a lawyer who deals with criminal cases all the time so he's well aware of what really goes on in this city."

"Did he mention that he'd had letters like yours?"

"No, Mr Lyman. He simply said that he was taking wise precautions. I wish I'd done the same."

"Perhaps you'd be kind enough to give me his address," said Lyman, taking out a pencil and pad. "I'll call on Mr Hazelhurst this very morning. Meanwhile, get as much rest as you can, sir, and tell you wife not to worry. I'm sure that this crime can be solved."

When Lyman arrived at the office, the lawyer was busy with a client so the detective was forced to wait. It gave him the opportunity to talk to the secretary in the outer office and gather a lot of information about the firm of Hazelhurst & Orme. The premises were well appointed and there was an air of prosperity about the whole enterprise. Lyman watched a number of clients come and go. He was eventually shown into a large office whose walls were lined with bookshelves filled with massive legal tomes. Behind the leather-topped oak desk sat William Hazelhurst. He rose to exchange a handshake with Lyman, then resumed his seat. The detective was waved to a chair opposite him.

Hazelhurst was a tall, thin, angular man in his forties with dark brown hair and mutton-chop whiskers. Impeccably dressed, he peered over eyeglasses perched on the end of his nose. Lyman explained the purpose of his visit and the lawyer was appalled.

"Attacked outside his own home?" he said. "That's dreadful."

"I understand that you live nearby, Mr Hazelhurst, and have thought it necessary to engage a bodyguard on occasion."

"Only when I'm returning home late at night – one can never be too careful."

"How long has this been going on, sir?"

"For a few months now," replied Hazelhurst. "Early in January, I had the feeling that I was being followed and that my house was being kept under observation. I never actually *saw* anyone, mark you, but I was nevertheless unsettled. Whenever she ventured out, my wife had the same sensation."

"Did you get in touch with the police?"

"Yes – they agreed to increase patrols in the neighbourhood but saw nothing untoward. Our sense of unease continued. Then one of the servants *did* see someone – a brawny individual, watching the house one evening. When he realized he'd been spotted, he vanished into the shadows. That settled it," said Hazelhurst. "I went in search of a bodyguard."

"Where did you find one?" asked Lyman.

"There was an advertisement in the *New York Times* for a company that offers a discreet but efficient service. I took them on a month's trial and was extremely satisfied. They've given me peace of mind, Mr Lyman. My wife and I are no longer afraid to venture out after dark. We feel secure."

"According to Mr Culver, your bodyguard also keeps an eye on your home at night. Does that involve a full-time presence?"

"No – he or a colleague goes past at regular intervals."

"That kind of protection must be rather expensive," said Lyman.

"I'd pay anything to ensure our safety. Yes," he went on, holding up a hand, "I know what you're thinking. You believe that the firm providing the bodyguard might have deliberately frightened me in order to get my business – that was *my* first thought as well. I'm a lawyer, remember. I check and double-check everything. I had one of my clerks look very closely at this firm and it turned out to be entirely trustworthy. It's run by a man of proven integrity. I can't speak more highly of him."

"In that case, perhaps I should recommend him to Mr Culver."

"That's for you to decide. I'm not here to advertise the firm. All I know is that they've helped my wife and me to sleep more peacefully at night. Nobody can put a price on that."

"Do you have the address of this firm, Mr Hazelhurst?"

"Yes," said the lawyer, opening a drawer to search inside it. "I have a business card somewhere. Ah – here we are," he went on, taking out a card and offering it. "The office is not in the most salubrious part of the city but don't be put off by appearances."

"I never am," said Lyman, getting up to take the card from him. "Thank you, Mr Hazelhurst. You've been very helpful."

"Please give my warmest regards to Culver."

"I'll make a point of doing so, sir."

"How badly was he injured?"

"I think his pride was hurt as much as his body. It just never crossed his mind that such a thing could happen to him. However, he seems to be a resilient man. I fancy that he'll be back on his feet again before too long."

Matthew Steen was a muscular young man in his twenties with a shock of red hair and a tufted beard. His fondness for whiskey, allied to a short temper, had got him into many tavern brawls and his broken nose was a vivid memento of one of them. Steen did a variety of jobs but his main source of income was Jeb Lyman. While he knew the man's weaknesses, the detective also appreciated his many strengths. Steen was alert, tenacious and fearless. More to the point, he was very reliable.

Lyman found him at his lodging, chopping wood in the garden. Having built up a rhythm, Steen was splitting the timber with power and accuracy. When he saw his friend, he broke off.

"You've got work for me, Mr Lyman?" he asked, hopefully.

"Yes, Matt," said the other with a friendly smile. "It's rather more subtle than swinging an axe. I need you to apply for a job."

"But I'm already employed by you."

Taking out the business card given to him by Hazelhurst, the detective explained what he wanted. Steen liked what he heard. It was the sort of assignment that appealed to him. He did, however, foresee a potential problem.

"What if they offer me a job?" he said, worriedly. "I can hardly turn it down."

"They won't do that," Lyman promised. "Even if they considered taking you on, they'd want to make enquiries about you first and your criminal record would deter them."

"I'm not a *real* criminal, Mr Lyman."

"I know, Matt, but the fact remains that you've seen the inside of the Tombs a number of times – mostly, I grant you, for being drunk and disorderly. But there was that sentence you served for wrecking all the furniture in a tavern."

"That was a mistake," claimed Steen. "They arrested the wrong man. All I did was to break a few chairs over people's heads."

"Be that as it may," said Lyman, "a firm like this one will think twice about employing someone with your history. If – that is – they're as thorough and honest as I'm led to believe. That's your first task. Sniff out the place. See if it really is a legitimate business. Even though it's not the prettiest part of your anatomy, you have a nose for villainy. Use it."

"What else must I do?"

"Get a sample of Barnett Lovell's handwriting. According to that card, he runs the firm. If my guess is right, some of the people on his payroll can barely write their names. Their assets are more physical."

"I'll do what I can, Mr Lyman."

"Come to my office in two hours. I should be back by then."

"Where are you going?"

"To the offices of the *New York Times*," said Lyman. "I need to look at an advertisement."

Matt Steen was punctual. He arrived on time at Lyman's office and wore a broad grin. Sensing that his friend had good news to report, the detective poured them both a shot of whiskey. Steen threw his down in one grateful gulp.

"I didn't need my famous nose," he said. "My eyes saw what kind of a business it was right away. As I walked towards the office, I saw someone leaving that I recognized."

"Who was it?"

"One of the guards from the Tombs – a vicious thug who liked to beat up prisoners for fun. I was always on the fourth tier where those of us charged with lesser offences were kept. O'Gara made our lives a misery, I can tell you."

"O'Gara?" echoed Lyman. "He was *Irish*?"

"As Irish as they come," replied Steen, "but so was Mr Lovell, though his accent was much slighter. I think he must have kissed the Blarney stone because he had the gift of the gab but O'Gara gave him away. If he's employing someone like that, then it's to do Lovell's dirty work. It's all that cruel Irish bastard is fit for."

"Did you get a specimen of Lovell's handwriting?"

"I did indeed. When I asked for a job, he turned me down, saying that he already had enough men on his books. So I told him I was desperate for work of any kind and that I'd be grateful if he could suggest anywhere else I could try." Steen fished a piece of paper from his inside pocket. "He gave me an address of a warehouse in Lower East Side. He said they might be able to use a pair of strong arms there." He passed the paper to Lyman. "This is what he wrote."

"Well done, Matt," said the detective, taking out the note that had been sent to Culver that morning. "I can now put a theory of mine to the test." Placing the two pieces of paper side by side, he beckoned Steen closer. "What do you think?"

"It looks like the same hand, Mr Lyman."

"It *is* the same hand – I swear it!"

"What does that prove?"

"It proves that Barnett Lovell is just as big a liar as a lawyer called William Hazelhurst. That's exactly what I expected."

"Did you?"

"Yes, Matt, they're in this together. It's the reason I sent *you* to Lovell's office. I had a feeling that Hazelhurst would send someone on ahead of me to warn his partner that I was coming. Lovell would've been on guard. He'd be less suspicious of you."

"What was that business about an advertisement?"

"I had a very productive visit to the newspaper offices. I not only found the advertisement for Lovell's firm in a back copy of the *Times*, I discovered the name of the person who's placed it there once a month since Christmas."

"Oh – and who was that, Mr Lyman?"

"William Hazelhurst – clear proof they're in this together."

"I thought you said that this man was a lawyer?"

"He's obviously found richer pickings on the other side of the law," said Lyman, thinking it through. "My guess is that he chooses the targets very carefully. They're wealthy men like Mr Culver who are first given a warning then a beating. Since they know that

Hazelhurst hires a bodyguard, they're likely to turn to him for advice, and what does he do?"

"He recommends Lovell's firm."

"And the victims pay up without realizing that their money is going to the very people responsible for the attack on them. As for keeping an eye on their properties at night, Lovell doesn't bother to do that. He withdraws the threat by standing one of his men – O'Gara, probably – down. It's easy money. I wonder how many frightened men are paying up."

"Are you going to report all this to the police, Mr Lyman?"

"No, Matt, we don't have enough evidence yet. Hazelhurst is a slippery customer and so is Lovell, by the sound of him. We need to catch them red-handed."

"How do we do that?"

"I think I know a way," said Lyman, thoughtfully. "We'll bide our time. We'll wait until they play right into our hands."

Steen beamed. "We'll do just that," he said, obediently, "but, while we're waiting, is there any chance I could have another shot of that whiskey?"

Henry Culver was not a man to hide his injuries. As soon as he felt well enough to get up again, he returned to work and braved both the physical discomfort and the horrified stares of his employees at the bank. Less than a fortnight after the attack, he was sufficiently recovered to accept an invitation to dine with some of the bank's directors. His wife Maria pleaded with him not to go but Culver was not dissuaded by her tears. He insisted on joining the others at a leading restaurant in the city.

"But the brute who attacked you might still be out there," said Maria with concern. "I'd hoped that Mr Lyman would have caught him by now but he has no notion of who the man can be."

"Don't lose faith in Mr Lyman, dear," cautioned her husband. "I have the greatest confidence in the fellow."

"Come home early," she begged, "and travel with someone else."

He gave her a farewell kiss. "Goodbye, Maria. There's no cause for alarm. I intend to return safe and sound."

It was an enjoyable meal. The food was delicious, the wine flowed freely, and Culver joined his companions in a cigar as they traded anecdotes about the financial world. When he left the convivial atmosphere of the restaurant, he was in a buoyant mood. He did not even see the horseman who was watching him from nearby and who waited until Culver had climbed into his cab before he kicked his mount into a canter.

Arriving in the street minutes before the cab, the man had time to tether his horse and take up his position. He pulled his hat down low and tightened his grasp on the cudgel. He heard the approaching cab well before it came into sight as the horse's hooves echoed down the long, empty thoroughfare. The vehicle pulled up outside the Culver residence and the passenger got out, tottering slightly. He paid the driver and the cab pulled slowly away. It was the moment to strike. The man rushed out of the shadows with his weapon held high.

But the assault was anticipated. Swinging round to face his attacker, the intended victim threw off his top hat and raised his cane to defend himself. Even in the half-dark, O'Gara could see that the man was not Henry Culver.

"Who the divil are ye?" he demanded, closing in.

"I'm an old friend of yours, Mr O'Gara," said Matthew Steen, slashing him across the face with the cane then kicking him hard in the crotch. "Remember me?"

Doubling up in pain, O'Gara cursed aloud then found the strength to swing his cudgel with murderous force. Steen ducked quickly beneath it and, dropping his cane, used both fists to deliver a relay of punches to the head and body. Dazed and bloodied, O'Gara staggered backwards. He was grabbed firmly from behind by Jeb Lyman, who'd been posing as the cabman and had stopped his vehicle a short distance away so that he could run back. In no time at all, the detective snapped a pair of handcuffs on to the Irishman's wrists, pinning his arms behind his back.

"I know ye," growled O'Gara, glaring at Steen.

"There's something else you'll know," retorted Steen with grim satisfaction. "You're going to know what it's like on the *other* side of the bars at the Tombs – because that's where you and your friends will end up."

By the time that Culver returned much later in another cab, it was all over. Liam O'Gara was in police custody and warrants had been issued for the arrest of William Hazelhurst and Barnard Lovell. The banker lapsed into a rare moment of generosity, praising Lyman for his expertise and paying him twice the agreed fee. Because it was Steen who tackled the man responsible for Culver's beating, he was given a sizeable reward. A protection ring had been smashed and the streets of the neighbourhood were safe once more.

"I can't thank you enough, Mr Lyman," said Culver, pumping his hand. "I'd recommend you to anybody."

"Thank you, sir," said the detective. "Matt and I are always ready to take on any assignment. Just remember that prevention is better than the cure."

The banker frowned. "I don't follow."

"You should've come to me when you received that first warning letter. Then we could've taken steps to ensure that you were never given that beating. It's always much more satisfying to nip a crime in the bud. That way," said Lyman, pointedly, "the only person who gets hurt is the villain."

CONFESSION

Paula Williams

This is the full written confession of Trevor Montgomery Pringle, aged fifty-five, of – well, there's not a lot of point me putting my address down because Trevor Montgomery Pringle is going away for a long, long time.

It's funny but I never really thought of what I was doing as stealing, more a question of building up my pension fund. It was, after all, the only one I was likely to get, in spite of the fact I'd worked for Fraddon and Son (Construction) Ltd for most of my adult life.

So I preferred to think of what I did more along the line of a redistribution of assets. And if that sounds like accountant-speak, that's because I am one. Or rather I was, for thirty-six tedious years.

But to be honest – and, in spite of everything, I am an honest chap – I'm not exactly an accountant. I'm what you'd call "qualified by experience". But I never took any exams or had any letters after my name, which was Roger Fraddon's excuse for paying me peanuts all those years.

"Let's face it, Trev," he said, back in the early days when I was still naive enough to believe him when he promised that next year my rise would be The Big One. "I pay you a fair wage considering you're nothing more than a glorified bookkeeper. And, of course," he jingled the loose change in his pocket, narrowed his eyes and looked challengingly at me, "if you don't like it, you can always leave."

Funny he should say that because my wife, Sandra, was always on at me to leave Fraddon's.

"Why don't you get yourself a job that pays a decent wage?" she grumbled when I got home, late as usual, one evening. "What you earn isn't enough to keep me in shoes and handbags."

252   Paula Williams

I stopped myself from pointing out that David Beckham probably didn't earn enough to keep her in shoes, handbags and anything else that took her fancy. It would only have caused an argument and Sandra doesn't like arguments when she's having one of her heads.

"That Roger Fraddon takes advantage of you," she said as I placed her supper tray – two eggs, lightly boiled, with bread and butter soldiers with the crusts cut off – on her lap so that she could watch *EastEnders*.

But how could I leave Fraddon's when there was old Bert Netherton to consider? Bert was night watchman at a disused fish-packing factory that Roger's father Arnold (now sadly no longer with us, having suffered a massive heart attack in the arms of the local floozy back in 1997) had once taken in lieu of payment on a re-roofing job that went over budget.

If I left, Roger, who was a bit casual when it came to what he contemptuously described as the "boring bits" of the business, such as staff welfare, wages and benefits, would look into files he hadn't looked in for years, discover the fish factory and want to develop it as luxury living for the discerning executive in a prime waterfront location. Poor old Bert would be history.

So I stayed – even when Roger took advantage not of me but my Sandra. Not that she minded being taken advantage of, because one Thursday morning, when I was up to my ears in lintels and roof trusses, it being the annual stocktake, she packed all her shoes and handbags and anything else she could stuff into half a dozen suitcases and moved in with Roger.

Things were surprisingly pleasant after Sandra and her shoes moved out. Not only did I gain space in the wardrobe, it meant I never had to watch another episode of *EastEnders* or *The Apprentice* ever again. I also started spending time at Bert's. Sitting on his front porch, watching the sun go down across the water, was very relaxing after a long day at the office.

After that, things rubbed along smoothly enough for a few years and nothing much changed at work, apart from the fact that I stopped asking Roger for a rise. I figured that now he had to keep

Sandra in shoes and handbags, he probably needed the money more than I did.

But I was worried about the company's financial future. Before Sandra moved in with him, Roger used to work long hours, particularly when it came to drumming up new business.

But even a glorified bookkeeper like myself knows that if you don't put in the hours, and you take more out of the business than you put in, then things don't look too good in the long term.

Which is why I was surprised when Roger called me into his office one day.

"You've been a loyal servant to the company, Trevor," he began in an unusually formal tone of voice that made my heart sink because the "you've been a loyal servant" bit is usually followed by the "but we're going to have to let you go" bit. And then the "this hurts me more than it hurts you" bit.

But it didn't happen like that. "Which is why I'm giving you a long-overdue promotion," he went on. "How does Finance Director sound? And there'll be a company car, of course, and a salary to match your new status."

My new status? I was astounded. Pleased, too, of course, but more than a little worried. That's not the sort of behaviour I've learned to expect from Roger and I couldn't help wondering what had brought about this sudden change of heart.

Could it mean— ? My mouth went dry and my palms began to sweat. Oh, no, surely not. Could it mean things were over between Roger and Sandra and she was packing her six suitcases, or probably more likely ten by now, and heading back to the marital home as we spoke?

But I needn't have worried because Sandra didn't come back. And Roger began spending even more time away from the business and I got on with my job in the same old way.

But I was getting increasingly concerned about the company's financial position, and every day I was taking calls from unhappy suppliers demanding to know when they were going to be paid as the bank balance was sinking further and further into the red.

"I'm out there getting new business," Roger said when I tried to tell him about the company's cash-flow problems. "In spite of what you may think, it's not all wining and dining and funny handshakes. It's damn hard work. So you do your job and leave me to do mine."

He turned to go but I called after him. "That large withdrawal you made last week," I said. "The bank says—"

He whirled round, his face flushed with anger.

"Listen," he said as if talking to a less than bright child. "You get back to counting beans or whatever it is you count and leave the higher financial stuff to me. I need hardly remind you, Trevor, that the title of Finance Director is, in your case, what they call a courtesy title. You leave the real directing of finance to me. OK?"

So that's exactly what I did. Until, that is, the day there was a knock on my office door and two grim-faced police officers stood there.

"Mr Trevor Pringle?" said the younger one, whose ears could have been used to direct taxiing aircraft. "We've a warrant to search your offices. We have reason to believe a major fraud has been perpetrated here."

"F-fraud?" I stammered, while my insides turned to water.

"If we could just go through your contracts files," he said. "We've been following the activities of this company for some time. It seems you've been putting in false tenders for council work, defrauding the local taxpayers out of tens, maybe hundreds, of thousands of pounds in the last eighteen months."

"I think you've made a mistake," I said, handing them the keys to my filing cabinet. "Mr Fraddon has some good contacts on the council but all the contracts have been won fair and square. He'd never do something like this."

"We know that, Mr Pringle. That's why we're here. Mr Fraddon has owned up to the odd irregularity, but it's not him we're after. It's your name on the contracts. You're the Finance Director, and I think you'd better see about getting yourself a decent lawyer. It looks like you're going to need one."

The police were quite right. I had committed a fraud. But where they'd got it wrong was that it wasn't against the local taxpayers but against Roger.

All those years ago, when he'd refused me a rise, made me work all those hours for peanuts, then stolen my wife and rubbed my nose in it, I, the bean counter in charge of the payroll, invented this old chap called Bert Netherton, gave him the job of night watchman at the old long-forgotten fish factory and began paying his modest wages into a bank account I'd set up in his name.

I'd always intended that, one day, Trevor Montgomery Pringle would disappear and I'd start a new life as Bert Netherton. I just hadn't planned on doing it quite so soon.

But when Roger's little scheme to get me to carry the can for his fraud kicked off, Trevor Pringle walked out of the office that Tuesday evening, never to be seen again – and Bert Netherton came to life.

That was five years ago now and I'm very happy here in Bert Netherton's ramshackle cottage, living the quiet life and enjoying watching the sun set over the salt marshes each night, with only the sea birds for company.

I'll have to move out soon, though, because I've just had a letter to say that Fraddon and Son (Construction) Limited are going into Receivership and all the staff are being laid off. I hear, too, that Roger Fraddon has had to sell his posh house and fancy cars.

I shall be all right though. Bert made some sound investments over the years and has a tidy sum tucked away, more than enough to buy a modest little bungalow down by the estuary that'll do me nicely.

As for the police, they've still got Trevor Pringle's name on file, of course, but they're not looking for him quite so hard since they received an anonymous tip off about a secret bank account that contained the proceeds of the council contracts fraud.

Poor old Roger never was much good at planning ahead, a necessary attribute for a successful fraudster. In order to stay out of jail, he'd had to deny all knowledge of the account, which meant he never got his grubby little paws on a single penny of his ill-gotten gains.

As for Sandra, she's left him and last I heard was living with a shoe salesman from Norwich and is, I imagine, as happy as she'll ever be.

So why am I writing this confession? Well, I have a lot of time for reading now – not to mention birdwatching, painting and listening to music – and it says in this book I've just finished about how confession is good for the soul so I thought I'd give it a try.

Writing this has taken longer than I thought and the evening has grown quite chilly while I've been sitting here. I think I'll light the fire. I scrunch up a piece of paper and toss it on to the kindling. Then I strike a match and hold my hands towards the flames, watching as the words I've just written writhe and twist before they disappear in a shower of sparks up the chimney.

What do you know? It works. The fire is drawing well and it feels good. The book was right after all. Well, nearly right. Confession, it seems, really is good for the coal.

TEN BELLS AT ROBBIE'S

Tony Black

THING ABOUT UNCLE Barry is eys no quite fukn right in the heid. Eys a scripto mad cunt the bastard tae tell the truth. Haufwey tae no bein the full fukn note, if ye ken what a mean.

Soas ahm straight wi ye, by the by, eys no ma real uncle. Ah ken that cos he's gein it tae ma maw. Ah rummilt the pair ay them years back, afore ah goat pit away likes, fukn at it like dugs so they wur, didnae even ken ahd clocked them ... uncle ma baws.

Ah tells him, the other night there ... stroll the fuk on wi yer heid the baw plans. Like ahm fir pleyin shoatie whilst that bawjaws is pittin eys bits intae fukn Scotbet.

Scotbet, aye, fuk tae fuk ... boy's scripto. Telt ye.

Ah but, wee man ... it's a piece ay pish, so it is. Ey goes.

Way tae fuk ... piece ay pish. Ye'll get fukn turned ower, think they're no set up fir that caper. Think they'll no clock ye strollin in there wi a pair ay Pretty fukn Pollys oan yer napper and flick a button fir the polis ... Away tae fuck, ya radge.

He gauns all cranky but, pittin oot that big fukn lip ay his. Eys goat een lik dugs' baws nawtae ... Ah think eys gonae stert greetin oan us. Widnae put it past him, fukn nut-joab thit ey is.

C'mon, Davie lad ... aws ahm askin is ye keep shoatie oot the back. Gis a wee blast oan the horn there if the polis or onay cunt shows. Ahm telling ye Rab fae the flats telt eys they're drawin some fukn poppy in there ... we'll be fukn laughin.

Tae fuk, man.

Ahm pure heyin nane ay it. Man's a fukn radge ... Standin ower Scotbet oan Leith fukn Walk fir fuksake. Ah gis him the haun, ken thon Trisha wan like they dae oan the telly and ahm gaun, talk tae the haun, talk tae the fukn haun. Ey disnae like that wan wee bit. Sparks up tae fuk. Should be taking eys prescription so ey should, ah ken eys no been ... far too fukn radge so ey is. Eys awa wi it, man. Ah shit ye not.

Ahhh ... might ay kent you'd hey nae boatil, Davie ... nae boatil fir the likes ay this. So ey says.

Whit's that supposed tae mean? Goat me a bit rattled that has, kens where all the buttons are likesay. Eys mental, but a right smart cunt nawtae.

Means whit it means, ey goes tae us.

Ahm no heyin this. Ey kens ah've goat tae clock in wi the proba-tioner every other fukn week ... eys at it. Kens ahm pleyin it cool the now, kens, normally like, ah catch any cunt getting wide wi us they'd be fukn leathert ... But like ah say, ahm big fukn Mr Frosty the noo. Goat tae be likesay ... ahm no gaun back inside. Fuk that all tae fuk.

Whit ye sayin, Barry? Sayin ahm some kind ay fukn pussy?

He does that shrug thing. Puts eys heid tae wan side and huffs. Ah watch him pittin the eye oan me and then he gobs oan the road. Ahm no heying this cunt makin oot ahm a fukn fannybaws. Cannae hey that. It's like day wan in the jail, goat tae gaun in smackin heids or ye'll get the erse rode aff ye worse than any Calton Hill rent boy. Shittin blood through the eye ay a fukn needle every day and night ay yer stretch ... fuk that tae fuk.

Alls ahm sayin is, Davie lad, that if ye had the baws ye wouldnae be shittin it.

That's me. Oaf the fukn page. Ah goes fir the cunt.

Shittin it ... whaes fukn shittin it, ya cunt?

Ah goes tae panel the cunt, but there's something stoping me, wouldnae be right tae ley intae yer uncle ... even though he's no ma uncle and eys gien a length oot tae ma maw. Ah stoaps masel in time, just kindae pushes intae him an sticks ma chest oot and that. Like they used tae dae at the skill. It's all pure daft as fuk and ey laughs it up. Ahm seeing red but, pure ready tae lamp the cunt ... even though a cannae, and dinnae.

Davie lad ... whit ahm ah thinkin? 'Course you've goat the baws ... we say ten bells at the Robbie's Bar?

Fukn right. Ahm there ...

Afore ah know it, that's me hauled intae anither wan ay Bad Barry's bawjaws plans. Ah'm up tae ma fukn nuts in all kinds ay shite awready wi the cunt and eys goat me farmin oot a shooter tae him, wan some cunt goat plugged wi no log ago doon Burdiehoose wey.

Ma maw would kick ma cunt if she kent. Pure kick Barry's nawtae.

So ahm staunin oot the back ay Scotbet watchin oor Barry pit the fukn tights ower eys heid and eys pure spraffin away like a mentaller ... oaf that medication, likes. Been that wey fir weeks, no supposed tae be a day aff the fukn Harry Hills but there eys fukn blowin eys heid aff wi the puff, powerin intae the Caly Specials and, fuk tae fuk, knockin ower Scotbet cos wee fukn Rab eys pal says there's bags ay poppy just sittin aboot.

Man's a pure cunt. But what can ye dae? Eys femly. Well, likesay, ma maw calls him femly ... Uncle Barry, isn't ey? Ah ken, eys a fannyrat. Ah ken eys... whit d'ye cry it nawtae... bio-fukn-polar, and eys no taking eys pills and that ... But man alive, it's no like eys ma faither. Ah dinnae owe the cunt fukn fuk all. Reallys, ah dinnae.

Ahm sittin at the fit ay the Walk and ah've goat the keys in the motor, nice fukn set ay wheels nawtae, big fukn 4x4 some horsey fukn square-peg cow left in Tesco car park wi the fukn keys in ... easy as fukn shootin fukn fish in a fukn barrel. Ahm waiting tae hear the shooter ah gied Barry go aff, or see some cunt come running oot the bookie's but there's fuk all gaun doon. There's nae fukn noise at all, except some auld jakey cunt pishin himsel and singing "Danny fukn Boy". Fuk me.

C'moan, Barry y'cunt ... whaur the fuk are ye?

Ahm gettin a wee bit restless now, beginning tae think this cunt's goat himself too fukn jaked tae pull this aff, that some cunt's panelled him in the heid and eys leyin oan the flair like some big fukn polar bear rug or sumthin wi every cunt in the place staunin ower him scratchin their heids. And then, fuk me, right oot ay naewhur it's fukn Barry chankin it doon the Walk and shouting tae get the fukn motor stertit.

Davie, y'fukn radge … Get they fukn wheels movin.

There's folk watchin, ah've telt this cunt afore aboot using ma fukn handle oan a joab but eys no gien two fuks … It's they pills ay his, needs tae get fired intae they pills and get eys fukn heid sortit. Ma maw said as much … Big daft cunt that ey is. Ahm pure ragin at the cunt so ah am.

Get the fukn door shut, Barry, I tell the cunt as he gets in the motor wi the bag and the shooter oot.

Ahm blastin the cunt fir using ma handle and ahm spinning they fukn tyres like fukn Pete fukn Tong oan the decks, but Barry's away wi the fukn pixies oan this massive fukn belter ay a high …

Shouldae seen the cunts man, faces oan them … pure fukn shittin it they wur, he goes.

Whit aboot the poppy? How much we get?

Uncle Barry's too fukn hypo tae gie two fuks aboot the poppy, eys fukn gaun scripto, eys jumpin oot eys heid n'all that. Ah have tae take the shooter aff the cunt, put it in ma jaicket pocket and tell him tae calm it fukn doon or ah'll be leyin intae the cunt. He disnae settle but. Cunt's radge. Pure mental.

Whit a fukn rush that wis, Davie … whit a fukn rush. Ah could dae anither yin! Ey says that like eys just had a fukn Chinkie or sumthin, no robbed a fukn bookie's. Eys totally fukn serious nawtae. Scanning aboot, taking a sketch oot the windae fir another fukn Scotbet.

Are you aff yer fukn scone? Ah says.

Naw … naw … serious, man. Oan a fukn roll so am are.

Ah take a deck at the cunt and eys fukn roarin oot the windae and screamin and gaun half fukn caked oot his nut, and ahm thinkin, whit the fuk is this cunt oan? Man needs eys fukn heid seein tae … Ma maw said the likes.

There's wan there, there's wan there, Davie. The cunt's clocked anither Scotbet – fukn rarin tae go nawtae.

C'moan, Davie ... pull ower, we'll dae anither wan.

He hauns me the bag wi the poppy ... There's aboot twenty grannies in there, ahm thinkin. Ah could fuk aff and get maself set up wi that, oot ma maw's hair fir guid. That's whit she needs, some peace and fukn quiet ... no all this shite wi me jist oot the jail and under her feet and Uncle fukn Barry aff eys Harry Hills.

C'moan, Davie ... c'moan, Davie ...

The cunt's up fir it. Fukn surein ey is. Fukn een sittin oan fukn stalks so they are ... eys goat this big red fukn set ay cheeks oan him nawtae. Looks like that fukn Hell Boy cunt. Radge is just as fukn daft likesay. Ah canne dey it but, eys femly and ye look efter yer femly don't ye? Ey is femly, kindae ... ah ken eys no ma faither and ah ken eys no even ma fukn proper uncle n'all that, really ... but femly's femly.

Awright, Barry ... get yerself oot the motor.

The cunt stomps oot, eys like a fukn dug wi two dicks, fukn rarin tae go so ey is ... pure shoutin at me fir the shooter. Fukn shooter some cunt fae Burdiehoose goat plugged wi, mind ey disnae ken that. So ahm oot the 4x4 and ahm telling him tae cool the fukn beans right doon. Eys gonae gie himsel a hert attack if ey disnae keep the heid.

Aye, aye ... gis the fukn gun, Davie, ey gauns.

So ahm passing the gun ower and eys getting the Pretty fukn Pollys oot again and telling me tae keep shoatie like the last time. Aye, aye, ahm gaun, and ahm thinking this cunt's away wi the fukn dizzy dippits. Needs proper fukn medical attention n'all that. Shouldnae be aff they Harry fukn Hills likes ah say. And ahm femly, well, likes as close as much, and ah need tae dae the right thing by the cunt. But mair so, ma maw. Ah need tae gie ma maw a breck here.

There ye go, Barry ... here's the shooter, mate. Now, mind ... keep the heid, eh? ah goes.

Eys oaf like a fukn rat up a drainpipe, disnae even look at eys. Just grabs the shooter and eys aff. Ah gie him tae the end ay the pavement thit eys taking like a fukn whippet, time tae get ootside the Scotbet, before ah tip the bullets ah took oot the shooter. Ah mean, cannae hey some cunt being shot if things gaun erse ower tit. Ah could've been a right cunt and left them in the fukn gun, ah mean, ah could, but ah didnae, cos ahm the kind ay cunt looks oot fir folk ... looks oot fir eys femly n'all that, eh?

Best move all round, Davie, ah says tae masel. Best move, aye, aye ...

Ah pulls open the phone box door in a oner. Goat the handle thing in ma haun as Barry steps intae Scotbet.

Eh, polis, please ... I want tae report a robbery in progress.

WILKOLAK

Nina Allan

K IP KNEW THE man was the monster as soon as he saw him. He was coming out of the convenience store attached to the garage at the bottom end of Lee High Road, his shopping in an old Tesco bag. Kip uncapped the Nikon and took his picture; the click of the shutter release sounded loud to him, even above the noise of the passing traffic. Kip lowered the camera, suddenly afraid the man might turn and see him, but that didn't happen. Instead, the man crossed the garage forecourt, ignoring the cars parked at the pumps and heading off up the road in the direction of Lewisham. He was of medium height, but skinny, with gangling limbs and a jutting Adam's apple, and reminded Kip of Tom Courtenay in *The Loneliness of the Long Distance Runner*. He wore tatty old Levis, and an army surplus jacket that was too big for him around the shoulders. He seemed lost in thought, cocooned in it, shut off from his surroundings, from Kip, from everything.

Kip raised the Nikon again and took half a dozen more shots in quick succession. Later, at home in his room, he downloaded the images to his hard drive, storing them in a file he tagged as *monster*. A fortnight ago an eight-year-old girl from Marischal Road had gone missing on her way home from school. The girl's name was Rebecca Riding. Her body was discovered a week later in a disused mobile home on the Isle of Sheppey. She had been raped and then suffocated. The police issued a photo fit of a man they wanted to question, a man with thinning hair and a scrawny build, and teachery little wire-framed glasses. The police said he was probably in his early forties, and living in the Lewisham area. Kip thought the man in the photo fit looked like a school nerd gone bad. He also looked exactly like the bloke he had seen coming out of the garage on Lee High Road. Kip remembered the man's walk, slightly knock-kneed, the Tesco bag bumping against his thigh as he moved along.

The tabloids had already dubbed him the Manor Park Monster.

Kip selected one of the photos and printed it out, the best one, showing the man's face in profile like the double agent in a spy movie. It was the kind of photo you could imagine flashing up on the TV news, or on the front page of the next day's papers. Rebecca Riding had been all over the news, always the same photo, a blonde kid with a demon smile and one of her top front teeth missing. Rebecca Riding had gone missing just before the start of the holidays and at school her name quickly became that summer's catchphrase: *What do you get if you cross Rebecca Riding with a rubber glove? What did Rebecca Riding's dad say when the cops asked him why his trousers were at the cleaner's?* The jokes were disgusting but you couldn't help laughing at them. One dork had laughed so hard Kip thought he was going to piss himself. Kip didn't want to think about the murder. It was the photograph of the murderer that interested him, some loser with a plastic carrier bag crossing the street. The image might seem ordinary but Kip knew it wasn't, that the very act of framing the man in his viewfinder and then choosing to release the shutter made the picture significant. The main point of a photo-graph was to invite you to *look*, to concentrate on the world around you a little harder. The photographer recreated the world in the way he saw it, and in this, Kip supposed, he was the master of his universe. A guy who worked for the *Star* and who had once come to the school to give a talk on photojournalism said that all photogra-phers were grubby-handed alchemists, pier-end magicians – words that stuck in Kip's mind like splinters of glass. Now that he had the photograph in front of him Kip found he didn't really care whether the man was the monster or not. The point seemed to be that he *could* be. He could just as easily be a hero. If you mounted a photo on a nice ground and gave it an interesting title then anybody could be anything.

He shut down his computer and went downstairs. The television was on in the back room, his mother slumped at the end of the sofa watching *The Weakest Link*. She was folding and unfolding a tea towel, one of the souvenirs she had brought back from their holiday in Tenby three years before. It had the Welsh dragon on it, in red.

"Your father won't be home for supper," she said. "He has work to finish."

"OK," Kip said. He sat down beside her, his eyes on the screen, careful not to look at her directly. This was a game they played together all the time now. She would tell him his father was working late at the site, and he would pretend to believe her and not care less. He would ignore the bunched, grasping look of her hands, her puffy eyes, and concentrate on Anne Robinson torturing a bank clerk from Cleethorpes over the identity of the currency of Argentina.

The thing he was not supposed to know but had known for six months was that his father was having an affair; that on at least three evenings a week Andrzej Kiplas would knock off work early and drive over to Streatham, where he would spend an unspecified number of hours with a woman named Grace Hemingway. Kip didn't know who she was or how his father had met her. Sometimes he imagined her as one of the peroxide Pirelli blondes on the calendar in the site Portakabin; at other times he saw her as a mousy little librarian with a flat full of dusty books, like the women in films by Wajda or Kieslowski.

Andy Kiplas sometimes didn't return until ten, eleven o'clock. On the nights when this happened, Kip would slope off to his room as soon as he heard his father's key in the lock. There would be a short interval without much happening, then his mother would start crying or his father shouting or both. This usually went on for about an hour. Then everything would go quiet, and later he would hear the headboard banging against the wall in his parents' bedroom.

Andy Kiplas was almost fifty, but his body was still lean and hard from his work on the site. Kip's mother Lynn was like an overblown rose. When she smiled and if the lighting was right she could still be beautiful, her heaviness transformed into a pink softness that put him in mind of strawberries, candyfloss, September sunsets. But when she was unhappy she turned pallid as lard.

Kip itched to photograph her. With her inflamed eyelids and the
ragged cloth in her hands she looked like a war victim, one of the
refugee women in the immigrant camps outside Calais. Sometimes
on evenings like this Kip would stay downstairs and play cards with
her, or backgammon. At some point during the game Lynn would
get up from her seat and pour them both a vodka, a double
Zubrowka straight from the freezer. The fumes rose up in a smoky
cloud as she unscrewed the cap.

"One little nip can't hurt you," she would say. She had been
saying that since he was thirteen. "Don't you go telling your
teachers." She would laugh then, a raucous, ribald sound, the same
laugh she used with her friends on the phone and that Kip loved to
hear. She would knock back her vodka in one, and two bright tears
would appear, squeezing like liquid crystal from the corners of her
eyes.

They sparkled there, jewel-bright, on the rims of her cheeks. Kip
wondered what he would do if she cried for real. No matter how
much he loved her he still hated her need of him, the way her fingers
twisted together when she told him the pointless lies about his
father.

The only thing to do was pretend not to notice. Once the truth
was out in the open it would be impossible for either of them to put
it back.

They ate supper off a tray, watching the news.

"I'm going out later," Kip said.

"Where to?" Lynn said. She glanced up from her plate. Her food
was still mostly untouched. "I don't want you roaming the streets
half the night, not with that man on the loose."

"I'm only going to Sonia's. I won't be late."

"Well, make sure you catch the bus coming home." She took her
plate through to the kitchen and Kip heard her scraping her supper
into the waste bin. It was the first time she had mentioned the
monster, at least to him. He thought it was probably her way of
trying to stop him from going out and leaving her by herself.

* * *

"I don't know," Sonia said. "It could be him, I suppose." She held the photograph in both hands, tilting it against the light. "They all look the same though, those photo fits. Just think how awful it would be for this man if you got it wrong."

They were sitting on the grass behind the garage in Sonia's garden. Sonia's hair was drawn back off her face in a ponytail. Loose strands glimmered at the nape of her neck like copper wire.

"I suppose," Kip said. There was a number you could ring, a police hotline. On the way over to Sonia's he had tried to imagine what would happen if he called it and told the cop at the other end that he had seen the monster. They would ask for his name and address, that would be the first thing, and later on they would make him hand over the photograph. He supposed it was evidence of a kind, evidence that linked him with the monster. The idea was disturbing, not so much because the link existed as because it might become known. Sonia's uncertainty about the photograph was a relief because it seemed to free him from the obligation of having to do anything.

He leaned in over her shoulder, pretending to look at the photo but in reality just wanting to get closer to her. She smelled of the coarse-grained pine soap the Vardens had in their upstairs bathroom. He imagined her at the sink, her bare feet on the coconut matting. The Vardens' house was like that, all polished wood and cream-coloured walls. Sonia went to Forest Hill Girls' School. Sonia's father Timothy had a good job in the City.

"I really like this photo though," Sonia was saying. "Can I keep it?"

"'Course you can," Kip said. "What are you going to do with it?"

"Nothing." She laughed. "I just like it, that's all. He looks lonely, don't you think? The kind of man who's always alone." She was still studying the picture, as if she had come upon it by chance in a magazine and was trying to decide whether she should cut it out or not. The way she looked at the photograph made him feel strange, weightless, as in the moments before an orgasm. There was part of himself that wished he had not shown it to her, that felt convinced it was dangerous. And yet the idea that she would want to keep something he had made, that she could like it that much, made his insides hurt.

He began to count the freckles on the back of her neck, concentrating hard to stop himself getting an erection. The freckles were red, like her hair, the glinting vermilion of the jagged patches of rust on the disused water tank around the back of the school toilets.

He'd had sex with Sonia twice, once up in Oxleas Woods, and once in her bedroom, when her parents were out for the day at some barbecue or other. The thought of being with her in her parents' house had made him almost sick with excitement, but it turned out not to be such a good idea. Every time a car went by on the street outside he thought it was the Vardens, returning home early. The time in the woods had been better. Sonia held his cock, clasping it in her fist and moving her hand cautiously up and down, as if she was afraid she might hurt him. He came too soon of course, but at least he managed to get inside her. He thought it would be embarrassing afterwards, trying to think of things to say, but it had been fine. Better than fine, in fact. They put their clothes back on and lay in the grass, watching planes soar in low overhead on their approach to Heathrow and talking about TV shows they had liked when they were younger. By the end of the afternoon he felt comfortable around Sonia in a way that went far beyond just wanting to fuck her.

He couldn't imagine what had driven the monster to fuck an eight-year-old. Almost the best part of sex with Sonia was knowing that she wanted it too, and that she liked him enough to want to spend time with him afterwards.

The rape of Rebecca Riding was something he was ashamed to think about, as if thinking about it somehow made him a part of what had happened. Had the monster killed the girl in the end because he wanted to cover his tracks, or because he could no longer stand the sound of her screaming? To erase what he had done, like pulling the wings off a fly and then crushing it beneath your thumb to put it out of its misery.

A crime like the monster's was so bad it had its own thumbprint, its own identity. If Kip thought about it hard enough he could feel it beginning to infect his imagination, cell by cell, like mildew creeping and spreading on a damp wall.

His stomach turned over at the thought, the same way it did when you went to pour milk in your tea and found it had gone off. He remembered seeing some kids once, larking around on a building site, using a broken-off branch to fish a dead rat out of a rain puddle. They had flicked the rat up in the air, then run away screaming as it plopped down again in the water. The memories repelled him and yet they persisted. You couldn't not watch them playing with the rat, couldn't not smell the curdled milk in its plastic container, even though it would make your guts heave and you knew that perfectly well before you started.

So long as you weren't forced to drink the milk or pick up the rat in your bare hands, it was okay. It was interesting even. The rat he remembered especially, because he had been back to the building site later to photograph it.

He leaned forward and kissed Sonia's neck. A strand of her loose hair tickled his lips, and a wisp of his own breath came back at him, rebounding off her skin in a puff of warm air.

She turned in his arms and kissed him. Her saliva tasted faintly of orange juice.

"I'll have to go in, in a minute. I'm supposed to be writing an essay on nuclear power."

"That's OK," Kip said. "I'll text you later." He stood up from the grass. He wondered when he would next get to have sex with her, then wondered if that was how it was for his father with Grace Hemingway. The idea of his father thinking about sex unsettled him even more than the thought of the rat.

"Thanks for the photo," said Sonia. "I'll buy a clip frame for it tomorrow."

"Be careful," Kip said, and then wondered what the hell he was on about. It was just a stupid photograph, nothing to be careful of there. He hurried away, leaving via the side gate without turning back, not wanting her to see that he was blushing.

He caught the bus from outside the old Capitol cinema on the London Road. He climbed up to the top deck, where he sat alone

apart from a gaunt and elderly black man reading a *Metro*. It was
just about beginning to get dark. Kip looked out at the amethyst
sky, the latticework of interlinked streets, shop fronts and garage
forecourts, the chequered fabric of gardens and railway lines. He
saw London as a labyrinth, with no way out. Even if you fled to the
edge, to the boundary posts at Morden or Edgware, there would
still be more roads, more alleyways, more cemeteries. *It was the
kingdom of the Manor Park Monster*. Kip wondered where in his
kingdom the monster was hiding at that moment.

The streetlights were coming on all over town, and soon it would
be dark for real. He got off the bus opposite the garage. Lee High
Road smelled of diesel fumes and dying hydrangeas. When he got
home he discovered his father had arrived there before him. The
back door was standing open into the garden. Lynn and Andy
Kiplas sat together at the kitchen table with their elbows touching.
Lynn was laughing, small creases at the corners of her eyes. Kip
looked at his father, not speaking. Andy Kiplas glanced quickly
away, then asked Kip if he would like a beer.

Kip saw the monster again three days later in Manor Park
Gardens. Some people thought that this was where Rebecca Riding
had gone missing, but it wasn't so. Manor Park Gardens was a land-
scaped park with a lake and ornamental waterfowl, popular with
families and joggers. As a kidnapping site it was close to useless. Kip
reckoned the only time you could get yourself kidnapped from the
gardens would be first thing in the morning before it got busy, but
even then there were the groundsmen and the dog walkers,
commuters using the park as a cut-through to Lee station.

Rebecca Riding had been abducted at around 3.30 in the
afternoon, not from Manor Park Gardens but from Manor Park
itself. Manor Park was a rough triangle of land sandwiched between
Weardale Road and Manor Lane, hemmed in on one side by a
swampy and narrow section of the River Quaggy. Sometimes you
would see rubbish floating in the water and once there had been a
child's tricycle but Kip liked Manor Park because it was quiet, the
tall terraces of Manor Lane backing directly on to the tussocky
grass and stands of nettles like the last, abandoned houses in a

zombie movie. Kip liked to photograph these houses, even though someone in one of the flats there had once leaned out of the window and called him a Peeping Tom.

This was the first time he had been back to Manor Park since Rebecca Riding's abduction. He had wondered if the place were still being treated as a crime scene but if there had ever been police tape or anything else of that kind it was gone now. To Kip the park seemed unnaturally quiet, *expectant*, but he knew he was probably imagining it. He took some photos of the park railings and the children's play area, hoping that no one would see him doing it and wishing he knew exactly where the abduction had taken place. He knew his interest in the monster was growing. He disliked this feeling, distrusted it, but was unable to let it go. He would have liked to discuss it with Sonia but was afraid she might start to think he was weird, one of the lonely serial-killer types who bought true-crime magazines and hung around Cromwell Road and the corner of the modern housing estate that had once been Rillington Place. The day after he gave her the photograph of the monster, Sonia told him an obscure theory some crime writer had concocted about how a famous English painter was really Jack the Ripper. The theory was connected with art, though, so it seemed it was all right to talk about it.

The monster was not connected with anything. He was just a monster.

Kip came out on to Manor Lane and crossed quickly into Manor Park Gardens. The sky was a high, dense blue, the sun dripped white light on the water. People sprawled on their backs in the grass, reading paperback thrillers. Kip knew he was invisible here. It was even OK to take pictures. He took a few shots of the fountain, a Dalmatian dog, some kid on a skateboard, but he knew already that the photos would not be much good. The park was not his thing. He preferred the tatty shop fronts and crumbling façades of the terraces on Lee High Road. He turned to go, walking across the grass in the direction of the park exit on Old Road. Then he saw the monster, sitting on one of the benches facing the lake.

He stopped where he was, raising the Nikon cautiously as if afraid the man might take flight, then fired off seven, eight shots, using the zoom lens to capture him in profile. As he lined up the final frame the man turned his head slightly, giving Kip a better view of his face. Seeing him again, Kip thought he looked less like the photo fit, less like a cornered rat and more like a ruined accountant who had just been fired. It was definitely him, though. Kip recognized him by his jacket. He appeared to be watching the ducks, plump mallards, a male and three females, dipping in and out of their limber reflections in a way that made the real ducks look blockish and unnatural as decoys. Kip wandered slowly in his direction, pretending to look at the lake. There were three children on the wooden landing stage, throwing bread crusts from a plastic bag. A horde of ducks surged towards them across the water. Kip slipped the Nikon back into its case and sat down on the bench. He watched the children, who had started to argue over who was in charge of the bread, and smoothed the leather case of the Nikon with the tips of his fingers. The park was full of people – onlookers, witnesses – and yet he could not escape the thought that he had put himself at risk somehow by coming here.

He turned to glance at the man beside him. He tried to make the glance seem casual, but was aware even as he did so that the movement was too rigid, too snatched, to appear anything but unnatural, the inept glance of a spy who was new on the job. The monster was staring right at him. His eyes were grey, the colour of tap water with a single drop of black ink dispersed in it. His expression was perfectly calm.

"Hello," he said. "I've seen you before, I'm sure. You're the boy with the camera."

Kip seemed to feel two worlds colliding, the world he saw through the lens of the Nikon spinning and crashing through the wall of reality like a wrecking ball through the shell of a condemned tower block. He noted the monster's clean, almost polished-looking nails, the small scar at the corner of his mouth that made it look as if someone had cut him there once with a razor blade. The idea that he was the watched instead of the watcher was enormous and fundamental and somehow awful.

He felt the air go out of his lungs, as if the world had expanded outwards, crushing his chest. Oddly enough it was the same feeling he'd had the first time he saw Sonia's naked breasts.

"I'm going to be a photographer," he said at last. "That's why I have the camera."

He saw the man's lips twitch, and Kip waited for him to laugh at him, or else demand to see the photographs he had taken. That was what people did, if they were interested at all that was, and then Kip would either have to refuse or hand over the Nikon, let the man see the multiple images of himself that were now locked inside the camera's memory, that final close-up, the sunlight flashing off his glasses and into the water.

Instead of asking to look at the pictures the monster smiled, his ridged and slightly yellowed incisors clearly visible.

"I thought as much," he said. "I recognized the signs, you see." He leaned back on the bench, his arms locked across his chest, his skinny wrists snaking out from the sleeves of his army jacket. Kip could not tell if the man was trying to patronize him in some way or if they were having a proper conversation.

"What do you mean?" he said. "The signs?"

"I mean I was the same at your age. Things were different then of course, none of this digital rubbish. I had a Minolta SR-7 and it weighed a ton. I didn't give a damn about that though. I took it everywhere with me. I got so used to the weight of it around my neck I felt wrong without it. Have you ever used film? A film camera I mean, rather than digital?"

Kip shook his head. It was a subject that embarrassed him, because his reactions were based on feelings and not experience. He knew that some people were obsessed with film, some of the younger photographers even were obsessed with it, and with something they called the *tangibility of the image*. Kip thought it was a load of crap. He liked to think of the Nikon as an extension of the eye, an optical application, the closest thing to actual seeing that there was. He loved the *cleanness* of digital, its lack of pretension. The idea of film, with its cumbersome processes, the unnecessary delay between the act of taking and the act of seeing, was something he hated.

He might have known the monster would be a film user. Everything about him suggested it, even his clothes.

"Are you a photographer then?" Kip said. "Do you work for the magazines?"

"I used to be. Not for the magazines though. I did other stuff."

"What kind of stuff? Would I know your work?"

"You wouldn't know my work at all. I worked for the police, as a forensic photographer. My work, as you like to call it, has the curious distinction of never having been seen outside a courtroom."

"You mean, you used to go and photograph crime scenes, things like that?"

The monster nodded. "It's not as glamorous as it sounds though, believe me. You see these American cop shows and think it's all about being rushed to the scene of some murder or other. Actually it's about having to get out of bed at two in the morning to take pictures of a sales rep who's managed to get his legs crushed in a motorway collision. It wasn't exactly the career I imagined for myself. Actually I got into it by mistake."

"By mistake?"

"It's a long story."

"Why did you give it up?"

"That's a long story, too. But my dad died last year, left me a bit of money. Not a fortune, but enough to give me some breathing space. You never know, I might even treat myself to a new camera." He sighed and stretched out his arms, cracking his knuckles in a way Kip found nauseating. "You should keep at it," he said. He got up from the bench. "You might even have what it takes."

Kip stared up at him, not moving. He hated the way most adults had of making you feel like a moron, almost as if they resented you for their own failures. It occurred to him that it might all be bullshit anyway, that the monster was trying to lure him with the talk of his defunct Minolta the way he had lured Rebecca Riding with sweets or *Jackie* magazine. Even here he was out of date; most perverts these days used the internet. He wondered why he hadn't used some of his father's money to update his wardrobe.

There was a restlessness that hung from him, baggy and shapeless as his ill-fitting jacket. Kip felt certain he was the killer, as he had felt certain when he first saw the man coming out of the garage. Instead of being afraid he felt a tense, nervous pleasure, knowing that he was ahead of him again, the watcher now instead of the watched.

"I'm Edwin Kiplas," he said suddenly. "Everybody calls me Kip."

"Dennis Croft," said the monster. "I'm sure we'll see each other around."

Croft held out his hand and Kip took it. Croft's hand was dry and rather small, but he had a strong grip, the wiry fingers grasping his own as if he meant to try and stop him getting away. Kip thought of Rebecca Riding and felt a tremor go through him. Then Croft was gone, striding along the tarmac path that skirted the lake then cutting across the grass towards the Manor Park library. Kip watched him merge with the other walkers, become one of them. In less than a minute he was out of sight.

Kip waited ten minutes and then followed him. As he came out of Old Road on to Lee High Road he looked both ways along the street, half convinced that Croft would be lying in wait for him, but there was no sign of him. He wondered what Croft had meant when he said he was sure they would see each other again. His words seemed to hang in the air, like a threat or a curse.

After supper he went to his room and browsed the internet for information about forensic photography. There was a careers website that told him most forensic photographers were non-professionals, police officers with only the most rudimentary training in the use of a camera. Of the others, those who had actually set out to become photographers in the first place, most worked for specialist agencies. Kip supposed that Croft had been employed by one of these agencies; he couldn't imagine him as a cop, of any description. He was too evasive, too much of a loner. You could say he had loner written all over him, that he was a loner archetype.

The agency guys were pretty well paid, because like doctors they were always on call. The careers website listed this as one of the job's main disadvantages, but Kip found he liked the idea. He thought a job that was that unpredictable would be difficult to become bored with. One of the agencies, a firm called Trulite Legal, had posted a series of photos of an office block gutted by fire. The photographer was named as Andrew Watson and the crime was a suspected arson. Kip liked the light in the photos, the strange dead whiteness that made the burned out windows look like portholes into outer space. Most of all he liked the way the pictures showed what was there and didn't tamper with it.

When he Googled Dennis Croft there were no relevant finds.

At a little after 11.30 he heard his mother coming upstairs. It was only then that he realized his father had still not come home. His computer whirred, fanning itself in the darkness. He could sense Lynn outside his door, listening to see if he was still awake. After a moment she sighed and moved away. A floorboard creaked. Kip jumped off his bed and went to open the door. His mother was standing right outside. She gazed at him stolidly, her expression caught midway between surprise and despair.

"You should be in bed," she said. "I thought you were asleep already."

"Where's Dad?" said Kip. The question hovered in the air between them, bobbing weakly like a deflating balloon. The hall light glowed a dull orange, reminding Kip of the light in the Midwestern motel rooms Stephen Shore liked to photograph. Kip stared at Lynn Kiplas in her quilted dressing gown and felt envious of Shore's talent, the way he had of making the most casual Polaroid snapshot look like the opening of a murder mystery. Kip had always hated Lynn's dressing gown, which was made of horrible fake mauve satin and reminded him of some naff sitcom set in an old people's home.

She had clearly been crying. Kip didn't know what he wanted most: to hug her or to slap her face. He became suddenly aware that he was dressed only in his underpants, that he was more or less naked in front of her.

"He's at Toke's," Lynn said. Lyonel Toklin was his father's business partner. "They've been playing cards and drinking, you know what those two are like once they get started. Anyway, he's not fit to drive." Her words sounded stilted, a speech she had prepared beforehand. Kip couldn't decide whether her lying was a sign of courage or idiocy. He took a step towards her, meaning to put his arms around her, but she flinched away as if afraid he might hit her.

"Go to bed now," she said. "And make sure that computer's switched off." She moved away towards the end of the landing. Kip watched her go into the bedroom then closed his own door with a bang. He picked his jeans off the floor and fished his mobile out of the pocket then brought up his father's number and depressed the call button. The call went straight to voicemail, which Kip knew meant precisely nothing. Andy Kiplas didn't like mobiles. He kept his phone on during work hours because it would hurt the business not to but as soon as he was finished for the day he switched it off. For the first time Kip saw this behaviour as thoughtless and selfish.

Andy's pet name for Lynn was the Gipsy Moth.

Kip realized he hadn't called Sonia that day or even messaged her. He supposed that made him as bad as his father. He felt a sudden, almost urgent need to speak to her, not about his father or monster but about Andrew Watson's photos of the burned-out office block, how the pictures looked to him like stills from a documentary about hell.

Still, it was too late to call. He sent a text message instead, *sleep well* and the letter *K* and then an *x*. He did not expect a reply, but a moment later his phone buzzed and there was a text from Sonia, the word *goodnight* accompanied by the little red heart graphic she sometimes used to sign off her messages.

The thought that she was awake and thinking of him made him start to get hard. Right after the second time they had sex he had jokingly asked Sonia what she wore in bed at night, and she had laughed, and said that when the nights were muggy like this she didn't normally wear anything except a pair of knickers.

He put his phone on to charge. He thought of the picture he had given Sonia, the photograph of the monster that she said she was going to mount in a clip frame. The idea of Croft on Sonia's writing desk or bookshelf looking down at Sonia's naked body made him feel queasy, and once again he found himself wishing he had never given her the photograph in the first place.

Two days later Rebecca Riding was on *Crimewatch*. They showed the same photo again, Rebecca Riding in her red school jumper and with the gap between her teeth, and then they staged a reconstruction of what they called her *last known movements*. A small girl wearing a red cardigan came out of the school gates on Manor Lane and trotted along Northbrook Road towards Manor Park. Just before she crossed to the park side she stopped to talk to another girl, a child actress playing the part of Rebecca Riding's friend Tanya Baker. The actress playing Tanya said she had to go home and change out of her school clothes but that she'd meet Rebecca in the park by the swings in ten minutes' time.

Then there was an interview with the parents of the real Tanya Baker. They looked dazed and spoke slowly, like people who had narrowly avoided being involved in a major road accident. After the interview with Tanya's parents they showed the photo fit of the monster again and repeated the number of the police hotline. Any information at all, they said, might turn out to be of vital import-ance in the search for the killer. Kip thought the word *killer* sounded worse even than the word *murderer*. Murder always sounded rather grand, something planned out in advance and with at least the semblance of reason to back it up. Killing was just an action, simple as that. A killer was brutal and thoughtless and probably stupid.

With Dennis Croft it was hard to tell where the murderer left off and the killer began.

"Just think of it," said Lynn Kiplas. "Those poor people."

"I'm going out," Kip said. He left the room quickly, before his mother had a chance to ask where he was going. As he unlatched the front gate he saw his father walking towards him up the road.

"Where are you off to, then?" said Andy Kiplas. "Anywhere exciting?"

"Just out." His father looked clean and smelled fresh, as if he had recently stepped out of the shower. His plaid shirt had been recently ironed. He spoke jauntily, with a kind of mock casualness, and Kip thought of the Toklins' dog, which always expected to be made a fuss of even when it had stolen the Sunday joint right off the table. He tried to imagine how it would be if his father left home, meeting him at the site and going off for supper somewhere, to Pashka's Kitchen in Brockley perhaps, where they would eat potato latkes with apple sauce and his father would tell him in blow-by-blow detail about his latest building project.

He thought he could cope with that. It was going to end up like that anyway when he went to college. But the thought of his mother alone at home made him feel trapped and scared.

He thought of packing his bags and leaving, just him and the Nikon, then realized he would never escape this shit, not even if he went to Australia.

For Christ's sake, Dad, he thought. *It's your problem. Leave me out of it*.

"Fancy a couple of rounds of Harris later?" his father said. Harris was a variant of rummy, something he and Toke had invented. The game was named after Bomber Harris, though the reasons for this had vanished into the past.

"OK, Dad, maybe. I'm not sure what time I'll be back though." He stepped carefully around his father and went off up the street.

"I'll save you a beer, then," Andy Kiplas called after him. Kip didn't answer. He felt for the Nikon around his neck then realized he had come out without it. Not that it mattered much. It was now almost dark, with just a narrow strand of pink chafing the horizon. Kip did not know where he was going exactly, only that he had needed to get out of the house. He decided to walk as far as the Lewisham clock tower and then turn back. Lee High Road was quieter now. The traffic was always lighter after the rush hour, and there were occasional moments of complete hiatus. Kip loved the houses on Lee High Road because they were always interesting to photograph. Most of them were pretty rundown, tottering decrepit terraces constructed from the dirty-looking yellowish brick his father said was called London stock. They reminded him of the Polish war widows in Pashka's, with their camphor-smelling clothes and their vanished hero husbands, their double rows of pearls hidden beneath their moth-eaten cardigans. There were still bomb sites along Lee High Road but not as many now as there had been. Mostly they had been built on. The Lewisham end of Lee High Road had suffered most but even that was being done up. It was all hairdressers and cafés now. Kip fingered the loose change in his pocket, wondering if he had enough for a burger or a sausage sandwich. Men and girls slid by in loud gaggles, pushing aside the darkness with their laughter, the glare from the bars and the street-lamps pooling in orange light slicks on their garish clothes. Kip liked being on the streets at night. There was a restlessness in people, the sense that anything might happen at any time. He wished he had brought the Nikon.

He stopped outside a kebab shop, drawn by the scents of sweet garlic and coriander. The yellow glow from the lighted window spilled out across the grubby pavement in a radiant trapezium, a distorted yellow shadow of the window glass. There were three men up at the counter. They all had their backs to him but one of them seemed vaguely familiar, and as Kip studied his worn-out jacket and tatty Levis he realized with a sudden start that it was Dennis Croft. His gut twisted in a mild spasm, and sweat broke out on his palms.

Distantly, as if it were something he was watching on a movie screen, he saw Croft turn towards the window and beckon him inside.

"Can I stand you a kebab?" Croft said. "They're always good here."

What the heck? Kip thought. *I was about to buy one anyway.* He found it difficult to explain to himself why he had obeyed Croft's summons, only that he was hungry, and that he wanted to see what would happen. Also, he resented the idea that Croft could make him afraid, that he might start avoiding places just because Croft happened to be there. He stood at the man's side at the counter, leaning against the angled glass and staring up at the television mounted on the wall behind. The reception was bad, and the sizzling of meat on the grill made the soundtrack all but inaudible. Kip gazed without much interest at the striking tube workers, the visiting president he had seen already on the early news.

When the picture of the monster appeared it seemed to come out of the blue, although if he had thought about it more carefully he would have realized it was coming. It had been on the early news also, only he had forgotten. If he had remembered he could have done something, turned away from the screen at the crucial moment. He could have watched the traffic outside until the news had finished. It would have been easy.

Now that Croft was there to compare it with, he realized the photo fit was not all that good. The glasses were the wrong shape, and they made the monster's face look squarer than it actually was. Also the real Croft's cheekbones were more pronounced, the eyebrows thinner and less unkempt-looking. He saw that Croft too was staring at the picture. He experienced a sinking feeling, the kind of sick resignation he remembered from all the times he had been handed the results of an exam he already knew he had failed, the dismal knowledge of having been *found out*. The silence between them seemed to deepen and increase, spreading through the air like some poisonous gas. After what seemed like a long time Croft turned to him, smiling the ratty little half-smile Kip remembered from when he had asked him about the Nikon.

"Weird likeness, isn't it?" he said. "I keep expecting them to come and arrest me."

The fry cook was wrapping their kebabs in greaseproof paper, folding it quickly and expertly, the finished parcels like tiny papooses. Croft tore the paper aside almost immediately and bit straight into the middle of his kebab. Kip watched, amazed, wondering how he was able to do that without burning himself. Croft nodded briskly as if in approval and started towards the door. His mouth was smeared with grease, the thin lips glistening. The shop was full now, there were half a dozen people in the queue behind them. The darkness of the street outside seemed deeper and more complete, though Kip knew it was most likely just the contrast with the bright lights inside the kebab shop.

"Your food okay?" Croft said.

Kip nodded. They were walking side by side in the direction of the clock tower. The seconds were passing quickly, and Kip knew he had to say something, that to say nothing would be dangerous, almost as revealing as coming right out and accusing Croft of being the killer. He took a small bite of his kebab. The meat was charred on the outside, pink and tender within. It tasted as delicious as it smelled.

"They all look the same, though, these photo fits, don't they? They could be anyone."

"I know you've been following me," Croft said suddenly. The tone of his voice had changed. There was something mean in it, a glistening menace that made Kip think of tensile steel: tripwires, garrottes. He turned to face Kip, forcing him back against one of the shop fronts. "You were taking pictures of me in the park the other day." He spoke in a harsh whisper, leaning in close, and Kip could smell the garlic on his breath. He stared at Kip fixedly, as if he would have liked to grab hold of him, strike him maybe, as if the effort of not doing so was placing him under a strain. Kip supposed he did not want to draw attention to himself, although no one passing by on the pavement was taking any notice of them and Kip realized they probably thought the monster was his father.

"I take photographs of people all the time. It doesn't mean anything. I don't know what you're talking about." His words came out in a rush, slipping over each other like coins spilling from a beggar's torn pocket. Kip replayed them in his mind more slowly, looking for loopholes. So far as he could tell there weren't any. He decided that so long as he stuck to his story he would be safe.

"Those pictures don't look like you anyway," he added. "It's the glasses, that's all." He looked Croft straight in the eye and thought about his father – the way he would come in from seeing Grace Hemingway and ask what was for supper, and his mother would tell him goulash and Kip would play along with her because he knew his world would explode into pieces if he didn't.

The point was to stick to your story. The murderers in the cop films all knew that and so did his father. It was more a matter of nerve than a matter of fact.

Croft took a step backwards, his face relaxing. Kip laughed to signal that everything was all right between them, and after a couple of seconds Croft laughed too. Kip took more bites from his kebab, still seeing in his mind's eye Croft as he had been moments earlier: the hard line of his mouth, the hollow cheeks, pale in the lamplight, the agitated posture, like that of a beast of prey about to spring.

He had seemed for those few minutes to become something else. At first it was rats Kip thought of, the way a cornered rat could kill a dog if it was desperate enough, or so he had heard. But then he found himself thinking of his Polish grandmother Dasha, and a story she used to tell him when he was younger that she called *The Wolf in Sheep's Clothing*. The story was about a monster that could change its shape at will to blend in with its surroundings. There was a special word she had for it too: *wilkolek*, or maybe *wilkolak*, the Polish word for werewolf. He had forgotten all about it until now.

It came to him that murderers, perhaps child murderers especially, were the ultimate shape-shifters. You could bump against one in the crowd, on the station platform, in a supermarket, and never suspect for a moment that what you were seeing was not an ordinary person but a *wilkolak*. It was only at certain moments that they revealed themselves for what they were. On a darkened street outside a kebab shop, for example. In the nylon-curtained back bedroom of a caravan on the Isle of Sheppey.

He did not believe in werewolves of course, not any more. But he knew the creature he had glimpsed in Croft's eyes was capable of anything.

It was important not to let Croft see that he knew that. It was his certainty over this – a cold feeling, but steady and clear, like the knowledge of his father's affair with Grace Hemingway – that kept him from panic, from simply dropping his kebab on the pavement and running away. He asked himself what he would do, what he would say to Croft now if Croft were not a monster but a human being.

I would talk to him about the murder, he thought. *I would want to find out what he thought.* This answer, the right answer, seemed to light up his mind like one of the illuminated boxes on *The*

Weakest Link. He knew also that it had to be now, right away, while the subject still lay open between them. If he returned to the matter later it would just look weird.

"It makes you think though, doesn't it?" he said. "That guy really is still out there somewhere."

Croft swallowed the last of his kebab then used the greaseproof paper to wipe his fingers. "There are always men like that," he said. "It doesn't matter how many you catch, there will always be more." He crushed the paper between his hands and dumped it into a waste bin at the side of the road. "Do you suppose he's really all that different from you?"

Kip shuddered inside his skin, the kind of quick involuntary movement he sometimes experienced just before falling asleep. It was as if Croft had read his mind, yet the way he had twisted his thoughts, turning them back on themselves so they pointed at him instead of Croft, filled him with outrage.

"You can't tell me that a guy who does stuff like that is normal?"

"What's normal?" Croft said, smiling. "Everyone has a side of themself they don't want other people to see."

"But this is different. This sicko killed someone. He murdered a little girl."

"Soldiers kill little girls every day. You don't see many of them getting arrested for murder."

Croft was staring at him intently, in a way that made Kip feel uncomfortable. The look was back, the fixed, crazy *wilkolak* look, not as bad as before but enough to remind Kip of what it had been like to glimpse that side of him, the side he didn't want other people to see. It occurred to him suddenly that it was his job that had made him that way, his work as a forensic photographer, that the sight of the dead and dying had unhinged him somehow, the way it had with soldiers in Vietnam. Kip had gone through a phase of watching 'Nam films, although he had grown tired of them in the end because they only ever seemed to show one side of the story. Nonetheless they might help explain Croft. For people like the 'Nam vets, killing was just another fact of life; they stopped being able to tell what was normal and what was not.

"Did you ever have to photograph a murder? A proper murder, I mean, with blood and everything?" Kip's heart pounded with a strange excitement. He was surprised and ashamed at how much he wanted to know the answer to his question. *Perhaps he's right*, Kip thought. *There's a monster in all of us.*

"Plenty of times," Croft said. "Do you want to see the pictures?" He moved a step closer, so close that Kip imagined he could feel the heat from his body, even though he knew it was just the night air he could feel, the warm night air mingled with the sharp scent of diesel. For the first time he felt really afraid. He knew there was nothing innocent about Croft's question, that it was indecent somehow, as if he were asking Kip if he wanted to go to a porn film with him, and the worst thing about it was that he *wanted* Kip to know this, he wanted to make him complicit.

Kip realized he hated Croft, that he loathed him in the way he loathed dog turds, or butter beans, with a vertiginous, sliding repulsion that grew out of instinct and not out of reason. Yet still he could not look away. It was the same as with the dead rat, the spoiled milk. It was not just because Croft knew how to use a camera that Kip felt drawn to him; he was drawn to Croft because Croft had seen terrible things.

"That would be great," he said. "I've been looking at some forensic stuff online actually. I was thinking I might want to get into it. Once I've finished college, I mean."

"Are you sure about that?" Croft said. "Most of it's pretty dull."

Kip shook his head. "Not for me. I like the idea of it. I like the idea of never knowing what's coming next."

Croft laughed. "That's one way of putting it, I suppose. Mind your back." He drew a ballpoint pen from his jacket pocket, and a small scrap of paper. When Kip examined the paper later he discovered it was a receipt from the DIY store at the bottom end of Lee High Road, that Croft had bought two tins of white emulsion and a bottle of turps. Croft placed a hand on Kip's shoulder, bending him forward and resting the paper on his back just below the left shoulder blade. Kip could feel the Biro moving over the paper, the pressure of Croft's hand firm and even and slyly insistent. Kip fixed his eyes on the pavement. The flagstones were filthy. The whole of Lee High Road was like that, but it couldn't help it. Most of the dirt was caused by traffic fumes.

"All done," Croft said, and Kip straightened up. Croft handed him the paper, which Kip saw now had an address written on it, and a mobile telephone number. "I'm busy over the weekend, but you can come on Tuesday afternoon if you like. We can have a chat and I can show you some photos. Don't forget to bring your camera." He slipped the Biro back in his pocket. "See you, then."

He walked off without looking round, heading back the way they had come. Kip took a few steps after him, thinking that he could trail Croft, see where he went, then realized he didn't need to because he had Croft's address already on the scrap of paper. It occurred to him that he could go to the police now, that he could tell them everything. He could have Dennis Croft arrested within the hour.

He knew almost at once that he wouldn't do it. If he went to the police he would be forced to explain himself, to tell them why he had Croft's address, why he suspected Croft of being the killer in the first place. He would also have to tell them who else knew, and that meant Sonia. He imagined a cop car drawing up outside the Vardens' house, Timothy Varden demanding to know what the hell Kip thought he was doing getting his daughter mixed up with a paedophile. It would be like telling his father he knew about Grace Hemingway, tearing his world apart in all the wrong places.

He also had the feeling that when the police went to arrest him, Croft would no longer be there. It was a feeling he couldn't explain but that he trusted completely, a deep itch, the same feeling he had sometimes during a game of Harris, when he knew the person sitting opposite had the ace of spades.

Still further back in his mind he was nagged by the sense that none of these things explained his refusal to act, that the real truth was that he didn't want Croft arrested just yet, because he was keen to get a look at his photographs.

All he knew for certain was that he wanted to talk to Sonia. He turned left into Brandram Road, walking until he was out of earshot of the main traffic. He keyed Sonia's number, convinced that she would not answer, that she was out with friends, or that she had left her phone in her bag and wouldn't hear it ringing. She answered on the third ring.

"Hey," she said. She sounded happy, and he seemed to catch a trace of her scent, the fresh, tangy scent of the pine soap she used with something else running beneath it, the dense musky smell that came from her armpits and between her legs. He wondered what she had been doing when he called.

"Hey, Son," he said. "You okay?"

"I'm fine. What's the matter, Eddie? You sound weird."

His dad called him Ed, his friends called him Kip, his teachers all called him Kiplas. Only his mother and Sonia called him Eddie. He had hoped that hearing Sonia's voice would make things better somehow, would get rid of all his crazy thoughts about werewolves and Dennis Croft being a murderer, but instead it was just making things worse. He couldn't get rid of the idea that she was in danger. He wished there were a way of keeping her safe without having to tell her anything. If he told her she might think he was going nuts.

"Have you still got that photo?" he said. His mouth felt dry and he swallowed. There was a back-taste of onion and charcoal.

"What photo? The one of the guy outside the garage."

He nodded, forgetting for a moment that she couldn't see him. "Yes," he said. "Did you keep it?"

"What do you think? You know I love your stuff. What's going on?"

He felt a surge of happiness, that she should treat him like a *real artist*, then fought to suppress it. "It's just that, well, I think I saw the guy again, that's all."

"What d'you mean, you saw him again? How long ago?"

"The other day, in Manor Park Gardens. And then this evening, up by the clock tower. I think it was him, anyway. He was too far away for me to see him properly."

The line went quiet, and for long awful seconds Kip felt certain she knew he was lying, that he was telling her only a small part of the truth. He pressed the phone hard to his ear, but all he could hear was his own breathing. When Sonia spoke again the sound was unnaturally loud.

"Can I tell you something, Eddie? Promise you won't laugh?"

"'Course I won't, Son. Just tell me, all right?" He wondered if she was about to dump him, although it didn't sound like that from her voice. *If you touch her I'll kill you*, he thought. *You rat-faced bastard.*

"He reminds me of someone. The guy."

"Someone you know, you mean?"

"Not really." She hesitated. "I think I saw him in a dream once. Only he wasn't really a man, he was some kind of monster. He could kill people, just by looking at them. I had problems sleeping after that, for a while. My mum thought it was all to do with my periods starting." She giggled, a light, tight sound that was not really like her. "It was ages ago now. I'd forgotten all about it until I saw the photo."

"A monster?" He could hear his voice rising in pitch, and he knew he sounded as if he was about to explode with laughter, only it wasn't that, it was the opposite. He felt like breaking down and telling her everything.

"Yes. You promised you wouldn't laugh."

"I'm not. So you reckon the guy in the photo is the guy from your dream?"

"Of course not. How could he be? They look the same, that's all. Something about the cheekbones. And those glasses."

"Like a rat."

"That's a strange way of describing it but I know what you mean." She paused. "I put the photo away in a drawer. Do you mind?"

"Of course I don't mind. I wish you'd chuck it out, though, get rid of it."

"I'm not binning your work over a stupid dream I had five years ago! The guy in the picture is just some guy anyway, he's no one. I was just a bit freaked, that's all."

"You'll keep the photo in the drawer, though, won't you?"

"If that's what you want. Are you sure everything's okay?"

"Everything's fine. Do you want me to come over tomorrow?"

Tomorrow was Saturday. Croft had said he would be busy over the weekend. Busy with what exactly? Kip found he didn't want to think about it.

"You'd better, or I might kill you. We can go to the woods, if you want."

Kip guessed what she meant, and felt himself blushing. "I'll bring my camera," he said absently. He remembered how she had looked the last time, afterwards, the yellow leaves in her red hair. If you could capture a moment like that then you were some kind of genius.

"Go home now," said Sonia. "It's getting late."

"How did you know I was out?"

"I can hear the road, silly."

"You're magic, Son," he said, and ended the call. On Lee High Road the buses sailed by like pirate ships, and from the gardens in Brandram Road there came a faint scent of honeysuckle. He realized it was night, real night, the bottomless tract of hours between dusk and morning. In his grandmother's stories this had always been the time of the *wilkolak*.

He met Sonia off the 122 bus at the bottom end of Lee High Road, then they walked up Lee Park to Blackheath Village, where they caught the number 89 to Shooter's Hill. Sonia had made a picnic: cheese sandwiches and flapjacks and orange juice. She had also brought a canvas holdall with a blanket in it. They spread the blanket under some trees and had sex again. It was better than the last time, different somehow, as if both of them had grown older overnight.

Neither of them mentioned the monster. Sonia talked about what might happen when they went away to college, and Kip supposed her need to make plans for them might have scared some people but it didn't worry him. He found he liked it. He closed his eyes and drifted. A sweet breeze played with the leaves, and Kip found himself thinking that they were safe here, that Croft wouldn't come to the forest, he was a city rat.

He was awakened by Sonia kissing him. She kissed him full on the mouth, pressing her lips carefully against his as if she meant to leave an imprint there, the way girls did with soldiers' handkerchiefs in the old war movies.

"I want you to know that whatever happens, today was real," she said. "That all of this really happened." Her top half was still naked. Her hair trailed in the grass, like runners of flame about to start a brush fire.

"What do you mean?" Kip said. "What do you think's going to happen?"

"Nothing," Sonia said. "I'm just saying."

He took some photos of her, just head shots. Her eyes were closed, her eyelashes cast spider-leg shadows on the curves of her cheeks.

Kip knew that someone would have had to photograph Rebecca Riding; that if he were serious about forensic photography he might soon be having to photograph dead girls all the time.

When he arrived home that evening he found his parents were going to dinner at the Toklins'. His mother had put on a dress Kip knew his father liked to see her in: cream-coloured silk cut low at the front and covered in large pink roses. She seemed nervously excited, as if she and Andy had only just met, and her nervousness made her beautiful. She was perched on the edge of the sofa, painting her nails with gold varnish and watching the news.

"Where's Dad?" Kip said.

"At the off-licence, I hope. He's supposed to be buying a bottle of that Bulgarian Merlot Toke likes. Be quiet for a moment, Eddie, I want to listen."

"What's the big deal?"

"It looks like they've caught that maniac."

Kip stared at the television. The photo fit of the monster was filling the screen. A man had been arrested and charged with the rape and murder of Rebecca Riding. The man's name was Steven Jepsom and he was from Brownhill Road, Catford.

"Thank God for that," Lynn said. "Good riddance to bad rubbish."

"We don't know it's him yet," said Kip. "Not until he's been convicted."

He wished they would show a picture of Jepsom but Kip guessed it was illegal to put someone's photo all over the news while there was still a chance they were innocent. He knew he should feel relieved but he somehow didn't. He wanted to know if Jepsom looked like Croft. It occurred to him that Steven Jepsom might be Dennis Croft's real name.

His mother glanced at him, her lips tightening.

"Aren't you pleased? At least it's some comfort for the family, knowing he's behind bars at last."

"I'm just saying," Kip said. "I hope they got the right bloke, that's all."

Lynn frowned, and looked as if she were about to say something else, but at that moment Andy Kiplas returned from the off-licence. He had the bottle of wine under one arm, wrapped in a sheet of green tissue paper. The ends of the paper had been twisted into a fan shape.

"Hurry up," Andy said. "I've got us a taxi."

Lynn's cheeks coloured to match the roses on her dress. "A taxi? What's all this in aid of?"

Kip's father was standing holding the door open like a butler in a television murder mystery. As Lynn got up from the sofa he bowed and began humming a tune from one of the opera CDs he sometimes listened to in the car. His mother laughed, and a look passed between her and his father that made Kip feel stupid and in the way, as if all his worrying about her had been for nothing. He wished they would keep their business to themselves.

He waited for them to leave, then turned off the television. He fetched the Nikon from his room and began to photograph the back room and the hallway, pretending that the house was the scene of a crime. He did a series of close-ups of the glass tumbler his mother had been drinking from. The tumbler was still half full of tonic water, and there was a fingerprint clearly visible near the brim. Lynn had changed her mind about her shoes at the last minute, and one of the discarded ones, a high-heeled pink sandal, lay on its side in the doorway. If you looked at things a certain way the dirty glass and the fallen shoe looked suspicious, as if someone had left the room in a terrible hurry.

He became so absorbed in the details that there were moments when he forgot he was in his own home. Eventually he laid the camera aside on the sofa and went through to the kitchen. There was potato salad in the fridge, some Polish salami, the remains of his parents' lunch. He piled it into a bowl and was about to put it all in the microwave when his phone rang. It was Sonia. He picked up at once.

"Did you hear?" she said. "They got him."

"Yes," Kip said. "I saw it on the news earlier."

"Do you reckon it's him? The guy in the photo, I mean?"

"I doubt it. I'd forgotten all about him, really." He was caught off guard by a memory of her, leaning against a tree as she pulled on her jeans. Her back was long, with a very slight curvature of the spine. There were exercises she was meant to do to stop it getting stiff but she was always forgetting. The skin over her vertebrae was taut and pearly white, the row of smooth bumps reminding him always of a saying of his mother's: *rare as hens' teeth, they are*. Quite suddenly the last thing he wanted to talk about was Dennis Croft.

"Can you call me back on the landline?" Sonia said. "They're showing *Donnie Darko* on Channel 4 in a moment. We could sit and watch it together, if you like?"

"What about your parents?" Kip said.

"They're out. With some people from Deutsche Bank. They won't be back for hours."

He finished microwaving the food then took the hall phone upstairs to his room. He dialled Sonia's home number and she picked up almost before it had a chance to ring. Halfway through the film Kip got undressed and lay down on his bed, clutching the phone between his neck and his shoulder to stop it slipping.

"You're taking your clothes off," said Sonia. "I can hear you doing it."

"I am not."

"Liar!"

"Shut up, I'm missing the film."

He closed his eyes and thought of Sonia lying on top of him. The fact that she was both far away and close made him feel breathless with excitement. He began to rub himself, focusing on the sound of her breathing and trying not to make any noise.

"Kip?" she said some time later. "You okay?"

"You're rare as hens' teeth, you are." A single tear ran diagonally across his face. "Watch the film."

When the film was over they said goodnight and ended the call. Kip pulled up the duvet and lay in the dark, watching the television with the sound turned down. Eventually he fell asleep. He woke briefly just after two. There was a light on downstairs and the sound of voices. For a moment Kip felt frightened. He remembered the dirty tumbler and the discarded shoe and thought something awful had happened. Then he realized it was just his parents coming home from the Toklins'. They spoke in loud whispers like miscreant school kids. He could tell from the way they were moving that they were both drunk.

He began to drift off again almost at once. His father was humming the Toreador Song out of *Carmen*. His mother stumbled against the box of newspapers in the hall, swore loudly and then stifled a laugh.

The box shouldn't even have been there. His father was supposed to take it out on Fridays for recycling.

Just before he fell asleep, Kip decided he would not go to Croft's house on the Tuesday, after all.

Croft's house was on Belmont Hill, the Lewisham end, one of a long Victorian terrace, the tall, gabled houses running away down the steep gradient like toppling dominoes. Kip photographed the house from both sides of the road, wondering if Croft were watching him from behind the curtains. He doubted it. He had already made up his mind on the way over that Croft would not be in when he called, that the address on the piece of paper was not even his. He told himself the only reason he was going there was to prove the whole thing was a fake. He pressed the bell, trying to work out what he would say if the door were opened by a complete stranger, a large woman in a flowered bathrobe say, or an old man in a saggy green cardigan with the elbows worn through.

Excuse me, but does Mr Gaumont live here? I promised my uncle I'd change his library books for him.

Kip liked the sound of Mr Gaumont. The idea of him was so convincing that when the door opened and Croft appeared, Kip had to think who he was. It seemed for a moment that Croft was the fantasy, not Gaumont, old Gaumont who was so harmless and so plausible. It crossed his mind that Croft had done away with Gaumont, just as he had done away with Rebecca Riding.

"Hi there," Croft said. "Come in."

He took a step back from the door. As Kip entered the house it occurred to him that nobody in the world knew where he was. He found himself wishing he had left a note in his room, or that he had texted Sonia. He wondered how often bad things happened to people because they were afraid of looking stupid, and supposed it was often, more often than you might think anyway.

"Excuse the mess," Croft said. "This was my dad's place. He left it in a bit of a state. It's taking me a while to get things straight."

There were some black bin bags at the foot of the stairs but other than that there was no mess that Kip could see. The hallway of the house was dark, made darker by the varnished wood panelling and dull red carpet. There was a smell of mothballs and furniture polish, reminding him of the Toklins' house, which was owned by Lyonel Toklin's ninety-year-old mother, Violet. Lynn Kiplas always joked that Violet Toklin was so stingy she hadn't had the place decorated since VE Day, and Kip felt half-inclined to believe her. Croft led the way through to a room at the back, home to an enormous buttonback sofa and a boiler on a tiled hearth protected by a square metal cage. There were piles of books everywhere. Kip noticed a stack of *Photography Now* and some issues of another magazine that he knew you could only get on subscription from America.

"Can I get you anything?" Croft said. "A drink maybe?"

Kip shook his head, then asked for a glass of water. It seemed safer to ask for something than nothing at all. He perched himself on the edge of the sofa and fiddled with the strap of the Nikon. He was desperate to photograph this room, with its stacks of old magazines and blacked floorboards, the sofa itself, leathery and vast as a beached whale. *Leviathan*, he thought, savouring the sound of it, a word that seemed to open its jaws and admit the world.

Croft disappeared into the kitchen, returning a few moments later with two glasses on a tray and two cans of Coke. He sat down next to Kip on the sofa, placing the tray on a low stool that stood close by.

"You can have water instead if that's what you want," he said. "But I thought you might like one of these. They're straight from the fridge."

"No, this is great," Kip said. "Thanks." He popped the seal on the can and poured the frothing liquid into the glass. He thought how typical it was of Croft, that he would drink Coke from a glass instead of straight from the can. It went with his old Minolta, his Oxfam clothes… and the thought that he could still predict Croft this way, that he could read him, made Kip feel calmer. He had come here of his own free will, after all. If he wanted to he could just get up and leave.

"Well?" Croft said. He took a sip of his Coke then wiped his mouth with the back of his hand. "Did you bring anything to show me?"

"You can have a look at these if you want. They're my most recent." Kip hesitated. "I didn't print them out. I don't think they're good enough." He handed Croft the Nikon. He had cleared its memory of everything except the pictures he had taken on the Saturday night, the mock scene-of-crime photos of his own living room. He wondered if Croft would have any difficulty operating the camera but he handled it as if he had been using digital cameras for years, and Kip supposed he probably had. He wondered if all the spouting about film was just guff, a pose that Croft had affected to impress him.

Croft scrolled quickly through the series of images and then worked his way backwards more slowly, taking time to examine each frame.

"These are good," he said. "Interesting. Did you take them at home?"

Kip nodded. "I was trying to look at the room in a different way, as if there'd been a murder there or something. It made me wonder what things might be important, you know, if you were photographing a real crime scene. I never thought about working for the police before but I think I might like it. It's interesting."

"Do you think you'd be able to handle seeing the bad stuff?"

Kip looked down at his hands. "It'd be my job to handle it, wouldn't it? I'd have to get used to it."

"Well, that's something you'd have to find out for yourself." Croft put his glass down on the floor and stood up. He leaned over, resting a hand briefly on Kip's shoulder and reaching behind the sofa. He drew out a large portfolio, black leather with a long brass zip. The zip gleamed in the black like a row of bared teeth. "I've got some shots here you can look at. Some of them are quite strong. I'd probably get into trouble actually, if anyone knew I'd been showing you these without your parents' permission." He caught Kip's eye and winked, though whether to show he was joking or trying to implicate Kip in his guilt Kip didn't know. Croft retook his seat on the couch, so close beside him now that Kip could feel his warmth through his jeans, Croft's leg resting against his own with a slight outward pressure. Croft smelled of the house, as if his clothes were not quite fresh. Kip unzipped the portfolio. It was crammed with images, photographic prints mainly though there were some newspaper clippings and photocopies, everything jumbled together like an insane montage. On top of the pile lay an enlarged shot of what had once been someone's living room, only now it was mostly reduced to a heap of ash. On the picture's right-hand margin stood a humped black thing about the size of a wheelie bin which Kip guessed had probably been an armchair. In front of this object was a single plate-sized patch of carpet that had somehow escaped being burned. Its colours were still bright, an interlocking pattern of blue and red diamonds. Kip thought there was something naked about the colours, something horrible. Underneath the photo of the burned-out living room there was a picture of a bicycle wheel, bent almost in half by the force of some impact. Its spokes jutted in all directions like shattered ribs.

"The lad on that bike was fifteen," Croft said. "He died at the scene." He pulled another picture from the stack, seeming to do it at random though Kip found time to wonder later if it had all been planned. The photograph, an enlarged detail, showed a pair of hands bound at the wrists with a coil of barbed wire. The thumb-nails were caked with blood, so thick in places that Kip thought at first it was mud. There were long vertical gashes around the wrist bones, showing clearly how the wire had been dragged into place before it was tied.

Kip could not tell if the hands belonged to a man or a woman though the crooked, rather ugly shape of the top thumb joint gave him the feeling it was probably a man. The photograph was horrible, yet it was also beautiful, immortal somehow, like a still from a documentary about the First World War. It was clear as life, with the kind of singing exactitude people meant when they talked about photographic clarity even when most photographs taken by ordinary people, Kip knew, were not clear at all. Most amateur shots were blurred or badly composed, off kilter in some way. The photograph of the bound hands was so true to life it leaked its atmosphere all over the room, the drizzle-grey of a cold morning in November when a man had died in pain with his face in the mud.

"This guy turned up on a building site in Charlton," Croft said. "He was dead when they found him. I took these pictures while we were waiting for the ambulance."

"Did they catch the killers?"

Croft nodded. "It was a gang crime. Seven men were arrested. Two of them got long prison sentences."

"And your photos helped to get them put away?"

"Maybe. Probably. But that's never the thing you think about, at least not until later. At the time all you care about is the picture, about getting it right. I hardly gave that poor guy a thought while I was taking these shots, he was just a subject. I despise myself for that, but it doesn't change anything. But you already know all this, Kip, you're an intelligent boy. If what you wanted was to help catch murderers you'd become a detective inspector, not a photographer."

Kip stared down at the photograph. He knew that what Croft said was true, truer even than Croft realized. If Kip's interest lay in solving crimes he would have reported Croft to the police a fortnight ago. Instead he had taken pictures of him, and now he was here in Croft's house, talking with him about photography. He did not care if Croft was the monster, only that he was here to have this conversation. He was glad the police had arrested Steven Jepsom instead of him. He wondered if Croft would help him with his college application.

"Can I use your loo?" Kip said suddenly. It was not just that he needed the toilet, although the can of Coke had filled his bladder to bursting. Mostly it was that he wanted to get away from Croft for a couple of minutes. Being with him was exhausting. He was also curious to see the upstairs of Croft's house.

"It's the first door upstairs, to your right," Croft said. "We could go for a curry later, if you like."

"That'd be good," Kip said. He got up from the couch. He tried to smile at Croft, but the smile seemed to slide from his face at the last moment.

He made his way back down the hall. He noticed that the door to the understairs cupboard had a bolt on it, wondered briefly why that was and then supposed that the basement floor was where Croft kept his darkroom. He went upstairs, stepping over the bin bags, which looked to be full of old clothes. There were four doors on the upper landing. Kip opened one at random and found Croft's bedroom, the bed unmade, a crumpled T-shirt strewn across the floor. The room next door was piled high with old furniture.

The bathroom, when he found it, was at least clean. The window was open, letting in the outside air. There was a faint smell of disinfectant.

He used the toilet and then washed his hands. He thought he would tell Croft that he had decided against the curry, that he should go home, that he had schoolwork to do, something or anything, he did not know why. He turned to go back downstairs, glancing as he did so into the one room he had not yet entered, a narrow room at the back, a spare bedroom most likely, or the bedroom that had belonged to Croft's dead father. There was a wooden bedstead, the mattress stripped to its striped cover, stained with age, the shallow depression towards the centre where the old man had lain. Kip wondered if he had died there. He felt instinctively for the Nikon, then realized he had left it downstairs. He pulled the door to, wondering if Croft might give him permission to photograph the room anyway, whether it would be rude or strange to ask.

He noticed there were some photographs propped by the skirting board, enlargements mounted on cardboard and protected by cellophane. They did not look like forensic shots. Kip bent to look at them, curious. He remembered how Croft had talked of using some of his father's money to buy a new camera. He wondered what kind of photography Croft was into, now that he was no longer working for the police.

There were six photographs, and they were all of Rebecca Riding. Two were in colour. Kip recognized her red jumper from the *Crimewatch* reconstruction, the fair hair hitched up on one side by a slide in the shape of a butterfly.

The rest of the pictures were in black-and-white, four miraculous, pristine prints that revealed the child for what she was: the only girl in the world at that moment, and Dennis Croft her only audience. In the final shot she looked straight at the camera, her gappy teeth bared in a sweet, shy smile that seemed to suggest she knew she was being looked at, but didn't mind.

She did not seem in the least afraid. Kip felt a rush of nausea, and then of cold, as if he were going down with a virus. The girl was so *there* in the photographs it was impossible to accept that she was no longer alive.

He turned the pictures around to face the wall then went back into the bathroom. He leaned over the toilet bowl, wanting to be sick, but the only thing that came was a kind of dry gagging. He ran water into the basin, turning both taps on full to make the maximum noise. Then he flushed the toilet again. He knew he had to go back downstairs, that his life might now depend on him being able to act as if nothing had happened.

He crossed the landing to the head of the stairs. He stared down into the hallway, at the front door with its stained-glass fanlight, the delicate leaded panes arranged in a design he believed was called *fleur de lys*. The door was probably not locked, Kip could not remember Croft locking it. The idea that he might have done was crazy, of course, but all Kip could think of was the image that had come to him before: worlds colliding, a wrecking ball spinning on its chain as it crashed through the wall of the known universe.

He heard footsteps at the end of the hall. A moment later Croft's voice came rising towards him up the stairs.

"You okay up there?" Croft said. "I want to show you the darkroom. Dad's cellar was part of the reason I moved back in here permanently."

Kip stayed where he was, paralyzed by the sound of his own breathing. He knew that what he did in the next few seconds would decide everything.

WHO KILLED SKIPPY?

Paul D. Brazill

ONE

"COULD BE WORSE, could be raining," said Craig, pretty much as soon as it started pissing down.

A big grin crawled across his flushed face like a caterpillar. He was sniffling away and wiping his runny nose with the sleeve of his leather jacket. Craig had just snorted a sugar bowl full of Colombian marching powder and popped a veritable cornucopia of multi-coloured pills. He was talking ten to the dozen and doing my napper in no end.

I forced a smile, though I was none too pleased. I was getting soaked to the skin in a vandalized cemetery after spending the last half-hour digging a grave while Craig turned himself into a walking pharmaceutical experiment.

"Let's get on with this," I said, grabbing the dead kangaroo by its legs. But Craig was away with the fairies again, watching a flock of black birds land on a cluster of graffiti-stained gravestones.

"A murder of crows," said Craig. "That's the collective noun for crows, you know? A murder." Craig was an autodidact, hooked on learning a word a day, as well as many other things.

"Yes, Craig, I did used to be an English teacher, you know," I said. My patience was getting frayed. The rain had slipped down the back of my shirt, trickled down my spine and crept into my arse crack.

"They say that crows are harbingers of death, eh, Ordy? Have you ever wondered why they never seem to talk about harbingers of good things?"

I was now inches away from picking up the shovel and twatting Craig, but thankfully he suddenly seemed to break out of his trance. He bent down and grabbed the kangaroo.

"Let's get a move on, Ordy, eh?" he said. "It's *Super Seventies Special* at the Grand Hotel tonight. We haven't got all day, you know."

TWO

The Grand Hotel, like a fair number of its clientele, was all fur coat and no knickers. It had lived up to its name once upon a time and its façade was still pretty impressive but the interior, however, left a lot to be desired. For many years, it had survived as a nightclub which was just about bog standard, with the emphasis on the bog.

Every Thursday it was *Super Seventies Special* because, unsurprisingly, the music that was played was from the seventies and all drinks were seventy pence. Unfortunately, most of the clientele were knocking on seventy, too, which was why it had the earned its reputation as a "grab a granny night". Which suited Craig Ferry down to the ground.

Craig was the youngest of the four Ferry boys and he'd been born premature and weak, leading his mother to become a tad overprotective of him. For most of his childhood he hardly left her side and had, it seemed, developed a bit of an Oedipus Complex. Hence, his regular attendance at the *Super Seventies Special*.

Which meant that I had to go there too, since, to all intents and purposes, I was Craig's minder. Not that I was anyway near a tough guy. And not that Craig needed a bodyguard. He was well over six foot with a physique worthy of Mike Tyson.

Craig had been a sickly child, as I said, but when he reached sixteen and his mother died, he transformed himself, in a manner akin to that of Bruce Banner turning into the Incredible Hulk, albeit at a decidedly slower rate.

When he was a kid Craig was almost anorexic, but with his mother off the scene he soon became a fast-food-and-beer-consuming monster. And that, combined with his scoffing of steroids and frequent trips to the gym, spawned the behemoth that was stood before me, gargling cider and blackcurrant and singing along to Sparks' "This Town Ain't Big Enough For The Both Of Us".

No, I wasn't employed by the Ferry family to protect Craig from other people. I was paid to protect him from himself.

THREE

I'd first met Craig when I was about twelve. We went to different comprehensive schools, so I didn't have much contact with him but I'd sometimes notice this gangling, scarecrow of a kid hanging around the local betting shop, which was owned by Glyn and Tina Ferry. He always looked lost, sat on the step reading *Commando* war comics and sipping from a bottle of Lucozade.

One day, during a long hot summer, bored and kicking a ball against a wall, I noticed Craig and asked him if he fancied a game of football. I never would have bothered normally, you could tell by the look of him that he'd be rubbish at football, but all my friends were away at Butlin's or Pontin's, or some other holiday camp, and needs must.

Craig must have been bored himself, I think he'd read the ink from the stack of comics he had next to him, and he said yes.

"Okay," I said. "We'll do penalties. You're in goal."

Craig shuffled over to the side of the garages. One of the walls had the wobbly-lined shape of a goal painted on it. He stretched his arms and legs wide.

I put the heavy leather ball on the penalty spot and stepped back for a run.

"Blow a whistle," I shouted at Craig.

"Eh?"

"A whistle."

He pursed his lips, looking more than a bit girly, and I started to giggle.

"No, like this, yer big girl's blouse," I said, and put my fingers inside my mouth to show him. But before I could start, I heard a shriek.

I jumped, but not as much as Craig. An overweight woman wearing a sleeveless, polka-dot dress was running towards him, her bingo wings flapping.

"Get here now," she said, clasping him towards a bosom that would be accurately described as ample, before pulling him back to the betting shop.

FOUR

It was now creeping towards the part of the night that I really hated. It was close to midnight and Craig was hammered.

"The pint of no return," he said. He downed a pint in one and staggered across the sticky carpet to the dance floor.

The Grand was crowded, hot and clammy. Billy Blockbuster, the DJ and quizmaster, was playing smoochy songs back-to-back. As "Betcha By Golly Wow" played, Craig canoodled with a couple of members of the cast of *The Golden Girls*. He could hardly stand up, and the pensioners were doing all that they could to support him, but it wouldn't be long before Goliath would crash down.

And before you could shout "Timber!" he was over, crushing one of the women beneath him. Two bouncers in Crombies, Darren and Dane Greenwood, ran over, but when they saw it was Craig they just stepped back and looked at me.

You could hear the screams of the old woman who was trapped beneath Craig so Billy Blockbuster quickly changed the song to The Jam's "Going Underground" and pumped up the volume.

"Well?" said Dane.

"Aye," I said.

Darren went back to the door and Dane bent down and grabbed Craig's ankles while I took hold of him by his, frankly minging, armpits.

He was a dead weight as we dragged him up, just enough so someone could pull the woman from underneath him. We struggled and turned him on his back. He was in a deep sleep, snogging with Morpheus and snoring like a Kalashnikov.

And then it was the hard part.

FIVE

Craig's father, Glyn Ferry, was a terrifying man by reputation although he was rarely seen in action. His foot soldiers were his boys: Alanby, William and Dafydd. William did most of the muscle work while Dafydd did the greasing of palms and the like. And Alanby, well, he was known as The Enforcer and he was in prison for murder for most of my childhood. But, of course, one day when I was about thirteen he got out.

I'd just finished my supper, cheese spread on toast, and was sitting with my mum watching *Callan*. My dad was on night shift at the Lighthouse and the house was calm until there was a rapid knock at the door. My mother, ever stoic and unruffled, slowly got to her feet and, keeping one eye on the television, looked out of the window.

"By the cringe!" she said. This was as much as she swore. "What does he want at this time of night?"

Callan and Lonely were arguing on TV and I wasn't really paying attention to her but I looked up when she came back from the door with Craig, who was white and shaking.

"It's Wednesday," I said, angrily. "Comic club is Thursday nights." It had been a tradition over the last few years that every Thursday, Craig and a couple of other waifs and strays came to my house and we swapped comics.

"It's our Alanby," stuttered Craig.

"What?" I said. My mother was giving him a sympathetic look, which was grating on me. There were another twenty minutes of *Callan* left.

"Why not sit down, luvvie?" said my mother. "I'll make you a cup of sweet tea and you can tell us all about it."

She pushed Craig down into Dad's armchair and went into the kitchen. I turned my attention to the TV until the adverts came on.

Mam gave Craig his tea in a Seatown FC mug and he took sips, making annoying slurping noises.

The story that tumbled out of Craig, in fits and starts, was that Alanby had been released from jail after ten years inside. And he'd come home with a bride, Trish, a Scottish prostitute he'd met two days after getting out.

Craig's parents were none too pleased and had kicked them out of their home shortly after they arrived. So, Alanby and Trish moved into a flat above one of the betting shops. Short of cash, and with a big heroin habit, Alanby had put Trish back on the game.

That night, she'd picked up a Dutch sailor down at the docks and sold him her wedding ring in the Ship Inn. Alanby had turned up at the pub in a drunken rage and sliced Trish to pieces. He'd then turned up at his parents' home covered in blood and wanting a change of clothes. Craig had opened the door to the blood-splattered Alanby and had freaked out.

He spent the next few nights staying at my house, working his way through my mam's *Reader's Digests,* and the Ferrys got into the habit of packing him off to stay with me whenever they wanted him out of the way.

Well, at least these days they paid.

SIX

I'd never set much stock on all that heredity cobblers. Bad blood and the like. I was more of a nurture over nature man. Though it did seem to me that the Ferry family were all born under a bad star.

Except Beverly, that is. Beverly was the only girl among the Ferry siblings. She was a qualified accountant who did the firm's books and worked in the local civic centre. And her business acumen was a real boon to the family, especially when their enterprises became more and more legit. And she was the one who had decided to hire me to keep a bleary eye on Craig.

Beverly was in her late-thirties. She was well read. She was good-looking. She was fun to be with. And I had been arse over tit in love with her for as long as I could remember. And, of course, she was married. To a local Councillor, to boot.

I'd managed to manoeuvre Craig in and out of the taxi and through the front door of his flat but was having trouble getting him up the stairs. I was still aching from all that digging I'd done and was considering giving up the ghost, and leaving Craig where he lay, when his mobile started to ring.

I took it out of his pocket and looked at the display. It was Beverly. I switched off the *Bonanza* theme and spoke.

"Craig's phone, Peter Ord speaking."

"Oh, God, is he trashed again, Peter?"

"Either that or he's rehearsing for his *Stars In Their Eyes* appearance as Oliver Reed."

A chuckle.

"All right, I suppose I'll see him tomorrow," she said. "It was just that he had a delivery job to do earlier and I wanted to make sure it had gone well. Know anything about it?"

"Er ... yeah, I think ..."

"Shit, he bolloxed it up, didn't he?"

"Well ..."

"Peter, I can tell when you're telling pork pies. I'll be there in bit."

SEVEN

Bev was looking very business-like in a sharp black suit and high heels, her blonde hair tied back. And she looked more than somewhat pissed off.

"So, who was the idiot with the Luger?" she said. She had to raise her voice slightly as Craig's snores were now echoing through the living room. We'd managed to get him on the sofa and left him there. We moved into the cramped kitchen and I took a can of Foster's from the fridge.

"Fancy one?"

Bev shook her head.

"So, the Shogun Assassin?"

"Dunno who he was. Craig said that the bloke pissed off on a motorbike before he could get his hands on him. Was dressed head to foot in black, like a ninja, apparently."

"Yeah, well, our Craig has always been blessed with an overripe imagination."

"True, true."

"A ninja with a Luger sounds like something from one of those comics you two used to read. Was he on anything?"

"Yeah, a motorbike," I said.

"Not the ninja, you plonker, Craig!"

"Ah, well…"

"Jesus. I thought you were supposed to keep an eye on him?"

"Hey, he was already as high as Sly by the time I met him."

The story was this: one of the Ferry family's occasional entrepreneurial activities was importing unusual animals through the docks and selling them to collectors of exotic pets. One such collector was Bobby Bowles, the former football superstar, who had a private zoo just outside Seatown.

Craig's job was to deliver a kangaroo to Bobby in exchange for a wad of dosh. However, on his way to Bowles's place, Craig's van was stopped by a ninja with a gun who shot the kangaroo and scarpered on a Harley Davidson. Craig phoned me to help him get rid of Skippy's body, of course, hence my fun day at the graveyard.

"This is a very bloody important time for the family business," said Bev. "Dad's very ill, Alanby is never going to get out of Wakefield nick since he spiked that warden's tea with ecstasy, and Dafydd is, well, Dafydd…"

Dafydd had, for many years, been so far in the closet he was in Narnia, but when he eventually came out he shocked the family by moving down south to open up a scuba diving club with an Australian. This was blamed for causing Glyn Ferry's first heart attack. The moving down south.

"So, Craig is being groomed to take over as head of the family business?" I said.

Bev raised her eyebrows.

"Supposedly," she said.

"Oh, dear," I said.

"Oh, dear, indeed," said Bev.

EIGHT

We were in Velvette's Gentlemen's Club, staring behind the bar at a stained-glass recreation of the famed poster of the female tennis player scratching her arse that many a teenage boy had on their wall in the seventies.

"Lesbians?" I said. I finished my pint of Stella. I was well and truly off the wagon now.

"Yep," said Craig.

"I've never heard that one before."

"Aye. Good With Colours is a euphemism for gay men, and Tennis Fans is for lesbians."

"Well, as always, Craig, you are an education."

"Well, you should read more, shouldn't you? Might learn something."

I finished my drink and went over to the bar. The dancers were starting to arrive at Velvette's. It was a couple of hours before opening time but Jack Martin, the owner, usually gave them a little booze-up on a Saturday night to get them in the mood. Jack was more of your benevolent kind of gangster.

"But I think you're avoiding the issue, Craig," I said, as I sat back down. "What are you going to do now?"

"Well, I'll see if Jack needs anyone for a bit of occasional strong-arm work. Him and Dad are on good terms. For the moment, anyway."

"But Bev's the family gaffer now?"

"Yep, pretty much. Head of the family. The Godsister. Dad's said he can't trust me after 'The Kangaroo Incident', as he calls it."

"You ever find out who shot Skippy? Or why?"

"Not a clue. And Bev doesn't seem too bothered about finding them, either. Thinks they were from out of town. Albania or some-where. She thinks we might have been encroaching on their territory."

"Oh, can't go around encroaching. Well out of order, that."

As the girls hovered around the bar there was a cacophony of foreign accents. It was nice. A welcome change.

Seatown had a population of less than one hundred thousand. It was on the north-east coast of England and its location meant that you couldn't really end up there by accident. All the main roads bypassed the place. People rarely left the town and not too many outsiders decided to settle here, either.

Contact with foreigners was once, in fact, such a rarity that, legend had it, during the Napoleonic wars, the people of Seatown hanged a monkey because they thought it was a French spy. Not an unreasonable mistake, in many people's minds. So, I suppose you could say that there was a track record of exotic animals coming to an unfortunate end in Seatown.

It was also very hard to keep a secret here.

Which was why I knew all about Bev's new Harley Davidson, even if the rest of her family didn't. And why I wasn't particularly shocked when she'd mentioned Craig's attacker using a Luger, even though I hadn't mentioned it to her before.

I did consider sharing this information with Craig, of course. Well, for all of five minutes, I did.

After all, it was pretty clear that the Ferry family were in safe hands with Bev ruling the roost. And it was a lot safer for me to have her on my side than against me.

After all, despite what Craig might have thought, it isn't what you know, it's who you know.

INHERITANCE

Jane Casey

Fʀᴏᴍ ᴛʜᴇ ʀᴏᴀᴅ, you couldn't see there was a house there at all. The granite gateposts still stood but the gates themselves were long gone, and the lodge beside them was dark and shuttered, derelict.

But there was a house, and Anthony Gallagher knew it. He knew a lot about it, in fact. He had done his research. And he had chosen a moonless night, a night when the rain was relentless – a night when you wouldn't turn a dog away from the door, no matter who you were – to make his move. He stood just inside the gate, tapping his fingers against his thighs like a footballer preparing to take a penalty. This was the worst bit. It was always the same. Once he got started, he'd be all right. But before, the nerves got to him. Every time.

The rain fell steadily, collecting in the potholes that pitted the gravel drive. He flipped up the collar on his jacket and started walking. A good half-mile in the dark, on a surface that promised a broken ankle or worse with one false step. He was swearing blue murder before he'd gone halfway, wishing he had his torch handy, but it was somewhere at the bottom of his bag. Besides, it would look suspicious to turn up with a torch. It wasn't the sort of thing a casual traveller would carry, probably, and he wanted to look like nothing more than a casual traveller.

The bag kept knocking against his legs no matter which hand he carried it in. It was light enough. Just a change of shirt, a tooth-brush, a razor and shaving foam, the torch and some odds and ends for later on. He needed to be presentable. Part of the game was looking smart. It was all about setting them at their ease. Making them trust him. Gaining their confidence.

Taking advantage.

There was a light on, he was glad to see as he rounded the last corner of the drive. It wasn't late, he knew. Half-past eight. Too late to send him away, not so late that the occupant would refuse to answer the door on principle. But there was always the danger they would have gone to bed early. Old people did. Especially in houses where central heating was an unfamiliar concept.

Framed between two straggling yew trees, the house looked grander than he had expected. It was a foursquare Georgian box, grey stone like the gateposts. Five windows ran across the upper storey. On the ground floor, soft golden lamplight shone through the two windows to the left of the porch. He moved towards the rectangle of brightness nearest him, careful to stay in the shadows, treading softly on the loose gravel that gave under him with every step. A lovely room: small, but elegant, with grey silk-covered walls, a marble fireplace carved with sleek, well-fed figures and Doric columns, and a ceiling ornate with swags and garlands of plasterwork. On the walls, landscapes and portraits and miniatures and hunting scenes hung three and four deep, as if there weren't enough wall for all of them, and pairs of gold-framed mirrors with dim old glass in them softened the room's reflection to a dream. And the furniture. He didn't know a lot about it – small items were his bag – but he'd spent enough time looking in windows on Francis Street to recognize the living glow of top-quality mahogany and the arrogant, springing sweep of an Irish Georgian table-leg. A fine breakfront bookcase filled most of one wall, and a pair of brassbound peat buckets flanked the fire. He was looking at wealth, generations of it, there for the taking by anyone who chose to walk up the dark drive.

She was alone anyway. There was a decent fire alight and she had a chair pulled up to it, a sagging armchair that looked comfortable. Her back was to the window, but he could see her head was bent over something. A book maybe or some sewing, he thought, stretching his imagination to the utmost. He had very little idea what an elderly woman might do on a winter's evening to entertain herself. No TV that he could see. No music playing. She wasn't asleep; he could see her head turning as she concentrated on whatever it was. A movement by the door set his heart thumping but it was nothing, it was just a dog walking over to her, a black yoke that looked like four bits of different dogs stuck together. The great lantern jaw belonged on a mastiff; the body was fat and barrel-shaped, like a Labrador succumbing to middle-age spread. Short little legs and a flailing tail that threatened to knock over the table beside her completed the picture. At a word from her it collapsed to the ground as if shot, the two stumpy legs that were uppermost paddling the air beseechingly until she leaned over and rubbed its stomach.

It wasn't much of a dog, he thought, but a dog nonetheless. It might hear him, or smell him. Better to knock on the door before he was discovered lurking outside. Peering in through the window would be hard to explain. He moved away. Trust was the key, he'd often thought. Establish that and they're yours. And they *want* to like you. He pressed the bell by the front door, hearing it jangle deep in the house. They want you to be nice and honest and decent. They want you to be like they are themselves. He took a couple of paces back so as not to crowd her when she opened the door. It had the effect of taking him out of the shelter of the portico, exposing him to the rain, flattening his hair to his head. The light went on in the hall. He assumed a doubtful expression, a wistful look that had worked like a charm many times before. The door opened – not wide, but enough.

"You'll have to forgive me for knocking on your door at this late hour," he began. Word perfect. Practised. All the consonants where they should be. A little too mannered to be credible, did he but know it, but a fair attempt at sounding well spoken. "My car broke down, I'm afraid. Just down the road. There isn't anywhere else around here – I was hoping I might get some shelter for the night."

"How unfortunate." Her voice was unexpectedly deep for such an elderly lady, such a slight frame. She had her back to the light and he couldn't see the expression on her face. "Have you no mobile telephone?"

"Out of battery," he improvised. "I would have asked to use your phone, but I don't know who to call at this time of night."

"A garage would seem to be the obvious choice."

He tried a laugh, spluttering a little on the rain running down his face. Jesus, he was getting drenched. "You're right there. But there's none of them at work at this hour."

'There is always the Automobile Association."

It took him a second. "Oh – the AA. I'm not a member. I should be, but I'm not." He sniffed. Time to turn it up a notch. "I don't want to put you to any trouble. If there is a barn, or an outbuilding of some kind …"

"This isn't Bethlehem, young man." A gravelly note of amusement in the throaty voice. "You may come in. But you must take the place as you find it. I can't promise you comfort."

"A roof over my head is all I ask."

"Well, I have one of those. Of a sort."

She stepped back, holding the door open, and he ducked his head as he passed her in an awkward kind of bow. He took up a position a few paces away from her on the stone-flagged floor, trying to appear unthreatening, but his mind was working at top speed. The air in the hall was freezing and damp, a damp that had nothing to do with the weather and everything to do with a couple of centuries of decline. Overhead, a brass hall lantern was blazing, shining brightly enough that he could see the wavering cracks in the floor, the worn treads of the carpet on the stairs, his breath misting in front of his face. Indoors. Jesus.

He was able to see his hostess properly too, and she him. She was old – of course, he had known that, but *so* old now that he looked at her skin, folded in hundreds of tiny wrinkles that looked powdery soft and delicate. She had high, slender eyebrows that she had drawn herself in an unlikely brown-pencil arc, and the remains of bright pink lipstick feathered the edges of her mouth. So she still cared about her appearance. You wouldn't have known it from the dress she wore – a shocking thing it was, black but you could still see the stains of food and God knows what down the front. A few inches of hem hung down at the side. She had a shawl around her shoulders pinned carelessly with a crescent brooch that had the yellowish, muted dazzle of filthy diamonds. No rings on the hands that still looked strong despite the veins that wormed across their backs, the loose skin dappled with age spots. That made sense. She hadn't ever married. He could smell cigarettes off her from where he stood. The front of her hair was yellow-grey with nicotine staining, and her teeth were as brown as if they'd been carved out of wood.

Unconsciously he ran his tongue over his own set: capped as soon as he could afford it, Persil-white and even. He was twenty-seven – almost thirty, which he couldn't believe personally, but at least he looked younger. Baby-faced was what they'd always said. He played up to it, with the big blue eyes and a smile he practised every time he was alone with a mirror. The smile said, trust me. The smile said, I'm only a young fella. The smile said, I'm harmless. He kept his hair short and his clothes neutral, dark, unmemorable.

He had a story prepared about being a pharmaceutical salesman but there was no need for it; she went past him to the door of the room where he'd seen her sitting.

"You'll be warmer in here." The handle was loose and rattled as she turned it – a bad noise, distinctive and hard to muffle. The dog had its nose up against the door, desperate to get out. He hadn't heard it bark but it was on to him all right. It pushed out past her, lunging towards him, wheezing aggressively. Without meaning to, he stepped back, away.

"Don't be frightened. He won't harm you."

"Good boy," Anthony said feebly.

"He's deaf. Getting old." She stood holding the door, too polite to tap her foot but impatience in every angle of her body. "You're letting the heat out."

"Sorry, I—" He gestured helplessly. The dog was standing between him and the door. He itched to kick it. A good punt in the ribcage. If she wasn't looking, maybe.

"Oscar." There was a whipcrack of command in her voice and the dog squinted back at her, reluctant to obey. She tapped her thigh and it moved at last, stomping past her on its short little legs, heading for the rug in front of the fire. He slunk after it, looking around with frank admiration once he had gone through the door.

"Beautiful room."

"It was once." She sat down in her chair and picked up the book that she had left on the floor. She was going to start reading again, he realized, wondering with a flare of panic what she expected him to do with himself.

"I suppose I should introduce myself. Graham Field." A nice Proddy name.

She looked up briefly. "My name is Hardington. Clementine Hardington."

Clementine Lavinia Hardington, daughter of Colonel Greville Hardington (d. 1963) and Audrey De Courcy Hardington (d. 1960). Last of her line.

"Pleased to meet you, Miss Hardington." *Shit*. "Or is it Mrs Hardington?"

"Miss."

No "call me Clemmie" he noted, sitting down opposite her and stretching his hands out to the fire. *Know your place, young man.*

She had gone back to her book. He scanned the room, seeing signs of neglect everywhere now that he was inside. The plaster ceiling was missing chunks of its frieze and had a huge water stain over most of it. The upholstery was frayed on every chair, the stuffing spilling out. The silk on the walls was in tatters. Long curtains at the window were two-tone from years of exposure to sunlight. They were threadbare along their folds, torn in places, probably riddled with moths. The rug was worn to its backing in places and the pattern was hard to distinguish, coated as it was in a thick layer of dog hair. And why was it that all dogs, no matter what colour their coat, seemed to shed grey hair?

"Have you lived here long?" He'd got the tone exactly right. Innocent curiosity.

"I was born in this house."

"Very good," he said, as if she had done something impressive. Pure chance was all it was. Pure chance had left her sitting in her big house with the grand paintings and the high ceilings. You couldn't respect that.

But you could respect the collection of eighteenth-century mini-atures on both sides of the fireplace. And you could respect the collection of Japanese figurines on the table beside him: topsy-turvy animals, twisted people, weird things like a plum being eaten by a wasp, a mouse fighting with a lizard. He itched to pick them up for a closer look but didn't dare. He looked around stealthily. What else? A pair of silver-mounted horns caught his eye but he could see the inscription engraved on the base: too identifiable. Blue-and-white china in various shapes and sizes, fragile and faded. Matching vases that were probably Meissen, but one was chipped. Forget it. The paintings now: they were worth a second look. Not on this trip, though. Too big, too awkward.

He turned his attention to the other side of the fireplace and choked despite himself. A pair of shotguns, the real deal, fine engraving on the silver side plates and polished walnut stocks.

She looked up at the noise and saw where he was staring.

"The guns? They were my father's. Purdeys. Quite the best game gun there is. They were made for him in 1936."

And nowadays they were worth about a hundred grand, easy. "Do they still work?"

"Of course."

"Can you shoot?"

"Of course,' she said again, turning the page. "My father taught me." My *faw*-ther. And that would be him in the silver photograph frame on the table beneath the guns, he presumed. Big moustache. Heavy jaw. Small eyes.

He looked at the guns again, longingly. No point in trying to take them. Twenty-eight inches long; he'd never get them out without being spotted. Another time.

She had lit a cigarette and now, without looking, she tilted her hand to tap the ash into a vast cut-glass ashtray at her elbow. She missed and a shower of grey flecks drifted down on to the floor. Easy to see why the carpet was in a jocker. It would be a long time before anyone pushed a Hoover around it either.

She must have noticed him watching her. "I didn't offer you a cigarette."

"I'm grand." He was gasping for one, but Graham Field was a clean-living non-smoker. He wouldn't have taken a drink if she'd asked him to. Not an issue so far, it had to be said. But he was obviously making progress, because she put down the book.

"Are you hungry?"

A polite answer was no. He hesitated for long enough that he was sure she got the message he was lying. "No. Not at all."

"Did you have your dinner?"

"No," he said again. "No. I don't need anything, though."

"You can't go to bed hungry." She stood up. "I can make you something. An omelette."

He couldn't stand egg in any shape or form. "Lovely. But I don't want to put you to any trouble."

She didn't bother to say it wasn't any trouble, but she didn't sit down again either. Bending with a sigh, she tweaked the fireguard across the hearth, then switched off the lamp beside her, leaving only the dying fire to light the room. Anthony got the message and stood too, letting the dog have a head start in the race to join her.

There was a pile of fur on a chair by the door. When she picked it up and shook it out, it resolved itself into a full-length coat that must once have been beautiful. It stank of mothballs, but by the looks of things they hadn't worked. Slinging it around her shoulders, she turned and gave him a sidelong smile. "Brace yourself."

It was good advice. After the heat of the drawing room, the cold in the hall struck into his very bones. His clothes had dried on him, more or less, but the chill found out the patches of damp behind his knees, along his shoulders, down his back. He would catch his death, he thought, not quite closing the drawing-room door before following Miss Hardington to the back of the hall, Oscar shambling between them with an occasional wary look in his direction. There was an archway leading to a short flight of stairs that twisted into a passageway dimly lit with a weak bulb. He thought at first that the walls were decorated with more pictures, frame upon frame jostling for space, but when he looked he saw beetles and butterflies and moths lovingly mounted on rubbed green velvet.

"Who likes the bugs?"

"My grandfather was a keen naturalist." Disapproval in her voice. A warning to him to watch himself and a timely one at that.

It had been an Anthony question, not a Graham one. He, Anthony, wouldn't fancy looking at a load of insects on his way to the kitchen, but Graham might see the point.

"Very interesting."

She didn't respond. She was grappling with the door handle, another brute that screeched with a nerve-shredding sound of metal on metal when it finally gave way. The door opened and he peered into the kitchen, which proved to be smaller than he had imagined and disappointingly prosaic – sterile white cupboards and a too-bright fluorescent light. No big Aga keeping the place warm, either. It was arctic. Nothing to interest him here. The gas cooker looked to date from the 1960s at the latest, but that didn't make it an antique – just a health hazard.

"Sit down there."

"There" was a plain wooden table with rotting feet from years of standing on a much-washed tile floor. He sat gingerly on a chair that threatened to give way under him, wondering if woodworm ever turned on humans. The table and chairs were riddled.

"Water?"

If that was all that was on offer. "Yes, please."

A glass landed on the table in front of him, a cheap tumbler. "There's a tap in the scullery."

And you can get it yourself, he filled in silently, taking it and going through to the next room where he found a sink and shelves weighed down with old Waterford glass: bowls, decanters, glasses, vases. They were dusty, untouched for years at a guess, and as he washed out his own glass fastidiously and waited for the water to run cold again, he found himself eyeballing a dead fly in the wine-glass directly in front of his face. *One that my grand-faw-ther missed*, he thought, allowing himself a small chuckle.

She had been busy; the omelette was almost done when he got back, and there was a fork and a folded napkin on the table. The napkin was starched linen, at least two foot by two foot when he unfolded it, and the folds were so stiff that it stood up in his lap as if he had an erection, which was far from being the case. The omelette was heavy on bits of eggshell and light on filling. He had an awful suspicion that the flecks in it were not black pepper but cigarette ash.

She sat opposite him, sideways to the table, smoking, and didn't seem to notice when he slipped the guts of the omelette into the napkin and flicked it under the table to the dog.

"That was very nice. Thank you very much. Were the eggs from your own hens?"

A blue glare. "I bought them in Supervalu."

Right. Enough of trying to make friends. Fuck it. He was only going to rob her anyway. "It's getting late. I don't want to keep you up. I can tidy up here if you just point me to where I'm to sleep."

"There's no need to tidy up. It can wait." The dog had dealt with his leftovers and was now investigating the frying pan. She had left it on the floor for him. Anthony felt his stomach heave. No cooked breakfast for him in the morning, thank you. She stood and it still came as a surprise to him that her posture was better than his, perfectly straight, not hunched over like the doddering old lady he'd expected. She should have looked ridiculous in the fur coat but she wore it as if it were the obvious thing, and so it was for the conditions. He'd have dressed like a fucking Eskimo if he'd lived in that house.

He'd expected to go back to the main hall so he could get his bearings, but there was another staircase, a wooden one that climbed up the back of the house. The creaks from it were chronic.

"I'll put you in the guest room. The bed isn't made up but the sheets and blankets are on the end of it."

"No problem."

"It may be a little cold."

"I'll be grand." *I'll be keeping busy ...*

"The bathroom is here." She indicated a room off the half-landing where they had paused. It reeked of Dettol, which was better than he might have hoped even if not exactly inviting. Anyway, he wouldn't be committing himself there. Face and hands only. Stripping for a bath was out of the question.

The bedrooms opened off a narrow central hall. His, she indicated, was at the very end of the house, and he went down the

hallway counting doors, noting creaking floorboards, marking out
his route. Opening the door, he recoiled as if someone had punched
him. He would not have thought it was possible for the air temperature to be so low in what was technically a sound structure. The
bed was a few inches shy of being a double and looked as if its last
occupant had died in it. The curtains on the window didn't meet in
the middle when he pulled them. The bow-fronted chest of drawers
listed to one side. The pictures were dismal flower studies, definitely
the work of an amateur. This was not a house that welcomed
visitors.

He made some attempt to make the bed, laying the sheets and
blankets over it. One blanket to protect him from the mattress
which was probably jumping with vermin. Two to go over him.
And his damp coat over that. He would still freeze. He huddled
under them, smoking, reckless of being caught as she would never
be able to tell it wasn't the smell of her own smokes. Usually he
would have been worried about falling asleep, but there was no
chance of that. He was shaking too much. At least it was no longer
raining. He hoped it would stay that way. He had to drive back to
Dublin the following day and it would be quicker if the roads were
dry. He would boot it the whole way, with the car's heater knocked
up to the max, he promised himself.

When he finally uncoiled himself and slid out from under the
blankets, he was stiff. He stretched, rolling his head from one
shoulder to the other, shaking out his arms, breathing deeply the
way he'd seen runners prepare before fitting themselves into the
starting blocks.

"Off we go." He slipped through the bedroom door into the
hallway. It was pitch dark. No streetlights. No moonlight. Just him
and his trusty torch, hooded so it only cast a speck of light. He
drifted down the hall, silent in his socks, holding his breath as he
went past the door of the woman's room. The stairs were an
unknown quantity which he didn't like, he didn't like at all, and he
took his time going down them, testing each tread before he put his
weight on it. Then the hallway, the stone floor cold under his feet
but solid, reliable, and he could pick up the pace.

He started in the dining room, playing his torch over the paintings on the walls, the long table, the fine chandelier and the twenty-four matching chairs, before he got down to business. Most conveniently, there was plenty on display that he liked the look of: silver, mainly. Serving spoons engraved with what had to be the family crest, a sauce boat standing proudly on tiny clawed feet, a pair of oval salt cellars with blue glass liners, a silver dish ring decorated with leaves and bunches of grapes. It was hard to stop himself from taking too much. He couldn't go mad. He had to take enough to make it worth his while but not so much that she'd notice straightaway. He wrapped everything that he took in strips of dusters, brand-new and soft, to cushion them from damage and keep them from banging together when he carried them upstairs. It was a matter of pride to make neat bundles, folding the material intricately. He should have been hurrying but he took his time over it.

In the drawing room he hesitated, suddenly struck by what he was doing, unsettled by the looks he was getting from the family portraits on the walls. Her ashtray was still there, her book over the arm of her chair. She sat in there day in, day out, surrounded by the things that had been passed down to her by her family. Who was he to take them?

Except that why shouldn't he? She and her family had had the best of everything through at least two Irelands: the one where they were top of the heap and the ordinary peasants were just there to admire them and pay them rent, and the one where the proles suddenly had the power, riding the crest of a wave of prosperity, buying up the old houses and furniture and art as if there would always be money, as if there were nothing but. She had held on to what was hers, even then. And in the third Ireland, the new one, the one where no one had a euro to their name, it was time to share out what there was. Specifically, with him. Why should she keep it anyway? She wasn't really Irish, Anthony thought, conveniently forgetting the generations of Hardingtons who had lived and died in the house. This was practically his duty as a proud Irishman.

He bagged a handful of snuffboxes, silver and gold, a pair of blue-and-white plates, a Dresden shepherdess of exquisite frailty accompanied by her would-be suitor plucking a lyre, and three of the little Japanese curios. God knows if anyone else would like them but he did, he thought, deliberating over which ones to take. He settled on a dormouse dozing inside one half of a walnut shell, a snake coiled into an evil-looking pyramid and an ivory samurai in full armour, his hands by his sides, his chest puffed out nobly. Six of the miniatures came with him as well: pretty girls in low-cut dresses, the sort of thing that appealed to collectors. They were easy to package up.

On his way out, he stopped by the shotguns. Putting his bag down, he lifted one of them off its hooks, feeling the heft of it, the lethal snugness of it against his shoulder, the *willingness* of the trigger. A thing of beauty. He put it back on the wall slowly, long-ingly, and winked at the black-and-white photo.

"Fair play, Greville."

There had been nothing in the kitchen for him – he didn't touch glass, too fragile – and although he looked into the library, he didn't fancy it. Dustsheets covered the furniture and the books were locked behind elaborate grating. He didn't know what he was supposed to be looking for, anyway. And he had a fair bit, he thought, hefting the shoulder bag that contained his night's work. Time to quit. He ghosted back into the hall and up the stairs, counting them under his breath and skipping the fourth, the ninth, the seventeenth …

Where he came a cropper was halfway down the landing. Seduced by the dim light from the window at the end that guided him towards his room, he had decided he knew his way well enough to dispense with the torch. He had no warning when he collided with something solid, something heavy, something that uttered a long-drawn-out howl as he nosedived into the ancient carpet, tasting the dust of ages and his own very modern blood.

It was as if she had been waiting behind her door. It slammed back against the wall, light spilling out into the hall so he had to shield his eyes for a second. She was still wearing the coat, he noticed, blinking up at her.

"Mr Field. What happened?"

"It was the fu— it was the dog. It was Oscar. I just – I needed the toilet. I was just looking for it. I got confused." *Stop talking. Start thinking*. He couldn't hit her. Not an old woman. But if he ran downstairs ... an image flashed into his mind. The shotguns. He curved his hand around an imaginary stock, practically feeling it against his palm. If he was quick, he could deal with her before she had a chance to phone the guards. That assumed she didn't have a phone upstairs, it assumed the shotguns were loaded, and it also assumed he had the nerve to do it. Murder. Kill her, in cold blood. Blow her away. Then spend a million years trying to wipe his prints and DNA off every bit of the house. It was a bit different from pocketing a few knick-knacks, when you thought about it.

He was still lying on the ground, grovelling in front of her. He got up slowly, picking up his bag as if it were nothing of note.

"It's the middle of the night. Where were you going?" She didn't sound panicked, which was something.

"I was looking for the toilet. I got confused about which stairs it was off."

"The back stairs." She pointed. "Down there."

"That explains why I couldn't find it." He tried a smile. "Sorry for disturbing you. And for stepping on the dog. Sorry about that, Oscar."

The mutt gave him a wall-eyed glare.

"I'll head down there, so. Sorry again." The toilet wasn't a bad plan, actually. The tension was squeezing his guts. He needed a crap. He walked away in the direction she had indicated, waiting for her to call him back to ask for a better explanation, or to tell him to empty his pockets, and what's in that bag?

She said nothing. He risked a look back at her as he turned the corner to go down the narrow back stairs, and she was standing in the light, leaning over, talking to the dog. He allowed himself a small grin of triumph as he headed into the dark. They were like children. They couldn't imagine you would do them wrong, so they believed every word you said to them. Fools. He was glad he had taken advantage of her now. He'd have kicked himself twelve ways to Sunday if he'd left empty-handed because of what? An attack of conscience? She wasn't even nice to him.

* * *

In the morning, he came downstairs carrying his bag to find his hostess in the hall. "Ah, you're up at last. Did you sleep well?"

What time she got up at, he couldn't imagine. It was only seven o'clock.

"I didn't, no. I think the roof is leaking, to be honest with you."

It had started raining heavily while he was taking his celebratory shit, the water gurgling in cast-iron drainpipes and spilling from unreliable guttering. He had got back to his room to discover the bed was saturated, the ceiling still dripping. The remainder of the night he spent curled up on the floor, trying to find a position where his bones didn't ache and the draught from under the door didn't cut through the one blanket he'd been able to salvage.

"Oh, dear." She didn't sound surprised. "I've had breakfast already. But there's some porridge if you'd like."

"No. Thank you." He'd yak if he tried. "I'll get something later."

She was looking thoughtful. "I don't suppose – I shouldn't ask, but maybe if you would – if you have a head for heights, which I must admit I don't—"

Payment for the night's board. He put the bag down, resigned. Always leave them grateful. "What can I do? Is it the roof?"

"Could you see if there are many slates gone? The man who looks after it is away."

"How do I get up there?"

"Through the attic. But you'll need to get the ladder. Cormac always uses his own."

"No problem. Where is it?"

"It's in the shed." She gestured vaguely to the back of the house. "Out there. The door is jammed, though. You'll have to go out the front door and walk around. And I think it might be quite near the back."

He was true to his promise, getting back to Dublin in record time with the radio blasting dance music and the heater blowing out a fug of hot air. He'd earned his money, that was for sure. First getting the fucking ladder out from what turned out to be a barn the size of a bus garage, full to the roof with junk. *"Shed" my arse.*

Then getting it into the house while Clemmie waved her hands and shrieked warnings to him every time he came near a light fitting. Then propping it up on the rotting floor of the attic, discovering that the rungs were shaky in the extreme, and making it out on to the leads of the roof in time for the rain to start again. He had taken shelter by a chimneystack and enjoyed an illicit cigarette, thinking of her waiting patiently for him to return. She would think he was doing a thorough job if he didn't hurry back. Another cigarette put manners on the hunger that was beginning to twist at his stomach. He didn't waste any time looking for missing slates. It was something of a surprise to find there were any up there at all. A deep breath, then back down the stairs with the ladder. He took it back to the shed, jamming it in as best he could between a knackered old Riley with deflated tyres and a load of rusty milk churns.

The relief of getting on to the M50, within reach of civilization. The joy of seeing Dublin spread out before him as he came over the mountains, the Pigeon House towers striped red and white in the distance, Howth Head glowing green behind them. The fucking sun came out and everything. Welcome to the Promised Land, my child.

In his case, welcome to the Sundrive Road. There was a house there, a small one, not the kind you'd notice, and it was the home of the finest fence he'd ever met, a fat man named Ken who had every book you could imagine on antiques and never needed to consult one of them. Anthony didn't ask what happened to the things he brought him. The fat man paid cash and that was all that mattered to Anthony. That and getting rid of the stuff before the guards came calling.

Ken's wife was a comically small woman, a little elf of a thing. Would he have a cup of tea? And a sandwich? He practically took the hand off her; he was desperate for something.

Ken was scratching himself in the front room, layered in cardigans and jumpers as if he were capable of feeling the cold. The room was hot anyway. He drew the blinds without getting up from his chair.

"Stick the light on there and let's have a look at what you've got."

Anthony sat on the other side of the coffee table and dug in his bag, setting out his bundled-up dusters where Ken could reach them. The fence tapped his fingers against his belly, waiting for his wife to come back with the tea.

"Tell me about the house."

Anthony described it in as much detail as he could. Ken listened, asking questions, thinking. The Purdeys had him shifting in his chair with what could only be excitement.

"Shame you didn't find out anything about the paintings. Never mind. I'll make a note."

Mrs Ken rattled in with a tray and handed Anthony a mug and a ham sandwich. Ken got the same, and a plate of biscuits. He needed to keep his strength up, Anthony reflected. Poor man couldn't be expected to wait until lunch.

As soon as the door closed behind her Ken's pudgy fingers went to work, unexpectedly delicate as he began unwrapping what Anthony had brought him. The first thing was the silver sauce boat. Even though he knew what was inside each parcel, Anthony still felt a thrill as the last fold of yellow cloth fell away – to reveal something that was definitely not an eighteenth-century sauce boat.

" ... the fuck?"

Reverently, Ken set a wooden teapot-stand down on the table. It had been crowned with a plastic measuring jug. "Well. Very interesting."

"I don't understand it. I don't know what happened."

The fat man was at work on the next parcel. He looked down at the contents without showing them to Anthony. "What's this supposed to be?"

"Two Dresden figurines."

'Two wooden dolls." He held them up. They were hideous things, homemade, with crudely painted faces.

The next parcel was the silver dish ring, or rather a stainless-steel dog bowl.

"I don't fucking believe this ..." Anthony picked up one of the smaller packages and started ripping, pulling it apart recklessly, careless of the contents, which was a mistake. It was not a fine little carving of a mouse asleep inside a walnut shell. It was a hen's egg, and it broke. He could feel the blood beating in his head, the rage pushing against the bones of his skull. "She sent me on a wild goose chase. She had me up on the roof cooling my heels while she was downstairs going through my bag. The fucking bitch."

"You wouldn't be up to them," the fat man observed in much the same tone as if he'd said the sky was blue.

Together, they unwrapped every parcel on the table, revealing every piece of junk that Anthony had carried away from Clementine Hardington's house. Chipped brown side-plates dating from the 1970s. A lump of coal. Two wooden spoons. Orange plastic egg-cups that were supposed to be salt cellars. Six green tiles masquerading as framed miniatures. Old matchboxes filled to the brim with rice to make them as heavy as the snuffboxes he'd assumed they were.

"This is a nightmare." Anthony couldn't stop staring at the junk on the table, as if he could make it change back into riches if he only looked hard enough. "I'm embarrassed, Ken."

"So you should be." He settled back in his chair, lacing his fingers over his paunch. "Ah, well."

"Is that it?"

"Doesn't make any difference to me. You're the one who's out of pocket." He yawned. "You shouldn't be surprised. There's a reason they've held on for so long. They don't give it up easily." He nodded at the last parcel, the smallest, which Anthony was clutching. It should have been the ivory samurai, upright and noble. "Open it."

It was tightly wrapped, folded in on itself, and he struggled to undo it, pulling the material apart eventually so what was inside bounced out and landed on the table where it spun around and around. Ken picked it up.

"What's this? A shotgun shell?"

Anthony shook his head, his mouth suddenly dry. "It's a message."

He knew in his heart that even if he had realized what she was planning – even if he had been as angry with her then as he was now – he would never have been able to pull the trigger. He knew it just as well as he knew that if she held the gun, she wouldn't hesitate. That was as much her legacy from her ancestors as the crumbling stones of the house, the acres of boggy parkland, the fine art and furniture and woodworm and all.

And as far as Anthony was concerned, she was welcome to the lot of it.

A MEMORABLE DAY

L. C. Tyler

IF THERE'S ONE piece of advice I'd like to pass on it's this. Keep a note of your alias. There's nothing worse than the sudden realization that you've no idea who you are

The young lady, whose name had also temporarily slipped my mind, was starting to look at me a little oddly.

"Mr Smith? Your tea …"

Smith – yes, of course. "John Smith", probably. My imagination is almost as bad as my memory. Hopefully they wouldn't ask me to confirm Smith's address, which was now forgotten way beyond any hope of recall. That's the good thing about being a hero, of course – people don't cross-examine you or expect you to provide proof of identity.

"Thank you," I said, accepting the steaming mug and wondering how many times she'd addressed me before I'd responded. "Thank you. That will go down a treat after all this afternoon's excitement. A treat." I tried to appear brave but modest – I've seen it done, so had a vague idea how it should look.

I took a first sip of the tea. Heroes clearly took plenty of sugar, or maybe the young lady had distantly remembered that a hot sweet drink was good for shock. We'd all had a shock, though possibly I'd had a bit more than the rest of them. Hopefully the worst was over. Fingers crossed.

"I'm sorry we can't offer our hero something stronger," said Mr Adewole, who I remembered was the Assistant Branch Manager (or was it Deputy?). He straightened his tie. I'd seen one like it in a shop earlier – pure silk, sixty quid. I'd been tempted, as they say, but not tempted enough.

"Tea's fine," I said. "The cup that cheers."

"You're a hero," said Mr Adewole.

"He's a hero," confirmed the young lady. (Arabella? Daisy? Lillwen? Some name like that anyway.)

"Seems like I'm a hero, then," I said.

We'd explored the present indicative quite well. I am a hero. Thou art a hero. He, she or it is a hero. Actually it was the first person plural we needed. We are heroes. I hadn't done it alone.

I'd been walking along the Holloway Road, head down, doing my level best not to get in anyone's way. My bag was a bit heavy and I'd stopped outside the bank briefly to check the contents and make sure all was well. I'd just put it on the ground and had scarcely begun to pull the zip when this large geezer with a stocking mask over his face and a sawn-off shotgun in his hands comes charging out of the door. I stood up and stepped aside respectfully, as you do with large geezers carrying shotguns. He went past at a fair lick and off down the Holloway Road. Then, stone me if his mate (small geezer, stocking mask, large nylon holdall stuffed with cash) didn't run straight into me from behind as I was stepping back. He wasn't big, as I say, but he was going fast enough to knock us both to the ground three or four feet from where I had been standing. I didn't bear him any ill will – he hadn't trodden on my bag or anything – so I suppose it was just a reflex reaction that made me lash out at him the moment we were both back in a sitting position.

With my arm fully extended, my fist just about made contact with his face. I'm not sure he even registered that I was trying to punch him, to be honest with you. It must have been simple curiosity that made him pause, looking at me as best he could through ten-denier nylon, for just a fraction of a second too long. A stocky member of the public had come running up and pinioned him in a pair of muscular arms. The small bank robber cursed me under his breath, but there was nothing more for him – or me – to do. Game over.

In the middle distance, the big guy with the shotgun had reached a conveniently parked Honda with its engine running. It was purple – a bit too visible as a getaway vehicle, but I'd already seen evidence that they weren't the brightest pair of bank robbers in North

London. He'd been about to jump into the fake-leather passenger seat when he turned and saw that his mate with the money was sadly no longer with him. The big guy too was still wearing ladies' hosiery on his face, and I couldn't read his expression, but from his body language he wasn't best pleased. For an instant I thought he might be about to come back and shoot a few of us, but fortunately all hell chose to break loose that very moment. The bank staff had been able to get their nervous little fingers to the alarm buttons and there were lights and noises and people running everywhere.

The young lady was already heading down the steps towards us, with Mr Adewole a few prudent paces behind her. Somewhere in the distance you could just make out a police siren – probably a squad car off to deal with a bad outbreak of graffiti, but it was enough to make up the mind of the guy with the gun. He was back in the purple Honda, which took off with a vicious roar of the engine and a screech of tyres – an event common enough on the Holloway Road not to draw much comment from passers-by.

The stocky guy could probably have hung on to the small bank robber all day if he'd had to, but the police were there within a minute of the alarm going off. They handcuffed the robber and then they wanted statements from the rest of us. Under the circumstances it seemed best that I come up with a false name and address, though the rest of my account was much as I've just told you. The stocky individual, who gave an address in Preston, proved to be called Shuttleworth. He was just visiting London and had expected Holloway to be a bit like that. Shuttleworth didn't seem the sort to lie about his name or anything else. He seemed pleased enough with his day so far, unlike the bank robber who shot me a glance before he was led away.

Mr Adewole, the Assistant or Deputy Manager of the bank, had congratulated us several times and then, possibly feeling mere words were inadequate, had issued a general invitation to tea in his office. I thought it might look a bit suspicious to say "no" and so said "yes". Shuttleworth, having as clear a conscience as need be, declined both tea and any suggestion that his had been more than a supporting role in the proceedings. I was, he said, the only hero and it had been his privilege to assist me. The way I'd landed that punch! Wow! He'd help me again, if I would just state where and when he would be needed.

I watched him depart with a degree of envy and proceeded to Mr Adewole's office, where we were joined by the young lady (Vicky? Martha? Faith?) and by the police inspector, who was taking a brief break from his questioning of staff and customers. The young lady had a nice smile. The police inspector didn't. I sat in one of the plastic chairs and pushed my bag under the seat as unobtrusively as I could.

"It was terrible," the young lady said. (Alis? Bubbles? Storm? Something like that.) "The two of them came running into the bank with stockings over their faces, yelling at the tops of their voices. Then the big one pulled a gun out of the holdall he was carrying."

"Did he?" I said.

"Yes," said the young lady. She frowned. "It was a bag ... a bit like that one under your seat."

"Like mine?" I said.

"Very much like yours," said the young lady. "I can't quite see it now you've moved your legs, but, yes, almost identical. They stuffed the money in it afterwards."

"Funny coincidence," I said. "He probably bought his bag in the market, where I got mine. At least, that's what I'd imagine. Small world."

"And do you know how much money?" asked Mr Adewole, uninterested in probability and coincidence.

Mr Adewole obviously wanted to impress me, so I guessed low. "Five thousand?" I suggested, as if I thought that was a whole heap of cash.

"*Seventy*-five thousand," said Mr Adewole. "That's what you saved us, Mr Smith, by your quick action. Seventy-five thousand pounds."

"He should get a reward," said the young lady, who not only had a nice smile but was clearly generous with the bank's money. I was beginning to like her.

"I'm sure he will," said Mr Adewole, slightly more cautiously. "Unfortunately we can't give you cash now to take away in your bag." He laughed.

"Shame," I said. I took another sip of tea. It was in a Charles and Diana Engagement mug – goodness knows where that had hidden all these years.

"I bet," said Mr Adewole, "that when you got up this morning you didn't expect you'd be preventing a bank robbery."

"No," I said. "Nobody told me to expect that. It would have been helpful if they had."

"In fact, a funny thought has just occurred to me," said Mr Adewole, who was quite chatty for a Deputy or Assistant Manager. "Maybe you too have a sawn-off shotgun in your bag, Mr Smith. Maybe you were coming *in* to rob the bank, as the other two gentlemen were coming *out*. That would be terribly amusing."

He was easily amused.

"Ha," I said.

"What *is* in your bag?" asked the police inspector, speaking for the first time. He put his own mug of tea down on Mr Adewole's desk. He'd got a yellow one marked "BOSS" in big red letters, possibly Mr Adewole's own, though he was really assistant or deputy boss.

"In the bag? Oh … er … this and that. Bits and bobs. Various stuff," I said, in a way that should have convinced even the most suspicious and untrusting of policemen.

"I didn't really mean …" Mr Adewole began. He looked from me to the inspector and back again. We weren't finding his joke as funny as he had hoped.

"Maybe you could just open the bag, Mr Smith, and let me have a look inside," said the inspector. "I'd better check it, just so that I don't look a total plonker if Mr Adewole is right."

I smiled to show that I understood he was only kidding and the heroes were not required to open their bags and justify what was inside.

"*Now*, please, Mr Smith," he said.

If I could give you a second piece of advice it's that you have to know when the game is well and truly up. My wife always says to me: "Benny," she says, "your face gives you away every time. There's no point in getting mixed up in any dodgy stuff because your normal expression is that of most people when they've just murdered their grandmother and cut her up for cat meat. My brother could lie his way out of anything and usually does. But not you. You have a naturally guilty conscience. Call it a curse. Call it a gift. But if you ever get caught, just own up. It'll save everyone time in the long run."

I opened the bag very slowly. The inspector looked inside and gave a low whistle.

"That's top of the range, that is," he said.

"Yes," I said. "Blu-ray, built-in hard drive – only just in the shops."

"Good picture quality?"

"I don't know yet."

The inspector looked at the unboxed DVD player in my bag, and frowned.

"I'm just returning it to Davies Brothers department store, down the road," I said. "I bought it there a couple of days ago and it doesn't seem to be working properly. I'm taking it back to check what's wrong. Probably I just can't programme it properly."

"You got kids?" asked the inspector.

"No," I said.

"Shame. They always know how to do these things. It's about all they're good for, but they do have that advantage."

He bent down and zipped up the bag for me.

"Thanks for the tea," he said to Mr Adewole. "I'd better finish what I was doing. Your people will want to get home."

"Me too," I said, seizing the moment. "I'd better get back. Home sweet home."

"Where is it you live?" asked the inspector.

"Close by," I hedged.

"Me too," said the inspector. "We'll bump into each again other soon, like as not. You'll probably have to give evidence at the trial, of course."

"Yes," I said. But only if they could find me. However much I might be to blame for what had occurred this afternoon, at least I'd not be giving evidence at the trial – a small blessing but one to be counted all the same.

"And there's the reward," said Mr Adewole again. "We'll be writing to you about that. A nice fat cheque, I should imagine." He smiled. He too had decided he could risk being open-handed with the bank's money. It was less of a risk than he imagined.

I wondered for a moment if there was any way of finding out what fictitious address I'd given, then going round there to intercept the cheque somehow and pay it into an account in the name of Smith ... No, maybe not. There is a limit to how far you should try to push your luck and I'd ridden mine quite nicely so far.

"Thanks," I said.

"And, Mr Smith, I do apologize if you thought we were in any way accusing you of being a bank robber. It was merely an inappropriate joke on my part. Neither I nor Fauzia would have wished to imply anything of the sort." (Of course, not Lillwen or Arabella – *Fauzia*, that was it.)

"No offence taken," I said to Mr Adewole.

"You're a hero," said Fauzia. "A have-a-go hero. You should get a medal."

I gave her a sort of regretful smile that might have meant anything. A medal too was something I'd have to pass on.

"You had better go to Davies's, before they close," said Fauzia helpfully.

"Yes," I said, though the store would be open for another two hours at least. "I'd better dash, hadn't I? Time and tide."

"And sorry about the robber thing," said Mr Adewole again. "Just a joke."

"I've already forgotten about it," I said.

In the banking hall everything was back to normal. People were queuing and paying in cheques. People were getting cash without the help of shotguns. People were being sold ISAs. Nobody gave me the slightest glance as I crossed the floor, which is how I like things. I walked through the doorway and out on to the street. I breathed a big sigh of relief. Davies Brothers was a couple of hundred yards down on the right and that's where I headed.

Oh, yes, I had something on my conscience but for once it wasn't dodgy gear that I was fencing for my brother-in-law. I wouldn't be fencing anything for him for … let's say, five years less time off for good behaviour. No, what I was worrying about was what I would tell my wife when I got home. Maybe I should just begin: "Funny thing, Tracey, I bumped into your brother coming out of the bank this afternoon." She'd laugh when I told her. Hopefully.

LAPTOP

Cath Staincliffe

I'D BEEN BOOSTING laptops for a couple of years but never with such bloody disastrous consequences. Up until then it'd been easy money. Two or three a week kept body and soul together and was a damn sight more conducive to the good life than temping in some god-awful office with all the crap about diets and Botox and endless squabbles over the state of the kitchen. Shorter working week, too. Eight maybe ten hours, the rest of the time my own.

I always dressed well for work – part of the scam, isn't it? People are much less guarded if I'm in a designer suit: something smart, fully lined, along with good shoes, hair and make-up. Helps me mingle. Looking like an executive, some high-flying business-woman, gives me access to the most fertile picking grounds: conference centres, business parks, commuter trains, the best restaurants and coffee bars. And, after all, if someone nicks your laptop who's going to spring to mind? Me with my crisp clothes, my detached air, snag-free tights ... or some lad in a beanie hat and dirty fingernails?

So, that fateful day, as I came to think of it, I was working at Manchester Airport. I do it four or five times a year; the train service is handy and with all the business flights I've plenty of targets to choose from.

As with any type of thieving, opportunity is all. The aim being to get the goods and get away with it. When I started working for Danny, he came out with me but I was quick on the uptake and after a few runs he left me to it. I'm one of his best operators but he reckons I'm lazy. You could make more, he tells me near enough every time I swap the merchandise for cash, a bit of ambition you could be clearing fifty a year, higher tax bracket. The last bit's a joke. No one in the business pays any tax. But I'm not greedy. I enjoy the time I have. Gives me a chance to indulge my passion. I paint watercolours. Surprised? So was I when I first drifted into it. Then it became the centre of my life. It was what got me out of bed and kept me up late.

That day when I spotted the mark I dubbed him The Wolf. He had a large head, coarse brown hair brushed straight back from his face, a long, sharp nose and lips that didn't quite meet; too many teeth for his mouth. Like a kid with those vampire fangs stuffed in their gob. I assumed he was meeting someone as he made no move to check in and we were near the arrivals hall. He had the laptop on the floor, to his right, at the side of his feet. He was in prime position at the end of a row of seats, in the lounge where people have coffee while they wait for the information boards to change or for a disembodied voice to make hard-to-hear announcements.

After walking about a bit, checking my exit routes and getting a feel for the atmosphere that day and the people hanging around (no nutters, drunks or surfeit of security guards), I settled myself on the end seat of the row adjoining his. He and I were back to back. I put my large bag down beside me at my left. My bag and his laptop were maybe five inches apart. On the seat next to me I put my own laptop and handbag. When I turned to my left I could see us both reflected in the plain glass of the offices that ran along the edge of the concourse. There were coloured screens behind the glass to mask the work areas so no danger of my being seen from in there.

Timing is crucial. I watched his reflection as he glanced down to check his laptop and I moved a few seconds after, just as a large family with raucous kids and two trolley-loads of bags hove into view, squabbling about where to wait. Keeping my upper body straight, I reached my left arm back and grasped the handle of his laptop, pulled it forward and lifted it up and into my big bag. I grabbed the handles of that, hitched it on to my shoulder, collected my other things, stood and walked steadily away. Belly clamped, mouth dry, senses singing.

Twice I've been rumbled at that very moment, before I'm out of range. Both in the early days. Turning, I look confused. "Sorry?"

"My laptop!" They are incandescent with outrage, ready to thump me. Except I don't run or resist. I gawp at them, look completely befuddled, furrowed brow. Mouth the word "laptop"? My hand flies to my mouth, I stare in my bag. "Oh, my God." Both hands to my mouth. I blush furiously. Wrestle the shopper from my shoulder. "God, I am so sorry." Withdraw the offending article, hand it back, talking all the time, on the brink of tears. "It's exactly like mine." I hold up my own laptop (case only: I'm not lugging around something that heavy all day – besides someone might nick it). "I was miles away... oh, God, I feel awful. You must think, oh, please I am so, so sorry. I don't know what to say." Deliberately making a scene, drawing attention, flustered woman in a state. Their expressions morph: rage, distrust, exasperation, embarrassment, and eventually relief tinged with discomfort. They just want me to shut up and disappear. Which I do.

With The Wolf, though, all goes smooth as silk.

Until I get the bastard thing home and open it.

I generally check to see if they're password-protected. Danny has a little code that cracks about fifty per cent of them, the rest he passes on to a geek who sorts them out. Danny appreciates it if I let him know which ones need further attention when I hand them over.

So I got home, changed into something more comfortable, had lunch on my little balcony. On a clear day, to the east I can see the hills beyond the City of Manchester stadium and the velodrome, and to the west the city centre: a jumble of Victorian Gothic punctuated by modern glass and steel, wood and funny angles, strong colours. It's a vista I love to paint. But that day was damp, hazy, shrouding the skyline. I polished off a smoked salmon salad, some green tea, then got down to business.

Danny's code didn't work. And I could have left it at that. I should have. But there was a memory stick there: small, black, inoffensive-looking. I picked it up and slotted it into the USB port on my own machine. There wasn't much on it, that's what I thought at the time, just one file, called *Accounts*. I opened it expecting credits and debits, loss carried forward or whatever. Perhaps bank details that Danny could milk. Overseas accounts, savings.

Not those sort of accounts.

12 June 2010

She was very drunk when she left the club. Falling into a taxi, falling out at her place. I let her get inside and waited for a while before I went in the back. She was stumbling about for long enough. When I judged she was asleep I crept upstairs. I had everything ready. She woke. But I'd done it by then. The colour flooded her face and she tried to get up, jerking, but couldn't, then the flush drained away and her eyes glazed over. I closed her eyes. She looked more peaceful that way. It was wonderful. Better than I'd imagined. A pure rush. Cleaner, brighter than drugs or religion or sex. On a different plane. I wish I'd stayed there longer now. I didn't want to leave her but I was being cautious. Everything meticulously done. Precise, tidy. I've waited all my life for this. I wasn't going to ruin it by being clumsy and leaving anything they could trace back to me.

18 June 2010

Lady Luck must be smiling down on me. No one suspects a thing.

The Wolf obviously fancied himself as a scribe. Some sort of crime thriller. I wondered if he'd got this backed up anywhere else or if he'd just lost his life's work. I read on. I mainly read biographies but it was intriguing. The next entry was a couple of months later.

```
23 August 2010


I'm getting restless again. Low after the
high? Things are difficult. I can't
remember her face any more. I should have
taken a photograph.


4 September 2010


I've found the next one. Not sure how to
get in but the good weather might make
things easier. An open window, patio
doors? She has a beautiful face; very
simple, strong mouth, wide eyes. I want
to see those eyes change.
```

A tinge of unease made me pause. I scrolled down the document – it was only four pages long. I scanned it all again. The dates spanned a nine-month period. The latest entry was from February 2011, only two weeks earlier. Four pages, hardly a novel. A short story maybe?

Or real?

The thought made my stomach lurch and my throat close. I switched the machine off, my hand trembling a little. Stupid. Just some sad bloke's sick fantasy. But like sand in an oyster shell the notion stuck. It grated on me while I tried to paint, making it impossible to concentrate.

I haven't picked up a brush since.

That evening I sat in front of the television flicking the channels. Nothing held my attention. The memory stick crouched at the edge of my vision, a shiny black carapace, like a malevolent beetle or a cockroach. I decided then there was one way to stop the flights of fancy. I just needed to prove to myself that the accounts were fictional.

24 September 2010

She never locks up when she goes next door for the morning paper. I hid in the spare room all day. The excitement was unbearable, delicious. And then I waited while she cooked herself a meal and bathed and watched television. It was after midnight before she turned out the lights. She'd been drinking whisky, I could smell it on her breath and from the glass beside her. I thought it would make her drowsy but she flinched when I touched her and struggled and almost ruined everything. She made me angry. I had to punish her. After all, it could have been perfect. She had robbed me of that. She soon learned her lesson and then I did it and the spasms started; the life bucking from her. I felt her go cold.

Then we were even. I still laid her out nicely, enjoyed her till the sun rose. Not long enough. With her spoiling it like that I had to cover my tracks. Everyone has candles around these days and some people forget to replace the smoke alarm batteries. Whisky's an accelerant. I want the next one to be perfect even if it takes me longer to find her.

I reread the entries and made a note of the dates. There were no names or addresses, not even locations, but I reckoned I could check those dates – for deaths. I looked online first, found the Office of National Statistics site. But their records only went up to the year 2009 and there were practically half a million deaths a year. That's getting on for ten thousand a week. Without more details there was no way to find out about a specific death on a particular date.

5 October 2010

Every day, going about my business, knowing that what I am sets me apart. I have gone beyond the boundaries and reaped the rewards. If anyone could bottle this and sell it they'd make a killing (hah!).

I tried the Local Records Office next. They had registered deaths for 2010 on microfiche. It took me several trips, booking the viewers for a couple of hours at a time. I started by eliminating all the men and then anyone under fifteen and over forty. Arbitrary, I know, but I had to narrow it down somehow. And I focused on Manchester. After all he'd been at the airport and he mentions the Metrolink when he talks about the third victim.

11 December 2010

She got on at Cornbrook. It was like recognizing someone. I followed her home. I can't wait – though I will. The antici-pation makes it hard to think straight.

Even then I still had lists with dozens of deaths for each of the two dates in 2010. It was hopeless.

Danny rang the following week. Had I retired? Or was I just being even more lazy than usual? A virus, I told him, couldn't shake it off. So I hadn't got anything for him.

It became harder to sleep. The Wolf stalked my dreams. I thought about pills but that frightened me more. If he did come and I was comatose, I might never wake up. I tried to imagine what he'd done to the women. He was never explicit in what he wrote.

I spent a fortune on increased security. I could have gone to the police then, I had rehearsed a cover story about finding the laptop, but I feared they would dig deeper. Want to know how I'd paid for my flat when I hadn't had any employment for over two years. They'd only have to check my bank records to see I handled a lot of cash. They were bound to be suspicious. I could end up in court for no good reason. In prison. So I delayed – hoping to find out it was all invented.

```
7 January 2011


Tomorrow I'll be with her. This has been
a long time coming, tricky with her going
away so often. But now she's back. She'll
soon be mine.
```

More than once I considered destroying the memory stick but what if it were all true and The Wolf was a killer? Then this was proof. In one dream the memory stick was missing, I searched the flat in a frantic panic and woke up, drenched in sweat. The fear forced me from my bed to check that I still had it. I copied it to my own machine for back-up.

I stopped going to bed. The doctor suggested sleeping pills but I lied and said that side of things was fine, I just needed something for my anxiety during the daytime. He prescribed Prozac. It didn't help. But they say it takes a while to have any effect. As it turned out, I didn't have that long.

```
8 January 2011


I was all ready but she brought a man home
and he stayed with her. I'd been looking
```

forward to it so very much. Everything
focused, concentrated. I won't let her
ruin it. I will not get angry. I won't
give up either. She's the next one. No
matter how long it takes.

Then I thought about trying the newspapers. Central Library was closed for refurbishment and they'd moved the archive to the records office so I went back there and trawled the newspapers they had on microfiche for the dates of the first two entries. 12 June 2010 had been a Saturday. Tucked away inside the following Monday's *Evening News* there was a paragraph headed *Untimely Death*. My pulse raced and my stomach contracted as though I'd been thumped.

The story identified her as Janet Carr, thirty-seven, an administrator who was discovered by friends when she failed to turn up for a social engagement and didn't answer her phone. Miss Carr was a chronic asthmatic. There were no suspicious circumstances. The only reason her death was in the paper was the fact that she was administrator of a charity involved in raising money for asthma research. It made good copy. Human interest.

I sat there in front of the microfiche reader, staring at the screen, feeling nauseous and the horror of it creeping across my skin like a rash. There was no mention of foul play. I'd imagined The Wolf strangling them but whatever he'd done, he'd done it in a way that avoided detection. Poisoning? Gassing? How else could he have killed and left it looking natural? Something to aggravate Janet Carr's asthma? Had he known she was asthmatic? Were the others? What else could he have used? I'd no idea.

I swapped that microfiche for the September one; the woman he had punished for flinching. It didn't take me long to find her. *Tragic Blaze Kills Nurse*. Fiona Neeson, twenty-four, a nurse at Wythenshawe Hospital. An address in Sale. A spokesman for the Fire Service urged everyone to check their smoke alarms and to be aware of the very real hazards associated with candles in the home. This was a preventable death, he said.

The newspapers for 2011 hadn't been put on to the system yet.

When I came out of the library the bright light made me giddy, my knees buckled and I had to hold on to a lamp post till it passed.

```
10 January 2011

Each time I reach a higher level. The
intensity is impossible to describe. As
if I'm able to fly, go anywhere, do
anything. I can. I am. What else is there?
Nothing else comes anywhere close. She
watched me. Her eyes flew open as she felt
it but she didn't move. No scream, no
begging, just those wide, wild eyes and
then her body took over and her eyes
rolled back in her head while she started
dancing. She was marvellous. And I was
even better than before. I never really
knew what joy was. Superb, sublime. I
stayed until dawn. Those precious hours.
Felt like shouting from the rooftops. My
dancing queen.
```

How had he killed them?

At home I tried the internet. I found myself at sites covering topics as diverse as assisted suicide, medical negligence and armed revolution. Surfing in the company of rednecks, criminologists, surgeons and serial-killer fans. Anything remotely useful I cut and pasted. I had also made photocopies of the relevant articles from the newspaper microfiche and read and reread them, hoping to find something that helped me make sense of the whole affair.

```
11 January 2011

All day I relive it. Feel the thrill
singing through my veins, every sense
heightened, each memory like a snapshot:
```

the terror in her stare, the grating
noise of her last breath, the final
tremors, the rhythm of her dance of
death, long limbs jerking so fiercely. I'm
put in mind of surfers, the ones who
ride the big one. On top of the world.
Invincible.

I was scared. I no longer ate. The textures felt all wrong. I'd take a mouthful and it would turn to dust or slime in my mouth.

20 February 2011

The hunger is growing again, already. But
I cannot risk it yet. I close my eyes and
see her, the last one, and it's the best
trip in the world. To hell and back.
Myself in her eyes. The last hopeless
suck of breath. Body twitching and
jolting. I can't stop. How could I ever
stop? This is my life now. Rich beyond
dreams.

Then I caught a news item: a young woman found dead in her Levenshulme flat had been identified as Kate Cruickshank. Don't ask me how I knew. I switched the television off but I couldn't get rid of the tension. My guts were knotted and I had an awful sense of foreboding.

I fell asleep in my chair. In my dream The Wolf came and I ran and locked myself in the shower room. I leaned back against the door to catch my breath and there he was reflected in the mirror. I was trapped. Waking with awful pains in my chest and my heart hammering, I knew I had to go to the police.

My timing was shot at. I planned to go at lunchtime, imagining that people would be taking lunch breaks and coming and going, and I could just leave it all on the doorstep without being noticed. The laptop and the memory stick. Enclose an anonymous note telling them about The Wolf, about Janet Carr and Fiona Neeson and a woman whose name I didn't know who had died around 10 January. Tell them to investigate Kate Cruickshank.

There wasn't any doorstep. I walked past the place a couple of times and realized if I left it outside on the pavement someone could take it and The Wolf would carry on. Killing women. Haunting me.

So, I went in through the glass doors. There was no one at the desk in the small foyer. I placed the laptop on the counter and was turning to go when a policeman came out of the door behind.

"Miss?"

I began to walk away.

"Is this your bag, Miss?"

"No." I moved more quickly. Ahead of me the doors clicked shut and then an alarm began to sound. I wheeled round in time to see the man disappear.

They thought it was a bomb.

Steel shutters began to roll down the glass frontage and I could see people evacuating the building from other exits, racing to cross the street. The alarm was deafening and then voices began shouting at me over the intercom. It was hard to hear above the din.

"It's just a laptop," I yelled. "Lost property." The sirens continued to whoop and screech. I went and grabbed the laptop, looked up at the CCTV camera in the corner. "Look," I yelled, unzipping the case, opening the cover, so they could see, lifting out the anonymous note I'd left.

There was a hissing sound, and smoke and a peculiar smell and it was hard to breathe. My eyes were streaming, I was choking.

I wasn't Miss Popularity.

Once the Bomb Squad had stepped down and the building was re-opened I was taken to a small interview room and waited with a woman officer until a man came to take my details. He was a short, skinny man with chapped lips. There was an order to the paperwork which he stuck to rigidly. Having established my name, address, date of birth, nearest living relative (none) and occupation (unemployed artist), he finally let me talk.

While I explained about "finding" the computer on the Metro and that it contained accounts of a series of murders, that the dates tallied with actual deaths in Manchester, his expression changed from weary to wary, then hardened. He hated me.

"Read it," I urged.

"It could be a journalist's – research."

That took me aback. I thought for a moment. "No facts or figures, no names or addresses. I'm sure it's a diary. And the deaths have never been seen as murders – so what are they investigating? Just read the memory stick."

"It was destroyed, along with the computer."

"What?" I was appalled.

"Procedure."

But there was still hope. "I made a back-up file, it's at home on my machine. I've copies of newspapers too, they match the accounts."

He still didn't seem to believe a word I said. "How long have you had it?"

"A couple of days," I lied. How could I explain I'd held on to it for nearly a month?

"You found this on Tuesday?"

"Yes, on the tram. The man who lost it, I can describe him, he got off at Mosley Street." I gave him a description of The Wolf.

"And you were going?"

"To the Lowry."

He rose without speaking, hitched his trousers up, left the room.

"Could I have a cup of tea?" I asked the PC.

She shrugged.

I began to cry.

The skinny man came back and grilled me some more, all about where I'd got the laptop. He seemed angry. I stuck to my story.

Looking back, it was all very fractured. Surreal even. Everyone still treating me like the mad bomber. Then they asked me to accompany them to my house. Show them the file and the other information.

I felt sick and light-headed on the way. I couldn't remember when I'd last eaten and the petrol fumes and the smell of fast-food grease on the air made me queasy. The traffic was terrible; it took us an hour to get there. The skinny man drove and the woman sat with me in the back.

At my flat it took a while to get in, with all the locks and that. I showed them the photocopies of the newspapers, and the back-up copy of *Accounts* on my laptop. They took me into the kitchen. I was shivering even though it was so close. I could never get warm any more. The woman poured me a glass of water but it tasted filthy.

There were more voices in the living room and a little hubbub of excitement in the interchange. At last, I thought, they were taking me seriously.

The Wolf came into my kitchen.

I knocked over my water in panic, scrambled to my feet, screaming, "That's him, that's the man, it's his diary!"

Someone grabbed my arms and pinned them behind me. Someone else tried to calm me down.

The Wolf raised his eyebrows and lifted his hand. He held a small plastic bag; inside was a syringe.

"Not very well hidden." His voice was soft.

"That's not mine," I yelled. "I am not a junkie." I turned to the woman holding me. "Check my arms. I've never taken anything like that."

"You slipped up, last time," The Wolf said. "Kate Cruickshank. We found the mark." He held up the bag again. Gave a wolfish grin. "Rebecca Colne, I am arresting you for the murder of Kate Cruickshank on …"

I didn't hear the end of the caution. The room spun then dimmed. I passed out.

They gave me four life sentences. They tried me for four murders. The third one, she was Alison Devlin. She was two months pregnant.

The Metrolink had been closed the day I claimed to have seen the man leave the laptop and get off at Mosley Street: a system failure. When I told them the truth about the airport, they raised questions about my delay. Why wait so long? If I honestly thought this was information about a series of murders, why wait at all? I'd stolen the machine, I told them, I was frightened that I'd be prosecuted, I wanted to make sure it was true. None of my excuses made any difference. My change of story made them even more convinced I was responsible. And when I repeatedly claimed that the man who owned the laptop was one of the officers investigating me, they clearly thought me deranged.

They seized my own computer and found all the other files. All the internet junk I'd copied: methods of murder. My defence counsel argued about the dates, demonstrating that I'd downloaded stuff long after the first three murders, but I could see the jury turning against me. Looking at me sideways. I was told not to make accusations about The Wolf, it wouldn't help my case. They linked me to Fiona Neeson. We'd been members at the same gym. It was news to me.

The clincher was the DNA evidence. A hair of mine at the scene of Kate Cruickshank's death. It didn't matter that I'd never been there. Someone had – with a hair of mine, or dropped it into the forensics lab. That coupled with the syringe "recovered" from my flat.

Juries love forensics, ask anyone. Never mind about logic or witnesses or other evidence – a bit of sexy science has them frothing at the mouth. Clamouring for conviction.

Like quicksand, the more I struggled for the truth the deeper I sank. Till I was swallowing mud day after day in the courtroom. The weight of it crushing my lungs.

A stream of acquaintances and people I barely knew were wheeled out to attest to my controlling, cold and dubious character. The prosecution harped on about my lonely and dysfunctional upbringing, my isolation, my prior mental health problems. They held up my severe weight loss, my Prozac use, my insomnia, as evidence of a guilty conscience. And my stunt at the police station as a cry for help. They never had a motive. How could they? I was a psychopath, I had a personality disorder – no motive required.

After the conviction, much was made of my lack of remorse and even more of the word murderess. The female of the species and all that.

They've turned down my application for an appeal. No new evidence. And no hope of being considered for parole until I admit my guilt.

Maybe I'm safer in here. The bars, the locks, the cameras. If they let me out he'd be waiting, wouldn't he? Lips slightly parted, hair slicked back, those lupine teeth. Waiting to get me once and for all. The sting of the syringe as he inserts the needle. The dull ache as he presses the plunger, forcing the air into a vein. The seconds left as the bubble speeds around my bloodstream. Zipping along as if in a flume. An embolism. Fizzing through my heart and on into my lung – tangling with my blood vessels. Making me gasp, claw for air. A jig of death. Stopping everything. Blowing me away.

BLOOD ON
THE GHAT

Barry Maitland

CHRISTINE WOKE BEFORE dawn. The night air was warm and sticky, and she threw off the cotton sheet and went over to the window. Opening it, she breathed in the unfamiliar smells of spices and pungent wood smoke and… well, something less pleasant. Down below her was the great river, the Ganges, which, very soon now, would begin to emerge from the darkness. She had arrived late the previous night with only a fleeting and confused picture of the city, of crowded narrow streets draped with electric cables and lurid signs, of old buildings tottering against each other, and of people everywhere, on foot, in tricycle rickshaws or sprawled on the footpaths. The glimpses of the people – the women wrapped in colourful saris and the men in white dhotis – had thrilled and also frightened her a little, for their strangeness and their sheer numbers. Her hotel, the Dubashi Guesthouse, was a modest affair of small rooms and limited facilities, but with spectacular views out over the ghats – the great cascades of stairs and platforms that descended from the edge of the city straight down to the river. The owners of the guesthouse, Mr and Mrs Dubashi, had welcomed her and offered her food, which she was too tired to accept, and shown her up to her room. There she had sat for some time at the window staring down at the spectacle on the ghat below, a line of priests performing a fire ceremony before a great crowd of worshippers and tourists, boats passing by on the edge of the darkness, the sound of chanting, bells and rhythmic clapping.

Now she quickly made use of the bathroom at the end of the short corridor, taking care not to swallow any of the tap water, and returned to get dressed and go downstairs to the lobby. An elderly woman wearing a bright orange sari and with white hair and pale European skin was there, talking to Mr Dubashi, who introduced them.

"Ah, Mrs Darling, please allow me to introduce Christine, another Australian. You are both going to visit the ghat at dawn, I think?"

Mrs Darling shook Christine's hand. "How nice to meet you. Your first visit to India?"

"Yes." She seemed a warm and enthusiastic woman, eyes bright with interest, although Christine thought that she detected some effort beneath the surface, as if perhaps she had been unwell and was struggling with fatigue.

"And this is your first day? How exciting for you. It is one of the great sights, dawn on the Ganges, the pilgrims drawn to the sacred river."

"Have you been here for a while?"

"A couple of days, but I have visited Varanasi many times before. And you? Do you have a special reason for coming here, Christine?"

Mrs Darling was giving her such a penetrating look that Christine felt compelled to tell her the truth. "I... would like to understand death better," she said, and saw the momentary look of consternation on the other woman's face.

"But you are so young," Mrs Darling said. "We must talk later." And Christine was saved from replying by Mr Dubashi, who said, "You should be going now, ladies. See, the dawn is breaking and the people are arriving."

Through the open door Christine saw that the street outside was filling with a stream of people heading for the ghat. The two women stepped outside and were immediately caught up in the crowd. Christine felt the excitement of becoming part of a great throng, and almost tripped over a woman sitting on the ground with a large basket of brilliantly coloured flowers. Nearby the driver of an ancient tricycle rickshaw was gesticulating to his two fat female passengers that they must get out now and walk because the way was becoming too congested. The crowd jostled and Christine found herself being squeezed back behind Mrs Darling. Ahead of them the street narrowed and the dark buildings on either side closed in, packing the crowd still more tightly together, and Christine felt a throb of panic as she tried to keep her companion in sight.

Suddenly the street came to an end and the sky opened up overhead. They were at the head of the ghat, the great flight of steps running down to the Ganges, which appeared ahead of them as a broad silver sheet. Through the press of bodies Christine saw orange flags and electric lights on tall poles overhead, and raised platforms on which bearded holy men prayed and priests held up offerings to the dawn. Along the margins of the concourse squatted beggars and hawkers selling garlands of flowers, bunches of sandalwood sticks and brightly coloured shawls and saris.

For a moment the press of people came to a stop, and she caught sight of Mrs Darling's orange sari ahead, about to begin her descent of the ghat, and then the crowd closed in between them again. Suddenly a shock seemed to pass through the crush. There were shouts, people staggered and fell into one another. In front of her, immediately behind where she had glimpsed Mrs Darling, a tall, thin man with a shaved head tripped backwards and tumbled against a brightly painted scarlet shrine, hitting his head with a crack against the stonework. Christine dropped to her knees beside him, trying to pull him to one side so that he wouldn't be trampled in the panic. She quickly took in the features of the unconscious man – his bare feet, his brown, weathered skin, his white dhoti and, the strangest thing, a piece of white muslin cloth tied with a string in front of his mouth.

"Miss Christine!"

She heard a shout, recognizing the voice of the hotelkeeper, Mr Dubashi, and saw him struggling through the crowd to reach her.

"What on earth is going on?" he cried. "Are you all right?"

"Yes, but this man was knocked over and hit his head."

Mr Dubashi squatted beside her. "Ah, it is a holy man, a Jain!"

"What's that covering his mouth? Is it a mask?"

"No, no. It is part of his philosophy of *aimsha* – non-violence to all creatures. It is to prevent him swallowing a fly by mistake."

Christine looked at him, wondering if he was teasing her, but he seemed perfectly serious. He was gazing around. "There must be... ah, there it is!"

He reached beside the shrine and raised what looked like a long-handled brush or flywhisk. "You see, Jain monks must sweep the ground in front of them to make sure that they don't tread on any insects."

"Well, unfortunately he's suffered some accidental violence himself."

At that moment the monk groaned and blinked open his eyes.

"Yes, we must get him back to the hotel and look after him. Sir! Can you get up?"

With some difficulty they helped the man to his feet, Mr Dubashi supporting him. Fortunately the monk seemed to be very light, while Mr Dubashi was stocky and strong.

"Look," Christine said, pointing to a bloodstain on the front of his white gown.

"Perhaps he has suffered a cut," Mr Dubashi said. "I shall take care of it. But what about Mrs Darling? Where is she?"

"I don't know, I lost sight of her."

"Find her. Make sure she is all right. I shall look after the holy man."

Christine agreed and struggled through the milling crowd at the top of the ghat. People were shouting and gesticulating to each other, as if trying to describe what had happened, but since they were speaking in Hindi, or perhaps Urdu, she couldn't understand a word. She looked around but couldn't see any sign of Mrs Darling's orange sari. About twenty metres further down the broad flight, a knot of people seemed to be the focus of much pointing and staring from people on the platforms and terraces above. She made her way down. As she approached, a man burst out of the throng, shouting into a mobile phone, "Dead, I tell you! Quite dead!" Christine felt a thump in her chest as she peered down between the legs of the clustered men and saw a head of white hair lying on the stone steps.

Christine cried out and the crowd parted for her, watching with bright eyes as she knelt beside the motionless body of Mrs Darling.

For a moment it almost seemed as if she were asleep, but there was something unnatural in her pose, one leg twisted awkwardly beneath the other, and when Christine stretched a tentative hand to her wrist she could find no trace of a pulse.

"The police have been called, madam," one man reassured her eagerly.

"Police?" Christine felt as if time were moving very slowly. "An ambulance, surely?"

"But she is quite dead!" the man insisted, and then, with an unnecessary relish, added, "Murdered!" and gestured with his hand up the flight of steps, where Christine saw a trail of dark stains. "Blood, madam. Blood on the ghat! The lady has been most atrociously stabbed!"

"But, who...?"

He broke off and everyone turned their heads back up to the city at the sound of a siren's wail, the scream of braking tyres, and then the clatter of boots as three men in berets and uniforms, carrying rifles, came down the steps of the ghat, followed by another man in a dark suit. Immediately the man who had been talking to Christine began speaking to them in a rapid stream of Hindi, while they frowned at the body, and at Christine, with suspicious glares. The man in the suit stooped to look more closely at Mrs Darling. He pressed his fingers to the side of her throat, then he lifted the back of her sari, and Christine saw that it was saturated with blood, and she gave a gasp.

The policeman looked up at her and got to his feet.

"Good morning. I am Sub-Inspector Gupta of the Varanasi CID. What is your name?"

Christine told him, watching him take out a notebook and write.

"And do you know this woman?"

"Yes," she said. "Her name is Mrs Darling." She felt absurdly exposed, standing like this surrounded by all those silent listeners as she answered his questions. He sounded very serious and severe, but this gravity was somewhat undermined by his youth, for he didn't look much older than Christine herself, who was twenty-four. "We are staying at the same hotel, the Dubashi Guesthouse."

"Aaah…" A murmur spread out through the crowd as the information was repeated.

The policeman coughed loudly and they fell silent. "And did you witness what happened?"

"No. I was behind Mrs Darling when we reached the top of the ghat, but I couldn't see her because of the crowd. Then something happened, people began struggling and shouting…" heads nearby were nodding their agreement "…and the man next to me fell down and I tried to help him. Then Mr Dubashi found us, and by the time I came looking for Mrs Darling, she was like this."

"Hmm." Sub-Inspector Gupta turned to the crowd and called in a loud voice, and in several different languages, for anyone who had seen what happened to the white lady in the red sari to come forward. A babble of conversation started up, but no one moved. The man who had spoken to Christine earlier did speak up, saying that he had been standing nearby when he saw the body tumble down the steps, "like a sack of potatoes", but confessed he hadn't seen her attacker. Nor, it seemed, had anyone else.

Christine had a thought. "Inspector," she said, "it's possible that the man I told you about, who was knocked down when it happened, may have seen something. He must have been very close behind Mrs Darling, and there was blood on his dhoti. He may have seen the murderer."

"Really? What was he like, this man?"

"He is a Jain monk. He was very shaken up, and Mr Dubashi was taking him back to his boarding house. He may still be there."

"Good!" The detective looked relieved and flashed Christine a broad smile. 'I'm only a sub-inspector, by the way. This is my first real murder case. The forensic people will soon be here to examine the scene. Let us go to Mr Dubashi."

He said a few more words to the uniformed men and then he and Christine set off, climbing back up the ghat.

When they reached the Dubashi Guesthouse they found the Jain monk sitting stiffly upright on a chair in the lobby, his flywhisk brush across his knees, while Mr and Mrs Dubashi fussed around him, applying a dressing to the back of his head. Christine introduced

Sub-Inspector Gupta and told them the terrible news about Mrs
Darling's murder, which caused much consternation, Mr Dubashi in
particular becoming very agitated, hopping around from foot to foot,
in contrast to the monk who maintained a stoic immobility.

Sub-Inspector Gupta called for calm, and began by writing their
names and addresses in his notebook. The monk's name was
Nemichandra, apparently, of no fixed address, since Jain monks
were wanderers, obliged by their faith to move constantly so as not
to become attached to any one place. Mrs Dubashi was able to
provide Mrs Darling's Australian passport from the hotel safe,
causing another wave of agitation in her husband.

"Mrs Darling's son is here in India," he cried. "He is in Kolkata,
she told me, on business. He must be informed."

A further search of the hotel safe yielded a package of other
personal items belonging to the murdered woman, including a diary
with a note of her son's Kolkata hotel number.

"I'll get on to it," said Sub-Inspector Gupta, who was having
trouble making them do things in the correct order. "First I must
know if you have any knowledge of what happened at the ghat.
You, Mr Nemichandra, were close behind the lady when it
happened, were you not? You must have seen the murderer."

They all stared at the mystic who, a man of few words apparently, said, "I can tell you nothing."

"But," the sub-inspector insisted, "Mrs Darling was stabbed in
the back at the same height as that bloodstain on the front of your
dhoti. The murderer must have brushed his weapon against you as
he withdrew it." This produced a gasp from Mrs Dubashi. "It was
probably he who knocked you down."

The monk said nothing, but flicked his whisk at a fly that might
have been planning to get into his mouth, which was no longer
covered by the muslin square.

"Perhaps the fall has erased his memory," Mr Dubashi offered.
"It may return with time."

"That's possible," the sub-inspector conceded. He thought about
this and then said to Mr Nemichandra, "I must insist that you stay
in the vicinity for a few days, until I agree that you can leave."

"He can stay here with us," Mr Dubashi said. "It would be an honour to accommodate a Jain saint in our house."

At that moment a man burst into the lobby from the street and said breathlessly, "B. K. Gungabissoon, assistant crime reporter for the *Aaj* newspaper." He looked at Mr Dubashi. "You are the detective in charge of the murder-on-the-ghat case?"

"No," Sub-Inspector Gupta said. "I am. I have nothing to say at this time."

"But it is said that you have two witnesses to the crime. You, miss?" He looked at Christine, who shrugged. "And the monk, yes? The word is that this is a terrorist attack on westerners. Is that right, Inspector?"

"No, there is no evidence of such a thing. You must not…"

"But there was the attack just last December by Indian Mujahideen here at Sheetla Ghat."

"That was a bombing. There is no suggestion that this is in any way connected."

"What is the name of the victim?"

"I have nothing further to say at this time. You must go now."

"At least give me a photograph, please. Everyone smile…"

They all posed stiffly and the camera flashed, then Mr Dubashi escorted the reporter to the door, giving him a handful of the guesthouse business cards and murmuring a few words in his ear.

Before he left, Sub-Inspector Gupta took Christine aside. "I must ask you to stay here where I can speak to you again, miss, but I am worried about your safety. Were you a close friend of Mrs Darling?"

"No, I only met her this morning for the first time. I'm sure I'll be all right.'"

Christine was touched by his concern. He seemed a very sincere young man, rather out of his depth, and she felt sorry for him. The truth was, she realized, that she didn't much care if she became a second victim. It shocked her a little to acknowledge that.

The next morning Christine went again to the ghat at dawn to see the sun rise over the Ganges. It was less crowded today, and she found a place to herself on the steps to watch the people passing by – the pilgrims and priests, the tourists with their guides, and the families of mourners who, Mr Dubashi had told her, came to have a dead relative cremated on the open fires beside the river. As she sat there she shed a tear for Mrs Darling whom she had known so briefly, and also for her own mother who had caused her to come to this place.

When she returned to the hotel, Mr Dubashi was proudly brandishing the morning's edition of the *Aaj*, in which was published the photograph the reporter had taken the previous day, the four of them standing grinning foolishly around the seated Jain monk, Mr Nemichandra. Since the paper was in Hindi, Mr Dubashi had to translate: "*Inspector Gupta of Varanasi CID grills witnesses to ghat slaying*. And it goes on to mention the name of our guesthouse. What a publicity coup!"

"What a piece of stupidity!" his wife snapped back. "We'll be sitting ducks if they decide to strike again. And what about Christine and Mr Nemichandra? They're named as witnesses. The murderer will have them in his sights now."

Mr Dubashi looked stricken – this hadn't occurred to him.

"Where is Mr Nemichandra?" Christine asked. "I thought I might have seen him at the ghat."

"He's in his room meditating on the soul of Mrs Darling," Mr Dubashi said. "Of course he spends most of the day meditating. He refuses to use the bed in his room, preferring to sleep on the floor, and is extremely self-denying, eating practically nothing."

"Actually he seemed rather peckish," Mrs Dubashi said. "He's already had breakfast. Are you ready for yours, Christine?"

"Yes, please." She felt suddenly ravenous.

They went into the small dining room and Mr Dubashi sat with her at one of the tables. "It's a little awkward feeding a Jain," he said. "They are vegans, and extremely particular about avoiding harming living things. That's why they have to sweep the ground in front of their feet, and in the monsoon season they have to stay indoors altogether so that they don't step in a puddle and inadvertently kill some tiny creature. We were going to have aloo paratha for breakfast this morning, but it contains potatoes, and Jains will not touch root vegetables, because you kill them when you dig them up, whereas with rice, for example, you can harvest it without killing the plant. So instead we are having mutter paratha, although without the ginger, which is also a root vegetable, of course."

"That is tricky," Christine said. "They sound very interesting, the Jains. Perhaps Mr Nemichandra would tell me more."

Mr Dubashi looked keenly at her. "Ah, you are looking for enlightenment, Christine! I remember that you told Mrs Darling yesterday that you wanted to understand death."

She'd forgotten that. It must have been the last thing she'd said to her fellow guest. Christine felt a surge of emotion and tears pricked in her eyes. "I lost my mother recently, you see," she said. "I nursed her at the end. We were very close, and I was heartbroken."

She hadn't meant to tell anyone about this, but suddenly it had just spilled out. It was this strange place, and being with people that she would never meet again.

"How terrible for you," Mr Dubashi murmured sympathetically.

Christine wiped her eyes. "Before she died, Mum told me about a trip to India she had made when she was my age, and about Varanasi. She said I should go. I think she hoped I might find some comfort here."

"Ah, well, you have come to the right place, and perhaps Mr Nemichandra is the right person for you to speak to, for the Jains are certainly much concerned with death."

Just then there was a knock on the door. An Indian woman wearing a bright orange sari just like Mrs Darling's was there. "*Namaste*," she said, pressing the palms of her hands together in greeting. "May I ask if this is the place where Mrs Darling was staying?"

"Indeed." Mr Dubashi rose to his feet. "*Namaste*. I am the owner of this guesthouse."

"My name is Dorothy Yanamandra. I am coming from Mrs Darling's ashram."

"Her ashram?" Mr Dubashi looked at her in surprise. "Mrs Darling attended an ashram?"

"Oh, yes, indeed, very much so."

Dorothy Yanamandra was a large, powerful woman, who took up a lot of space in the small dining room. She said, "Mrs Darling was a regular visitor to our Atmapriksa Ashram and a devoted follower of our Swami Bhatti. Unfortunately we were full up when she arrived this time and she had to stay here until her room was ready, otherwise this terrible thing might have been avoided."

Mr Dubashi bridled at this and said, "Madam, it was hardly the fault of the Dubashi Guesthouse that Mrs Darling was murdered."

Mrs Yanamandra dismissed this with a wave of her hand, flashing the gold and diamonds of her rings. "I have come to collect Mrs Darling's things."

"Impossible! They must stay here until her son arrives to collect them."

"He is coming here?"

"He is flying in from Kolkata this morning."

Mrs Yanamandra made a sound like a low growl. "Hmm... Well, I believe Mrs Darling left some documents which must be examined urgently, concerning her death."

"Her death?"

"Yes, she spoke at length with Swami Bhatti about it. Are you aware of any documents?"

"She did leave some in the hotel safe," Mr Dubashi admitted reluctantly.

"Fetch them."

Mr Dubashi looked for a moment as if he might say something rude, but then relented and left the room. Mrs Yanamandra turned to Christine. "You are a tourist?"

"Yes."

"Perhaps you have come to Varanasi for spiritual enlightenment?"

"I believe I have."

"Then you should speak to Swami Bhatti." She reached beneath the folds of her sari and produced a business card. "That is the address of the Atmapriksa Ashram, and on the back is a map of how to get there. Call in any time."

"You work there?"

"Yes, I am Swami Bhatti's PA and Business Manager."

Mr Dubashi returned, accompanied by his wife, who wanted to see what was going on. He carefully opened the large envelope he was carrying and emptied its contents on to the table. "The police took her passport," he said. "Here is her notebook and her airline tickets..."

"What's that?" Mrs Yanamandra pointed at a plain white envelope, sealed.

"I don't know. The police didn't open it."

"Well, we must," Mrs Yanamandra insisted, and reached for it, but Mr Dubashi was quicker, snatching it up.

"Certainly not. It may be confidential."

However Mrs Dubashi promptly took it out of his hand, reached for a knife on the table and sliced it open. There were several documents inside, and when she opened the first she read its typewritten title out loud: "*Instructions in the event of my death.*"

"Aha!" Mrs Yanamandra cried.

Mrs Dubashi read on: "*When I die I wish to be cremated in Varanasi in the traditional manner according to the instructions of Swami Bhatti, and my ashes cast into the Ganges.*"

"There you are," Mrs Yanamandra said. "It was important to know that, wasn't it?"

"It is signed by Mrs Darling and witnessed by a Mr Nath, of Prasad Nath, Notary Services, Advocates and Lawyers," Mrs Dubashi said, and opened the second document. "Oh, goodness, it is a will..." She looked at the foot of the page. "It is dated two days ago, and also witnessed by Mr Nath."

Mrs Yanamandra grabbed it and read it greedily. "Ah!" Without another word she folded it up again and returned it and the other document to the envelope and handed it to Mr Dubashi. "You must put this back in your safe until Mrs Darling's son arrives. You are responsible for its safekeeping."

"Yes," Mr Dubashi said, looking quite put out. "I was before."

Mrs Yanamandra left, and Christine watched her march across the street, sari flowing, other pedestrians ducking out of the way of her relentless progress. Christine thought that she was undoubtedly a bully, but perhaps her abrasive manner was just her way of being businesslike and getting things done. In any event Christine felt that there was something fortuitous in her appearance. She read the business card again, wondering if Swami Bhatti might have been Mrs Darling's gift to her.

When Mrs Darling's son arrived at the Dubashi Guesthouse later that morning, Christine was in the dining room where Mr Nemichandra had interrupted his meditations to get a glass of water from Mrs Dubashi. She had strained it through muslin in the prescribed manner, to avoid the possibility of the monk killing any tiny creature in the water. She had also washed his dhoti overnight and got rid of the bloodstain.

Jeremy Darling looked disgruntled and out of sorts, as if he'd had a disagreeable journey from Kolkata. He accepted the Dubashis' commiserations with an indifferent grunt, and gazed around at the guesthouse with a look of disgust. "She stayed here, did she?"

"Oh, yes, sir." Mr Dubashi nodded enthusiastically. "She was very comfortable here. She told us how much she enjoyed staying with us."

Darling muttered, "Good grief," then did a double-take when he noticed the monk sitting in the corner.

"Mr Nemichandra was a witness to your mother's murder, sir," Mr Dubashi explained. "The police have insisted that he stay here until they have finished their enquiries."

Jeremy Darling stared at Mr Nemichandra. "He... saw who did it?"

"Possibly, sir, but he received a bump on the head and cannot remember."

"I see. The police have questioned him, have they?"

"Oh, yes. And the police examined some documents your mother left in the hotel safe. Perhaps you would care to see them?"

He fetched them and they all watched Mr Darling turn them over and pick up the envelope of documents. He opened the first and gave a snort of disgust. "Apparently she decided she wanted to be cremated here. Oh, well." He shrugged and opened the second document, the will, and his face darkened, and then he roared, "What!"

Mr Dubashi took a step back. "Bad news, sir?"

Darling swore, read the document again and snarled, "Prasad Nath, lawyers. Where the hell can I find them?"

Mr Dubashi checked the address and showed Mr Darling the city map. "Near the jail, sir."

"I'll need a taxi. Look after my suitcase, will you?" And Jeremy Darling rushed away.

"Oh, dear. Oh, dear," Mr Dubashi said. "He is very upset."

"I wonder what was in the will?" Christine said.

"I believe," Mr Dubashi said vaguely, "that Mrs Darling decided to leave all her wealth to Swami Bhatti and the Atmapriksa Ashram."

"You read it?"

Mr Dubashi gave a guilty little smirk, then looked at the monk, who had risen unsteadily to his feet, a worried frown on his face. "Are you all right, Mr Nemichandra?"

"I must go back to my room and meditate," he said, and shuffled off, sweeping the floor before him with his brush.

At that moment the policeman, Sub-Inspector Gupta, knocked at the front door and came in. "Ah," he said, seeing the suitcase, "has Mr Darling arrived?"

"He arrived," Mr Dubashi said, "and then left in a great hurry, very upset after reading the will that his mother had left in the hotel safe, to see the lawyers who drew it up."

"Really? Any idea why he was upset?"

So Mr Dubashi told him.

"To an ashram? Golly. Do you know which one?"

Mr Dubashi told him that too, and then added, with a disingenuous air, "By an amazing coincidence the business manager of that ashram came here earlier this morning, insisting on reading that will, which gave her a great deal of satisfaction. Well, it would, wouldn't it? What amazing timing! Mrs Darling writes a new will in their favour and they only have to wait two days until her fortune drops into their laps, like a ripe mango, before her son arrives and has the chance to talk her out of it."

"Are you suggesting...?"

"Oh, dear me, no! But you know what some of these ashrams are like, Inspector, only interested in milking tourists for their dollars, and I must say that business manager was a pretty ruthless type. If I weren't such a trusting man I might imagine her capable of, well, almost anything."

"Hmm." Sub-Inspector Gupta pondered that. "Well, my superiors have taken over the running of the case now. Clearly it is very high-profile, and they are worried about the possible terrorist angle. I only came by to meet Mr Darling, and also to make sure that you were all right, especially you, Christine."

"That's very kind of you, Sub-Inspector."

He gave her one of his beautiful big smiles. "I was extremely concerned by the report in the *Aaj*. I want to give you my mobile number, and you must contact me, day or night, if you see anything suspicious." He gave her a card.

"Thank you."

He grinned, looking suddenly coy and very young. "Promise you will contact me."

"I promise."

"Good. Now, Mr Dubashi, perhaps you can give me the details of this dodgy ashram."

"With the greatest pleasure, Inspector."

That afternoon Christine set out to explore Varanasi, using the map and guidebook given her by Mr Dubashi. She took a tricycle rickshaw to the Kashi Vishwanath Temple, a complex of shrines dedicated to Shiva, the destroyer god, and one of the most sacred sites in the Hindu religion. The place was crammed with visitors, its entrance protected by armed guards. It left a vivid impression, but she found it hard to penetrate its meaning. From there she walked through narrow streets to the river, and followed the great terraces of the ghats along the shore of the Ganges, seeing the columns of smoke from the funeral pyres rising into the hot still air. After a while she found herself not far from the ashram, which Mr Dubashi had marked with a cross on the map, and she struck back into the densely packed city, trying to maintain her bearings until she came to a sign with a painted image of a venerable figure squatting in the lotus position beneath the name *Atmapriksa Ashram*.

She cautiously pushed through a screen of beads and entered a dark corridor down which echoed a sound of distant chanting. She came to a door marked *Office*, and was confronted by the impressive figure of Dorothy Yanamandra scolding a typist. She whirled around and beamed at Christine.

"Ah! The lady from the Dubashi Guesthouse. You have come to us!"

"Yes. I thought I should find out more about the ashram."

"Excellent. Come into my office."

It had rough whitewashed walls, but contained smart office furniture and the latest computer equipment.

"Atmapriksa is Hindi meaning *soul-searching*, Christine," the business manager said. "That is what we do here, following the ancient spiritual tradition of *guru-shishya*, in which *shishya*, or disciples, are mentored in their soul-searching by a guru, which in our case is Swami Bhatti. I have many leaflets here that will be of interest to you, but first I would ask you to fill in a questionnaire."

Christine filled in the sheet asking for basic information about herself, but with a blank space left at the end to answer the question, *Why are you here?* Christine wrote, *To come to terms with the death of my mother*, then wondered if that was really the right way to put it. Could you come to terms with death? Perhaps Swami Bhatti would tell her.

Mrs Yanamandra studied her answers, nodding sagely over the final reply. "You have come to the right place, Christine." She typed into her computer an appointment time for the following morning for her to meet the guru. "Now I shall take you on a quick tour of our facilities."

They followed the corridor to an open courtyard paved with stone flags. In the arcade that surrounded it Christine saw about a dozen people, mostly young and Western in appearance, performing exercises or domestic chores – washing sheets by hand in a large tub, sewing and cleaning.

"It is part of the discipline by which the *shishya* learns respect for the guru," Mrs Yanamandra explained. "There are other Australians here, and Americans, and people from all over."

They moved on to a wing of rooms, very simply furnished, in which disciples slept, then to a yoga class and another courtyard in which people sat in meditation. As they moved on again Christine tried to imagine Mrs Darling here.

"Now we'll collect your leaflets and say goodbye until tomorrow," Mrs Yanamandra said, and led her back to the street door. Christine went out with a feeling of hope that this peaceful place in the heart of the ancient city might be able to help her.

Unfortunately the map wasn't able to help her find her way back to the hotel, and she became lost in the labyrinth of narrow streets. At one point she stopped, realizing that she was going around in circles, and turned to go back, and as she did so she saw a man watching her from a doorway. She had a split-second image of an evil-looking face, a grubby dhoti and a red turban, before he darted away into the shadows and disappeared around the corner of an alley.

Christine took a deep breath, feeling her heart pounding, and wondered if she should ring Sub-Inspector Gupta, but by the time she got back to the hotel she decided that she had been overreacting.

Mr Dubashi and his wife were having an argument when Christine came down after breakfast the next morning. She gathered that it had been sparked by her mentioning her appointment to meet the Swami Bhatti.

"Christine is here to learn," Mrs Dubashi said. "Why should she not find out what the ashram has to offer?"

"All I'm saying is that she should be careful what those people's motives are," her husband said stubbornly.

"You should never have said those things to the police inspector yesterday. You made it sound as if Mrs Yanamandra had stabbed Mrs Darling with her own hands."

"Well, that wouldn't surprise me!" Mr Dubashi insisted truculently.

"Rubbish! I admired Mrs Yanamandra's nitty-gritty approach. She calls a spade a spade. I bet she keeps those mystics in line."

"A strong woman," Mr Dubashi groaned.

Christine left them to it. She found her way to the ashram more easily this time, with only one disturbing moment, when she thought she caught another glimpse of the dirty red turban belonging to the evil-looking man she suspected had followed her the previous day, but she couldn't be sure.

She was met by a young woman of about her own age, with an American accent, dressed in an orange sari. She was one of the Swami's *shishyas*, she explained, and launched into a gushing account of the life of the ashram, the sense of comradeship among its guests, and the profound experience of its spiritual life. By the end of it Christine felt that she had been thoroughly softened up.

She said, "Did you know Mrs Darling?"

"Oh, poor Elizabeth. We were so devastated. She was like a second mother to me – well, a first mother actually. I had some problems back home with my mother and her fourth husband."

"She was happy here, was she?"

"Oh, yes. She's been coming here every spring for quite a few years. She and the Swami were very close... in a spiritual sense, I mean. He's been in deep retreat ever since it happened. You're about the first person he's agreed to see since then. Come along, I'll take you to him."

Swami Bhatti was a small man with a large white beard, wrapped in an orange shawl and with a matching orange bindi on his forehead. He was sitting in the full lotus position on a plain cotton mat, and gestured to Christine to sit facing him. His eyes gleamed at her through large rimless spectacles, which reflected the flames of candles set up around the room.

"Christine," he said, in a voice so soft that she had to lean forward to hear his words. "You have set out on a great spiritual journey. You feel like a traveller without a map, a sailor without a rudder, a bird without a sense of direction."

"Yes."

"You grieve for your mother."

"Yes."

"You are deeply troubled by your loss."

'Yes."

"You seek closure."

Christine hesitated. She wished he hadn't used that word.

"Here we can help you to find closure, and to put this behind you, so that you can move forward in your spiritual journey."

The Swami closed his eyes and a deep murmuring sound filled the room. It took Christine a moment to realize that it was coming from him. It stopped and he opened his eyes again.

"Often there are impediments to closure – a feeling of guilt, for example."

"Oh, yes!" Christine nodded vigorously.

"Property, for example. Things that the dead beloved left behind."

"My mother left me her house."

"Exactly. It weighs upon you, like a debt, it fills you with guilt."

The guru blinked and gave a little cough, as if he were getting ahead of himself. "But we can speak of that later. For now it is enough to recognize your need for forgetfulness and closure, so that you can begin again your spiritual journey, here, with us."

He was interrupted by a sudden commotion outside in the courtyard. A woman – Mrs Yanamandra perhaps – was shrieking and then a man shouted, "Where is that thieving bastard!"

The door of the meditation room in which Christine and the guru were sitting crashed open and Mrs Darling's son stood there, a furious expression on his face. "Ah, there you are!" He glared at Swami Bhatti, who was scrambling to his feet in alarm. "Come here, you little scumbag. I'm going to wring your bloody neck!"

Christine watched in alarm as Jeremy Darling charged into the room. The candle flames flickered and the Swami stumbled back against the wall as the furious interloper lurched forward, hands bunched into fists, and then several young men, some in dhotis and some in jeans, came running in and grappled him, falling to the floor in a struggling heap.

Mrs Yanamandra appeared, wild-eyed. "Swami! Are you hurt?"

Swami Bhatti had pulled himself together. He took on the dignified stoop of a martyr. "I am perfectly fine, thank you, Dorothy. This poor man is sadly deluded."

"Yes, yes." Mrs Yanamandra pulled out a mobile phone from beneath her sari and called the police. On the floor the bodies had stopped struggling. The young men got to their feet, hauling Darling upright. "What shall we do with him, Dorothy?"

"Lock him in the store room," she snapped. She turned to Christine. "Come with me."

As she waited in the office, Christine thought back over her meeting with Swami Bhatti. There had been the disconcerting mention of property just before Jeremy Darling had appeared, but the guru's words before that had also made Christine feel uneasy. All that talk of closure – he seemed to want to numb her feelings about the death of her mother and cover them up. But she didn't want forgetfulness. She was angry at its unfairness and she wanted to hang on to her anger and fight against those awful memories, not blank them out.

"Christine!"

She looked up and saw Sub-Inspector Gupta in the doorway.

"Are you all right?"

"I'm fine." She described what had happened.

"So you heard Darling make threats against Swami Bhatti's life?"

She nodded reluctantly. "He was very angry. He said the Swami was a thief."

"That's absolute rubbish," Mrs Yanamandra said, coming out of her office. "The man's a menace. You must arrest him for attempted murder."

"Where is he now?"

"We have locked him up in a store room. I'll show you."

Sub-Inspector Gupta followed her out to the corridor, where two uniformed policemen with rifles were waiting, and they set off to make the arrest. A little later they were back, the sub-inspector giving orders to the other two, who ran out into the street.

"He broke through the tiled roof of the store room and climbed down into the alley behind the ashram,'" Gupta said, getting out his phone. "He'll be miles away by now."

When he finished his call to headquarters, Christine said that she felt sorry for Jeremy Darling. In a way they were both the same, seeking answers to the death of a mother, both angry at the unfairness of it. And although Mr Darling's anger at Swami Bhatti might be financial in nature, that may just be a mask for his deeper feelings of loss.

Sub-Inspector Gupta looked at her with a smile. "You try to see the best in people, Christine, although in this case I think Mr Darling's motives are straightforward. His mother's legacy consisted almost entirely of her house, in an expensive part of Sydney Harbour, worth many millions of dollars. She left it to Swami Bhatti to establish an ashram there, to further his work."

A house, Christine thought – another parallel.

"So long as Mr Darling is free, we shall have to post a guard here to protect the Swami."

"And meanwhile Mrs Darling's killer is on the loose."

"That's true. My superiors who have taken over the case are not making much progress. The autopsy has shown that she was stabbed by a long, narrow blade, but we have no record of such a weapon, no terrorist group has claimed responsibility, and we still have no eyewitnesses coming forward, even though she was surrounded by dozens of people when she was killed. It is a baffling case. If only I could solve it, I could make a considerable name for myself."

Christine remembered the impression that Mrs Darling had made on her when they had met so briefly before her death. "It would be nice to think that some good might come of it," she said.

Christine returned to the Dubashi Guesthouse feeling disappointed by her visit to the Atmapriksa Ashram. Perhaps she hadn't given Swami Bhatti a fair trial, she thought, but his words had not resonated with her.

Mr Dubashi called out to her when she stepped inside. "You do not look uplifted by your meeting with the guru, Christine."

She told him what had happened, and he nodded smugly. "You confirm my suspicions. He is all right for gullible tourists who want to pay a lot of dollars for a mild taste of Indian mysticism, but not for a serious pilgrim like yourself."

"What should I do, then?"

"If you ask me, fate has brought the answer right here to your side. Here, under this very roof, is a true student of the mysteries of life and death."

"Mr Nemichandra?"

"Exactly, a Jain monk. If anyone can help you it is surely he. And do you know, Christine, it may help us in another matter if you talk to him."

"How is that?"

"Jain monks and nuns live by the five *mahavratas*, the five 'great vows', which are non-violence, truthfulness, honesty, asceticism and celibacy. Of these, the first, *ahimsa*, non-violence, is the most important, and if there is a clash it takes precedence over all the others. So, what if telling the truth would cause someone to suffer violence? A Jain would then have to remain silent, and I am wondering if this, rather than the knock on his head, is what is preventing Mr Nemichandra telling us who he saw kill Mrs Darling, for the Indian Penal Code prescribes death as the penalty for murder."

"I see," Christine said. "Yes, that would be a terrible dilemma, wouldn't it?"

"Indeed. Come, let us pay a visit to Mr Nemichandra, and ask him to instruct you in his philosophy, and perhaps we may find a way to discover what he knows about Mrs Darling's death."

So they climbed the stairs and knocked on the door of Mr Nemichandra's room. Christine heard a slight scuffling inside, and then the door was opened by the monk, dressed in his usual white robe, a square of muslin hanging in front of his mouth. Mr Dubashi explained their purpose and, reluctantly Christine felt, Mr Nemichandra invited them into his room. He and Christine sat on wooden stools by the window overlooking the Ganges, with Mr Dubashi perched on the end of the bed, and Christine explained about the death of her mother, and her search for a way to come to terms with it.

Mr Nemichandra cleared his throat, making the muslin square flutter. "A Jain believes that death is an inevitable part of the cycle of existence, by which each soul passes from life to death to rebirth in a form according to its karma, as some new living being. We believe there is no god, only the endless cycle of nature, of birth, death and rebirth, which a soul can only escape through the complete shedding of its karmic bonds to attain divine consciousness. Therefore your mother's soul has already been reborn and there is no purpose to your grieving for her in her old life. We must learn to give up all such bonds and concentrate on living a pure life without attachments for people or things or places in this world."

Christine tried to absorb this stark view of life. She could see that it might have its appeal as a way to cope with the chaos and pain of the world, but still, she found it rather chilling, and knew she could never abandon her mother's memory. She was about to say something along these lines when Mr Dubashi jumped in.

"Tell me, Mr Nemichandra," he said, 'is it not the case that a murderer – say the murderer of Mrs Darling – will be reborn as one of the hellish beings, and must suffer the torments of hell until he has paid for his crime?'

Mr Nemichandra turned to look at him, eyes narrowed. "Yes, it is so," he said softly.

"Therefore, would it not be merciful to him to help him on his way to the next life as rapidly as possible, since it cannot be avoided and must be endured?"

Mr Nemichandra clearly didn't like this ingenious argument, but as he pondered an answer Christine had a sudden feeling that Mr Dubashi had been right. She said, "Mr Nemichandra, you know who murdered Mrs Darling, don't you?"

The monk stared at her, a look of shock on his face. "You must go now," he said sharply. "I have nothing more to say."

The coroner having released Mrs Darling's body, it was arranged for her cremation to take place the next day as specified in her final instructions. That morning Christine rose before dawn as usual to join the pilgrims on the ghat below the guesthouse. Today she decided to take one of the boats that plied up and down the river, and joined three Indian women in bright saris in a boat rowed by an old man and a boy. They went upstream first, along the great wall of buildings that formed the edge of the city on the river's left bank, passing the succession of ghats, the flights of steps that spilled down to the Ganges, some crowded with people and boats, some with just a few people sitting on the steps and bathing in the sacred river, and others with women washing laundry and spreading it out on the bank to dry. The far side of the river was quite different, a low bank of silt that vanished into the hazy morning light.

The boat turned at a place that the old man said was the Harishchandra Ghat, one of the two burning ghats, where bodies were brought to be cremated on the shores of the river. This one was open to people of all religions, he explained, while the other, Manikaran Ghat downstream, was for Hindus only. Christine looked at the stacks of timber piled up on the shore, and realized that this was the place where Mrs Darling's body would be brought later in the day. She swallowed, wondering how she would deal with that, and the old man, seeing her expression, reached under his seat and offered her a bottle of water with a toothless smile.

They took up the oars again and pulled, gliding downstream more quickly, as far as the Manikaran Ghat, a darker place with many weirdly shaped temple domes wreathed in smoke, where they turned to go back to their starting point. As they approached the quay they became aware of a commotion at the foot of the ghat, below the flight of steps where Mrs Darling had been murdered. Men were shouting and gesticulating, and the boy leaped up on to the prow of the boat to try to see what was going on. Then they heard the howl of a siren and the boy pointed to the top of the ghat, where the crowd was parting for a group of men who came charging down the steps – three of them in uniform and one, who looked very like Sub-Inspector Gupta, in a dark suit. Christine blinked, feeling as if she were having a dream, replaying the scene of Mrs Darling's death but now seen from a distance, from the river.

The old man said something to the boy and they began to pull strongly towards the shore, and as they came close they saw the police emerge through the mob at the water's edge and go to one of the boats tied up there, where, accompanied by a great murmur from the crowd, they heaved a limp body up on to the stone steps.

The old man steered his boat to a clear space further along and they all jumped out. It was impossible to get through the crush on the waterfront, and instead Christine climbed to the top of the ghat and watched from there as an ambulance arrived and two men carried a stretcher down. They returned after a while, followed by the man in a suit.

"Sub-Inspector Gupta!" Christine called, for it was he, and he turned and came to her.

"Christine! My goodness."

"What's happened?"

He took her to one side, shooing away the people nearby. "It is Mr Jeremy Darling, the murdered lady's son. His body was found floating in the river by one of the boats."

"He's dead?"

"Very much so. He has a stab wound through the heart. Since the incident at the ashram we have been looking for him without success."

"That's terrible!"

"Indeed. I must make my report." He hurried away.

According to Indian custom, cremation should occur within twenty-four hours of death, and Mrs Darling's ceremony could not be delayed. Christine and Mr and Mrs Dubashi took tricycle rickshaws to the Harishchandra burning ghat at the appointed hour and made their way down to the shore where they recognized Sub-Inspector Gupta talking to Dorothy Yanamandra, business manager of the Atmapriksa Ashram, among a cluster of people. As they got close Christine recognized some of the young people from the ashram, and discovered that they were witnessing the Swami Bhatti having his beard and head ceremoniously shaved.

Mrs Yanamandra greeted her and explained, "Since Mrs Darling no longer has any family here for her cremation, following the tragic death of her dearly beloved son, the Swami has decided to represent her family and go through the rituals on their behalf."

She pointed out a man who was supervising the arrangements. "He is a member of the Dome caste, who were given the sacred flame four and a half thousand years ago by Lord Shiva to light the first funeral pyre, and have been its guardians ever since. When the Swami has been shaved he will bathe in the Ganges to purify himself and will change into a pure white gown. Then he will go to the Dome temple nearby to buy the holy fire to light Mrs Darling's pyre. Meanwhile his disciples from the ashram have been buying wood logs to build the pyre – three hundred kilos are required, at one hundred and fifty rupees a kilo, would you believe, not to mention some sandalwood at a thousand rupees a kilo, which is a necessary part of the rituals." Mrs Yanamandra was tapping numbers into her iPhone. "Such a lot of cash, but we must do this properly for Mrs Darling. Anyway, the pyre is ready now, and Mrs Darling's body has been placed on it, face up, and covered by a final layer. You do not look well, Christine. Do you need to sit down?"

It was the oppressive humid heat, Christine thought, coupled with the heavy smell of burning timber down here on the ghat, not to mention that glimpse she had just had of Mrs Darling's white foot sticking out from among the logs.

"Are you all right?" Sub-Inspector Gupta had taken hold of her arm and was offering her a bottle of water. His face was full of concern.

"Yes, thank you, Sub-Inspector…"

"Please, it is time you called me Deepak. That is my first name… much shorter.'

Christine smiled at him. "Thanks, Deepak. I was just thinking of my own mother's funeral, not long ago but very different from this."

"Ah, I understand how you must feel, this is all a bit confronting. But that is the point, I think, to fully embrace the reality of death. And although people are sad, they also find relief. They believe that the fire sets the dead person's soul free. Often the souls are so happy to be set free that you can see them dancing in the flames. Sadly, though, I must go. This second murder is causing turmoil. Australian diplomats are here from Delhi to be briefed, and my bosses are trying to persuade them not to issue a tourist travel warning about Varanasi."

Once Swami Bhatti lit the pyre from the sacred flame it took over three hours for the fire to burn down and for Mrs Darling's ashes to be scattered in the river. During that time Christine had a chance to consider Deepak's words. They seemed convincing, and the cremation was certainly a powerful experience, yet she couldn't feel that it had much to do with the living Mrs Darling she remembered.

Eventually she got to her feet and made her way up the ghat, planning to walk back to the hotel. As she approached the head of the stairs she saw a man who appeared to have been watching the ceremonies turn away and disappear down an alleyway. She thought he looked like the Jain monk, Mr Nemichandra, who hadn't come to the funeral, and she decided to follow him.

The man pacing through the crowded streets ahead of her looked very like the monk, but Christine couldn't be sure. They came to a place that was wide enough for street food sellers to set up their stalls down one side. The man had stopped by the first vendor and was buying something. He paid and as he turned to go she caught his profile and was convinced it was Mr Nemichandra – why, yes, he had his whisk tucked under his arm, although he wasn't using it to sweep the street in front of him.

She made her way to the food seller and said hello.

"Hello, madam. I am your aloo tikki walla. You will have some?"

"What's in it?"

"Potatoes, madam, with mint harri chutney. Very tasty."

That was odd, for Mr Dubashi had told her that potatoes were forbidden to Jain monks. Christine handed over a few rupees and took the snack, which was indeed delicious. As she ate she saw that Mr Nemichandra, or his double, had stopped at another stall further along and was eating something else. She worked her way closer and was surprised by a delicious smell of frying meat. This time the vendor explained that the man had bought several shami kebab mince patties. "Lamb mince, lady, filled with green mango. He is very hungry, your friend. He comes here every day."

Meat? That was impossible, surely. Mr Nemichandra was a vegan. Christine saw the man disappear down a narrow alleyway ahead and went after him, but just at that moment she saw something else that gave her a sudden fright – a figure very like the sinister-looking man in the dirty red turban whom she had seen watching her several times before was lurking in a doorway. He turned away as she caught sight of him, and she wondered what to do. Should she phone Deepak? But he would be tied up in important business and anyway she didn't want to lose sight of Mr Nemichandra, so she hurried on, into the alleyway.

The buildings closed in around her – old blackened stone walls, heavy timber doors, timeworn paving stones and steps. She turned a corner and was confronted by a cow, blocking the lane. She was forced to climb a few steps up to the door of a tiny temple, then squeeze around the cow's haunches and step down, straight into the puddle of dung it had freshly dropped.

"Ah." She stared at her shoes, then looked up and saw Mr Nemichandra, twenty metres away, staring intently at her with blazing eyes.

"Excuse me."

Christine turned at the sound of a girl's voice behind her – a small girl, smartly dressed in clean white socks and tartan skirt, with a backpack, on her way home from school. Christine let her pass and when she turned back found that Mr Nemichandra had vanished.

She hurried on, determined now to speak to the Jain. She turned a sharp corner and gave a cry as a hand closed tightly on her arm and yanked her through an open doorway and began to drag her down a narrow passage into a tiny courtyard, half filled with stinking rubbish. The man was incredibly strong, his panting breath filled with the fumes of lamb kebab.

"You stupid woman," the monk hissed, crushing her back against the wall. "You should have minded your own business.'

Christine looked with horror at the weapon in his free hand, the handle of the monk's whisk, from which protruded a long narrow blade.

"You killed Mrs Darling…" Christine croaked as he clutched her throat "…and her son."

"And now you," he growled.

Eyes swimming, Christine looked over his shoulder and saw the man in the red turban watching them, an evil smile on his lips.

She didn't see the club in the turbaned man's hand, but she heard it as it landed on Mr Nemichandra's head with a shocking crack. Mr Nemichandra released her and dropped to the ground.

"Christine!" the turbaned man cried. "Are you all right?"

She knew the voice, but could hardly make sense of it. "Deepak? Sub-Inspector Gupta? It's you?" She fell forward into his arms in a dead faint.

Later, after Deepak had called for armed police to take Nemichandra away, and after he had escorted her back to the guest-house for a long bath and several cups of Mrs Dubashi's rejuvenating tea, he returned, dressed now in his usual dark suit, to see how she was. She couldn't help noticing how elated he was, barely able to contain himself.

"I am a hero, Christine, the man of the hour. My bosses are over-joyed. They are talking about promotion, a medal, a Bollywood movie… and all thanks to you. How did you do it? What made you suspect him?"

She had to confess that it had been a matter of luck, seeing him eat the forbidden food, and following him so that he panicked and gave himself away. "And you've been following me in that… amazing disguise."

"Yes. My bosses took over the case straight away, putting me back on routine duties, but I was worried that Mrs Darling's murderer might target you as a possible witness, and I decided to keep an eye on you."

"You gave me the willies in that outfit."

"You spotted me?" He looked downcast.

"You saved my life, Deepak," she said, reaching for his hand. He cheered up immediately.

"Anyway, he has made a full confession. He really was once a Jain monk, apparently, until he lost his calling and resorted to thieving to survive, becoming a hardened criminal and a paid assassin. We will probably never know how many people he has killed during his criminal career. When Mr Darling realized that his mother was intent on giving away all her money to the ashram, he made contact with Nemichandra on one of his business trips and arranged for him to kill her on her next visit. Unfortunately for Mr

Darling she had already made her new will when she was murdered. When he realized Nemichandra had bungled things they had a furious row and Darling said he wouldn't pay him. They fought and Nemichandra killed him and dumped his body in the Ganges. The Jain monk was a perfect disguise for a murderer, of course, no one believed him capable of violence, but in the end his appetites betrayed him. Pretending to be virtuous is not so easy."

His mobile phone rang and he listened for a while. "Yes, sir!" He rang off and said, "They want me for a news conference, Christine. TV! The world's media! But you will not leave now, will you? I must see you again. If necessary I shall have you detained!" He gave an excited laugh.

"No,'" she said. "I won't leave. Good luck with the media."

"I shall be cool, like James Bond."

When he had gone, Mrs Dubashi came and sat with Christine. "I'm afraid your spiritual journey in Varanasi has not been a conventional one," she said. "Are you disappointed?"

Christine thought, then nodded sadly. "The Swami, the Jain, the burning ghat – they were all powerful experiences and gave me much to think about, but none of them have changed the hurt I feel when I think of my mother's death."

Mrs Dubashi said, "When I lost my first baby, I was heartbroken. Nothing could ease my pain. Then my mother told me that the pain was from the labour of creating a place inside myself for my baby. When I had finished doing that, the pain would ease and my baby would live for ever in my heart."

"Oh." Christine pondered her words, and as she did so it occurred to her that they might be the truest thing she had heard on her journey.

Later that evening they watched television together, to see the news. The lead item was the arrest of Mr Nemichandra, with Sub-Inspector Gupta the star. He spoke to the cameras in a clear, confident voice, more mature now, Christine thought.

Mr Dubashi said, "My goodness, he's talking to the whole world," but his wife corrected him. "No, look at his face, he's talking to just one person – you, Christine. You'd better watch out," she chuckled, "that young man's in love with you."

VANISHING ACT

Christine Poulson

"ONE OF THESE men is a murderer."

Edward looked at the grainy black-and-white photo that Edith held up. Three men smiled out at him.

"What's this all about?" he asked. "Who are they?"

"I'll give you a clue. One of them's my brother – and he's not the murderer."

Edward gestured impatiently. "I need a better look."

She brought her wheelchair closer to his bedside and leaned forward, bringing with her a gust of perfume, something warm and spicy.

Theirs was a new friendship and it would inevitably be a short one. The doctors were careful not to offer any predictions, but Edward knew that he didn't have more than a week or two. He was bedridden now. The morphine took care of the pain, but what he hadn't expected was the boredom. Strange that time should drag, when there was so little of it left, but so it was. That was why Edith was such a godsend. She was in the hospice for a week's respite care. They had taken to each other and she visited him every evening, scooting down the corridor in her wheelchair. She was an interesting woman, had spent most of her working life in Canada as a museum curator. He enjoyed her "take no prisoners" attitude without feeling it was one he could adopt himself.

"Your brother is the one in the middle," he decided. They had the same nose: that bump on the bridge was unmistakable. "Who are the others?"

"Let's call that one Dr X and that one Doctor Y." She pointed with a red-varnished fingernail.

Edward studied the photograph. Doctor Y was tall and fair with something irresolute about his mouth, the kind of man who is a little too anxious to please. Dr X was short and dark with a widow's peak and full, sensuous lips.

"When you say murder … ?"

"This all happened a long time ago – say, twenty-five years, even thirty? A surgeon had an affair with a theatre nurse. When it turned sour, he murdered her to save his marriage – and his reputation. There was a conspiracy of silence amongst his colleagues and he was never brought to book."

"Then how do *you* know?"

"My brother told me. He was one of the doctors who kept quiet. Fred died a couple of months ago." She gave a caw of laughter. "He's beaten me to it. Just. He was very near the end when he let the cat out of the bag. It preyed on his mind. You know how it is …" She shrugged.

When you're near the end? Yes, he did know – who better? – and counted himself lucky. On the big things, marriage, children, work, he'd done just fine. He did rather regret that he'd never got round to reading Proust, but you can't have everything.

"Fred told me what I've just told you," Edith went on. "'One of these men is a murderer.'"

"Did he say how …?"

"She was found dead in bed. Healthy young woman, never had a day's illness in her life. One of those unexplained deaths. Hospital dispensaries are full of things that could bring that about. They weren't as strict about keeping track of drugs in those days."

Edward thought it over.

The stillness was broken only by the slap of sleet on the window. The curtains hadn't been drawn against the November night. Streaks of rain gleamed on the glass and overlaid the smeared lights of the town in the valley below.

At last he said, "After all this time, it's pretty academic …"

"Is it though? What about all these breakthroughs in forensic science and what they can do with DNA? If the police reopened the case, who knows what they might find?"

There was a knock at the door.

They both started, caught each other's eye, and laughed.

"Edith?" A nurse, a thickset man that Edward hadn't seen before, was standing at the door. "It's time for your injection."

Edith swung her wheelchair round.

"Hey! You can't just leave it at that! Which one is it?"

"You decide. Observing criminals was your job, after all." As she headed for the door, she raised a hand in farewell. "Let's see how good a judge of character you are." The words rang out like a challenge.

He watched as she disappeared through the door. Helpless and exasperated, he slumped back on his pillows. That was Edith all over. Surprising that someone hadn't murdered *her* before now.

She had left the door open, but it didn't matter. He liked to see people coming and going up the corridor.

His glance strayed to the clock on the wall. Only nine o'clock. An hour until he could expect his daughter's phone call. He sighed and picked up the photo again. Yes, he had seen many killers in his time as a court artist. But he had long ago learned that, as Shakespeare put it, "there's no art to find the mind's construction in the face". Appearances could indeed be deceiving.

The men were standing on the steps of a building – neo-Georgian – and now that he looked more closely he saw that one of them had a glass in his hand. Some kind of celebration? Had this been taken before the murder? If indeed there really had been a murder. The three men were much the same age, somewhere around the mid-thirties. The clothes and the body language – it was surprising how much you could learn … Was Doctor X or Doctor Y wearing a wedding ring? If only he had a magnifying glass …

When the phone rang, he was surprised to see that an hour had passed.

Jennifer cocked her head. Her ear was so attuned to the night and the silence that she was alert to the smallest unusual noise. She wasn't the nervous type – never had been – and she was used to working nights, but … what *was* that sound?

She put her paperwork to one side and went out into the corridor. It stretched in both directions. There was no one there, but she had the feeling that she had just missed someone. She listened again. The silence was unbroken. On a quiet night like this the hospice must be one of the most peaceful places in the world. No visitors, no phones ringing, no consultants' rounds. And tonight she wasn't expecting anyone to die while she was on duty.

She looked at her watch. Nearly one o'clock. She'd got into the habit of sitting with Edward for a while around now. He didn't sleep well and enjoyed the company.

She brought him his tea and settled down for a chat. This was what nursing should be, really getting to know and care about your patients. It was a privilege and so often you saw the best of people at times like this. People sometimes asked her, did that make it harder, when they died, but strangely enough it didn't.

"Any news about the baby?" she asked. Edward's only daughter, Laura, was in New Zealand waiting for her own daughter to give birth. It had been a difficult pregnancy with enforced bed-rest.

He shook his head. "Laura rang earlier. She's still fretting about not being here. I've told her not to be so silly. Melanie needs her mum with her. And as for me, I don't want any harm to come to my first great-grandchild, do I? Just so long as he or she arrives before I go."

"I'd put money on it," Jennifer said.

She would, too. Edward would hang on for that, though afterwards it would be a different matter. The real question was whether Laura would get away in time to be with him at the end. She could guess how sorely he yearned for his daughter, but it remained unspoken between them.

"I'm not short of visitors," he said, as if he had read her mind.

"The day staff tell me you've made quite a hit with Edith."

He winked at her. "Oh, I'm not so far gone that I don't have an eye for a good-looking woman. Kathleen popped in earlier on, too."

Kathleen was the hospice chaplain, a Church of England vicar who came in four afternoons a week.

"I thought you Quakers didn't have any truck with clergy?"

He laughed. "Oh, I'm happy to chat to anyone. And anyway we don't talk about religion. We've discovered that we're both keen on classic crime fiction. She's promised to lend me a collection of Ellery Queen short stories."

Jennifer nodded. She wasn't a regular church-goer, but her own faith was simple and secure. She was certain that the souls of her patients found safe harbour. She didn't know how she knew that, but she did know it.

They talked for a while longer. When she saw that his eyelids were drooping, she arranged his pillows for him and put the emergency buzzer within reach. She dimmed the lights and went quietly away.

As she walked back to the nurses' station, she glanced into each room in turn. She had actually passed Edith's room before she registered that something was wrong. She turned back and went in. What she had seen was the light reflected off Edith's eyes. They were half-open. She moved without haste to the bed and touched the pulse-point at the throat. The skin was cool under her fingers. Sometime in the last couple of hours, Edith had slipped silently away.

Jennifer closed Edith's eyes and said a short prayer.

"You weren't expecting it, were you?" Edward said. "I know Edith wasn't. She thought she had a while to go yet."

It was the following night and Jennifer was rearranging his flowers. "Well, yes. But these things don't always go according to a timetable."

"I can't believe it. She was so full of life."

Jennifer gave him a compassionate look. He had no difficulty in interpreting it. Funny: the more his body wound down, the greater seemed to be his insight into what other people were thinking. He could almost see the thoughts flitting through her head. Poor old boy, she was thinking. It brings home the fact of death. Bound to be upsetting.

What she actually said was, "The doctor says her heart gave out – it could have happened at any time."

"I know, I know. 'Death in Hospice': hardly a banner news headline, but all the same ..."

Jennifer plucked out a dead carnation and dropped it into the bin. "To go without any fuss or pain, that's not a bad thing."

He snorted. "Maybe not. But it sure as hell wasn't Edith's style. I can't imagine her ever taking the easy way out. I'll miss her," he added, suddenly realizing he was close to tears.

Jennifer put her head on one side and tweaked the arrangement to conceal the gaps.

"The family didn't expect it either," she admitted. "And that reminds me. According to her niece there was a bag of family photos that she'd brought in to sort out. We can't find them. She didn't leave them in here, did she?"

"Not a bag full, no, but she did leave one." Edward fumbled on his bedside table for the photo of the three men.

She came over, took one look and said, "Doctors."

He was taken aback. "You recognize them?"

"No, no, but they have that look about them, and it's obvious what the occasion is."

"It is?"

"Of course. They've just set up in practice together. Look." She pointed to something in shadow on the left-hand side of the picture. "That's their new name-plate. They're drinking a toast."

To think that he had missed that! But of course he had been concentrating on the faces. He squinted at it, trying to make out the letters. They were tantalizingly out of focus.

"Who are they?" Jennifer asked.

Edward hesitated. But what was there to lose?

He told Jennifer what Edith had told him.

She thought about it for a while. Again he could read her thoughts: should she pooh-pooh the idea, or be honest?

She decided to be honest. "D'you know the joke about the man who dies and goes to heaven? He sees someone rushing around in a white coat and asks St Peter who it is. St Peter says, 'That's God. He thinks he's a doctor.' Some of those old-style consultants did pretty much think they were God."

"Some still do," Edward said wryly. "So you're not going to say it couldn't happen?"

"We both know that it could. As long as nothing was said, people could pretend they didn't know."

"And after a while they'd be able to tell themselves that it really *didn't* happen, and that if there were any real evidence, the police would have been on to it. But, you know, he could still have a lot to lose. What about those murders in Finland? At Lake Bodom. Someone was brought to trial over forty years later. And Edith wasn't the kind to let sleeping dogs lie. If he felt threatened by her …"

But that was one step too far. He saw that he had lost Jennifer. He felt a stubborn determination to press on. "You think I'm letting my imagination run away with me, morphine dreams …"

He saw from the slight flush on her face that he was right.

"There's something you're forgetting," she said. "Even if someone *wanted* to murder Edith, how would they get in here? All visitors have to sign in and this isn't like a huge hospital. I know everyone who works here. It just wouldn't be possible for anyone to masquerade as a doctor."

"They wouldn't be masquerading as a doctor, they would actually *be* one. I asked one of the friends from my Quaker meeting to bring in my pastels." His sketchbook was lying on the bed. He opened it to show her. "I've tried to age them," he said. "Doctor Y – that sort of fair hair tends to get thin. It's already receding a bit in the photo. By now he's probably bald on top. And the face – he's the kind of man who gets gaunt with age. With that long jaw, he'll look a bit skull-like.' He had her full attention now. She was studying the drawings, fascinated.

He went on. "Dr X is the type who puts on weight easily. Not just because of his build, he likes his food and drink. He's a bit greedy. His hair might recede a bit, but not a lot, it'll just make the widow's peak more prominent. He'll have some grey in his hair by now. It's a distinctive face – with that strong nose."

"How old would they be now?" Jennifer asked.

"In their sixties."

"Neither of them is on the staff." But she was frowning, narrowing her eyes as she stared at the drawings.

"You're not certain?"

"Yes, I am, but ... no." She shook her head. "I don't know either of them."

A bell rang from a nearby room and she got up to leave.

"Take them with you – the photo and the drawings – please. Something might come to you."

She hesitated, and this time he wasn't sure what she was thinking. A shutter had come down.

Was it just to humour him that she did what he asked?

Things got busier for Jennifer after that. Mrs O'Shea, who had been lingering for several days, took a turn for the worse. There are no set visiting hours in a hospice and her large and devoted family were in and out all night. Not one but two priests arrived to give her the last rites. She was still hanging on when Jennifer went off duty.

At home there was the fuss of getting the kids ready for school and then she flopped into bed. She woke up at two o'clock, put on her dressing gown, and made a strong cup of coffee. She took it back to bed. The cat followed her up and stretched himself beside her. She stroked him absent-mindedly. The idea that Edith might have been murdered almost made her snort with laughter. In the cold light of day it seemed absurd, it *was* absurd. Like something in one of those old-fashioned detective stories that Edward liked so much, and maybe that was even where it had come from. Patients on high doses of morphine did get strange notions.

She rummaged around in her handbag and found Edward's drawings. She stared at them again. The uneasy feeling she'd had earlier came back to her. That widow's peak ... and that bag of photographs going missing ... not so odd in itself perhaps, but ... She saw again the look of surprise on the duty doctor's face. He really hadn't been expecting it, though he had signed the death certificate willingly enough. And – face it – how hard would it be to get away with murder in a hospice? Just one more needle mark in someone who was already having several injections a day.

Her eye fell on the bedside clock. Oh, Lord, she was going to be late collecting the kids. She threw her clothes on and was out of the house in two minutes. Then it was non-stop: supervising piano lessons and homework, simultaneously cooking the dinner and listening with half an ear to a convoluted story told by the twins. Five children under the age of nine. Whatever had they been thinking of? Then Matt was home and it was all right again just as it was every evening. He was a computer person, worked in hospital admin, nine to five, which was what made the whole thing possible. Then dinner was over, it was 8.30, and the kids were in bed.

This was their time. She told him everything and so she told him about Edward.

"Of course it's all nonsense," she said, hoping he'd agree.

"Interesting little problem, trying to identify these chaps," Matt said, looking at the photo over the top of his glasses. "That name-plate – I could scan the photo and fiddle about with Photoshop, increase the contrast. The one who was Edith's brother – do you know his name?"

"I don't think she was ever married – so I expect it's the same as hers: Johnson."

"You can do wonders with online records and Google. Leave it with me, love."

"Of course there can't be anything in it. Can there?"

"Nah. But if I find out who they are and they're both long gone, well then, you can put the poor old boy's mind at rest, can't you?"

Edward was restless. Kathleen had brought in the collection of Ellery Queen short stories, but they failed to hold his attention. He found himself looking at the clock every other minute. Laura always rang at ten o'clock to say goodnight to him. It was now eleven o'clock. There must be something wrong. He sent his thoughts winging off to the Bay of Plenty, held in the light his daughter and his granddaughter and the child waiting to be born.

Jennifer had popped her head round the door to say she'd do her best to pop in for a chat around one o'clock. So there was that to look forward to, but he had the feeling it was going to be a long night.

When the phone rang he was startled. As he stretched out his hand, he knocked a slew of things off the bedside table.

The moment he heard Laura's voice he knew that it was all right.

The words came tumbling out. "Dad, it's all over! She went into labour naturally – and after all those problems it couldn't have gone better, only a few hours – amazing for a first baby. Didn't have a chance to ring you—"

"The baby—?"

"She's perfect…oh, Dad, she's perfect. They're going to call her Alice after Mum." He heard tears in her voice. "And Melanie's just fine. She'll speak to you herself tomorrow. And that's not all. The airline rang ten minutes ago. There's been a cancellation. I've got a seat on a flight leaving in three hours."

"So soon …"

"Look, I've got to go. John's waiting to take me to the airport. When he gets back he'll send some photos through to the hospice. Just hang on! I'll be with you the day after tomorrow."

The day after tomorrow. A little girl called Alice.

The happy news lit up the room and tears filled his eyes. Now that he knew Laura was coming he could let himself yearn for her. He thought of the day that he had held her in his arms as a newborn baby. It was only right and fitting that her dear face should be the last he would see.

There was a far-off muffled boom. A couple of days to go until Bonfire Night, but someone was setting off early fireworks. There was a flash of light and above the town a firework unfolded like a big blue chrysanthemum. There were more distant bangs and whizzes: coloured lights blossomed and chased each other across the sky.

He had always loved fireworks. He settled back to enjoy the show.

Paperwork, paperwork. The downside of modern nursing. Jennifer sighed. One day she might actually clear her desk. She looked at her watch. 12.20. Forty minutes until her tea-break and her chat with Edward. She put her head down and ploughed on.

She was puzzling over a questionnaire from the local health trust when the computer gave the little ping that meant there was incoming mail. She ignored it. It wouldn't be anything that couldn't wait.

When the phone rang ten minutes later, she reached for it with her eyes still on the form.

Matt's voice brought her head up with a jerk. Something wrong with the children? She breathed a sigh of relief when he said the kids were fine.

"What are you doing still up?" she asked.

"Got a bit carried away on the computer. Didn't you get my email? I've managed to work out who they were, the men in the photo. Charles Ballantyne – distinguished career – Southampton hospital, big wheel in the BMA – you won't care about all that. Thing is, he died last year. The other one, Robert Cleaver, went to Australia, returned about ten years ago, he's an Emeritus Professor of Oncology, specializing in a rare form of cancer at—" Matt named a London teaching hospital.

Out of the corner of her eye she saw someone pass the open door. She caught a glimpse of a dark suit and a clerical collar. The footsteps went on down the corridor.

She opened Matt's email.

He was still talking. "There's a photo of him on the hospital website. If you want to see what he looks like now, click on the link."

She did and a face stared out of the screen at her. It was uncanny how right Edward had been, except for—

Her instincts were telling her that something was wrong. The footsteps had stopped further down the corridor. Who was he visiting? Not Mrs O'Shea. She had died earlier that evening and her body was in the hospice mortuary waiting to be collected by the undertakers.

And he wasn't visiting Edward. Edward was a Quaker.

Jennifer dropped the phone and sprang to her feet.

* * *

Edward's eyes were heavy, but he forced himself to stay awake. He wanted to hang on until one o'clock so that he could ask Jennifer if an email had arrived with photos of the baby and Melanie. He wished he could tell Edith. Funny how much he missed her. That story of hers – he couldn't quite understand how he had let himself get so carried away by it. Perhaps he had been groping for a reason for her death, unwilling to believe that she had simply disappeared, given him the slip, pulled off the vanishing act he was so shortly to pull off himself.

Just for a moment he had the feeling that she was somewhere close by. He seemed to catch a whiff of her perfume.

When the man in the clerical collar appeared in the doorway, Edward's first thought was that he had come to the wrong room.

His second thought as the man closed the door behind him was that he had done a good job of updating the photo, but he couldn't possibly have guessed about the beard.

His third was that he wouldn't be seeing Laura after all, because among the things he had knocked off the bedside table was the emergency buzzer.

Jennifer punched the panic button to summon help.

Nurses aren't supposed to run, and Jennifer was a big woman, but she flew down that corridor.

She reached the room in time to see the man standing by Edward's bed.

Light glinted on a hypodermic.

Another moment and she flung her arms round him from the back. She squeezed. He struggled, but years of manhandling toddlers at home and lifting patients at work had given her arms like steel hawsers. He didn't stand a chance.

The hypodermic went clattering to the floor.

Then Paul, the burliest of the hospice nurses and an ex-soldier, appeared in the doorway and it was all over.

"Just a black shirt and strip of plastic cut from a bottle of washing-up liquid," Edward marvelled for at least the tenth time.

Jennifer nodded. "That was all it took. Dressed like that he could walk into any hospice – or any hospital ward – claim to be visiting a parishioner and no one would bat an eyelid."

It was nearly the end of Jennifer's shift on the following night and she hadn't been able to resist popping in to talk it over one more time. It was as if she needed to go over and over it again to convince herself that it really had happened.

"Only sorry I won't be here to follow the trial," Edward said with an effort. "But it's clear enough what happened."

"His bad luck that Edith had the same rare cancer that he'd made his speciality, and consulted him privately."

"Johnson's such a common name – no wonder he didn't make the connection."

"But she did. I wonder if she really had anything on him. She certainly made him think she had."

"And that she'd shared it with someone in the hospice."

Edward closed his eyes. He claimed that the excitement had given him a new lease of life. Jennifer wasn't so sure. The disease was progressing fast now. He was too weak to sit up and his face was very pale against the pillow. She wondered if he would be alive when she returned in the evening. She hoped so. She'd like to be there at the end and she wanted to meet Laura.

Her eyes strayed to the colour printout of a beaming young woman with hair plastered to her sweaty forehead. She was cradling a tiny baby with a face like a crumpled rosebud.

She patted Edward's hand and was getting up to leave when she saw that he had opened his eyes. He was gazing past her into the corridor.

She turned her head and saw a handsome middle-aged woman approaching.

"Laura," Edward murmured. "You're here."

"Dad! I hired a car at the airport."

"This is Jennifer."

The two women clasped hands as they passed in the doorway. Laura gave a smile of recognition that made her look very like her father.

Jennifer closed the door behind her and went to get a Do Not Disturb sign.

No one would be needed here for a while.

THE BETRAYED

Roger Busby

"IT'S IMPOSSIBLE," DENNIS Jewel said, "even if you'd got a case of JD tucked under your arm there, I'd be telling you the same thing."

Mark Fletcher placed the bottle of Jack Daniel's Old No. 7 he had brought along as a sweetener on the desk between them. "Dennis," he said, "what say you lock the door there, we pull a couple of glasses out of your bottom drawer, and we sip a little of this amber nectar and see if you don't change your mind?"

"There's no way I'm going to do that," Jewel replied, "not while we've got an operation running. You think I can conjure blokes up out of the air or something? I'm not a bloody magician, Fletch."

Fletcher sighed. He'd come to the Borough for a favour and he'd expected to have to haggle, but here was Jewel sitting on his backside just acting stubborn. "What operation trumps a murder?"

"Zatopek. You know, the lorry hijacking thing."

"Zatopek?"

"Don't you start." Jewel took a pack of cigarettes out of his pocket and glanced wistfully at the image of a rotting lung on the packet. The only place he could light up these days was skulking in the station yard with the last of the diehards. "Some comedian up at the dream factory came up with that stupid name, something about it's got to run the distance."

"Christ," Fletcher said. "Now I've heard everything."

"Well, it don't change a thing," Jewel insisted, turning the cigarette packet over in his hand. "I'm committed a hundred per cent, and if they get wind up the road that I'm even thinking of loaning blokes to you on the old pals act, they're going to have my balls. It's as simple as that."

Mark Fletcher regarded his friend for a moment as he marshalled his thoughts for a new gambit. Jewel was a heavily built man, solid with beefy shoulders which bulged under his shirt. He had a head of tight grey curls and his face wore a permanently perplexed expression. They were the same rank, detective chief inspector, only Jewel was a guv'nor on the Borough-wide CID under the wing of the Metropolitan Police Major Crime Directorate, with his own complement of detectives. He took his orders from New Scotland Yard. Normally the Borough would be only too happy to oblige on tricky investigations which stretched the limited resources of the Divisional CID, but now that Fletcher wanted his help here was his old oppo bellyaching about some Zatopek nonsense.

"Look, Dennis, it's not like I'm asking for the earth, just a couple of decent blokes would do. You know I wouldn't come begging if I wasn't really up against it. I've got the big bin murder running away with me and the guv'nor already shouting the odds on overtime."

"Yeah, I see your problem, Fletch," Jewel agreed. "Sounds like you've got dead meat there all right. Not many like that get cleared these days."

"That's what I like about you, Dennis, always the optimist."

"Well, you've got to be a realist sometimes," Jewel said. "Sounds like it's stacked against you. If I was you, Fletch, I'd think seriously about coasting and leave those eager beavers up at dream factory to take the shit when it all hits the fan."

"Come off it," Fletcher said. "You never took a soft option in your life, and I'm the same. We're just a pair of thick-skinned Ds at heart who happen to think clearing crime still matters, particularly a swine like this one. That's what I pin my reputation on, not ducking and diving and playing politics. And don't try to kid me you're not the same."

Jewel shrugged. "You don't get any medals for pissing in the wind these days."

"I'm talking about in here." Fletcher tapped his chest. "Call it personal satisfaction or professional pride... call it what you like.

And I'm buggered if I'm going to let some lunatic who'd stick a screwdriver into a kid like that until she looked like a colander, then dump her body in a recycling bin, get away with it. If I start back-pedalling this one I wouldn't sleep nights, and you know it."

Jewel rolled his shoulders again. "All you'll get yourself is an ulcer, my friend. Tell you what, run it by me and maybe something'll come to mind. What've you got so far?"

"Well, first off, we've got the car spotted on the street camera, old Astra. Lots of blood in the boot that's a DNA match to the vic and the back seats are missing, so that could be where it happened before she was dumped. Doc reckons she was dead best part of five days before the bin men found her, so matey's got a head start."

"How about the motor... any good?"

Fletcher pulled a face. "You'd have thought so, wouldn't you? We got the owner right away and put him through the mincer. His story is he was away on holiday and left the car in the street outside his drum, and somebody must've nicked it because the first thing he knows is he comes home and there's the law beating down his door."

"Sounds like a good enough story to put him in the clear. How's it stand up?"

"That's the trouble," Fletcher said. "It's cast iron and watertight. He's got about a thousand witnesses backing up his alibi and we can't shake 'em. Looks like he's telling the truth or he's got a lot of clout somewhere to rig a thing like that."

"What's he like?"

"Tasty, CRO with form as long as your arm," Fletcher said. "Rape, indecent assault, drug dealer by trade. Complains against the police for a pastime. Hits you with harassment if you look sideways at him. A right charmer – was one of the brothers who used to run with the Ace of Spades crew. If his story wasn't so rock solid he'd be right there in the frame. I'd have him strung up by his thumbs. But after the riots we've got to treat 'em all with kid gloves. Came down on tablets of stone."

"That's the way it goes," Jewel said. "Tough on crime, tough on the causes of crime."

"Ha-ha, don't make me laugh. Burn down a furniture store, kick in a few shops, throw a few petrol bombs… and our lords and masters are having a ginger fit. How about associates? Maybe he's got some running dogs of similar persuasion. Maybe he loaned some face his motor."

"Well, if he did," Fletcher replied, "he's not about to be telling us. He's as cunning as a barrel-load of monkeys so we're not going to be able to pull any flankers with him or he'll just lawyer up and there'll be white forms coming down like a blizzard."

"What else've you got?"

"What would you like?" Fletcher asked. "We've got hours and hours of street CCTV to wade through, a few possible witnesses to boot, and background on the girl to go through. But once it hit *London Tonight* the brass suddenly took an interest, leaping about trying to put on a big show of dedicated police work. Every bugger so busy hustling their image, I can see this job going right out of the window."

"Don't take it so personally," Jewel said, "you're going to lose your objectivity."

"Advice like that I can do without," Fletcher said. "Now are you going to stop playing with your fags and give me some help on this or not?"

"I'd like to." Jewel softened a little, gazing reflectively at the image of the rotting lung. "Only I can't see any way I could squeeze it without some joker upstairs noticing."

"Bottom line, Dennis," Fletcher said "Just one decent D would do me. All my blokes have been yanked off on this Weeting thing and I just need someone to watch my back."

"That phone hacking nonsense is a total balls-ache all right." Jewel turned the pack over in his hands as the craving for a nicotine hit increased. He'd tried the patches, gum and even hypnosis, but the addiction of a lifetime was stubborn. "One D, eh?"

"At a pinch, yes."

"Tell you what, Fletch," Jewel said, "I've got a transferee come in from Kent who hasn't been assigned yet. Bloody good detective by all accounts." A hint of a smile touched his lips. "I could maybe loan you Helen Ritchie."

Fletcher felt the blow in the pit of his stomach coupled with a sudden lightness behind the eyes. "Oh, Christ, Dennis, that's below the belt."

"Best I can do." Jewel was grinning openly now. "Take it or leave it. Do you want her or not?"

Fletcher groaned. "I've got no choice, have I?"

"Nope."

Fletcher reached across the desk and retrieved the bottle of whiskey. "For a low trick like that, you don't deserve my hospitality."

"That's all right," Jewel said, amused at his friend's discomfiture. "I switched to gin anyway... smoother on the old tubes."

Fletcher stared at the bottle; felt like he needed a shot. "How is Helen anyway?" he said. "I haven't seen her in years, not since she left the Met."

"How'd you mean?" Jewel asked, still enjoying himself. "Job-wise or what?"

"You know what I mean, Dennis," Fletcher said. "How the hell is she?"

"Well," Jewel said, "I always got the feeling something must've soured Helen way back. Oh, she still looks terrific, but inside," he tapped his temple, "hard as nails...who knows what goes on in there? I just get the impression that somewhere along the line some smooth-talking bastard slipped her something nasty and she's never got over it. I heard she was a sweet kid back along, but you'd know better'n me, eh, Fletch? You were on the old Peckham robbery squad with her in those long-gone days, weren't you?"

"Sure," Fletcher said, still staring reflectively at the bottle, "back when we were young and impressionable and everybody was breaking their neck to prove what a great thief-taker they were."

"Good times, eh?" Jewel said. "So who'd you think slipped Helen a crippler?"

"How would I know?" Fletcher said. "I was only on the squad six months before I got posted to the Yard."

"Oh, yeah, I recall," Jewel said. "You were a flier in those days. We used to sit here in the weeds, chewing on our straws watching your career take off. First the Yard, then Bramshill and all that clever stuff...you were the blue-eyed boy back then, all right, Mark."

"Didn't last though, did it?"

"Oh, come on." Jewel settled back in his chair. "Don't tell me you're getting bitter and twisted too?"

Fletcher crossed to the door and Jewel followed him with his eyes. "So how about Helen," he called after him, "d'you want her or not?"

"I'll let you know," Fletcher said as he went out.

Marian was putting the kids to bed. He knew that from the familiar noises in the house, a nondescript semi on Brunel Road just down from Rotherhithe Overground station. Mark Fletcher sat at the IKEA desk in the spare bedroom, which served as his study. It was after eight when he got home from the job and he was tired to the point of exhaustion. He'd told his wife that all he needed was half an hour's peace and quiet, and he'd gone up to his study taking the bottle of Old No. 7 with him. After a few minutes he'd broken the seal and poured himself a drink. He nursed the glass for a moment, reflecting on his thickening waistline, the result of too many beers, too many snatched sandwich lunches, the unmistakable evidence of approaching middle age, then swallowed the whiskey in one gulp. Fletcher poured himself another.

It was unusual for him to act in this way. Normally he would never shut himself away from his family, he had precious little time with them anyway. Neither would he dream of drinking alone, he'd seen too many go down that road, but then tonight was different. Tonight he was fortifying himself against a deep melancholy as his memory transported him back across the years and conjured up images from the past... images of Helen Ritchie. Had all those years really slipped by in the blink of an eye? All those years she had dwelt somewhere deep in his memory, waiting for the right moment to return and settle the score. Mark Fletcher massaged the moisture from his eyes. It all seemed like yesterday.

It was back in the heady days of his youth that Mark Fletcher, billeted in the single men's quarters of a Southwark section house, began to get the feeling that a bright young man could make a name for himself in London's Metropolitan Police Force. The old adage "in the country of the blind the one-eyed man is king" seemed more and more appropriate as he assuaged his sexual appetite on an ample diet of nurses and manoeuvred himself into the CID. It was a time of plenty, a time of golden opportunity, and for Fletcher, breathing the sweet clean air of ambition, promotion to Detective Sergeant in record time seemed a natural reward for his talents.

Within a month he had engineered himself a transfer into the free-wheeling Peckham robbery squad, had moved into a stylish bachelor pad and was driving a sports car. His star was well and truly in the ascendant. The squad appealed to his vanity: the swashbuckling image of the elite crime fighter, the absence of regimented routine. He began to affect sharp suits, and allowed his hair to grow longer than regulations permitted. Brash, flashy, aggressive and conceited, that was the veneer, and it gave him a glow of satisfaction, when he walked into a bar for a quiet drink, that a proportion of the patrons would slink away in the direction of the rear exit. In his own impressionable eyes, Mark Fletcher was a "bloody good D" who put the fear of God into the criminal fraternity. So when a policewoman named Helen Ritchie joined the squad for a plainclothes attachment, it seemed only natural in the incestuous world of "the job" that an affair was on the cards.

Helen Ritchie was a doll, no two ways about it, and plainly she had been selected for CID because she bore not the slightest resemblance to the archetypal policewoman. She was petite, fine-featured, with a model's figure and a natural walk with pelvis thrust forward which brought a chorus of wolf whistles from building sites. She wore her coppery hair in a mass of finger curls, like a burnished halo around her elfin face. Her nose wrinkled delightfully when she smiled. Her first day on the squad produced a desperate contest to see who could tempt her out to lunch. DS Mark Fletcher won by a long head. Pretty soon they were seen regularly together, driving out of town in the MX5 for evenings in country inns. After a surfeit of nurses Fletcher was enchanted, felt a fluttering sensation inside himself when they were together, a mild anxiety when they were apart. It was a unique experience. Like the time they lay together on the Habitat settee in his flat, her head cradled against his chest, Ella and Frank duetting on the hi-fi. A wave of romantic imagery suddenly washed over him.

"Helen…"

"Hmm?"

"I love you."

"Uh-huh."

"No, I really do."

"What?"

"Love you."

"Oh, yeah?"

"Come on, I'm serious."

"All right." Her eyes were closed as she listened to the music. After a moment Fletcher said: "Helen, I really love you."

"Howd'you know?"

"What?"

"How d'you know you love me?"

"It's how I feel, I just feel it." Mark Fletcher floundered for the right words.

"How do you feel it?"

"Oh, come on."

"Mark," she said, opening her eyes and smiling as she teased him. "What on earth makes you think you love me?"

"I just know it."

"You think you love me," she said a little more seriously. "We'd need to know each other a lot better before you'd really know it."

"Oh, come on, Helen."

"Believe me, Mark," she said, really serious now, "you love yourself more than you love me, and when that changes, I'll know it."

"That's a pretty cruel thing to say."

"There's no sense in kidding ourselves," she said, "give it time, don't rush it."

"But I love you now."

Helen closed her eyes again. "Relax, Mark," she said, "listen to the music."

* * *

Times like this, he thought to himself, she could be infuriating, but he swallowed his injured pride and tried to imagine what it would need to convince her. He had no way of knowing that the convoluted process of female courtship required edging forward slowly, consolidating each move before surrendering further precious resources of emotion. He had no way of knowing that Helen was already enmeshed in the complicated emotional web that he had spun within her. His feelings were still too shallow for that kind of comprehension, and Helen Ritchie, playing the game dictated by her instincts, would never admit it. As if that weren't enough, sometimes the job intruded.

They were driving home from a restaurant when Helen, who had been in a pensive mood all evening said, "Let's just park over there, Mark, and talk a minute."

Fletcher steered the Mazda into a layby and cut the engine. They sat for a moment in absolute silence.

When he could stand the suspense no longer, Fletcher said: "Penny for 'em then?"

Helen, who had been staring out of the window, turned to face him. "How serious is withholding information?"

Fletcher was taken aback. "How d'you mean?"

"In the job."

"Depends."

She bit her lip. "I mean, do you switch off when you're off duty, Mark? Can you have a personal life as well?"

Fletcher smiled. "We're like the Pinkertons, we never sleep."

"Mark, I'm serious."

"Well," he said, "you know the score as well as I do, Helen, particularly on the squad. A good D's supposed to put the job first."

"What about us?"

Fletcher shrugged. "We've done all right so far, there's no regulation says you can't live your own life." He felt a sense of foreboding, like stepping on to shifting sands. "You'd better tell me what's on your mind," he said finally.

* * *

Helen was staring out of the car window again, her face turned away from him. "How important is Bernard Goodman?" she asked softly.

Fletcher jerked upright in his seat. "What d'you know about Bernard Goodman?"

"Only that he's a squad target."

"Jesus, Helen, that's the understatement of the year. The top brass at the Yard have been busting a gut over him for the past six months or more."

"Big deal then, eh?"

"Helen," Fletcher said, "Bernie Goodman and his little team ripped off two mill in bullion and artefacts from the vaults of the Bank of Japan in the Strand. He's not just a big deal, he's the Met's number one most wanted."

"I'm the new girl," Helen said, still without looking at him. "Tell me what makes him so special."

"Look, love," Fletcher said, "Bernie's a star villain, best lance man in the business. He went though the vault of that bank like butter and damn near caused an international incident. The Japanese Embassy went ballistic. Went in from an old sewer nobody knew was there, clean as a whistle, left us with egg on our face. Vanished into thin air. We never got a sniff on that job."

"I know where he is," she murmured.

Fletcher was stunned. "Say that again?"

"Bernard Goodman. I know where he is, Mark." She turned to face him, her expression sombre.

"Come on...you're kidding me?"

She shook her head. "I wish I were."

Fletcher took her hand in his. "Look, Helen," he said carefully, "this is serious. Are you telling me you know where Bernie Goodman is, right now, this minute?"

She nodded.

"Jesus Christ," Fletcher exclaimed. "You'd better tell me all about it."

"It's not that simple."

"Look, Helen, we're not talking about some toerag here, you know, Goodman's a major league villain. Any D worth his salt would give his eye teeth to nail him. That's the stuff reputations are made of."

"I know," she said. "That's what worries me."

Fletcher was still holding her hand. "If you know anything about Bernie Goodman's whereabouts, you need to tell me right now."

"As you and me, or as detectives?"

"As you and me. God's sake, if we can't trust each other now, it's a poor lookout."

"All right," she agreed. "It's funny how it happened, you know, Mark. I mean me getting a whisper on a thing like this."

"Go on," he urged her, the hairs on the back of his neck starting to prickle, "tell me about it."

Helen frowned. "Well, when I was doing my initial training at Hendon there was a girl in my class called Carol Dunne. How she ever got past the selection board I'll never know, you could see a mile off she'd never make it. Anyway, I felt sorry for her and we became friends. Weekends I used to go and stay with her family in Devon. She was a strange girl and I got the impression she joined the police in desperation, to try to bring some sort of order to her life. But it didn't work and after Hendon she did a couple of months as a pro con then packed it in. We kept in touch for a while but when she started working as a croupier in the clubs I didn't hear from her any more and I presumed she was breaking all her old ties, one by one, and I was the last. Anyway the years went by, then last week, right out of the blue, she phoned me and said she wanted to see me about something important, something she couldn't talk about on the phone. She sounded so desperate I agreed to meet her, but you know, if she hadn't made the first move, I'd never have recognized her. She'd changed completely, and let's say the years hadn't been kind."

Helen paused for a moment and then continued, "Well, to cut a long story short, she told me she was living with this Greek and working nights as a croupier and hostess at the Desert Island Club at the Elephant. She said this boyfriend of hers was a right piece of work who'd get juiced up and knock her about then come crawling back and plead with her when he was dried out again. She said she stuck with him because he needed her, and besides..."

"The Desert Island," Fletcher interrupted. "That's Danny Hood's place – a real nutter. Used to be a pretty fair heavyweight boxer before he got punchy and drifted into bad company."

"Well anyway," Helen picked up the thread, "Carol told me she was terrified because this boyfriend had got in over his head with Hood. So I told her I couldn't help unless she was more specific and she came right out with it. She told me they've got Goodman locked up in a back room at the club and they're squeezing him dry. She said the deal had started off as a hideout, but now he was a prisoner and the thing was getting out of hand."

Fletcher was suspicious. "How'd she know all this?"

"Apparently the Greek's inclined to brag when he's had a skinful and she's scared stiff they're going to find out and do something to keep him quiet."

"Well, she knows the score there all right," Fletcher said. "That's about Hood's barrow."

"She said she couldn't think of any way out, and then she remembered me and tried the phone number I'd given her way back."

"OK, Helen." Fletcher was still sceptical. "So she comes to you and spins you this yarn. What's to say it's not just some fairy tale she's dreamed up to give her man a hard time? What's her angle?"

"There's a kid," Helen said. "I finally got it out of her. She had a baby by the Greek, that's what's eating her up. Just one of our little feminine quirks."

"All right," Fletcher said, "you get her to come in and we can put something together. We're going to need a warrant and that means reasonable grounds...do you think she could handle a wire?"

"Mark," Helen said, "you haven't understood a word I've said, have you? There's no way Carol can be involved, or me either. They'd put it together in no time flat. Why do you think I was asking you about withholding evidence?"

"On a thing like this," Fletcher said, "we could get her into a witness protection scheme, safe house, new identity, new life, and you're a squad officer so you're fireproof."

Helen shook her head. "No way," she said. "That bunch of maniacs would be on to Carol like a flash and she'd be in worse trouble than she is now. You know witness protection is Mickey Mouse."

"I could go to the guv'nor, lay it on the line."

"Oh, Mark, don't you see? Then I'd have to deny this conversation ever took place. She's put me in an impossible position just because I felt sorry for her. We were good friends once."

Helen looked so troubled that Fletcher cupped her face in his hands and kissed her lightly. "Well, you got it off your chest, that's a good thing. Now you leave it to me, I'll work something out."

But the prize of Bernie Goodman, the gold robber who had outwitted the Yard's finest, was too much to resist. The following morning DS Mark Fletcher called his team together for a little off-the-record conference. Laid it on the line for them without revealing his informant.

"The only way around this," he told them, "is to take that pillock Dan Hood out of the frame and soften him up a bit, then we hit the club and collar Goodman."

"Nick 'im official, Skip?" one of the DCs asked, and Fletcher shook his head. "No, this one's a foreigner. We'll do it off our own bat and see how it shapes. The fewer know about this the better especially as we'll be off our manor. We'll book out on general enquiries tonight, two cars will do... oh, and one of you draw a shooter. Give 'em the usual rigmarole, OK?"

Working to Mark Fletcher's instructions they pulled Daniel Hood that night, sandwiched his Merc between unmarked police cars as he left the Desert Island shortly after midnight. The exchange in the New Kent Road was brief and to the point. After forcing the Mercedes to stop, the armed detective thrust a 9mm Glock through the driver's window into the face of the bodyguard behind the wheel whose eyes immediately took on a glazed thousand-yard stare. Fletcher opened the passenger door and invited Hood to step out. "Congratulations, Danny," he told him. "You're the star turn for tonight."

They took Hood to an undertaker's off the Walworth Road just as Fletcher had planned and in the prep room, which reeked of death and embalming fluid, stripped him naked and laid him out on one of the freezer drawers. Daniel Hood was a hard man. He had a tough smooth face drawn taut by scar tissue, a legacy of his days in the ring. His heavy body had begun to run to fat and looked strangely vulnerable stretched out on the slab. His cold eyes betrayed no emotion. Daniel Hood was accustomed to playing games with the filth.

Fletcher twisted a toe tag around his finger. "Heard you've got yourself a lodger down at the Island these days, Danny."

"What makes you think that, Mr Fletcher?"

"Just a whisper, Danny."

"Someone's pulling your leg, Mr Fletcher."

"Name of Bernie Goodman."

"Bernie Goodman? Never heard of him."

"And he's outstayed his welcome, Danny."

"I don't know where you get 'em from, Mr Fletcher."

Fletcher gave the drawer a shove with his foot and it slid back into the freezer. He waited a moment or two and then rolled Hood out again.

"About this lodger of yours, Danny."

Hood's teeth chattered when he spoke through clenched jaws. "I already told you, I don't know what you're talking about."

"You'll remember soon enough, Danny," Fletcher said, and he repeated the treatment, wheeling Hood in and out of the freezer, leaving him in the icebox just a little bit longer each time. The hard man's lips were turning blue, but his eyes remained expressionless.

"See, the way we reckon it, Danny, you've had your pound of flesh out of old Bernie. Now it's our turn. So how about it?"

"Get stuffed, copper," Hood replied flatly.

The interrogation followed the same pattern for a while longer with the drawer carrying Hood in and out of the freezer, and finally, when he could no longer feel his extremities, the hard man began to relent.

"This cock and bull story of yours, Mr Fletcher, just supposing it was true... I'd be daft to admit it without some safeguards, wouldn't I?"

"We're not interested in you, Danny," Fletcher reassured him. "You know our motto, always save something tasty for another day. You're not due yet."

"So what's in it for me?"

"Insurance, Danny."

"Come again?"

"You play ball with us and we won't tell Bernie's firm what a diabolical stroke you've been pulling with their main man. Because if we did..." Fletcher took the body tag off his finger and tied it to Hood's big toe "...we might have to make you a permanent reservation."

"Who put the bubble in?"

"Be your age, Danny."

Hood breathed a sigh. "All right, you've got me cold."

Mark Fletcher smiled down at him. "More like on ice," he said.

The crime squad hit the Desert Island mob-handed at four in the morning and lifted Bernie Goodman with the dew still on him. It was a textbook operation.

"You should've seen the poor bugger, guv," Fletcher told his DI when they returned to the station. "Squatting there in his underpants and blubbering like a baby. A few more days of that kind of treatment and I reckon he would've been a goner."

"You got a good snout on that one all right, Mark," the DI told him admiringly, "do you a bit of good too."

Fletcher shrugged. "Good intelligence," he replied, "could have happened to anyone."

"Pull the other one," the DI said, "the guv'nor's delighted with you, a real feather in your cap. You could be going places on the strength."

Basking in the glory of the moment, Mark Fletcher went back to his flat to freshen up. The phone was ringing.

"Quite the little hero, eh?" It was Helen's voice, sharp and brittle.

"Helen," Fletcher exclaimed. "I was going to call you...it worked like a charm...I'm just off to the Yard for a briefing so I've got to dash..."

"You bastard...you bastard, Mark!" Her cry cut through him like a knife. "You rotten lousy selfish bastard." Her voice started to break as pent-up emotions boiled over. "I had a call from St Thomas's A and E. They just brought Carol in, hit and run. She didn't stand a chance, dead on arrival."

Fletcher gripped the phone. "Helen," he said, "listen...I didn't..."

"You really take the prize, Mark." She was crying now. "You know that. You killed her as sure as if you'd done it yourself. You signed her death warrant, you bastard. You'd stiff your own mother for a pat on the head."

"Helen, listen to me..."

"And you know what? She was carrying a note in her pocket saying to call me in case of an accident. How's that for a laugh!"

"Hey, Helen, you don't think I had anything to do with that?" Fletcher protested desperately. "I never even mentioned her name, or yours either. I kept you both out of it, you've got to believe that. Helen...Helen..." But he was talking to the dialling tone.

Fletcher stared at the phone for a moment, his mind in turmoil. It must have been a coincidence, a quirk of fate. He thought of calling the traffic officers to get details of the accident that had killed Carol Dunne, contemplating going immediately to Helen and somehow convincing her that he hadn't broken his word. He looked at his watch. He was expected at the Yard. There just wasn't time.

So Mark Fletcher seized his chance with both hands and was whisked off to NSY to join the elite brotherhood of the legendary Flying Squad. It was the sort of once-in-a-lifetime opportunity that any ambitious detective would have happily cut off an arm for. Helen Ritchie was expendable.

Now, sitting in his makeshift study, reflecting upon a glass of whiskey with the benefit of hindsight, Mark Fletcher knew it had all been a charade and that his early promise had burned out like a shooting star. Had the guilt that gnawed within him for turning his back on Helen's tragic outburst eventually eaten him away? Was that the answer? At moments like this he would concede the possibility. At moments like this he would sacrifice his home life, career, everything, for the chance to roll back the years and somehow make Helen Ritchie understand that he'd had no hand in her friend's death.

His wife was calling from downstairs and it was time to cap the bottle and put aside such maudlin thoughts. He couldn't change the past. Never look back, that was the hard lesson of reality. In the morning he would call Dennis Jewel and tell him to forget it.

TURNING THE TABLES

Judith Cutler

WAS GRIFF DYING? What if it was only those flashing and blinking machines that were keeping him alive? I didn't dare count the number of wires and tubes that greeted me when I was summoned to his hospital bed.

Oh, Griff.

I kneeled beside the bed, and gently clasped the hand that wasn't bandaged, pressing it to my lips. Griff, my rock, my stay, my dearest friend – how dare you leave me like this? My tears dripped on to the mottled old flesh.

"I'm sure someone could find you a chair, Lina dearest, even in this benighted hole," he said querulously.

It wasn't just machines then – it was Griff's willpower that stopped him dying.

"I look a lot worse than I am, dear heart," he continued. "I always did bruise easily, you know. Now, if you keep crying, your eyes will be puffy and bloodshot and you won't look your best for this darling young registrar who's keeping watch over me. I thought he was my guardian angel at first. Then he bent over me and I found that he smokes. A doctor, too. I told him off, believe me."

"And what did he say to that?" I asked, diverted as he knew I would be.

"Told me to save my breath to cool my porridge. Dr Rankin. A fine young man, though his hair is more ginger than gold." The hand I was holding shook mine gently. "Your mascara's run, sweet one. Quickly – he wants to speak to you about me as my next of kin."

Next of kin? As far as I knew Griff had no living relatives, but he often introduced me as his granddaughter. We both wished I could be, but in legal fact I wasn't, since I was the natural daughter of some crazy Pot Noodle-eating lord. But I wasn't about to tell a medic that, was I?

"What about?" I asked, my throat closing again. They didn't want to harvest Griff's organs, did they? I wanted him back, alive and kicking, not switched off so that others might live.

"Oh, you know…" He waved vaguely and fell asleep. Or so he would have me believe. If I knew Griff, he'd be watching and listening for every nuance of my encounter with the smoking quack.

Tough.

Perhaps Dr Rankin was on to him and his eavesdropping ways, or perhaps it was medical etiquette that prevented doctors talking across the patient as if he were already dead. Whatever it was, I was summoned by a sweet-faced Filipina nurse to a little room decorated so tastefully it would have made Griff scream with rage.

It was empty. I had to wait another seventeen minutes before Dr Rankin arrived, seventeen minutes I could have spent with Griff. And the damned peach and magnolia room wasn't even big enough to pace.

Just when I'd got fed up waiting for one man, blow me if two didn't arrive, practically getting jammed in the door. Both in their late-twenties, both tallish and trim – as if they both worked out. The first – Dr Rankin, I presume – was wearing not a white coat and a serious suit but a set of hospital scrubs. The other wore a washable polyester suit as if it were a uniform, and had a short haircut and big feet. Medicine, the law – all it wanted was the hospital chaplain to make the set.

They looked like two men after the same parking space.

"Ms Townend," they began together. And stopped and glared. At each other. One fingered his stethoscope, the other waved his ID.

Despite not having had a drop for several days – Griff thought we should respect Lent and I was in favour of anything that cut back his drinking – I was decidedly tired and highly emotional.

At least the policeman should recognize a stop signal, so I held up my hand in his direction and pointed at the doctor. "You first. Before you say anything, I am not prepared to have Griff switched off." I turned to the cop. "You'll bear witness to that, won't you?"

He nodded.

"What's this about switching off Mr Tripp?" Rankin demanded.

"For his organs." To show I wasn't against the idea in principle, I flashed my donor card.

Rankin snorted. "Mr Tripp's? We want fresh not pickled ones, Ms Townend. And we do in general prefer to wait until the patient dies. And – despite his poor hobnailed old liver – that could be for many years yet. I wanted to talk to you about taking him home, that's all."

It took a doctor to do that? My eyes narrowed in disbelief.

"Not so much home, perhaps, as somewhere he can get a moderate degree of care, with medical back-up if need be."

"And won't bed-block the dear old NHS," I observed.

"Or," put in the policeman, "be so likely to catch MRSA."

I began to warm to him. "One of Griff's friends," I began – for *friend* read *long-term partner* – "might fund him a few days in a nursing home." A very upmarket one, if I knew Aidan and his bank balance.

"Just the ticket. Let the ward clerk have details and she can set it up." His bleeper went before he could frame any tender words, let alone say them, but I had the feeling that he was as little interested in me as I was in him; Griff's perennial matchmaking had been inspired by his desire to get me safely married off (oh, yes, properly, in a long white dress in church) before he shuffled off, as he always put it, this mortal coil. One day I'd get round to looking up the quotation, but not yet, just in case it brought bad luck.

So now it was PC Plod's turn – actually Detective Sergeant Will Barnes, according to his ID. "I understand Mr—"

"Griff. Do call him Griff. Everyone does. And in the circumstances, calling him Mr Tripp seems a bit too appropriate."

"Except that he didn't, Ms Townend. Trip, that is. He was pushed, very hard. And kicked, according to the medics. All after he'd been dragged from his van. And we'd like to know why." His tone was decidedly less friendly; I'd no idea why.

"Have you asked him?"

"He says he'd been to a house sale.'

I nodded. "Yes, at Forley Towers, that ugly Victorian pile. It belonged to some recluse, and now her executors are selling everything up."

"And you were—?"

"Not with him, obviously." Or his attacker might not have lived to tell the tale. "I've been at our shop all day, repairing some Regency china." The customer who'd asked me to restore the lovely Worcester chocolate cup wanted it done urgently, or I would never have let Griff go on his own. "What's this all about, Sergeant? You're not thinking that I might beat Griff up like that? Me? I'd die for him... if he'd let me, that is."

He shuffled his feet, but coughed pompously. "Our information is—"

"That I have a criminal record. Well, check out how long ago it was, and see how long I've been a decent hard-working member of society. I've been with Griff through thick and thin for six years now. He'd have adopted me if he could." He was a much better parent than my own father had ever been. "Why should I want to hurt the person I love most in the whole world?" My voice only went and cracked, didn't it? Now I sounded more tearful than outraged – but perhaps, in the circumstances, that's what I actually was. I grabbed a handful of tissues from a convenient little box someone had left on the arm of an easy chair for slightly different circumstances and scrubbed my eyes. For good measure I sat down heavily. And nearly disappeared in the squidgy upholstery.

Barnes fidgeted with embarrassment. "Has he any enemies? Do you know any reason why anyone else should attack him?"

"No enemies that I know of. You don't need enemies to be robbed of something precious, do you? Just an opportunist thief or two. Someone who wanted what Griff had bought. And if Griff isn't well enough to tell you, the auctioneers would know more about that than I do. All I had was this call saying Griff was here and I came

straight over." Though not without setting all the state-of-the-art
alarms and locks that Griff insisted on, I have to admit. Even as he
knocked on Heaven's Gate he'd have wanted our precious stock
protected – everything from Jacobean stumpwork to Victorian
filigree. "I'd like to go back to Griff now."

My attempts to get out of the chair made him drop his grim
professional glare. Smothering a laugh, he even went so far as to
help me lever myself out. He had nice firm hands, with a grip that
you could rely on. And he let go the instant he ought.

So I said, "If he's awake, I could ask what he bought. Otherwise,
as I said, you'll have to ask the auctioneer – only," I added, looking
at my watch for the first time since I'd arrived at the hospital, "it's a
bit late, isn't it?" It was. It was nearly eleven at night.

"Can I offer you a lift home?"

I shook my head. Nothing short of an earthquake would get me
more than ten yards from Griff's side. I'd sleep on the floor beside
his bed if necessary.

Griff looked much better the next morning, but was inclined to be
tetchy, hardly surprising since there was nowhere this side of his
hospital gown that wasn't purple or red. Goodness knew what else
his poor old body had suffered. I think he was relieved to hear that
on receiving my phone call Aidan had booked him in for a week's R
& R at an exclusive nursing home to which a private ambulance
would convey him.

"But it will be such a long way for you to come and see me, my
loved one," Griff observed wistfully. "And you know I don't like
you driving after dark."

"If it makes you happier, I shall take up Aidan's offer to stay
overnight with him as long as you're away from our cottage."
There! Griff would know the extent of my self-sacrifice, and possibly
of Aidan's – we'd never hit it off, maintaining an armed truce for
Griff's sake. "Now," I said briskly, to cover any emotion, "it'd help
the police if you told them what you'd bought at yesterday's sale. It
was obviously something that someone else couldn't keep their
hands off," I joked.

"They could have had it and welcome. You know Mrs Davenport was asking for a games table to replace the one she had stolen? Well, I found one – pretty cheap, as it happens. A Victorian affair, with goodness knows how many drawers and curves wherever nature wanted a straight line. Rather vulgar, if you ask me, but then so was Mrs Davenport's original. You might tell her I did my best, if she should happen to call. Lina, there'll be a picture of it in the catalogue, won't there? And I'm sure I left that in the glovebox."

"You hadn't been trying to carry the table on your own, had you?" I demanded, arms akimbo.

"What, when there were a couple of gorgeous well-muscled lads to put it straight into the van for me?" His poor swollen mouth headed for winsome, but didn't quite reach it.

"So when was it stolen?"

He went to scratch his head but evidently thought better of it. "I can't … yes, I remember! My mobile phone rang, and I pulled into a layby to answer it." He flashed an almost impish smile – how many times had I had to shout at him when he'd tried to use his mobile when he was driving? "Someone opened the driver's door – and Bob's your aunt."

"How did they know the number?" I asked, looking for a conspiracy.

"Because it's painted on the side of the van, of course! Oh, Lina – it's I, not you, who had the bang on the head."

The door opened to admit a young man pushing a wheelchair.

"Ah, my transport of delight!" Griff exclaimed, submitting to having a nurse check that the number on his wristband matched that on the young man's paperwork. Lest I feel a frisson of alarm, with wild fears of the attackers taking him where they could finish off what they had started, Aidan made a dramatic appearance, pressing me to somewhere fairly near his bosom and then hindering rather than helping the porter in his efforts to get Griff into the wheelchair. Aidan would go with him in the ambulance. I would follow in my car.

As soon as DS Barnes had finished with me, that is. He had just pulled his unmarked car up alongside mine, and was checking for the right change to feed to the meter. He pulled a face when I told him Griff was no longer at the hospital, but listened disbelievingly when I told him what had been stolen.

"Try and kill an old man just because he's bought a table you wanted?" he squeaked. "You're joking. Was it made of gold and lined with silver?"

"Wood inlaid with more wood, from what I can gather. There's a picture of it in the auction catalogue – and that, according to Griff, should be in the glovebox of the van."

"Which is currently in one of our car pounds. If you came with me, you could tell me all about it." His smile was agreeable, but I had this rule never to trust anyone till I'd had Griff's opinion of them. So I muttered something about not affording any more time in the car park – well, they charged as if lives depended on the parking fees – and told him I'd follow him, provided he would phone one of his police cronies to make sure Griff had arrived safely. He looked at me very hard. "You really are worried they'll have another go at the old guy, aren't you? OK, I'll get on to it."

The *Tripp and Townend, Antique Dealers* van sat rather sadly in the corner of the pound, as if it felt personally responsible for the trickles of blood on its paintwork. DS Barnes had already donned disposable gloves and was fossicking round inside, displaying a neat bum to the world. But he came up with nothing, and, seeing me the far side of the barrier, waved to his mate to let me in.

"Are you sure about the catalogue?"

"Griff was. But then, he's over seventy and has been beaten about the head, so he might have got it wrong. In any case, it hardly matters – the auctioneer must have loads left over."

"If I get hold of a copy and bring it over to your shop, can you tell me all about the table? Not until you've seen that Griff's all right and tight, of course. And he has arrived safely – well, he would, with a couple of our lads riding shotgun, as it were."

"You set up motorcycle outriders?" Forgetting my manners, I reached up and gave him a smacking thank-you kiss – but only on the cheek.

* * *

Much as I would have liked to spend the day holding Griff's hand, he pointed out that we had a business to run. As luck would have it, it was a very quiet day, and I could have stayed. However, since I had time on my hands, I could spend a lot of it texting or emailing fellow-dealers, asking if they had ever had similar experiences to Griff's. Of course, the police were probably checking through their records for exactly the same information, but I had an idea that some of our colleagues would only have called in the fuzz if they'd had the Crown Jewels stolen.

I never spent much time at school, and Griff's best efforts to help me write what he called a lady-like script had failed. But he had taught me keyboard skills, so I could run off a list for DS Barnes. Neat columns: *items stolen; when; where; value; from whom* (I nearly typed *who from* but that would have made Griff grind his teeth); *police action.* As I'd suspected, only about half of the twenty or so robberies had been reported to the police, and none of the objects had ever been recovered. Nor had they shown up elsewhere in the UK, at auctions or at antiques fairs.

Just as I was locking up for the day, Barnes appeared, looking, in a much more expensive suit, rather sleeker than he had yesterday. His expression of concern told me that I didn't. Well, the floor beside Griff had proved harder than I'd expected so I'd not slept a lot.

"What I thought was," he began, "is that I could run you over to see Griff, we could all have a chat, then I could run you back here and we... Well, maybe we should have a bite to eat somewhere."

I didn't directly reply but said, "If Griff sees me looking like this he'll have an instant relapse. Can you give me five minutes to change?"

"An hour if you like. So long as you leave me in here to look round... it's like a museum, isn't it? An Aladdin's cave?"

But he still hadn't had Griff's approval so I said, truthfully, "It'll be freezing in here in five minutes. Come into the house – there's some nice stuff in there, too."

And I didn't let him see what burglar-alarm code I tapped in either.

What we kept in the house was stuff we couldn't sell in the shop because it was slightly damaged or the provenance was dubious or else was so lovely neither of us had the heart to sell it. So while I was taking a risk, it was smaller than leaving him with all the highly collectable items in the shop. In any case, I hadn't told him about the CCTV that operated even inside the house if we wanted it to, so I could watch him while I was putting on a better top and applying what Griff, after years in the theatre, always called slap. It took longer than five minutes, but no more than eight, and I even had time to brush my hair. Will had done no more than gaze with what looked like open-mouthed wonder at a couple of small Impressionist oil paintings – standing back, getting close to, but never touching. Which was fortunate, since they were wired into a very loud alarm system indeed.

It only took forty minutes or so to reach the nursing home, which looked and smelled far more like a posh hotel than the repository for incontinent old codgers Griff had always feared ending his days in. He had a single, en suite room, with a TV and couple of easy chairs, in addition to the upright one on which he was enthroned and a bed that did its best to disguise its high-tech lifting and tilting mechanisms. The décor was almost as bland as that in the bad-news room at the other hospital, but the standard of the reproductions on the wall was much higher.

Aidan was sitting beside him reading aloud, something his consciously mellifluous voice was well suited to. He stopped, inserting a bookmark and closing the volume with just enough of a snap to show he was not used to being interrupted in mid-paragraph. My smile and his were as bland as the wallpaper, something I suspected Will noticed.

He shook hands first with Aidan and then very gently with Griff. "The bruises are coming out, I see."

"Why not? *I* did years ago," Griff said with a beam. Then he touched his cheek. "I've not seen my face yet – they sent a minion to shave me and throw in a haircut as a bonus."

The expression on Aidan's face told me he expected to see the freebie added to his bill. But he had the decency to make himself scarce so that both Will and I could sit down. Will produced the auctioneer's catalogue.

"My reading glasses hurt my nose," Griff complained. "That's why dear Aidan was reading aloud."

"What a good job I remembered these," I said, burrowing in my bag. "Here, try these lorgnettes. They came with that job lot of spectacle cases, remember? They may not be quite your prescription but they have a certain something, don't you think?" I waved the pretty turquoise-and-white-enamelled Victorian hand-held specs before me, pressing a little button so that the lenses popped out.

"My sweet girl, what a gem you are!" Griff took them and peered this way and that. "You see, you adjust the focal length by moving them closer to or further away from your eyes. How clever. And how very pretty. Dear child. Now I can see whatever it is you wish to show me, young man," he added, taking the catalogue and opening it. "Ah – there's the wretched games table. What on earth could there be about such a monstrosity that someone should go to such lengths to get hold of it? Why, a quiet word to me beforehand and the promise of a drink afterwards and I wouldn't have bid so high. Or indeed at all. Mrs Thingy could have waited for another – as indeed she will have to now."

"And why indeed should they have stolen twenty or so others in the last twelve months?" Will asked. "At least, that's what Lina's research shows."

Griff shot me a keen glance. "Do our friends know that the police might see this list?"

Will coughed. "Just at the moment we're interested in the thieves, not their victims, Mr – Griff. And I gave Lina my word that I would only interview people who had already reported the thefts to their local police."

"Very well. I hope you will keep it."

"Of course." He sounded sincere enough. He patted the catalogue photo. "Now, if these are gaming tables, am I right in thinking that they would have been in casinos or clubs?"

"*Games* tables. Probably in private homes – no TV in those days so you made your own entertainment," Griff explained.

Will jotted. "Okay. Now, to me this just looks like an ordinary table with a chessboard inlaid on the top. Am I missing something?"

"Sometimes the chessboard part swivels round to reveal a backgammon well. Or some have side drawers for pieces and counters. I dare say some even have secret drawers, so that someone who knows where they are can cheat. None are terribly valuable, not unless they're made by a famous manufacturer." Griff didn't volunteer how much he had paid, still less how much he would have asked Mrs Davenport to pay.

"Yet someone wants shedloads of the dratted things. And hides them away."

"Or, more likely, young man," Griff said, closing the lorgnette and waving it to emphasize the point, "has had them out of the country within the hour. Look at the places they were stolen... Ipswich; Plymouth; Southampton; loads round here in Kent."

"But why on earth should they want them abroad?"

"It seems to me," I said, as Will and I walked back to the car park, "that the only way of finding out why these tables are going abroad is to buy one and follow it."

"Follow?" He frowned. "I suppose we could always hide a tracking device in it. So how could we make sure that there'd be a games table on the market soon?" He let me into his car before going round to the driver's side, just as if Griff were watching to make sure he had good manners.

"Easy," I said. "So long as you don't want a kosher one."

"Do I want to know what you mean by that?" It was hard to tell in the darkness whether he was serious or not.

"No names, no pack drill. I know a couple of dealers who would put together – using authentic bits and pieces – a games table that would convince most punters. And so long as it was me – it was I – who bought it, knowing it was a fake, that wouldn't be a problem, would it? In fact," I added, "wouldn't it be all the better for being dodgy? It would mean that whoever bought it just wanted any old rubbish, not a really good one."

"I'm not sure I follow your logic." he grinned. "But I don't think you'd be involved. It'd be one of our officers."

"In the antiques world everyone knows everyone else. You put a police officer in there and whoever wants the table would be on to him in thirty seconds."

"Or her," he corrected me. "Someone who looked like you. You could do the bidding and then the officer could take your place in the van. There's a whole department at Scotland Yard devoted to fine art theft – I'm sure they'll want to be involved."

I wrinkled my nose. "Games tables aren't exactly fine art. And I have this feeling that it's not the art value the thieves are interested in." Griff always insisted that I had a bit of the divvy about me, in other words an instinct for what was real and what was fake.

"What do you mean?"

"I don't know… But maybe we'll find out."

Smudger Smith operated at the shady end of antiques dealing. If asked, he might say he was into recycling before it even got fashionable. What he did was take a nice table top, say, the legs of which had been ruined by something like a fire or woodworm. Then he'd find a set of legs of the same wood, but not necessarily even from a table, and marry them up. He might even make his own table legs, and artificially age them, or make them from old wood from yet another item.

We met in a pub in a town some way from both our bases, and cash was exchanged in the used fivers and tenners he demanded, all courtesy of the police. What they'd say when I couldn't provide a receipt I'd no idea – but ask Smudger to put anything on paper and he'd have disappeared before you could blink.

"How soon d'you want it?"

"The next furniture sale in Canterbury." I was dead sure that if I'd asked him how he was going to fix it he'd have been outraged. "Plenty of little drawers and a couple of cupboards, if you can manage it," I added. "'You know the sort of thing." My hands conjured the sort of mini-turrets and curlicues and cabriole legs that Griff particularly loathed.

But that was all right because I made sure Griff knew nothing about it.

A week later Will popped into the shop with some news. "We've had a couple of writing bureaux reported as missing," he said. "Could there be any connection?"

"What period?"

"One's seventeenth-century Italian."

"Wow, you're talking serious money there. Collectors would have your hand off." I tugged an idea from my brain. "It would have one thing in common with those tables – it would almost certainly have secret drawers. Very secret. Will, has anything else gone missing over the last few weeks? So valuable your specialized squad would be on to it?"

He jotted in his notebook. "I could find out. Any news of your table?"

"It'll be ready for next week's sale." I handed him the money I hadn't had to spend, thanks to my haggling skills. "Sorry – my contact doesn't do receipts."

"So you could have kept the whole lot and I'd have been none the wiser."

"*I* would," I said shortly. When I was younger I'd have taken the lot and lied myself blue in the face. But not after six years with Griff. I changed the subject. The problem would be keeping Griff away from the auction now he was back on his feet. I might have to talk to Aidan.

"You don't think Will's a bit too good to be true?" I asked Griff, when Aidan, always the perfect host, had gone to bring fresh toast.

Griff was staying with him for an extra week's convalescence when he'd been signed off by the private hospital. Then Aidan – prompted by me – thought they might go for a nice cruise somewhere exotic. Half of me was delighted: a break was just what Griff needed. The other half was desolate. But at least it meant he wouldn't be at the sale.

"You're not losing your heart to him, are you, sweet one?"

I licked my index finger and collected a few crumbs from the pristine cloth. "It'd be very easy to." Eventually I looked him in the eye. "You wouldn't recommend it?"

But Aidan was returning.

"Just make haste slowly," Griff whispered.

Having bought Smudger's games table – he'd actually done such a good job I would have had to look twice to see it was a wrong 'un – all I had to do was deliver it to a smallish, brownish man at another remote location. Having shown him the hidden drawer, a cunning device that made him suck in his breath quite sharply, I gave it a farewell pat, and tried to think no more about it. After all, I had a few questions of my own to ask. Smudger wasn't the only one with skills he didn't talk about. There were people out there who could copy the Kohinoor Diamond, others who could knock up a Leonardo cartoon the man himself would have been proud of. I didn't dare approach them directly, of course, because I wasn't supposed to know of their existence. But I did discover that a guy known as Provo, since he could even provide a convincing provenance for his fakes, had been especially busy recently, though no one knew why anyone should want a whole load of Nicholas Hilliard miniatures. There was another rumour that there was a glut of games tables up in the north, something I could with a clear conscience tell Will, who made another note and sucked his pencil.

Being trussed up in the back of the van wasn't supposed to be part of the deal, was it? Not that I'd be trussed up very long. There's a trick to bracing your wrists when you're tied up – I told you I didn't go to school much, but I learned a lot of things not on the national curriculum. While I worked on the rope, I seethed with anger. The police were supposed to have replaced me as I left the auction rooms with a lookalike, because though I may now be law-abiding, I didn't see that my getting beaten up like Griff needed to be part of the deal. But the cop they sent was a woman who'd played rugby for England, all five foot eleven of her and goodness knows how many stone. Twice what I carry, that's for sure. Will and a couple of other plainclothes officers had been hard put not to laugh. So I'd been the tethered goat, after all. I'd seen the table loaded into the back of the van, driven off, and someone had called on our business mobile – the one with its number painted on the side of the van.

Everything had gone more or less according to plan. Possibly less, actually.

The difference was that when I'd pulled over to a layby to take the call and been rushed by a gang of heavies, they hadn't duffed me up and left me for dead, taking just the table. They'd picked me up and shoved me in the back of their van.

The only light came round the edge of a badly fitting door.

I'd no idea where they were taking me. I couldn't very well ask them because they'd taped my mouth when they'd tied up my hands. And for good measure one of them had stamped on my mobile phone.

So what would they do with me? They didn't want me, just the table. What if they decide to dispose of me? I had a sudden vision of disappearing from the face of the earth, never being found for Griff to grieve over and bury. But I couldn't indulge in tears, self-pitying or otherwise, because something was happening.

The van slowed, went over a cattle grid, drove up a gravelled drive, and stopped. Feet walked round to the back doors. I lay as if I were still unconscious. There was a scrape and a curse as the table was removed. I was locked in again.

While I knew in my head that Will and his colleagues must know exactly where I was, my heart told me I wanted to be free as soon as possible.

Should I get my hands free now?

No. Already footsteps were approaching the van, heavily, as if they were carrying the table, so I went back to inert mode. I didn't even protest when one of them kicked me to make sure I was still out cold. I just flopped back into the position they'd found me.

But the moment the van started – down that drive and over the grid again – my hands were free. Then my feet. I didn't bother with my mouth. There wasn't any time for that. It was time to check out that table.

I had to hand it to Smudger; if I hadn't known exactly how to unlock that hidden section, I'd never have managed it. But I did. And found the little device, not much larger than a flattened pea, was sharing the space with another small object, small as the palm of my hand, wrapped in chamois leather. It fitted in my bra, not comfortably but at least unobtrusively. The chamois bag went back where I'd found it, a handkerchief inside folded to roughly the right size and shape. It wouldn't fool anyone taking more than a casual glance, but perhaps that was all they would give it.

Then – miracle of miracles – I realized that you could open the doors from the inside. I could leap out the moment the van stopped. Or I could if it wasn't locked from the outside.

At last we drew to a halt and I decided it was time to make a run for it. I ran at the doors, pulling on the handles and pushing outwards as hard as I could. Free!

Someone was trying to grab me. Fist-fighting was something I knew all about, and I winded one of them and kicked another so hard he might not need family planning for a week or so. It was only as the red mist in my head cleared that I realized that I'd only gone and assaulted a couple of police officers – and was now pinioned very firmly myself. It was the somewhat breathless arrival of Will that saved me the inconvenience of being arrested.

"Ostensibly they were only exporting furniture, you see," I explained to Griff on the phone that night, pleased to have used a word he'd spent a long time explaining to me. "No one was interested in the odd bit of Victorian mahogany or burr walnut. And even if Customs had gone poking around, they wouldn't have found the secret compartment. So the thieves could transport all sorts of small items that would never have got export licences. Some jewellery, but mostly miniatures. I've never had a Hilliard in my hands before, Griff. You should see the colours!" I didn't embarrass him by telling him where else the tiny painting had been.

"Are you sure you're all right, dear heart?"

"I'm absolutely fine."

"Which means you're not."

"It means this time I am. I might even be in line for a reward. Because not only were the gang using the tables they stole to get priceless stuff out of the country, replacing them with copies, they then used the tables to bring in the drugs that are sloshing around Glasgow and Newcastle at the moment."

"Well, I'm blowed. So how are you going to celebrate?"

"I shall have a very good haircut. When they taped my mouth they got some of my hair stuck too and I look a bit patchy. Griff, you're breaking up," I lied. "I love you!"

And then it was an early night for me and the teddy bear Griff had given me. Will had invited me to dinner, but I never did like threesomes. And in my heart I still resented his wife for being so much larger and taller than me that I'd had a very nasty few hours.

Still, I told myself as I applied cream to my sore face, it's not every girl who can say that she's clasped Robert Devereux, Earl of Essex, to her bosom, and lived to tell the tale.

HANDY MAN

John Harvey

IT WAS HIS hands I noticed first. Really took in. Broad, dependable hands. A ring on the wedding finger, dull gold. And the nails, surprisingly even, rounded, no snags, not bitten down; no calluses on the fingers, such as you might expect from a working man, a man who worked with his hands. Only the suggestion of hard skin around the base of the thumb, hard yet smooth.

Harry.

A simple name. Straightforward, simple.

The things I knew about him later: time he'd spent in the army, Northern Ireland, Iraq. Things he would never really talk about, just hints, nightmares, dreams. His anger. Not so simple really. Harry.

Nine years I'd been living in the house then, the first time I set eyes on him. Nine years since the divorce and then all that business with Victor, and I suppose it's true to say for the last two or three years I'd let things go. Easy enough to do when you're living on your own. The cupboard door that won't open without a tug, and once the handle's snapped off, won't open at all; the window that's permanently stuck; the shower that leaks; the wardrobe rail that keeps collapsing under the weight of all too few clothes.

I must have mentioned something to Marie over lunch, just as a way of making conversation, how things seemed to be falling apart. The second Tuesday of each month, that's when we meet. Years now. The Yacht Club, where she's a member, or the Blue Bell down by the river. Every month, save for November when she and Gerald go off to their timeshare in Florida, and, recently, June, which these days they tend to spend with their daughter and her family somewhere near

Lake Garda. Otherwise, it's a nice white wine, not too dry, chicken escalopes, pumpkin risotto or Dover sole, and then rather too much about Gerald's progress, greasing his way up the slippery pole of investment banking. Although, to be fair, she's been quieter on that front of late. What we've had are the grandchildren instead. First words, first steps, potty-training disasters that are meant to elicit laughter, photos of chubby faces, each, to me, indistinguishable from the other. Isn't he gorgeous? Isn't she lovely?

I do my best, I really do. Make an effort to show some interest, manifest concern. Marie is my best friend, after all. Just about the only one I still have since all the hoo-hah of the divorce, the dirt that Squeegeed out on to the front page of the local paper. What kind of a woman is it who argues for financial parity over the custody of the children? A woman who was clearly no better than she should be, that's what. A husband's long-term adultery with his secretary more acceptable than a wife's dalliances with a PR client on a jolly to Cap d'Antibes. All of that before Victor had slithered on to the scene.

And so because she's stuck with me all this time, I do try, between the crème brûlée and the coffee, to share Marie's delight in her burgeoning family. But children, other people's children, I've always found it hard to warm to, and where grandchildren are concerned, well, I'm just not ready. I mean, I am, of course. Chronologically, biologically – but mentally …

It's one of the great advantages of marrying early, Marie says, not like so many women today: you have your grandchildren when you're young enough to enjoy them. Maybe. But there are other things I feel young enough to enjoy and they don't include a return to nappy changing or singing "Baa-Baa Black Sheep" for the umpteenth time.

Which led, I suppose, to Victor, a black sheep if ever there was one, though a wolf in sheep's clothing.

And then to Harry. Poor Harry.

"What you need," Marie told me solemnly, after yet another report of some small domestic malfunction, "is a handy man." Straight-faced, not a trace of innuendo. "Here, look …" And from her bag she took a business card, not new, turned down a little at the corners.

CARPENTER/HANDY MAN

Shelves, doors, locks, windows, floors

Good work, friendly service

Estimates free

References available

Harry Campbell

"We've used him once or twice," Marie said, "just for little things. Not too expensive, I'll say that for him. Turns up when he says he will, too. Not like some. And quiet. All I could do to drag a word out of him." She smiled. "Tea with milk, no sugar. You could do worse."

I started fishing around for something to write down the phone number, make a note of the email, but Marie said to keep the card, so I slipped it into my bag and that's where it lay for quite a while. Until one afternoon when I pulled hard at the cutlery drawer and the whole front came away in my hand.

All I got at first was an automated message on his answer phone; then when he called back that evening I was just on to my second glass of wine and settling down to watch Kenneth Branagh in something Swedish and bracing.

"Mrs Francis? It's Harry Campbell. I'm not disturbing you? It's not too late to call?"

His voice was a trifle slow, but sure; traces of an accent I found hard to place.

"No. No, Harry, it's not too late."

Harry. First-name terms from the start. For me, at least. He would continue to call me Mrs Francis for quite some little time.

Eight o'clock, he'd said, and there he was on the doorstep, true to his word. Brown cord jacket and denim shirt, grey-green trousers – chinos, I suppose they were; canvas tool bag slung over his shoulder, grey van parked on the street behind. Broad-shouldered, tall. Imposing, is that the word?

"I'm not too early?"

"No, no. Not at all."

I hadn't quite finished dressing when he rang the bell; the wretched zip on my skirt had stuck, not for the first time, and I'd scarcely had time to run a brush through my hair. Standing there, I fastened another button on my blouse before stepping back to let him in.

"You'd like a cup of tea, I dare say?"

He'd set his bag down in the middle of the kitchen floor.

"No, I'm all right for now, thanks. Maybe in a while."

I hadn't been meaning to stare.

"Something about a busted drawer?" he said. "A few other things that needed sorting?"

I showed him what required attention and left him to it for the best part of an hour. Made the bed, fixed my face, watered the plants and riffled through the pages of a magazine. A voice I didn't recognize burbled away between songs on Radio 2. The *Telegraph* still lay, folded and unopened, on the table in the hall.

"How about that cup of tea?" I said.

He was stretched out on the floor, ratcheting something underneath the sink.

Slowly, his head eased back into sight. "Thanks. Just a drop of milk and ..."

"... and no sugar."

"That's right." When he smiled, the skin crinkled around his eyes.

"I would offer you a biscuit, but ..."

"It's okay." He patted the flat of his stomach. "Got to watch the weight."

The cup seemed so small in his hand I thought it must break.

"I suppose you're kept busy," I said aimlessly, unable to sit there saying nothing.

"Busy enough."

His eyes were pale blue; his hair, quite wiry, was starting a little prematurely to go grey. I supposed it was prematurely. He was what? Late-thirties, forty, little more. Not so great a gap. His other hand, on the breakfast bar, rested innocently close to mine.

"These units," he said, glancing round, "I'll do what I can, but it's a bit like, you know, shifting the deckchairs on the *Titanic*."

"You mean we're going to drown?"

"In a manner of speaking."

Kate Winslet, I thought. Leonardo DiCaprio. Little more than a boy.

"You could get them replaced. IKEA. B&Q. Needn't be expensive, if you don't want."

"I don't know. This place, I'm not sure how much longer I'm going to stay."

"Well, just a thought." He set down his cup and was quickly to his feet. "Thanks for the tea."

"You've not finished already?"

"Good as. I'll sweep up those shavings if you've a dustpan and brush."

"Only I was wondering …"

He looked at me then, waiting.

"The shower, upstairs, it's been leaking. Quite badly now."

"Seal's gone, I dare say, needs replacing. I'll take a quick look, but I've not got the right stuff with me now." He glanced at his watch. "I could probably drop back later."

"Yes, all right. Do. I mean, if that's okay with you?"

It was raining hard when he returned. A darkening across the shoulders of his jacket and, as he came into the hall, careful to wipe his feet, a few drops fell on to his face from where they'd caught in his hair and I wanted to wipe them away.

Desperate Housewives, I thought. I was in danger of becoming a cliché.

The next time he came, a week or so later, I was careful to make myself scarce, dropping a set of keys into his hand the minute he arrived and asking him to pop them back through the letterbox when he was through.

"Off to work, then?"

"Something like that."

The one good thing that came from my distant divorce, as long as I avoided undue extravagance and was careful to tread within my means, there was no more need for nine to five, not regularly at least. The occasional bit of market research, filling in from time to time at the agency where I used to be employed, and that was enough.

So instead I loitered over a latte and Danish at the local coffee franchise; gave over some time to a manicure and polish change; finally took a stroll down by the river, just as far as where they're starting to fill in one of the old gravel pits, turn it into a country park.

As I neared home I tried to ignore the soft flutterings in my stomach, the lingering hope that he would still be there. In his stead, he had left some catalogues showing various styles of kitchen cabinet, appropriate pages turned down.

I stowed them in the bottom of a drawer. Pushed Harry to the back of my mind. Even flirted momentarily, crazily, with the idea of getting back in touch with Victor. One stupid, desperate day I even got as far as the door of the club – part bar, part casino – where he used to spend much of his time.

"Victor? No, he's still away, I think. Out of the country. But if you want to leave a name?"

I shook my head and turned away, legs unsteady as I walked back to my car. Nothing – no promise of pleasure, however strong, however intense – could make me want to go through all of that again. Better by far to stay home with a good book, something comforting on the TV, Valium and a large G & T. The fleeting fantasy of a working man's hands.

Just a few mornings later, as I left the house, my breath caught in my throat; across the street, at the wheel of an almost brand new Merc, window wound down, cuff of his white shirt turned back just so, sat Victor. Victor Sedalis. Smiling.

I should have walked away as if he weren't there; gone back inside and locked the door. Instead I continued to stand there like a fool.

"I hear you've been looking for me," he said.

"No."

"A couple of days ago. Wanting to welcome me back home."

"I don't think so."

An eyebrow rose in that sceptical, amused expression I knew so well. "All right," he said, "but you will." He slid the car into gear. "Either that or I'll come looking for you."

I had to lean back against the door and grip my arms hard to stop myself from shaking. Right from the first, there had been something about him that had made me squirm, made me crawl; something that had made it impossible for me to say no. The loans asked for so casually and never returned; the three in the morning phone calls after the club was closed, when he would come to me with cigarette smoke in his hair, brandy on his breath and another woman's perfume on his skin, and still I could never turn him away.

But then, without warning, he disappeared. Minorca, some said, Porta Ventura. Cyprus. Spain. Money he owed, gambling debts that had been gambled again and lost – something shady, dangerous, underhand. Of course, he had gone off before, weeks, months sometimes. But this seemed more definite, complete.

I floundered, came close to falling apart. It took an overdose and months of psychotherapy, but with help, I put myself back together, bit by bit.

It wasn't going to happen again.

I called Harry and left a message on his machine: one or two things, I said, in need of your attention. The wardrobe, the chest of drawers.

When he arrived, I was busy in the kitchen; a wave and a few quick words and, tool bag over his shoulder, he was on his way up to the bedroom. When I followed, some little time later, my feet were quiet on the stairs.

He was standing at the open wardrobe, running his hand along the silk of a black slip dress I'd bought from Ghost, eyes closed.

I touched my fingers to his back and that was all it took.

There was a scar, embossed like a lightning flash, across his chest; another, puckered like a closing rose, high on his thigh.

"Harry?"

Sweaty, the surprise still lingering in his eyes, he touched my breast with the tip of each of his fingers, the ball of his thumb.

After he'd gone, I bathed, changed the linen on the bed, saw to my face and hair and wondered how I would spend the rest of the day till, as promised, he returned. A little light shopping, lunch, perhaps an afternoon movie, a quiet stroll.

He was there at the door at eight o'clock sharp, freshly shaved, a clean shirt. Before kissing me he hesitated, as if I might have changed my mind, filed it away under Big Mistake. And when I kissed him back I could feel something shift within him, a deliverance from some small fear or doubt.

We made love and then we talked – I talked, in the main, and he listened. Marie had been right. Though as this night gradually became a second and a third and he felt more at ease, at home, he let slip bits and pieces of his life. How his wife had told him she was leaving him in an email because she was too scared to tell him face to face. That had been when he was on his second tour of Northern Ireland, in Belfast. She was living in Guildford now, remarried; he saw the two boys quite often, though less often than he'd have liked. The eldest was away at university in Stirling, studying animal biology, the youngest was hoping to take up the law. Bright kids, he said, take after their mother. If either of them had gone into the army, she'd threatened to slit her wrists.

We started to fall into a routine: Fridays and Saturdays he would spend the evening, stay the night. If ever he came round mid-week, he would go home and sleep in his own bed so as to make an early start. The ring from his finger had disappeared to be replaced by a pale band of skin.

When finally I told him about Victor, the way he had made me feel, powerless, used, as if I had no will, no skin, there was something in his face I hadn't seen before. Something that made his body tense and his hands tighten into fists.

"People like that," he said, "they don't deserve to live."

Victor sent me texts, left messages on my phone, to none of which I replied. He didn't like to be ignored. When finally he came round, it was not much after one in the morning, early for him. Possibly he'd been watching the house to see if Harry were there, I don't know. I opened the door partway and held it fast.

"What's the matter?" I said. "Lost your way?"

"I wanted to see you."

"All right, you have. Now you can go."

He was wearing a new suit, expensive, six or seven hundred at least; his face still tanned from his time abroad, eyes small and dark and rarely still. The same old smile slipped into place with practised ease.

"It's been a long time," he said.

"I hadn't noticed."

"Liar." His tongue showed for an instant, lizard-like, between thin lips.

"Goodnight, Victor."

I leaned against the door to push it closed and he pushed back. Whether he meant it to or not, the edge of it caught me hard in the face, just alongside the eye, and I stumbled to my knees.

"Careful," Victor said, shutting the door behind him. "You could get hurt."

He touched his finger to the well of blood and drew it down, slowly, across my cheek.

When he left, an hour later, all I could do was curl myself into a ball, cover my head and wish for sleep.

That was how Harry found me next morning, a surprise call on his way to work.

"This was Victor? He did this?"

Gingerly, I touched the side of my face. "It was an accident... sort of an accident. I don't think it was meant."

"Then how ...?"

"Last night, he was here. I was trying to stop him from coming in."

"He forced his way into the house, that's what you're saying?"

"Yes, I suppose so."

"Suppose?"

"Well, yes, then. Yes."

"And forced himself upon you?"

I turned my head away.

"He raped you."

"No."

"Then what else would you call it?"

I had begun to shake.

"I'll kill him, so help me, I will."

"Harry, don't, please. Don't say that."

"Just tell me where I can find him."

"Harry, no."

"You want this to happen again? Keep happening?"

"No, of course not."

"Then tell me. And I'll put a stop to it once and for all."

I didn't tell him, not then. Not right away. The last thing I wanted was for him to go off angry and emotional, acting impulsively, without properly thinking it through. That he could kill a man, I had little doubt; he had killed men before, after all; men he didn't know, men at close range, men he couldn't – didn't – see. It was what he'd been trained to do. He could kill a man, I was sure, with his bare hands. Those hands.

"The Concord," I said. "You know, that place out towards the estuary. That's where he spends a lot of time. Victor. If you still did want to see him. Talk to him. He'd listen to you."

It was the next evening, the two of us propped up on pillows after making love; Harry's head resting on my shoulder, my fingers combing through his hair.

"What if he doesn't?" Harry said.

"Hmm?"

"What if he doesn't listen?"

I reached down and kissed the palm of his hand. "Maybe the club's not the best place to talk. Somewhere quieter might be better. Where he's less likely to make a fuss. The park, perhaps. Up river. Where they're filling in the old gravel pit. Somewhere like that."

"He'd never come."

"He might if he thought I was going to be there."

I didn't say anything more about it; neither did he. Several more days passed. A week. Then ...

"I'm meeting him this evening. Later. Where you said."

"You're sure?"

His arms slid around me and I pressed my face against his chest.

"Don't trust him," I said. "Don't turn your back."

I didn't see him again that night, nor for several nights after. I texted him to make sure he was all right and he was. Just busy. See you soon as I can.

When he did come round there was some bruising I noticed, now fading, to the back of his hand; his knuckles were grazed. An accident, I thought, while working, a chisel that had slipped, a length of timber that had leaped back at his face.

"You saw him?"

"Yes, I saw him."

He didn't tell me what had happened, what had been said. The only time I asked, weeks later, he said, "You just don't want to know."

Victor Sedalis had disappeared again, into thin air. Nobody asked questions, bothered to report him missing. After all, he'd done it before. Cyprus, this time, that was the story. Limassol, somewhere. Gambling debts he couldn't pay, the interest rising, compounding day by day.

"I shouldn't be surprised," said the barman at the Concord, "if this time he's gone for good."

I continued to see a little of Harry, but after that it was never quite the same. The last I heard, he'd upped sticks and started a little boatbuilding business down near Southampton. One of his sons lives near there while he's studying for his doctorate. Biotechnology? Something like that?

At first there was the odd postcard or two, but Harry's not much of a one for writing and, I suppose, neither am I.

I did think about moving myself, got as far as putting the house on the market, but in the end I stayed. Too late to dig myself up, perhaps, too much effort, transplanting myself, at this stage of my life. And, besides, I like it here. Where I know. It suits me. My little lunches with Marie. The tennis club. I can just about hold my end up at doubles, much to my surprise. And on a sunny day like today, I'll sometimes take a stroll down along the river to the country park.

A few dog walkers, kids kicking a ball; quite often, weekdays, I've got the place to myself. Not that I mind. I feel safe there, secure. The ground, fresh and firm beneath my feet.

My thanks to Amy Rigby and Bill Demain, whose song, 'Keep It To Yourself', as sung by Amy, provided the initial idea for this story.

http://amyrigby.com/

THE INVISIBLE GUNMAN

Keith McCarthy

IT WAS 7.50 on a warm May evening in 1976 and Max and I were running late. Dad had invited us for a meal at 7.30 and he did not normally like to be kept waiting. The reasons we were late were many and varied; firstly, I had been kept at the surgery by the mother of a small boy who had stuck a wodge of masticated chewing gum up his nose that would not come back down (when I inserted a pair of forceps so far up there, I fully expected to see his eyes being pulled back into his sockets), and Max – a vet by trade – had been overrun by an outbreak of diarrhoea and vomiting in a local kennels; then the car had refused to start for ten minutes because I managed to flood the engine.

Dad had told us to come round the back because he was planning a barbecue. I had feigned enthusiasm for this idea but had suggested that he should avoid doing pork or chicken. I thought I'd done this tactfully but clearly not for he had asked at once and rather sharply, "Why not?"

I groped for the correct form of words. "Because chicken and pork don't barbecue particularly well." Actually, on Dad's barbecue, no meats did particularly well, but at least you were relatively safe with lamb or beef that had fourth-degree burns on the surface yet still, miraculously, a beating heart within. Similar cooking conditions when applied to chicken or pork were apt to lead to terminal food poisoning.

"I've never found that," he pointed out.

"How about sticking to beefburgers?"

"Horrible, pre-digested pap. Wouldn't feed them to my dog."

I tried the last gambit in my arsenal. "I know that Max likes lamb…"

A pause. "Does she?"

"Loves it."

"Oh, well…I'll see what I can do, then." In the eyes of Lance Elliot Senior, retired general practitioner, Max Christy could do no wrong. Accordingly, I was hoping for an evening meal that, if not destined for gastronomic legend, would not at least see Max and me spending the next forty-eight hours threatening to overwhelm the sewers of Thornton Heath.

I hurriedly opened the wooden door by the side of the garage that led down a narrow pathway to the back garden. I would judge that I had the door open about six inches when it happened. There was a heavy thud, and simultaneously the door was pushed violently back into a closed position while I found my right eye about two inches from the metal-tipped point of an arrow that protruded through a small explosion of splinters from the door. I jumped back, colliding with Max who squealed then fell over.

I said, "Bloody hell!" while Max said, "Ow!"

As I turned around to help her back up, the garden door opened and the heavily beard-encrusted face of my father looked out. "What's all the fuss?"

It took a moment to straighten Max out, who also had a few questions to ask me – like why I had decided to assault her – so it was not immediately that I turned to my aged parent. In this interlude he had pulled the arrow out of the door and was examining it. "What in the name of all that's good and holy are you doing?" I demanded.

I knew his expression well. It was a perfect blend of innocence and reproach, and it asked me where I had learned to speak to my elder and better in such a way, because it certainly hadn't been from him. "Practising."

"Practising? Practising what? Trying to kill me?"

"No, of course not. Practising archery."

There would once have been a time when this reply would have left me not only short of things to say but also short of breath to say

them with. But no longer; I knew him too well. My father collected
new hobbies like small boys collect pictures of first-division foot-
ballers, only he tired of them considerably more quickly. Over the
last year he had taken up campanology, astronomy, carpentry,
metalwork, juggling and karate; admittedly, the last he had been
forced to give up after two days when he broke his fifth metacarpal
trying to chop firewood with his bare hands, but all the rest had
arrived with a rush of enthusiasm, stayed for a few weeks, then
dwindled to indifference in the space of perhaps five days.

"You were aiming at the door to your garden," I pointed out.

"Of course I was," he said, his voice betraying doubt that I was
using my brain about the matter. "That's where I pinned the target."
He gestured behind us and we turned to see a large paper archery
target peppered with holes – none in the bull – on the inside of the
garden gate. "The pathway down the side of the garage makes a
nice shooting gallery."

"But you knew we were coming in that way."

He frowned. "So? Oh, don't worry," he said airily. "I wouldn't
have fired the arrow if the door had been any more open than it
was."

I didn't believe that for one moment but knew better than to
argue the point, so tried another one. "As it was, the bloody thing
went through the wood and nearly got me in the eye."

"I know," he said with real enthusiasm. "Very impressive, you'll
have to agree. And all with a home-made bow. Come over here and
look at it."

He toddled off and all Max and I could do was proffer each other
a despairing smile and follow him. I have never been able to decide
whether my father is a madman pretending sanity, or a sane man
pretending madness. He was standing just in front of his home-
made, oil-drum barbecue from which the distinct odour of burning
meat was rising. He was cradling his bow with the kind of love that
is normally only seen in mothers with their first-born. "Isn't she
beautiful?"

It was, I have to admit, a fairly impressive item; about five foot
long and an inch in diameter at the middle, it was highly polished

and had a handle made of a crepe bandage wound tightly round. Just below this there was some sort of thin bolt protruding forwards, on the end of which was welded a five-pound kitchen weight. Just above the handle was a slight notch on the left-hand edge.

"I made it myself." My father said this in the tone of voice that dared you not to be impressed. Max complied with, "Wonderful craftsmanship, Dr Elliot. You're clearly very talented." I merely said, "Mmm...."

"I got this book on archery out of the library and I suddenly thought what a brilliant idea to make my own longbow."

"Have you killed anyone yet?"

He took offence. "What do you mean by that?"

"You came close with me. If that arrow had hit a knothole in the wood, at this present moment I'd be doing a fairly lifelike imitation of King Harold on the field at Hastings."

He turned to Max. "He does go on so, doesn't he?"

At which point, with a faint "whoosh", the whole barbecue went up in flames and, what with trying to save the food and stop the overhanging sycamore tree from burning down, the subject wasn't raised again that evening. As we ate meat that varied from cremated to raw in the space of two mouthfuls, I remember vaguely wondering whether I should try to argue him out of his current obsession but, what with nearly being killed and then having to play at fire brigades all in one evening, I didn't feel strong enough to ask.

At 7 o'clock on Thursday, 3 June, on a hot and sticky day, I parked my car in Fairlands Avenue, which stretched and curved away behind me, rather upmarket terraced houses staring at each other across the road. The reason I was there was not because of the day job as a general practitioner, but because I had newly become a Police Surgeon. I had not wanted the post but had been badgered into it by Brian, my practice colleague, who had been doing it for ten years and was now about to retire; he had been assisted in this coercion by my father – himself a Police Surgeon in his day – who painted a rosy-hued picture of the life, one that, inevitably, was as true to reality as my father's recollections of his war exploits. It was not a pleasurable thing to do – although it did supplement my income quite nicely – and it had the amazing knack of doing maximum damage to my social life. I was becoming seriously afraid that Max would soon forget how beautiful I was.

I walked up to the top of the road where Fairlands Avenue met Thornton Road, which was where a lot of coppers were thronging. I had been doing the job long enough to be let in to what I discovered to be a clockmaker's shop – proprietor Harvey Carlton, Esquire – without hindrance, where I found Inspector Masson. I wish I could say that he and I were buddies of the bosom kind, that we spent many a long night chatting cosily about our mutual hobbies, how we both quite liked ABBA (although all their songs tend to sound the same) and how we were delighted that Southampton had trounced Manchester United in the FA Cup final. In truth, though, I was slightly scared of him, and he was completely contemptuous of me; this was not the basis for a deep, lasting relationship.

There was an even greater concentration of constabulary blue behind him as he turned to face me. "Doctor," he said, as he usually did, his tone suggesting that he had hoped for better.

"Inspector."

"We normally wouldn't have bothered you, but the pathologist's been taken with diarrhoea and vomiting."

Maybe he meant this well, but I had the impression he found my presence only slightly more welcome than an attack of either. "What's happened?"

He turned and gestured me forward. I followed him through the uniforms that parted as we moved amongst them to reveal the body of a man dressed in brown overalls. He was on his back and his left eye was gone, replaced by a bloodied pulp. In falling, he had knocked over a whole shelf full of clocks, watches, barometers and weather stations, many of which appeared to have shattered, so that he was surrounded by an astonishingly intricate array of cogs, wheels, wood splinters, coils and spherules of mercury.

"Ouch."

"Did that kill him?" asked Masson.

I rather hoped that it had, but I couldn't say for sure immediately. "Can I move him?"

"SOCO have got all the photos they need for now," he assured me, so I gently took the head in my hands and lifted it, feeling the scalp with the tips of my fingers. There was a soft boggy patch that would do for an exit wound. Then, having laid it back down, I quickly looked over the rest of the body, enlisting a constable to turn it so that I could look at the back; I tested the limbs for rigor mortis and gross bony injuries, checked for bruising around the neck and ligature marks around the wrists and ankles. Then, telling myself that a corpse has no dignity to lose, I undid his belt, pulled down his trousers and pants, and inserted a thermometer where not only the sun didn't shine but there was no starlight either. I left it there for five minutes, pulled it out and examined it, noting the temperature before wiping it with a tissue and putting back in its holder. Without completely stripping the body, it was as good an examination as I could make.

"Well?" Masson's tone suggested that he was fed up with watching me footle around pretending to know what I was doing.

"The body's only lost two degrees and it's still limp, so I'd estimate he's been dead about three to four hours…"

If I thought I was doing well, Masson soon put me right. "I know when he died, Doctor. As he fell he broke at least eight clocks and all of them stopped at the same time – three-fifty-two."

It appeared that I was not even to get credit for being accurate in my estimate, so I swallowed some bitterness and went on, "I can see no other evidence of serious trauma apart from the injury to the eye for which there is an exit wound. I would say that there's no doubt it was that injury that resulted in his death."

"What made it?"

"My first impression is that it's a relatively small-calibre bullet, but until a full post-mortem can be done, that can only be a guess."

He nodded but forgot to thank me as he turned back to his troops and barked, "I want the bullet found."

I appeared to have been dismissed, but I thought I ought to issue some Health and Safety advice. "Be careful of the mercury from the barometers. It's poisonous."

Masson turned to look at me. "Is it?" He sounded suspicious that I might be having him on.

"Everyone should wear gloves."

He snorted, looked at me for a moment, then said to the room in general, "You heard the man. Get some disposable gloves."

I asked conversationally, "Is that Harvey Carlton?"

He shrugged. "Who knows?"

I hung around for a bit but no one had anything more to say to me, so eventually I slunk away. No one even seemed to notice. On my way out I noticed the shop on the opposite corner. It was some sort of bespoke furniture shop. The name above the window said that the proprietor was Peter Carlton, Esquire.

Inspector Masson always evinced nothing but impatience and exasperation in his dealings with me, but I like to think that he had a soft spot for me nevertheless because he seemed to gravitate towards me when things were not going well in his capacity as a sleuth. Max and I had followed the case in the *Croydon Advertiser*, although we were well aware that this fine organ did occasionally get its facts quite startlingly wrong.

Peter and Harvey Carlton were brothers, and they hated each other. Harvey became a master watchmaker, Peter a highly skilled joiner and carpenter making furniture that was snapped up as soon as he finished it. Apparently they had fallen out over twenty years before because of a woman, Mary. They both fell in love with her and only one could win; they matched each other in terms of looks, skills and prospects, but she chose Harvey. Peter tried to commit suicide, failed, and became an eternally angry man. He had a reputation as an unforgiving, hard and unscrupulous businessman. The paper didn't say so, but it was clear that Peter was the number one suspect, though there were problems.

"Of course he's guilty," Max said with complete conviction.

"Is he?"

She nodded. When I enquired how she knew, she said, "He was a nasty man."

I saw no point in debate.

It appeared that although a bullet had been found, there were no reports of a shot being fired, despite extensive house-to-house enquiries. Peter had been interviewed for several hours, had been cooperative and open, portraying shock but no remorse at the death of his brother. He assured the police that he had not left his shop all day and no witnesses could be found to contradict this. Harvey Carlton's financial affairs were reported as being sound, and all enquiries regarding his private life returned nothing but the utmost propriety. The paper, inevitably, reported – perhaps more appropriately, crowed – that the police were "stumped".

The case slipped from public – and our – consciousness.

When the doorbell rang on the evening of Sunday, 27 June, Max and I were sitting in the garden partaking of some Pimm's. I cannot say that the appearance of Masson's sunny visage as I opened the front door produced anything close to a whoop of delight from my vocal chords. "Doctor Elliot," he said. "Mind if I come in?"

I showed him through to the garden. He was graciousness itself as he nodded at Max and said, "Miss Christy. Are you well?"

She smiled at him because that was Max; she would probably smile politely at the Grim Reaper when he came to call. "I'm very well indeed, thank you."

He sat down and, in not asking for a drink, made it plain that he would quite like one. "Pimm's?" I asked.

A shake of the head. "Can't stand the stuff. Poncey in the extreme." Only Masson could have refused the offer so graciously; only Masson could have then said, "I'll have a bitter, though."

After I had accommodated him and we were all sitting around the table looking at the midges and mosquitoes dancing over the garden pond, I was afraid the conversation might prove a tad desultory, but I had reckoned without Masson's forthright character. "I expect you're wondering why I'm here."

"Not a social call, then?"

He looked at me and I found myself wondering if he disliked everyone as much as he appeared to dislike me. "I don't seem to get the time for social calls." With which, somehow, he seemed to imply a puritanical disapproval of anyone sitting in the garden on a summer's evening.

Max, bless her, asked, "Would it be to do with the death of Harvey Carlton?"

To which he said curtly, "After we'd got the pathologist out of his bed, he confirmed what you had told us – that Carlton died of a single small-calibre bullet wound that entered through his right eye and exited through the back of his skull." He didn't seem inclined to applaud my diagnostic skills so I said nothing. "We eventually found it embedded in the corner of a wooden cabinet. It's a small-calibre revolver round."

"That's good," I said.

He didn't snarl because he didn't make a sound, but it was the look that big hairy men were always giving Charlie Chaplin in the golden age of silent movies. "You think so?"

"Isn't it?"

Masson said nothing; I looked covertly at Max and she did likewise at me. I think that we were both unsure of what to say, or whether to say anything at all, since it would almost certainly be taken amiss by our guest. Silence therefore ensued between us and there was the faint sound of a cuckoo in the distance. Masson drank more beer and we did similar damage to the Pimm's.

He said at last, "It has to be Peter Carlton. It just has to be." He snorted. "We've found out that a few weeks before Harvey's death the two brothers met unexpectedly at Mary's grave. There was some sort of fracas. It was witnessed by one of the gardeners at the crematorium; he didn't hear everything that was said, but he swears that he heard Peter threaten to kill his brother."

Max asked, "Does Peter Carlton own a gun?"

Masson shook his head. "No, but that means nothing. Fifty pounds is all you need, if you know the right people."

Max enquired, "And does he know the right people?"

He snorted. "Not as far as we can tell."

"So maybe he didn't do it."

He shook his head immediately. "He did it. I know he did."

We waited a while as Masson stared at a dragonfly as if he would quite like to give it what for with a truncheon. It was starting to turn to dusk, the light becoming golden and soft as opposed to harsh; the very first stirrings of a breeze played about the tops of the trees. Eventually, Max pointed out gently, "That doesn't seem very logical to me. Are you sure you're not just being a bit headstrong?"

Coming from me, he would probably have got out his rubber cosh at this and given me a good talking-to, but Max had this way with people and he merely glanced briefly up at her and then said thoughtfully, "I don't think so."

"Why not?"

"Peter Carlton employs a young man called Colin Bell as general assistant and runaround. Bell says that he was in the shop with Carlton almost all of the day that Harvey died, except for a thirty-minute period when Carlton asked him to make a delivery of a foot-stool to a house in Gonville Road. That was between three-thirty and four."

I said softly, "Blimey."

He smiled. "Sounds significant, doesn't it?"

"I'd have thought so."

"So would I," he agreed, but then stopped. It was as though a fuse had blown and he was no longer functioning.

"And we've found the gun. It had been thrown into the grounds of St Jude's Church about two hundred yards down the road."

All of this seemed like good news and we waited patiently until he said suddenly, "One problem is that ballistic analysis of the bullet's trajectory places the point of origin as the opposite side of Thornton Road, at ninety degrees to the position of Peter Carlton's shop. To be precise, from a rather neat and tidy end-of-terrace house called *Dunhiking*. A newly married couple live there, Mr and Mrs Homan. She's pregnant and he's a plasterer; we've searched the house and investigated them thoroughly – and, in the process, scared the bejeesus out of them. And found nothing."

"Ah…"

"As you've probably read in the papers, Carlton claims not to have left his shop all afternoon, and all the witnesses we've talked to support that; we have no positive sightings of Carlton outside his shop during the critical time. Certainly no one saw him with a gun."

"Did anyone hear the shot? Surely someone did."

He shook his head. "A silencer was used."

"Well, that's something…"

He pointed out sourly, "A silencer doesn't make the marksman invisible."

"Perhaps he was in a soundproofed van or something, parked in the road in front of *Dunhiking*."

Masson was becoming impatient. "He didn't leave the shop all day, remember?"

"An accomplice?" Max suggested, but it was with such timidity that she was almost cowering as the words came out. Masson didn't even seem to hear, though. He merely repeated, "He did it. I know that, I just don't know how."

"Why are you so sure?"

He drained his beer, then put the glass down hard. "I've been staring at him across an interview table for the past nine days and he radiates smugness because he knows he did it, and I know he did it, but I can't show how."

Max, as usual, came to the point. "Why are you here, Inspector?"

It took him a while to answer that one, and when it came it did so with a degree of reluctance that was quite entertaining to behold. While we waited, I poured more Pimm's for Max and myself and asked him, "Another beer?"

He shook his head. More silence. He seemed to have forgotten the pleasurable prospect of delivering a beating to the dragonfly and was contenting himself with staring at the bird table. Max and I drank some more Pimm's.

Then, "You're his GP, right?"

Pennies – several of them – dropped. "Yes," I replied warily.

He glared at me. "I know all the crap about patient confidentiality, Doctor, I've been there before. You silly sods have no idea how difficult you make my life, but I'm not talking about that."

"No?"

"I don't want to know about Peter Carlton's medical conditions – I want you to tell me if he ever mentioned anything that might be relevant to the death of his brother."

Which was different. The doctor's waiting room is not a priest's confessional; I only have to remain schtum about medical things. "I can't recall anything," I said.

He was suspicious. "Really?"

"Yes, absolutely. He's never mentioned his brother, or the history between them."

He breathed heavily for a bit, possibly angry at me, possibly at the fates that he felt goaded him, then nodded. "It was worth a try." More silence and more Pimm's.

He began to speak again after a while. "In pursuit of this case, I seem to have uncovered a secret coven of loonies in the area. I've been told about midnight prowlers, UFOs, ghosts and goblins. One old woman saw a man indecently exposing himself, although she only told anyone when we came to call, and another was visited by her ex-husband, except that he was lost at sea in 1948."

As crusty and irritable as Masson was, Max managed to find empathy within herself. "Surely you've been in situations like this before? Cases that seemed insoluble, I mean."

"Oh, yes. Too many, in fact. And, in some of them, I've known who did it, too, but I've never felt so bloody *taunted* as I do in this one. He thinks I'll never prove that he did it, and he's quite happy to crow about it."

The phone began to ring in the house, which was something of a relief. I went to pick it up and heard Dad's dulcet tones. "Lance? I just wanted to tell you that it's back."

"What is?"

"The book."

The way he said it, the word might have had a capital letter; he might have been talking about a holy writ or a long-lost first edition. "What book?"

"From the library."

Which did not answer my question nor, indeed, did it answer any question at all. "Dad, could you be more explicit?"

He tutted; I was used to my father's tutting and he was undoubtedly good at it, but this was better than most. He followed it up with, "The next stage." When I said nothing, he went on, "Of my project."

I was slightly exasperated by the way that the evening had gone and so was slightly acerbic as I asked, "What on earth are you talking about now?"

"The next step on from the longbow."

"What does that mean?" As I asked this, I felt something furtling around in my bowels.

"Although the longbow undoubtedly revolutionized the art of war..." A shiver of cold horror blossomed within me. I could see that this meant trouble; knowing my father, I now appreciated that "the next stage of the project" probably meant building his own nuclear weapon and then testing it in the greenhouse while he took shelter in the kitchen with a large saucepan on his head. He droned on, "I am of the opinon that for sheer elegance, it is inferior to its predecessor, the crossbow. The crossbow was more powerful and easier to use, see. A great sniper's weapon."

"But you can't," I protested.

"Why not?"

"Because you really might kill someone with one of those. Where will it end? A do-it-yourself cannon?"

To my horror, there was brief silence and I just knew that he was storing this for future reference before he said, "You really are so melodramatic, Lance. Anyone would think you were talking to an irresponsible child."

"Dad, is this wise?"

"Wise? Why shouldn't it be?"

I had taken in a deep breath with all the arguments poised and ready to spew forth, but then thirty years of experience told me to keep quiet. Nothing I would say – nothing anyone would ever say – was going to stop my father doing what my father did. I let it all out in a long sigh. "It doesn't matter."

"Lance, are you all right?" he asked with genuine concern. "You seem a bit out of sorts."

It took me a moment to find my voice. "I'm fine, Dad. Just fine."

When I went back out to the garden, Max was looking severely strained and Masson was looking as he always did, which was morose. He stood at once. "I must be going," he announced as if anyone was going to argue.

As I showed him out, I tried to cheer him up. "I'm sure you'll break the case soon."

He didn't even reply.

For two months nothing happened and everyone forgot about the death of Harvey Carlton, even the *Croydon Advertiser*. Dad went quiet, too; I asked him how his crossbow was coming on, but all he did was mumble something about "technical problems". I remember nodding sympathetically whilst giving thanks to God. Then, quite abruptly, Peter Carlton was found one morning unconscious on the floor of his shop by a woman who was interested in purchasing a set of dining chairs. An ambulance was called and he was taken to Mayday Hospital where a severe, left-sided stroke was diagnosed; he regained consciousness within a day but he remained severely compromised – paralyzed down the right-hand side, unable to speak, dribbling constantly. I visited him after two days and saw in him what I had seen in so many stroke victims – severe depression. Who could blame him? In the space of a second, his entire life had been taken from him; he had not just been placed in a cage but gagged and restrained by a straitjacket as well. There would be some improvement if he could find the will to work at it, but it would not be much, unlikely ever to bring him to an independent existence, definitely never enough to allow him to work again. I could see within his eyes that he knew it, too, and that was agony to behold.

On a walk in Norbury Park, I told Max that evening. She was uncharacteristically unsympathetic. "Perhaps it's a punishment," she said. There was a kestrel hovering in the air above us and to our right; it was about fifty yards up and the only movements that it made were at the ends of its wings. Something was about to die.

"What for?"

"For killing his brother."

"We don't know he did."

"Inspector Masson seemed to think he's guilty. Anyway, nobody liked him."

I sighed. "I have to say, I'm not sure that we can automatically assume any form of infallibility on the good Inspector's part." Still the kestrel hovered. It was a symbol of patience. "And unpopularity is not normally considered a firm foundation on which to bring a conviction."

"No," she conceded. "But he mistreated Mrs Kerry's Georgie, and that's a sure sign of an evil man." I knew Max well enough to decipher this cryptogram at least partially. Georgie was a dog and Max would never forgive someone who mistreated an animal.

"It's a long way from kicking a dog to murdering a man."

"No, it's not," she replied at once, and I knew better than to argue. She said thoughtfully, "He'll be stuck in hospital now..."

I didn't like the sound of that. "What's going through your head, Max?"

She frowned for a moment, then smiled; it was a sweet smile, and all the more worrying because of it. "Nothing," she said. A movement in the sky caught my eye, but I was too slow to see the kestrel dive and I never found out if it was successful.

Despite my constant questioning, Max would say nothing more.

The next evening I was on call but it was a relatively quiet night and so the following day I didn't feel too bad, especially after a short afternoon nap. I was awake by six, had a sandwich and then called Max but got no answer. She was occasionally called out at night because of a veterinary emergency, although her practice did not have a formal on-call rota, so I wasn't too concerned. I decided that I would spend the evening watching television and try her later; as it happened, I fell asleep to be awakened at eleven o'clock when the phone rang. Before I had a chance to speak, Max said, "Lance?"

"Oh, hi, Max." I yawned.

"Are you busy?"

"Well...no..."

"Do you think you could come and fetch me?"

"Sure. Where are you?"

She didn't even hesitate. "In Peter Carlton's shop."

Life with Max had never been boring and I would not have wanted it any other way, but her propensity for breaking into premises – or, for variety, inducing me to do it – did prove a trifle wearing at times. I was not, therefore, in the best of moods when I stopped the car at the end of Fairlands Avenue and walked to Peter Carlton's shop. It was in darkness but she must have been watching out for me because the shop door opened a fraction as soon as I walked up to it. "Come in," she hissed urgently, although I couldn't see her. As I squeezed through, Max shut it at once, making barely a click. I could just make out the crouched form of my girlfriend.

"Max?"

"Come with me."

She scurried off to the back of the shop, making a fairly good imitation of a chimpanzee as she did so. As a respected member of the community and feeling it unlikely that anyone could see me anyway, I chose to walk more normally. She led me into an office at the back of the shop, closed the door behind me and then switched on a lamp on the desk. "There," she said, straightening up at last.

"Max, what the bloody hell are you doing?"

"Investigating."

"That's one word for it. Others would be breaking and entering."

She looked pained. "Surely not. I haven't broken anything."

"How did you get in, then?"

"I got the key from Mrs Kerry who lives next door. She cleans the shop for Peter Carlton and I've been treating her poodle. She's ever so grateful to me."

"What did you tell her?"

She had no shame. "I told them you had been to see Peter Carlton and you had asked me to collect a few things for him in hospital."

I breathed very heavily, told myself that I loved her. "Listen, Max. Peter Carlton might be in hospital and likely to be there for quite a few weeks, but that doesn't mean you can waltz into his shop and search through whatever takes your fancy."

She looked outraged. "Lance, he's a murderer."

"Max, there are rules…"

She sighed. "It doesn't matter. I didn't find anything."

I said at once, "Exactly. There's no point in charging in until you know what you're charging into. What did you think you'd find? A confession signed in blood? A gun with one bullet missing?"

"You never know…"

"Life's not that simple, Max."

She nodded. "I see that now." My mouth was open and I was about to continue my philosophizing when she said, "You're absolutely right. There's nothing here at all." I was about to sound even more pompous when she said, "It's all rather pathetic, really. Just lots of invoices for different types of wood and thngs."

"As you'd expect."

"Of course," she said forlornly.

It took a few minutes but I led her after a while from the shop through the darkness and then out into the cooling air of Fairlands Avenue, Thornton Heath. Having pushed the key through Mrs Kerry's letterbox, we hurried away, looking around us all the while, seeing no one. In the car on the way back, Max said, "He must have been very eccentric."

"Why do you say that?"

"Because he bought lots of fluffy dice – the things that you hang in the car."

It was a relatively new craze then, but I was taken aback by this news. "You're sure?"

"I saw the receipt. He spent eighty pounds on them in May."

"Eighty? He must have bought a hell of lot of them." The picture I had of Peter Carlton was one of a desperately unhappy and driven man, but not a loony. I imagined that eighty pounds' worth of fluffy dice would occupy an entire room and I could not for the life of me imagine why a dedicated and expert furniture-maker should start a sideline selling novelty gifts. "How peculiar," I said.

"And he was branching out into his brother's territory."

"In what way?"

"He bought a consignment of barometers at the same time."
Which at least to me sounded less barmy than buying several crates
of fluffy dice. She continued, "Maybe that's the reason he killed
Harvey – because they argued about selling barometers."

"I would have thought that would be more reason for Harvey to
kill Peter, not the other way round."

These were mysteries for sure, but they weren't of great import
when compared with the central conundrum of who had killed
Harvey and why.

Max and I were gardening when Dad came visiting that evening. I
hate gardening but Max is quite enthusiastic, which makes me feel
just guilty enough to show slightly willing and pull the odd weed. The
familiar sound of Dad's bright red Hillman Avenger – if you can
imagine Chitty Chitty Bang Bang crossed with a Flying Fortress trun-
dling down the runway, then you have some idea why it is not hard to
identify my father's presence in the neighbourhood – interrupted the
serenity of a warm summer's evening. Max led him through to the
garden; he was carrying a battered brown suitcase and for a moment
I thought that he was planning on staying for a while.

"Hello, Dad."

"Good evening!" Like Masson, he was noticeably happier than
usual, which led me to wonder if there was something in the air.
Before I could offer him refreshment, he asked, "Is this the way you
treat your guests? Nothing to drink? Are you suddenly teetotal?"

Max said, "What would you like, Dr Elliot? Beer, wine, or something soft?"

"If my son has a decent bottle of beer, I'll have one. None of that
gnat's pee you call lager, though."

She found him a bottle of bitter that he sniffed at somewhat – he
only liked beers that stripped the stomach of its lining and then
knocked out your bone marrow – but eventually deigned to try.

"What's in the suitcase?"

"Aha! I thought you'd never ask." He sighed with happiness.
"It's finished." With which he pulled the suitcase on to his knees

and flicked the catches. From within it he withdrew a crossbow draped in a white cloth, much as a Stradivarius is cosseted by its owner. He placed it on the garden table, exposed it fully and sat back.

Max said at once, "It's wonderful." Even I had to admit that he'd done a good job on it. The stock was beautifully shaped and deeply varnished; the bow was of burnished metal, the trigger mechanism finely etched with filigree. There was a sight at the front and small handle towards the back with which to wind back the bowstring. It looked lethal.

"Gosh," I said softly.

"I'm rather pleased with it." He picked it up, put it to his shoulder, at which Max and I ducked instinctively. He looked at us. "What's wrong with you two?"

"Is it loaded?"

A look of irritation passed across his face. "Don't be stupid, Lance. I wouldn't point it at someone if it had an arrow in it, would I?" I thought about responding, saw the futility of this at once. "Anyway, I haven't made any arrows yet. I've only just finished the bow."

"Let me know when you do," I suggested, half to myself. He didn't hear and continued, "Mind you, I might not just stick at arrows."

"No?" asked Max.

"It's quite versatile. You can even fire things like marbles. They could be just as lethal."

He had put it back down and Max was inspecting it carefully. "How easy is it to use?" she asked.

"Very. That was the beauty of it; unlike the longbow, it doesn't require much training to be very accurate. The disadvantage is that it has a low rate of fire – at most one or two arrows per minute as opposed to a dozen with a longbow. But as a sniper's weapon, it's superb. Accurate and lethal over nearly two hundred yards."

As he prattled on, I remember wondering whether to ring his neighbours and warn them that it would be in their best interests to remain indoors during daylight hours for the next few weeks. Dad was clearly in love with his new creation and I could not criticize him for it, but the memory of my close encounter with death a few weeks before was strong within me.

Suddenly, I was brought back to the present as he was talking about the troubles he had had in making it. "To think that I had to wait so long to get hold of the book from the library. Some people are just so selfish. The librarian got very angry that this chap, Carlton, held on to it for so long. The fine was quite astronomical…"

"Carlton?"

"Yes. As I was saying…"

"Peter Carlton?"

"I'm not sure."

I was looking at Max who was returning the compliment. Dad drank his beer and carried on talking.

When I rang the next morning and asked the librarian if it had been Peter Carlton who had kept the book on making crossbows out of my father's hands, he was at first slightly surprised to be asked, but eventually confirmed that, yes, it had indeed been Peter Carlton. He made some comment that he was glad that the book had been returned before he had had his stroke, which I thought was a bit tasteless though I said nothing.

What, though, was I going to do with the information? This question occupied me as I worked my way through morning and evening surgeries, sandwiched by the midday home visits. By the time I was finished, though, I had made up my mind and, trying to avoid feelings of hypocrisy, I knocked on Mrs Kerry's door. She was a delightful old lady who swallowed every lie that I told her about wanting to look in Peter Carlton's shop for his cheque book, happily handing over the key.

What was I looking for? I suppose, to be truthful, I was thinking I might just find a crossbow, but I was not optimistic. If Peter Carlton had any sense, he would have burned it immediately, and I suspected that he had had a lot of sense indeed. The theory that had percolated its way through my brain cells was that he had shot the bullet with the crossbow, but that left some important questions unanswered; firstly, why had he used an old bullet – one already fired from a gun with a silencer – and secondly how had he managed to fire the crossbow in broad daylight when there were potentially a hundred people to see him?

I spent several hours looking but without success. The only vaguely suspicious thing I found was in the back garden where there were the remains of small bonfire. By the light of a torch I looked through it and came up with several pieces of charred metal but none of them looked like they might be from a crossbow; I raked them together, though, and put them in a plastic bag. I finished by searching the office, as Max had done, which was when everything fell into place as I came across those peculiar receipts for fluffy dice and barometers.

With Max, I went to see Peter Carlton the next evening. He was sitting out by his bed, dressed in pyjamas and dressing gown, a urinary catheter snaking surreptitiously out from beneath the ensemble. The right side of his face was drooping, a faint shiny line of dribble coming from the corner of his mouth. His right arm was flexed on his lap; his eyes were bright but it was with the light of tears held back. After the niceties of introduction and questions about his welfare that he could only answer with nods and winks, I said gently, "Peter, I want to talk to you about your brother's death." There was no reaction. "I'd like to suggest to you what might have happened that day."

If he wanted to hear what I had to say, he didn't show it. I glanced across at Max who encouraged me with a smile. "I think you did something that was quite ingenious, quite outrageously clever."

The flattery had no effect either. "I think that you made yourself a crossbow. You borrowed a book from the library to help you construct it, but you would have managed with your skills to make a very, very good one, I suspect." For the first time there was something in his eyes that suggested a reaction – pride, perhaps. I continued, "As my father has told me, it's a perfect sniper's weapon. Silent and very deadly over long distances. Also, it can fire anything, not just arrows. The problem is, of course, that it's difficult to conceal.

"Also, since the murder occurred in broad daylight – at three-fifty-two in the afternoon, to be precise – and the trajectory of the bullet suggests that the killer must have been standing in open view of scores of witnesses, it is spooky that no one saw him."

For the first time he made a noise; it was no more than a gurgle and incapable of being comprehended. I said, "The clever thing was that it wasn't the bullet the police found that killed your brother, was it? That was just a decoy, so that they would work with completely the wrong trajectory. You fired that the night before, didn't you? You put a silencer on the gun, walked across Thornton Road and stood in the garden of the Homans' house. You knew that he worked late into the night, and more or less when he would leave. What did you do? Wait for your brother to leave the shop and then fire over his shoulder? You must be a good shot, Peter. Are you?"

He didn't answer, of course, so I went on, "It must have been tempting to kill him there and then, but you were patient. Your target was the wooden shelving behind him, and you hit it; it was small-calibre ammunition so that it wouldn't do too much damage. You knew the police would find it and you knew that they'd jump to all the wrong conclusions.

"With that piece of misdirection, you could then proceed with the murder. You shot him using your crossbow from the safety of your own shop, through the open door. You waited until he was standing in front of the place where you had shot the bullet and then you killed him."

He was trembling, I noticed. Was that something new?

"But what of the bullet you used? The police found only one, of course, so where is the other?"

Which, since I hadn't told her, was when Max joined in. "Yes, Lance, where is it?"

I had brought the charred metal fragments with me and, opening a newspaper on the bed, I poured them out. "I was hoping that these might be parts of a crossbow, but I think not. I think that they're pieces of barometers. You ordered several in May, didn't you?"

"And fluffy dice," pointed out Max

I shook my head. "No, Max. Not fluffy dice. Not car dice, but cardice."

She looked none the wiser so I explained, "Cardice is solid carbon dioxide. It has a temperature of minus seventy degrees centigrade, and that is quite cold enough to freeze mercury solid; mercury that you might get out of barometers, say."

She saw the implications of what I was saying, and gasped. I looked at Peter Carlton and for the first time I knew that he was listening to me and that I was right. She said, "He made the bullet out of solid mercury."

"He made several, I should think, just to be on the safe side. He fired the mercury bullet with the silent crossbow through the open doors of both shops as Harvey stood in front of the shelves where he kept his barometers. It passed through his eye, through his brain and through his skull, and then melted to join the rest of the mercury on the floor around the body."

There was silence for a moment, and it took a while before I realized that Peter Carlton was crying.

Officially Masson solved the case but he hid his gratitude well. The next time I saw him, he rather curtly confirmed that, with the aid of a speech and language therapist, Peter Carlton had been helped to make a voluntary confession that fairly accurately mirrored what I had conjectured.

"I don't know, Doctor, but I'd be worried if my brain were devious enough to have worked all this out."

That sounded suspiciously like sour grapes to me but I smiled sweetly and pointed out, "It's just as well somebody's devious enough, isn't it?"

I walked away before his scowl could excoriate me.

My father had invited us to another barbecue but I only accepted after his reassurance that he would not get his crossbow out of his suitcase until we arrived. Nevertheless, I had a faint feeling of trepidation as I opened the back garden gate and peered carefully around. Dad was sitting reading, apparently completely weaponless, but he jumped up at once as we walked up to him and produced his beloved crossbow. "I decided on arrows," he announced. "Much more aesthetically pleasing than solid projectiles."

He showed us his arrows; as usual with my father, they were exquisitely well made.

"Now, what you do is turn this handle, which draws the bowstring back, then you press that switch there and, by doing that, you lock the string into place under tension. You place the arrow there, and then pulling the trigger releases the string which projects the arrow forward."

Max said, "Go on, then."

He began to turn the handle. At first, it was quite easy, but it quickly became harder and harder. Within a few seconds there was a frown on his face and the string was only two-thirds of the way back. He persevered, though.

"Careful," I advised.

He looked up at me whilst continuing to wind. "Lance, don't fuss. This is a precision instrument and I know exactly the tolerances that can be applied. There is no danger…"

The snap was loud and sudden and somehow sad. Dad looked down to see his precious crossbow in two pieces, split through the stock.

A moment of silence ensued; if any neighbours were watching, that was the moment they would have opened the champagne.

"Bugger," said Dad.

THE GOLDEN HOUR

Bernie Crosthwaite

---

17 August, 20.05 hours

THE DOMESTIC IS a real downer. Wife attacks husband with a cricket bat. Apparently it's been going on for years. It started with punching him, then pulling his hair out in handfuls, then stubbing cigarettes on his bare back. While he's telling us all this the guy is sitting on the floor, whimpering like a dog. That really gets to me.

"What a loser," says PC Lowery on the way back to the station.

I don't say anything, just take one hand off the wheel and release a strand of hair that's got trapped in my plait. I glance out of the window. After a wet day it's turned into a beautiful evening. The sun is streaking out from under the clouds like fingers. I feel sorry for the kids on their school holidays. It's been a lousy summer.

The duty officer is talking on the phone as we come in. He puts a hand over the mouthpiece. "Helen – you can take this one. A misper. Caller's name – Mrs Sally Hunter. Try and get some sense out of her."

He hands me the phone. Brett Lowery pushes past me on his way to the canteen.

"Hello, Mrs Hunter? My name's Sergeant Brandling. What seems to be the—"

"My little – girl – my little – girl ..." There's a catch in the woman's voice like hiccups.

"Hold on, Mrs Hunter." I signal for a notepad and pen. "Tell me exactly what's worrying you."

"She was playing outside – she's – not there – I don't know – I don't know where—" The words are being pulled out of her forcibly. "She's ... disappeared.' I can barely hear the last word. It's whispered like it's an obscenity.

"Is there anywhere she might have gone?"

"She knows not to leave the garden."

"Did you check up and down the street?"

"She's as good as gold."

"Have you looked for her indoors, Mrs Hunter?" It's surprising how many don't, how quickly panic sets in. They're on to the police before they've even searched the house.

"I called her. She always comes when I call." Her voice is getting higher, close to hysteria.

Obsessive mother, rebellious child? Maybe. But my gut twists. I have a feeling about this one.

"Okay, Mrs Hunter. I need a few details. What's your address?" All I get is a weird noise like a howl. "Try and keep calm, for your little girl's sake."

She takes a deep breath. "Thirty-seven Gunnerston Road."

"And your daughter's name?"

"Natalie."

"How old is she?"

"Eight and a half."

"Can you tell me what clothes she's wearing?"

"A pink-and-white sundress and pink sandals."

"And what does she look like?"

"She's quite small for her age. Light-brown hair. Green eyes." Her voice falls away as if realizing she'll never see those green eyes again.

"Okay. I'll get her description circulated straight away and I'll be with you in about ten minutes. Please listen carefully, Mrs Hunter. As soon as you put the phone down I want you to have a good look round the house, and check the garden and any outbuildings or sheds. Will you do that, please?"

"But she isn't—"

"The most likely thing is that Natalie's hiding. Let's hope you find her before we get there. That'll be the best outcome for everyone."

As soon as the call ends I give the duty officer my notes and he starts logging them into the system. "And can you check the database for known paedophiles in the Gunnerston Road area?"

I'm up the stairs two at a time. Brett's in the canteen, just about to stuff a bacon sandwich down his neck.

"Forget that. You're coming with me."

I give Brett the few details I have as we clatter down the stairs. The duty officer looks up from his computer and shakes his head.

No leads then. Nothing to point us in the right direction. We'll have to start from square one.

As we run towards our patrol car I check the time. Quarter-past eight. If we can find Natalie Hunter within the hour the odds are she'll still be alive. As time passes the odds worsen. A day without a sighting and it's fifty-fifty. After that we could be looking at a murder investigation. The next sixty minutes are crucial.

The golden hour starts now.

I've been waiting for an evening like this for a long time.

I had planned to take the Norton to the coast today. I got all my equipment ready last night. But when I woke up this morning it was wet and the rain was forecast to last for hours. It was almost certain there would be a sea fret, a "haar" as they call it in Scotland, and the thought of riding all that way in the rain to find nothing but thick white fog was unappealing and I abandoned the trip.

It's been a frustrating day, spent staring out of the window and reading my monthly photography magazine. I read the many articles on digital techniques with deep misgivings. I'm not against the new technology. I recently invested in a very expensive digital camera and I've played around with images, but it feels like a form of cheating. Capturing my subject in all its natural perfection has always been the challenge for me.

With dinner eaten, the dishes washed up and put away and nothing on television but wall-to-wall rubbish, I'm lost for something to do. Since I retired from the college, if I can't get out with my camera, time hangs heavy.

When I take the bin bag out I see that the sky is no longer a uniform grey pall. The clouds are beginning to break up and rays of sunshine, like the spokes of a fan, shoot out and touch the ground with gold. The correct name for them is crepuscular rays. Some people call them the fingers of God.

My camera bag is already packed. The motorbike has a sidecar, which Lynette never liked, but she isn't here any more and that means there's more room for bulkier equipment like the tripod. I'm ready to go within minutes. And all the time the sky is changing, the clouds dissolving and re-forming in unpredictable patterns.

I feel my excitement rise. Along with dawn, around sunset is one of the best times of day to take pictures. Among photographers there's a particular term for it.

We call it the golden hour.

20.19 hours

Gunnerston Road is a steep street with houses built against the slope. The garden of number 37 is terraced to cope with the gradient – concrete beds filled with bushy heathers. There's a steep winding flight of steps up to the front door. We're both breathing hard by the time we get there.

The door is opened by a small plump woman around forty.

"Mrs Hunter? Sergeant Helen Brandling. And this is PC Lowery."

She doesn't look us in the eye. She seems mesmerized by our uniforms. Then her gaze darts behind us, up and down the street.

"Can we come in?"

She steps back. A grandfather clock takes up a lot of space in the narrow hallway and we have to shuffle past it to close the door.

"Any sign of Natalie?"

"No. I've searched the house. I can't find her anywhere."

"I want you to call her friends. She may have gone off to play with someone without telling you."

"She'd never do that."

"It's worth a try." I look at Brett and nod. He starts to climb the stairs.

"Where's he going? I told you – I've looked all over!"

"No harm in double-checking."

I've known kids hide in the tiniest spaces – the drawer under the bed, behind the bath, the gap between the wardrobe and wall. Sometimes they're not hiding at all – they've been hidden. What's left of them.

"Is your husband at home?"

Her eyes flicker nervously, looking everywhere but at me. "No."

"Working late?"

"He left us. About six months ago."

"I'm sorry." I wait no more than a heartbeat before I ask, "Have you got a recent photo of him?"

She leads me into a small cramped living room and points to the mantelpiece. "I keep it for Natalie's sake."

Florid complexion, receding hair, rimless glasses.

"Is he fond of Natalie? Does he miss her?"

"Of course." She looks at me directly for the first time. "You think Gary might have...?"

"What's his current address?"

She finds it for me. I write it down and ask her what car he drives and the registration. Then I point to the phone in the hall. "Try everyone you can think of – friends, relatives, neighbours, anyone Natalie might have gone off with. But don't ring your husband, okay?"

I hurry down the hall to the kitchen, a gloomy sunless room with units made of dark wood. I open the back door. It's warmer outside than in the cheerless kitchen. I phone HQ and give them Gary Hunter's description, address and details of his car, a silver Honda Civic.

The back garden slopes upward to a high fence. It has a crowded neglected feel. A search in the thick shrubs reveals a rubber ball, the arm of a doll and a pink scrunchie, muddy and sodden as if it's been there a long time.

The door of the rickety shed gapes open. There are empty plant pots, old bikes, a rusty pushchair. I shift the heavy bags of compost. An enormous spider runs out and scuttles across the wooden floor.

There are no locked cupboards or old fridges, no hidden trapdoors.

I walk through the kitchen as Brett comes down the stairs. Mrs Hunter puts the phone down. We stare at each other blankly. Natalie's mother is the first to look away.

"PC Lowery and I are going to start knocking on doors up and down the street."

The grandfather clock strikes the half-hour. Fifteen minutes into the enquiry already and we have nothing.

"Don't give up, Mrs Hunter. Somebody must have seen her."

They call it a lake but in reality it's a flooded gravel pit. It has a slightly bleak artificial look about it – too symmetrical perhaps and the steep sides are banks of pebbles rather than vegetation. But it has a certain wild appeal and over the years it's become a beauty spot, a bird sanctuary, even the sailing club uses it.

I drive along the rough path beside the water. Motor vehicles are not strictly allowed but I'm in a hurry and take the chance that at this hour the place will be deserted. The rain-washed sky is filled with furiously active cloud formations which I long to capture, not to mention the shot I've come here for – the water gleaming like satin and boiling clouds backlit by the setting sun.

I don't see anyone, but just in case, I park the bike off the track in a copse of trees. I can't wait to get started. I'm not a professional photographer. I'm not interested in profit. The paps are always looking for the "money shot" – a drunken politician or a celebrity half-naked on a beach. It doesn't seem to matter how blurred or badly composed the picture is, they can still make a small fortune from it. But that's not my way. I only want perfection. With me it's a labour of love.

20.37 hours

I'm doing the evens, Brett Lowery the odds. Climbing up and down the steep steps to each house is exhausting and time-consuming. This is only the third house I've tried. Number 24.

Male, twenties, wearing a loose tee-shirt and baggy shorts. His legs are deeply tanned and muscular, tattoos on each arm, shaven head. He smells clean and soapy as if he's just had a shower. There's a dog too, an Alsatian. The man hangs on to its collar even though it looks old and tired. A retired police dog perhaps. I don't ask. There isn't time.

While I introduce myself and get his name he looks shifty. "What's this about?"

"A missing person enquiry. Just a routine house-to-house, Mr Corby. Nothing to worry about."

He relaxes slightly and I ask him if he's seen anything unusual in the neighbourhood today.

"What time?"

"This evening, around seven or eight o'clock?"

"I went to the off-licence at half-seven." A yeasty gust of beer from his belly confirms this.

"Did you see any children playing?"

"Yeah, suppose. But I couldn't tell you which ones. I don't take any notice of kids."

"Okay. Thanks, Mr Corby." I flip my notebook shut.

"Hold on." He scratches his neck with his free hand. "There was a car driving dead slow. Old guy on a motorbike nearly went into the back of it. I saw it on the way to the offy and again on the way home. It was going the other way then, like it was lost or something, looking for a house number. They're hard to see 'cos of the steps—"

"A silver Honda?" I shouldn't have said that, put words in his mouth.

"No. It was red. A Vauxhall. It was making a chugging noise, like there was a hole in the exhaust or something. Maybe that's why I clocked it."

"Any chance you noticed the car registration?"

"Nah." Mr Corby lets go of the dog and it flops down with exhaustion, its tongue lolling sideways. "Apart from the letters."

I open my notebook. "What were they?"

"E-T-C. Etcetera. Geddit? That tickled me, don't know why." His grin reveals even white teeth, apart from one missing canine, lower right.

"How many people were in the car?"

"Just the bloke driving."

"Can you describe him?"

"Just a bloke, nothing special about him as far as I can remember."

"Okay, Mr Corby."

He comes down the top few steps to see me off the premises. That's when he notices the police car, parked outside the Hunters' house.

"It's not little Natalie, is it? Has she gone missing? Has some bastard taken her?"

I fetch the tripod from the sidecar and begin to set it up. The sky is dissolving from blue-gold to mauve. As I hastily release the telescopic legs of the tripod I catch the skin of my finger and reel back with the intensity of the pain, only eased by sucking on the wound. The skin is inflamed but not ruptured, which is a great relief. I once ruined a shot of snowy mountains with a bloody fingerprint on the lens.

I attach the camera to the tripod. I've decided on my new digital model, a Canon that is capable of shooting eight frames a second and has an inbuilt spirit level to make sure the horizon is straight. Then I begin to compose the shot. I fiddle with the equipment until I have the exact angle I want. A sudden ray of bright sun from behind a cloud causes a burst of flare, which is normally regarded as a fault. But it can create unexpectedly interesting effects so I take the shot anyway.

The sky is tinged with pink now. It's becoming more dramatic every second. I take a few more shots but I'm simply flexing my muscles for the big one, the image that will combine the elements of sky, cloud, water and the blood-red light of the final moments of sunset. I suppose it's a bit like capturing the last breath of someone dying.

20.41 hours

My phone rings as I reach the bottom of the steps of number 24. They've traced Natalie's father. He's been fifty miles away all day on business. No sign of a little girl in his rented flat or in his car.

"Shit."

Brett Lowery runs across the road towards me.

"Have they found her?"

"No such luck."

He swivels away from me, a grim look on his face.

"Anything from the door-to-door?"

"Nothing. You?"

"Not much. A cruising car, half a registration."

"It's worth a try, isn't it?"

"Why not? We've got bugger all else."

Redness is staining the sky, most intense near the horizon, then becoming paler, like ink in water. My finger rests lightly on the shutter.

Then I hear something, a faint rattling noise that disturbs the tranquillity of the lake. It sounds like a car whose engine isn't tuned properly. It's getting louder. I look up from the viewfinder. After a few seconds I see it, a red car bumping along the same track I used earlier. I shrink back into the gloom of the trees. The car drives past but to my horror it stops a little way along the track, just where I have angled the camera towards the lake to capture the finest view.

I'm almost ready to shoot and there is a bright red car slap bang in the middle of my carefully composed shot.

20.49 hours

We carry on knocking on doors, all the while on tenterhooks, waiting for information on the Vauxhall. An old man keeps me talking. He doesn't know anything, He's just glad of the excitement. A couple of others resent being taken away from the footie on telly and can't wait to shut the door in my face. No one except Mr Corby saw a red car cruising up and down the street around half-past seven.

My phone rings.

"I've got a trace on a red Vauxhall Astra, G92 ETC, probably stolen as the car is registered to a spinster lady of seventy-five."

"Last seen when?"

"CCTV on Victoria Road at ... 20.10. Again at the Mill Lane roundabout at 20.14."

"Could you see which exit he took?"

"Going towards Steelbridge. We lose sight of him after that – he doesn't appear on the retail-park camera a mile down the road."

I wave frantically at Brett Lowery across the street and he comes running. We jump into the car at the same moment and I drive off with a screech of tyres.

"There's a map on the backseat. Find the Mill Lane roundabout."

Brett studies the map then jabs it with his finger. "Got it."

"Take the Steelbridge exit. Now tell me what's off that road before you get to the shopping mall."

He traces the route. "There's a big housing estate. He could be taking her to where he lives."

My heart sinks. If he's garaged the car then it's going to be a needle and haystack job. "OK. We'll come back to that possibility. What else?"

"Industrial park. Sixth Form College. Further on there's a narrow lane down to a lake but it's not much more than a track."

"The gravel pit?"

"It says *lake* here."

"Same thing."

The roundabout is coming up. I swing on to it, taking the Steelbridge exit. I know the track to the lake. I used to go there years ago with my mates. Lager and ciggies and skimming stones on the still flat water.

"What do you think?" asks Brett.

I'm not thinking, not really. I'm relying on instinct, experience, gut feeling. All I know is that time is running out and I've got to make a choice.

It's still there, a bright red blot on the landscape. And all the time the sky is changing, deepening like a developing print, rushing towards the perfect moment.

I'm tempted to go and remonstrate with the driver, but what if he turns nasty? No doubt he's come here to see the sunset too, but I just wish he would move fifty metres along. There's movement inside the car. Are there two of them? For God's sake. If they're lovers they could be here for ages. And once they start snogging they'll miss the sunset anyway. I stand there helplessly, watching my hopes die.

But the shadow puppets inside the car shift. The door opens, a man wearing a grey tracksuit gets out. He's pulling something. No. Someone. A little girl in a pink-and-white dress.

Father and daughter then. What are they doing here? The child is dragging her footsteps. It's way past her bedtime. Surely they aren't going for a walk at this time of night, leaving their car stuck in the middle of my shot?

They enter the wood just a few metres away. Now is the moment to confront him and calmly state my case, but he's striding along with a glazed expression that unnerves me and I draw back, crouching down into the undergrowth. Perhaps the little girl just needs a pee in which case they won't be long. Maybe I can salvage something from this disaster after all.

From my hiding place I watch them approach. The man looks tense, even angry. The child is being pulled along unwillingly. Why is she resisting if she needs to go to the toilet? She seems tired and scared. There's something wrong here but I'm not sure what it is. Saliva rushes into my mouth. I swallow. I have an odd feeling that I should do something, but what?

They pass by so close I can hear his laboured breathing and her moans of distress. They disappear into the wood behind me.

The sky is beautiful – scudding pewter clouds against scarlet, deepening every second. That's my business, that's what I'm here for. The man, the little girl – they have nothing to do with me. I just wish they would go away.

21.04 hours

The track around the lake is rough and bumpy, not meant for motor vehicles. The exhaust bangs on a stray rock.

"Over there." Brett points across the lake to where a red car is parked next to a clump of trees.

"Get on the Airwave and call for back-up," I tell him. "And ask them to put the helicopter on standby."

We rise inches into the air as I take a curve too sharply. Brett gives me a look but I don't care if I trash the car. I don't care if the driver of the red car hears us coming. I know the track becomes impassable beyond those trees except on foot so he can't escape in that direction. If he drives towards us we'll throw a stinger in his path and wreck his tyres. Personally I would happily crash into him and bring him to a halt that way. But it's not an option. Natalie might be in the car. She's what matters. She's all that matters.

Even before I've come to a standstill Brett is out of the car and running. He yanks open the doors of the Astra then the boot.

"Empty!" he shouts.

I stand between the two cars and scan the scene. The track is deserted up ahead. The water is silky-smooth, unruffled. I turn towards the trees. Something glints in the light from the bright red sunset. Metal? Glass? There's movement. A man. Grey hair, beard, leather jacket. He looks startled, steps back and disappears.

Brett's seen him too. He rushes ahead of me into the bushes.

"Get him!" I scream. "Get the bastard!"

I can't believe it when I hear the second car, coming fast along the track as if this is Silverstone or something. Joy riders, no doubt. I expect to hear loud music coming from the car's speakers, but as I stand up I see with a shock the jazzy blue and yellow flashes. Police.

A young man in uniform leaps out and checks the red car. A female officer joins him. The car is empty. I could have told them that. They look round in desperation.

Sky and water have almost reached the moment of perfection I have been waiting for so patiently. If they find what they're looking for and go away, I might yet capture a truly glorious shot.

I take a few steps forward. When they see me, both of them have the same look of disgust and hatred in their eyes. The man hurtles towards me. Some deep blind instinct tells me to turn and run.

Bernie Crosthwaite

I can hear him close behind me, crashing through the bushes. He grabs me round the waist and knocks me to the ground. I feel my right shoulder bone crunch. I lie there winded and shocked.

"Where is she?" he yells. "What have you done with her?"

Now the woman is towering over me, her face tight.

"Tell us where she is."

"Who?" My voice is shaking. It sounds weak and pitiful but all my strength has drained out of me.

"The little girl. Natalie. What have you done with her?"

I raise my left hand – the right one seems to have lost all connection to my body – and point to the trees. "In there. Both of them."

They glance at each other.

"Both?" asks the woman. "You mean … there are two girls?"

"No. A child and a man."

The male officer sets off but she calls him back.

"You stay with him. I'll go."

21.07 hours

The bit of daylight that's left barely penetrates in here. I switch on my torch, pointing it down, and inch my way forward. I strain my ears, listening for human sounds beneath the rustle of leaves, the movement of small creatures, the soft breeze that cools the sweat on my back.

I go deeper and deeper into the wood, searching for a ribbon, a strand of light brown hair caught on a bush. Anything.

There's a sudden commotion behind me. I swing round and bring the torch level. I see a man running through the undergrowth, arms flailing, heading back towards the lake.

"Brett! He's coming your way!"

"We saw something shining," says the policeman. He swipes at the tree branches.

I struggle up from where I'm squatting on a patch of damp moss.

"It's my camera."

"Show me."

I lead him to where the Canon still sits on the tripod.

"Did you take pictures of them?"

"No, of course not. I specialize in landscapes." I point to the lake and the spectacular sunset. "I was all set up and ready when that man, not to mention you and your colleague, came along and ruined my shot."

"Ruined your shot?" His voice is full of contempt. "You saw a man take a little girl into the woods, and all you care about is taking snaps?"

"It's none of my business."

He bunches his fist and draws his arm back. But at the last moment he slaps his arm down by his side. He takes a running kick at the tripod. It keels over and smashes on to the ground.

" Have you any idea how much that camera cost?"

From the look on his face he's going to tell me what I can do with my precious camera. But in the distance we can hear the woman shouting. The man in the tracksuit bursts through the trees. The policeman barges him in the stomach. He collapses, grunting loudly. The officer kneels on him, takes handcuffs from his pocket and secures his wrists behind his back. The man utters an obscenity then lies quiet.

21.13 hours

"Natalie?"

She's lying very still under a tree. Her dress is muddy and torn. She's wearing one pink sandal. The other lies on the ground, exposing a smooth pale foot.

"Natalie," I whisper. "It's all right. It's all right now."

But my throat is thick. It's not all right. It will never be all right.

I gently touch her leg. Still warm. Her arm, her cheek.

Her eyelids flutter.

"Natalie!" I don't mean to shout but I can't help it. She flinches. Her eyes shoot open with terror.

"I'm a police officer," I say quietly. She puts her arms out to me and my heart buckles. I hold her tight.

* * *

The world has gone mad. The air is filled with the sound of sirens. Two more police cars arrive and the man in the tracksuit is bundled into the back of one of them.

The female officer emerges from the woods, carrying the little girl. The child clings to the woman, arms circling her neck, legs gripping her waist, the way a young chimp clings to its mother. The woman walks past me, without so much as a glance, but when she reaches her colleague I hear her tell him to get my details. She places the child in the back seat of her car and gets in the front.

The young man takes my name and address. "We'll be in touch," *he says, and spits on the ground. Not a word of apology for the injuries I've suffered or the damage he's done to my equipment.*

There's a lot of noise as the cars perform complicated turning manoeuvres on the narrow track. Then they roar off towards the main road.

Peace at last.

I tentatively swing my arm. There's some pain, but it's not, after all, a broken clavicle. I should be able to handle the bike. I pack up the camera and tripod. If the Canon is ruined it will be a great loss. But in some ways the greater loss is my failure to get the picture I crave. These opportunities don't occur very often. I have other cameras but who knows when there will be another evening like this?

Now the clouds have lost all definition and interest. The lake is a dark pool, and in the sky there's just a prosaic red glow. I watch, filled with regret, until the sun goes down.

Night falls.

The golden hour is over.

THE HABIT OF SILENCE

Ann Cleeves

NEWCASTLE IN NOVEMBER, Joe Ashworth thought, is probably the greyest city in the world. Then running up the steps from the Westgate Road he realized that he'd been to this place before. His seven-year-old daughter had violin lessons at school and he'd brought her here for her grade one exam. They'd both been intimidated by the grandeur of the building and the girl's hand had shaken during the scales. Listening at the heavy door of the practice room, he'd heard the wobble.

Today there was rain and a gusty wind outside and the sign *Lit and Phil Library open to the public* had blown flat on to the pavement. Taped to the inside door, a small handwritten note said that the library would be closed until further notice. Mixed messages. The exams took place on the ground floor but Joe climbed the stone staircase and felt the same sense of exclusion as when he'd waited below, clutching his daughter's small violin case, making some feeble joke in the hope that she'd relax. Places like this weren't meant for a lad from Ashington, whose family had worked down the pit. When there *were* still pits.

At the turn of the stairs there was an oil painting on the wall. Some worthy Victorian with a stern face and white whiskers. Around the corner a noticeboard promoting future events: book launches, lectures, poetry readings. And on the landing, looking down at him, a tall man dressed in black, black jeans and a black denim shirt. He wore a day's stubble but he still managed to look sophisticated.

"You must be the detective," the man said. "They sent me to look out for you. And to turn away members and other visitors. My name's Charles. I found the body."

It was a southern voice, mellow and musical. Joe Ashworth took an instant dislike to the man, who lounged over the dark wood banister as if he owned the place.

"Work here, do you?"

It was a simple question but the man seemed to ponder it. "I'm not a member of staff," he said. "But, yes, I work here. Every day, actually."

"You're a volunteer?" Joe was in no mood for games.

"Oh, no." The man gave a lazy smile. "I'm a poet. Sebastian Charles." He paused as if he expected Ashworth to recognize the name. Ashworth continued up the stairs so he stood on the landing too. But still the man was so tall that he had to crick his neck to look up at him.

"And I'm Detective Sergeant Ashworth," he said. "Please don't leave the building, Mr Charles. I'll need to talk to you later." He moved on into the library. The poet turned away from him and stared out of a long window into the street. Already the lamps had been switched on and their gleam reflected on the wet pavements.

Joe's first impression, walking through the security barrier, was of space. There was a high ceiling and within that a glass dome. Around the room a balcony. And everywhere books, from floor to ceiling, with little step-ladders to reach the higher shelves. He stared. He hadn't realized that such a place could exist just over the room where small children scratched out tunes for long-suffering examiners. A young library assistant with pink hair sat behind a counter. Her eyes were as pink as her hair and she snuffled into a paper handkerchief.

"Can I help you?"

The girl hadn't moved her lips and the words came from a small office, through an open door. Inside sat a middle-aged woman half hidden by a pile of files on her desk. She looked fraught and tense. He supposed she'd become a librarian because she'd wanted a quiet life. Now she'd been landed with a body, the chaos of the crime-scene investigation, and her ordered life had been disrupted. He introduced himself again and went into the office.

"I suppose," she said, "you want to go downstairs to look at poor Gilbert."

"Not yet." As his boss Vera Stanhope always said, the corpse wasn't going anywhere. "I understand you've locked the door?"

"To the Silence Room? Oh, yes." She gave a smile that made her seem younger and more attractive. "I suppose we all watch *CSI* these days. We know what we should do." She gestured him to sit in a chair nearby. On her desk, behind the files, stood a photo of two young girls, presumably her daughters. There was no indication of a husband.

"Perhaps you should tell me exactly what happened this morning." Joe took his seat.

The librarian was about to speak when there were heavy footsteps outside and a wheezing sound that could have been an out-of-breath hippo. Vera Stanhope appeared in the doorway, blocking out the light. She carried a canvas shopping bag over one shoulder.

"Starting without me, Joe Ashworth?" She seemed not to expect an answer and gave the librarian a little wave. "Are you all right, Cath?"

Joe thought Vera's capacity to surprise him was without limit. This place made him feel ignorant. All those books by writers he didn't know, pictures by artists whose names meant nothing to him. What could Vera Stanhope understand of culture and poetry? She lived in a mucky house in the hills, had few friends, and he couldn't ever remember seeing her read a book. Yet here she was, greeting the librarian by her first name, wandering down to the other end of the library to pour herself coffee from a flask set there for readers' use, then moving three books from the only other chair in the office so she could sit down.

Vera grinned at him. "I'm a member of the Lit and Phil, pet. The Literary and Philosophical Society Library. Have been for years. My father brought me here to lectures when I was kid and I liked the place. And the fact that you don't get fined for overdue books. Don't get here as often as I'd like though." She wafted the coffee mug under his nose. "Sorry, I should have offered you some." She turned back to Cath. "I saw Sebastian outside. You said on the phone that he found the body."

The librarian nodded. "He's taken to working in the Silence Room every afternoon. We're delighted, of course. It's good publicity for us. I'm sure we've attracted members since he won the T. S. Eliot."

Vera nudged Joe in the ribs. "The Eliot's a prize for poetry, Sergeant. In case you've never heard of it."

Joe didn't reply. It wasn't just the smell of old books that was getting up his nose.

Cath frowned. "You know how Sebastian hates the press," she said. "I do hope he won't make a scene."

"Who else was around?" Joe was determined to move the investigation on. He wanted to be out of this place and into the grey Newcastle afternoon as soon as possible.

"Zoë Wells, the library assistant. You'll have seen her as you came in. And Alec Cole, one of the trustees. Other people were in and out of the building, but just five of us were around all morning." The librarian paused. "And now, I suppose, there are only four."

The Silence Room was reached by more stone steps at the back of the library. This time they were narrow and dark. The servants' exit, Joe thought. It felt like descending into a basement. There was no natural light in the corridor below. The three of them paused and waited for Cath to unlock the heavy door. Inside, the walls were lined with more books. These were old and big, reference texts. Still no windows. Small tables for working had been set between the shelves. The victim sat with his back to them, slumped forward over one of the tables. There was a wound on his head, blood and matted hair.

"Murder weapon?" Vera directed her question to both of them. Then: "I've been in this room dozens of times, but this is the first time I've ever spoken here. It seems almost sacrilegious. Weird, isn't it, the habit of silence?" She turned to Joe. "That's the rule. We never speak in here."

"I wondered if he could have been hit with the book." Cath nodded towards a huge tome lying on the floor. "Could that kill someone?"

Vera gave a barking laugh. "Don't see why not, with enough force behind it. Appropriate, eh? Gilbert Wood killed with words."

"You knew him?" Why am I not surprised? Joe thought.

"Oh, our Gilbert was quite famous in his own field. Academic, historian, broadcaster, writer. He's been knocking around this place since I was a bairn and he's turned out a few words in his time." She turned to Cath. "What was he working on now?"

"He was researching the library's archives. The Lit and Phil began its life as a museum as well as a library and there's fascinating material on the artefacts that were kept here. Some very weird and wonderful stuff. We thought it might make a book. Another boost to our funds."

Outside there were quick footsteps and a man in his sixties appeared in the doorway. He was small and neat with highly polished black shoes, a grey suit and a dark tie. Joe thought he looked like an undertaker.

"I was working upstairs," he said. "The accounts for the AGM next week. Zoë had to tell me that the police had arrived." There was a touch of reproach in the voice. He was accustomed to being consulted.

"Please meet Alec Cole." Cath's words were polite enough but Joe thought she didn't like him. "He's our honorary treasurer. It's Alec who makes sure we live within our means."

"A difficult task," Cole said, "for any charitable organization during these benighted times."

"You knew the deceased?" Joe had expected Vera to take charge of the conversation, but she was still staring at Wood's body, apparently lost in thought.

"Of course I knew him. He was a fellow trustee. We were working together on the restructuring plan."

Now Vera seemed to wake up. "What did you make of Gilbert? Got on all right, did you?"

"Of course we got on. He was a charming man. He had plans to make the library more attractive to the public. His research into the archives had thrown up a variety of ideas to bring in new members."

"What sort of ideas?"

"He wanted to develop a history group for young people. History was his passion and he was eager to share it, especially since he retired from the university. He thought we could run field trips to archaeological sites, invite guest lecturers."

"Aye," Vera said. "He tried something like that once before. I remember an outing to Hadrian's Wall. My father thought it would be good for me. It was bloody freezing."

"It's not so easy to set up field trips these days," Cath said. "There are implications. Health and Safety. Risk assessment. I wasn't sure it was worth it. Or that we could justify the cost."

Joe sensed that this was an argument that had played out many times before. He was surprised at Vera allowing the conversation to continue. Today, it seemed, she had no sense of urgency.

"Perhaps we should go upstairs," he said, "and talk to the other witnesses."

"Aye," the inspector said. "I suppose we should." But still her attention was fixed on the dead man. It was as if she were fascinated by what she saw. She bent forward so she could see Wood's face without approaching any closer. Then Ashworth led them away, a small solemn procession, back to the body of the library.

They sat around a large table with the vacuum jug of coffee and a plate of digestive biscuits in the middle. There were six of them now. Sebastian Charles had been called in from the landing and Zoë had emerged from the counter. Joe Ashworth thought she looked hardly more than a child, her face bare of make-up. He saw now that she was tiny, her bones frail as a bird's. The pink hair made her look as if she were in fancy dress.

"This is where the old ones sit," Vera said. "The retired men and the batty old ladies, chewing the fat and putting the world to rights. Well, I suppose that's what we're doing too. Putting the world to rights. There's something unnatural about having a murderer on the loose." She looked at them all. "Who was the last person to see him alive?"

"I saw him at lunchtime," Zoë said. "He went out to buy a sandwich, and for a walk, to clear his head, he said. Just for half an hour."

"What time was that?"

"Between midday and twelve-thirty." Zoë wiped her eyes again. She made no noise, but the tears continued to run down her face. Like a tap with a dodgy washer, Joe thought, only leaking silently. No irritating drips. "He brought me a piece of cheesecake from the bakery. A gift. He knew it was my favourite."

"Any advance on twelve-thirty?"

Joe found it hard to understand his boss's attitude. She'd known the victim yet there was this strange flippancy, as if the investigation were a sort of game, or a ritual that had to be followed. Perhaps it was this place, all these books. It was easy to think of the murder as just another story.

"We had a brief discussion on the back stairs," Alec Cole said. "Just after Gilbert had gone out for lunch, I suppose. He was on his way down to the Silence Room to continue his work on the archives. I'd just gone to the gents. I asked how things were going. He said he'd made a fascinating discovery that would prove the link between one of the early curators of the Lit and Phil Museum and the archaeology of Hadrian's Wall. Esoteric to the rest of us, I suppose, but fascinating to him."

"Did you notice if anyone else was working in the room?" Vera asked.

"I couldn't see. The door was shut and I was on my way upstairs when Gilbert went in."

"And if there *were* anyone inside he wouldn't greet Gilbert," Vera said. "Because of the rule of silence. So you wouldn't hear anything either way." She paused. "What about you, Cath? Did you see him?"

"Just first thing when he arrived. He must have passed the office when he went out to lunch and I always have my door open but I didn't notice him. I'm snowed under at the moment and I only left my desk to go to the ladies or to pour myself a coffee."

"And then you found him, Sebastian."

The poet gave a slow, cat-like smile. "I went down to start work and there he was, just as you saw him. It was a shock, of course, and rather horrible even though I've felt like killing him myself a few times."

"You don't seem very shocked!" At last Zoë's tears stopped and now she was angry. "I don't know how you can sit there and make a joke of it."

"Not a very good joke, sweetie. And you all know I couldn't stand the man. It would be stupid to pretend otherwise just for the inspector."

"Why didn't you like him?" For the first time Vera seemed mildly interested.

"He was creepy," Sebastian said. "And self-serving. All this work with the archives was about making a name for himself, not raising funds for the library."

They sat for a moment in silence. They heard the insect buzzing of the central heating system in the background. Joe waited for Vera to comment but again she seemed preoccupied. "Is the only access to the Silence Room through here?" he asked. Again he felt the need to move things on. The library was very warm and he found the dark wood and the high shelves oppressive. It was as if they were imprisoned by all the words.

"Yes," Cath said. "The doors downstairs are locked from our side when the music exams are taking place."

"So the murderer must be one of you," Vera said.

She looked slowly round the table. Joe thought again that it was as if she were playing a parlour game, though there was nothing playful in her expression. Usually at the beginning of an investigation she was full of energy and imagination. Now she only seemed sad. It occurred to Joe that the victim would have been just ten years older than her. Perhaps she'd had a teenage crush on him when he'd led her on the field trip to the Roman wall. Perhaps the earlier flippancy had been her way of hiding her grief. Vera continued to speak.

"You'd better tell me now what happened. As I said before, it's unnatural having a murderer on the loose. Let's set the world to rights, eh?"

Nobody spoke.

"Then I'll tell you a story of my own," she said. "I'll make my own confession." She leaned forward so her elbows were on the table. "I was about twelve," she said. "An awkward age and I was an awkward child. Not as big as I am now, but lumpy and clumsy with large feet and a talent for speaking out of turn. My mother died when I was very small and I was brought up by my father, Hector. His passion was collecting: birds' eggs, raptors. Illegal, of course, but he always thought he was above the law. Had a fit when I applied to the police..." Her voice trailed away and she flashed a smile at them. "But that was much later and perhaps Gilbert had something to do with that too.

"Gilbert was kind to me. The first adult to take me seriously. He was a PhD student at the university. A geek, I suppose we'd call him now. Passionate about his history. Alec was quite right about that. He listened to me and asked my opinion, more comfortable with a bright kid than with other grown-ups maybe. He bought me little presents." She looked at Zoë. "Some things don't change it seems."

Vera shifted in her seat. Joe saw that they were all engrossed in her story and that they were all waiting for her to continue.

"These days we'd call it grooming," she said. "Then we were more innocent. Hector saw nothing wrong with entrusting me to the care of a virtual stranger for days at a time while we scrambled around bits of Roman wall. He couldn't believe, I suppose, that anyone could find me sexually attractive. And, to be fair, he assumed that other kids would be there too. At first I revelled in it. The attention. Gilbert had a car and, sitting beside him, I felt like a princess. He brought a picnic. Cider. My first taste of alcohol. And the arm around my shoulder, the hand on my knee, what harm could there be in that?"

She came to a stop again.

"He sexually assaulted me." Her voice was suddenly bright and brittle. "One afternoon in May. Full sunshine and birds singing fit to bust. Skylarks and curlew. We'd climbed on to the moors beyond the wall, to get a proper view of the scale of it, he said. There was nobody about for miles. He spread out a blanket and pulled me down with him. There was a smell of warm grass and sheep shit. I fought back, but he was stronger than me. In the end there was nothing I could do but let him get on with it. Afterwards he cried."

She looked up at them. "I didn't cry. I wasn't going to give him the satisfaction."

For a moment Joe was tempted to reach out and touch her hand, but that of course would have been impossible.

"I never told anyone," Vera said. "Who would I tell? Hector? A teacher? How could I? I refused to go out with Gilbert again and Hector called me moody and ungrateful. But I should have told. I should have gone to the police. Because the man had committed a crime and the law is all we have to hold things together."

Vera stood up.

"I don't believe he's changed," she said. "He wasn't stopped, you see. He got away with it. My responsibility. We'll find images of children on his computer, no doubt about that." She turned to Sebastian Charles. "You were right. He was a creepy man."

She paused for a moment. "So who killed him?" Her voice became gentle; at least, as gentle as a hippo's could be. "You look like a twelve-year-old, Zoë. Did he try it on with you?"

"No!" The woman was horrified.

"Of course not. It wasn't a child's body he wanted as much as a child's mind. The need to control and to teach."

Vera turned again, this time to the middle-aged librarian, who was sitting next to her. "Why don't you tell us what happened?"

Cath was very upright in her chair. She stared ahead of her. For a moment Ashworth thought she would refuse to speak. But the words came at last, carefully chosen and telling.

"He befriended Evie, my elder daughter. When my husband left last year she was the person most affected by our separation. She's always been a shy child and she became uncommunicative and withdrawn. Gilbert had been part of our lives since I first took over here. I invited him to family parties and to Sunday lunch. I suppose I felt sorry for him. And I thought it would be good for Evie to have some male influence once Nicholas left. He made history come alive for her with his stories of Roman soldiers and the wild border reivers. On the last day of the October half-term he took her out. Like your father, I assumed other children would be present. That was certainly the impression he gave. Like your father, it never occurred to me that she could come to harm with him."

"He assaulted her," Vera said.

"She won't tell me exactly what happened. He threatened her, I think. Made her promise to keep secrets. But something happened that afternoon. It's as if she's frozen, a shell of the child she once was. The innocence sucked out of her. I should be grateful, I suppose, that she's alive and that he brought her home to me." Cath looked at Vera. "The only thing she did say was that he cried."

"So you killed him?"

"I went to the Silence Room to talk to him. I knew he was alone there. Zoë was busy on the phone and didn't notice that I left the office. I asked him what he'd done to Evie. He put his finger to his lips. 'I think you of all people should respect the tradition of the Silence Room,' he said in a pompous whisper, barely loud enough for me to hear. I shouted then: 'What did you to my child?'" Telling the story, Cath raised her voice so she was shouting again.

She caught her breath for a moment and then she continued: "Gilbert set down his pen. 'Nothing that she didn't want me to do,' he said. 'And nothing that you'll be able to prove.' He was still whispering. Then he started work again. That was when I picked up the book he was reading. That was when I killed him. I left the Silence Room, collected a mug of coffee at the top of the stairs and returned to my office."

Nobody spoke.

"Oh, pet," Vera said. "Why didn't you come to me?"

"What would you have done, Vera? Dragged Evie through the courts, forced her to give evidence, to be examined? Don't you think she's been through enough?"

"And now?" Vera cried. "What will happen to her now?"

Joe sat as still as the rest of them but thoughts were spinning round his mind. What would he have done? *I wouldn't have let my daughter out with a pervert in the first place. I'll never leave my wife.* But he knew that however hard he tried, he could never protect his children from all the dangers of the world. And that he'd probably have killed the bastard too. He stood up.

"Catherine Richardson, I'm arresting you for the murder of Gilbert Wood." It was Vera, pre-empting him. Taking responsibility. Putting the world to rights.

THE UNKNOWN CRIME

Sarah Rayne

I'VE NEVER BEEN a high-profile thief. I'd better make that clear at the start. But I'm moderately prosperous and over the years I've developed my own line in small, rare antiques. An elegant chased silver chalice from some obscure museum, perhaps, or a Georgian sugar sifter.

But I've always had a yen to commit a crime that would create international headlines. The removal of the Koh-i-noor or St Edward's Crown or a Chaucer first folio. You're probably smiling smugly, but there are people who will pay huge sums of money for such objects. (I'd be lying if I said the money didn't interest me.)

And then my grandfather died, leaving me all his belongings, and the dream of a theft that would echo round the world and down the years suddenly came within my grasp.

He lived in Hampstead, my grandfather, and the solicitors sent me the keys to the house. I didn't go out there immediately; I was absorbed in a delicate operation involving the removal of a Venetian glass tazza from a private collection – very nice, too. A saucer-shaped dish on a stem, beautifully engraved. So between tazzas and fences (yes, they *do* still exist as a breed and I have several charming friends among the fraternity), it was a good ten days before I went out to Hampstead. And the minute I stepped through the door I had the feeling of something waiting for me. Something that could give me that elusive, longed-for crime.

I was right. I found it – at least the start of it – in a box of old letters and cards in the attic. I know that sounds hackneyed, but attics really are places where secrets are stored and Rembrandts found. And, as my grandfather used to say, if you can't find a Rembrandt to flog, paint one yourself. My father specialized in stealing jewellery, but my grandfather was a very good forger. He was just as good at replacing the real thing with his fakes. If you've ever been in the National Gallery and stood in front of a certain portrait… Let's just say he fooled a great many people.

At first look the attic wasn't very promising. But there was a box of papers which appeared to have been my great-grandfather's. He was a bit of mystery, my great-grandfather, but there's a family legend that he was involved in the theft of the Irish Crown Jewels in 1907. My father used to say he had never been nearer the Irish Crown Jewels than the pub down the road, but I always hoped the legend was true. And it has to be said, the Irish Crown Jewels never were recovered.

It wasn't the Irish Crown Jewels I found in that house, though. It was something far more intriguing.

Most of the box's contents were of no interest. Accounts for tailoring (the old boy sounded as if he had been quite a natty dresser), and faded postcards and receipts. But at the very bottom of the box was a sheaf of yellowing notes in writing so faded it was nearly indecipherable.

How my grandfather missed those papers I can't imagine. Perhaps he never went up to the attics, or perhaps he couldn't be bothered to decipher the writing. If your work is forging fine art and Elizabethan manuscripts, it'd be a bit of a busman's holiday to pore over faded spider-scrawls that will most likely turn out to be somebody's mislaid laundry list or a recipe for Scotch broth.

But the papers were neither of those things.

They were an account of Great-grandfather's extraordinary activities during the autumn of 1918.

October 1918

I've been living in an underground shelter with German shells raining down at regular intervals for what feels like years, although

I believe it's actually only three weeks. But whether it's three weeks or three days, it's absolute hell and I'd trade my virtue (ha!) to be back in England.

You'd expect a battlefield to be cut off from the rest of the world, but we get some news here: how the Germans have withdrawn on the Western Front, how the Kaiser's going to abdicate, even how a peace treaty is being hammered out. It's difficult to know what's truth and what's propaganda, though. And then last night I was detailed to deliver a message a couple of miles along the line.

I'm not a coward, but I'm not a hero either and it doesn't take a genius to know that a lone soldier, scurrying along in the dark, is a lot more vulnerable than if he's in a properly dug trench, near a gun-post. But orders are orders and I delivered the message, then returned by a different route. That's supposed to fool the enemy, although I should think the enemy's up to most of the tricks we play, just as we're up to most of theirs.

I was halfway back when I saw the château. The chimes of midnight were striking in the south and there was the occasional burst of gunfire somewhere to the north. It was bitterly cold and I daresay I was temporarily mad or even suffering from what's called shell-shock. But I stood there for almost an hour, staring at that château. It called out to me – it beckoned like Avalon or Valhalla or the Elysian Fields.

I was no longer conscious of the stench of death and cordite and the chloride of lime that's used to sluice out the trenches. I could smell wealth: paintings, silver, tapestries...

But I can't drag a Bayeux tapestry or a brace of French Impressionists across acres of freezing mud. Whatever I take will have to be small. And saleable. There's no point in taking stuff that hasn't got a market. I remember the disastrous affair of the Irish Crown Jewels...

The present

That's as far as I read that first day. The light was going and the electricity was off, and it's not easy to decipher a hundred-year-old scrawl in an attic in semi-darkness. Also, I had to complete the sale of the tazza. That went smoothly, of course. I never visualized otherwise. I'm very good at what I do. That night I celebrated with a couple of friends. I have no intention of including in these pages what somebody once called the interesting revelations of the bedchamber; I'll just say when I woke up I was in a strange bed and I wasn't alone. And since one can't just get up and go home after breakfast in that situation (*very* ungentlemanly), it was a couple of days before I returned to Great-grandfather's papers.

November 1918

For two weeks I thought I wouldn't be able to return to the château. You can't just climb out of the trenches and stroll across the land-scape at will.

Then last night I was chosen to act as driver for several of the high-ranking officers travelling to Compiègne, and I thought – that's it! For once the British army, God bless it, has played right into my hands. I'll deposit my officers in Compiègne, then I'll sneak a couple of hours on my own.

We set off early this morning – it's 10 November, if anyone reading this likes details.

Later

I have no idea where we are, except that it's in Picardie. I've been driving for almost an hour and it's slow progress. We've stopped at an inn for a meal; the officers are muttering to one another and glancing round as if to make sure no one's listening.

I'm in the garden, supposedly taking a breath of air, but actually I'm staring across at the château and writing this. I can see the place clearly, and it's a beautiful sight.

The present

I was interrupted by the phone ringing. A furtive voice asked if it had the right number and, on being assured it had, enquired if I would be interested in discussing a jewelled egg recently brought out of Russia. Yes, it was believed to be Fabergé. No, it was not exactly for sale, simply considered surplus to requirements. A kindness, really, to remove it.

"Considered surplus by whom?"

"A gentleman prepared to pay very handsomely. He could see you in an hour."

I hesitated. On the one hand I had Great-grandfather's exploits. On the other hand was the lure of a Fabergé egg.

Fabergé won. Thieves have to eat and pay bills like anyone and I had recently bought a very snazzy dockside apartment.

I rather enjoyed that job. There were electronic sensors in the floor, so I used a simple block and tackle arrangement, which I slid along by means of a suspended pulley-wheel. I scooped the egg from its velvet bed, stashed it in the zipped pocket of my anorak, then wound the pulley back and hopped out through the window.

The client was a charming and cultured gentleman of complicated nationality and apparently limitless funds, and we celebrated the transaction liberally with vodka and caviar. After that we discussed Chekhov and explored the causes of the Russian Revolution until he fell off the chair while making a toast to the House of Romanov and had to be taken to the local A&E with a fractured wrist.

A&E were busy and we were there all night. But my client was polite and civilized during the whole time.

10 November 1918

We're all being very polite and civilized during this journey, whatever its purpose might be. We're even being civilized to the enemy – half an hour ago we were overtaken by a car carrying three Germans of unmistakable high rank. I didn't panic until we came upon them a few hundred yards further along, parked on the roadside.

"They've got a puncture," said the colonel in the back of my car, and told me to stop in case we could help.

"Are you mad, sir?" said the major next to him. "It'll be a trick. They'll shoot us like sitting ducks."

"We're all bound for the same place, you fool. There won't be any shooting."

I don't pretend to much mechanical knowledge, but I can change a wheel with the best – although it felt strange to do so alongside a man with whose country we had been at war for four years. I expected a bullet to slam into my ribs at any minute, and I promise you I kept a heavy wrench near to hand. But we got the job done in half an hour, with our respective officers circling one another like cats squaring up for a fight.

I stowed the punctured wheel in the boot.

"Not too close to that case," said the German driver, pointing to a small attaché case.

"Why? It hasn't got a bomb in it, has it?"

"Oh, no," he said, earnestly. He had better English than I had German.

"It contains a— I have not the word—" He gestured to his own left hand where he wore a signet ring.

"A ring? Signet ring?"

"Signet ring, ach, that is right."

"From a lady?"

He glanced over his shoulder, and then, in a very low voice, he said, "From the Kaiser. I am not supposed to know, but I overhear... It's for the signing of the Peace Treaty."

I didn't believe him. Would you? I didn't believe a Peace Treaty was about to be signed, and even if it was, I didn't believe Kaiser Bill would send his signet ring to seal the document. Nobody used sealing wax and signet rings any longer.

Or did they? Mightn't an Emperor of the old Prussian Royal House do just that? In the face of defeat and the loss of his imperial crown, mightn't he make that final arrogant gesture?

"So," said the German driver, "it is to be well guarded, you see."

I did see. I still didn't entirely believe him, but I didn't disbelieve him. So, when he got back into his car, I reached into that attaché case. I expected it to be locked and it was. But it was a flimsy lock –

not what you'd expect of German efficiency – and it snapped open as easily as any lock I ever forced. No one was looking and I reached inside and took out a small square box, stamped with a coat of arms involving an eagle. I put the case quietly in my pocket, got back into the car, and drove on.

The present

Infuriatingly, the next few pages were badly damaged – by the look of them they had been shredded by industrious mice or even rats to make nests. I didn't care if the Pied Piper himself had capered through that attic, calling up the entire rodent population of Hampstead as he went. I needed to know what came next.

Clearly Great-grandfather had driven high-ranking officials to that historic meeting in a railway carriage in Compiègne Forest, at which the Armistice ending the Great War was signed. And on the very threshold of that iconic meeting, he had planned to go yomping off to some nameless château to liberate it of easily transportable loot! Carrying with him what might be Wilhelm II's signet ring.

I carried the entire box of papers home, but after several hours poring over the disintegrated sections I gave up, and hoped I could pick up the thread in the pages that were still intact.

11 November 1918

Well! Talk about Avalon and Gramarye! I got into that château at dawn, and it was so easy they might as well have rolled out a welcome mat.

And if ever there was an Aladdin's cave…

The family who owned it must have left very hastily indeed, because it didn't look as if they taken much with them. The place was stuffed to the gunnels with silver and gold plate, paintings, furniture… But I kept to the rule I had made earlier and only took small objects. Salt cellars, sugar sifters, candle snuffers. Some Chinese jade figurines, and a pair of amber-studded snuff boxes.

Beautiful and saleable, all of them. I thought – if I survive this war, I shall live like a lord on the proceeds of this.

And so I would have done if the military police hadn't come chasing across the countryside. You'd have thought that with a Peace Treaty being signed – probably at that very hour – they'd overlook one soldier taking a few hours extra to return to his unit. But no, they must needs come bouncing and jolting across the countryside in one of their infernal jeeps.

I had the stolen objects in my haversack, and I ran like a fleeing hare. I had no clear idea where I was going and I didn't much care, but I got as far as a stretch of churned-up landscape, clearly the site of a very recent battle. There were deep craters and a dreadful tumble of bodies lying like fractured dolls half-buried in mud. The MPs had abandoned their jeep, but I could see its lights cutting a swathe through the dying afternoon, like huge frog's eyes searching for prey. Prey. Me.

The haversack was slowing me down, so eventually I dived into the nearest crater and lay as still as I could. It was a fairly safe bet they would find me, and probably I would get a week in the glass-house, but if they found the château loot I would get far worse than a week in the glass-house. And find it they would, unless I could hide it...

I'm not proud of what I did next. I can only say that war makes people do things they wouldn't dream of in peacetime.

There were four dead men in that crater. I had no means of recognizing any of them, partly because they were so covered with mud and partly – well, explosives don't make for tidy corpses. I chose the one who was least disfigured, and tipped the stash into the pockets of his battledress, buttoning up the flaps. He was a sergeant in a Lincolnshire regiment. I memorized his serial number.

One last thing I did in those desperate minutes. I slipped the Kaiser's signet ring out of its velvet box and put it on the man's hand.

Then I stood up and walked towards the MPs, my hands raised in a rueful gesture of surrender.

* * *

I didn't get a week in the glass-house. I didn't even get forty-eight hours. Armistice was declared at eleven o'clock that morning, and four hours filched by a soldier who had driven the colonel to the signing of the Peace Treaty was overlooked.

And after the celebrations had calmed down, those of us who had survived had to bury the dead.

They say every story is allowed one coincidence and here's mine. I was one of the party detailed to bury the bodies from the very battlefield where I had hidden. That Lincolnshire sergeant was where I had left him, lying in the mud, his jacket securely buttoned, the signet ring on the third finger of his right hand. I promise you, if I could have got at any of the stuff I would have done, but there were four of us on the task and I had no chance.

But when they brought the coffins out, I watched carefully and I saw my Lincolnshire sergeant put into one with an unusual mark on the lid – a burr in the oak that was almost the shape of England.

The present

The journal ended there. Can you believe that? I felt as if I had been smacked in the face when I realized it, and I sat back, my mind tumbling. What had my great-grandfather done next? Had he tried to get into the coffin later? But he couldn't have done. If the signet ring of the last German Emperor had been up for grabs after the Armistice, I would have known. The whole world would have known.

I went back to Hampstead next morning. I intended to scour that house from cellar to attics to find out if Great-grandfather had recovered the Kaiser's signet ring from the coffin—

I've just reread that last sentence, and it's probably the most bizarre thing I've ever written. Hell's teeth, it's probably the most bizarre thing anyone has ever written. I hope I haven't fallen backwards into a surreal movie or a rogue episode of *Dr Who*, and not noticed.

But there were no more journal pages. Eventually, I conceded defeat, and returned to my own flat. This time I ransacked the few

family papers I possessed. I don't keep anything that could incrim-
inate any of us, of course – there's such a thing as loyalty, even
though my family are all dead. But there were birth certificates,
carefully edited savings accounts – burglars have to be cautious
about investments. Too much money and the Inland Revenue start
to get inconveniently interested. My father used to buy good antique
furniture; my grandfather invested in gold and silver. I don't know
what my great-grandfather did.

There were letters there, as well, mostly kept by my parents out of
sentiment, and it was those letters I wanted. I thought there might
be some from my great-grandmother and I was right; there were
several. Most were of no use, but one was dated September 1920,
and attached to it was a semi-order for Great-grandfather to report
to the HQ of his old regiment. He had, it seemed, been chosen "at
random" to be one of the soldiers who would assist in exhuming six
sets of "suitable" remains from battlefields in France.

Random, I thought, cynically. I'll bet he contrived it, the sly old
fox.

The six coffins, said the letter, would be taken by special escort to
Flanders on the night of 7 November. A small private ceremony
would take place in the chapel of St Pol, and Great-grandfather
would be one of the guard of honour.

By that time a pattern was starting to form in my mind, and I
unfolded my great-grandmother's letter with my blood racing. It
read, *"My dear love... What an honour for you to be chosen for
that remarkable ceremony. When you described it in your last letter
it was so vivid, I felt I was there with you... The small, flickeringly
lit chapel, the six coffins each draped with the Union Jack... The
Brigadier General led in, blindfolded, then placing his hand on one
of the coffins to make the choice..."*

That was when my mind went into meltdown and it was several
minutes before I could even get to the bookshelves. Eventually,
though, I rifled through several reference books, and in all of them
the information was the same.

*"From the chapel of St Pol in Northern France, the Unknown
Soldier began the journey to the famous tomb within Westminster*

Abbey... The man whose identity will never be known, but who was killed on some unnamed battlefield... The symbol of all men who died in battle no matter where, and the focus for the grief of hundreds of thousands of bereaved..."

Great-grandmother's letter ended with the words, *"How interesting that you recognized the coffin chosen as one you had helped carry from that battlefield shortly before the Armistice. I wonder if, without that curious burr, you would have known it? It's a sobering thought that you are probably the only person in the whole world who knows the identity of the Unknown Warrior."*

All right, what would *you* have done? Gone back to your ordinary life, with the knowledge that the grave of the Unknown Warrior – that hugely emotive symbol of death in battle – contained probably the biggest piece of loot you would ever encounter? The signet ring of the last Emperor of Germany – the ring intended to seal the Peace Treaty that ended the Great War. Wilhelm II's ring, that never reached its destination because a German car had a puncture.

The provenance of that signet ring was – and is – one hundred per cent genuine. It's documented in Great-grandfather's journal and Great-grandmother's letter. Collectors would pay millions.

It's calling to me, that iron-bound casket, that unknown soldier's tomb that's the focus for memories and pride and grief every 11 November. It's calling with the insistence of a siren's seductive song... Because of course it's still in there, that ring, along with the loot taken from the French château. It must be, because in almost a century there's never been the least hint of anyone having tried to break into that tomb.

I'm ending these notes now, because I have an appointment. I'm joining a party of tourists being taken round Westminster Abbey. Quite a detailed tour, actually. After I come home I shall start to draw a very detailed map of the Abbey. Then I shall make precise notes of security arrangements and guards, electronic eyes, CCTV cameras...

THE LADDER

Adrian McKinty

Donald sighed as the university loomed out of the rain and greyness. All morning he had hit nothing but red lights and now, although it was green, he had to stop because a huge gang of students was crossing the pedestrian walkway in front of him.

It was rag week and they were wearing costumes: animals, Cossacks, knights, milkmaids. Predictable and drab, the outfits had a home-made look and they depressed him. The students were laughing and some were actually skipping. It was raining, it was cold, it was November in godforsaken Belfast so what the hell had they to laugh about?

The traffic light went red and then amber and then green again and still they hadn't all got across. He was tempted to honk them off the road but no doubt from hidden pockets they would produce flour-and-water bombs and throw them at him. He sat there patiently while the car behind began to toot. He looked in the rearview at a vulnerable, orange VW Microbus. Yeah, you keep doing that, mate, he said to himself, and sure enough half a dozen eggs cut up the poor fool's windscreen.

He chortled to himself as the mob cleared and he turned into the car park.

"Jesus, is that a grin?" McCann asked him when he appeared in the office.

He nodded.

"What, have you got a job offer somewhere?" McCann wondered.

"No, old chap, I am doomed to spend my declining years with your boorish self and my cretinous students in this bombed-out hell-hole of a city slowly sinking into the putrid mudflats from which it so inauspiciously began."

"Bugger, if I'd known I was going to get an essay..." McCann said, not all that good-naturedly.

Donald took off his jacket and set it down on the chair. "Is this coffee drinkable?" he asked, staring dubiously at the tarry black liquid in the coffee pot.

"Drinkable yes. Distinguishable as coffee, no."

Donald poured himself a cup anyway, added two sugars and picked up the morning paper.

"Before I lose interest entirely, why were you smiling when you came in? Some pretty undergraduate, no doubt?" McCann asked.

"No, no, nothing like that, I'm afraid. The students went after some hippy driving a VW Microbus... talk about devouring your own."

"Aye. I've seen that thing around. New guy. Been parking in my spot. Kicked his side panels a few times. Buckled like anything. It's an original. Those old ones are bloody death traps."

"A windscreen covered with eggs and flour won't make it any safer."

McCann took out his pipe and began filling it with tobacco. Donald went back to the paper. "So what's on the old agenda today anyway?" McCann asked.

"Nothing in the morning. Playing squash at lunchtime and then we're doing *The Miller's Tale* after lunch."

"*The Miller's Tale*? Which one's that?"

"Do you actually want to know?"

"Well, not really, I suppose," McCann replied, somewhat shamefaced.

The hours passed by in a haze of tobacco smoke, bad coffee, worse biscuits and dull news from the paper.

At twelve Donald slipped off, only to be intercepted by a student outside the gym.

"Dr Bryant," the student began in a lilting voice, and Donald remembered that he was a Welshman called Jones or Evans or something.

"Mr Jones, how can I help you today?"

"Uh, actually my name is—"

"Yes, Mr Jones, how I can help you? Come on. Out with it, man. I'm in a hurry."

"Uhm, Dr Bryant, I'm supposed to do a presentation next week on Jonson..."

"Ben or Sam or, God save us, Denis?"

"Uhhh, the playwright."

"They all wrote plays, Mr Jones."

"They did? Uhm, well, it's Ben. Yeah. And, well, the library doesn't have the secondary sources... someone took them all and I don't know what to do really. I tried to borrow them from the University of Ulster library but they're out too. I've read all the primary stuff, but I want the secondary sources to do a good job."

Donald felt a pinprick of guilt. Mr Jones seemed like a nice, sincere young man. One of the few good students. He was studying engineering but was taking English as an elective. Perhaps that explained his curious dedication. The BAs in English were all perverts and drug fiends. "All right, Mr Jones, come by my office at four today and I'll lend you my own books, they should be sufficient for a half-decent presentation. You'll be careful with them, won't you?"

"Oh, God, yeah, thank you, thank you very much," the student said.

Donald arrived at the gym feeling unnaturally buoyant – two quite pleasant incidents in one morning.

He showed his ID to Peter Finn, the ancient security guard at the reception desk.

"Afternoon, Dr Bryant," Peter said in his rough country accent.

"Afternoon," he replied curtly.

"Going to give the wee muckers another hiding, eh?"

"One tries, Peter, one tries."

"You still at the top?" Peter asked, knowing full well the answer. Donald swelled a little. "Still plugging away."

"Sixteen straight months, Professor Millin says. Yon's a record, ye know," Peter said very seriously.

"Is it indeed?" Donald said, and this time it was his turn to pretend.

"Aye."

"Well, all good things must come to an end sometime. This new crop of lecturers is giving me a run for my money," Donald said magnanimously.

Peter winked at him as if he didn't quite believe him.

Donald grinned, went to the basement, found locker 201 and changed quickly into his gear: a casual blue tee-shirt, white shorts, white socks and an old pair of Adidas squash sneakers. He looked at himself in the mirror. He was in the prime of life. His eyes were clear, his cheeks clean-shaved, his hair jet black with only a few strands of invading grey around the ears.

Fenton was late and Donald tried hard not to show his irritation. Fenton was a slightly younger man and he was nimble. He was number three on the squash ladder and by no means an unworthy opponent. Fenton playing above his game and Donald playing beneath his could pretty much even out the field. Fenton changed into his kit: pristine white shorts, Fred Perry top and a brand new racket.

They walked to the court, stretched, warmed up the ball.

Donald won the racquet spin.

He served a high looping ball that died in the corner. Fenton made an attempt to return it but he had no chance. Donald served five more like that before Fenton managed to get one back and by that time it was too late – his confidence was broken. Donald won the match three games to one, Fenton's sole game coming from Donald's largesse. When he was in control it was Donald's policy always to let an opponent win at least one game so that no one would ever know the true picture of his ability.

They showered and had a quick gin and tonic in the bar before Donald went off to his lecture. It was nearly a full house, the students didn't ask stupid questions and he was in good form when he set off for home at four o'clock. Halfway to the car he remembered about young Jones and went back to his office. Amazingly the undergraduate was on time and he gave him the books without further ado.

"Quite the day," he said to himself as he walked to his Volvo Estate under a clearing sky. Susan noticed his good mood immediately as he picked her up outside the Ulster Bank on Botanic Avenue. "You're in a good mood," she said.

"Yes," he said. "Let's eat out at the new Italian."

"What about your aubergine lasagne?"

"We'll give it to the dog."

"What dog?"

"Any dog."

The drive to Carrickfergus was easy, the new Italian was acceptable, the sommelier complimented him on his choice of wine.

He parked the Volvo outside his neat, mock-Tudor detached house near the Marina. After another cheeky bottle of Tuscan red he and Susan had sex only slightly less exciting than that he'd been lecturing about this afternoon in *The Miller's Tale.*

As days go, it wasn't bad and when the university loomed out of the mist next morning, this time he didn't sigh.

Susan, getting a lift to Belfast for the shopping, smiled at him.

"It's growing on you," she said.

"Perhaps," he agreed.

"You're playing Fenton today in your silly squash thing, aren't you?"

"Oh, no, that was yesterday. And it's not silly. He was the third seed. Psyched him out completely, poor chap. Went to pieces. Had to go easy on him."

"So you're still top of the ladder?"

Donald was a little surprised at the question. Of course he was still top. Did she seriously think he could take her out to the expensive new Italian restaurant, get the priciest plonk on the menu and be happy as a clam if he was off the top? My God, what kind of cipher did she think she'd married?

"Oh, yes, I think so," he said casually.

She started talking about something or other but he was replaying the game in his mind, wondering if his backhand was still quite as strong as his lob. He left her outside the bank.

"So you'll drive me to the soup kitchen on Saturday?" she asked, getting out of the car.

"I'll drive you," he said, and then after a pause added: "What soup kitchen, what are you talking about?"

"Haven't you been listening? Our reading group. That book really affected us and we're volunteering at the soup kitchen on Saturday. Christmas is coming, you know."

He tried to think what the book could be. Something by Orwell perhaps, or Dickens, or some ghastly novel set among the poor of India.

"Of course I'll drive you. In fact, I think I'll even go. Help out."

"You?" she said incredulously.

"Me, yes. Why so shocked? I'm a Labour man through and through. Help the common people, each according to his needs and from, uh, you know...that's my motto," he said with only semi-sarcasm, for she had hurt him a little with her surprise.

The week went by like every other week and on Saturday he did help out in the soup kitchen and it was by no means completely unpleasant. Some of the indigent were witty and grateful fellows fallen on hard times and he felt, if not happy, at least content.

The following Monday morning Mr Jones gave his presentation and it wasn't bad and that afternoon he played squash with Professor Millin in the gym. Millin was number six on the ladder, not a serious opponent. An older man, a physics lecturer, well into his forties, although last week he had taken a game off Dunleavy who was currently in second place and Dunleavy was the sort who never let anyone have a game, ever.

"Heard you gave old Fred Dunleavy a run for his money," Donald said conversationally as they walked down to the court.

"The big Scots ganch, I showed him! He's slipping, he's really slipping, getting a paunch. I tell you, you'll cream him next time you play him, cream him," Millin said.

Donald was happy to hear this. Dunleavy was a young Physical Education lecturer and for some time it had been his fear that Dunleavy would one day pull a superb game out of the bag and beat him.

"He's been avoiding me for weeks, I suppose that's why," Donald said with satisfaction.

They paused outside the court to stretch. Donald looked at the squash ladder and was surprised to see a new name way down at the bottom, at number sixteen: V. M. Sinya.

"Who's that?" he said, pointing at the name. Millin was the Ladder Secretary for this term, so he should know.

"Oh, yes, new fella, foreigner, bloody Pak...er, I mean, uh, an Indian gent, I think. Initials stand for Victor Mohammed so I suppose he's a Muslim. He's from Computer Science. A lot of those boys do computers nowadays."

"Is he any good?" Donald asked with a hint of nervousness in his voice. Anyone new could be trouble and several world champions had come from Pakistan.

"How the hell should I know?" Millin replied with great indifference.

"All right, let's go in," Donald said putting all ominous thoughts of the newcomer out of his mind.

He let Millin have a few points early before cruising to an easy victory in four games. He showered, picked up Susan and drove home.

On Thursday the Dean told him that his student evaluations were up since last term and, after buttering him up, asked if he'd ever considered standing for the University Council. He had no such intention but the thought that the Dean was interested in him pleased him immensely.

On Friday he had a game with McCann who was number twelve on the ladder. McCann had been quite a useful little player until the drink had become the dominant force in his life. Now all he was left with was a powerful serve and a few trick shots. He had no stamina and he couldn't get about the court. Donald never usually bothered to play anyone this low down but McCann was a friend. When he got to the court he was pleased to see that Mr V. M. Sinya was still at number sixteen. He hadn't even been able to beat old Franklin at fifteen, clearly the man wasn't much of a threat. He found that he was tremendously relieved by this. Was the ladder so important to him that the thought of a mysterious stranger had given him the jitters? He laughed at himself. What a dunderhead you are, he said to himself, and to prove his good humour he let McCann take a couple of games.

On Saturday he was still feeling sufficiently good to help out at the soup kitchen. Also at the weekend he received a letter to say that one of his papers on Chaucer was going to be anthologized in the new collection by Dalrimple. Things, in fact, were going so well that he began to be suspicious that something terrible was about to happen. Perhaps he would be informed that he had some dreadful illness or maybe he would crash the car.

Just in case, he took the train to work on Monday, sitting in a back carriage near the emergency exit and steeling himself for a sudden derailment.

Nothing happened except for fifty gum-chewing, messy, obnoxious children getting on at Greenisland who tormented him all the way to Central Station with their music and pointless celebrity gossip.

His fears of impending disaster were somewhat realized when he showed up at the court to play Dunleavy and he saw that the mysterious Mr Sinya was at number ten on the squash ladder. The man had demolished five opponents in a week! This meant, of course, he had displaced McCann, so at least he could interrogate his friend at lunch.

In an unusually brutal and hurried match he thrashed Dunleavy, showered quickly and found McCann in the office, eating toast and drinking tea mixed with whisky.

"What's Sinya like?" he blurted out before even saying hello.

"Sinya, I've no idea, mate."

"You played him."

"I gave him a bye, he wanted to play me on Friday lunchtime and I just couldn't be bothered."

"You gave him a bye?"

"Yes."

"So maybe that's why he's jumped up the ladder? People have been giving him byes."

"Aye, could be," McCann said, not at all interested.

Relief sank over Donald like chloroform and again he chastised himself for the importance he attached to something so silly as the squash ladder.

The relief lasted until Wednesday when he bumped into Millin coming out of the university bookshop. Millin informed him that

Sinya had demolished him and that he, Sinya, was now number five on the ladder.

"What's he like?" Donald asked, trying not to sound frantic or panicked.

"Oh, he's good. Going to give you a pretty tough game."

"What's he like?" Donald insisted.

"Don't get your knickers in a twist. He's Pakistani. I suppose forty, perhaps older, it's hard to tell with them. He's fast, and my God...that serve, those returns! It's a nightmare. You give him any opportunity and he destroys you. Our match was over in half an hour."

Donald went home that night in a state of distress. He barely talked to Susan and he couldn't concentrate on his proofs for the Dalrimple book.

From his upstairs study he stared at the boats in Carrickfergus marina and the grey castle beyond. The halyards were muzzled by the wind, the granite castle walls kept their own counsel.

Could it be that the squash ladder was perhaps the one thing that gave him any satisfaction, any sense of accomplishment, in what was really a rather pathetic, little, nondescript life?

Not the teaching, not the writing, not even Susan.

And now, inevitably, he was going to face his Nemesis. It was a melodramatic thought but he couldn't shake it.

A few days later the phone rang in his office. With a sense of dread he picked up the receiver. Naturally it was Sinya. He had beaten Fenton and Dunleavy and he would like to play Donald whenever it was convenient.

His voice was pleasant enough, foreign but not very foreign, and gentle. Aye, that's how they get you, Donald thought. Softly softly. Lull you and then go for the jugular. Bastards. Well, he wouldn't let them. He wouldn't take this lying down. This was his league, his campus. Who did this guy think he was, for Christ's sake? He'd been going easy on these chumps, he could take them all with one hand behind his back. This guy was no different. Try to spook me? See about that. He realized that during this prolonged internal soliloquy Sinya had been waiting for a reply on the other end of the phone.

"This afternoon's fine with me. One p.m." he said quickly, hung up and attempted to bury himself in work until just before the match.

He arrived early but Sinya was already there, changed, waiting for him. They shook hands. Sinya was tall, bearded, good-looking. He had a very charming way about him. He smiled easily and was polite. He asked Donald how he was and enquired about Donald's new (bought yesterday) super-light, super-strong, carbon-fibre, state-of-the-art Khan Slazenger Pro racket.

Sinya won the spin, served, and launched a tremendous dying serve that Donald barely returned, but of course Sinya was already at the front wall waiting to volley Donald's weak backhand. Donald, anticipating a crushing return, ran to the back right of the court, but Sinya placed a perfect drop shot in the left front corner, flat-footing Donald and winning the point. Sinya won the next four points and then missed one. On Donald's serve, Sinya volleyed the ball back so fast Donald didn't even see it until it was too late.

The whole match went that way, Donald's play grew worse and forty-five minutes later it was all over. He had managed to take a game but Sinya had easily beaten him: 9-5, 9-4, 7-9, 9-1. Shell-shocked, he let his opponent prattle on about this and that and then watched with horror as Sinya stopped at the noticeboard outside the court and had the cheek to take out Donald's name from the top of the ladder and substitute his own. Couldn't the bastard even have the decency to wait until he was showering?

He drove home and after four hours of silence Susan got it out of him, and of course he agreed that it was only a stupid game and it meant nothing. The next day he went to the court with his new racket and practised serves and drop shots for an hour and called Sinya and asked him for a rematch.

The rematch was on a Friday and this time Sinya took him in straight sets. He realized with horror that Sinya had given him the game he'd won last time as a courtesy, just as he had condescendingly done with the lesser players in his bouts.

They walked back to car park and Sinya stopped at the repulsive Volkswagen Microbus Donald had seen egged by the rag week students.

"Do you want a lift?" he asked. "You're in Carrick, aren't you? I drive all the way to Larne so it would be easy to drop you."

The fact that Sinya lived in Larne, one of the grimmest towns in Ulster, gave Donald no comfort on the silent ride home.

Sinya's reign at the top began and seemed unbreakable. He was miles ahead of all the players. In fact, if he'd been younger he could well have been an international. Weeks went by and Donald played him on and off with little effect. On a weekend game with Fenton, Donald unexpectedly lost, and after another fortnight he was only at number four on the ladder.

Despite the repeated assurances of his wife, his friends and even, on one humiliating occasion, the university's psychological counsellor, that it was only a senseless cardboard list of names, he felt that his work, his health, his libido and his mental outlook were all suffering terribly as he slipped down the ladder.

Christmas came and went, term ended and began again.

McCann was no comfort but Donald found himself spending a lot of time with him in Lavery's or the Bot, enjoying increasingly frequent liquid lunches.

At the gym he noticed now that Peter Finn was cool to him at the door. On a miserable Tuesday morning he played a man called Jennings, lost in straight games and found that he was now last on the ladder. He almost relished this final embarrassment. Now there was no place lower to go.

He slipped upstairs to the cafeteria, called Susan and asked if she could get a lift back to Carrick with one of her friends. He sat, nursing a coffee, watching the sky darken and the lights come on street by street, Sandy Row, the Shankill, the Falls, the illumination moving north to the old shipyards and then down around the university and the City Hospital. In Belfast tonight there would be violence and love and passion and death. People in the hospital would be passing away from cancer, accidents, heart disease, and in other wards dozens of babies were being born. New lives for old.

"It really isn't that important, you know, old man," he said to himself.

"What isn't important?"

He turned. It was Mr Jones, his student from last term's course on the Elizabethans. He was holding a book called *Automotive Engineering Mistakes*.

"Oh, I was just talking to myself. Join me. Have a seat. What on Earth are you reading?"

Jones sat. "It's about design faults in cars. Not just the Ford Pinto. Some pretty famous cars. Even brilliant designers make mistakes."

He got Jones a coffee.

Something McCann had once said came floating back into Donald's mind.

"I heard those Volkswagen Microbuses are a death trap," he said.

Jones grinned. "Oh, yeah! No crumple zone at the front to absorb a crash and the exhaust pipe runs the full length of the floor...oh, boy, you get two holes in the rust and your vehicle's filled with carbon monoxide. Death trap isn't the..."

But Donald was no longer listening.

It would be the easiest thing in the world.

Punch a hole through the floor and the exhaust.

Punch a hole. Let fate take over. If nothing happened, nothing happened. But if Sinya got into an unfortunate accident in the long drive from Belfast to Larne, well, it wouldn't really be Donald's fault. It wouldn't be murder, or attempted murder. It was a design flaw in the vehicle, he was helping nature take its course.

He said goodnight to Jones, ran six flights to the ground floor and out into the wet, cold January darkness.

He knew that it would have to be now. Tonight. If he thought about it, he wouldn't do it at all. He conscience would kick in. His middle-class sensibility. His cowardice.

It would have to be now or never.

He reached the car park. It was six o'clock. Most of the vehicles had gone but the putrid orange Volkswagen was still there. Sinya often worked late. Trying to get ahead no doubt, Donald thought spitefully. He went to his Volvo, rummaged in the boot and found a torch and his toolkit. He locked the boot and walked to the Volkswagen.

"I'm not going to do this, it's not me," he said to himself.

He checked that the coast was clear. No one was within a hundred yards.

"I don't even know what to do. Should have asked Jones for details. Doesn't matter, I'm not going to do anything. I'm not a killer. What I *will* do is take a look underneath, just to see if it's possible."

He scanned the car park again, turned on the torch, squatted on the wet tarmac and looked under the VW. A great hulking exhaust pipe ran almost all the way from the front of the cabin to the back of the car. The pipe was rusted, the chassis was rusted. A few taps from a screwdriver might do the trick...

He stood, checked the car park one more time.

No one.

He was calm.

He lay back down again.

In five minutes it was done.

He had punched a hole in the top of the exhaust pipe and another through to the cabin. He had connected the two holes with a paper coffee cup he had found lying around – squeezing the cup into a tube. If an accident did occur the cup would burn in the fire, and if it didn't it was an innocent enough thing to find stuck under your car.

He wiped himself down, got in his car, sped to the Crown Bar, had two pints of Guinness to calm his nerves and drove home.

In his study he had a double vodka and a cognac but he couldn't sleep.

Susan went to bed and he checked the radio for reports of road accidents, deaths.

He really didn't want Sinya to die. If the poor man was injured that would be enough. Then Donald could resume his march back up the squash ladder and get his life back in order. Get to the top, stop drinking with McCann, start writing his book, have that talk with Susan about kids again...

Finally he drifted off to sleep on the living-room sofa at about three. He woke before the dawn in the midst of a nightmare. Sinya's Volkswagen had plunged off the cliff at the Bla Hole just outside Whitehead. Two hundred feet straight down on to the rocks below. The car had smashed and it was assumed to be an accident but the police had found a paper cup wedged in the exhaust. The murderer had left fingerprints all over it.

Five years earlier Donald had been arrested for cannabis possession at Sussex University. His prints were in the database.

"Oh my God," he said.

He turned on the radio, found the traffic report: a road accident in Omagh, another in County Down, nothing so far on the Belfast-Larne Road.

He paced the living room. What madness had overtaken him? To try to kill a man over something so preposterous as a squash ladder? He had obviously taken leave of his senses. That's what he would do at the trial. He'd plead temporary insanity.

Insane was the right word. Macbeth crazy. Lear crazy.

Susan woke and he was such a mess that she drove him to Belfast.

He thanked her and ran to the car park.

The Volkswagen wasn't there.

"Oh, Christ," he said to himself.

He cancelled his lecture, went to his office and waited for the telephone to ring. He imagined the phone ringing, the resulting brief conversation:

"Is that Dr Bryant?

"Yes."

"This is Detective McGuirk, we'd like to come over and ask you a few questions if that would be okay..."

He found an ancient packet of cigarettes, lit one and sat in his onyx Eclipse Ergonomic Operator Chair waiting. The phone lurked in its cradle...

There was a knock at the door but it was only McCann come by to see if he wanted to go for lunch. He said he wasn't feeling well. It wasn't untrue. He felt sick to his stomach. McCann left. He closed the door and turned the light off. He sat there in the dark. Perhaps they wouldn't ring him. The first he would know about it would be them marching into his office with guns drawn.

He wouldn't go with them. He wouldn't let them take him. His office was on the sixth floor. The window. A brief fall through the damp air. A crash. And then ... nothingness.

He waited.

Waited.

He sank beneath his desk and curled foetally on the floor.

The phone rang.

"Dr Bryant?"

"Sinya?"

"Yes."

It was Sinya. He was alive!

"Yes?" Donald managed.

"Dr Bryant, Professor Millin cancelled with me today and I was wondering if you could squeeze in a quick game?"

"A game? A squash game? Yes, yes, of course, I'll be right over."

He sprinted the stairs.

Sinya was already in the court warming the ball.

He waved to him through the glass, ran to the locker room, changed into his gear and ran back to the court without stretching or getting a drink of water.

He didn't care how suspicious or unsubtle he sounded. He *had* to know.

"I didn't see your car this morning. You're always in first," Donald said.

Sinya grimaced. "That thing tried to kill me. I was halfway home last night and I realized the whole car was stinking of exhaust fumes. I pulled over just before Whitehead. Would you believe it? The whole exhaust is rusted away next to nothing and a paper cup had blown in there and gotten stuck between the exhaust and the car. I left it at the garage in Whitehead and got a taxi home. I suppose I'll have to get it fixed."

Donald grinned with relief.

Emotions were cascading through him: relief, happiness, gratitude.

He would inform Susan tonight that she should go off the pill. He would start going to that soup kitchen again. He would give to charity. He would really get cracking on the book.

This would be his last squash game ever.

"I have really screwed up my priorities, darling," he'd tell Susan. "That silly squash ladder! Something as banal as that. I'm going to be more Zen. Live in the present, live in reality. Real things. You, me, life, stuff like that. It's corny but, well, I've had a moment of clarity. It's about perspective. It all seems so bloody stupid now. God. I mean can you believe how obsessed I was?"

Sinya hit him a few practice shots which he returned with ease.

"Well, I'm sorry about your car, old chap, but I think you can afford a new vehicle with the money they're paying you in computers. And Larne isn't the priciest place in the world to live. You should be more like me. Enjoy life. Live for the moment. Get yourself a Merc or a Beemer. You deserve it," Donald said.

Sinya laughed. "Are you kidding? The university only gives me three hundred a week, you know. A BMW on my wages?"

"Three hundred a week? What are you talking about? A junior lecturer makes twenty-five grand a year. It's more in computers, I'm sure."

Sinya grinned. "I'm not a lecturer. I'm a technician in the computer department. I fix the machines, man. Hardware, software, you name it."

Donald gasped but said nothing.

The game began and Sinya took a mere thirty-five minutes to beat him.

They showered, talked about the weather, shook hands, parted ways.

Donald walked to the English department building.

No one knew, *no one had to know.*

When he got to his office he called Millin and told him. Millin was outraged.

"Doesn't the fellow know that the ladder is only open to faculty? My God, the effrontery."

"You'll do something about it?"

"Of course I will. Right away. I'll scrub the last two months' results and put it back to the way it was at the beginning of December."

Donald hung up the phone. Leaned back in his chair.

Grey sky.

Black sky.

Night.

Stars.

In the car Susan talked about the soup kitchen, birth control. He avoided giving direct answers. They ate separate microwaved meals from Marks & Spencer.

When he got into work the next morning he went straight to the gym. V. M. Sinya's name had disappeared and he, Dr D. Bryant, was again in the number one spot, for the first time in nearly two months.

"The once and future king," Peter said at reception, startling him.

"Yes," he attempted to reply, but his throat was dry and no sound came.

THE HOSTESS

Joel Lane

NOT LONG AFTER I moved to Birmingham in the 1980s, a family feud led to one of the worst crimes in my experience. It happened in Digbeth, an old industrial district now taken over by warehouses and wholesale businesses. The narrow backstreets and rotting factories hid a multitude of stolen goods. But most of the actual crimes happened elsewhere. The Digbeth police station was busier with drunks fighting in the Barrel Organ and the Railway Tavern than with professional villains.

For two decades, the O'Kane family had been significant players in the black economy of Digbeth. They were a family of craftsmen: one could hide the pieces of a stolen car in a dozen vehicles; another could work stolen gold and silver into brand new jewellery. Three of them had done time, but they were a close family and we'd have needed something much nastier to put them out of business. I think the Digbeth team had a sneaking respect for their dedicated work on the wrong side of the disused tracks.

The Marin family were something else again. New money, well-spoken, an attitude you could break a glass on. The three brothers formed the core of an under-achieving but vicious gang that specialized in drugs and prostitutes. Its informal office was the back table of the Bar Selona, a dive frequented by people who'd been banned from the Little Moscow. There were some severe beatings around that time, of men we knew to be involved in similar business. But the victims weren't talking even when their mouths healed.

I saw the youngest Marin brother one night in the Railway Tavern, when I was relaxing off-duty at a rhythm and blues gig. The band finished late, and when I came out of the function room a lock-in was in progress. I might have been tempted to buy a drink, but just at that moment a thin-faced man in a suit entered the pub in the company of a young policewoman. Who wasn't, of course. It was some lad's birthday, and the girl put handcuffs on him before starting a strip-tease. I walked out, but the girl's minder shot me a look that could have frozen vodka.

We had an informer at that time who warned us that the Marin and O'Kane families were at odds. There was a fight outside a pub near the Parcel Force depot that resulted in a close ally of the O'Kanes being glassed: a classic "Belfast kiss". He lost an eye. Then the house of the elder Marin brother burned down when he and his wife were away for the weekend. We found the charred remnants of a petrol-soaked blanket inside a broken rear window. Just after that, something scared our informant so badly that he relocated to the Netherlands.

While we were struggling to get to grips with the situation, Theresa O'Kane went missing on her ninth birthday. She was the only daughter of one of the family's more law-abiding members. He and his wife didn't hesitate to call us. Theresa had been walking home from her school in Highgate with a friend when a car had stopped and two men had got out. One of them had hit the friend with a cosh, and she'd blacked out. When she'd recovered consciousness Theresa was gone.

That night, we put out an appeal on local TV and radio. Nothing. A day of frantic searching and questioning followed. The Marin brothers didn't have perfect alibis – that would have been too obvious – but we had nothing on them. Another night fell with Theresa's parents – both of whom were under thirty – in a state of numb desperation. Then another dark November day. Another night.

The call came at six in the morning. A homeless man, looking for a place to sleep, had wandered through the viaduct off Digbeth High Street after a troubled night. The mewing of seagulls had caught his attention. Behind one of the arches, near the porn cinema, he'd found a heap of dead rats and a few dying gulls. There was an acrid smell in the air. Using a stick, he'd pushed the rats aside – and then run to a phone box.

Theresa O'Kane had been garrotted with wire. Her body cavity had been opened up, packed with rat poison and sewn shut again. Poison had also been forced into her mouth and throat. We were shown post-mortem photos. The body had only been under the viaduct a few hours, but our pathologist estimated the time of death as the evening of the abduction. She hadn't made it through her birthday.

Of course, the murder was in the papers for weeks – though we managed to keep the rat poison quiet. The O'Kane family had to go through the standard press cycle of bogus sympathy, suspicion, revelation, blame, abuse and final indifference. Twenty-eight per cent of *Daily Mail* readers thought the O'Kanes were tragic victims, while seventy-two per cent thought their criminal record was directly responsible for the child's death. It was business as usual: the memory of a dead child being tainted, circulated to the masses and put to work on the streets.

Small wonder that the O'Kane family sold their homes and were scattered overseas before the end of the year. The Marins continued their operations. We never managed to prove their connection to the murder, let alone the vicious symbolic gesture that followed it. But within a couple of years, we had some luck with their drugs racket and put the two elder brothers away. They weren't sufficiently big-time to own the police or local authorities. Then the youngest brother died of a septic ulcer, and the gang was finished. Other bastards replaced them, of course.

Years passed. I moved to the Acocks Green station and lost interest in Digbeth. The area slipped further into silence, with old houses and even churches being used as storage space for construction materials. As rents fell and concern for preservation became increasingly absurd, the ground was laid for the area's colonization by offices – but that was still a decade off. Turf wars were still going on: pubs were set on fire, building projects were subject to overnight "accidents". The only people living in the district were in hostels or on the streets.

I'm not sure when it started – some time in the early nineties. We thought it was one of the new gangs making its presence felt. An old

man who'd been drinking in the Eagle and Tun was found dead in
Lower Trinity Street, a few yards from one of the arches of the
railway viaduct. Two days later, a homeless woman was seen dying
in convulsions under the railway bridge by the Taboo cinema. Both
deaths were the result of strychnine poisoning. Which could be rat
poison, though we found no sign of it in the area.

A week after that, three children aged nine or so were found dead.
They'd been playing with a ball in a disused car park near the Digbeth
viaduct. Again, it was strychnine. Some of the powder was found
smeared on their mouths. The local police station went into overdrive,
trying to find a drug dealer who might have sold them (or given them)
a wrap of painful death. They arrested every addict they could find. It
was late October. A few days before Theresa O'Kane's birthday.

Childhood memories are strange things. Who can predict when a
buried memory will come to the surface and cause harm? It could be
at puberty, or on leaving home, or after a broken marriage, or after
the loss of a child. And when the trauma is profound enough to tear
you out of the world… what then? I'm not de Richleau, I don't have
those certainties. The best I have is guesswork. There was no way I
could banish Theresa unless I could stop the ruthless from
controlling others. But maybe I could make her back off.

We kept a police watch on the viaduct, and no one was going
there at night any more. At 3 a.m. we packed up and left the poorly
lit brickwork to whatever crept in the shadows, picking over scraps
of litter. An hour later, I came back alone, wearing a black tracksuit, surgical gloves and a scarf over my face. Under the scarf, I was
wearing a flesh-toned Latex mask I'd got from a Soho colleague
with underground contacts. The eyes and mouth were narrow slits.

A half-moon was just visible through a skin of cloud. There was
frost on the pavement. Miles away, fireworks were slamming doors
in the night. I paused under the bridge where the homeless woman
had died. Rain had drawn spikes of lime from the brickwork. Then
I walked slowly on, past the private cinema to the viaduct.

From the pub in Lower Trinity Street, you can see three railway
arches. I stood in one of them and lit a cigarette, then dropped it and
stamped it out. A trace of smoke filtered through the cold air. The

smell of rotting brick was overwhelming. About twenty yards away, against the wall, a Victorian iron urinal had been closed up for decades. She was standing there, watching me. Her face looked slightly out of focus, as if one of us were shivering.

I waited under the viaduct, cupping my hands over my mouth to trap the warmth. She was hesitant, but determined. It was her birthday and no one else had come. *Did they tell you it was a surprise party?* I thought. Her hair was dark and tangled. Her face was as white as the frost. Her school blouse and skirt were torn and smeared with oil or tarmac. As she moved towards me, looking sick, I held out my arms. Then I turned my face so her lips would touch my cheek.

Her small hand pressed into mine. I felt her grip more as intent than as sensation, since her hand was as weak as fresh snow. Her mouth fastened on the slick non-flesh of the mask. Then she let go of me. Her face closed in on itself, flickered like old celluloid. I watched her turn and walk slowly away, back into the shadows of the industrial estate.

When there was no further sign of movement on the street, I peeled off the mask and gloves and slipped them carefully into a plastic bag. I'd dusted them with strychnine powder before putting them on. I wasn't sure if I'd told her a kind of lie or a kind of truth. Either way, she'd got the message.

There were no more unexplained deaths in the Digbeth area for a while. A few more children died from poisoning, but that was just a result of the amount of toxic waste in the ground. If police work teaches you anything, it's that gradual death is very rarely a crime.

COME AWAY
WITH ME

Stella Duffy

11 April, 7.30 p.m.

CAROLINE COMES HOME to a quiet and empty house. This is no surprise, Pete has been working late most nights for the past month. He's on a tight deadline, his own boss, and in this economy any work is good work. When Pete started out film editors were special, those with his broad training rare; now any kid with a Mac and half a brain can call themself an editor – and frequently do. Pete is that rare thing, old-school trained, with an old-school work ethic. This current job is taking much longer than he'd planned, longer than he quoted for as well. But he gets on fine with the director, and he says the project will be astonishing when it's done. That's all he says; Pete firmly believes that the director is the author of the piece. His job is to help the director bring the dream they once held in their mind to reality through the mess of rushes and retakes. He never talks to Caroline about the work until after she's seen the final edit. He never talks to anyone but the director about it. Not even the writer. Old-school, pecking order, playing the game.

Some nights Pete doesn't come home at all, texts Caroline at ten or eleven or later, when he's finally managed to sneak out for a fag – a fag he promises Caroline he doesn't have – and when he's outside he texts to say he loves her, it's looking like an all-nighter, he'll sleep in the spare room if he comes home, sleep tomorrow if not, kip on the divan in his office if he gets a chance. Pete is twenty-three years older than Caroline, and more thoughtful than any of the young men she knew and loved before she met the one who calls himself her old man. He is not old at fifty-seven, but even Caroline sometimes wonders how it will be when she is fifty-seven and Pete is eighty. She thinks he might be her old man then.

7.35 p.m.

Caroline opens the fridge. It's been a good day, lots done, lots ticked off on the to-do list. Caroline is a manager for an events company. She doesn't do the running around, the charming and cheering of people, she does the ordering, the sorting, the arranging. Booking taxis and vans, planes and trains, ensuring deliveries get there on time, ensuring people get there on time. She and Pete met when he was editing a corporate video for one of her company's clients. One of those ghastly ra-ra-ra corporate videos, inevitably underscored with Tina Turner belting out "Simply The Best". The screening time had been brought forward by a day because the CEO had some emergency he had to attend to in the wilds of middle America and, with the client company terrified that online delivery wasn't secure enough for their ground-breaking yay-us video (underscored with Tina Turner singing "Simply the Best"), Caroline had offered to go and pick up the edited video herself, take it directly to the conference centre the next morning. Which she duly did, having spent half an hour with Pete laughing at the absurdities of corporate paranoias, then another half-hour enjoying a small glass of the single malt Pete always allowed himself on completing a job, and then six hours in Pete's studio, laid out on the divan he kept there for late-night naps, laid out for Pete, with Pete, Pete laid out for her.

She opens the fridge for a glass of the cold white left over from yesterday and finds instead a typewritten note, tied to a half-bottle of champagne with a thin red ribbon. The note says : "Drink Me. Drink Me First. Do Nothing Until You Have Drunk Me. Then Go Upstairs".

Caroline smiles. He remembered. Today is the anniversary of that first night, that night in his studio, that night before the morning when she drove along the M40, exhausted, delighted, smiling and singing to herself, singing "Simply the Best". What Pete has never known is it's also the anniversary of the day she ran out on The

Bloke Before a year earlier, Pete's presence that night the perfect antidote to her anniversary-inclined mind.

She takes out a glass, opens the champagne, sits at the kitchen table and drinks it. Does as Pete's asked. She knows he'd expect her to rush upstairs, she usually would, but this is so sweet, such a lovely gesture. She'll drink the fizz and then go to see what's next. What Pete has waiting for her.

The half-bottle lasts two and a half glasses; on the half she decides it's time to go up. It's 7.55 p.m. now and she's slightly fuzzy. Happily fuzzy. Loving her old man, sure no man her own age would have remembered, made such a gesture, known how much she enjoys these games.

She does enjoy games. Pete and Caroline enjoy games.

7.58 p.m.

Caroline turns on the bedroom light. In the middle of the bed, slightly on Pete's side of the bed actually, is an open suitcase. The small, wheelie suitcase they use when one of them goes away for a night for work. Caroline hates going away for work, Pete even more so, they both try to get out of it whenever they can, but sometimes needs must, and sometimes they have to go. They have been sharing this suitcase for almost five years; it doesn't get a great deal of use.

Sitting in the open suitcase is an A5 envelope, and inside the envelope are tickets and her passport. Caroline's name on first-class return tickets to Venice.

There is another note with the tickets, printed in blue this time. It says a car will be there to pick her up at 9 p.m. She has an hour to pack, bring clothes for two days, bring clothes for warm days and slightly chilly nights by the water. Bring herself. Bring love. Bring five years of them.

8.55 p.m.

Caroline has showered and packed. She is ready. She carries the little case downstairs, her handbag already on her shoulder, and a thought occurs to her. It's a wonderful, wonderful gesture, but there is a tiny part of her that thinks it's also a very little bit odd. They have played games before, ever so slightly scary games. Caroline doesn't want this to be a game, she wants it only to be fun. She runs back upstairs, opens the drawers on Pete's side of their shared chest of drawers. She checks. His passport is gone, good. She looks in the drawers below. She's not sure, but she think some pairs of his boxers are missing, a couple of pairs of socks. The doorbell rings. She opens the wardrobe; his suit is missing, the not-quite-best suit he likes to wear out for a nice dinner. Not that they go out that much, his work, her work, recently they've been thinking it's as nice to stay in for the night as go out. The doorbell rings again and Caroline calls that she is coming. She feels good now. Safe in the knowledge that, if this is a game, it's one he's playing with her. Safe in the knowledge that Pete will be waiting for her, at the airport, in the hotel maybe. Safe.

9.05 p.m.

Caroline is in the car, the driver knew her name and which airport she is going to – Heathrow, Terminal 2. Lucky, as she hadn't checked herself. She wonders if the driver will hand her a package, more instructions, more messages. She texts Pete to tell him he is brilliant; there is no reply but she wasn't really expecting one. She knows Pete likes to maintain the mystery of his games, when he plays games. They are on the M4 and almost at Heathrow before she has stopped wondering where Pete is now. She worries that perhaps she is meant to pay the driver. Pete's not as good as she is with cash, with always making sure she has enough cash. Caroline has just-in-case ten- and twenty-pound notes tucked in the back of her wallet, in the zipped section of her handbag, in a little plastic purse in her make-up bag. Just in case. So Caroline knows she has enough cash, but she wonders if Pete has paid the driver anyway; she's usually the one to pay the driver. They arrive at Heathrow. Pete has paid.

10 p.m.

This is the last flight to Venice tonight. There is no queue for First Class and Caroline slips through security quickly and easily, is directed to the first-class lounge.

10.45 p.m.

Boarding is announced and just as she walks the easy distance to the boarding gate a text comes. It is from Pete. "There will be a water taxi waiting for you. Look out for the sign with your name on it. I love you. Pete".

A water taxi. Caroline and Pete haven't used the water taxis before, they seem so extravagant, so unnecessary, when the journey on the vaporetto is easy and smooth anyway; when that round trip via Murano, past the cemetery, is so easy. They have been to Venice three times before now, have stayed in San Marco and Dorsoduro. She wonders if the taxi will take her to one of those hotels or some-where new. Caroline is tired and boards the plane, happy to lean back in her seat, to take the meal offered, the wine, to eat and drink, and then she sleeps.

12 April, 1.15 a.m. local time

Caroline sleeps most of the flight and wakes groggy; the champagne and the wine have muddied her mind. And she's very tired. It's been a long week, tonight was meant to be Friday night nothing, Saturday sleep in. But her bag is the third off the carousel, and then she is through the green lane and out into arrivals where the nice young man holds a broad card with her name on it. CAROLINE HUNTER. He speaks almost no English and she has even less Italian but they know the international signs for yes, that's me, and follow, and please take your seat, here, in this ludicrously luxurious little speedboat that is also a taxi, all wood panelling and lace curtains. And then they are off, he is driving the boat and Caroline is wide awake, can't keep the grin from her face, they are powering down the channel to the island and she can see the old lights, and the towers, walls and there, just peeking over the wall, a spire, the top of the campanile perhaps, it might be San Marco, it might be another church, it is there and gone as the taxi speeds over the waves thrown by the boats it passes. He is a young man and he drives like a young man.

1.45 a.m.

The ride, the water, the waves, the wind are successful in their conspiracy to please; Caroline is wide awake and delighted. The taxi enters the Grand Canal; the Guggenheim palazzo is on her left. Caroline remembers when she and Pete went there, how they spent the whole dinner that night talking about what they'd do with a house like that, what it must be like to live in such a place, to have the water so close, so part of your home.

She thinks about the first time she came here, with The Bloke Before, with John. So many mistakes with him and then that last mistake, coming to Venice, agreeing to come away with him when she'd already had enough of his possessiveness, arguing with him and running out of the nasty little bed and breakfast he'd booked for her birthday treat, running out and leaving him. Calling the B&B owners and struggling for the right words, the language to pass on the message that she'd gone back to London, heart-wrenching messages from John begging her to come back, to try again, and then, as the days and weeks wore on, angrier messages, messages she has tried hard to forget.

She hadn't gone back, she stayed on in Venice, furious with John for being so demanding and yet calling her possessive. Caroline was certain something had been going on and, sure enough, the next day, watching him across a square she'd seen him chatting with a couple of girls, chatting and then laughing and then, yes, just as he'd accused her of the day before, there was the exchange of numbers, then the kiss on both cheeks, too friendly, too lingering. John was the slut he'd called her, and she knew he was.

Caroline looked down at her handbag, Pete's notes inside, with her return ticket. God, she was lucky she'd run from John. But that first time here with him, when they'd arrived at the airport and walked down to catch the vaporetto and she'd assumed they were riding the waves to an island... she hadn't quite understood, not from the books or the movies, that it really was all water. No roads, no cars. Caroline had not been able to imagine no cars. And all those bridges, the dead ends, the alleyways that appeared to go somewhere and just returned to water instead.

That was then, with John. Caroline knows better now, knows Venice better. A little at least. She knows it with Pete, where they like to stay, to eat, to drink.

Caroline is now with Pete and this is a lovely gesture on his part, but actually she is starting to feel a little lonely. It is dark and colder than she expected and Pete's surprises, his games, are all very well, but she prefers to play with him rather than for him. She will explain this, tomorrow perhaps, over breakfast; that she is grateful for his romantic gesture, and maybe, anyway, it would be more fun to be together than apart, in touch than not.

San Marco is on the right now, they are closer to the southern shore, so maybe the taxi is turning off soon. The boy-racer driver has slowed a little, Caroline is sure there must be laws about driving too fast here, though the canal is wide and virtually empty. It is late, later than at home. The Accademia Bridge and then an opening. The taxi turns south. He drives her down one wide canal then into another more narrow, then there are smaller turns, dizzyingly fast. Even though she realizes, technically, they must be driving slower, the boat's speed seems faster. The canal is so narrow here she could reach out and touch the sides. The tide is out and the taxi is low in the water. The edges of the canal loom over her. Caroline does not want to touch the sides. It is dark, cold, wet. She looks ahead and now it seems as if they must have come back on themselves. If she leans to the side, if she looks past the young driver's head, she can see the Doge's Palace, more distant now, it is down one, two, maybe three widenings of this narrow canal they are in. Then under another bridge, very low this time, another left turn, another left, back in on themselves again, and then the taxi stops. It is dark, and the silence is sudden. He turns and smiles. Here.

2.20 a.m.

Here. There is no hotel that she can see, no welcoming light. There is no light, just the faint milky sheen from a half-moon high above night-white cloud. Caroline repeats the boy racer's words as he picks up her bag and jumps up on to the canal side. There is apparently no dock either. Caroline had been envisioning one of the pretty little side-canal docks she'd seen from the Grand Canal, the lovely hotels with their own landings. She takes the boy's hand and he hauls her up on to the waterside. She slips a little, grazes the hand he isn't holding, brings it to her mouth without thinking, partly to stem the yelp she doesn't want to let out, partly the animal desire to lick a wound. She tastes a little grit, unravelled skin, maybe a tiny touch of blood, but the predominant taste is the dark silty water of the lagoon, a flavour of algae too, that particular soft pale green that is the water of Venice on a bright blue day. Pete's ex-wife had those light green eyes, the colour of the water. He told her, once, only once. She didn't want to know and Pete never mentioned Susannah's eyes again. The young man is standing her up straight now, looking into her eyes, she doesn't understand the words, but she knows he is concerned. Caroline is exhausted, she has half-fainted, swooned – has she swooned? She thought women only did that in old romance novels, but then, she is in Venice, Venice is an old romance novel in itself – she stands straight. She is fine, assures the young man in English he, in his turn, does not understand. But the hotel, where is the hotel? she asks.

These are words he knows. He smiles, nods, leans down to tie up the boat, a rope procured in semi-darkness from a corner. He takes her bag with one hand and guides Caroline with the other. He holds the hand she has grazed and there is almost comfort in feeling his skin on her ripped skin, the sting of his hand's moisture seeping in to the flesh of her own. One corner, another, and then, just at the point Caroline was going to dig in her heels, say no more, try to call Pete again, call out for anyone, worried, frightened, not wanting to follow this young man, with his warm hand and insistent yes/*si*/yes/follow/*andiamo*, there it is, the Hotel Angelo. Tiny sparkling lights around a door and the windows on either side. A discreet sign and an older man in a dark coat in the doorway, waiting for her. He thanks the driver and pays him, taking Caroline's bag and ushering her in, welcoming her, expecting her. "*Benvenuta*, Signora Caroline." He pronounces the "e". The man knows her name, her room is ready, come in.

2.30 a.m.

The man takes her passport, she signs a form, they show her to a room. Pete is not there. Caroline wants to cry. The room is beautiful, a suite not a room, a sitting room opening on to a bedroom opening on to a bathroom, all soft lighting and cool minimalism but warm too, comfortable, balconies from both sitting room and bedroom. There is a locked door, just off the sitting room, an extra bedroom for a family of guests, Caroline assumes. It's more a small, elegant apartment than a hotel room, but there is no Pete. Caroline even goes outside on to the balcony, just in case he is hiding. He isn't.

She sees the boy racer below, on his phone, talking in quiet, fast Italian, smoking. He unhooks the rope and, without putting down the phone, without taking the cigarette from his mouth, without stopping talking, he sets the boat into gear and drives away. She watches him go, then there is silence. Water, lapping, only just, and silence. Caroline shakes her head. This is insane, she is angry now, Pete's just being stupid. It's no fun without him. She will go in and call him and shout and they will have a row but it doesn't matter, she wants to hear Pete's voice. She wants Pete.

A knock at the door and she runs to answer it, calling his name, believing him to be on the other side of the door. A young woman stands there smiling, pushing a trolley. There is a huge bunch of flowers, spring flowers, a half-bottle of champagne – Caroline shakes her head, half-bottle again, a single glass she notes, her anger rising further, and an envelope. She points to the envelope and asks the girl about it. Did he leave this? My boyfriend? But the girl shakes her head, *mi dispiace, non parlo* ... She pulls out a plate of fruit from the bottom layer of the trolley, bread too, some cheese, and then leaves. *Buona notte.* Caroline doesn't want her to go. She doesn't want to be alone. The girl closes the door behind her and Caroline opens the envelope.

There is a single piece of paper inside, and a small pill, just one, in a foil wrapper. There is no writing on the foil.

The paper is a printed email : *Sorry, I meant to be there waiting for you. Impossible delays here. I'm getting the first flight out in the morning. Eat, Drink, Sleep. Sleeping pill if you want. I'll be there by the time you wake up.*

Caroline opens the champagne, she eats a chunk of melon. She is close to tears. She tries Pete's phone but it goes to answer. Tries again, leaves a message, trying not to sound angry, needy. Pete hates needy. Hangs up realizing she probably sounds both. She is lonely and tired; Caroline is not very good at her own company, not at night. In the day she can happily spend twelve hours at a stretch alone, but once dusk hits she hungers for other people, for noise, interaction, warmth. Pete. She turns on the TV and turns it off again. The middle-night Italian talk-show, women with their porn-star make-up and brash clothes, are not the warmth she wants. Caroline sighs.

She goes to the bathroom, takes off her make-up, checks all the doors and windows are locked, double locked, drops her clothes on the floor and takes the sleeping pill and the half-bottle of champagne to bed.

Caroline drinks, swallows, sleeps.

12 April, 11.15 a.m.

Caroline wakes, disoriented. Her head is fuzzy from champagne and the sleeping pill and no water, no food. No Pete. She has woken up and he isn't here. Caroline sits and then falls back on to her pillows, these big, soft, white-cottoned pillows that are so ready for her tears. And then Caroline is standing and rushing for the bathroom, dizzy head and stumbling feet, arms out to find walls, doors, knee smashing into bedside cabinet. The blackout blinds kept night light, street light out last night, now they turn the room into a labyrinth. She finds a door, runs a sweaty hand up and down the wall, clicks a switch, light blinding, mouth open, kneeling at the toilet, throwing up. After she has washed her face, cleaned her teeth, Caroline takes the white towelling gown from the hook in the bathroom and walks into the bedroom.

She finds her phone and there are three texts from Pete, all saying the same thing. Sorry. Sorry. Sorry. Each one giving a later departure time. The last text says 6.15 p.m. arrival. He will be there for dinner. He. Will. Be. There. For. Dinner. Caroline is not sure why Pete is still trying to promise, when clearly he has no power to do so. Caroline knows how angry he must be, how Pete hates delays at the best of times. She wants to text him back, to placate him, to tell him it's fine. And she doesn't want to as well. She wants him to miss her as she is missing him, she wants to cry and shout and stamp her foot and complain. She texts back simply: Don't worry. I love you. See you later.

Caroline is hungry. She has an afternoon in Venice, alone. She will go out, she will eat, she will enjoy herself. There are things she knows she wouldn't do if Pete were here, tourist shops full of pretty little bits of Murano glass Pete would never go into, windows of carnival masks he loathes. Pete hates all that tourist crap. Caroline is sure he's right, and yet a part of her, the part she doesn't dare show Pete, is still attracted to it, to being – more honestly – the tourist she is. She will walk over the Rialto Bridge and go to San Marco and she will order insanely expensive coffee and cake that Pete believes only stupid American tourists would eat and leave the kind of tip Pete never would and look at all those shops that spin off the square. And when she has finished wasting money she will come back to the hotel and get dressed up and she and Pete will have dinner and they will come back to that big fluffy bed and fuck and sleep together and it will all be fine. She can bear being alone in daylight and Pete will be here by night.

12.55 p.m.

Caroline walks downstairs. There is no one at Reception, no one to leave her key with, to return her passport. There is no bell either; it is all quiet, cool, the place feels empty. She imagines this is a good time for the staff to take a break, grab a rest between breakfast and checkout and cleaning the rooms and then the after-lunch rush as the morning flights that left London and Paris and Madrid land and the new guests check in. She puts the heavy room key in her bag and leaves the hotel, the door locking behind her.

1.00 p.m.

Caroline turns right. This is not the way she came in. She makes a note of the street name, and where the door is in relation to the water, to the canal off-shoot where the taxi dropped her. She looks up and can see, past the narrowing perspective of tall buildings on either side of the small street, that the sky is very light blue, high white cloud filtering the pure blue she remarked on the last time they were in Venice, and the first time in Venice too, that time with John. A city girl, Caroline always looks up to the sky. Not for her the checking of fields or flowerbeds or hedgerows to judge the weather or the season, it is all in the sky. She likes a high sky, and a lot of it. These narrow streets, narrow canals, make her claustrophobic.

   She heads out of the small street and into a larger one and then another wider still. Across a bridge she finds a footpath leading alongside a canal, into another canal, broader now, and then sees what she is looking for, walks along and up to the Grand Canal. This is how she will find her way around, this is how she will orient herself. She will not get lost. She looks across the water, north-east to the Doge's Palace, to her right the span of the Accademia Bridge; she knows the Rialto is all the way round to her left. She will go to the Rialto, because Pete would not. She will cross it and may even buy herself a mask, something that hides her eyes, with feathers perhaps, because Pete would not like it. She will waste money on things only stupid tourists do. Pete isn't here and Caroline is.

2.15 p.m.

Caroline has eaten ice cream – cherry, rich, syrup dripping from the creamy vanilla ice, fat cherries squirting sweet juice into her mouth when she bites into them. She has stopped for coffee twice, both times an espresso, both times standing at the bar, paying the cheaper price, the price she cannot pay with Pete who likes to sit, take his time to look around. She has stood at the bar and talked to no one and sipped the bitter coffee made easier with sugar and been glad, almost glad, to be alone.

2.45 p.m.

Caroline is standing in front of the four horses, the ones from Constantinople they keep here, upstairs in San Marco. She's been here with Pete but he wouldn't let her touch them. He was right, no one is supposed to touch, there's a sign saying no photos, no touching, and Pete wouldn't let her take their picture either, led her outside to get close to the copies standing above the front doors to the big church. But Caroline has wanted to touch the originals since then, and now she does. She walks around the barrier, ignores the camera she knows is watching, and stands before each horse. There are a few other tourists in here, not many, it's as if no one really cares about these horses. That's one of the reasons Caroline wants to touch them. She thinks they should be outside, that they shouldn't have to mind about the weather and the pigeons, wants them to be open to the world as they must once have been, long ago, far away. The other tourists are tutting, one uses it as a chance to take a photo, his camera flashes just as Caroline turns her head, a hand reaching out to the fetlock of the first horse, and from the light, from behind the light, blinded by the flashlight, Caroline thinks she sees a face she recognizes.

A security guard comes and Caroline is asked in very polite English to leave the building. The man with the camera is asked to leave too. She does as she is told.

2.58 p.m.

Outside, in the square, the bells about to ring, people gathering to listen, Caroline rubs her eyes. Behind her palms, behind her lids, she sees the negative image of the man with the camera that made the flash and also the man standing behind him, watching her, the man she thought she recognized. Caroline doesn't know what John looks like now. The man she thought she saw looked like John might look, now.

Caroline feels sick. The ice cream and the bitter coffees and the adrenaline rush of getting kicked out of the church, it is that, it's definitely that, it can have nothing to do with thinking she saw John behind the man, behind the light of the flash. That would just be paranoid.

3.01 p.m.

The bells have begun to ring and it's too loud for her here, ears fuzzy with ringing, bile in the back of her throat. Caroline walks across the square, beneath the portico, takes a right down a street, any street, it doesn't matter. She walks for ten minutes, fifteen. The afternoon sun is beginning its descent; light angles into the narrow paths between buildings, the high white clouds of earlier are burned off, and every now and then the sunshine catches a window, bouncing sunlight back into her eyes, and each time it's like the flash going off, the man taking the photo and the man behind him, and now Caroline is sure it was John, looking, just looking, not surprised to see her, just there. Looking. Watching.

3.35 p.m.

The turn she just took has led her down an alleyway between two houses and to a dead end. Caroline stops as the alley peters out, falling into water. She can see where it would continue. Over there, across a narrow canal, just wide enough for two small boats to pass each other, over there is a café where people sit and chat, drinking coffee and wine, drinking spritz, the Aperol bitter in the bubbles. They are close enough for her to hear the American accents of the group of young people, talking about where they will go tomorrow, about a friend who will join them later. Two middle-aged women sit side by side. They speak more quietly, but even so, the canal here is so narrow that Caroline thinks she can hear their Italian lady voices, their soft, discreet murmurs in someone else's language. Both women are beautifully groomed, each with a dog in her lap. The dogs should match the women, they too are beautifully groomed, coiffed hair poking out from little dog-shaped coats on their small, round bodies, but the women look as if they are holding the wrong dogs, each one holding her friend's.

The street continues past the café, but Caroline cannot walk down it, the water is in the way. To her left, past a row of houses, is a bridge, but the houses are right on the water, there is no walkway alongside them. There are two boats moored here at her feet. For other people, for locals, this would not be a dead end at all, this would be an opening, an exit, a way out, a way home. For Caroline there is nothing to do but go back. She begins to turn, looking down the alleyway behind her, into a cooler darkness now. The lower sun can no longer reach down here and the alley looks dark, its distant opening into a broader street hidden in shadow. There is nowhere else to go but back and as she turns Caroline hears a loud laugh from the group of young people on the other side of the water. She doesn't know why, but she feels like they are laughing at her. She twists around, and now she's sure the young woman at the rear of the group, head thrown back in laughter, head leaning forward to kiss the young man beside her, kiss him long and hard... Caroline is sure she's the chambermaid who brought the trolley last night, with champagne and food and the sleeping pill, the young woman who spoke no English. But the young woman's face is obscured, by the young man she is kissing, and they were all speaking English she is sure, speaking with American accents.

Caroline takes a deep breath, she feels tears behind her eyes and she does not want to cry, doesn't want to feel sick, is in danger of doing both. She plunges back into the alleyway, pushes past a Spanish couple who are clearly walking in the wrong direction, who are lost and start to ask her directions, pull out their map, and then they take a closer look at her face, step back, allow her to pass. Caroline rushes on, walking down streets and along narrow canals and across bridges, everywhere other accents, Spanish and French and English and American, is no one here Italian? She thinks of an Italian friend at home whose family come from Venice, who said no Italians can afford to live there any more. And then she shakes her head again. What is she thinking of her friend for? Why is she thinking of John?

3.55 p.m.

Caroline stops. She is in a small square. There is a bar at either end, a church in the middle. She goes to the closest bar, sits down, orders a coffee and a glass of prosecco. Her hands are shaking. What is she thinking of? She isn't thinking at all. This is insane. Of course that girl wasn't the same girl from the hotel, there must be hundreds of young girls in Venice, all of them tourists or students or here with boyfriends and girlfriends. All the young girls look the same anyway. Caroline is on the edge of calling herself a woman, not a girl any more. These days, when she sees a young woman she sees the fine skin, the fresh eyes, sees the new. Sees what Pete saw in her at first and what he maybe sees no longer. Sees what John saw in her. She smiles, the coffee and wine arrive, she takes a long slow sip of both, one after the other. Stop it. Stop it. Her hands slowly stop shaking. John always said she was paranoid, that he was not possessive, as she thought him, just loving, wanting to take care. Pete's the other way; accuses her of jealousy sometimes. He says she has no reason for it, that she's imagining things, imagining flirtations, potential. There must be hundreds of young girls in Venice, thousands. Caroline finishes the prosecco, orders another.

4.10 p.m.

Her phone beeps. She is low on battery, should have plugged it in last night, wasn't thinking, must start thinking. It's Pete again: About to turn off my phone. Plane taxiing. Air steward has glared at me twice. I love you. Coming.

Caroline smiles, nods to herself, breathes out a breath she didn't even know she had been holding. She rubs her neck, downs the now cold coffee, orders a third prosecco. She texts back, it doesn't matter that Pete won't get this, it doesn't matter that he will only pick it up when his plane lands, it matters that she tells him. I love you. I'm waiting for you.

4.40 p.m.

Caroline pays for her drinks, stands; she's actually a little drunk now, enjoying feeling a little drunk now. She should probably eat, will get back to the hotel, find her way through these insane streets and canals. She'll stop on the way and buy something to eat from one of those shops that sell fat-filled breads to tourists hungry from sight-seeing, something with cheese and aubergine and courgette and salami. Antipasti in bread, that's what Pete calls it, disapproving. He likes long Italian meals, each course an adventure in itself, doesn't think the Venetians should accommodate tourist desires, doesn't think of himself as a tourist at all. Caroline probably has three hours before she needs to be ready for Pete, two to be on the safe side. She will make her way back slowly, eat, sober up, wash and dress and be ready for the surprise he has been unready for. All will be well.

5 p.m.

Caroline has found her way back to the Grand Canal. She didn't realize she'd come so far; there are signs for the Ghetto back behind her. She and Pete came here the first time they were in Venice together. It was sad, and lovely, to see the old synagogue, to see where the word came from, and then Pete found an amazing restaurant that night, quite close to the Ghetto, and they'd eaten so well, so happily. When they walked out into the night she was amazed it was so late, and so very quiet, so different from other parts of the city, busy until late at night. It's quiet here now, too, quieter anyway than back where she thought she'd been heading, to the Rialto. She heads east again, a falling sun behind her, in and out. Unable to walk directly alongside the Grand Canal here, she tries to keep the sun behind her, even when she has to turn north again. Eventually there are more people, and signs, and a vaporetto stop, and Caroline buys her ticket, boards it, the beginning of a headache coming with sunset.

Caroline gets off at San Toma, between the Rialto and Accademia, it must be close to the hotel. She wishes she'd thought to bring a map, to ask the man at Reception for a map, but she didn't. At home Caroline never gets lost, prides herself on knowing her way round London, even the farthest reaches, or the most winding parts down by Greenwich and Canary Wharf, prides herself on always knowing where the water is. Here she is where the water is, always. Her compass is waterlogged. She will wander and she will find it. She remembers the street name, the canal name, she will find it.

5.10 p.m.

Caroline has a feeling she is close. She is walking alongside a narrow canal, the footpath here is narrow too. She is behind two men, one older, greyer than the other. They have Australian or New Zealand accents, she can't tell the difference, and they're laughing about a girl they both know. You should have seen her face, one says. Mate, I don't need to see her face, I can see *your* face! And they laugh and the greyer one slaps the other one on the back and they stop for a moment. One is lighting a cigarette and Caroline needs to get past them. She says, excuse me, excuse me, can I get past here? They shuffle to the side, she hears the match strike, the flare of warm light, and Caroline turns to thank the two men. She recognizes one of them. The older one, with greying hair, is the man from the hotel's Reception. She knows for sure he is from the hotel and she knows this because he sees her, sees her looking, and nudges his friend and they both look up. Shit! the older one says. And he turns away, his head to the wall, but it's too late and Caroline wants to throw up again, wants to grab him and ask what the fuck is going on, wants to reach out to the man, but her legs don't want that at all, her legs and her gut are terrified, and she runs instead, runs away from them, rushing on to where she thinks the hotel is. Her head doesn't want to go to the hotel at all, it isn't safe, can't be safe, but her legs and gut propel her. Now pushing past a young couple, Caroline shoves them both out of her way. They are English and yell at her in surprise, yell that she should be careful, there's no need for that, what's her problem?

Caroline doesn't know what her problem is. And then she does. Running on, slowing, walking now, breath catching, a stitch in her side, walking towards the hotel anyway, sure she knows these streets now, sure she knows where she is... Caroline does know what her problem is. She knows she hasn't been able to believe those messages from Pete, not really, knows Pete would never let her down like this, knows he would have been at the airport, in the hotel, would have been waiting. And now she stops, cold, sick to her stomach and bile rising again in her throat. Because she knows, actually, that Pete doesn't really do surprises, that while they have their games, Pete has never really done surprises, that the real surprise she came home to on Friday evening was that it was so out of character for Pete. So in character for John.

5.40 p.m.

The sun is still lighting the sky, but it's darker and cooler in the narrow street leading to the hotel. On the other side of the small canal just here, beneath a shop awning, standing with his back to her, Caroline sees a man texting. She sees the man and she is sure she knows who he is, knows the back of him. The man stops texting, watches his phone's screen. A few seconds later her own phone beeps. A text comes through, from Pete's phone. I'm here. Landed. Won't be long. Can't wait to see you. It's been way too long.

The man turns; he doesn't see Caroline looking. It's John, Caroline is sure it is John. He looks in through the window of the shop, waves, walks on, away down the little walkway alongside the canal, down to a bridge that will bring him back to this side of the canal, where the hotel is.

The hotel has her bag and her things and her passport and Caroline wants nothing more than to run from here, run from this place, but her phone is almost out of battery and the charger is in her room and her stuff is in the room, and maybe, maybe she is as paranoid as John always said, maybe she's just exhausted and maybe it will be all right, but whatever it will be she needs to charge her phone and she needs to get her things and so she runs back down the street to the hotel and opens the front door and lets herself in.

5.50 p.m.

There is no one in Reception, just as there was no one earlier. She runs upstairs and into the sitting room of the suite, slamming the door behind her, locking it. Caroline looks around. She takes in the room properly, sees that while it is a beautiful room, cool and clean, lovely lines, it is missing some of those things even the finest hotel rooms must have. The sign on the wall about emergency exits. The list by the telephone of charges, useful numbers to call. The explanation in five different languages of how to work the TV and satellite. She remembers there were no signs downstairs either. Nothing on the reception desk that was, after all, just a counter really, a plain counter, with nothing on it, no message about breakfast or checkout, no handy pile of maps and leaflets for unprepared tourists. Caroline realizes she has seen no other guests. The only people she has seen are the chambermaid and the man behind the desk. And that she did see them when she went out today and they were speaking English, she wasn't mistaken. Caroline has let herself believe. And now she lets herself understand. She walks over to the locked door; it opens. Behind it is a kitchen. A normal, elegant, newly fitted kitchen. This is not a hotel room. It is an apartment.

Her phone beeps. She doesn't want to look. Can't stop herself looking.

I'm in the bedroom. Waiting.

And even though she doesn't want to go, and even though her gut and legs are trying to hold her back, Caroline overrules them this time and walks herself to the bedroom door.

She opens the door.

Pete is on the bed. And a lot of blood. Pete's blood, on the bed, bloody Pete.

And the phone beeps again and she hears the sitting-room door, the door from the corridor, the door she locked, she hears it being unlocked.

And she looks at the phone as the door handle turns and her phone says: See? I told you it was a surprise.

And Caroline wants to move, to scream, to run, but nothing is working, her legs, her mouth, nothing is working, nothing can move her, she is stuck staring at Pete, Pete's blood, stuck waiting as the steps come closer behind her

And then a hand is on her shoulder and still her mouth won't open, her voice won't come and John says, See? I told you I'd always remember you.

BEDLAM

Ken Bruen

I'VE BEEN OUT of the hospital, near three weeks.
I know because I precisely counted and oh, so.....................
delicately counted the days.

I wish I knew how long I was incarcerated.

The heavy medication, the padded room, you lose all sense of nigh everything.

A room designed to drive you............madder.

It did.

I alas, remember, months gone by, weeks, years?

Curled up in the foetal position, and cackling to me own self.

They'd just hosed me down, those fucking lethal sprays of water that bounce you off the freaking walls.

A day came when I managed to feign taking the pills and slowly, oh, so fucking slowly, I began to get back to me own self. Now play the game.

I became the model patient.

It mostly worked.

I was released into the general population.

One slight hiccup.

One of the orderlies didn't buy my new act.

Kept on my case, pushing me to reveal my real self.

I did.

When she was least expecting it.

I got her on the early morning of the night shift, drowned her in the toilet. Took a time but then I didn't have anywhere else to be yet, so I drew it out a bit.

Heard the bitch plead.

Then, when I got bored, hung her from the socket, put a placard round her neck, in nice neon yellow.

It read:

I can't take it any more.

Looked at her for a brief moment then put my hand on her hip, pushed her hard to get that swing going, said:

"You're a swinger, babe."

The Government cutbacks were biting, they were releasing patients all over the fucking place, and with my new model patient status...

I was freed.

The mad bastards.

Gave me a bucketful of pills to keep me on an even keel.

Good luck with that.

Four of us CURED patients were bundled into a minivan. Due to be dropped at four separate hostels in Galway city.

The driver had the look of an ex-bouncer/boxer.

The drive to Galway was silent, the other three so medicated they were comatose.

I acted similar; had been doing the zonked gig for so long it was effortless.

He dropped the other three at their designated hostels.

He checked his list

Said:

"They have you in a hostel............lemme see, yeah, in Woodquay."

I said in my meekest tone:

"Thank you so very much."

He was surprised, asked:

"What were you in for?"

I near whispered.

"Alcoholism."

My head bowed in shame.

He near smiled, in recognition, said:

"Yah poor devil, it killed me mum."

I thought:

Gotcha.

Said:

"I'm afraid, though."

He gave a look of part sympathy, mostly curiosity.

Said:

"Ary, it will be okay. What are you most afraid of?"

I hesitated, as if it was too agonizing to say.

He was in control now, urged:

"Spit it out, maybe I can help."

Oh, he was helping all right. Tentatively, I ventured:

"My old apartment is still in my name and I know I'll have to go there sometime but……………"

He was full hooked. I said:

"There's six bottles of fifty-year-old Black Bushmills there."

I could literally see the Euro signs in his bloodshot eyes, a serious amount of cash there.

His drinker's face, the bulbous nose, the rescreen, the broken veins, the mint pills on his breath nearly disguising the effects of last night's bash, he drooled at the mouth then all chivalrous, offered:

"Now that we can fix, right now. I'll take them away for you."

I protested, said:

"I couldn't ask you to do that."

He put the van in gear, said:

"I insist."

I told him my apartment was at the end of Long Walk and he jumped right in with,

"I know them, Jesus, I'll have us there in, like, four minutes."

He did.

Parked at the end of Long Walk, facing the ocean.

I pointed at his feet, asked:

"Is that twenty euro?"

He bent down and I plunged in the glass shard I'd smoothed to a fine point.

I moved back as the spurt of blood gushed. He muttered:

"Sweet Jesus."

I had to stab him a few more times till he bled out. I took his wallet, nice bit of cash there. I looked round, no witnesses I could spot. Found a black watch cap in his glove department. Pulled it right down over my face. Then I jammed his foot on the accelerator, used a piece of wood to hold it in place. I turned the ignition then slipped out as the van rolled towards the water.

I didn't look back, moving fast. Thought I heard the van hit the water, muttered:

"Quite a splash you made, fellah."

I made it into the shadows of the large office complex, turned in the direction of Wolfe Tone Bridge and was on Dominic in jig time.

A skip and a jig and I was passing The Samaritans' office...and a hundred yards later, I was in Nun's Island.

Where I owned a small apartment. Against all the odds, I'd managed to retain it as a bolt hole. No one else knew about it, I never even killed anyone there. The neighbours were a snotty bunch, never spoke or acknowledged my existence.

Perfect.

I don't do............cordiality.

Putting the key in the lock was a real rush. I said:

"I'm home, dear."

Absolute silence answered.

Bills were paid by direct debit, not in my own name of course. I'd more aliases than Puff Daddy.

I did have a bottle of Jameson. Who can afford Black Bush?

I poured a large one.

Sank into the battered sofa, took a lethal wallop of the Jay, and waited for the burn.

Come it did.

The fire in my gut a pale echo of the blast from gutting the van driver, I raised my glass, toasted him, said:

"Don't forget to feed the swans."

Perhaps they'd see him as takeaway. That amused me hugely. Truth to tell, nobody amuses me like me own self. You could call it......killer comedy. I poured a another wee dram of Jay then went to brew some coffee. One of my passions is real coffee. Real

Colombian beans, and the aroma alone gets me amped. Took a while as all real art does. When it's brewed just right, with the Jay as outrider, I feel almost human.

Well, at least an Irish one, which allows huge flexibility.

Once I'd eased the cricks out of my body, I stood, pushed the sofa.

It didn't move.

Terrific.

I leaned under it, found the switch and hit it. The sofa moved as easy as the River Corrib, without the poisonous face. Beneath it the wood floor appeared seamless.

One.

Two.

Three.

Lifted the third panel with the glass shard. All intact.

Money.

Mobile phones.

Coke.

Taser.

Weapons.

I took a thousand euro, the taser, a few grams of coke and my old reliable Glock, a leather band wound tight around the butt for controlled grip. Tested it, primed and ready to go. Added two clips of ammo in case. Put the rest back in place then positioned the sofa, resecured it with the lock and heard the click as it engaged. I laid out a few lines of coke and snorted them fast. The icy trickle down my throat was near-instant and I could feel the clear focus building behind my eyes.

My bookshelves are laden with books.

All poetry.

No true crime or serial killer shite.

I know my game and, better, I know my act.

My early days in the asylum, one of those interviewing me had read all the relevant books.

Me too.

He asked:

"As a child, did you ever torture or kill small animals?"

Gimme a fucking break, the most basic question.

I said:

"I love animals, why would I hurt them?"

Then the freaking classic.

"Did you ever set fires and receive sexual gratification as a result?"

God almighty.

I said:

"But we had central heating."

He'd caught on to my mind-fucking and didn't like it.

Not one bit.

Asked in icy tone:

"Does killing give you sexual release?"

I stared at him, said:

"You're a wee bit obsessed with sex and violence. Have you spoken to anyone about that?"

He lost it then.

"I know what you are."

"Pray tell?"

He took a deep sigh, said:

"You are a narcissistic psychopath, and highly dangerous."

I looked at his name tag. Now he had my attention. I said:

"Dr Williams, I don't understand those big words."

4 A.M., WHEN THE WALLS ARE THINNER

Alison Littlewood

STUMPY ELLIS TOLD a lot of stories about how he lost his thumb, and they always seemed to involve violence, and grinding, and eyes. I was the only one who heard the real story, and I never would have told. Stumpy had a temper, and a man with a temper in prison is like a powder keg in a room full of lit matches.

He had a shine in his eyes, Stumpy Ellis: a cold, dangerous kind of shine. It was like seeing a flat, wide sky in there, a grey sky, although the sun was shining in the yard when he stuck out his hand – the one with only half a thumb – and asked if I had a smoke. I looked at those eyes and took a cigarette from my pocket, without seeing what he had to trade. If I'd learned one thing inside, it was when to resist and when to bend.

He muttered around the cig in his mouth, to my back.

"Payment."

I turned and waved his words away: no problem.

"I always pay," he said. "I always pay and I always expect to be paid. Sit down."

I felt stiffness working up my back and into my knuckles, but he sat down himself, so I sat next to him and smelled the burning in his lungs.

"I'll tell you a story," he said. "As payment."

I waited.

He thrust out his hand in front of me, palm down, but I didn't jump. Another thing I learned in prison: it doesn't pay to be jumpy.

"See that?" he said, and I grunted. His left thumb was missing from the first knuckle to the tip, leaving a thick, blunt, flexible mound.

"Want to know how I did that?"

I grunted again.

"There was a guy thought he could cross me," said Stumpy. "We worked together for a while. Building jobs, mainly. I'd get the business in, he'd mobilize the troops. Whoever was hiring us, they paid me, and I paid him. Only this one time, he came to me, he said, 'Ellis – help me out. I need something extra.'"

He glanced at me, so I nodded.

"He took the money and the next time I see him, he's coming out of the jeweller's, and he sees me and he turns red-faced. And I knew, you know? You don't fool Stumpy Ellis. Not when it comes to his missus.

"A picture, my missus." He breathed out a long, jagged breath of smoke as he laughed. "Blonde. Tits out here. Legs up here." He stared off into the distance, pulling hard on the cigarette.

"I didn't follow him, didn't need to. Told him I was off to see about a job, something out of town. And then I doubled round and went home. Knew as soon as I got there. Window was open, and this laughing floating out."

I nodded, wondering why he would tell this story, why it didn't bother him what his wife had done.

"She had him on his back when I got there. Her arse stuck up in the air." He sucked noisily on the cigarette. "Know what I mean?"

I nodded.

"Got the shock of her life when I shoved her off the bed. Took half of it with her, and her looking all wide-eyed and surprised, trying to tell me she didn't do nothing, with his blood running down her chin."

He laughed, but I didn't.

"So he was there, practically begging, so I start punching, and she's digging in the cabinet and comes at me with the gun."

I raised my eyebrows.

"My gun. My own gun. Keep it for – special occasions, you know? And she's holding it with her hands, shaking everywhere, and screaming, and then she points it in the air, only she's still shaking, and then she squeezes too hard and she fires it. And the only person more surprised than her is me, cause half my thumb's gone, and there's blood everywhere. All over the sheets, all over me, and all over the little prick who started it all. And I figure, she's my missus, and what sort of a man hits his missus? So I turns round to him, my old mate, and he's laughing at me. 'See that?' he says, and his voice is high as a girl's. 'See that?' And he keeps looking at me and laughing."

He stubbed out the cigarette, then spread his hand and stared at his thumb. "Put his eye out," he said.

"What?"

"I said, I put his eye out." He hooked his thumb and mimed gouging. "Didn't even feel it. My thumb all covered in blood, and half missing, and I didn't even feel it. Seems it wanted it, you see. My thumb knew what it wanted and it took it."

He looked up. "Fucker never looked at my wife again." He spluttered laughter and nudged me in the ribs.

I laughed. It wasn't funny, but I laughed anyway.

He nudged me again. "See him?" He indicated an older man, thin, with white hair. He walked in a wide circle around the yard, his eyes fixed on the ground. "Librarian," Stumpy said, and chuckled. "If you want to know anything, ask a librarian. He's the one'll get you out of here."

"What?" I said.

"*What*?" he says. "Escape, that's what. That's the man'll show you how. Just climb right out." He gave a dry laugh. "Climb right out."

I waited for him to say something else, but he shook himself.

"Another story," he said, and stood. "You'll have to pay me for that one. You'll have to pay me good." And he walked off without saying anything else, swaggering his way across the yard just as the guard called time.

I knew Stumpy hadn't told me the real story about his thumb, and I didn't care. What he'd said about escape, though; it stuck in my mind, and that was dangerous. Curiosity could get you killed in prison as well as anywhere else.

I didn't approach Stumpy again, but when I got my lunch I saw an empty seat by the librarian, and I took it. If Stumpy knew something, he was a middleman. I didn't deal with middlemen.

I nodded to the white-haired man next to me. "Si Jameson," I said to him in a low voice. "Short for Simon." He glanced at me, looked away, and said nothing.

"Hear you're the librarian," I said, but he went on grinding something over and over in his teeth.

"If you want to know anything, ask a ..." I began again, but he stood, pushing his chair back so hard it rocked on two legs before slamming down behind him. He picked up his tray and was gone.

It took a moment for the sound of eating to resume, the scrape of cutlery, the low buzz of conversation. I didn't realize Stumpy had sat down on the other side of me until I heard his voice.

"He won't give it up, that one," he said. "You can't just introduce yourself to the librarian."

I almost laughed, then remembered the flat metal shine in Stumpy's eyes, and swallowed it down.

"You have to earn it," he said. "It don't come cheap."

"What does he want?"

"Ah," Stumpy said, smiling around a mouthful of sausage and mash. "Not like that. Smokes and money – they won't cut it. You have to do something for him."

"What?" I said, although the real question, the one I was thinking, was "Why?" He was nothing but an old man who spent his days sorting battered paperbacks.

"Nothing you can do for him, not in here. On the outside, though. Once you get out."

Stumpy sat back in his seat and pushed his tray back with a scrape. "Old scores," he said. "You might have noticed, but in here old scores go around and around. They don't break up and they don't fade. Just go round and round in a man's head, never getting any smaller. Looking for payment. And him, he'll never get out. He's a lifer, like you."

"Why doesn't he just climb out?" I said, and smiled.

Stumpy grinned. "He'll never leave, not that one. He likes it here. He's fed, he's watered. Says he'd be happy to stay here for ever, only he's scared someone would notice eventually."

I snorted. I guess the shine in Stumpy's eyes didn't seem so dangerous when he wasn't looking straight at me. And I had been wrong to ask, wrong even to think about getting out. Some people shouldn't think about some things, and I was one of them. I'd forgotten that, all for one stir-crazy psycho and an old man – the joke was on me, that's all.

But Stumpy was off again. He waved a hand and the whole table turned to listen. "But anyway," he said. "Did I ever tell you the story of how I lost my thumb?"

There were groans, splutters, and laughter. He began, some story about how he'd had the tip of his thumb removed because it was easier to grind out a man's eye that way, because it was shorter, squatter, stronger. And I knew that this wasn't the real story either, but I also knew something else: if anyone got to hear that story, the real story, it was going to be me.

I didn't say anything, though. I just sat and ate and listened, because prison was like that. You learned when it was time to wait. You did a lot of waiting: I guess you got a feel for it.

I left Stumpy alone after that, but I always had cigarettes in my pocket, so I was ready the next time he put his hand out in the yard and asked me for a smoke.

"Never leave home without them," I said, and passed one over.

"You don't even smoke," he said, "but I'll help you out, don't you worry. You don't even have to pay me." He scraped a match on the ground and lit the cig, shielding it against the breeze, which blew occasional spits of rain in our faces.

I was about to walk away when he gestured towards something. "He's never short," he said.

I turned and saw the librarian sitting on the ground nearby. His knees were drawn up under his chin, his posture that of a younger man. His eyes were a pale, piercing blue.

Then I saw him reach out with one hand and he did something with his fingers. I couldn't quite see what it was: some kind of twist, some kind of flurry, and I lost sight of his hand for a split second. Then it was back and the librarian put a cigarette to his lips. It was lit, and battered-looking, half-smoked.

"Never lacks for anything, that one," Stumpy said. "Just reaches out and takes it."

I shook my head. I couldn't see how he'd done it, and I didn't know what to say.

"Climb right out," said Stumpy. "That's what he says, only I don't quite have it yet. But one day I will. They'll wake up and I'll be gone." He turned to me, eyes agleam. "I'll show you," he said. "You'll be there. You can listen, anyway, and you'll know I've done it. I'm moving cell."

I raised my eyebrows and he nodded. "Guard owes me a favour. I'm moving tonight."

"What do you mean?" I asked. "About climbing out. You got a plan?"

He shook his head, narrowing his eyes against the smoke of his cigarette. "Don't need a plan," he said. "I've got a book. *His* book." He nodded towards the librarian. "And I made a promise. Gotta score to settle."

There was something about the way he looked. "Is it true?" I asked. "Are you going?"

He shook himself. "Everything I tell you is true," he said. "Didn't I tell you how I lost my thumb?" And he was away, waving the stub of his cigarette in the air, his eyes flat and grey and staring off into the distance, focused on nothing. He told me how he'd lost his thumb when he ground it so deep into a man's eye it severed against the skull. The man had been screwing his wife, who was tall and brunette and had tits Stumpy paid a year's salary for.

When Stumpy pulled his thumb out of the man's eye he left the tip behind, protruding from the socket, all the evidence the pigs needed to put him away.

***

That afternoon I lay on my bunk, staring at the ceiling. I wasn't sharing the cell but had taken the top bunk, so the ceiling was close. I listened to the quiet from below and the noise from the corridor, the banging, half-shouts, the footsteps.

I heard it when Stumpy moved into the cell next to mine. He was talking to the guards, loud and cheery and familiar. Setting things down, doors sliding and slamming. Then, after it had gone quiet for a while, I heard his voice at my door.

"Come in?" he said.

"Be my guest."

The cells weren't locked and he came in, his walk quiet and steady. His jauntiness had gone. I sat up on the bunk, and when I saw his face, I jumped down. "Smoke?" I offered.

He waved his hand. "Not this time. This one's on the house." He turned and his eyes looked pale, the shine in them absent, leaving them watery and somehow naked.

"I – I thought someone should know," he said. "I'm going, later. Tonight. I thought you should know." He pushed something into my hand. It was a crumpled photograph of a woman. She looked about forty, her hair mousy, clothes nondescript. She had a good smile and laughter lines around her eyes and no kind of tits at all.

"My wife," he said. "That's my wife." He looked down and I saw that his eyes were full of tears.

"I got her a gardener," he said. "I got her a house and a big garden, and she was always going on about it, so I got her a gardener. But she kept saying how she wanted this gazebo, a love seat she said …" He paused. "A love seat, and I couldn't expect a gardener to build it, she said. *I* was the builder, and she wanted me to do it.

"So I did. I got this – this – gazebo. A stupid word for a stupid thing. It was just a frame that wouldn't even keep the rain off, and a bench. Big enough for two, she said. She said…"

I didn't say anything.

"So I started putting it together, only the damn thing wouldn't go straight. And I was nailing one side together when the other one slipped, and it fell, right on my thumb." He looked at his hand.

"Blood everywhere," he said. "And I screamed. She took me to hospital, and they took the end off. But she kept looking at me, like, I dunno ..."

I waited.

"She looked at me like I was a little kid who'd wet his pants, you know? All the time. Like I'd let her down. And then later, when we got home – later, after – when they took me away. She looked at me then, too. Like something the dog had shat out on the carpet. She looked.

"The last time I saw her, and she looked at me like that. She never visited me, you know. Never did, not once." His face twisted. "She said she was leaving. I was in the fucking hospital, and she tells me this. She'd been seeing him. Her and the fucking gardener. All the time. Fucking."

I put my hand on his arm, and he looked at it, and shook it off.

"I sorted it," he said. "I sorted him. I had a gun, remember me telling you that? And they took me away and they put me in here. But I'm not staying. I'm going to see her again."

He punched his fist into his palm, over and over. "I can still see her," he said. "The way she looked at me with those eyes. Those eyes."

He sat there for a long time. Finally, he stood and turned to me, although he still wasn't looking at anything, not really.

"You know, people think it's just a bit of your thumb," he said. "But it hurt. It hurt."

He walked out of my cell, then. That was the last time I saw Stumpy Ellis alive.

I woke, staring into the dark. I got the feeling something had woken me, but I didn't know what. The night was full of noises. Men muttering to themselves; rasping snores; guards' voices; metal on metal. Prison is never silent, even at night. It was one of the things I missed about the outside – real silence.

Then there was an almighty, shocking bang from the cell next to mine. And a shudder, as though I could feel whatever it was through the walls, the floor, the bunk. The banging noise seemed to hang in the air, echoing.

After that came a wet splatter, like rain, heavy droplets landing on concrete. It seemed to go on for a long time.

Prison was never quiet at night, but it was quiet then, like never before or since. The texture of the air grew heavy with listening, turning to grey speckles before my eyes.

I was the one who broke the silence.

"Stumpy?" I said. "Stumpy? You there?" And there was nothing, not one sound coming back. Not one.

I slipped down from my bunk and went to the bars, looked out into the corridor. There was a wet gleam on the floor outside Stumpy's cell. I couldn't see any further, but I heard the footsteps of the guards when they came running. They stopped. Then there was the nearer splatter of one of them losing their lunch outside Stumpy's cell.

"They say his insides turned to soup," someone said. "As though he'd taken a dive off a building. Everything smashed up."

"They say his skull shattered."

"Every bone in his body, broken, just like that."

"He must have jumped off his bunk, only they say it wasn't high enough to do that kind of damage. Even if he'd hung from the ceiling, it wasn't high enough for that kind of damage."

It was lunchtime, and it was all anyone could talk about, although I said nothing at all. I just kept replaying those sounds in my head, the bang echoing on and on, and the long splatter that came afterward. The thing Stumpy had said, over and over: "Climb right out. That's what I'm going to do. Just climb right out." And the way his eyes had shone when he said it.

I kept glancing around, looking for the librarian, but he was nowhere to be seen.

It was late before they allowed us back to our cells, and when they did there was a black cloth hanging across Stumpy's bars. It must have been some kind of mess in there if they felt they had to hide it from the likes of us.

I climbed into my bunk and tried not to listen to the silence coming from the next cell, but I did, for a long time.

Something woke me later. It was deep night and my head was thick with the confusion of it, night seeping in through my eyes and ears. Then came a distant snore and I remembered where I was. If there was one thing I wanted on the outside, it was to sleep somewhere out of earshot of other men's snores.

I looked into the dark, the walls and the bunk taking shape. I looked at the door of my cell. As I watched, the lock pulled back with a loud metallic clang.

After a time, I resumed breathing. The door was unlocked, but no one came to lock it again. It was just there in the dark, an open door, and no one to stop me walking out. Except of course there were guards at the end of the corridor; more locked doors.

All the same, I slipped off the bunk and went to the door. I didn't touch it, though, not at first. I put out a hand, saw the thick, open bolt, but didn't touch it. When nothing happened I gave the door a gentle push. It moved easily under my hand, sliding without a sound.

I put my head out into the corridor. I could see a shape further down, a door, more bars, dim light, long shadows. And then I saw the dull mark on the concrete outside Stumpy's cell, a dark stain where the wet gleam had been. I moved out further and saw the curtain hanging across his cell suddenly fall, billowing as it filled with air, finding its way to the floor.

Stumpy's cell was much the same as mine. The same bunk, the same box for a wardrobe. But everything was covered in those same dark spatters. The curtain came to rest on the floor, leaving humped whorls and shapes. At first it seemed there was the form of a body beneath it, but then it settled and was only a curtain.

Stumpy's door, too, was open.

I stood and swallowed for a while. Then I went in, trying not to step on that stain in my shoeless feet.

There was stuff all over the floor, and those little number tags the forensics boys put down before they take pictures. It was like seeing two rooms: the one they had been over, investigated, and underneath it the room where Stumpy lived and slept and shat. Used to, I corrected myself. There was a radio on the floor, and I half expected the little dial to light up and some song to creep into the room, under my feet, and that was when the hairs on my arms started to prickle. But it didn't light up, it didn't make a sound. I looked some more. Stumpy's uniform hanging in the box, just like mine. His stuff underneath that, a couple of pictures, a newspaper, a book.

A book.

I picked my way over there, half expecting to hear the door lock behind me, but nothing happened. I just went over there and nothing happened and I picked up the book. The cover was some kind of cloth, rough under my fingers. I ran my hand over it and felt grooves, lettering I couldn't make out. A dark sliver of thread was tucked into the pages. I stroked the cover. A stain had soaked into it and I pulled my hand away. My thumb felt damp, just the tip, and I stared at it.

I turned, and that was when I saw the rope. It hung there in the middle of the room. When I looked straight at it, though, it was gone.

I tilted my head. I could feel those prickles again, but this time they ran all the way down my back, like little hands, unwelcome hands.

I started to edge my way back out of the cell, trying not to step in anything that looked wet. All the time I looked at that space in the middle of the room. Looked up. The ceiling was featureless. There was nothing to hang a rope from. Anyway, it had been low down, as though hanging upwards from the floor, just a few of feet of it and then nothing.

As I pieced it together in my mind I thought I saw it again, just for a moment.

My arm pressed up against the cell door and I almost cried out. I tucked the book under my arm and slipped out of Stumpy's cell, down the corridor and back into my own. I tucked the book under the sheets of the bottom bunk and climbed into bed, pulled the sheets over my body and lay awake, this time trying not to think of the book, somewhere beneath me in the dark.

* * *

The book was a joke, it had to be. I turned it over in my hands. There was no stamp inside, nothing to show it belonged to the prison library, no publisher's mark. The first pages were blank. All of them were yellowed and foxed, the edges rough and uneven. Inside the writing was tiny, and it was in script: handwritten, not printed. The ink had faded to a pale brown.

The pages seemed to be full of magic tricks. There were small, hand-drawn diagrams of cards and dice and coins. Coffin-shaped boxes and saws. Ropes and knots and the means of escaping them. And there, on the page with the bookmark, *The Indian Rope Trick and Secrets Thereof*.

How to make space where there is no space, rope where there is no rope. How to feel with your mind for what you need, and reach out and take it. There was a lot of stuff about dimensions, about how the things you needed were all there, somewhere. Somewhere there was a rope, somewhere a door. About bending things with your mind, until what's there is also here.

Think of a reason, it said. Think of a reason and the rope will answer. Hold it in your mind as you climb, and the rope will not fail. Hold it in your mind: not the rope itself, or the journey, but the destination.

At the bottom, a note had been added. It was in rough, spiky writing and blue ink, and I could almost picture Stumpy forming the letters, his tongue poking out of his mouth: *Go at 4.00 a.m., when the walls are thinnest.*

I snapped the book closed and stared at the wall of my cell. Smiled and shook my head, as though Stumpy were having one last laugh. *Did I ever tell you how I lost my thumb?*

And then I started to dream of it, walking with my back straight, looking people in the eye, a free man. Tasting the air. Just – climbing out. Climbing right on out. And a rope, seen for a moment from the corner of my eye, hanging from nothing in the middle of a cell.

Think of a reason and the rope will answer.

What reason had Stumpy had that could be strong enough? All he had was revenge. I saw again the way he'd talked about his wife, and eyes, and grinding, all the time staring at that thumb of his. His obsession. But it hadn't been strong enough to get him out.

I had no thoughts of revenge. Everyone I hated was already dead. I had no love either, no one waiting. So I tried to think about why. And what came into my mind was a park, a soft, green park, where people sat in the sun. They splotched the grass in twos or threes or fours, talking and laughing, the girls wearing white halter-tops so you could see their shapes beneath. I stood there. I would stand there, and I would turn my face up to the sun, and breathe. Only that.

His insides had turned to soup.

In the cell next to mine was a rope. It hung in the air beneath a blank ceiling.

I looked again at the book and in that second, just in the corner of my eye, it looked as though the tip of my thumb was gone. My left thumb, from the middle knuckle to the nail, leaving only a thick, flexible stump.

I pulled my hand back, dropping the book. I should burn the thing, I thought. Take a match, strike it on the concrete floor, and burn the damn thing right here in my cell. But I didn't strike the match, and I didn't burn it. What I did was slip it back beneath the sheets of the bottom bunk; then I sat down and stared at the wall for a long time.

Some people shouldn't think of some things, I knew that. I was one of those people. Waiting: I was good at waiting.

But somewhere, in the cell next to mine, was a rope. *Go at 4.00 a.m., when the walls are thinnest.* I swallowed.

However stupid the idea of the rope, it was too late. I knew I couldn't let it go, and it wouldn't let go of me.

The cell door wouldn't open. I tried to slide it, and it wouldn't move. I got my weight behind it and pushed, hard, but it wouldn't move. Of all the things that occurred to me that might go wrong, I never once thought the door wouldn't open.

I glanced at the clock. It was 4.03 a.m.

I kicked the door. It still wouldn't open.

I sat down on the bottom bunk, and felt the book beneath the sheets. All the air went out of me and I sat like that, my head down, for what seemed a long time. When I looked at the clock again, though, it said 4.07.

The rope, I thought. I had to get to the rope. Now, when the walls were thinnest. I reached out and put my palm to the wall between my cell and Stumpy's. It felt thick and solid and cold.

And then it came to me: it had to be mine. Whatever this was, whatever crazy game, it had to be my reason and my rope.

I closed my eyes and saw the park. A group of kids were playing Frisbee by the lake. The Frisbee spun, too high, out over the water – and was snatched from the air by a young lad, who fell back to earth, laughing.

I opened my eyes and the rope was there. It hung in the middle of the floor, a strong, thick rope, in a little pool of spring light. I dropped to the floor and kneeled by it, but I didn't touch it, not yet. I put my hand into that light, feeling it on my skin.

And then I saw my hand, really saw it, and drew in a sharp, hissing breath.

My thumb was gone. My left thumb. Not all of it, just the part from the middle knuckle to the tip.

I turned it in the light and it was a short, thick stump. Pulled it out and my hand was whole again. I grabbed the rope, pulled on it, and it held. It was a strong rope, a good rope. But there was a sour, sick taste in the back of my throat, and I wondered just how far away Stumpy was.

Dimensions, the book had said. Bending things with your mind, so that what is there is also here. What if Stumpy didn't fall, not really? What if he climbed until he found a door, only it didn't lead to a park, or a house, or a gazebo: it led to a place a little like this, and through the door was someone a little like him. And he bent things with his mind, and turned them, and he changed places.

Because at this time of night, at 4.00 a.m., it seemed the walls between were thin. I could feel it, like I could taste that sour taste in my mouth. They were thin, and in that moment, it didn't seem like Stumpy had gone very far at all.

I swallowed. Stumpy believed in payment. You always had to pay for things, even if it was just a story. It was what he saw as right, his way of slapping meaning on the world. What had he said? *I always pay. I always pay and I always expect to be paid.*

Now I had to pay. I had Stumpy's book, after all. And I thought of his wife with the gardener, grinning, laughing, while Stumpy worked on her gazebo, making a love seat just big enough for two. I closed my eyes, and thought of hitting, and eyes, and of grinding. And in the middle of it all, a rope.

I thought then how lucky it was that Stumpy had shown me that picture, the photograph of his wife; how lucky it was I knew what she looked like. Because I had a feeling I'd be paying her a visit real soon. And then we'd have a chat, a quiet little chat, me and Stumpy's wife. *Payment.*

I looked up, swallowed hard, trying to get rid of that taste, and I tried the rope once more. It was solid. So I took hold, and lifted my feet from the floor and wrapped them around it. I closed my eyes, then opened them again, but didn't look down. I saw only that park, the sunshine, felt the clean air in my lungs. I saw them, and held them in my mind, and I started to climb.

THE CASE OF DEATH AND HONEY

Neil Gaiman

It was a mystery in those parts for years what had happened to the old white ghost man, the barbarian with his huge shoulder bag. There were some who supposed him to have been murdered, and, later, they dug up the floor of Old Gao's little shack high on the hillside, looking for treasure, but they found nothing but ash and fire-blackened tin trays. This was after Old Gao himself had vanished, you understand, and before his son came back from Lijiang to take over the beehives on the hill.

This is the problem, *wrote Holmes in 1899*: ennui. And lack of interest. Or rather, it all becomes too easy. When the joy of solving crimes is the challenge, the possibility that you cannot, why then the crimes have something to hold your attention. But when each crime is soluble, and so easily soluble at that, why then there is no point in solving them. Look: this man has been murdered. Well then, someone murdered him. He was murdered for one or more of a tiny handful of reasons: he inconvenienced someone, or he had something that someone wanted, or he had angered someone. Where is the challenge in that?

I would read in the dailies an account of a crime that had the police baffled, and I would find that I had solved it, in broad strokes if not in detail, before I had finished the article. Crime is too soluble. It dissolves. Why call the police and tell them the answers to their mysteries? I leave it, over and over again, as a challenge for them, as it is no challenge for me.

I am only alive when I perceive a challenge.

***

The bees of the misty hills, hills so high that they were sometimes called a mountain, were humming in the pale summer sun as they moved from spring flower to spring flower on the slope. Old Gao listened to them without pleasure. His cousin, in the village across the valley, had many dozens of hives, all of them already filling with honey, even this early in the year; also, the honey was as white as snow-jade. Old Gao did not believe that the white honey tasted any better than the yellow or light brown honey that his own bees produced, although his bees produced it in meagre quantities, but his cousin could sell his white honey for twice what Old Gao could get for the best honey he had.

On his cousin's side of the hill, the bees were earnest, hard-working, golden-brown workers, who brought pollen and nectar back to the hives in enormous quantities. Old Gao's bees were ill-tempered and black, shiny as bullets, who produced as much honey as they needed to get through the winter and only a little more: enough for Old Gao to sell from door to door, to his fellow villagers, one small lump of honeycomb at a time. He would charge more for the brood-comb, filled with bee larvae, sweet-tasting morsels of protein, when he had brood-comb to sell, which was rarely, for the bees were angry and sullen and everything they did, they did as little as possible, including make more bees, and Old Gao was always aware that each piece of brood-comb he sold meant bees he would not have to make honey for him to sell later in the year.

Old Gao was as sullen and as sharp as his bees. He had had a wife once, but she had died in childbirth. The son who had killed her lived for a week, then died himself. There would be nobody to say the funeral rites for Old Gao, no one to clean his grave for festivals or to put offerings upon it. He would die unremembered, as unremarkable and as unremarked as his bees.

The old white stranger came over the mountains in late spring of that year, as soon as the roads were passable, with a huge brown bag strapped to his shoulders. Old Gao heard about him before he met him.

"There is a barbarian who is looking at bees," said his cousin.

Old Gao said nothing. He had gone to his cousin to buy a pailful of second-rate comb, damaged or uncapped and liable soon to spoil. He bought it cheaply to feed to his own bees, and if he sold some of it in his own village, no one was any the wiser. The two men were drinking tea in Gao's cousin's hut on the hillside. From late spring, when the first honey started to flow, until first frost, Gao's cousin left his house in the village and went to the hut on the hillside, to live and to sleep beside his beehives, for fear of thieves. His wife and his children would take the honeycomb and the bottles of snow-white honey down the hill to sell.

Old Gao was not afraid of thieves. The shiny black bees of his hives would have no mercy on anyone who disturbed them. He slept in his village, unless it was time to collect the honey.

"I will send him to you," said Gao's cousin. "Answer his questions, show him your bees, and he will pay you."

"He speaks our tongue?"

"His dialect is atrocious. He said he learned to speak from sailors, and they were mostly Cantonese. But he learns fast, although he is old."

Old Gao grunted, uninterested in sailors. It was late in the morning, and there was still four hours' walking across the valley to his village, in the heat of the day, ahead of him. He finished his tea. His cousin drank finer tea than Old Gao had ever been able to afford.

He reached his hives while it was still light, put the majority of the uncapped honey into his weakest ones. He had eleven. His cousin had over a hundred. Old Gao was stung twice doing this, on the back of the hand and the back of the neck. He had been stung over a thousand times in his life. He could not have told you how many times. He barely noticed the stings of other bees, but the stings of his own black bees always hurt, even if they no longer swelled or burned.

The next day a boy came to Old Gao's house in the village, to tell him that there was someone – and that the someone was a giant foreigner – who was asking for him. Old Gao simply grunted. He walked across the village with the boy at his steady pace, until the boy ran ahead and soon was lost to sight.

Old Gao found the stranger sitting drinking tea on the porch of the Widow Zhang's house. Old Gao had known the Widow Zhang's mother, fifty years ago. She had been a friend of his wife. Now she was long dead. He did not believe anyone who had known his wife still lived. The Widow Zhang fetched Old Gao tea, introduced him to the elderly barbarian, who had removed his bag and sat beside the small table. They sipped their tea. The barbarian said, "I wish to see your bees."

Mycroft's death was the end of Empire, and no one knew it but the two of us. He lay in that pale room, his only covering a thin white sheet, as if he were already becoming a ghost from the popular imagination, and needed only eye-holes in the sheet to finish the impression.

I had imagined that his illness might have wasted him away, but he seemed huger than ever, his fingers swollen into white suet sausages.

I said, "Good evening, Mycroft. Dr Hopkins tells me you have two weeks to live, and stated that I was under no circumstances to inform you of this."

"The man's a dunderhead," said Mycroft, his breath coming in huge wheezes between the words. "I will not make it to Friday."

"Saturday at least," I said.

"You always were an optimist. No, Thursday evening and then I shall be nothing more than an exercise in practical geometry for Hopkins and the funeral directors at Snigsby and Malterson, who will have the challenge, given the narrowness of the doors and corridors, of getting my carcass out of this room and out of the building."

"I had wondered," I said. "Particularly given the staircase. But they will take out the window frame and lower you to the street like a grand piano."

Mycroft snorted at that. Then, "I am fifty-four years old, Sherlock. In my head is the British Government. Not the ballot and hustings nonsense, but the business of the thing. There is no one else knows what the troop movements in the hills of Afghanistan have to do with the desolate shores of North Wales, no one else who sees the whole picture. Can you imagine the mess that this lot and their children will make of Indian Independence?"

I had not previously given any thought to the matter. "Will India become independent?"

"Inevitably. In thirty years, at the outside. I have written several recent memoranda on the topic. As I have on so many other subjects. There are memoranda on the Russian Revolution – that'll be along within the decade, I'll wager – and on the German problem and ... oh, so many others. Not that I expect them to be read or understood." Another wheeze. My brother's lungs rattled like the windows in an empty house. "You know, if I were to live, the British Empire might last another thousand years, bringing peace and improvement to the world."

In the past, especially when I was a boy, whenever I heard Mycroft make a grandiose pronouncement like that, I would say something to bait him. But not now, not on his death-bed. And also I was certain that he was not speaking of the Empire as it was, a flawed and fallible construct of flawed and fallible people, but of a British Empire that existed only in his head, a glorious force for civilization and universal prosperity. I do not, and did not, believe in empires. But I believed in Mycroft.

Mycroft Holmes. Four-and-fifty years of age. He had seen in the new century but the Queen would still outlive him by several months. She was almost thirty years older than he was, and in every way a tough old bird. I wondered to myself whether this unfortunate end might have been avoided.

Mycroft said, "You are right, of course, Sherlock. Had I forced myself to exercise. Had I lived on bird-seed and cabbages instead of porterhouse steak. Had I taken up country dancing along with a wife and a puppy, and in all other ways behaved contrary to my nature, I might have bought myself another dozen or so years. But what is that in the scheme of things? Little enough. And sooner or later, I would enter my dotage. No. I am of the opinion that it would take two hundred years to train a functioning Civil Service, let alone a secret service ..."

I had said nothing.

The pale room had no decorations on the wall of any kind. None of Mycroft's citations. No illustrations, photographs, or paintings. I compared his austere digs to my own cluttered rooms in Baker Street and I wondered, not for the first time, at Mycroft's mind. He needed nothing on the outside, for it was all on the inside – everything he had seen, everything he had experienced, everything he had read. He could close his eyes and walk through the National Gallery, or browse the British Museum Reading Room – or, more likely, compare intelligence reports from the edge of the Empire with the price of wool in Wigan and the unemployment statistics in Hove, and then, from this and only this, order a man promoted or a traitor's quiet death.

Mycroft wheezed enormously, and then he said, "It is a crime, Sherlock."

"I beg your pardon?"

"A crime. It is a crime, my brother, as heinous and as monstrous as any of the penny-dreadful massacres you have investigated. A crime against the world, against nature, against order."

"I must confess, my dear fellow, that I do not entirely follow you. What is a crime?"

"My death," said Mycroft, "in the specific. And Death in general." He looked into my eyes. "I mean it," he said. "Now isn't that a crime worth investigating, Sherlock, old fellow? One that might keep your attention for longer than it will take you to establish that the poor fellow who used to conduct the brass band in Hyde Park was murdered by the third cornet using a preparation of strychnine."

"Arsenic," I corrected him, almost automatically.

"I think you will find," wheezed Mycroft, "that the arsenic, while present, had in fact fallen in flakes from the green-painted bandstand itself on to his supper. Symptoms of arsenical poison are a complete red herring. No, it was strychnine that did for the poor fellow."

Mycroft said no more to me that day or ever. He breathed his last the following Thursday, late in the afternoon, and on the Friday the worthies of Snigsby and Malterson removed the casing from the window of the pale room and lowered my brother's remains into the street, like a grand piano.

His funeral service was attended by me, by my friend Watson, by our cousin Harriet and – in accordance with Mycroft's express wishes – by no one else. The Civil Service, the Foreign Office, even the Diogenes Club – these institutions and their representatives were absent. Mycroft had been reclusive in life; he was to be equally reclusive in death. So it was the three of us and the parson, who had not known my brother, and had no conception that it was the more omniscient arm of the British Government itself that he was consigning to the grave.

Four burly men held fast to the ropes and lowered my brother's remains to their final resting place, and did, I daresay, their utmost not to curse at the weight of the thing. I tipped each of them half a crown.

Mycroft was dead at fifty-four, and, as they lowered him into his grave, in my imagination I could still hear his clipped, grey wheeze as he seemed to be saying, "Now *there* is a crime worth investigating."

The stranger's accent was not too bad, although his vocabulary seemed limited, but he seemed to be talking in the local dialect, or something near to it. He was a fast learner. Old Gao hawked and spat into the dust of the street. He said nothing. He did not wish to take the stranger up the hillside; he did not wish to disturb his bees. In Old Gao's experience, the less he bothered his bees, the better they did. And if they stung the barbarian, what then?

The stranger's hair was silver-white, and sparse; his nose, the first barbarian nose that Old Gao had seen, was huge and curved and put Old Gao in mind of the beak of an eagle; his skin was tanned the same colour as Old Gao's own, and was lined deeply. Old Gao was not certain that he could read a barbarian's face as he could read the face of a person, but he thought the man seemed most serious and, perhaps, unhappy.

"Why?"

"I study bees. Your brother tells me you have big black bees here. Unusual bees."

Old Gao shrugged. He did not correct the man on the relationship with his cousin.

The stranger asked Old Gao if he had eaten, and when Gao said that he had not, the stranger asked the Widow Zhang to bring them soup and rice and whatever was good that she had in her kitchen, which turned out to be a stew of black tree-fungus and vegetables and tiny transparent river fish, little bigger than tadpoles. The two men ate in silence.

When they had finished eating, the stranger said, "I would be honoured if you would show me your bees."

Old Gao said nothing, but the stranger paid the Widow Zhang well and he put his bag on his back. Then he waited, and, when Old Gao began to walk, the stranger followed him. He carried his bag as if it weighed nothing to him. He was strong for an old man, thought Old Gao, and wondered whether all such barbarians were so strong.

"Where are you from?"

" England," said the stranger.

Old Gao remembered his father telling him about a war with the English, over trade and over opium, but that was long ago.

They walked up the hillside, that was, perhaps, a mountainside. It was steep, and the hillside was too rocky to be cut into fields. Old Gao tested the stranger's pace, walking faster than usual, and the stranger kept up with him, with his pack on his back.

The stranger stopped several times, however. He stopped to examine flowers – the small white flowers that bloomed in early spring elsewhere in the valley, but in late spring here on the side of the hill. There was a bee on one of the flowers, and the stranger kneeled and observed it. Then he reached into his pocket, produced a large magnifying glass and examined the bee through it, and made notes in a small pocket notebook, in an incomprehensible writing.

Old Gao had never seen a magnifying glass before, and he leaned in to look at the bee, so black and so strong and so very different from the bees elsewhere in that valley.

"One of your bees?"

"Yes," said Old Gao. "Or one like it."

"Then we shall let her find her own way home," said the stranger, and he did not disturb the bee, and he put away the magnifying glass.

```
The Croft
East Dene, Sussex
11 August 1922
```

My dear Watson,

I have taken our discussion of this afternoon to heart, considered it carefully, and am prepared to modify my previous opinions.

I am amenable to your publishing your account of the incidents of 1903, specifically of the final case before my retirement, under the following conditions.

In addition to the usual changes that you would make to disguise actual people and places, I would suggest that you replace the entire scenario we encountered (I speak of Professor Presbury's garden. I shall not write of it further here) with monkey glands, or a similar extract from the testes of an ape or lemur, sent by some foreign mystery-man. Perhaps the monkey-extract could have the effect of making Professor Presbury move like an ape – he could be some kind of "creeping man" maybe? – or possibly make him able to clamber up the sides of buildings and up trees. I would suggest that he could grow a tail, but this might be too fanciful even for you, Watson,

although no more fanciful than many of
the rococo additions you have made in
your histories to otherwise humdrum
events in my life and work.

In addition, I have written the following
speech, to be delivered by myself, at the
end of your narrative. Please make certain
that something much like this is there,
in which I inveigh against living too
long, and the foolish urges that push
foolish people to do foolish things to
prolong their foolish lives:

There is a very real danger to humanity, if one could live for ever, if
youth were simply there for the taking, that the material, the sensual,
the worldly, would all prolong their worthless lives. The spiritual
would not avoid the call to something higher. It would be the
survival of the least fit. What sort of cesspool may not our poor
world become then?

Something along those lines, I fancy,
would set my mind at rest.

Let me see the finished article, please,
before you submit it to be published.

I remain, old friend, your most obedient
servant,

Sherlock Holmes

They reached Old Gao's bees late in the afternoon. The beehives
were grey wooden boxes piled behind a structure so simple it could
barely be called a shack. Four posts, a roof, and hangings of oiled
cloth that served to keep out the worst of the spring rains and the
summer storms. A small charcoal brazier served for warmth, if you
placed a blanket over it and yourself, and to cook upon; a wooden
pallet in the centre of the structure, with an ancient ceramic pillow,

served as a bed on the occasions that Old Gao slept up on the mountainside with the bees, particularly in the autumn, when he harvested most of the honey. There was little enough of it compared to the output of his cousin's hives, but it was enough that he would sometimes spend two or three days waiting for the comb that he had crushed and stirred into a slurry to drain through the cloth into the buckets and pots that he had carried up the mountainside. Finally he would melt the remainder, the sticky wax and bits of pollen and dirt and bee slurry, in a pot, to extract the beeswax, and he would give the sweet water back to the bees. Then he would carry the honey and the wax blocks down the hill to the village to sell.

He showed the barbarian stranger the eleven hives, watched impassively as the stranger put on a veil and opened a hive, examining first the bees, then the contents of a brood box, and finally the queen, through his magnifying glass. He showed no fear, no discomfort: in everything he did the stranger's movements were gentle and slow, and he was not stung, nor did he crush or hurt a single bee. This impressed Old Gao. He had assumed that barbarians were inscrutable, unreadable, mysterious creatures, but this man seemed overjoyed to have encountered Gao's bees. His eyes were shining.

Old Gao fired up the brazier, to boil some water. Long before the charcoal was hot, however, the stranger had removed from his bag a contraption of glass and metal. He had filled the upper half of it with water from the stream, lit a flame, and soon a kettleful of water was steaming and bubbling. Then the stranger took two tin mugs from his bag, and some green tea leaves wrapped in paper, and dropped the leaves into the mug, and poured on the water.

It was the finest tea that Old Gao had ever drunk: better by far than his cousin's tea. They drank it sitting cross-legged on the floor.

"I would like to stay here for the summer, in this house," said the stranger.

"Here? This is not even a house," said Old Gao. "Stay down in the village. Widow Zhang has a room."

"I will stay here," said the stranger. "Also I would like to rent one of your beehives."

Old Gao had not laughed in years. There were those in the village who would have thought such a thing impossible. But still, he laughed then, a guffaw of surprise and amusement that seemed to have been jerked out of him.

"I am serious," said the stranger. He placed four silver coins on the ground between them. Old Gao had not seen where he got them from: three silver Mexican pesos, a coin that had become popular in China years before, and a large silver yuan. It was as much money as Old Gao might see in a year of selling honey. "For this money," said the stranger, "I would like someone to bring me food: every three days should suffice."

Old Gao said nothing. He finished his tea and stood up. He pushed through the oiled cloth to the clearing high on the hillside. He walked over to the eleven hives: each consisted of two brood boxes with one, two, three or, in one case, even four boxes above that. He took the stranger to the hive with four boxes above it, each box filled with frames of comb. "This hive is yours," he said.

They were plant extracts. That was obvious. They worked, in their way, for a limited time, but they were also extremely poisonous. But watching poor Professor Presbury during those final days – his skin, his eyes, his gait – had convinced me that he had not been on entirely the wrong path. I took his case of seeds, of pods, of roots and of dried extracts, and I thought. I pondered. I cogitated. I reflected. It was an intellectual problem, and could be solved, as my old maths tutor had always sought to demonstrate to me, by intellect.

They were plant extracts, and they were lethal. Methods I used to render them non-lethal rendered them quite ineffective.

It was not a three pipe problem. I suspect it was something approaching a three hundred pipe problem before I hit upon an initial idea – a notion, perhaps – of a way of processing the plants that might allow them to be ingested by human beings.

It was not a line of investigation that could easily be followed in Baker Street. So it was, in the autumn of 1903, that I moved to Sussex, and spent the winter reading every book and pamphlet and monograph so far published, I fancy, upon the care and keeping of bees. And so it was that in early April of 1904, armed only with theoretical knowledge, I took delivery from a local farmer of my first package of bees. I wonder, sometimes, that Watson did not suspect anything. Then again, Watson's glorious obtuseness has never ceased to surprise me, and sometimes, indeed, I had relied upon it. Still, he knew what I was like when I had no work to occupy my mind, no case to solve. He knew my lassitude, my black moods when I had no case to occupy me. So how could he believe that I had truly retired? He knew my methods.

Indeed, Watson was there when I took receipt of my first bees. He watched, from a safe distance, as I poured them from the package into the empty, waiting hive, like slow, humming, gentle treacle.

He saw my excitement, and he saw nothing.

And the years passed, and we watched the Empire crumble, we watched the Government unable to govern, we watched those poor heroic boys sent to the trenches of Flanders to die, all these things confirmed me in my opinions. I was not doing the right thing. I was doing the only thing.

As my face grew unfamiliar, and my finger-joints swelled and ached (not so much as they might have done, though, which I attributed to the many bee-stings I had received in my first few years as an investigative apiarist) and as Watson, dear, brave, obtuse Watson, faded with time and paled and shrank, his skin becoming greyer, his moustache becoming the same shade of grey, my resolve to conclude my researches did not diminish. If anything, it increased.

So: my initial hypotheses were tested upon the South Downs, in an apiary of my own devising, each hive modelled upon Langstroth's. I do believe that I made every mistake that ever a novice beekeeper could or has ever made, and in addition, due to my investigations, an entire hiveful of mistakes that no beekeeper has ever made before, or shall, I trust, ever make again. "The Case of the Poisoned Beehive", Watson might have called many of them, although "The Mystery of the Transfixed Women's Institute" would have drawn more attention to my researches, had anyone been interested enough to investigate. (As it was, I chided Mrs

Telford for simply taking a jar of honey from the shelves here without consulting me, and I ensured that, in the future, she was given several jars for her cooking from the more regular hives, and that honey from the experimental hives was locked away once it had been collected. I do not believe that this ever drew comment.)

I experimented with Dutch bees, with German bees and with Italians, with Carniolans and Caucasians. I regretted the loss of our British bees to blight and, even where they had survived, to inter-breeding, although I found and worked with a small hive I purchased and grew up from a frame of brood and a queen cell, from an old Abbey in St Albans, which seemed to me to be original British breeding stock.

I experimented for the best part of two decades, before I concluded that the bees that I sought, if they existed, were not to be found in England, and would not survive the distances they would need to travel to reach me by international parcel post. I needed to examine bees in India. I needed to travel perhaps farther afield than that.

I have a smattering of languages.

I had my flower-seeds, and my extracts and tinctures in syrup. I needed nothing more.

I packed them up, arranged for the cottage on the Downs to be cleaned and aired once a week, and for Master Wilkins – to whom I am afraid I had developed the habit of referring, to his obvious distress, as "Young Villikins" – to inspect the beehives, and to harvest and sell surplus honey in Eastbourne market, and to prepare the hives for winter.

I told them I did not know when I should be back. I am an old man. Perhaps they did not expect me to return. And, if this was indeed the case, they would, strictly speaking, have been right.

Old Gao was impressed, despite himself. He had lived his life among bees. Still, watching the stranger shake the bees from the boxes, with a practised flick of his wrist, so cleanly and so sharply that the black bees seemed more surprised than angered, and simply flew or crawled back into their hive, was remarkable. The stranger then stacked the boxes filled with comb on top of one of the weaker hives, so Old Gao would still have the honey from the hive the stranger was renting. So it was that Old Gao gained a lodger.

Old Gao gave the Widow Zhang's granddaughter a few coins to take the stranger food three times a week – mostly rice and vegetables, along with an earthenware pot filled, when she left at least, with boiling soup.

Every ten days Old Gao would walk up the hill himself. He went initially to check on the hives, but soon discovered that under the stranger's care all eleven hives were thriving as they had never thrived before. And indeed, there was now a twelfth hive, from a captured swarm of the black bees the stranger had encountered while on a walk along the hill. Old Gao brought wood, the next time he came up to the shack, and he and the stranger spent several afternoons wordlessly working together, making extra boxes to go on the hives, building frames to fill the boxes.

One evening the stranger told Old Gao that the frames they were making had been invented by an American, only seventy years before. This seemed like nonsense to Old Gao, who made frames as his father had, and as they did across the valley, and as, he was certain, his grandfather and his grandfather's grandfather had, but he said nothing.

He enjoyed the stranger's company. They made hives together, and Old Gao wished that the stranger were a younger man. Then he would stay there for a long time, and Old Gao would have someone to leave his beehives to, when he died. But they were two old men, nailing boxes together, with thin frosty hair and old faces, and neither of them would see another dozen winters.

Old Gao noticed that the stranger had planted a small, neat garden beside the hive that he had claimed as his own, which he had moved away from the rest of the hives. He had covered it with a net. He had also created a "back door" to the hive, so that the only bees that could reach the plants came from the hive that he was renting. Old Gao also observed that, beneath the netting, there were several trays filled with what appeared to be sugar solution of some kind, one coloured bright red, one green, one a startling blue, one yellow. He pointed to them, but all the stranger did was nod and smile.

The bees were lapping up the syrups, though, clustering and crowding on the sides of the tin dishes with their tongues down, eating until they could eat no more, and then returning to the hive.

The stranger had made sketches of Old Gao's bees. He showed the sketches to Old Gao, tried to explain the ways that Old Gao's bees differed from other honeybees, talked of ancient bees preserved in stone for millions of years, but here the stranger's Chinese failed him, and, truthfully, Old Gao was not interested. They were his bees, until he died, and after that, they were the bees of the mountainside. He had brought other bees here, but they had sickened and died, or been killed in raids by the black bees, who took their honey and left them to starve.

The last of these visits was in late summer. Old Gao went down the mountainside. He did not see the stranger again.

It is done.

It works. Already I feel a strange combination of triumph and of disappointment, as if of defeat, or of distant storm-clouds teasing at my senses.

It is strange to look at my hands and to see, not my hands as I know them, but the hands I remember from my younger days: knuckles unswollen, dark hairs, not snow-white, on the backs.

It was a quest that had defeated so many, a problem with no apparent solution. The first Emperor of China nearly destroyed his empire in pursuit of it, three thousand years ago. He died. And all it took me was, what, twenty years? I do not know if I did the right thing or not (although any "retirement" without such an occupation would have been, literally, maddening). I took the commission from Mycroft. I investigated the problem. I arrived, inevitably, at the solution. Will I tell the world? I will not.

And yet, I have half a pot of dark brown honey remaining in my bag; half a pot of honey that is worth more than nations. (I was

tempted to write, *worth more than all the tea in China,* perhaps
because of my current situation, but fear that even Watson would
deride it as cliché.)

And speaking of Watson …

There is one thing left to do. My only remaining goal, and it is
small enough. I shall make my way to Shanghai, and from there I
shall take ship to Southampton, half a world away.

And once I am there, I shall seek out Watson, if he still lives – and
I fancy he does. It is irrational, I know, and yet I am certain that I
would know, somehow, had Watson passed beyond the veil.

I shall buy theatrical make-up, disguise myself as an old man, so
as not to startle him, and I shall invite my old friend over for tea.

There will be honey on buttered toast served for tea that
afternoon, I fancy.

There were tales of a barbarian who passed through the village on
his way east, but the people who told Old Gao this did not believe
that it could have been the same man who had lived in Gao's shack.
This one was young and proud, and his hair was dark. It was not
the old man who had walked through those parts in the spring,
although, one person told Gao, the bag was similar.

Old Gao walked up the mountainside to investigate, although
he suspected what he would find before he got there. The stranger
was gone, and the stranger's bag. There had been much burning,
though. That was clear. Papers had been burned – Old Gao recognized the edge of a drawing the stranger had made of one of his
bees, but the rest of the papers were ash, or blackened beyond
recognition, even had Old Gao been able to read barbarian
writing.

The papers were not the only things to have been burned; parts of
the hive that the stranger had rented were now only twisted ash;
there were blackened, twisted strips of tin that might once have
contained brightly coloured syrups.

The colour was added to the syrups, the stranger had told him
once, so that he could tell them apart, although for what purpose
Old Gao had never enquired.

He examined the shack like a detective, searching for a clue as to the stranger's nature or his whereabouts. On the ceramic pillow four silver coins had been left for him to find – two yuan and two pesos – and he put them away. Behind the shack he found a heap of used slurry, with the last bees of the day still crawling upon it, tasting whatever sweetness was still on the surface of the sticky wax.

Old Gao thought long and hard before he gathered up the slurry, wrapped it loosely in cloth, and put it in a pot, which he filled with water. He heated the water on the brazier, but did not let it boil. Soon enough the wax floated to the surface, leaving the dead bees and the dirt and the pollen and the propolis inside the cloth.

He let it cool.

Then he walked outside, and he stared up at the moon. It was almost full.

He wondered how many villagers knew that his son had died as a baby. He remembered his wife, but her face was distant, and he had no portraits or photographs of her. He thought that there was nothing he was so suited for on the face of the earth as to keep the black, bullet-like bees on the side of this high, high hill. There was no other man who knew their temperament as he did.

The water had cooled. He lifted the now solid block of beeswax out of the water, placed it on the boards of the bed to finish cooling. He took the cloth filled with dirt and impurities out of the pot. And then, because he too was, in his way, a detective, and once you have eliminated the impossible whatever remains, however unlikely, must be the truth, he drank the sweet water in the pot. There is a lot of honey in slurry, after all, even after the majority of it has dripped through a cloth and been purified. The water tasted of honey, but not a honey that Gao had ever tasted before. It tasted of smoke, and metal, and strange flowers, and odd perfumes. It tasted, Gao thought, a little like sex.

He drank it all down, and then he slept, with his head on the ceramic pillow.

When he woke, he thought, he would decide how to deal with his cousin, who would expect to inherit the twelve hives on the hill when Old Gao went missing.

He would be an illegitimate son, perhaps, the young man who would return in the days to come. Or perhaps a son. Young Gao. Who would remember, now? It did not matter. He would go to the city and then he would return, and he would keep the black bees on the side of the mountain for as long as days and circumstances would allow.

ACKNOWLEDGEMENTS

"The Bone-Headed League" © 2011 Lee Child. First appeared in A STUDY IN SHERLOCK, edited by Laurie R. King and Leslie S. Klinger. Reprinted by permission of the Darley Anderson Literary Agency.

"This Thing of Darkness" © 2011 Peter Tremayne. First appeared in ELLERY QUEEN MYSTERY MAGAZINE. Reprinted by permission of A. M. Heath.

"Big Guy" © 2012 Paul Johnston. Reprinted by permission of the author and the Broo Doherty Literary Agency.

"The Conspirators" © 2010 Christopher Fowler. First appeared in CRIMEWAVE. Reprinted by permission of the author.

"Squeaky" © 2011 Martin Edwards. First appeared in ELLERY QUEEN MYSTERY MAGAZINE. Reprinted by permission of the author.

"Fists of Destiny" © 2011 Col Bury. First appeared in MANCHESTER 6. Reprinted by permission of the author

"Nain Rouge" © 2012 Barbara Nadel. First appeared in ELLERY QUEEN MYSTERY MAGAZINE. Reprinted by permission of the author.

"The King of Oudh's Curry" © 2011 Amy Myers. First appeared in ELLERY QUEEN MYSTERY MAGAZINE. Reprinted by permission of the author.

"London Calling" © 2011 Ian Ayris and Nick Quantrill. First appeared in CAFFEINE NIGHTS. Reprinted by permission of the authors.

"The Curious Affair of the Deodand" © 2011 Lisa Tuttle. First appeared in DOWN THESE STRANGE STREETS, edited by George R. R. Martin and Gardner Dozois. Reprinted by permission of the author.

"God Moving Over the Face of the Waters" © 2011 Steve Mosby. First appeared in OFF THE RECORD, edited by Luca Veste. Reprinted by permission of the author.

"Stardust" © 2011 Phil Lovesey. First appeared in ELLERY QUEEN MYSTERY MAGAZINE. Reprinted by permission of the author.

"He Did Not Always See Her" © 2011 Claire Seeber. First appeared in GUILTY CONSCIENCES, edited by Martin Edwards. Reprinted by permission of the author.

"Method Murder" © 2011 Simon Brett. First appeared in ELLERY QUEEN MYSTERY MAGAZINE. Reprinted by permission of the author and his agent, Michael Motley.

"The Man Who Took Off His Hat to the Driver of the Train" © 2011 Peter Turnbull. First appeared in ELLERY QUEEN MYSTERY MAGAZINE. Reprinted by permission of the author.

"Together in Electric Dreams" © 2011 Carol Anne Davis. First appeared in GUILTY CONSCIENCES, edited by Martin Edwards. Reprinted by permission of the author.

"Last Train from Desprit" © 2011 Richard Godwin. First appeared in MEDIA VIRUS. Reprinted by permission of the author.

"The Message" © 2011 Margaret Murphy. First appeared in GUILTY CONSCIENCES, edited by Martin Edwards. Reprinted by permission of the author.

"Tea for Two" © 2011 Sally Spedding. First appeared in RADGE-PACKET. Reprinted by permission of the author.

"Safe and Sound" © 2011 Edward Marston. First appeared in ELLERY QUEEN MYSTERY MAGAZINE. Reprinted by permission of the author.

"Confession" © 2011 Paula Williams. First appeared in WOMAN'S WEEKLY. Reprinted by permission of the author.

"Ten Bells at Robbie's" © 2011 Tony Black. First appeared in CRIME FACTORY. Reprinted by permission of the author.

"Wilkolak" © 2010 Nina Allan. First appeared in CRIMEWAVE. Reprinted by permission of the author.

"Who Killed Skippy?" © 2011 Paul D. Brazill. First appeared in NOIR NATION. Reprinted by permission of the author.

"Inheritance" © 2011 Jane Casey. First appeared in DOWN THESE GREEN STREETS, edited by Declan Burke. Reprinted by permission of the author.

"A Memorable Day" © 2012 L. C. Tyler. Reprinted by permission of the author.

"Laptop" © 2011 Cath Staincliffe. First appeared in BEST EATEN COLD, edited by Martin Edwards. Reprinted by permission of the author.

"Blood on the Ghat" © 2011 Barry Maitland. First appeared in THE CANBERRA TIMES. Reprinted by permission of the author.

"Vanishing Act" © 2011 Christine Poulson. First appeared in ELLERY QUEEN MYSTERY MAGAZINE. Reprinted by permission of the author.

"The Betrayed" © 2011 Roger Busby. First appeared in eBook format. Reprinted by permission of the author.

"Turning the Tables" © 2011 Judith Cutler. First appeared in ELLERY QUEEN MYSTERY MAGAZINE. Reprinted by permission of the author.

"Handy Man" © 2011 John Harvey. First appeared in AMBIT. Reprinted by permission of the author.

"The Invisible Gunman" © 2011 Keith McCarthy. First appeared in ELLERY QUEEN MYSTERY MAGAZINE. Reprinted by permission of the author.

"The Golden Hour" © 2011 Bernie Crosthwaite. First appeared in GUILTY CONSCIENCES, edited by Martin Edwards. Reprinted by permission of the author.

"The Habit of Silence" © 2011 Ann Cleeves. First appeared in BEST EATEN COLD, edited by Martin Edwards. Reprinted by permission of the author.

"The Unknown Crime" © 2011 Sarah Rayne. First published in GUILTY CONSCIENCES, edited by Martin Edwards. Reprinted by permission of the author.

"The Ladder" © 2011 Adrian McKinty. First appeared in CRIME FACTORY: THE FIRST SHIFT, edited by Keith Rawson, Cameron Ashley and Jimmy Callaway. Reprinted by permission of the author.

"The Hostess" © 2011 Joel Lane. First appeared in CRIMEWAVE. Reprinted by permission of the author.

The Mammoth Book of New CSI

by Nigel Cawthorne

Thirty-one accounts of the fascinating work of the crime scene experts
who let the evidence speak when the victims cannot.

Crime scene investigators rely on cutting-edge technology, including
genetic fingerprinting, blood-spatter analysis, laser ablation, toxicology
and ballistics analysis. Here you will find detailed accounts of high-profile
contemporary investigations and older cases recently reopened as a
result of advances in forensic science.

Madeleine McCann – the young girl
abducted in Portugal

Snowtown – body parts found in a disused bank
in South Australia lead the police to mass murderers

Amanda Knox – who *did* kill Meredith Kercher in Perugia?

Josef Fritzl – the secrets of the cellar in Austria where
he incarcerated and raped his daughter

Marilyn Monroe – was she murdered by the Mafia,
the FBI or the CIA?

Visit **www.constablerobinson.com** for more information

The Mammoth Book of Bizarre Crimes

by Robin Odell

You couldn't make it up!

A gripping collection of stories of human criminality at its most bizarre. These unusual, sensational murders recall not only gruesome historical crimes, but also touch on shocking and macabre modern murders. Included are details of ground-breaking advances in crime detection, law enforcement and forensic science. This is the top-secret report on the most grisly, and unusual, criminal activity of our time.

Incredible and bizarre true crimes include:

Krystian Bala – Polish writer who killed a rival,
then used the murder as the plot for a novel

Alexander Pichushkin – Russian man stopped one short of
killing the sixty-four victims he needed to "fill a chess board"

John Lee – "the man they could not hang", who survived three attempts
to execute him at Exeter prison

Robert "Rattlesnake" James – Californian barber who used two snakes
in a box to kill his wife

Visit **www.constablerobinson.com** for more information

The Mammoth Book of Historical Crime Fiction

Edited by Mike Ashley

Our dark past brought to life by leading contemporary crime writers.

A new generation of crime writers has broadened the genre of
crime fiction, creating more human stories of historical realism, with
a stronger emphasis on character and the psychology of crime.

This superb anthology of 12 novellas encompasses over 4,000 years
of our dark, criminal past, from Bronze-Age Britain to the eve of the
Second World War, with stories set in ancient Greece, Rome,
the Byzantine Empire, medieval Venice, seventh-century Ireland
and 1930s' New York.

A Byzantine icon painter, suddenly out of work when icons
are banned, becomes embroiled in a case of deception;
Charles Babbage and the young Ada Byron try to crack a
coded message and stop a master criminal; and New York detectives
are on the lookout for Butch Cassidy and the Sundance Kid.

Steven Saylor, Anne Perry, Peter Tremayne, Tom Holt, Charles Todd, Richard
A. Lupoff and many more

Visit **www.constablerobinson.com** for more information

The Mammoth Book of
New Sherlock Holmes Adventures

Edited by Mike Ashley

26 unrecorded cases solved by the great Holmes himself.

The biggest collection of new Sherlock Holmes stories published
since Sir Arthur Conan Doyle laid down his pen – superb fiction
featuring the great detective by masters of historical crime.

The 26 cases are presented in the order in which Holmes solved them,
with a continuous narrative alongside the stories which identifies
the gaps in the canon and places the cases in their correct sequence.
The book includes an invaluable, complete Holmes chronology.

- Derek Wilson's discovery of the great detective's
  forgotten first case

- L. B. Greenwood on a stratagem to stop the
  First World War

- Amy Myers's revelation of why Holmes refused
  a knighthood

- Peter Tremayne describes Holmes's first confrontation
  with Sebastian Moran

Visit **www.constablerobinson.com** for more information

The Mammoth Book of the Mafia

Edited by Nigel Cawthorne and Colin Cawthorne

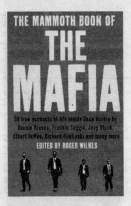

19 inside stories of the American Mafia and the Sicilian Cosa Nostra.

Images of life in the Mob pervade our film and TV screens, some glamorous, some horrific – what is the reality? Nigel and Colin Cawthorne have put together the largest-ever collection of insider stories from prominent ex-mafiosi, infiltrators and award-winning writers.

Richard 'The Iceman' Kuklinski, the contract killer who claimed to have murdered over 200 people in a career lasting 43 years.

Frankie Saggio, who 'freelanced' for all five of New York's Mafia families, narrowly escaping assassination before being busted for a major scam.

Joey Black, the 'Hitman', chillingly professional murderer of 38 victims and regarded by many as 'the original Soprano'.

Albert DeMeo, the son of a gangster, who later became a lawyer.

'Donnie Brasco', real name Joseph Pistone, the FBI agent, who worked undercover in the Bonanno and Colombo crime families in New York for six years

Tommaso Buscetta, the Sicilian mafioso – the first *pentito*, or informant, of real significance to break *omertà*. The two judges with whom he worked, Giovanni Falcone and Paolo Borsellino, were both later killed by the Mafia.

This is the reality of the world of men you wouldn't want to cross.

Visit **www.constablerobinson.com** for more information

The Mammoth Book of Undercover Cops

Edited by Paul Copperwaite

True stories of high-risk undercover police work where the smallest mistake can lead to certain death.

From the initial growth of plain-clothes and undercover policing in the 1930s and 1940s through to the major undercover operations against the Mafia, organized crime and corrupt cops in the 1970s and 1980s to contemporary police work in the age of terror, the Internet and online predators, this collection presents 19 extraordinary true stories of police officers facing, sometimes for years on end, the threat of a deadly end-game.

The Wire creator David Simon provides a gripping account of attempts to counter ruthless drug dealing and murder on the streets of Baltimore.

Ex-LA cop Joseph Wambaugh, whose 1971 novel *The New Centurions* prefigured realistic TV cop dramas from *Hill Street Blues* to *The Wire*, writes about events surrounding the abduction of two plain-clothed LAPD officers.

Joe Pistone, with Charles Brandt, tells the riveting story of his life undercover as Donnie Brasco. Holding his nerve through six years of living a lie, he played a key role in weakening the Mafia's hold on American society in the 1980s.

Visit **www.constablerobinson.com** for more information